The Forbidden City Series

MELISSA ADDEY

Table of Contents

Spelling and Pronunciation 5

Maps 7

Main Characters 11

The Consorts 13

The Fragrant Concubine 75

The Garden of Perfect Brightness 333

The Cold Palace 509

Biography 666

Current and Forthcoming Books 667

Bonus: Thoughts on Research… and Magic 669

Spelling and Pronunciation

I have used the international Pinyin system for the Chinese names of people and places. The following list indicates the elements of this spelling system that may cause English speakers problems of pronunciation. To the left, the letter used in the text, to the right, its equivalent English sound.

Therefore, the Empress' name, Lady Fuca, is pronounced Foo-cha.

c = ts
q = ch
x = sh
z = dz
zh = j

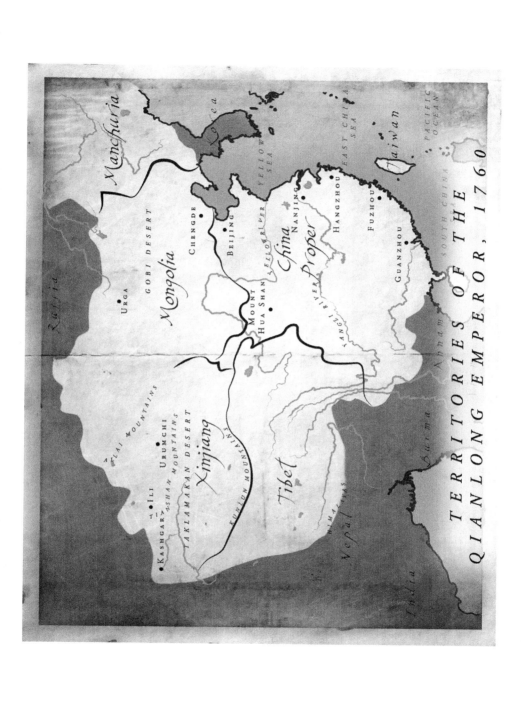

TERRITORIES OF THE
QIANLONG EMPEROR, 1760

Manchuria

Korea

Russia

GOBI DESERT

Mongolia

URGA

CHENGDE

BEIJING

YELLOW SEA

YELLOW RIVER

MOUNT HUA SHAN

China Proper

NANJING

HANGZHOU

EAST CHINA SEA

Taiwan

PACIFIC OCEAN

FUZHOU

GUANZHOU

YANGZI RIVER

SOUTH CHINA SEA

ALTAI MOUNTAINS

URUMCHI

ILI

KASHGAR

TIAN SHAN MOUNTAINS

TAKLAMAKAN DESERT

Xinjiang

KUNLUN MOUNTAINS

Tibet

HIMALAYAS

Nepal

India

Burma

Annam

1 Engraved Moon and Unfolding Clouds:
The Peony Terrace

2 Hall of Fulfilled Wishes:
Castiglione's Painting Studio

3 Grand Palace Gate
to the Garden of Perfect Brightness

4 The Rear Lake
And the 9 Continents Clear and Calm

5 Sea of Blessings

6 The Maze

7 The Western Palaces

Yuan Ming Yuan: Garden of Perfect Brightness

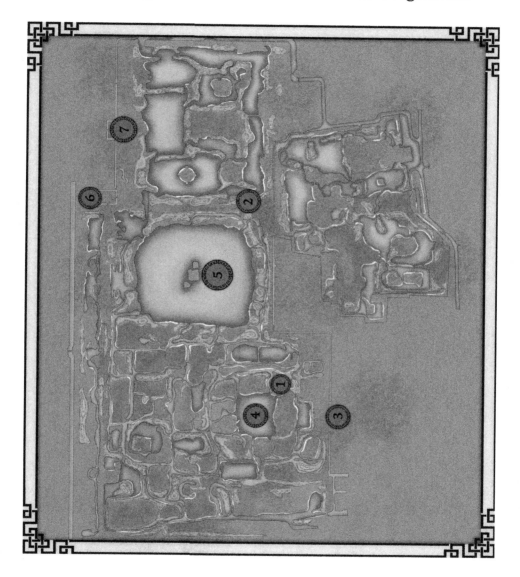

Main Characters

Emperors, main concubines and children

The Kangxi Emperor
- Multiple concubines including Lady Que Hui
- Over 30 sons, including the Crown Prince, Prince Yong and Prince Zhi

Prince Yong, later the Yongzheng Emperor
- Lady Nara, Primary Consort, later Empress
- Lady Niuhuru, concubine to Prince Yong, later Empress Dowager, mother to Hongli,
- Lady Qi, mother to Hongshi

Hongli, later Prince Bao, later the Qianlong Emperor
- Lady Fuca, Primary Consort, later Empress
- Lady Ula Nara, later Step Empress
- Lady Ling
- Lady He (the Fragrant Concubine/Hidligh)
- Lady Qing
- Lady Ying
- Lady Wan

The Jesuits

- Giuseppe Castiglione, painter, also named Lang Shining (Shur-ning) (Italian)
- Laura Biondecci, painter (Italian)
- Brother Costa, surgeon (Italian)
- Brother Michel Benoist, engineer (French)
- Brother Jean-Denis Attiret, painter (French)
- Father Friedel, Superior of St Joseph's (Austrian)
- Brother Michele Arailza, painter (Italian)
- Brother Ferdinando Moggi, architect (Italian)
- Brother Matteo Ripa, copper-engraver (Italian)

- Giovanni Gherardini, painter and Castiglione's predecessor in China (Italian)

Servants

- The Chief Eunuch
- Bao, head eunuch to Lady Qing
- Huan and Jiang, eunuchs to Lady He
- Mei, maid to Iparhan
- Yan, maid to Niuhuru
- Kun, eunuch gardener, later husband to Yan
- Chu, adopted daughter of Yan and Kun
- Feng, head eunuch to Lady Ula Nara
- Ping, chief maid to Lady Ula Nara

Other Main Characters

- Iparhan, (acting as maid to Lady He), from Xinjiang
- Nurmat, (acting as cook to Lady He), from Xinjiang
- Nian Xiyao, court official introducing Castiglione to court life
- Madam Guo, a Chinese Christian
- The Lei family of imperial architects, including Jinyu Lei, head architect

MELISSA ADDEY

The Consorts

The Consorts

For my own little prince, Seth

The Forbidden City, China, 1700s

Honoured Ladies

BAO IS FUSSING. "PERHAPS THE pink is better," he worries, lifting first one and then another flower to my already laden headdress and frowning at both. First attendant amongst my eunuchs and maids, head of my household, Bao is always worrying about something.

I sigh. "Bao, what does it matter?"

"It *matters*," insists Bao. "It always matters when the new ladies are brought into the Forbidden City. The Emperor may be taken with their novelty, but he must not forget the ladies who already reside here."

I make a face at him in the mirror of my dressing table. "The Emperor is besotted with Empress Fuca as well you know," I point out. "He barely notices the rest of us." This is true, although I also know that I too readily use this truth to mask my own failures.

Bao is not put off so easily. "The Empress is a wonderful woman," he says dutifully, "but the Emperor is still young and a young man has need of variety. He will come to call upon his other ladies more often, you will see. And when he does, he needs to remember your face."

I look into the mirror before me while Bao concedes to the last of the early spring's pink camellias and busies himself tucking them securely into my hair, fastening them with jade pins and rearranging multiple strands of pearls to his satisfaction.

"And think," says Bao, stepping back and regarding his handiwork with a beaming smile, "If His Majesty should look upon you with favour then you might have a child. Such a blessing."

I've heard this too often, though I know loyal Bao means well. I would like a child of my own, to share my life here, but I doubt it will ever happen.

In the mirror I see a young woman's face. A pretty face, certainly after Bao's careful ministrations. An elegant face, of course, for the Honoured Ladies of my rank are always elegant in their grooming.

A lonely face.

My palanquin bobs its way through the tiny passageways of the Inner Court. We pass by many other small palaces, each close to the next, separated only by their gardens. Here reside all the women of the court. We are a world of women, children, maids and eunuchs. Amongst our femininity towers the palace of the Emperor himself, the only man allowed to reside in the Forbidden City.

There is a change in our pace as we come through the gates to the Outer Court, the public face of our lives. Here are mighty temples and receiving halls, watchtowers and endless courtyards, golden lions guarding marble plinths. Everywhere there are scurrying or imposing officials of varying ranks, armoured guards, colourful flags, noise. I let the curtains of my palanquin drop. I am unused to all of this. I hardly ever venture into the Outer Court except for the greatest of occasions.

We arrive at the grand receiving hall and I join the other ladies of the court there. Most I know only at a distance. I begin by making my obeisance to the Empress Fuca. She's older than I and is known as a kindly woman but she is so exalted that I see little of her. Still, she inclines her head and smiles when I bow to her. She was only sixteen when she married the Emperor and although it was an arranged marriage, still Heaven must have smiled on their union, for the two young people fell in love and have remained devoted ever since. There are many other women here at court but few have had much opportunity of advancing, since the Emperor's affections lie so firmly with his Empress. Other ladies are called to his chambers from time to time, but not as often as any of them would like and so very few have risen through the ranks. Amongst our numbers there are only two women whom everyone knows and watches, for it is clear that they are the most ambitious amongst us. I look about me and quickly spot them.

Lady Ling was only a lady-in-waiting, not even a chosen concubine, when I first came here but two years ago she caught the Emperor's eye and within a year had been promoted twice – first to an Honoured Lady like myself, then to an Imperial Concubine. I am not sure what she has done to be so liked, for she has not yet born a son, only a daughter. Whispers wondered if, being Han Chinese, she offered variety from many of the other ladies who are Manchus, but I am Han by birth myself and it has not made me a favourite. The whispers went on to suggest that she must therefore be very accomplished in the bedchamber and those who whisper watch her to see how high she can rise on such skills alone. Today she stands with her head held high, her body held erect, full of confidence. Her robes are a rich purple with complex embroidery and her hair is full of silken flowers.

The other woman whom all the court knows is Lady Ula Nara. Already a Noble Consort, only two ranks lower than the Empress herself, Ula Nara has been at court since before the Emperor was enthroned. There are others more senior to her, but Ula Nara is known to be a jealous woman. She craves the position of Empress, though that is unlikely to ever happen, for Empress Fuca has been the Emperor's Primary Consort since he was a prince and he did not hesitate to make her Empress once he ascended the throne. Today Ula Nara is in full court dress, her robes a rich yellow: not quite the imperial yellow to which she aspires, but certainly close to it. Her posture is immaculate but there is a tension in how she holds herself that speaks of something hidden below, a fear or even an anger, it is hard to tell. Her hair glitters with gems. Ula Nara is fond of jewellery.

We have gathered to mark the end of the Daughters' Draft, the lengthy selection process for new concubines, when every Manchu girl between thirteen and sixteen must be presented at court so that the Emperor may have his pick of them. Today those chosen will enter the Forbidden City and join our ranks. This is a day when the ambitious and the jealous are watchful and afraid. They scan the new faces for future rivals. The rest of us wonder what use the Emperor can have for more women when he makes little use of the ones he already has.

I find a space to stand but as other ladies arrive after me I find myself edged forwards until, to my dismay, I am side by side with Lady Ula Nara. I keep my eyes low so as not to meet her gaze and try not to move too much, so that I will not draw her attention to me. But perhaps I need not worry. Ula Nara's face is tight with tension, her eyes are locked firmly onto the great doors through which will enter first the Emperor and then each of the new arrivals.

There is much rustling and jostling for a good viewing position before a loud call announces the Emperor and we all fall to our knees to complete the sequence of kowtows required as he strides past and takes up his place on the imperial throne. By his side is the Empress Dowager, his mother, who gives him a brief smile before nodding to the Chief Eunuch to begin the naming of the girls who are about to become concubines. In theory it is the Emperor's mother who chooses each girl. In practice the choices have mostly been made through the endless checks that are made into everything from each girl's lineage and family to her body odour, height, quality of hair and demeanour. Any found wanting will have been sent away long before now. Any actual choosing the Empress Dowager has done was from a bevy of already-perfect beauties.

The naming goes on for a long time, tedious in its elaborate detail. Each girl advances, kowtows, has her family announced before being given a new name which wipes out her past and brings her like a fresh empty scroll to our world, ready to have a new destiny written upon it. There are not even that many new women this year but the proclamations are so slow there might as well be hundreds. Endless titles and allocations of silver, jewels, servants and palaces are read out for each new face. I shift in boredom and stifle a yawn. To amuse myself I do not look at any of the new girls until I have guessed by the look on Ula Nara's face how beautiful each one is. I almost laugh when her face darkens in rage and I turn to see a very beautiful girl join us. The more senior ranks are called first, before we slowly work downwards.

We have reached the Honoured Ladies, my own rank: higher than a lady in waiting but not by much. A few girls are named and enter our strange lives. I'm surprised as Ula Nara's face lightens with relief and I turn to see what manner of ugly girl has somehow slipped through the rigorous selection process.

She is not Manchu, nor Chinese. She is a Mongol, something of a rarity amongst us, with high broad cheekbones and very white skin. Her cheeks are painted pink, for the Mongols prize pink cheeks on their pale-skinned women. She seems older than many of the girls, at least sixteen and perhaps closer to seventeen. They have taken away her own traditional clothes and dressed her in the Manchu style. She will have been used to striding about in sturdy boots and now she must sway precariously on our cloud-climbing shoes, raised a full hand's width above the ground on a tiny platform requiring a good deal of practice to walk in. Her black hair has been pinned with the first white almond blossoms and she is tall, taller than many of the women here. Her eyes are dark and I think at once of a hawk or falcon, perhaps even a young eagle such as the Mongols use for hunting. Fettered by her high shoes, the heavy silken robes, her almond blossom hair, but fierce and longing to be free. This is no dainty girl who will fly to the Emperor's command. This is a wild bird. No wonder Ula Nara is relieved. She is not ugly, but no-one could imagine this girl trying hard to please the Emperor, simpering and longing for his attention. I will be surprised if she does not die here, fading away as wild birds often do if you try to cage them.

"Honoured Lady Ying," announces the Chief Eunuch and I stifle a laugh. Her new name denotes intelligence but also brings to mind the eagle. She has been well named. She looks about her, twisting her neck and shifting uneasily on her cloud-climbing shoes. As she is led past us to leave the ceremony she stumbles and a eunuch has to catch her before she falls. She stands again, flustered and angry at her loss of dignity. I smile at her, wanting to reassure her and she gives me a small tight smile in return, unsure of my intentions.

"I am Qing," I tell her before she has a chance to move away, hardly even knowing why I am addressing her. "Welcome to court," I add, almost blurting out the words.

She hovers, uncertain whether to follow the gesturing eunuch or speak with me.

"I'd follow the eunuch, if I were you."

I startle. Lady Ula Nara has been watching us and now she has intervened. I bow my head to her and Lady Ying awkwardly follows suit.

"You are new to court," says Ula Nara, speaking only to Ying and ignoring me. "You cannot be expected to know with whom you should associate. But I would suggest that you do not waste your time on those who may bring you ill luck through being supremely ill favoured." As she finishes speaking she sinks into a gracious bow to the Emperor and leaves the hall.

I stand still in front of the new arrival. I can feel heat rising up my neck and know that an ugly blotchy stain is creeping from my collarbones up into my face. I know now why I spoke to her: because I hoped that an outsider would not know what there is to know about me, that someone here might overlook my failings. I struggle to meet the curious gaze of the newcomer before she is hurried away by her guide.

Somehow I make my way from the hall and back into my palanquin, where I have a few moments of solitude to force the rising tears out of my eyes and to cool the flush of shame that has scarred me. Bao waits in my courtyard garden, eager for gossip.

"Well?" he asks before I've even alighted from my chair.

"The usual," I say. "Mostly pretty, one very beautiful that annoyed Lady Ula Nara." I pause, thinking of angry eyes under delicate almond blossom, of my crushing shame at Ula Nara's words. "And a Lady Ying," I say, despite myself.

"Who, my Lady?"

I don't even know why I said her name. I don't want to tell my loyal Bao what Ula Nara said. I have heard it too many times before from other lips and he will only hurry to reassure me, to comfort me that her truthful words were false. I shrug. "She looked cross," I say. I don't want to tell Bao that she was like a fettered eagle. He will think I have gone mad.

Bao tuts. "What has she to be cross about?" he says. "She has been chosen as a concubine for the Son of Heaven. What more could a woman wish for?"

"A glimpse of him from time to time?" I say.

Spring passes away and as the weather grows warm we move from the high red walls of the Forbidden City into the open green spaces and wide lakes of the Summer Palace. On our first day there I set out early to walk alone along the lakeside, one of my favourite pastimes.

"You spend too much time alone," sighs Bao. "You should at least walk with one of the other ladies to pick fruit or flowers. I can send a maid with you to carry baskets if you need one. Or go down to the lake house where they play card games. Why don't you spend time with the ladies there? Some are quite pleasant, I'm sure."

I shake my head. "I'm happy alone," I say with a bright smile. Bao lets me go, but not before he lets his hand rest on my head a little longer than is necessary to check my hairpins are in place and I hear him murmur a blessing for me under his breath. I leave quickly so that he will not see the sudden welling up of tears in my eyes. Bao is like a father to me but I never tell him that I am not brave enough to bear the whispers of the ladies when I draw close. What Ula Nara spoke out loud, they only mutter to one another. I would rather be lonely than ashamed.

There's a violent splashing nearby and I turn to see what is causing it. A boat is drifting on the lake, its sole occupant a concubine who is trying to master the oars. She pulls hard on one side and the boat twists round rather than gliding forward, the lesser-used oar crashing into the water so that her silken robe is splashed. She tries again and this time the boat swings the other way, turning towards me, so that she finds herself back where she was before and splashed once again. I recognise the newcomer, Lady Ying, her pale skin now pink-cheeked through her efforts alone. She is enraged.

"You stupid, stupid... useless *thing*!" she yells, her voice far louder than any lady's should ever be. She jerks at the oar, which has now become stuck in the watery depths, perhaps entangled in the lotus roots below. Her face contorts with anger and effort.

I can't help it, I laugh out loud. She is so angry, so much how I remember my first glimpse of her. Several months in our gilded cage have not tamed this eagle.

She hears me and looks up, her boat by now close to the shore. At the sight of me she tries to stand up, using one oar as a support. "Help me out of this ridiculous thing," she calls.

I start towards her but she has already pushed too hard on the oar, trying to move the boat closer to me, and the boat comes forward faster than she expected, the oar pulling her arm, unbalancing her altogether. There is a moment when she tries and fails to regain her footing and then she is in the water, spluttering and gasping. I run to her and kneel, holding out my hand from the very edge of the lake and grasping her as she reaches for me. Our hands interlock and I am conscious, for a brief moment, of the warmth from her tight grip. It is an effort to pull her out but I manage it somehow and in a few moments she stands before me, her sky blue robe now soaked to a murky grey, waterweeds clinging to her delicately embroidered silk sleeves. Her hair had been decorated with the first peonies of summer in rosy pinks but now they look bedraggled. We stand for a moment, staring at each other before she speaks.

"Thank you," she manages, in an effort at politeness, before turning to look at the boat, now drifting out of reach. "Wretched thing," she bursts out. "Now it's lost!"

"The eunuchs will bring it back," I tell her, used to having my every need met. I look her over. "You're very wet. Do you want to come to my palace – it is just over there – and have some dry clothes? My first attendant, Bao, will take care of everything."

She nods, chastened a little by her failure. I make my way towards my palace and she follows me, her robes making a stiff wet sound as the soaked silks rub together. "I am Lady Qing," I say to her, the word I use for Lady indicating to her that we are the same rank.

"They have named me Ying," she says by way of introduction.

I nod. "I saw you when you arrived," I say. I do not know if she remembers me from the day when she arrived here. I am not sure I want her to.

But she is looking away from me, across the lakes and I think that on the day she arrived she saw nobody and heard nothing, wrapped up in her own fears as each of us was when we first came here. "I didn't think I would be chosen," she says. "Not many Mongol girls are. I thought I was too tall – the other girls all looked tiny." She is quiet for a few moments. "But here I am," she says finally and her voice is flat.

Bao is appalled. A dripping wet concubine bedecked with waterweeds is a sight he has probably never encountered in his many years of service and he calls for every servant I have to help him. She is led away to my bathroom to be washed with warm water before she catches a chill. Servants are sent running to her own palace to collect dry clothes and inform her household of what has befallen their mistress.

"So careless," opines Bao, as he directs maids to fetch hot tea and little cakes, while calling for another eunuch to ensure Lady Ying's hair is properly reassembled. "Really, they should be whipped, letting their mistress go off alone. Why, anything could happen."

"I walk alone," I say.

"And I watch you from the palace to be sure nothing happens to you," retorts Bao. "She could have drowned. Why wasn't a eunuch rowing the boat for her? A lady has no need to row."

We are interrupted. Freshly dressed in a pale pink robe with tiny rosebuds from my gardens nestled in her hair, Lady Ying now seems younger and less sure of herself, hovering in the doorway. Bao excuses himself.

"Come and have tea," I offer.

She sits opposite me, takes up a small bowl of tea and sips it uncertainly. "Thank you again," she says. "You've been very kind."

"It's nothing," I say and then can't help laughing. "You've been my entertainment this morning."

She smiles, rueful. "They said a eunuch should row me. But I wanted to do it myself, like riding a horse. Only a baby would ride on a horse with someone else holding the reins," she says, some of her fierceness returning.

I think of her home in Mongolia, where they say they have fearsome warrior queens and endless flat grasslands where they can ride at full gallop. "Do you miss your home?" I ask.

She shrugs. "I will never return there, so it's as well not to think of it," she says as though repeating something she was told when parting from her family. Her tone is still fierce but her lower lip trembles.

I try to change the subject. "Perhaps we can go boating together," I find myself offering, although I have never rowed in my life and can only picture Bao's face at the thought. "It might be easier to row with two of us?"

She brightens at once. "Yes," she says. "I would like that." She looks about the room and then at me. "How long have you been at court?" she asks.

"Seven years," I say.

She nods. "Do you see the Emperor often? I mean as a companion," she adds, a small blush rising on her neck.

"Not often," I say.

"How often, though?" she asks, too new to this world to have caught my tone.

Something in me wants to tell her the truth. "Three times," I say.

"A month?" she asks, no doubt thinking this to be quite a lot considering how many women the Emperor may command to his rooms.

"In seven years," I say and see her eyes widen at the reality of her possible future here.

Only a few days passed before I emerged from my bedroom to find Lady Ying waiting for me, Bao providing her with tea but no doubt taken aback by the earliness of the hour and the boldness of a visit that was not even arranged. She waited impatiently while I got dressed – "Why bother with all that decoration in her hair if the Emperor's not going to see her?" she threw at the horrified Bao – and then all but dragged me to the lakeshore. Since then she has arrived every day and every day we flounder on the lake. When we pay attention our rowing improves, but Ying spends most of her time quizzing me about the new world she has joined, which means she does not look at what she is doing and I get distracted.

"But he can't *only* call on the Empress," she protests one day. "Otherwise what is the point of all of us other ladies?"

"Please will you pay attention to the rowing and stop talking about the Emperor?" I ask her, struggling with my own oar while hers trails uselessly in the water.

"So who else does he call on?" she persists.

I sigh and sit back, loosely holding the oar and abandoning any pretence at rowing for the day. "There's a Lady Ling," I offer.

"Who is she?"

"A nobody," I say. "She was just a lady in waiting, there are hundreds of them. She managed to catch the Emperor's eye and got promoted twice inside of a year, first to an Honoured Lady like us, then an Imperial Concubine."

"Children?" asks Ying.

I shake my head. "Only a girl."

"Can't be long till she has a son, if she's a favourite."

I shrug.

"Any other ladies in favour?"

I screw up my nose. "Not really. He and Empress Fuca really do love one another, everyone says she was the perfect match for him. He likes Lady Ling. There's Noble Consort Ula Nara – she's very highly ranked and desperate for his favour but he doesn't seem keen on her. She's very jealous, she's always throwing tantrums because of other women and he finds it annoying. She goes creeping round the place spying on the other ladies and trying to find faults with them that might get them demoted. You need to keep clear of her, she'll make things up that aren't even true if she can't find any real faults."

"Why?"

I shrug. "She was in love with a man before she was chosen as concubine," I say. "She wouldn't let go of the idea of him. It turned her bitter. She wants everyone to be as unhappy here as she is and she's spent so much time spying and making accusations that now I think she finds pleasure in making other people suffer."

Ying throws scraps of cakes to the ever-eager fish below the boat and sighs. "Do you mean to tell me I'm going to spend the rest of my life here and never even see him?"

"You might," I say. "He might take a liking to you."

"He's never seen me," she scoffs. "I was in a crowd of girls at the selection and in the presentation. I could disappear and he'd know nothing about it."

I laugh. "He would notice a disappearing concubine, even if he didn't know who you were," I say. "Now *row*."

Ying finally sees the Empress up close when we attend a silkworm-raising ceremony. Each of the ladies of the court is required to attend, for silkworms are a precious industry for our empire and the Empress sees it as her duty to request that Heaven looks kindly on it, ensuring that the delicate threads will continue to flow from the tiny corpses into the great looms that provide us with our most prized fabric. The ceremony involves much in the way of mulberry leaves being personally offered to the silkworms by the Empress and all of us ladies with our own hands, as well as many prayers.

"She's not as stuffy as I expected her to be," acknowledges Ying as we are finishing. She's right. Empress Fuca does not over-dress in jewels and imperial yellow. Today she wears a delicate blue robe embroidered with a mulberry design and her hair is bound with summer meadow-flowers rather than the formal headdresses to which she might lay claim.

"And now that we have finished our honours to the gods it is time for us to eat the fruits of this great tree," she says, laughing and waves us towards great platters heaped with ripe mulberries, their flesh sweet and juicy, so that the ladies cluster around, laughing and chattering more freely than usual. The Empress moves amongst us, smiling and speaking easily with each woman, although we can see that her conversation with Ula Nara is brief and the one with Lady Ling briefer still.

"How must it feel to know that everyone wants your throne?" murmurs Ying.

I shrug. "No-one will be getting it any time soon," I say. "So she can be light-hearted."

This year the summer days seem to pass more quickly with Ying at my side. Instead of hours of tedium, pacing by the lakeshores alone, now I have all manner of diversions. We play card games and drinking games and attend ceremonies and rituals that I used to find tedious with no-one to talk to. Ying gives me a puppy, a foolish lolloping thing that has no sense but loves to swim and throws himself into the lakes without a second thought. I name him Fish and swear he has flippers rather than legs. In turn I find her a kitten we name Golden Peach, who seemed fond of caresses at first but slowly turns into a most disdainful animal, preening and posing on the rooftops, soaking up the long summer days into her fur and wholly ignoring us unless we offer titbits. The two creatures keep us busy, either drying the foolish pup or beseeching the cat to grace us with her presence.

We get better at the rowing by the time summer comes to a close, even managing well enough so that we can talk and row at the same time. I take Ying to my favourite parts of the gardens and she terrifies my servants by standing on a swing and swinging so high we are all certain she will fall and harm herself.

"You're a scaredy," she taunts me, flying almost above my head, petals falling from her hair, robes fluttering.

"Yes I am," I call back. "You're mad!"

She forces me to stand on the swing that I have been used to idly sitting and rocking on, one foot safely on the ground. Against Bao's protestations she pushes me until my knuckles are white on the ropes. I feel the terrifying thrill of the ground rushing past me too fast to stop. My mouth opens to protest but I am unable to speak, both for fear and the air that fills my throat. Ying runs from her place behind me so that she can see my face and laughs out loud at my expression, her eyes bright, her pink lips formed into an O mimicking my own. She frowns when she sees my expression suddenly change and turns to see approaching eunuchs. Behind her, I manage to stop the swing and climb down, stumbling then rising dizzily to my feet. I know what this visit means but she does not and I do not know for whom the summons has come.

"Lady Ying?" asks one of the eunuchs.

"Yes?" she says.

"You are the chosen companion for this evening." The eunuchs bow and walk away.

She turns to me. "What do they mean?"

"You've been summoned to the Emperor's bedchamber," I say, blushing a little at having to explain. "You have to tell your first attendant," I say. "He will arrange everything and prepare you. You have to go back to your own palace at once, it'll take all day," I add, vaguely recollecting the last time I was summoned myself.

She stands confused, a little fearful. I try to smile encouragingly and she responds although it's only a half-smile. "Goodbye, then," she offers.

"Goodbye," I say.

She walks away from me and I stand alone but for Bao. He pats my shoulder. "Do not be jealous, my lady," he says. "She is new, he has to call for her at least once. Your time will come again," he adds, staunchly ignoring seven years' worth of evidence to the contrary. "I will prepare you a tea now," he says.

I nod but do not follow him. Instead I stand still, trying to understand the feelings rising up in me. I *am* jealous, but not because of the Emperor's affections. I have no craving for his company, since I barely know him. Instead I find myself angry that he has taken my new friend from me, this wild eagle who has, in one summer, made me laugh more than I have done in the seven years I have spent alone here. He has taken my playmate away so that I have no-one to splash me with muddy lake water and push me too high and too fast on a swing.

I must be going mad. It happens to the women who have been here too long. Most of them end up tending to silkworms as though they were children, or talking all day to their songbirds. The ones who have really gone too far, the ancient concubines of former emperors, live in the most distant palaces and carve gourds into strange misshapen faces.

I must stay away from gourds, I tell myself as the rest of the day passes in a haze of unending boredom, a boredom I foolishly thought had disappeared forever.

A few days pass and I don't see her. Well, it has happened as I expected, I think to myself, kicking a stone as I walk along the lake's edge. She is gone – sucked into the scheming world of the court women, plotting and planning how each of them may get a little closer to the Emperor, how they may draw attention to themselves and obscure their fellow concubines. Even Ying, who I thought was wild and different and would be hard to tame to this strange world. Even she has succumbed, the fettered bird of prey coming to the call of its master, flying to his hand without question.

More days pass and then Ying appears in my rooms. She is subdued, quiet. She turns down my offers of refreshments and silently shakes her head when I half-heartedly ask if she would like to go rowing. I feel my spirits fall further. It is as I thought. She is gone but has called on me out of a dreary, well-meant politeness, a favourite pitying a nobody.

"May we walk in your gardens?" she asks at last.

I rise. The silence indoors has grown oppressive and at least if we walk I can make meaningless small talk regarding flowers or the weather. I hope she will leave soon and return to her own palace and then leave me alone, as I used to be. No doubt I'll grow used to it again, after all I managed not to carve gourds before.

We walk a little in silence and then sit down beneath a small canopy of flowers, on cushions left there for my comfort. I say nothing about her night with the Emperor (or perhaps there was more than one night, I think sadly. Perhaps she is already a much-desired favourite). It would be unspeakably vulgar to discuss matters of the bedroom so I keep quiet. But now that we are away from the servants Ying regains her voice.

"I doubt he'll call me back again," she blurts out suddenly as we sit in my garden. Her face is turned away from me as she ostentatiously smells some flowers.

I'm desperate to know more, however improper it is to ask. I wait but she is silent. I'm blushing furiously but I have to know. "Why not?" I ask her violet-silk back.

She shrugs, hot colour creeping up her neck as she turns back to face me. "I didn't know what to do," she says. "He had to show me everything I should do and I wasn't very good at it. I think – I think I bit him," she adds in a half-whispered rush, head down.

I gasp back a laugh. "What?"

She's giggling now, looking up at me, her hands covering half her face, only her eyes peeping at me. "I didn't mean to!"

And we're both laughing helplessly, rocking back and forth on the soft cushions until she falls into my lap, her hands pressed over her mouth in a desperate effort to stop. I look down at her wide eyes and feel her whole body shake with her barely suppressed, spluttering giggles. The petals from the late roses in her hair are coming loose and drifting over my robe onto the grass and suddenly I am happy. My days of lonely boredom are over at last. She does not shy away from my bad luck with the Emperor. She has not been stolen away into the scheming world of the other women, as I had feared. She is still here – my only friend – and she is mine.

Empress

THE AUTUMN LEAVES BEGIN TO fall and we are removed from the freedom of our summer home and brought back within the high red walls of the Forbidden City, where the cold winds and hard frosts soon force us to retreat still further until we are trapped indoors. Unable to venture out, there seems to be nothing to do but play board games or drinking games. I quickly tire of both.

As ever it is Ying that changes our routine and Bao that mutters and huffs at her presumption. I am barely even dressed one chilly day, my hair hangs loose and my feet are bare, when there is an unexpected pounding on our door and Ying bursts into my rooms, still in her sleeping robe, her hair loose and ruffled from her bed, cheeks pink from the cold. Our two palaces sit side by side, only a walkway separates them.

"I couldn't bear the thought of a whole morning of dressing alone!" she exclaims. "It takes hours and I get so bored. It will be more fun together!"

Bao's face makes me giggle but I overrule his pleading glance. "Tea for Lady Ying," I instruct a maid, who gawps at the sight of the undressed visitor.

Ying is too clever not to know that it is Bao that must be won over, not I. "Bao, will you oversee my hair too?" she begs. "I had them send over my clothes. You always know what hairstyle should accompany each robe. You have such good taste."

Bao very nearly blushes. "You have no idea how to manage your servants," he says crossly. "You should whip them all for being so lazy. Sit here and I'll pin your hair first. It hasn't even been brushed!"

Ying sits, a picture of meek obedience although her eyes catch mine in the mirror and there is mischief in them.

Now there is a new rhythm to our winter days. Ying takes to her palanquin as soon as she rises from her bed. Still in her night robes, wrapped in blankets to keep her warm, she is carried all of fifty paces to my rooms, a servant trotting alongside to carry her clothes for the day. Once in my palace, she emerges from her silken cocoon and settles herself in my bedroom, where the maids help us both to dress and Bao sees to our hair. We do not rush, for what is there to hurry us? We slurp bowls of hot rice porridge and munch on warm honey buns, sip hot tea and talk endlessly of nothing. We giggle for no reason, while whoever is not being attended to lolls on my bed, night robe and blankets draped carelessly over bare legs and arms. It takes us till the middle of the day to be correctly attired for anyone to see us. We quickly lose any shyness at seeing one another half-dressed, playing silly games of catch around the rooms while the maids giggle at our foolishness and Bao holds his hands up in horror when our hair, only half-pinned, falls back down our backs, gemstones hitting the floor as maids scurry to collect them.

"Why doesn't she just *live* here," Bao grumbles, but after a while he finds out how to prepare Mongolian specialities and has them made for her as a surprise. He keeps stocks of her favourite teas and sweets ready and waiting for her daily visits and is grudgingly proud that she would rather spend her time in my palace – or his household, as he no doubt thinks of it, than her own. She flatters him while he mutters about her being a nuisance to dress. "Always on the move, always giggling and being foolish, leading my mistress astray with your nonsense. She never used to cause me half the trouble *you* do. Be off with you now," he adds, as darkness falls and the lanterns are lit in my courtyard. "Back to your own rooms, shoo. I cannot imagine what your good-for-nothing servants do all day, since you are always here."

Ying only ever laughs at him and waves as she enters her chair. She grins at me before pulling the curtain closed over her tiny palanquin window and I lift my hand to bid her farewell from where I stand inside the doorway of my rooms. Bao drags me away. "Too cold! You will catch your death and I shall be blamed for it, oh yes, it is always the servants that are blamed when their mistresses are so stubborn."

"I miss her when she goes," I say sadly. "My rooms seem empty without her."

"*Miss* her?" echoes Bao. "How can you miss her? You know very well she will be here tomorrow morning before I have even had a chance to have the fires lit. What do you want her to do, stay the night? Sleep in your bed? The two of you are inseparable. At least you are happy now you have a friend," he adds. "Though you don't talk to your poor old Bao any more, oh no. Too busy with your precious Lady Ying to remember your loyal servant."

I laugh and slap away his hands that are held up in mock pity. "You should be pleased," I say. "You used to tell me off for complaining that I was bored."

"Oh heavens yes," agrees Bao. "I can do my work now that I don't have you following me about like a lost puppy. Thank goodness the two of you have each other. It's not as though either of you has the Emperor's eye," he can't help adding.

"No, we don't," I say flatly. "I'm glad you've stopped hoping."

"One should never stop hoping," says Bao piously.

"I can't stay indoors anymore," says Ying early one morning, as soon as she has arrived. "Let's go out."

"Out where?" I ask, looking at the whirling snow that has been falling all morning and the thick drifts that have piled over the plant pots in my courtyard.

"Out!" she laughs. "In the snow. The servants say that the streams have all frozen up and the snow is as high as a man's knees or more."

"You are *not* going out," says Bao. "And that is final. You will catch a chill and die."

But we insist and he has to content himself with our hurried dressing, our half-pinned hair, heaping both of us up with fur-lined robes and boots until we look like bears, before standing at the window wringing his hands to watch us venture into the increasing snowstorm.

It's freezing. I stand on the walkway of my garden, catching my breath at the shock of the cold after my cosy rooms, where *kangs* burn day and night to keep me warm.

"Come!" says Ying, holding out her hand to me. I take it and step gingerly down from my covered walkway onto the cobbles. I sink to my knees at once, my boots making walking hard going.

We teeter along the tiny lanes of the Inner City, breaking off icicles to suck on, giggling when we slip and fall backwards, staggering to pull one another back up. When we come to the gateways leading to the Outer City I hesitate. But Ying, still tugging at icicles behind me, urges me on and I step forwards alone.

I have never seen the Forbidden City like this. The vast public courtyards, usually so busy with officials and servants, palanquins and guards, stand silent and empty. Whiteness is everywhere and the once-golden rooftops now sparkle with icicles, their imperial colour lost to the might of the snow that has drifted down from Heaven.

I'm about to cautiously step out into the vast space when I'm nearly knocked over by a blow to the head and jerk round to see Ying, doubled over with laughter, her hands forming a second snowball to lob at me. But I'm too fast for her, grabbing a handful of snow and throwing it at her, a straight hit to the belly. Soon we are running round the endless snow-filled landscape, hurling snowballs and laughing so hard it hurts. I slip and fall and she holds out a hand to help me up, clasping me to her as I try to stand, unsteady on the icy flagstones beneath my feet.

"What good friends you are," says a low voice.

I turn from Ying's arms to see Ula Nara standing in the gateway between the Inner and Outer Courts, blocking our way back to the safety of our palaces. Dressed all in a dark blue silk, trimmed with thick brown fur, her face white from the cold, she stands, framed by the spent red lanterns and the whiteness all around her, making her seem an even darker figure than she already is.

We manage to bow, feeling the cold seep back into us after our exertions. "Lady Ula Nara," I manage. "Are you well?"

She doesn't move, doesn't respond to our bows although a strange smile curves her lips. "I was told the two of you were friendly," she says. "I did not know you were *such* good friends."

I feel Ying stiffen beside me and her hand slide away from where she was gripping me by the elbow, trying to keep me upright a moment ago. Unsure of what to do or say I remain silent and Ula Nara's smile grows broader. "I'll take that silence as agreement, shall I?" she says. She turns away and is gone in a moment, nothing but whirling snow where she was standing, as though she was a vision, a ghost.

I turn to Ying. "Ignore her," I say.

But Ying's face has lost its happiness. "It is as you said," she replies, her voice devoid of emotion. "She wants to find fault, even if it means braving a snowstorm to do her snooping."

I spread my hands. "What fault could she find?" I ask. "We were having a snow fight!

What is wrong with that?" I know, even as I say this, that I am not quite being honest. There is something between us that Ula Nara can sense, something she has seen before I have even given it a name.

Ying looks at me for a moment and then smiles. "It's cold," she says and puts her arm about my shoulders to lead me back inside. "Bao will be beside himself at how long we have stayed out."

The darkest days of winter are upon us and the Empress is closed away from view. Smallpox visited Beijing and made its way inside the Forbidden City. Despite the inoculations practiced so assiduously within the imperial household, her young son has died. He was her second son to die young and she has no others. The Emperor is grim faced at court although very gentle to his Empress and for now she keeps to her rooms, where he has sent every kind of gift to ease her sorrow: from winter berry branches artfully arranged to platters of sweets and poems in his own hand. This child should have been their heir, all of us know that it would have been his name kept in the golden box behind the throne. After the Emperor's death it would have been opened to reveal the name of his successor, the little boy who has now been taken away. Now the box is empty, awaiting another name. The court waits to see what battle-lines will be drawn. Will the Empress rally herself to bear more children, even though she is now fully thirty-six years old? Or will a younger concubine provide the future Emperor and in so doing supersede the current Empress to become, one day, that most important of all the women at court: a Dowager Empress?

The Emperor is not about to give up hope of an heir from his beloved Empress. When the astrologers tell him that the Empress must not remain in the palace, for fear of evil influences in her chart, he orders that a tour be arranged to Shandong in the south-east. This, he has determined, will be of benefit to her wellbeing. She surely cannot fail to be stirred by such sights as Mount Tai and the birthplace of Confucius himself. The tour is organised with all due speed and before the first month of spring can reach us a party of courtiers, concubines and our accompanying servants have been selected. I am surprised to find myself and Ying amongst the party, but pleased not to have be left behind as some of the older ladies have been.

"You are to provide gaiety and entertainment," the Chief Eunuch lectures us. "His Majesty wishes for Empress Fuca to be surrounded by happy faces."

I can't imagine that a woman who has just lost her child much wishes to be surrounded by the cheerful countenances of younger concubines, each plotting for their own ascent, but if that's what the Emperor wants, it is what he will get. Servants rush back and forth packing fur-lined robes and thick boots as well as lighter clothes should spring come early. Guards and officials ready themselves and soon thousands of people flood out through the gates of the Forbidden City, leaving it quiet behind us.

The tour is pleasant enough and seems to improve the Empress' wellbeing as planned.

She prays at the temple of Mount Tai and the Emperor spends much of his time by her side, their heads tenderly together, her every wish granted. As we move from place to place we accustom ourselves to the new lodgings in which we are placed each time. Ying and I are often placed in nearby houses and enjoy visiting new gardens. Uncalled for, as usual, we spend our time together.

One garden we visit draws most of the ladies, for its large pond and fountains create an attraction. We gather the first flowers of spring and enjoy the warm rays of the sun. I lean over the edge of the pond feeding the eager fish while Ying sits beside me. Most of the other ladies sit nearby, playing board games or chattering amongst themselves.

"When we return to Beijing we will have moved back to the Summer Palace and can go boating again," says Ying and I nod eagerly.

"Always together, always planning to be alone?"

The two of us sit silent, not looking up at Ula Nara's too-loud voice but down at the darting orange fish. Slowly I raise my head and see the eyes of all the other ladies on us. My heart sinks at the unwanted attention.

"You are welcome to join us, Lady Ula Nara," says Ying boldly. I feel a shiver of fear. Ula Nara cannot be so easily got rid of, she can use anything you say against you. It would be better to stay silent but I do not know how to signal this to Ying.

Ula Nara's smile broadens, as though Ying has given her an unexpected opportunity. "I wouldn't dream of it," she says. "Two is so romantic. Three – well that is just clumsy, don't you think?"

Ying's face is growing thunderous. I frown at her to keep quiet but she ignores me and rises to her feet. Ula Nara, even in her highest shoes, is shorter than her. "Is there an accusation you wish to make, Lady Ula Nara?"

The women around us have been quiet, watching while seeming not to watch too closely. Now the silence is absolute and no-one feigns indifference.

Ula Nara's smile doesn't fade. "Accusation? Is there an accusation to be made?" she asks. "I had not meant anything by my remarks but if there is something you would like to tell me, Lady Ying…"

Ying's mouth opens but I grab at her hand and she closes it again, stands silent, her eyes narrow and angry.

"Holding hands," says Ula Nara, still smiling. "How sweet."

I let go of Ying's hand and watch as Ula Nara moves away, still smiling. The other ladies pretend to look away and begin to whisper amongst themselves, still darting glances our way. Only Lady Ling is silent, gazing at Ying and I with an expression of curiosity and interest, head tilted to one side. When she sees me watching her she smiles, not unpleasantly, and holds my gaze too long before I drop my head and return to my rooms, Ying stubbornly remaining where she is. Bao tuts when I relate the story and mutters unpleasant things under his breath about Ula Nara and her devious ways. "Pay no attention to her," he says as he tucks me into my bed. "She will forget about you soon enough and bother someone else."

In the early morning I am still only half-dressed when Bao hurries into my bedchamber. "Lady Ula Nara is here," he hisses.

I can think of no reason why she would call on me at this hour and my belly knots at the thought of yesterday, of her words aimed like poisonous arrows at Ying and I.

"She says she wants to see you."

"Like this?" I say, indicating my loose hair, my bare feet.

Bao gestures helplessly. "She insisted," he tells me and I know that even Bao, for all his loyalty to me and commanding ways in my household, for all his muttered words about her, is afraid of Ula Nara.

I make my way to the living room, where I find Ula Nara standing by the window looking out into my garden.

"My lady," I say, bowing. "You find me unready for visitors."

She turns to look at me, her eyes taking in every part of me from my ruffled hair down to my feet, now encased in little silk shoes to at least keep me warm. She towers over me, wearing cloud-climbing shoes far higher than those of most of the ladies. Her lips curve into something approaching a smirk. "Were you... *busy*, Lady Qing?" she asks.

"I was asleep," I say, "and not expecting visitors." I want my voice to sound cool but I hear my words tremble.

"I came to give you a gift," she says.

I wait, silent. I will not give her the satisfaction of showing curiosity.

She gestures towards a silk-wrapped parcel on my table.

I don't move towards it. Whatever game she is playing, I want no part of it. There is no gift Ula Nara could give me that I would want to receive, of this I'm sure.

"A gift for you," she says. "Something to peruse in your bedchamber, perhaps? Or with ... a *friend?*"

I stay silent.

"Well, I will be going," she says.

I bow and gesture to Bao that he should show her out. Left alone, I pick up the parcel and slowly unwrap it.

It is an album of paintings. I have seen such albums before. I was shown them before I joined the court, as part of my education as a future bride for the Emperor and I saw them once in the Emperor's rooms. In such an album there are many depictions of what goes on between a man and a woman. They can be used for private titillation, for the education of young women and men, for lovers to look at together and be aroused. I bite my lip. Why would Ula Nara give me this? I turn to the first page. It is a painting of two women, standing by a tree in full blossom. The robes of the first woman are loose, the second cups her breast in one hand. I feel my cheeks grow warm and turn to the next painting. Two women kiss, their arms wrapped around one another while ripe fruits hang above their heads. I turn each painting faster and faster. Women embrace, kiss, touch one another. They lie in bedchambers among crumpled sheets, undress in gardens, reach out for one another in flower-filled pavilions. They throw back their heads in pleasure and laugh intimately together, their naked bodies entwined.

There are hardly any men. Every album I have ever seen depicts men and women together. Sometimes there are women pleasuring one another, but mostly under the gaze of a man. Here there are almost entirely women, in painting after painting. I stand, holding the album, my eyes unseeing as I gaze at the garden outside. Ula Nara means to imply things about Ying and I with this gift, she means to taunt, to threaten, to make me afraid that she will reveal something about me, about us, Ying and I, to others. She seeks to find the weak point of every woman here at court and press so hard upon it that those women crack under the pressure, withdraw from any competition for the Emperor's gaze. She makes each woman afraid, uncertain, ashamed that her secrets will be found out, however foolish and unimportant they may be.

I try to comfort myself. I *have* no secrets, I think. Ying is my friend. There is nothing of this forbidden intimacy between us, as Ula Nara implies. The gift is meaningless. Why does she want to target us anyway? I have no interest in the Emperor and have been shown no favour. Ying may be new here but already she has been found wanting. Ula Nara's threat, masquerading as a gift, is without strength, without power. A tiny voice inside me says that this is not true, but I push it away. I am afraid of Ula Nara finding anything in me that she can use against me.

But I find myself hiding the album away. I slip it inside my own personal travelling box of belongings, where my servants will not find it. Even as I hide it I wonder why I do not just hand it to Bao to be disposed of, but I have no answer, even for myself. I do not mention the album to Ying but I am conscious that in the presence of the other ladies now I am stiff and silent with her and I do not allow so much as our robes to brush one another. The days pass and I feel a sad ache for something easy between us that has been lost.

We are reaching the end of our tour and there is a grand banquet, a tedious affair as usual, for there is nothing to do but wear even more elaborate clothes, eat ever greater amounts of food and be admired by the officials and courtiers, whilst speaking mostly only amongst ourselves. Almost everyone is in place, mostly chattering about an unexpected snow flurry, too late in spring to be usual, that chased us all indoors yesterday, but there is a notable absence.

"The Empress has caught a chill and will not be attending the banquet," explains the serving eunuch closest to me, when I raise a questioning eyebrow.

We nod, uninterested. Few of us are close friends with the Empress, for she is always by the Emperor's side. Only Ula Nara brightens and avails herself of the space closest to the Emperor, as she is the highest-ranking amongst us. Ling watches her with a small smile. Ula Nara may be higher-ranked, she can edge her way closer to the Emperor at any banquet or public event she chooses to, but it is Ling who is called again and again to the Emperor's rooms, seemingly without even trying.

The banquet is long and slow. Seated amongst the women there is little conversation, for too many women here think of nothing but how to make their way into the Emperor's affections and do not want to make friends with a possible rival.

In the morning we are informed that the Empress' chill has not improved, so there are few plans for the day and we are left to make our own choices, a rare occurrence on this journey. I wrap up in furs and walk in the gardens, nod to a few of the other ladies. We are bored, we thought we would be heading home by now, but we cannot leave if the Empress is still unwell. I see Ying in the distance and rather than hurry to her side I find myself edging away, wondering whether I can return to my own rooms without her noticing. I am afraid of the other ladies' too-bold stares when Ying and I are together, their curious looks and sometimes the whispers between them, as though we were some sort of object of curiosity, some rare breed rather than two among the many women here. But Ying is too quick and she catches me up as I reach my rooms.

"You have to tell me what Ula Nara has done to you," she says, exasperated and out of breath. "You're silent when we are in company and you move away from me any time I come near you. Did she see you again after that time by the fish pond?"

I don't need to ask who 'she' is. I nod unwillingly.

"Well?"

"She gave me a gift," I say.

"Gift? Ula Nara? Why?"

I shake my head at her, for there are maids present. I go to my room and fetch the album of paintings, then lead Ying out into the gardens with me. I hand it to her at arm's length and watch her face as she looks through it. She blushes when she sees what it is but as she leafs through the pages I see her face grow still and her lips part. I wonder if I have shocked her very greatly, if perhaps they do not have such albums in Mongolia. I am about to ask for it back, to say that it is stupid and I will have it thrown away, when I hear footsteps nearby. Too late I see a figure approaching and see Ula Nara approaching. I grab at Ying and all but drag her inside the shelter of a huge willow tree that falls, cavern-like, over a secluded part of the garden. "Shush," I hiss. "Shush!"

We stand pressed closed together, arms about one another trying to make ourselves smaller, listening for Ula Nara's footsteps. She does not call out to find me, nor summon a servant. Instead her steps are slow and cautious, soft as she can make them. I try not to move. I cannot see Ying's face but I can feel her warmth slowly seeping into me through our robes, feel her breath on my neck. She does not hold me stiffly but rather embraces me as though it were the most natural thing in the world, allowing her head to rest on my shoulder, her body soft against me rather than stiff with fear as I am. I take a deep breath to try and calm myself and find myself inhaling her perfume, a delicate thing of light flowers and fresh air after the rain. For a brief moment I forget about Ula Nara and simply enjoy the sensation of being embraced. Bao often clasps my hands and sometimes rubs my back if it aches but I don't believe I have been embraced since I enter the Forbidden City, since I left my family behind, never to see them again. The Emperor perhaps embraced me on those three occasions when I was in his rooms but I was too awkward and afraid to relax into his arms. I have been here seven years without feeling love from another person and now I am embraced. I think for a moment of the paintings, of two women standing beneath a fruiting tree, embracing as we are, their arms about one another, their lips upon one another's lips and I feel a heat rise up in me. I begin to pull away.

But the footsteps have stopped. There is complete silence, broken only by a bird, singing. A brief trill and then silence again. I try to see but all I have sight of is leaves and the grass beneath our feet. Then I see two feet. Perched on blue silken cloud-climbing shoes, their owner shifting from one to the other as she turns about. It is Ula Nara and she is so close she must be able to hear our breathing. In a moment she will see us, for if she looks down she will surely see our feet.

"My Lady Ula Nara!"

It is Bao's voice, his tone surprised, his voice very loud. I see the blue shoes turn away from us towards him and then see Bao's face near the shoes as he falls to his knees before Ula Nara. "My Lady! We have been remiss in welcoming you. Are you lost in the gardens? Are you here to visit my Lady Qing?"

"No – no," I hear Ula Nara reply, her tone reluctant. "I was only wandering. I was – lost, as you say," she adds.

"Let me accompany you back to your own palace," says Bao, all concern. He raises his face from the ground and as he does so catches my eye for a moment. His face does not change at the sight of Ying and I embracing. He rises, and I see him accompany Ula Nara out of the garden, their footsteps fading.

I release Ying. "She was about to find us!" I say. I laugh a little, embarrassed at how long we have been embracing. "If she'd seen us she would have thought all her silly comments were true!" I add, my voice a little too loud.

Ying doesn't laugh. Her eyes are serious as she meets mine. Her gaze flickers for a moment to my lips and then she smiles and looks away, shrugging a little. "Ula Nara sees what she wants to see," she says.

I walk behind Ying as she makes her way back to my palace. Outside it she stops and turns to me. "I will return to my rooms for now," she says, her voice quieter than usual. "I am a little tired."

I nod and smile, then wave to her as she makes her way out of my garden to where her bearers await. Only as I turn back to my own rooms do I think that, in all the time I have known her, I have never heard Ying say she is tired.

We do not speak of Ula Nara again, nor of the album, which I return to its hiding place. But it is as though a heavy burden has been lifted, and we no longer act oddly amongst the other ladies, instead we spend time together as usual, as though daring Ula Nara to comment, but she does not. She has other concerns.

The Empress has grown gravely ill. Her chill may have been of little concern at first but she seems to have had no strength to fight it and now one physician after another visits her rooms and the Emperor is seen pacing the floor. Banquets and other events are cancelled and we are told to pray for Her Majesty's good health, which we do, somewhat bemused by the sudden change in our party's nature – we have gone from pleasure-seeking diversions to carers for an invalid in a matter of days.

At last the Emperor orders that we should embark onto the imperial barges to take us back to Beijing. He is dissatisfied with the Empress' care and decrees that we must return to her own palace, where she will feel more content and recover quickly. Servants hurry to prepare everything and we make our way into the small cabins that will carry us back toward Beijing. Ahead of us is the barge carrying the Empress, swaddled in silken covers and surrounded by concerned physicians.

Night falls and still we have not set sail. Ying is in her own cabin and I feel as though I cannot breathe in my own. I wish she was at my side so that I could talk to someone but we have been told to remain within our own quarters. Lanterns begin to glow along the edge of the canal and looking out from the barge windows I see swaying, shadowy forms lining the banks and hear distant chanting. The air seems full of foreboding.

"Officials and monks, praying for Her Majesty," Bao tells me as he undresses me for bed, shooing away too-curious maids. "Stop peeping out, you silly girls. How unseemly," he tuts.

He doesn't stop me though and I watch as the kneeling shadows bow and bow again. "Is she very ill, Bao?" I ask. The chanting is beginning to grate on me, I want to stuff my ears with something to escape its endless repetition.

"Who can tell," he says, wrapping a sleeping robe about me. "She has been well enough until now. And it was only a chill, she should have recovered by now. But the loss of a child…" He sighs and shakes his head. "Now into bed," he adds, all but pulling me towards the heavy blankets he has arranged for me on my already-heaped up bed. "I will not have you catching a chill as well."

I lie awake for a while. This has been a strange journey for me. I have seen more of Ula Nara than I care to and she has frightened me, for to have her follow you like a dog scenting its quarry is a fearsome thing. I worry for Ying and I, that we will be somehow tainted by her suspicions, and yet I cannot stay away from Ying. She is my friend, my companion, the person who has made my life here more pleasant than it has been in the past seven years when I was alone and forgotten. I am too weary to strategise. Instead I fall asleep and dream strange dreams, of dark shadows that may or may not be Ula Nara watching me, of lips too close to mine which are not the Emperor's but those of an unseen woman.

In the darkness of my bedchamber the barge rocks unsteadily and a hammering at the outer doors wakes me. My household stirs. I sit up in bed, straining to hear. Bao loudly demands to know what is the meaning of this disturbance at such an hour and receives a muttered reply, which leaves him without words. I wait, as the eunuch on guard lights a lantern. I pull a cover about my shoulders, hearing Bao's quick footsteps. The door opens and he stands framed in the shadows.

"What is wrong?" I ask.

"The Empress is dead," pants Bao and with those four words our whole world changes.

Emperor

W E DRESS IN WHITE AND our hair hangs loose down our backs, flowers and gemstones forgotten, a sign of respect and mourning for the Empress. The men's queues are cut short. We look like ghosts wandering about the court, hungry for news, for gossip, for direction now that our hierarchy has been smashed, its glittering shards dangers on which the unwary may tread.

The Emperor is red-eyed with grief. I have never seen him like this. He refuses to carry out his usual tasks of administration, leaving important papers, official appeals and the generals of his vast army without response or direction. The only rituals he will carry out are those involving prayers. He stumbles his way from temple to temple, bowing and praying, praying and bowing, white-faced, his every move surrounded by clouds of incense and chanting monks. He commanded that his Empress' body should be brought back to Beijing without leaving the imperial barge. Sailing up the canal was accomplished readily enough but once close to Beijing the entire barge had to be dragged out of the water on a hastily-constructed wooden track greased with vegetable leaves. Hundreds upon hundreds of labourers were needed to pull the barge through the streets of Beijing to the Forbidden City. The Palace of Eternal Spring, once her own magnificent home, now acts as a mausoleum for her to lie in state, before she is interred. Each of us must visit to pay our respects and more often than not the Emperor is by her side, tears flowing down his face. When my turn comes I don't know where to look or what to say, so I perform the most formal of kowtows both to him and to the Empress' body, my forehead knocking on the cold hard floor, my face hidden from view. When I rise I hesitate, wondering whether I should offer words of comfort or reach out to touch his heaving shoulders. But although I am his concubine, I barely know this man. He might as well be a stranger to me and so I retreat, my footsteps as quiet as I can make them. He does not raise his head.

I see him again in one of the grand receiving halls as he reads out memorials and poems sent by officials and noble houses throughout his empire. They offer tribute to the 'loyal and wise' Empress, praising her beauty, her goodness, her love for the Emperor and his for her. He cannot stop tears falling and has to pause often, but he will not allow his officials to take over the task. I stand silent, amidst the other women of the court, each of us taken aback by the strength of his grief. Even the Chief Eunuch, chosen for his abilities to manage any and every situation, looks lost. How to handle the Son of Heaven when his godlike exterior has shattered like some exquisite porcelain shell and revealed the Emperor to be only a man after all?

There is a pause in the readings and the Emperor sits more upright. He gestures to the Chief Eunuch and there is a consultation, during which his face darkens. We watch, too far away to make out what is being said, all of us women and courtiers straining to make out what is making the Emperor angry.

"It seems," he announces suddenly, his voice stronger, "that certain officials, whom I believed loyal to me, have not seen fit to offer their condolences to me, nor praise our beloved Empress."

"They must be mad," whispers Ying to me. "Why would you not send your condolences? Everyone knows it is the correct thing to do, surely?"

I dip my head in a small nod. Whoever these officials are, if they could see the Emperor's face at this moment they would deeply regret their oversight.

The Emperor stands. He is a tall man. Now he is angry. The court stiffens, no-one daring to move, to draw attention to themselves at this dangerous moment.

"We have been given a list of over fifty names," he says. "Those who have not seen fit to pay homage to our Empress will be punished for their lack of respect. Those from the Han Chinese families will be demoted by two grades."

There's a murmur of sycophantic assent from the court, although nobody cares to meet the Emperor's eyes.

"They have been shown leniency because they are not Manchu," he adds. "They cannot be expected to show the proper behaviour expected of our own people."

Silence. We had all thought that it was the Manchu officials who would be shown leniency. Now courtiers turn their heads to meet one another's eyes, wondering what will happen to those who will receive a harsher punishment. Greater demotions? Exile perhaps?

"These people should have been howling in sadness," declares the Emperor. His voice is growing louder and less controlled, wavering as his eyes fill with tears. The Chief Eunuch looks afraid. The Emperor has never behaved like this before. "They should have rushed forward to beat their breasts in sorrow and make their pain known to us."

The Empress Dowager, sitting close to the Emperor, reaches out a hand and gently touches his, perhaps attempting to calm him, but he takes no notice.

"We have also heard that there are people who have not followed the regulations of mourning. There have been weddings and music within the prohibited period. There have been men who have not shaved their queues and women who have dressed their hair with adornments. There are those who have not worn mourning clothes."

I glance at Ying and both of us shake our heads slightly. There may not have been many of these people but they have been fools. They are about to be punished for something they could so easily have avoided.

"It is intolerable!"

We jump. The Emperor has shouted – no, screamed this last. The sound of over two hundred people falling to their knees is followed by absolute silence, each of us wishing to be anywhere else but here. None of us can see his face when he speaks again.

"They will forfeit their lives for this affront to the Empress Fuca," says the Emperor, his voice breaking on her name.

The court tiptoes. The Emperor, even though he holds the power of life and death, has until now in his reign been known as a peaceable man. Devoted to his duties as ruler, pleasant and even loving to his women, filial to his mother and kindly towards his young children. Now he has shown another side to his character and it is one that none of us wishes to see again. Mourning efforts are redoubled. Ever more tributes are made to the Empress. The courtiers spend as little time at court as they can manage, fearful of making some error, some blunder that will unwittingly earn the Emperor's wrath. The great halls are silent and only the monks in the temples can feel safe, endlessly chanting for the Empress while the Emperor kneels among them.

The bamboo name chips denoting each concubine go untouched on their silver tray in the Emperor's bedchamber. None of the women is called to his side. The days and weeks wear on and still no lady is named as a companion. The women who used to be called on occasionally are lost. They worry, they fret. They glance sideways at myself and Ying, at the older concubines, those of us who were never called upon and are afraid they will be forgotten too.

But two women among us have spotted their chance. Even amidst mourning and fear, the court cannot help but speculate on the path that each will now choose. There are only two names on the lips of the gossips. Ling. And Ula Nara.

Ula Nara shows her hand first. She is Manchu by birth, even if her family is nowhere near as exalted as the late Empress'. An Empress should be Manchu and Ling, however much a favourite, is Han Chinese by birth, even if her family have been made honorary Manchus. Does this give Ula Nara an advantage? Could she become the next Empress? Or will Ling be preferred and her Chinese origins be brushed aside? Ula Nara knows that if she wishes to be seated at the side of the Dragon Throne, she has to move – and move quickly. This may be her only chance.

She is seen to offer herself up for the rituals that must be performed. Empress or no Empress, there are tasks that must be undertaken. Prayers at certain temples on certain days. Rituals must be continuously carried out to ensure good crops, good weather, strong children, a powerful empire, a strong dynasty. Some of these tasks fall to the Emperor. Others traditionally fall to the Empress. In the absence of a living Empress, a senior woman of the court must undertake them and now Ula Nara shows that she has not been idle during the many years that she has resided in the Forbidden City. She may have spied on every other woman at court but she has also been learning court etiquette. The days go by and it becomes plain that there is not one ritual that Ula Nara does not know how to perform. Where one of the other women among us, even one of high rank, might stumble or be uncertain, might need some guidance, Ula Nara never falters. She must have watched the Empress at every event she has ever attended, for Ula Nara knows the correct day and time to perform every ritual. She knows every move and word, the correct offering to each deity, each motion to be made. She makes her way from one event to another, flawless in her execution. Her bows are immaculate, her prayers clear and well-spoken.

"But he's never cared for her," objects Bao. "And surely the Emperor will make the choice of who is to be his next Empress?"

But for once it seems Bao is wrong, for it becomes known that even against the Emperor's grief-stricken and stubborn refusal to appoint another Empress, a higher authority has made herself known. The Empress Dowager, the only person alive whom the Emperor himself must bow to, has made a decision. She insists that a new Empress must be appointed, that a court without an Empress is no court at all. She has forced this request on the Emperor and he has unwillingly acceded to her authority as his mother. And for some reason it seems she favours Ula Nara. She praises her for her grace and poise, for her knowledge of court etiquette, for her extraordinary ability to produce from memory every possible lineage of the Qing dynasty and every dynasty before them. To recite poems appropriate to the moment, to speak with elegance and confidence on any topic. Ula Nara is a seeker and keeper of secrets. Now her own secret knowledge is revealed and it might just earn her the imperial yellow she so badly craves.

"It can't just be because of her knowledge of etiquette," opines Ying. "Ula Nara knows something about the Dowager Empress. Trust me."

I think of the solemn-faced Dowager Empress and can't imagine what possible secrets she could have. "Like what?" I ask Ying.

Ying shakes her head. "She knows something," she insists. "And if she doesn't know then she has made something up."

I think of Ula Nara standing in the whirling snow, her dark eyes watching Ying and me throwing snowballs and laughing. Her secret smile and insinuating words.

"Well whatever she knows, she's about to get what she wants," I say. "She'll be made Empress, you wait and see."

Ying nods slowly. "Maybe then she'll be happy and stop spying on other people," she says, but she sounds doubtful.

But while Ula Nara has boldly shown her hand and made it clear that nothing but the imperial yellow robes will do for her, that she will not be satisfied until she is seated at the Emperor's side wearing the kingfisher-blue feathered headdress of an Empress, Ling seems to have all but disappeared.

"I thought she was ambitious," I say to Bao.

Bao is pinning up my hair. His hands pause in mid-air. "Lady Ling has chosen a different path," he says.

"What other path is there for a lady at court?" I ask. "There's only one path here and it leads upwards to the Empress if you are popular and down to those poor crazed wretches in the back palaces if you're forgotten about or widowed. Every woman wants to be the Empress or as close as they can get. And how many times in a lifetime does the possibility of becoming Empress open up before us?"

Bao shakes his head. "How many Emperors have been born to an Empress?" he asks me.

I've never really thought about it. "I don't know," I say.

"None," he tells me. "Every Emperor has been born to a concubine."

I think about this.

"And," says Bao, "who is the most important woman at court?"

"The Empress," I say without thinking.

Bao shakes his head. "No, she's not," he says. "The most important woman at court is the Empress Dowager. The Empress must bow to her, even the Emperor must bow to her."

"So?"

"So," says Bao. "I don't believe Lady Ling wants to be the Empress. She has a greater plan. She wants to bear the next Emperor, and become the next Dowager Empress. Look at the Emperor's mother, how well she is treated: he does everything for her, she has only to utter a desire and it is done. She's not even that old, she might live for years and years and be treated always as the most important woman at court."

I shrug. "Good luck to her," I say, thinking of the imperial children who have already died, those whose names were inscribed with such care in the golden box and are no longer living to claim their place as future heirs. "If Ling wants children she'd better make the Emperor start calling women to his chambers again."

The gossip begins slowly, as the autumn leaves turn from green to blazing colours. It seems that at last a woman was called to the Emperor's rooms, and it was Lady Ling, as any of us might have expected. But the next night another woman is called for and this time it is one of the youngest recruits, a girl named Jasmine, whose delicate body and child-like features marks her out as the newest amongst us. Another night and it seems Jasmine has been found wanting, for now a more senior woman is called in and then another. Women are being called every night to the Emperor's rooms and their servants are kept busy, but the gossip grows ever greater, for it seems that the chosen women are returning to their palaces silent, a little downcast, unwilling to boast of their new-found attention.

"And Lady Ling was called last night," says Bao.

"I heard it was one of the others," I say, puzzled.

Bao shakes his head. "She has been called every night," he says.

"No she hasn't,'" I object. "It was Jasmine and then that other girl, the tall one, and then it was..."

Bao shakes his head at me in the mirror where he is unpinning my hair. He takes away the last golden pins and wipes away my makeup. I look into the mirror, my hair loose, my shoulders bare before Bao wraps my sleeping robe about me. His voice is very low. "It seems Lady Ling is at the Emperor's side every night," he says.

"But..." I begin again.

"Every night," says Bao. "No matter who else is called."

I frown. "Are the other ladies lying?" I ask, fumbling at the truth. "Are they not really being called to his rooms?"

Bao looks at me, his head tilted, in silence. I think about what he is saying and can feel a blush beginning as I remember Ula Nara's gift to me. How, leafing through the pages, I had seen the image of an older woman, her robes loosened to expose her breasts, standing by the side of a man, guiding him inside a young woman who was lying back on a table, her body fully naked.

"You may go now," I tell Bao and he leaves me with no further words.

Alone, I climb into my bed and lie still for a few moments before I reach down the side of the bed to find the album of paintings I hid there when we returned from our journey. In the dim light of the two lanterns left burning in my room I open the album and look through the pages. The flickering light casts shadows onto the images, so that they seem to move. I feel my breath come a little faster at the thought of being discovered with such a book and yet I keep turning the pages, looking at each image longer than I have ever looked at them before. When I have finished I hide the book again and try to sleep but it is a long time before sleep comes to me and when it does it brings dreams of entwined bodies and kissing lips, of gardens where petals fall from fresh flowers and breasts ripen like fruits. I awake in the darkness of the night with one hand pressed to my sex and the other tangled in my long hair, my body drenched in sweat, filled with a desperate unfulfilled desire that grips me in its claws.

Morning comes and I sleep longer than usual after my restless night. I wake to the sounds of the servants hurrying about and assume Ying must have arrived. But when I peep out of my room, wrapped in my sleeping robe, hair still ruffled from my tossing and turning of the night, there is no sign of her. Instead, maids are rushing to carry hot water to my bathroom while Bao, red-faced and sweating, is looking over my very finest clothes and seeming none too pleased with them.

"Is something wrong?" I ask, standing in the doorway, ignored by everyone.

Bao turns to me, flustered. "You are called on."

"What?"

"You have been summoned."

"Summoned where?" I ask, still stupid from lack of sleep.

"To the *Emperor*," says Bao, exasperated. "You are his chosen companion for tonight. And there is *nothing* suitable for you to wear," he adds, almost in tears.

I stand, silent. I can feel myself swaying slightly in shock. "I am to be the Emperor's companion tonight?" I repeat. "In his bedchamber?"

"Yes of course in his bedchamber, where else?" splutters Bao. "Now go and be bathed. I have important things to prepare if you are to be ready in time. And tell them to do something about the dark circles under your eyes," he adds, grabbing another handful of clothes and beginning to sound hysterical. "You look *old*." It is the only unkind thing

Bao has ever said to me and it makes me realise that this is real, this is actually happening, it is not some strange dream or practical joke.

Why have I been called on now? How has the Emperor even remembered me after all this time? I had assumed I had been forgotten forever, that I would live out the rest of my life here untouched, uncalled for. I feel my skin turn to gooseflesh and my hands shake. I can barely remember what will be expected of me, only that the few times I was called on I cannot have been found satisfactory, for I was not called on again. And yet now… now I am the chosen companion. Why? What has caused the Emperor to choose my name chip from the many dozens presented to him? Was it a mistake? Is there another lady with characters similar to my own name? Did he believe he was calling for another woman? Will he be disappointed when I arrive?

"Where is Ying?" I ask, wanting to tell her what is happening, wanting her to tell me what to do, not wanting her to know at all and yet needing her near me. I need her to give me strength and courage, to make me laugh rather than be fearful.

"Who cares where Lady Ying is!" cries Bao. "Why would we want her here now? Will you go and be bathed? At once!"

I make my way to the bathtub and while eunuchs and maid fuss about me and the hot water turns my skin pink, I am silent and afraid. I emerge, dripping and worried and still Ying does not appear. She has been warned off, I think, someone has told her that I have been called for and now she is staying away, perhaps unhappy that she has not been called on herself and wondering what I have done to draw the Emperor's attention to me. I find myself wondering whether I *have* done anything to draw attention and yet what could I have done? The Emperor is wrapped so tightly in his grief he barely sees any of us, his eyes look beyond us to his own private vision of Lady Fuca's goodness and beauty. The rest of us are nothing but an annoyance to him in comparison to her exalted memory.

Darkness has fallen when the palanquin comes for me. I am shaking in fear and Bao's own hands tremble even as he tries to encourage me. "You are beautiful," he murmurs. "Do not forget that. The Emperor may have been sad at the loss of his Empress but now he is coming out of his grief. He has cast his mind back and remembered your beauty and grace."

I think Bao is wrong but at least he has fabricated an explanation for my being called. I have none. I hold Bao's hand too tightly and he has to pull away so that the bearers can lift my palanquin and take me to the Emperor's chambers. I look back at Bao, see him standing in the dark, lit only by lanterns, his hands wringing against one another in his fervent prayer that this is the beginning of a new chance for me, that I may suddenly, incomprehensibly, rise in the Emperor's favour.

I sit in the rocking darkness, the only sound that of the bearers' feet as they run towards my fate. I am not proud and excited, as a concubine ought to be as she is taken towards the Emperor's rooms, dressed and groomed to reach the very heights of her beauty. Instead I feel like a small fearful animal, crouched and cold in my heavy silks, dreading what is to come.

All is brightness. Lanterns are everywhere, in every size and shape. Unknown servants surround me. I am led to an antechamber and undressed without ceremony, their hands skilful and quick. I look surreptitiously at their faces but they are bored. This is a tedious, daily task for them. One women or another, what does it matter. It might matter were I Lady Ling, of course, or some other exalted woman. But I am a nobody. My clothes are gone in moments and I stand waiting to be taken to the Emperor, ready to be found wanting once more. I try to think back to the pillow books I was given as a girl, what sorts of delights I might offer up to the Emperor in an effort to please him, but all that comes to mind is the book Ula Nara gave me. I think of the two women in a bedchamber, one naked in a bath, the other kneeling by her side, one hand caressing the breast of the first, her other hand hidden beneath the depths of the water. I must stop thinking of those images. What use are they to me in what is to come now?

A eunuch stands before me and indicates with a brusque nod that I should follow him. I walk behind him, cold and breathless, eyes down. He stops and bows to someone before him, then leaves the room. I daren't raise my eyes.

"Welcome."

A woman's voice. I look up, startled.

A large bed sits within the alcove of the wall, dark red curtains draped around it, tumbled silk coverlets falling from it. On the bed sits Lady Ling, naked. Her loose hair is long and lustrous, her body firm for her age, pleasing enough to the eye. She is watching me, her face amused at my slowly rising colour.

"I said welcome," she repeats.

I don't know what to say. Why is she here? Where is the Emperor? I stare at her, mute.

She laughs. "You were expecting the Emperor, of course," she says. "Your Majesty," she adds, looking behind me.

I turn quickly and find myself standing in front of the Emperor, also naked. He stands an easy head above me and I fall to the floor.

"Rise, rise," he says.

I stand before him. I don't know what is happening here. I do not know what to do. My head whirls. Does the Emperor intend to have us both – Lady Ling and I? Together? I have never done such a thing, have only seen it in the pillow books, as some strange fantasy. I never expected to have to take part in such an act. What will I do? I want to turn and run.

The Emperor walks past, ignoring me. He joins Lady Ling on the bed, settling himself back as though about to watch a play, one hand lazily caressing her hair. He does not look filled with passion, rather a little tired, perhaps a little curious, but not about to ravish either of us. I look, helpless, to Lady Ling.

She smiles, reaching behind her to stroke the Emperor's thighs, her hand practiced and confident, her face serene. "Lady Qing," she says. "His Majesty wishes for some… variety in his companions, and so he – we – have been exploring the delights of the many ladies of the court these past nights."

This explains it, the silences, the many women sent for, their unwillingness to speak of what happened behind these closed doors.

Lady Ling continues. "There are the more mature women and those who are… new to court. There have been those who are differently shaped in their bodies. And now His Majesty is intrigued to find that there are those who have – different tastes – amongst his ladies."

I look at her. I don't know what she means. Tastes in what, I want to ask, but I'm not sure I want to hear the answer. I am cold and afraid and I wish I was anywhere but here. I feel as though I am being mocked. The lavish room feels tight, as though it is too small for our bodies, for our thoughts, for my fear.

"I have asked for a friend of yours to join us here tonight," says Lady Ling. "I believe you know her well. Perhaps the two of you can enjoy one another's company, while the Emperor and I observe you."

I frown at her. A friend? What does she mean?

Lady Ling's eyes flicker to a shadow that moves in the darkest part of the room. I flinch and then feel my shoulders slump in aghast amazement. The shadow is Ying. Naked as I am, her body tightly held at its full height, her eyes fixed on me as though trying to tell me something I cannot hear. Ying.

I lower my eyes at once. My mouth has gone dry. My heart is pounding so hard that I think it may kill me. What am I to do now? The Emperor and Lady Ling want me to cavort with Ying under their eyes, as though we were pages come to life from a pillow book? They want me to caress her – everywhere, to put my lips to hers, her hands to touch parts of me that – that – I cannot bear it. I feel tears come to my eyes, which fortunately no-one can see, so low is my head bent. This night, this demand of Ling's, it will destroy my only friendship. How can this night happen and Ying and I then continue as friends, to somehow ignore what is to come and act as though nothing happened? It is not possible. This night, this very moment now is about to take away the only person who has made my life here more than bearable – has made it happy.

"You friend is more eager, Qing," comes Ling's voice. I raise my eyes a little and find that while I have stood still, Ying has slowly approached me. Now she is only a hand's breadth away from me. She looks at my face, at the tears glistening in my eyes and her face is sad. I think, she knows this is the end of our friendship too, and at that thought a tear falls.

Ying lifts her hand at once and touches my cheek, stopping the tear and brushing it lightly away with her thumb. She does not lift away her hand, she leaves it there, cupping my face and now I feel her other hand cup my other cheek, so that she holds my face between her hands. Her hands are warm, they do not tremble as mine are doing. Her gaze on me is steady and as each tear falls from my eyes she wipes it away gently, without hurrying. Then she leans forward and kisses me on the lips so lightly that I wonder if she has touched them at all. But my lips sting, they burn as though she had pressed herself against me with urgency. Wondering, I lift a finger to my own mouth and touch my lips, but my touch does not burn like hers.

I find I cannot meet Ying's gaze, I cannot look at Ling to see what she wants of me now, what I should do.

"Well," says Ling's voice, sounding as though she might laugh, "Aren't you going to play with your companion a little, Lady Qing? Offer her at least a caress, an embrace?" Her voice is light, teasing, but I can hear the undertone. I am here by command and I must perform. I raise one shaking hand and place it against the warm skin of Ying's shoulder, without daring to look at what I am doing. I will lose my friend, I think, my only friend, for how can we face each other again after tonight? Gently I draw my hand downwards, stroking the skin of her arm, which has grown goose fleshed. I feel her tremble a little at my touch. Is it worth it, I wonder. Is it worth staying here, satisfying the Emperor and Lady Ling's orders, if I never see her again? If she will not look at me again after this night, nor speak with me? I pause at the thought. If she will not laugh with me, row the boats across the lake with me, push me too far and too fast on the swing, giggle when it is not appropriate, allow her hair to grow rumpled in my lap so that the petals in her headdress fall down across my robes when I rise, then perhaps I would rather run from here and be disgraced, forever set aside.

But Ying's hand is on mine and she lifts it and places my fingers against her breast. My hand stiffens but Ying presses her hand over mine so that I have no choice but to cup her breast in my hand. My fingers might be carved in stone, they are so rigid, so unmoving. My skin is cold all over, but Ying's is warm to the touch, indeed she feels hot, as though she is feverish. I draw back a little so that I can see her eyes and they are bright, shining as though she is truly ill. But her lips are curved in a smile and her movements are soft and relaxed, as though she does not find this moment a torture, rather a pleasure. I feel something inside me unfurl. If she will protect me at this moment then I will protect her from the situation that surrounds us. I cup both her breasts in my hands, that they should not be seen by the Emperor and Ling, I lean into her so that my body covers hers and I rest my head upon her shoulder, my hair falling down her back as though it belonged to her head, not mine.

And Ying sighs. It is a tiny sigh, meant for my ears only. Her whole body relaxes under my touch and she pulls me to her, her warm bare arms wrapped around me, her smile upon my neck and then upon my lips, her own soft hair caressing me as she moves. I find myself thinking that if the Emperor had smiled like this, if he had held me like this, I would have been more graceful in lovemaking; I would have known what to do. I find myself caressing Ying as though it were natural that I should do so and slowly I feel a smile grow on my own lips. Is this what I have waited for, then? Is this what it is to love and be loved? I have waited seven years here to be favoured and thought I had failed and yet it seems I have succeeded without even trying. I think back to my laughter with Ying, our adventures together and the petals falling from her hair and suddenly I know that I have loved her, all of this time. Ying's mouth is sinking below my breasts and I stop her, I cup her face in both my hands and look down at her in astonishment at my own thoughts. She gazes back at me and then buries her face in my belly.

She kneels before me as though I were an empress and before I know what is happening her mouth is on me and I feel my whole body tense with the excess of sensation. It is too much. I cannot bear it. I have gone from not being touched, year after year to this... this... I cannot even name it but every part of my body is shaking both with a tight desire and the fear of giving way to it. I cannot succumb. I must stay upright. I must manage my emotions, these sensations, or I will be overwhelmed by them. Only when I feel her hands on me, when her hands clasp my thighs and her long loose hair sweeps my feet do I hear myself cry out and know that I am lost to this – to her – forever. I find myself kneeling too, grabbing Ying roughly, as though she might suddenly escape me and holding her so tightly she cannot move, can only pant against my mouth, my tongue, my teeth as I try to make every part of her my own, to taste every part of her so that I will never forget this moment, however short it is. In the dark light of the lanterns I hear Ling groan and over Ying's shoulder I see the Emperor enter her, his eyes closed, his body thrusting against Ling, whose smile holds the fierce joy of victory. I close my own eyes, not wishing to see either of them, wanting only to be lost in this moment.

It is over so soon. I do not have time to look into Ying's face again before there is a whispered command from Ling and the eunuchs stand ready. The Emperor, sated and held in Ling's arms, is half asleep. Ying and I are led away in different directions. I want to call after her but I have not yet spoken to her in this place and I don't know what to say to her. I want to ask if she is mine, if this moment is a truth between us or only a lie, a play enacted at the behest of the Emperor's favourite that she was powerless to refuse. In the cold courtyard I am helped into my chair and the bearers lift me just as Ying emerges, led to her own chair. I feel every jolt, every movement of silk against the still-wet parts of my body and want to call out to the men to stop, to take me to Ying, but I know that her own chair is bobbing along in the darkness, back through tiny paths to her own palace where her servants will await her, will wait to hear how it went and she will respond with what? With the silence that has marked each woman that has returned from a night orchestrated by Lady Ling? Will she weep to herself for having been made to do something she hated, or will she have a tiny secret smile on her mouth, the mouth that I cannot stop thinking of? I want to tell the bearers to take me to her palace but I cannot do that. I have to return to my own rooms, where Bao awaits.

"Is all well, my Lady?" he asks. Bao knows that he cannot ask what happened, but he is hoping that I will tell him.

"I am well," I say.

Bao shoos away every other servant and sees to my bedtime ministrations himself. As he undresses me he looks me over with care, as though trying to see what happened while I was away, as though he expects to see markings where I have been touched. In truth I am surprised he can see nothing, for I feel as though every part of my skin is marked by Ying's touch, as though I could look down and see the trails of her fingertips across me like streaks of paint on a silk canvas, pale colours where she caressed me lightly and dark stripes where she clasped me with something approaching rage.

I stand alone in my bedroom, wrapped only in a sleeping robe and gaze with unseeing eyes at my surroundings. Was it a dream, I ask myself? It cannot have been reality. Forgotten for seven years, only to be summoned to the Emperor's bedchamber, ordered to cavort in front of him and his favourite – filled with shame and fear and then to find myself held in a lover's arms, looking into eyes filled with desire… I feel as though I could laugh out loud and yet I am afraid that all of it was nothing, that I misread what I saw in Ying's eyes and that our friendship will now vanish under the weight of this new burden, this unbearable truth. I shiver. Last night was everything I thought I could never have. The price I must pay for it may be too high to bear.

Imperial Concubines

"**I** SEE YOUR FRIEND YING DOESN'T want to know you now," says Bao crossly. "Still," he adds, meaning to be kind but unable to stop himself being a little smug on my behalf, "It cannot be easy for her to know that you are a favourite with the Emperor now and that she is not."

I sit silently by the window and watch the breeze tug at the falling leaves.

"Girl, hurry up!" exclaims Bao, cuffing a maid on the side of the head as she passes him. "Your mistress' bath must be ready at once or there will be no time to prepare her. And she is in favour now, she must not keep the Emperor waiting!" Even when speaking to the maids Bao cannot keep himself from mentioning my new status, the words tumble eagerly from his mouth every time he opens it.

I am sent for every night. Every morning the summons is sent and with each day that passes Bao grows prouder of me. He spends the day preparing me for my time with the Emperor and I spend the day watching the flowers in my garden and thinking of Ying until I see her.

We never speak. Naked, we walk towards one another as though there were no-one else present. In the dimly lit room we know that Lady Ling uses our embraces to titillate the Emperor until he takes her in his own arms but we might as well be alone. Our caresses grow more tender, our eyes lock together, our kisses are gentle, but we do not speak. I do not know how to say what I want to say and if I did, I would want no-one else to hear it. We used to spend our days together and our nights apart and now all is changed. I barely sleep at night, for I am either entwined in Ying's arms or I lie sleepless in my own bed afterwards, whispering words to her imagined self that I have not the courage to utter when she is close. I sleep fitfully in the daytime, a heavy but broken sleep, desperate for sleep and yet unable to rest. By evening I am pacing my rooms with eagerness, my eyes circled with my own dark desire.

"I know you are called for nightly," whispers Bao, trying to stop my constant movement. "I have had sacrifices made in all the temples so that you will continue to be favoured, but I must also warn you against falling too deeply in love with the Emperor. You know that another lady may be called for one day and I do not want you heartbroken when that moment comes. You must be loving and willing in all ways but do not get too swept away."

I want to laugh. I want to tell Bao that I barely glance at the Emperor, that all I can see are Ying's eyes, her body's lines shifting in the lanterns' flickers, that all I can focus on is the touch of her skin, her hair, her lips. That I cannot even hear Lady Ling cry out from the Emperor's bed because all I hear is Ying's soft breath on my skin. I feel the colour rise in my cheeks and nod at Bao, as though I understand his warning and will take it to heart.

Each night I think that tonight I will whisper to Ying, that I will tell her what is in my heart and hear what she replies. And each night I do not speak, afraid of her silence. I wish she would come to me in the daytimes, as she used to, so that we could speak together and I could know the contents of her heart for sure but she does not and I tell myself that she must be ashamed of our nights, that she must go through with them because she has been ordered to and for no other reason. I look into her eyes and think that she looks at me with love and desire and I open my lips to speak but then dare not and when day comes I look back on the night and think that all I saw was fear and anger at her circumstances. I berate myself for a fool and tell myself that all it would take are a few steps from my palace doors to hers, a question, a glance even but I am not brave enough and as the days pass and Ying never comes to me, my night-time bravery fails me. I sit on my porch, rub Fish's long furry ears and hope for a glimpse of her, but she never appears.

And then comes a different morning. The servants prepare for the evening, confident that I will be called for as companion and yet no eunuchs arrive.

"They're late," huffs Bao, still chivvying the maids to prepare my clothes for later on, but time passes and still there is no summons. I catch Bao looking out of the windows and then standing on the walkway and still I am not named.

"Well," says Bao at last, "it seems clear you are not to be called on for tonight. There will be some ceremony for which the Emperor must remain chaste, I suppose. We could all do with a rest, Heaven knows," he adds.

But the days come and go and I am no longer called for. I see Bao passing small coins to servants from other households and his face grows anxious when it is known that other ladies have been called to the Emperor's rooms.

"When you were last summoned," he says cautiously to me, "did anything untoward happen? Anything that might have somehow offended His Majesty?"

I kissed Ying's lips until my own stung, I think. I slipped my hand between her legs and… "No," I mutter. "Nothing unusual happened."

Bao shakes his head and mutters things under his breath, whether promises or threats to the gods, I don't know.

"Is there word of Lady Ying?" I ask casually, as though she is of little importance to me.

"Oh now you remember your old friend," sighs Bao. "Now that you are all alone again? She will not think much of your loyalty."

I feel tears rush to my eyes and have to turn away at the heat in my throat. Does Ying think I do not love her? Does she think I held her in my arms and kissed her because

I was told to? Does she sit, now, in her palace and weep because I do not visit her? My hair undressed, still in my sleeping robe, I make my way out to the walkway between our palaces and take a few steps before I pause. She has never come to me since that first night, I think. And she used to come every day, it was she who made herself at home with me and now she does not wish to see me. Whatever I feel for her, she does not reciprocate it. I turn back and make my way to my bed. I refuse Bao's horrible medicinal teas and pull the curtains close around me, cry into my pillows and eat nothing for days at a time until the gnawing hunger is too great and then I eat and eat until I am almost sick with food, as though eating will somehow fill the void that Ying has left in my life.

There is a ceremony at one of the great temples. I do not even know or care what it is but I am required to attend, as are all the ladies. Now, I think. I am too much of a coward to seek Ying out in private but at the ceremony I will see her and when I do I will know by her face, by her glance…

I am up and bathed and dressed too early and sit watching the sun move round until I can at last set off in my palanquin to join the other ladies of the court. My throat is dry when I step out of the chair and I stumble gracelessly, saved from the cobbles only by the quick wits of a bearer. I blink in the brightness of the day and look about me. Ula Nara, of course, edging closer to the Emperor. The other ladies of high status, each hoping that she might somehow shine forth in his eyes, although he seems oblivious to us all. Ling, a secret smile on her lips as she observes the unending pushes for power unfolding around us. I choke a little on the clouds of incense and play my part, looking, looking for Ying but I cannot see her.

"Missing your friend?" Lady Ling has come close to me without me noticing.

"Yes," I say, without hesitation or shame. What shame can I have before Ling, who has seen me do things I never knew I was capable of? "Where is she?"

"Ill, apparently," says Ling. "Nothing serious," she adds with a smile, seeing my face grow pale. "Just enough to keep her from this ceremony. Not enough to worry anyone."

She turns to move away but I grab at her arm. Her eyebrows raise.

"Lady Qing?"

"Call us back," I whisper frantically.

"Call you? To where?" asks Ling, smiling as if playing a game.

"Call us back to His Majesty's rooms," I say, as quietly as I can. "I need to see her again, Lady Ling. I need to speak with her. I need to…"

"Why don't you visit her?" asks Ling.

"I – I cannot," I say and I can feel the tears forming in my eyes. "I beg you, Lady Ling," I add, using her full title. If we were alone I would kowtow to her. "Call us back."

Ling shakes her head. "I cannot do that for I am not called upon myself," she says.

"You must be," I say desperately, my voice a little louder. "You are His Majesty's favourite!"

Her smile is wide. "Oh yes," she says and her hand strays to her belly, hidden below her silken robes. Her hand caresses her own body and for a brief moment I see her belly outlined beneath her robes, its proud curve. "I am indeed a favourite, Qing, but I am no longer called on as a companion. Perhaps in due course," she adds, her smile confident.

I stumble away from the ceremony, mutter something about a headache to the eunuch in charge, clamber into my palanquin and return to my own palace. My head is full of calculations that make no sense. Lady Ling is with child. She will not be called back to the Emperor's rooms again for many months and even when she is, she may not need Ying and I to entice the Emperor into her arms. I have heard that other ladies have been called to his rooms, he must have regained his interest in the women he has available to him. I wonder briefly whether I could somehow seduce him and make him call for me but I do not want him to call for me without Ying and if he called for both of us and wanted to touch us, to – to – I do not want that. I do not want him to touch either Ying or myself. By the time I reach my own rooms I truly have a headache and I retire to bed even though it is barely past midday, sending poor Bao into a frenzy of concern. I wave him away, turn my face to the pillow and weep again.

I'm woken by Bao hovering near me. From the light I guess that I have slept through the afternoon and the night, for it is early morning.

"I don't want any more of your vile concoctions," I mutter, my mouth dry. "Bring me water and tea and then leave me alone. I am not getting up."

"Nonsense," says Bao, and I can hear that he is smiling. I struggle to open my eyes and see him bustling about the room humming.

"What have you to be happy about?"

"We are all happy," says Bao, turning to me with a beaming face. "As will you be when you hear the news."

I don't ask what news. I suppose he has heard about Lady Ling's pregnancy. It's hardly something I wish to celebrate.

"You are to be promoted," says Bao.

"What?" I ask, thinking that I have somehow misheard him.

"You won't be an Honoured Lady for much longer," he says with great satisfaction. "You are to be named Imperial Concubine. There! Aren't you happy now? Will you stop your moping?"

I go through the motions of getting up, being dressed and having my hair done, while wondering why I am being promoted. Is this from the Emperor's hand, or Lady Ling's? Am I being rewarded for getting Lady Ling with child? "Are there others being promoted during the ceremony?" I ask.

Bao nods briskly, his mouth full of jade pins for my hair. When he can speak he tilts his head towards Ying's palace. "Your friend," he says. "Though I see you two are no longer speaking. I suppose she was jealous of your attention from His Majesty. But I don't know why she's being promoted. An Imperial Concubine, same as you."

I grab at Bao's hand. "Make me beautiful," I say.

"I always make you beautiful," says Bao, but my clasp must be a little too tight, my voice a little too desperate, for he nods more gravely. "Never fear," he reassures me. "The Emperor will see you at the height of your beauty and he will call you back to his rooms."

I feel hot in my heavy court robes. The too-many layers of silk weigh me down, turn my movements slow and clumsy. I fan myself but the air feels warm, no matter how much it moves. I am surrounded by eunuchs, waiting in the dark recesses leading into the receiving hall, which is full of courtiers and the other women of the court, as well as the Emperor and his mother. Court matters are being attended to before my promotion is announced and I know that somewhere in the darkness is Ying, also weighed down in her court robes, teetering on her cloud climbing shoes. I look about me but I cannot see her and I wonder if she has fallen ill or will be led in on another occasion.

"Lady Ying!"

Even as her name is called, I feel her pass by me. She had been somewhere behind me and her silken sleeves brush past mine too fast for me to clasp her hand. I can only watch in the shadows as her new status is announced.

"Lady Ying is promoted, she is made Imperial Concubine!"

The usual list of privileges is read out, the additional jewels and silks she will receive from the imperial warehouses, the servants she will be able to command. She is given a new *ruyi* sceptre to hold, white jade carved into the complex swirls of a mushroom, wishing her longevity and joy. Her ceremony complete, she turns and is guided away into the crowd of women, her own face pale as the jade she carries. I keep my eyes fixed on her face, hoping she will glance my way but her gaze is kept low and I am already being pushed forwards by the eunuchs managing the ceremonial matters of the day.

"Lady Qing is promoted, she is made Imperial Concubine!"

Facing the Emperor, I hold out my hands to receive my own *ruyi* and find that I am holding a reddish wood, carved with the same emblem of a mushroom as Ying's. Our sceptres match, one dark and one light, but twins. I glance at the Empress Dowager, who looks tired and bored. The Emperor smiles at me but his brief glance tells me nothing. As I step aside to listen to the privileges being read out for my own household I look towards the women. Standing side by side are Ula Nara and Ling. Ula Nara's face is confused. She looks from me to Ying and her eyes narrow. She can find no official source for our promotions, only the rumours she has no doubt paid good silver to gather. Lady Ling catches her eye and smiles. Her hand drops to her belly and I see the shock in Ula Nara's face as she realises that her greatest rival is with child and not only that, but has somehow used Ying and I to achieve her goals. When Ula Nara's glance turns back to me I feel myself grow cold under her unyielding gaze. Ula Nara now counts me as her enemy. I had better pray Lady Ling rises further in court so that she can protect me. By my side I feel one of the eunuchs, escorting me back to the folds of the women. I look about me to see if I can get closer to Ying, but the eyes of the court are on the imperial throne, where the Empress Dowager, sitting beside her son, has risen to her feet.

"My son's loyal and wise first Empress has left us bereft at her passing," she announces in a surprisingly carrying voice. "He is, naturally, full of grief at this loss. But a court without an empress is not a proper court and therefore I have chosen a new empress for my son."

The court rustles and murmurs with anticipation. It seems the Emperor's mother has won after all and he will have to accept her choice out of filial duty. I glance towards Ling and Ula Nara but neither face shows me anything.

"Lady Ula Nara will be the successor to the first Empress," announces the Empress Dowager. "Her own ceremony of promotion will be held in due course."

I swallow. Ula Nara has just reached the pinnacle of power for a concubine and in her mind, I am an enemy. As is Ying.

Step Empress

"STEP EMPRESS?" I SAY. "WHAT'S a Step Empress?"

"The title the Emperor is going to grant Ula Nara," says Bao, ready with the latest gossip.

"Not just Empress?" I've never heard of a Step Empress.

"No," says Bao, certain of his facts. "He said he would not have the title of Empress given to another lady."

I sigh. "Will that be enough for her?" I ask.

"I doubt it," says Bao. "Nothing is ever enough for Ula Nara."

He's right of course, Bao's sources are always correct. Ula Nara is made Step Empress and although eyebrows are raised at the title nobody dares to comment. Ula Nara behaves as though she has not heard the full title and since she is mostly called Your Majesty now, it doesn't much matter to the rest of us.

"Not the same sense of style as Empress Fuca," sniffs Bao. "You could hardly fit any more gemstones onto her."

It's true. Where Empress Fuca was not given to ostentation, preferring headdresses decorated with fresh flowers or straw woven into delicate shapes and wearing robes in delicate hues of peaches and pinks, Ula Nara is determined that there should be no doubt as to her status. Almost all her robes are now made in imperial yellow, signalling clearly to each of us that she is the only one of us who may wear this colour aside from the Emperor and his mother. She is elite, different to us. She wears formal headdresses on almost every occasion, towering blue birds and pearls trembling above her head, kingfisher-feather hairpins gleaming in the light. Ropes of pearls are draped over her, her fingers glitter with golden nail shields.

"No one can doubt she is the new Empress," I say.

Bao is not won over so easily. "Empress Fuca didn't have to prove she was Empress," he says. "The Emperor loved her."

I shrug. "Maybe he'll come to love Ula Nara," I say. "In due course." I say it more with hope than conviction. Maybe if Ula Nara felt loved she might stop her incessant jealousy, her watching and fault-finding. She might not notice her rivals so much if she were more secure in her position.

Bao shakes his head. "The Emperor does not care for her jealousy," he says. "He has always liked women who are different, who hold their own in some way. Like Empress

Fuca, like Lady Ling. Ula Nara isn't different. She's an Empress of China, chiselled from jade, moulded from clay. Nothing more nor less."

I don't care how much yellow Ula Nara wears. She can flaunt every jewel in the imperial warehouses if it will make her happy, if it will finally stop her spying and sneaking, her looking out for trouble in every possible way, if it can somehow assuage her need to make others unhappy. I wait, anxious, for her to make a move.

"Lady Ula Nara is made Step Empress," calls out the Chief Eunuch and all of us fall to our knees to offer her kowtows. High on her throne, seated to one side of the Emperor while his mother sits on the other side, Ula Nara's huge headdress of blue birds made from kingfisher feathers and gently dangling pearls sits atop her unsmiling face. Only when all proclamations have been made does she motion to the Chief Eunuch, who nods his head at her reminder and turns back to face us.

"Her Gracious Majesty has asked that one of the Imperial Concubines should be moved from her current palace to one within the grounds of Her Majesty's own residence. This privilege is given to one of Her Majesty's closest companions."

Closest companions, I think, who might they be? Certainly Ula Nara does not have friends amongst the women of the court. But already something inside me is growing heavy and when I see a faint smile on Ula Nara's lips, see where her gaze is falling, I feel a sharp acid rise in my throat.

"Imperial Concubine Ying is granted this privilege," continues the Chief Eunuch and I see Ula Nara's triumphant glance at Ling and Ling's grim face as Ying is brought forward to stand just below Ula Nara's throne, like a prisoner of war on display by a conquering general.

By the time I reach my own palace she is already gone. Golden Peach prowls the rooftop, yowling. The servants must have been packing while I stood motionless for the never-ending tedium of Ula Nara's promotion and the cat refuses to follow her mistress to a new home. I can't help myself. I stand on the walkway, trying to peer inside. I try the door and finding it unlocked I go from room to room, each of them stripped bare. In her bedroom I find one small jade hairpin and sink to my knees, hearing a strange sound echo around the empty palace. I half-wonder what it is until I realise it is me, keening. Watching my tears fall onto the floor I rock back and forth holding the tiny pin, all I have left of her, all I will ever have of her again if Ula Nara has her way.

"She was still your friend?"

Bao has found me. Gentle old Bao, who held me many years ago when I first came here aged just thirteen, little more than a child weeping with homesickness. He promised me then he would make me a home here and has spent every day since proving himself both loyal and kind to me. He is the only person in whom I can confide.

"She was still my friend," I sob. "Oh Bao, she was more than my friend. She was my love."

Bao is quiet for a time while I sob, although his hand does not stop stroking my back, each gentle stroke a comfort. When my sobs have quietened he turns me to look at him and his eyes are curious.

"We were both called," I stumble. "To – to the rooms. Both of us. Because Lady Ling wanted to – to encourage His Majesty. And – and – " my sobs return. "She is my love," I manage once again "And Ula Nara has taken her from me to hurt Lady Ling, to show her that she has more power, that Ling may promote us but Ula Nara can keep us apart. Oh Bao!"

Bao says nothing. He pulls me to my feet and lets me keep Ying's little pin. He walks with me back to my own rooms, where he removes my heavy court robes and has teas and sweetmeats brought to me. He does not insist on one of the usual dreadful concoctions from the physician but treats me as he might a child, hand-feeding me little cakes and wrapping me in a silken coverlet. He unpins my hair from its tight fastenings and only when darkness comes does he wrap me in a furred robe, lift up a little lantern and gesture to me to follow him. I open my mouth to question him but he shakes his head and I follow him in silence, grasping his hand when he holds it out to me.

In darkness we walk through the tiny streets of the Inner Court, our steps lit by Bao's quivering lantern and by the larger lanterns that mark out each palace. I have never walked these streets except the time Ying ran with me in the snow. I have always been carried. I have never gone out after darkness, I have always been safely installed in my rooms, my servants in attendance. The Inner Court at night seems like an unknown land, a place of shadows and fears. More than once I startle at a noise or a movement but Bao's warm hand holding mine keeps me from turning back.

We stop outside the gates of Ula Nara's palace. She was moved here only recently, acknowledging her promotion. Her courtyard garden is larger than mine, her palace far bigger. Tall lanterns burn outside her gates and guards are posted nearby. Bao turns away towards a smaller palace nearby and I wonder at his knowing exactly where to find Ying. I open my mouth to ask him but he must hear even my intake of breath, for in the wavering light he shakes his head and gestures to me to be quiet before taking my hand again and moving quietly to a half-open gate.

And I see her. A hunched figure, wrapped in a crumpled sleeping robe that shows how often its owner has turned and turned again in her bed before rising to sit here, in darkness, alone. No servants to comfort and care for her, no guards to protect her. Alone.

Quickly I step forwards, my hands already outstretched towards her when Bao's hand suddenly wrenches my arm back and pulls me into the shadows. Standing behind Ying's hunched shape is the forbidding height of Ula Nara, recognisable even in the flickering light of lanterns. She stands over Ying, looking first one way and then another, as though she stands on guard over her. I hear her speak although I am not close enough to hear what she says and at her voice Ying gets wearily to her feet and follows her indoors, each step an unhappy shuffle.

"What is she doing in Ying's palace?" I hiss at Bao once we are back in the little lane outside Ying's garden.

"She knows that you would seek one another out," says Bao. "She is punishing you for something. What is it?"

"Lady Ling is pregnant," I murmur, leaning against a wall for support, my heart still beating too fast at the brief glimpse of Ying. "Ula Nara hates us for helping her to give the Emperor a child."

In the dark, Bao's voice is serious. "You had better pray Lady Ling has a son," he says. "Or Ula Nara will torment you for the rest of your lives here."

Prince

"**L**ADY QING IS PROMOTED, SHE is made Consort!"

Once again I stand in full court dress, heavy with silk and flowers. Details are read out of my promotion. In my hands I twist the *ruyi* granted to me to mark the occasion: a dark wood inset with pearls, which take the shape of flowers, something akin to the almond blossom I first saw in Ying's hair. I feel dizzy and am grateful when I have to make way for the second announcement of the day.

"Lady Ying is promoted, she is made Consort!"

I watch as Ying passes me, stiff and awkward as ever in formal court dress. She has never yet learned to be at her ease at court. I doubt she ever will. I want to help her, to step forward by her side and smile encouragingly as she approaches the throne but instead I stand like a statue, my face unsmiling, watching as the Emperor hands her another ceremonial *ruyi*, this one green jade studded with floral-carved gemstones to mark her promotion. Ying's own announcements are made, granting her all that I have been given, with one difference. She is to move palace again. I startle, but a hand brushes my own and I turn to see Ling standing close by me. She smiles as though to comfort me and when the name of the palace is read out I bow my head to her in gratitude, for I know this is her work. Ying is to be moved back to the palace adjoining mine, our walkways interlinked. Somehow Ling has seen to it, has whispered in the Emperor's ear or that of his senior eunuchs, and now Ying and I are to live as close as is possible here. Ling smiles, confident in her wishes being carried out to the letter. Above us, high on a golden throne by the Emperor's side, Ula Nara's scowl is terrifying to see but the announcements go on and her objection goes unspoken. Ying will move.

Lady Ling bore the Emperor a son. There were fireworks all night long. Ula Nara may have been named Step Empress, she may sit on a golden throne and be laden with gemstones forever but a son has lifted Ling far higher than Ula Nara has yet to accomplish. Ling has but to say the word and all is done as she commands.

I return to my own palace and Bao, all smiles at my new promotion, chatters as he helps to remove my court robes. "Consort," he says, relishing the word. "Not just a concubine anymore. A Consort. I always said you would do well, didn't I? Didn't your poor old Bao always say that?"

I want to smile at him and agree that his loyalty to me has been absolute, that he has never voiced any of the doubts he must have had when I spent my first years here neglected and forgotten. In his mind he has re-told my story and now, to hear him tell it, I was never forgotten, only waiting for my moment to shine, which has surely come to me in the past year. Promoted twice following a brief moment of favour with the Emperor. Who knows, I may rise even further, and if not, well then at least I am now a Consort, lifted above the common throng of concubines. Now I can retire with grace to a quiet corner of the Forbidden City, not abandoned by any means but simply living a quieter life, as befits a lady of my stature and growing age. I try to nod and force something that looks like a smile, but now Bao is worried.

"You are trembling," he says. "What is the matter? Did you catch a chill? I have always said those ceremonies are too long," he adds, dispatching maids in all directions for teas, medicines, blankets and furs. "Any lady of refinement would naturally catch a chill standing about for hours in those draughty receiving halls."

I let him put me to bed early. I let him stoke up the fires to bring the heat of my kang to near-burning levels, I allow him to force vile medicinal drinks down me. Anything so that he will leave me alone.

It is dark and I am alone. The bed is like a firepit and yet I am still trembling, even as sweat trickles between my breasts. I know that Ying and all her household will have returned to the palace next door. I know that she is there now, that she is lying in her own bed, that if I were to step out of my own palace and make my way along the walkway… if I were to be brave…

The cold outside takes my breath away after the bed. But I breathe in the frosty night air as though it will take away all my pain and fear, all the love I have felt and been unable to speak of. I step down onto the walkway with a sudden quick boldness. I will see her. I will go to her palace now. In the dark, dressed only in my sleeping robe, I will demand to see her. I will tell her all that I have felt for her from the very first moment she came here, an angry fettered eagle. I will tell her everything I remember of her. Dripping and enraged climbing out of the lake, laughing above me on the swing. Her head in my lap as petals fell all around us as we laughed. And that night, the night I first saw her in the Emperor's bedchamber. All I feared and all I felt. The aching unbearable loneliness that has filled my every day since we were forced apart. I will tell her everything. And if I am wrong in how she feels, I will not care. I will have said what is true and my heart will be set free.

A shadow moves ahead of me and I stop, expecting a guard, a eunuch on duty. I am about to command them to stand aside when I see the ripple of a silk robe and Ying steps into the light of a lantern. Her arms are wrapped tight around herself as though she is cold, her face looks pale and her eyes look as though she has been crying. For a moment we simply stand and look at one another. She has lost all her boldness, her bravery, her passion. She looks afraid and lonely and somehow smaller than she really is.

I step forward and take her in my arms and as I do I feel her arms close tight about me, her shallow breath turn to sobs. I hold her so tightly she must struggle to breathe. The words I meant to say, the speech I had prepared, have gone. I have forgotten everything except that we are together again. I loosen my hold on her for a moment and she clings to me. I half-laugh. "I will never let you go," I say and I hear from her gulped sob that she was afraid of this. Instead I take her hand and lead her back along the walkway to my own palace. As we enter I see Bao, coming to investigate what the noise is, a small lantern in his hand. I do not stop and as we pass him he holds out the lantern and Ying takes it from him with a tearful smile, which he returns.

I lead Ying to my bedroom and close the door behind us. In the light of the lantern I remove most of Bao's excessive covers from the bed, before turning to Ying, who is watching me. I laugh and hold out my hands. Setting down the lantern, she steps towards me and I lead her to the bed, helping her into it as though I were Bao before I lie beside her. She turns to me and something of the bright flame has returned to her eyes. She lifts a hand and places it against my cheek as she did that first night and I close my eyes and feel tears run down my face. "Oh my love," I whisper to her. "My love."

The days pass so fast that the sun rises and sets in moments. The nights go on forever. Ying's household must be the laziest in the Forbidden City, for she does not stir from my own palace, until at last Bao arranges things to his own satisfaction so that all our servants come under his jurisdiction and our home is always here. Ying's palace sits empty, dusted when Bao can be bothered with sending a maid there and otherwise used only for storage and servants' sleeping quarters. We spend our days talking, walking in the snowdrifts of our gardens and the courtyards beyond, eating, unable to leave one another's side. We do not venture far from the safety of our own little world. We avoid the great court rituals and stay away from the other women and their planning and plotting, their constant scheming for a greater destiny. We came close enough to the burning flames of ambition to feel our hairs grow singed and feel our flesh grow hot. I cling to the happiness I have found and seek no other greatness. We are happy, and here in this strange world we inhabit, that is a greater destiny than might ever be wished for.

The pale spring sun warms us as we play a board game. Ying's hair is full of my favourite almond blossoms. We are interrupted when an unknown eunuch is ushered into the room, Bao scowling behind him. He addresses me.

"You are commanded to the palace of Lady Ling," he says.

I stand, heart thumping. "For what reason?" I ask.

"Her ladyship wishes to entrust you with a task," he says.

I look at Ying, who has grown pale. Am I to be taken back to the Emperor as a companion for the night? Are we both to be summoned? I had thought, had hoped, we would be left alone at last, safe in our tiny world within a world, away from the eyes of the court. I do not want to be a piece in the high-stake games Ling and Ula Nara play. They frighten me.

I make my way outside. A chair is already waiting for me, the bearers know that a summons from Lady Ling is to be obeyed at once. I look back at Ying as she stands on the walkway, framed by the doorway. She is afraid of what is to come. I try to smile at her but I can feel that my face is shaped into a twisted grimace, not the easy reassurance I was trying to give her. I close the curtain and feel the chair lift.

Lady Ling's palace is sumptuous. An Imperial Noble Consort may have anything she desires and Lady Ling's tastes lean towards cheerful, colourful excess. Her courtyard is filled with early blooming flowers of all possible shades of red and yellow, her rooms are full of colour and decorative objects. Servants bustle about. I am shown into a receiving hall, given tea and sweets and told to wait.

I can feel my feet tapping and try to still them, only for my fingers to begin clenching and unclenching. I try to breathe more deeply, to think of what I can say if she requests my presence in His Majesty's bedchamber again. Can I bargain with her to avoid the task? I have nothing to offer that she wants.

There is a sudden scurry as multiple servants enter the room ahead of Lady Ling. I kneel and kowtow to her. She strides to her chair, a magnificently carved red lacquered wood, seats herself, accepts a bowl of tea and only then looks down at me, her eyes gleaming. I feel my hands shape into fists.

"Sit," she says. "You and I know one another too well to stand on ceremony, Qing."

My throat feels very dry and I try to swallow again. But if I don't speak now Ling will issue some form of order that I daren't refuse. "I must speak, Lady Ling," I say, still on my knees before her. "I ask you not to call me back to the Emperor's rooms. Nor Lady Ying," I add.

Ling's smile is broad, amused. "I have not called you here for that," she says. "But I see you have grown bolder, Qing. You would not have dared make such a request a year ago."

I stay kneeling. "I do not wish to offend," I say. "I seek only a quiet life."

"A life away from the Son of Heaven?"

"A life away from the games women play here," I say.

"The games can be hard," she says. "But there are great rewards to be won."

"I have my reward," I say softly.

Ling nods and is quiet for a moment. "You are lucky, then," she says at last. "Some of us must continue to play before we win the rewards we desire. I have a task for you," she adds.

I swallow.

"The Step Empress is with child," says Ling.

This moment had to come, of course. The Emperor may not greatly care for Ula Nara but she is his Empress now and he has done his duty by her. She is called to his rooms on a regular basis. Lady Ling is afraid of losing her newly established status as imperial favourite and mother to a possible future heir. But she has a plan, I can see it gleaming already in her eyes. Lady Ling is nothing if not a strategian. She should have been a man, she would have made an excellent general.

"The Emperor is most happy with the birth of our son," she says. "Prince Yongyan is strong and growing quickly."

"I wish him all health and happiness," I say automatically.

"Indeed," says Lady Ling. "But it is as well, don't you think, Qing, to have more than one son for the Emperor to love?"

I can see she is thinking of the Empress Fuca, whose beloved sons, so certain to be the heirs to the throne, died, one after another. She does not intend her game to be lost in this way.

"I wish to have more children," she clarifies. "Ula Nara may be Step Empress, but what really matters, as you know, Qing, is children. Sons. Heirs."

I bite my lip. "I wouldn't know, Lady Ling," I say.

She smiles. "Your lack of children may be of advantage to you now," she says. "I need a woman whom I can trust to raise my son so that I can turn my attention back to the Emperor and give him more heirs."

I hesitate. Has she just said what I think she said? I don't dare to hope for such an honour as she seems to be suggesting. "My Lady?"

She makes a small gesture and a eunuch, already instructed, moves forward from the recesses of the room. He is carrying something and at a nod from Lady Ling he makes his way to me and places a heavy, warm bundle in my arms. I can't even look down, so conscious am I of the burden I am being given. Instead I look up at Ling, who smiles, satisfied at my dumbfounded expression.

"You will raise my son, Lady Qing," she says, her voice loud enough for all to hear. "You will give him every care. Who knows, he may be an Emperor one day."

"Yes, Ling," I murmur, not even remembering to use her proper title. "I will raise him as my own."

She nods. "You may go now," she says.

I rise unsteadily on my high shoes, clasping the warm silk to me, scared that I will overbalance with this unexpected weight. How can she bear to let the child out of her sight, I wonder. But Ling is a practical woman. The only thing better than one son is another son. I have no doubt she will ensure the Emperor gives her more than one son. When I look back at her she has already turned away.

When I reach my palace Ying is waiting for me, her face pale. From the windows I see maids and eunuchs peeking out, no doubt against Bao's strict instructions, too curious to mind his threatened punishments. She frowns when I step out of the chair. "What's that?"

I have no words. I walk past her, nearly tripping over Fish, who gambols around my feet, his tail wagging with interest at the new smell he scents in the air. I indicate with a nod of my head that she should follow me. When we enter my bedchamber, Ying just behind me, I motion to the door. She closes it. Cautiously, I settle myself on the bed and draw back the silk wrappings that all but cover the baby's pale face. He is silent, still, his small face motionless, eyes closed. I have a sudden moment of cold terror. Is he dead, I wonder? Have I managed to kill a prince of the imperial bloodline in the short distance we have travelled together from his birth mother's palace to mine?

But the prince stirs. His eyes open once, twice, fluttering with bleary confusion. At last they open fully and he gazes up at me, his dark eyes demanding to know his whereabouts.

Ying is leaning over my shoulder. "Who is it?" she ask, her voice a whisper.

I find my voice at last, although it is hoarse with emotion. "Prince Yongyan," I say. "I am to raise him." I look up at Ying and see that her eyes are filled with tears.

"He is so tiny," she says, reaching out one finger to touch his cheek. She looks at me, sees that my face is still anxious. "Are you happy?"

"I am afraid," I whisper. "How will I know what to do? How will I know if he is too hot or cold, or if he should be fed or… and what if he falls ill," I add miserably. "I am so afraid, Ying."

Ying shakes her head and laughs, although it is half a sob. "You are happy," she tells me. "You are only afraid because you love him already."

I hold the tiny prince closer to me and he lets out an indignant wail at my too-tight embrace. The unusual noise brings Bao to investigate and he stops short at the sight of a baby in my arms and Ying's happy tears.

"The prince?" he asks. Only Bao would know at once who this child is, why I am holding him instead of his mother. "Are you to raise him?"

"Yes," I say, rocking the baby to try and stop him crying. He snuffles and rubs his face against me.

Bao clasps his hands. "You are a family!" he says in a choked whisper. I see his eyes glisten with sudden pride. If we are going to be a family, I think, then Bao is going to spoil this child beyond all measure.

I feel Ying's arm curve around my lower back as she gently sits down beside me.

The baby prince looks up at us – Ying and I, our heads together, faces awestruck, Bao's beaming face hovering above us – and he smiles.

Author's Note on History

Because this is a novella I have considerably condensed the time period and the events that happened within it. From Consort Qing first entering the Forbidden City to the birth of Prince Yongyan would have been about twenty years. Consorts Qing and Ying were not lovers as far as anyone knows, although erotic paintings of the time often show two women together and men with more than one woman, as depicted in the story. At the time when this novella is set homosexuality had been made a recent offence in China, but it had been quite widely accepted until this time. There are various stories of concubines having affairs together or with their eunuchs.

It was common practice for a concubine not to raise her own child but for it to be given to another concubine. Consorts Qing and Ying each brought up one of Lady Ling's sons. Prince Yongyan (entrusted to Lady Qing), became the next Emperor of China. Both of them were posthumously promoted for their care of the two children, Lady Qing in particular ending up being an Imperial Noble Consort, the highest rank below Empress.

The two women were promoted in the same year from Honoured Ladies to Imperial Concubines and then Consorts, after the death of Qianlong's first Empress. I could not find any obvious reason why they were promoted (there was no coronation, birth of a child, etc.). Neither of them ever had children of their own, implying they were not great favourites, yet they were given charge of Lady Ling's children, who was herself most definitely a favourite of the Emperor.

Empress Fuca, the first Empress, died suddenly after what seemed to be a minor chill following the death of her son and the Emperor was stricken with grief, reacting very badly to anyone that he did not deem to be mourning properly for her. They had been together since they were teenagers and seemed to have had a genuine and loving relationship. He was very unwilling to appoint another Empress but his mother insisted and forcefully backed Ula Nara.

Ula Nara eventually went mad (rumour had it with jealousy over another woman) and was banished from court. The Emperor refused to appoint another Empress.

Ling was the birth mother of the next Emperor of China (Prince Yongyan), but did not live to enjoy the role of Empress Dowager. She was posthumously made Empress. I have made Prince Yongyan her first son, although she actually had a previous son who died very young.

In 1760, about two years after this story ends, the Emperor conquered a territory to the West (Xinjiang), from which arrived a new, Muslim, concubine. Her legend is told in *The Fragrant Concubine,* in which the Emperor, Ula Nara, Ling, Qing, Ying and little Prince Yongyan appear again.

The names of concubines were regularly changed throughout their lives, usually at each promotion, so tracking one person can be tricky! I have chosen to keep the same names for each concubine regardless of their promotions and the names given are those I used in *The Fragrant Concubine,* so they reflect the names they held as Consorts. These names are actually their family names, not personal names, which were often not set down in the official court records. I have therefore used them as though they were personal names rather than invent names for each woman.

Thanks

Thank you to Joanna Penn and Nick Stephenson (and the 10k FB community) whom I consider my virtual mentors, for massively speeding up my learning process. Thank you to Ryan, who goes way above and beyond being supportive and my children for letting Mamma have a little bit of writing time here and there. Thank you as ever to the Streetlight Graphics team, who let me get on with the writing!

MELISSA ADDEY

The Fragrant Concubine

The Fragrant Concubine

For Ryan

Legends of the Fragrant Concubine

THERE ARE MANY VERSIONS OF the legend of the Fragrant Concubine.

It is true that in 1760 the Chinese Emperor Qianlong conquered Turkestan. A Muslim woman from that region was sent to the Forbidden City as his concubine and named Rong Fei. It seems she was something of a favourite, being promoted twice and given many gifts.

Over time, other stories have grown up around her.

In China they say that her body emitted an irresistible natural fragrance and that the Emperor was besotted with her. She was homesick, but he gave her many gifts, including a bazaar, a mosque and a cook from her homeland named Nurmat. At last she fell in love with the Emperor and they lived happily ever after.

But in her homeland they say that the woman was named Iparhan and born to a family of rebels. Brought to court by force, she kept daggers hidden in her sleeves to protect her honour. Finally she took her own life rather than submit to the Emperor's desire for her.

I found myself wondering which woman was the real Fragrant Concubine. Which ending was true: the sad one or the happy one?

This novel is about what might have happened.

Before

HE TRAILS MY FOOTSTEPS LIKE *a whipped dog. When I turn to him his eyes flinch away from the cut, the ragged edges now held together with crude stitches, still seeping pus. He looks down, away, over my shoulder, fixes his gaze on the fastenings of my sheepskin jacket.*

But I have just seen something that took my breath away, that numbs both the stinging pain and the crushing defeat of all my plans. Something – someone – that makes my head lift up again.

"Did you see her?"

Nurmat's eyes flicker to my face and then hastily away. "Who?"

"That beggar girl."

He shakes his head, uninterested.

I turn away from him, look about. "She was begging outside the mosque after prayers. We have to find her again."

"Why?"

"So you can see her."

"Why would I want to see her?"

I ignore him, scan the crowd, twist my neck this way and that, oblivious to the passersby who stare at my face. But the girl has gone, slipped away somewhere. I turn back to Nurmat, catch him looking at the cut, his eyes filled with tears he cannot hold back. "We will stay here tonight."

"Why?"

"Find us an inn."

He obeys me without further questioning. He does whatever I ask of him now, since that one moment, the sharp blade's quickness against my skin. His shame is too great to rage against my plans as he used to. This morning, looking in the mirror, my fingers tracing the open wound before it was clumsily sewn back together, I had thought that all was lost, that I must resign myself to a different life. And there was a part of me that was glad. I thought of Nurmat's arms about me, of his mouth upon my lips, and I felt such desire for him, for my new life. But rising from my prayers I heard a plea for alms. When I turned to place a coin in the outstretched palm I looked into her eyes and my heart leapt in recognition. I must see her again, to know if I saw true.

When we rise the late summer morning is cool and the traders have not yet found their voices. We walk through the warren of the city streets until I am dizzy and sick with turning my head this way and that to find her. The market-day crowds began to grow all around us.

Nurmat lays his hand on my arm. "Iparhan," he begins. But I pull away, breaking into a run, pushing my way through the people. I stop so suddenly that Nurmat collides with me and sends me sprawling but I rise at once, ignoring the sting of my grazed palms.

"There!" I say. "There!" Her ragged skinny frame making its way through the crowds. Her face… I wait for her to turn my way and when she does I feel my body begin to shake. Her face is my face. From before the quick blade swept across my cheek. I pull at Nurmat's arm. "There!" I say.

Nurmat turns his head, blinks in confusion as he tries to follow my pointing finger. Then he sees her and grows very still. When he speaks his voice trembles. "No," he says. "No, Iparhan. You said it was over."

I lie to him then. I have never lied to him before. "She will take my place," I say. "I will use her as a spy. Nothing more. If I have information from the City then I – we – can bring about a rebellion. It is a new plan."

Nurmat grips my arm so hard it hurts. But not as much as the hope in his voice. "Swear," he says. "Swear you will not…"

I put my hand on his and I lie again. "I swear," I say. "A spy, nothing more. Bring her to me, Nurmat," I said. "Make sure she has no one: no family or friends to seek her out. Then bring her to me."

He nods and begins to follow her, moving away from me. In that moment I know that our happiness is lost. I could call him back to me, could change my mind and live a gentle loving life by his side.

But it is too late to turn back now.

Market Day

"**R**EMEMBER, MY FRIENDS — ALL legends are true, even the ones that never happened. For in them we find ourselves."

The spit bubble I'm idly blowing bursts unexpectedly. I wipe the spittle off my chin with my sleeve and watch the crowd around the old storyteller disperse; a few small coins tossed his way by the more generous. He always begins and ends with this phrase when telling his far-fetched tales of wild adventure and passionate love, savage monsters and epic journeys. I don't know if he truly believes it or whether he just thinks it adds an air of mystery — after all, all storytellers need an air of mystery about them or they'd just be common beggars with a fanciful imagination. You need to stand out from the crowd here, have something special to make people seek you out. Market day is the day when such storytellers earn their living, and the market of Kashgar, sitting on the trading routes, draws more crowds than most. Being known as a good storyteller here is important.

Now he tucks the coins away and prepares himself for another performance, scratching his balls through his layers of ragged clothing and taking a long drink of water from a dirty old jug, chipped round the edges. He wanders off to find a quiet spot where he can relieve himself before beginning another tale of mystery and romance. His eyes are growing milky but he would know his way round these streets by memory alone. His space is stolen by a troupe of acrobats, flipping this way and that, walking on their hands as though it were the easiest thing imaginable. It isn't. I tried it once when I was a child. I had strong arms even then but I fell over almost immediately and struck my face on an old root. Got a nosebleed for my effort rather than applause.

I start my daily rounds at the mutton dumpling stall of old Mut, tucked down a little corner street on the edge of the market. "Anything for me?"

He shakes his head. He'd give me the split or burnt dumplings but he doesn't care for me enough to give me dumplings that he could sell. "You're too old to still be wandering the streets, girl," he admonishes me. "Find a husband and settle down."

He's been saying this for years. "I don't need a husband, Mut, I manage well enough on my own."

"No one can manage on their own," he says, keeping his eyes on the bobbing dumplings. "Everyone needs a family. People to look out for you."

I shrug and start to turn away when I feel a hand stroke my behind. I smack it away without even looking. "Get your hands off me, you fat good-for-nothing."

Mut's son leers at me through a half-chewed mouthful of meat and bread. "I'll marry you," he says thickly, not bothering to swallow before he speaks.

I make a face. "Spend my life as your slave? No, thank you. Why don't you help your father earn a living instead of sitting about pawing women and stuffing your face?"

Dejected, he goes back to his food as I head towards the main square. I'm almost out of earshot when he calls after me. "Someone was asking about you earlier!"

I ignore him. Maybe someone who caught me stealing food wants to find me and give me a hiding. I'm hardly going to seek them out. I thread my way back through the crowds and settle down to watch the acrobats.

"Tell your fortune?"

I jump. The voice is right by my ear. I turn and there's an old woman behind me. Her clothes are nothing so much as layers of rags, and there's a thick sweet smell about her which I know is opium, though where she gets enough money for it I don't know; perhaps she uses the cheap stuff mixed with even cheaper tobacco.

I raise my eyebrows. "Slow day?"

She shrugs, her eyes darting about to either side of me, looking at the market-day crowds over my shoulders. "Once they see one person being told their fortune they all come running."

I laugh. "Only if it's a good one, eh?"

She grins, showing a surprisingly good set of teeth still in her head. "Of course."

I grin back. A slow day for her means a bowl of noodles for me. "You'll give me the usual?"

She looks about and lowers her voice. "I've something will make your day brighter?"

I shake my head. "No flowery dreams for me, thank you. Noodles are what I want."

She agrees, grudgingly making it clear it's to be a *small* bowl. If I refuse her offer she'll soon find someone else who will accept.

I settle down on a crumbling wall nearby and present my face for her inspection.

She picks up two wooden rattles and hits them together rhythmically, indicating a fortune-teller at work. The noise attracts people's attention, and two or three bystanders wander over to listen in on my fate.

She runs her hands over my face and looks at me intently. Her voice is louder when she starts to speak, my fortune apparently being of more interest to the complete strangers hanging about than to me.

"A dainty face," she starts. "What a fine face for a poor ragged girl. Her face may bring her great good luck."

I've heard this fortune so many times I roll my eyes. She pinches my ear hard. I'm supposed to look rapt, not disbelieving. I try harder, fixing my eyes devotedly to her face and thinking of hot noodles. This seems to give my face the necessary attentiveness; she pats my cheek and carries on. "Good luck will come from this face," she practically shouts. "A great man will love such a face."

I try not to snort and she grabs my hands, lifting and turning them so the crowd can see. "Such coarse little hands here, so rough. Perhaps your face will bring softness to your hands one day. I see a great man, a man who will let your hands rest only on silk."

I can feel the onlookers getting closer; a few giggles tells me that the old woman's favourite kind of customers, silly young girls with more cash than sense, are edging forward, beginning to hope for their own turn.

"Silk, yes," she goes on. "Dress you in fine silks, he will, and give you jade pins for your hair. Your face will be your fate."

I know she's almost done with me. The real customers are lining up. She likes to keep my fortune short enough to draw them in, not long enough to let them wander away again. I can hear the chink of little coins being turned in impatient hands. My bowl of noodles is getting closer.

"Who amongst you can guess your own futures? What turns of fortune may come your way? Even now the Emperor of China, so far away in Beijing, sends his armies here and claims our lands for his own, from one day to another. Now we are his subjects, his to command. Our people have fallen, our leaders lie silent in their tombs, their heads taken as trophies."

There are some mutterings in the crowd. Quickly she brings their attention back to my shining future rather than their uncertain present. These people are tired of wars. There's been too much fighting in recent years. If the Emperor has taken our lands now, let him have them. Life goes on here on the streets as it always did. Our taxes go to a new master; different officials oversee the trade routes. What difference is there? Wars bring death; taxes bring the same old hardships that can be borne more easily. They want to forget the sorry past and dream of a richer future, so she presses on. "This young girl now, so raggedy and with rough hands, who but I could know she is destined for silks? Are there others who wish to know their fates?"

There are murmurs and little excited pushings amongst the nearest girls. She lets go of me so I stand up, ready to make way for fee-paying customers. She slips me enough for a small bowl of noodles as agreed and I nod, pretending that I am the one paying her. I move past her towards the nearest noodle stall when suddenly she turns and grabs my arm. Behind her sits an eager girl, clutching a coin and lifting up her face, hopeful of another rich generous man appearing in her own future. The fortune-teller ignores her. Her eyes are fixed on me but they seem glazed and her voice is slow. I suppose it's the opium taking effect.

"Where'd you get a perfume like that?" she asks.

I stare at her. "What?"

She leans into me and I pull back a bit for she certainly doesn't smell like perfume. She inhales deeply, her eyes closed. "That. That's…" She thinks for a moment and then shakes her head, almost losing her balance. She clings more tightly to my arm to keep herself upright and opens her eyes. "Don't know what it is, never smelt anything quite like that. Expensive, though. That's the kind merchants bring from a long way off and what rich ladies wear. Not the likes of you. Where's it from?"

I shake my head and pull away. "I'm not wearing perfume. I carry nightsoil, if you like the smell of piss. Where would I get perfume?"

"Some rich man?"

"I'm not that kind of girl."

Her eyes lose their glazed look and now she's focused on me rather than her restless customers. She's never looked at me so steadily or for so long.

I stare back at her. "What?"

She shakes her head, confused. "Don't know. I smelt a perfume on you."

"I told you, I don't wear perfume."

She's frowning. "I know. But I could smell it. It was very strong and then it faded away."

I wink. "Maybe the great man'll give it to me. You know, the one who's going to dress me in silks and have me sitting around doing nothing all day."

I think she'll laugh and let me go, or tell me to keep it down so her customers don't hear me being flippant about her fortunes. She doesn't, though. "Maybe," she says slowly, and turns away.

I puzzle over it for a moment, even sniff my own arm to see if I can smell an expensive perfume. I can't, of course. I smell of a faint stench left over from the dawn when I carried pails of nightsoil to be dumped away from the city walls. The tight-fisted foreman only gave me a thin vegetable broth for my troubles, though, instead of the coin he owed me. I made sure to be clumsy after that so that one of the buckets fell over, leaking a foul mixture of piss and shit all over the doorway of one of his best customers, a fancy house in the centre of town. The broth's all I've had today, so a bowl of noodles is more interesting right now than the opium-raddled ramblings of a so-called fortune-teller.

I order a small bowl and smile nicely at the vendor, hoping he might add a bit more. He doesn't. I take the bowl and squat nearby, scooping noodles into my mouth as quickly as I can. They're gone before I've had time to savour them.

I hand my bowl back to the stallholder and make my way through the crowds. It's slow work to move about on market day. The warren of narrow city streets, squeezed in by high sand-coloured buildings and lined with stalls, swarms with people. I'm surrounded by the bleating of sheep, bellowing of camels, the slow wooden wheels of carts and above all the chattering of people. Cages of live hens and partridges are everywhere, cackling and shrieking as they're lifted out by their feet. The women gossip their way from stall to stall making a simple purchase of dried fruit or nuts last hours. Meanwhile their menfolk are no doubt claiming to be equally busy buying stock – sheep or camels, perhaps even a horse. This, too, seems to take up a great deal of the day. There are acquaintances to nod at, relatives to embrace, wrestling to watch or even take part in, perhaps a spiced lamb pie to eat, bartering being hungry work even if you don't do much of it.

Here and there the Emperor's officials make their way about, consulting records that show them the names of merchants who owe them taxes. They have guards with them in case there's any reluctance to pay up. We're used to the sight of soldiers by now. Young men who fancied themselves rebels used to attack them in the narrow streets after dark – and paid with their lives. Most people kept their heads down and avoided trouble. But now the fighting is over. The Emperor has won and if all he wants is glory and taxes, then so be it. A little boy sticks out his tongue at the soldiers as they pass by but they don't notice him. They wouldn't care if they did. They don't expect us to love them.

I wriggle past two gossips and find myself close to a dried fruit stall where a rich lady is buying whole handfuls of dried raisins. My mouth waters for their sweetness. The lady is fussing over their quality, looking them over disdainfully as though she might command finer things. But raisins in Kashgar are the very best that money can buy and so she can sniff and look down her nose for only so long before she graciously permits the stallholder to sell them to her. Now she turns away, her servants bobbing alongside her carrying many baskets and bundles. She has been busy spending her money today. As they pass me I follow behind the most stupid-looking servant, the one who is carrying foods rather than being entrusted with the more delicate pottery or silks. One quick pull and a handful of raisins is mine. The motion makes the basket rock, though, and a twist of spices falls to the ground. I've already slipped away from them and found a low wall to crouch behind, the raisins hidden inside my too-big man's jacket, so I can watch the lady's fury as others might watch a play.

"Fool!' she shrieks.

Someone ought to tell her she sounds like a common peasant woman instead of the gracious lady she likes to imagine herself. The servant ducks, expecting the slaps coming his way. The first blow catches his shoulder instead of his head, which doesn't satisfy his mistress, so she goes for him again and this time, perhaps realising it is better to get it over with quickly, he doesn't move much and the blow of her hand knocks off his little cap. "Useless, good-for-nothing! The very next market I shall buy a new servant, for you're not worth the sorry few coins I paid for you!"

I grin and settle down in the dusty street behind the wall, cramming sweet raisins into my mouth till every last one is gone, even the ones that fell in the dust when they slipped through my fingers. A little scruffy white cat with a shrivelled leg rubs against me and I stroke it till it purrs and settles down to sleep on my legs, a small embrace from a living creature, a warmth I am unused to. For now my belly feels at least partly full and I sleep for a while in the afternoon sun, hidden from passersby.

It's early evening when I'm woken by drunken singing nearby. I hurry to the nearby mosque, anxious not to miss evening prayers. I pray at the back of the women's room and loiter about afterwards. Sometimes praying gets you a coin from a wealthy woman, it makes them feel pious to give alms to a poor street girl. I've never been taught to pray properly but I can join in with everyone else, go through the motions and murmur scraps of the right words. The bright tiles decorating the mosque are cold to kneel on without a prayer mat but I make do. When winter comes the mosque's a brief respite from the wind. But today no one feels generous and when prayers are over I move off through the crowds, which are now less focused on bargaining for household goods and are happily settling down to the real business of the day: entertainment. I can hear old tunes being sung, gasps at the acrobats who have moved on from their warm-up of walking on their hands and are showing off finer skills with juggling and injury-defying leaps and twirls in mid-air, using all manner of poles and ropes to thrill the crowd. In nearby inns there are drinking games being played, which start off with a literary bent involving reciting poems but become decidedly bawdy as the night wears on. Men sit in the street with their heads tilted back, being shaved or massaged, their tall felt hats on the ground beside them. They munch on almonds and figs, risking their throats being cut when they swallow too close to the strokes of the sharp blades.

I wander away, down other streets. There's one more place to visit before the day is over.

"So, can a pretty girl show me the many delights of Kashgar, eh?"

My grumbling belly has brought me to a small lane with a tall pole at one end, embedded in a yellow earthen wall. It's one of the women's lanes, a place where they wear more ribbons and silks than you'd think would fit on one body and where local men and merchants from further afield come to see what pleasures their money will buy. When I was a little girl I used to come and stare at them, till I found the customers began to stare at me too closely for my liking. These days I have to be careful round here, but sometimes it's a risk worth taking.

The man is fat and balding, and very drunk. He's barely standing straight. He has his cock in one hand, supposedly ready for action, though it looks a bit limp to me. If he were less drunk he'd see I'm not even dressed like a serving maid to one of the pleasure-women, let alone being one of them myself, but he's a merchant and this is what he is looking for. Merchants come here from all over and it is said that in Beijing they sing rude songs about the girls of Kashgar and their supposed charms. He's just right for me, though, too slow and drunk to grab hold of me. I push him away and he sways dangerously, grasps the pole to keep his balance and fumbles in his robes.

"Got cash," he burbles. "Got strings of it." Sure enough he pulls out a string of coins with his free hand. "How much, then?" he says, because even in his drunken state he can see I'm not running off, that all my attention is fixed on the many swaying coins threaded together on a red string.

I look at the dangling string of cash. Usually they hold up a single coin and I can sometimes grab it and run. I'm too quick for them to chase. But a whole string of coins… I could eat meat instead of noodles every day till next market day.

"Well?" says the man, and then he falls over and lies there at the foot of the yellow wall.

I'm scared he's died for a moment, but then he starts snoring. Much to my disappointment he's fallen on top of the string of cash, so I can't even grab it. I'm a strong girl but he's huge; I'd never roll him over in his state.

I look down the lane. A stout woman I've seen before, who runs one of the brothels, has come out of her doorway and is watching me. "Help you?"

I gesture to the man lying by my feet. "He's got cash and he wants a good time."

"You going to show him it then, are you?'

I shake my head.

She comes a bit closer. "Ah, you again. You keep coming back to look down the lane. Made up your mind to come and work for me?"

I shrug.

"Thinking about it?"

Of course I have been. What other choices do have? Winter will be here soon and how many more winters will I be able to survive alone on the streets? Last year I thought I would die in the cold. By spring I was nothing but bones, my skin stretched too tight across them. The lanes would mean warmth, food. But the price I'd pay for them… I stand silent before her while she waits for the answer I'll have to give one day. I can't bring myself to give it yet. I keep hoping I will think of some other way.

The woman laughs. "Well, some men like a quiet girl." She squints at me and makes her voice softer, coaxing. "I look after my girls. They wear silk, you know. Not all the girls do."

I look down. The fortune-teller's words about my hands resting only on silk come back to me and I wonder if this is what she sees for me each market day. If she really sees anything at all.

"I feed them well too," she says. "Doesn't do to have a scrawny girl about the place."

I look up and she smiles, seeing the first flicker of real interest. "Come and see."

I step back.

"Just a peek," she says.

"I won't stay," I say.

"Of course not," she says. "But a peek won't harm you."

I hesitate, then step forward. She smiles and takes my hand, but I snatch it away.

"All right," she says, laughing at me. "No touching."

We get closer to the house and she points me to a small door. I put my hand on the doorframe for a moment, then step inside.

There is a little courtyard with the house built around it. There's a terrace above us. In the yard are cushions, a table or two and a scrubby little oleaster tree, its fruit slowly turning to gold from grey-green. There are customers here already, half-naked girls sitting on their laps. I step back and bump into the woman who is right behind me.

"Don't worry about them," she says. "Come and see the other girls."

We step away from the courtyard into a room. It's painted in bright colours and there are a few women sitting about on cushions. One is having her hair combed; two are mending clothes. One is smoking a waterpipe, staring into the air.

"My girls," the woman says, waving a hand at them and smiling.

They turn round to look at me.

They're not girls. They look old and tired. The bright silks they wear are cheap and thin, with patches of faded colour where the poor quality dye has dripped away on laundry days. Here and there are stains that haven't washed away so easily. The smell of tobacco is thick in the air.

I turn to face the woman.

"Want to eat with us?" she says, smiling. "There's good food cooking."

I've already smelt the air for food and what I smell is old fat, used again and again. I shake my head and walk towards the door.

She grabs my arm a little too tightly. "Won't you stay?"

I shake my head.

She smiles. It's not the nice smile from before; it's wider and shows her missing teeth. "You'll come back one day," she says. "They all do. You can't last much longer on the streets, a girl your age. A child might receive alms; a young woman might get more than she bargains for. We'll be here when you come back. When the autumn sun's gone and winter gets cold."

I pull away from her and walk out, through the courtyard and back down the lane. I walk slowly, my back very straight because I'm afraid someone will chase me if I run, but my heart beats fast until I find myself in the safety of the market crowds again. The familiar sights – the knife stall with the decorated handles, the delicately balanced piles of eggs, the hat stalls adorned with every colour of velvet and felt shining with bright embroidered threads – surround me and I breathe deeply.

"Thief!"

The man grabs at me but I've already stuffed the hot *naan* into my mouth and made my way down a side street, the bread flapping down over my chin like a giant tongue. The market of Kashgar is no place for a grown man to try to chase a girl who can slip through the crowd at speed. I hear him shout again but it's already a distant sound. I'm safe.

I've found a dark corner between two buildings to crouch in while I eat. Not that there is much left to eat now for I can run and eat at the same time. Hands are better used to make my way in the crowd. My face contorted grotesquely as I made my way down the narrow back streets and now there is barely half a *naan* left. I finish what is left of it in seconds, barely chewing, struggling to swallow great chunks of it. It doesn't do to take your time with food when you might get caught.

I yawn. The earth walls here are hard but the area is growing quieter as the traders finally pack up, grumbling about a poor day's takings. The wind grows a little chill and I pull my hands into my sleeves. I could just stay here for the night I suppose; the earth is still warm from the day's sun and I can't easily be seen by anyone. I stretch out my legs in front of me and yawn again.

"You took some finding."

I leap into the air and come tumbling down, my knees hitting the ground so hard that I cry out. A strong hand slips over my mouth and another pulls me upright and steadies me, for my feet are somehow bound together, though I can't see by what. I try to turn to see my attacker but he doesn't let me move.

"Stand still," he says, his voice low in my ear. "I'll loosen your feet but you're to walk with me as though you were my servant, do you understand?"

I don't reply. There's a hiss before I feel a tiny patch of cold on the nape of my neck. It pricks and I know it's a knife. A sharp one. I nod, downwards only, keeping my head bowed so that my neck no longer touches the knifepoint.

"Good."

The man moves his hand from my mouth to my shoulder, stoops and cuts whatever was tying my feet together. I tense, ready to run.

"Don't," he says. He sounds calm, not angry, which somehow is more frightening. "I found you this time, I'll find you again."

I lift my chin. "Don't count on it."

He tightens his grip. "A man's holding you at knifepoint and you're talking back instead of trembling like a good girl should?"

"I'm not a good girl."

"No," he agrees. He sounds amused. He keeps a hand on my shoulder. I still haven't seen his face. His hand, though, I can see out of the corner of my eye. It's well formed and smooth, not calloused. A young merchant's hand perhaps, not a peasant's. "Now," he says. "I'm not sure I trust you to walk behind me like a servant girl should. Maybe you ought to pose as my wife instead. That way I could keep a hand on your shoulder as we walk."

I don't reply.

"Awkward one, aren't you," he says. "Never mind, we'll soon cure that."

He keeps one hand on my shoulder and with the other puts away the blade and I feel him twist to grasp at something. He pulls away my ragged jacket in one hard movement.

I gasp. "Don't – don't!"

I struggle under his hand and at once he pins me tight again, his arm across my collarbone. I bend my neck and bite down into his arm as hard as I can. He's wearing good thick clothes but still he jerks away and curses. He cuffs the side of my head and I stumble to the ground. He hauls me to my feet again. "Stand still and be quiet," he says. "If you do that again you won't be standing up again in a hurry."

"Please don't touch me," I say. I try to keep the tears out of my voice but I can hear them trembling on my lips.

"Oh shush," he says. "As if anyone would want you for *that*, the way you look. And smell," he adds, with distaste.

Warmth steals over me. I look down to see he is draping a knee-length waistcoat over my shoulders. It's velvet, a finer thing than I've ever worn, embroidered with little flowers, split to panels over my hips. A rich woman would wear a pretty, full skirt under this and a gauzy-sleeved shirt. My stained trousers peep out from the bottom, spoiling the effect. Over the top of this he adds a thick sheepskin jacket, warming me further. It's growing dark now and there are few people left to see the young man with his well-clad wife as they leave the main market square and make their way slowly towards a pair of horses, tethered in the far corner, close to a narrow street. A lantern shines nearby but its flame is flickering, about to burn out.

Now the man turns me towards him. He's tall. I only reach his shoulder and have to tilt my head up to look at him. Broad-shouldered, with wide cheekbones, red-brown skin from a summer of sun and thick dark hair, he's a local. His mouth is wide while his nose is a little askew. His eyes are large and dark. He's looking at me as though I were a ghost.

Keeping his hands firmly on my shoulders so that I can't move he turns my face towards the lantern and peers into my eyes, then over every part of my face, as though looking for something. I stand rigid, waiting for him to throw me to the floor. What else would a man grab a girl for? I try not to shake but I am so afraid. I should have made my home with the brothel owner. At least I would have known what was coming and there might have been someone nearby to watch out for me if a man were too rough. Now I am alone with this stranger and no one will protect me from whatever he wants to do with me. My eyes begin to fill with tears.

He notices. His eyes come back to meet mine and he pulls away from my face a little, stopping his close scrutiny. He loosens his grip on my shoulder and his voice is soft when he speaks. "I am going to put you on this horse. I will take the other. Can you ride?"

I look down and slowly shake my head. Ride? Where is he taking me?

He nods. "Good. Then you won't be tempted to ride off without me, will you?"

He lifts me up onto the closest horse in one smooth movement, as though I weigh nothing. He fiddles with the saddle, shifting my legs to make me sit better. I sit rigid and wait. If I move quickly enough I can dismount and run into the alleyways while he is busy with his own horse. As soon as he turns away to mount I throw myself forward, yanking my legs upwards to get out of the saddle.

I find myself dangling headfirst, my face a hand's breadth from the ground. He bound my legs to the saddle's straps while he was adjusting my seat.

The man gets down from his horse and helps me back up. He doesn't speak until he's back in his own saddle. Then he looks over his shoulder at me. "Your horse will follow mine," he says, and urges his horse forward.

I almost lose my balance as we move.

"Keep your legs tighter together," he advises. "You don't want to fall from that height. And hold the reins, don't just let them drape over her neck like that. Stop holding her mane. Sit up straight."

I let out a little whimper as I let go of her mane and clutch at the reins and he nods with satisfaction.

"Doesn't take much to stop your cheekiness, does it? Now come on, do as I say, you'll have a better journey if you learn to ride a little at least." He narrows his eyes when he sees my hands, so tight on the reins that the horse's neck is pulled down, her chin against her breastbone. "Try not to yank on her mouth like that with the reins, she'll think you want her to stop. We've got a long way to go so you'd better learn fast."

I'm not sure how far we've ridden.

It's dark out here. It must be a few hours since we left the city walls behind us. I could smell the sweet ripe scent of the grapes and the mustiness of the overripe melons, rotting at the sides of the fields outside the city. We headed out east, towards the desert, I suppose, although no one heads straight for that, they go round it, so maybe I'm just confused. I'm tired and scared, although I still can't think what this man would want with me that he couldn't have had in Kashgar or immediately outside the city walls.

As we rode out of the walls I sat rigid on the horse, waiting for him to throw me to the ground and rape me, or kill me – though why he'd want to take my life I've no idea. I thought of calling out to him to ask him why he'd taken me but I was too afraid of the answer. Has he taken me for a slave girl? My shoulders slump at the thought. It seems the most likely reason. A life of drudgery and beatings awaits me, then, with perhaps the odd rough fumble when the mood takes him. My shoulders tense again as another thought occurs. Perhaps he is only a servant and his master has told him to bring a girl to him, one no one will miss, with whom he can – can do as he wishes? I try to stop thinking, my hands are shaking too hard and my lips are trembling with the approach of more tears. I try to think of anyone who will miss me in the market – but why would they? Who would miss a scruffy street girl – and if they did, if they briefly wondered where I was, they wouldn't come looking for me. No one cares what happens to me.

I am alone.

My horse suddenly stops, pushing her nose up against her companion's backside. The man has pulled up without warning and now he is dismounting. "We'll stop here," he announces.

I look around. It's thick darkness now. I can barely see his outline. I'd hoped we might go to a village or even a city, somewhere I could slip away from him. But this is nowhere. Why would we stop here? He approaches and I feel rather than see him untie my legs. Then he offers a hand to help me down. I don't take it. My hands are shaking but I don't want him to see how scared I am.

"Where's 'here'?" I ask, stalling for time.

"Part of the way there."

My fear makes me angry. "And where exactly is 'there'?" I ask.

"You will see when we arrive. Do you wish to eat or not?"

I climb down ungracefully, ignoring his guidance and nearly falling on the ground as a result.

"Make yourself useful," he says. "Pick up some kindling and wood."

I'm about to ask where from but stumble on a stick. I almost have to feel my way around the horses and nearby ground but I put together a few sticks and old brushwood, which he uses to start a fire.

He lifts down his saddlebags and squats beside them, reaches in and takes out some cold hard *naan* breads and a big yellow melon, a long oval in shape, heavy with seeds and thirst-quenching, tongue-tempting flesh. I love these fruits. They're from Hami, where the best melons grow. I've only had them occasionally, the odd bruised slice given as a kindness from a stallholder. He sets it on the ground and rummages about again, emerging with a wrapped up package, bloodied on the outside. Inside are thick chunks of fat lamb. I swallow as saliva rises in my mouth at the thought of it. I rarely eat meat. A doddery old *naan* vendor might not chase you far; a seller of richly spiced skewers of roasted meats most certainly would – and your ears would be ringing if he caught you.

He roasts chunks of lamb over the hot flames and warms the *naans* so that they soften up and taste fresh again. He slices the melon into crescent moons of pale golden sweetness. When the meat is spitting hot he tosses a *naan* to me and I hold it like a bowl, into which he lets fall chunks of the rich meat as it slides off the skewer on which it cooked.

I eat with both hands, taking unfeasibly large bites of the parcelled up bread and lamb, which I nevertheless manage to cram into my mouth. I finish one *naan* in moments and am given another and then still one more. The man raises his eyebrows but I ignore him, my eyes on the food. Whatever this man intends to do with me, he is at least feeding me and I know better than to turn down food. If I am to get away from him, I will be stronger and think better for having eaten well. When my belly aches with fullness I turn to the melon slices, heaped up so that only their skins touch the bare earth. The flesh is juicy-ripe and I eat more than my fair share, slurping at it till my chin is wet and sticky. The man watches me. He's eaten some of the bread and lamb, but not much.

"You'll have to learn better manners than that," he remarks, passing me the melon slices that should have been his share. I devour them and scrape the rinds with my teeth until not one bit of the sweet flesh is left.

The food has given me some courage. Perhaps he won't be a harsh master. I have never eaten a meal as good as this one. "Why do I need good manners? They just slow you down so you get less to eat."

"There will be enough to eat," he says, but his voice sounds odd when he says it.

"Where?"

He doesn't answer the question. He just looks at me. "How long have you been without a home?"

I frown at him while thinking quickly. I must make him think that people will be out looking for me. "What are you talking about? I live in Kashgar with my grandmother. My mother is a sickly sort, so she doesn't go out much. The two of them sit there all day cracking nuts and munching on raisins; the shells everywhere drive me mad. And the gossiping! So I spend most of my time outdoors. I'm to get married soon, though, so I suppose my husband won't fancy me going off here there and everywhere without so much as a by-your-leave. I expect I shall have to stay at home a bit more and mind some babies."

He shakes his head slowly.

"What?"

"Not what I heard."

My lies haven't fooled him. My voice was too light, too unconcerned. "What did you hear, then?"

He tilts his head, looks at the fire instead of me. He sounds like he's reciting a lesson. "You're fifteen. Your name is Hidligh. Old-fashioned name, from before we were Muslims here. Means fragrance. Your mother came from a poor peasant family near the city of Turpan. Your father was a young merchant from Kashgar. Met your mother on a market day in Turpan. Besotted with each other. Good match for your mother, of course, not quite so good for your father. His mother was a widow and she objected to the match. He was always travelling so your mother came to live in Kashgar, in the family home, much against your grandmother's wishes. Treated her poorly when your father wasn't there, fussed over her when he was. Local people felt sorry for her but no one did anything."

He stops and looks over at me. "Right so far?"

I think of this morning, of Mut's lazy son calling after me about the person who was trying to find me. I should have listened to him, should have been more careful. This man knows too much about me. "I wasn't there. Before my time."

He nods. "Your mother fell pregnant, your grandmother became more reconciled. Hoped for a grandson." He stirs the coals. "Cold winter. Your father got sick travelling in the cold and rain, the snow, the winds. Died. Your mother was devastated; his mother nearly went mad. Went to every fortune-teller in town and they all promised the same thing. A boy, yes, of course, a grandson to replace her son. They saw daggers, a palace, horses, power. A boy for sure."

I look up and meet his gaze. I have to brazen this out, make him doubt what he's heard. I cross my arms. "Do I look like a boy to you?"

He shakes his head with a small smile. "A boy with plaits?"

I make a face at him but he's not watching me, he's staring into the flames.

"So: the big day came, your mother had the baby – and it was a girl. Any care your grandmother was taking of her vanished. She dismissed the servants and turned your mother into a maid. She ranted at her day and night, how she'd brought nothing but shame and bad luck to the family, killed off its only living son and turned what should have been a boy to a girl in her womb out of spite." He stops, falls silent.

My earliest memories are of scrubbing floors. My hands were too small to hold a scrubbing brush properly in one hand so I had to use both. Sometimes the brush would run away from me and I'd lose my balance and fall forwards. A floor that needs scrubbing seems endless when you are very small. My mother died eventually, coughing and coughing while I scrubbed and scrubbed. Not long after that I stole a bunch of grapes at the market, too tiny to be noticed as my hand crept over the edge of the stall. When no one saw me and I knew I had been fed better that day than any other since I was at my mother's breast, I ran away and took up my life on the streets of Kashgar.

He stands, stamps out the few remaining coals so they won't start a fire while we sleep, then repeats his first question. "So, how long have you been without a home?"

He knows the answer anyway, no use in lying. "Always."

"What happened to your grandmother?"

I look up at the outline of his shape, faceless in the dark. "You must know that if you know everything else about me."

"She died a few years later. There were some things missing from the house on the day of the funeral."

When I heard the wrinkled old bag was dying I went back to the house and took everything that might be useful to me, mostly clothes which were too large but were warmer than my tight and shredded rags, plus a few coins I found and a small threadbare velvet pouch which I tied round my neck under my clothes to keep money in. Not that I ever had any for long. That was my whole inheritance. I heard her ranting in her room and stood in the doorway. She saw me, thought I was a ghost. Afraid, she told me she never meant to drive me away. When I came closer to take her hand, feeling sorry for her all alone in that empty house, she felt my cold little hands, saw I was flesh and blood. She spat then and cursed me, told me I'd get nothing when she died. Her house had been promised to some distant relatives who had sons. I dropped her hand and left her there. Four days later I heard she was dead.

I sit in silence, remembering the smell of dust and her ranting echo in empty rooms.

He throws me a blanket that smells of horse. I wrap it round myself and lie down. The blanket's thick but I grow cold as he walks closer and stands over me. I suppose he'll take what he wants now. I wait. My teeth and fists are clenched. I know it will hurt.

"Got a lot of riding to do," he says. "So get some sleep." He turns and walks away, takes a blanket and settles himself a little way off.

I lie in the darkness. Slowly I unclench my fists but my hands start trembling, so I ball them up again. When I'm sure he won't touch me I finally risk asking what I really want to know. "Why did you bother finding out all that about me? What do you want with me?"

He doesn't answer.

I wait until I'm sure he is asleep. He knows a lot about me, but there's one thing he doesn't seem to have realised. My poor posture, whimpers and clutching at the horse's mane have fooled him.

I'm a good rider. I've worked with horses since I took to the streets. Scraped their hooves clean and brushed them down, held them for rich merchants and fed and watered them for everyone from farmers to noblemen. Sometimes all the thanks I got was the muddy impression of their fat master's boot in my hand from helping them to mount. I got used to them, though, was unafraid even when I was so small they towered over me. When no one was looking I'd hoist myself onto their backs, even when it meant climbing up a wall to reach them. I'd sit there, feeling their warmth seep into my cold body, whispering to them. Later I'd have them walk a bit, when my legs were long enough for my commands to get their attention. A few times, out in the fields away from the main city, I'd find horses pasturing and learnt what it was to ride at a full gallop, terrified by the speed the first few times but always wanting more, till a farmer would inevitably notice his horse galloping around the field with a girl on its back. I got yelled at plenty of times and got a beating twice, but it didn't put me off. So here I am, a poor girl, who should never have been on a fine horse in her life, and I can ride.

My horse is fast but it's not long before I hear hoofbeats behind me, and although I urge her on I know she can feel my defeat because she's not really trying. If he caught up with us that quickly when I had a good head start then there's not much hope. I slow her down and finally stop, then sit there waiting in the darkness for him to reach me.

I wait for him to pull me down from the horse and beat me but he just pulls up alongside. He leans towards me without dismounting and takes the horse's bridle. His voice is flat. "You're going to be hard work," he says, and turns both horses back the way we came. Now he knows I can ride we go faster.

I try not to wonder why he needs us to hurry. The possibilities frighten me.

We ride the next day and night too. I've never been on a horse this long and I'm tired of the jolting and the ache in my thighs. We stop a couple of times. Walking when you've been on horseback for hours is agony: I stagger when I dismount and then hobble like a wounded duck to relieve myself behind bushes. The food runs out and now all I am given is a handful of raisins. Here, in a scrubland far away from any landmark except the odd blackened stump of a dead poplar, with no idea of a destination, there's something gritty and wan about them, as though they need the noise and hustle of a market to give them their true flavour.

It's dawn and I'm drooping over the neck of my horse, half-awake, when at last we stop again. We're in the most barren place I've ever seen. Rocks, sand, rocks, sand, some more rocks and more sand. A huge old dead poplar tree, its bark shredding away. Its branches are decorated with tiny scraps of cloths, tied as symbols of past wishes made. Probably wishes to escape death in the desert. Nothing else. There are sand dunes in the distance but my eyes must be not working properly through lack of sleep, because they're taller than houses, many many houses stacked on top of each other.

I think this madman has actually brought us into the Taklamakan Desert. Any thoughts I might have had of trying to escape from him again fade away. No one can survive out here alone.

We're going to die for sure.

"Here we are," the man says. He dismounts and approaches my horse, then stands for a moment, looking up at me, his eyes tired and somehow sad.

I'm wary. "Where are we?"

"Home."

"Live under a rock, do you?" I ask. I try to sound sharp but my voice comes out shaky.

He doesn't laugh. "Get down," he says. "That's home." He points.

I was mistaken. Rocks, sand, rocks, sand – and a house. It's only one storey high, built low and broad, quite big. Sand has piled up on one side almost as far as the flat roof, and it's made of earth so your eye passes over it thinking it's just a strange shape for a dune. I can only see two windows and they're quite small. It must be dark in there.

I look back at the man and he's watching me. "Is it what you expected?"

I don't know. I don't know what I was expecting. I think I'd stopped expecting anything. "You live here?"

"Yes."

I stare at him, eyelids aching, hands trembling, for once unable to come up with a quick-witted response. "Why?"

It's the only thing that comes to mind. Why would someone with the money for clothes and food and horses live here? No one lives here. They struggle through here only if they get lost, mostly they take their goods along the well-worn trading routes no matter how long the detour, doing their very best to avoid this place.

He takes hold of my reins, turns the horse and then lifts up his hands to me. "Get down."

I almost fall off the horse into his outstretched arms.

Arrival

I SEE HER FROM THE WINDOW. *Drooping in the saddle, skinny as a twisted stick. Her face pale with tiredness, looking at the house and seeing nothing until Nurmat speaks. I cannot hear his words but she looks again at the house – and sees it. She blinks, startled by its sudden appearance but still too exhausted to be as wary as she wants to be. Nurmat speaks again and she looks down at him, tries to refuse to enter. He holds up his arms to her then, a coaxing gesture like a man with an untrained colt, promising kindness and good food in return for obedience. Grudgingly she relaxes her legs, slips down from the horse's hot flanks. She almost falls into his arms and I see them tighten about her for a moment, to stop her collapsing onto the sand as her legs give way beneath her. For one brief moment Nurmat holds another woman in his arms and I cannot help myself: I draw back a little, shocked by even the illusion of betrayal.*

She stands, shivering, her arms close by her side, seeking to contain what little strength and warmth she has left. She does not look about her. When Nurmat gestures her forwards she stumbles towards the door and I draw back from the window, tilt my head to hear Mei's bustling steps going to welcome them in.

I saw the traitors' army come too, our own family, their banners held high, their soldiers fresh and fierce, heading towards the walls of our fortress, coming to join the Emperor, to pass on our family secrets. Our men were weary from fighting, our women and children wept with fear at this treason, this new onslaught from the Emperor, emboldened by his new allies.

I stood, halfway between child and woman, longing to be a man, to carry weapons and join the fight. I watched the fighting from high up until my mother, a gentle woman, drew me away.

I hear footsteps as the girl passes by my room, blindly following Mei.

For one moment I think of Nurmat's arms about her, her weakness held up by his strength, and something cold comes over me. Perhaps I should turn her out into the desert. To starve or die of cold, whichever comes first. Something in me is afraid of her somehow, as though she is stronger than me.

Then I hear Mei's steps pass my door and behind her the shuffling steps of the girl, being led to a room where she will be put to sleep. Every step is an effort to her and I chastise myself for my foolish fears.

She is mine, for what other choice does she have?

The Taklamakan Desert

I WAS WRONG ABOUT THE HOUSE being dark inside. The windows are small and outside the desert is still a pale grey, but this room shines.

There are candles and lanterns everywhere, burning brightly. There are ornate and colourful wooden carvings all the way round the walls. Large silk and velvet cushions, heavily embroidered, are scattered so extravagantly I could sit down anywhere and find one ready for my horse-sweaty backside. There's a long low table, which a very small old woman is busily filling with little bowls of raisins, almonds and honey. There's a larger bowl filled with yoghurt and I can smell hot bread cooking.

The little woman has a back that is bent forward so far that it's an effort for her to look up at us as we enter. Her deeply wrinkled face is like a tortoise craning up from under its shell. I stare at her. Beneath the layers of wrinkles her features are different to ours. She's Chinese, her old skin paler, more yellow-tinged than reddish-brown, her eyes slanted more deeply than ours.

She nods to my captor and then looks at me. Her eyes widen and she takes a little step backwards. Then she takes in my ragged clothes topped off with the velvet and sheepskin the man provided. She looks down at my dirty nails, up at my frightened, exhausted face and her own face grows sad. "Welcome," she says. She speaks our language well, but with a strong accent, which I've heard before in the market. Merchants who hail from Beijing speak like her. She indicates that I should sit down. "At peace?"

It's the local greeting. The simple, ritual reply that I ought to be giving is: *At peace – and you?*

I've never felt less at peace in my life and even a standard response I've given a thousand times in my life eludes me. I stand, swaying, in the doorway. This room is too much for me, too many colours and patterns, too much warmth and comfort, the smell of fresh hot food too great an assault. It seems I've arrived but I don't know where I am, nor why I've been brought here.

The man pushes me forward. "She is tired," he says. "A good enough horsewoman, but unused to such distances and I have not been able to feed her as well as I would have done had we not been heading this way. Feed her up, then she can sleep."

The tortoise woman nods and heads through a doorway, emerging in moments with a platter of hot *naan* breads in one hand. "Sit," she says.

I take two hobbling steps forward, then sink down onto a pile of cushions. The man steps quickly to the table, takes a hot *naan*, smears it with honey, throws a fistful of almonds into it and accepts a bowl of tea from the tortoise.

"I'm going to bed," he announces, and leaves the room through another doorway.

If I were less tired I'd follow him, even to his bed. He's the only person I know here and he's treated me well so far, whatever his future intentions. But I don't have the strength to stand.

I sip burning hot tea and slowly eat a soft *naan* with honey but even I can't manage much. When she sees my eyelids drooping and my chewing slow down the old tortoise gently takes the bowl of tea away and offers me her hand. She pulls me up, then shuffles off ahead of me into an equally colourful and comfortable room, but with fewer candles, making it glow softly rather than gleam like the first room. There's a *kang* made up with blankets. I sit down and shudder at the unaccustomed warmth coming from the heated bricks. The tortoise mistakes my reaction. "Not warm enough?" she asks. "I can put more wood on the stove."

I shake my head, dazed by the heat and food.

She crouches down in front of me, pulling off my worn boots. "What's your name?"

I try to speak but hardly any sound comes out and I have to try again. "Hidligh," I manage in a croaked whisper.

"My name is Mei," she says. "Let me take your clothes. I will give you new ones. These will be full of lice."

I clutch at my clothes but I'm so tired that her little calloused hands pull back my fingers one by one from the cloth and in the end I sit, slumped, as she strips every bit of clothing off me.

"Sleep," she says, and pushes my shoulder so that I lie down. She seizes my legs and swings them up. Then she heaps blankets over me. She stops for a moment, looks down on me, frowning. Then she shakes her head and leaves the room. I can hear her little puffs of breath as she blows out each candle she passes, the room growing dark as she leaves me.

I try to focus, to think about where I am and how to get away again, but the heat of the *kang* seeps into me and I close my eyes.

In the warm darkness two things wake me: the rustling of clothes and a fragrance. Someone is moving about in the room. I lie very still. The rustling comes closer and my nostrils fill with perfume, muddling my thoughts. I feel a person sit on the bed, close to me.

I swallow. "Who's there?" I manage to whisper, hoping it is the little bent woman, Mei.

A flame flickers and a lantern is lifted. At first the light blinds me but when it gets closer to my face I blink and shrink back. In the darkness, a hand's breadth from my nose, is a young woman's face.

She's beautiful. I see that, but only after I've drawn away from the huge scar that runs across her face. It traverses her whole cheek and comes too close for comfort to her left eye. Her skin elsewhere is smooth. She looks like an overripe peach split open by too much rain in the height of summer, perfection ruined.

She still smells perfect, though. Like a wondrous fruit warm in the summer sun and yet somehow like its own delicate springtime blossom as well: an impossibility.

Her dark eyes are fixed on me. Slowly she reaches out a hand and touches my cheek, lightly stroking my whole skin where hers is damaged. She looks over every part of my face in silence. Behind her another lantern is lit and I see my captor standing, watching us.

Their silent scrutiny is unnerving. "What do you want with me?" I blurt out.

The woman sits back a little. Her voice is soft. "What did you think Nurmat wanted you for when he took you?"

I shake my head. "A slave. A…" I stumble over the word wife; no one would steal a raggedy street girl to be a wife. "A concubine?"

She nods and speaks over her shoulder to the man, Nurmat. "She's not stupid. I can train her."

Her voice has a cold eagerness that makes me wriggle backwards, edging up against the wall so that I'm sitting upright. I pull the blankets around my naked body as though they might protect me. "Train me for what?"

The woman ignores my question and gets up. I'm relieved she's no longer so close to me and hope she'll move further away, but she stands still, looking me over. She has long thick hair, arranged as several fine plaits that fall down her back from under a little embroidered cap. She wears a full skirt and a velvet waistcoat. Her scar is worse than I first thought, a throbbing red on her pale skin, still fresh, made only days ago. Rough stitches and scabs are still in place, crusting brown bridging the pale silk skin. Her perfume is extraordinary, though. I can't help my nose stretching out towards her a little.

Nurmat, behind her, speaks. "We don't have to go ahead. We could be free of all this."

He can't see the woman's face from where he stands, but I can. Her eyes glisten with tears for a moment and then her face hardens. There's a rage in her eyes that scares me so badly I feel a trickling on my thighs and know that I've pissed myself in fear. I press my spine up against the hard wall trying to lean away from her.

The woman composes her face, then turns away from me and walks past Nurmat. "I have made my choice," she says, and leaves me alone with him.

Nurmat looks at me and then down at the dagger on his belt. I wait. I wonder how quickly I could move if he came for me but he's standing between the door and me. I can't feel my legs.

After a long moment his shoulders slump. He nods at me with an unhappy smile. "Looks like I have no choice," he says, "So we'd better learn to work together so we can get this over with quickly. My name is Nurmat. Are you hungry?"

The sudden reversal leaves me trembling. My lips are cold. "A little," I manage, although my stomach rumbles loudly, giving away my lie.

He nods. "I'll send Mei to you so you can be washed and dressed."

I've barely time to unwrap myself from the soaked blanket when Mei the tortoise drags in a heavy tub, steaming water, cloths, combs and rose scented soaps. She strips and remakes the bed without comment, then turns her attention to me. I'm scrubbed down in a very short space of time, kneel to have my hair washed and by the time the soap's been rinsed away she's laying out fresh clothes for me to wear. I reach out to touch them. A soft white cotton shirt with long billowed sleeves, a floor-length intricately patterned skirt woven in bright blues and reds, a thigh-length waistcoat in red velvet which fits me better than the one Nurmat covered me with in the market of Kashgar and a pair of good quality leather shoes with little heels which make me walk like the acrobats on their ropes.

Mei nods when I've finished putting it all on. "A good fit," she says. "Tiny bit loose but you'll fill out when you've eaten a few good meals. Now let me do your hair. Then you can go to eat with Nurmat and Iparhan."

"Who's Iparhan?" I ask.

Mei's voice goes flat. "The woman with the scar."

"Why does she want me here?"

Mei's wrinkled tortoise face is guarded. She opens her mouth as though to speak, then thinks better of it and closes it again. She picks up a comb. "Time enough to talk of why you are here later," she says and starts work on my hair. She drags a comb through it with a few choice words on my part. Days on horseback against a desert wind have made it even more tangled than usual. Once it's smooth she braids it tightly into many tiny plaits.

I protest. "I usually just have two."

"Nonsense. Only married women have two plaits – too busy to be braiding so many every morning. A young girl like you should have lots."

Once the plaits are done she finishes each end with a tightly wrapped blue ribbon and then puts a little velvet cap on my head. It's blue and has red flowers embroidered around the band. I reach up and feel its stiff newness. I had a black cap before, a man's one because it was bigger and kept my head warmer than this one, but it was worn and frayed. I don't ever recall having new clothes. My skin feels tight with cleanness.

Mei gazes at me without speaking. She looks a little afraid.

I try to break the silence. "Do I look nice, then?"

She nods, a slow reluctant movement.

I frown. "Can I see? Do you have a mirror?"

She hesitates too long. "No," she says. "Come and eat now."

I think she's lying but I make my way to the door. There's a quick flash of silver light behind me. I'd swear Mei has just hidden away a mirror.

The main room is laid out for a meal again, this time with thick *lagman* noodles, roast lamb and vegetables. I stand in the doorway, awkward in my new clothes and clean skin.

I'm not sure who else might be around, but the room is empty apart from Mei, who starts bustling in and out with more plates of food. Above the smell of the cooking I breathe in that scent again, the one I now associate with the woman Iparhan. I look about the room but can't see her.

Nurmat appears from the doorway opposite me, the one that leads outside. He sees me and his eyes widen.

"What?" I ask.

He pauses, then shakes his head. "Nothing," he says, although his eyes stay fixed on me.

I don't like being stared at. "What's that perfume?" I ask, hoping to distract him. It fills the room. Not even rich women smell like this.

Nurmat looks pleased. "The perfume is Iparhan's. She always wears it."

"Is that why you call her Iparhan? What's her real name?" Iparhan just means Fragrant Girl. It's not a real name; it sounds like a nickname, like being called Little Melon if you're a bit plump.

He shakes his head. "She's been called Iparhan for years. No one uses her real name any more."

I step further into the room, thinking she must be there somewhere for her perfume to be so strong. But it's just Nurmat and me in the room. "She's not in here."

He grins suddenly, looking younger and more cheerful. "She is, you know. You just can't see her."

I look at him to see if it's a joke but he's looking round the room carefully, at the hangings and the long curtains hanging either side of the small window. He even looks at the larger cushions as though she might be inside one or underneath it.

I make a face. "What is she, a magician?"

There's a cold hard sharpness on the back of my neck.

"Too slow."

I move fast to the other side of the room and look back. Standing where I was standing is Iparhan. She's the same height as me, and she's holding a dagger where my neck was.

By my side Nurmat is laughing. "You always beat me at this. Were you behind the door? I thought I checked."

She doesn't answer, just reaches up to a rafter and pulls her whole body upwards so that it lies flat against the ceiling above where I was standing, just her arms holding her in place. I can see them trembling with the effort but she stays in place for several breaths before she swings back down again.

Nurmat looks impressed. "That's a new one."

She ignores his praise and sits down.

Nurmat nudges me and I sit, as far away from both of them as I'm able. I don't like their sudden changes of mood, from the soft voice and then eyes full of rage I saw on Iparhan's face to Nurmat staring at his dagger and then his tired joviality towards me. I don't know what might come next. I find myself holding my breath and flinching when they move. I try to sit still and force myself to breathe. All I'm thinking is: how do I get out of here when the desert surrounds me?

They wash their hands and start to eat. I hesitate, but food is food. Mei joins us, passing little bowls of food to each of us, making sure our plates are full. The food is good, I'm clean and warm and well dressed. I ought to feel comfortable, but I'm too anxious and on edge.

Iparhan turns to Nurmat and indicates me as though I'm not even in the room. "It's going to take longer than I'd like. She speaks like a peasant." She gestures at my sticky fingers and chin. "She eats like one too."

Nurmat looks me over and smiles. "Perhaps you should explain why she is here," he suggests. "Then she might know why she needs to behave differently."

I cross my arms and sit back against the cushions, chin up. My heart's pounding. My mouth is dry with curiosity and fear. "Yes," I say, trying not to let my voice tremble. Instead I sound too loud and almost cheerful, as though we were talking about someone else. "What *am* I doing here?"

Silence. I look at Iparhan but she seems to be ignoring all of us, gazing into her bowl of tea as though mesmerised. It takes a moment before she begins, her voice too quiet after my loudness. "What do you know about the besieging of Yarkand?"

I blink. This is not the beginning I was expecting. "What?"

She looks up, suddenly impatient. Her voice is sharp. "The siege. Of Yarkand."

"Not much." I try to think fast, afraid of arousing her anger. Yarkand? The end of the war, when the Emperor of China finally claimed our land as his own? What does that have to do with me? "I know that the Sultan cut off the heads of Burhan ad-Din and Khoja Jihan and showed their bodies to the commander of the Emperor's army." I begin tentatively. Iparhan's face contorts in a painful grimace and I hurry on, unsure whether I'm saying the right thing. "I know that pretty much ended any rebellions, and now Altishahr is the 'New Dominion' – *Xinjiang*." I shrug and try to end my piecemeal history. I don't think I'm saying what she wants me to say. "We all belong to the Emperor of China now," I finish lamely. I wait for her response.

She's staring at me, appalled. "Is that the whole of your understanding of the conquest of our homeland?"

What more does she expect of me? I spread my hands. "What else would I need to know to live on the streets of Kashgar?" I say, which is the truth, but she glares again, so I try to do better: "We were one of the great cities of Altishahr. Now we're one of the cities of Xinjiang and part of the Empire. So what? I see Emperor's Bannerman officials hanging around all the time, collecting taxes and swaggering about looking pleased with themselves. But trading goes on as it always did. Life goes on as it always did. Not much changes. Not for real people."

She's frowning. Suddenly I'm almost angry with her. She may be strange but clearly she wants for nothing, not even out here in the desert, sitting on her fat cushions and being fed mountains of food. "Real people need to eat." I tell her. "Only rich people worry about who is ruling them. Rich people who want the power for themselves."

She shakes her head, as though she can't even think where to begin in correcting me.

"You still haven't answered my question," I tell her. "What has any of that to do with me? I've never had anything to do with the war. I've been too busy trying to feed myself and stay out of trouble. Why would you bring me here?"

"I need you to do something."

I don't like the sound of this. What could I do for her? She has money, she could ask anyone to do anything for her if she offered them enough money. What does she need doing that cannot be bought with silver? Why does she need me and not anyone else she could have chosen?

"I don't understand," I say, although I'm not sure I want to hear her explanation.

She takes a sip of the cooling tea and looks down into the bowl as she speaks. "Two hundred years ago—"

I stop her at once. "Two hundred *years* ago?! I don't want a history lesson! I want to know why you brought me here! Who *are* you?"

She looks at me for a moment. "My family is of the White Mountain brotherhood. My grandfather was Khoja Afaq."

I blink. I may have lived on the streets but everyone knows her family. They are – or were – effectively our rulers. Her family lived in Kashgar on a great estate, guiding both religious and secular affairs. All their lands were seized by the Emperor's officials, turned into grain storage or offices for his administrators. "But I thought your family was…" I stop. I was going to say 'dead'. They were wiped out. I thought they'd all been killed and yet here is one of them. I'm gaping at her. "How did you escape?"

She ignores me. "To rule we had to have the support of the Zunghars, but they grew too demanding and we rebelled against their control. When we did, the Zunghars captured my grandfather Khoja Afaq, my uncle Khoja Jihan and my father Burhan ad-Din, and imprisoned them in Yili."

"That was four years ago," I say. "There was plenty of coming and going in Kashgar when that happened. But trading goes on. Doesn't matter who rules the cities, they always want them to keep trading. That's how they get their money, by taxing merchants. Can't be frightening off the merchants, even if you are the Emperor of China."

She looks as if she might strike me. I draw back. Perhaps I should keep my mouth shut. This is a woman who's lost every member of her powerful family and who no doubt has a price on her own head. Not a person to be trifled with.

She's speaking again. "The Emperor of China had been trying to take Altishahr for many years. Now he believed he had a chance to do so. He offered us our freedom and the rule of both Yarkand and Kashgar if we would be his tributaries. But my family refused. We had heard that the Zunghar had rebelled in the North and so we too rebelled."

I make a face. "Why be allies again with the Zunghar when you'd rebelled against them in the first place?"

Her voice goes cold. "We are the people of Altishahr. We would rather join forces with the Zunghar than allow the Emperor of China to reach out his greedy hands and take away our freedom. His empire cannot take over the entire world. He had to be stopped."

I hold up my hands. I'm not about to argue with her. I think I might not even live to regret it if I do. "Whatever you say."

"The rebellion angered the Emperor. He sent a huge army to take Altishahr by force. He would not accept failure this time. In this he was aided by a traitor."

I don't understand any of this. It's turning into a history lesson after all and I keep searching for my place in it. But these are emperors and rulers and noble families she's talking about, the people who make history. Where does a street girl fit into it? I try to hang on to the last thing she said. "A… traitor?"

"My father's cousins, greedy for influence and resenting my father's command, refused to support our rebellions. Instead, hoping for privileges from the Emperor, they sent their forces to support the Emperor's army. My uncle Khoja Jihan was killed. The Emperor threatened the local Shah, demanding my dead uncle's head and that my father Burhan ad-Din should also be handed over, to do with as the Emperor pleased. The Shah was a coward and he handed over both the head of my uncle and the body of my father, whom he had executed himself." She stops, her breathing a little too fast.

I sit up straight, my attention finally caught by something she's just said. "The Shah handed over your uncle's *head* and your father's *body*?"

"Yes."

"Why not two heads? Or two whole bodies, come to that, with the heads still on?"

Nurmat cuts in. "The Shah said that the head of Burhan ad-Din had been mislaid."

"Mislaid?"

Nurmat nods.

How you can mislay a head is the least of my concerns. "So your father and uncle were both killed and you came here to hide?"

Iparhan nods.

"And Nurmat?"

She hesitates, flushes. For one moment the red scar disappears into the rose of her cheeks and her face is perfection.

Mei stands and begins to clear the table. "They are promised to one another. Their families were friends. Nurmat and Iparhan are to wed one day."

I raise my eyebrows. "What's stopping you getting married now?"

Iparhan's face is hard, but her voice is quiet. "I will not marry until I have exacted revenge."

She sounds like she's said this more than once. I look to Nurmat. "You don't mind waiting?"

Nurmat smiles. It's a sad smile. "I'd wait for ever for her, of course," he says.

I think he's said this more than once too but it sounds as if it's beginning to grate on him. "So you're hiding here," I repeat, then ask the question that's still burning in my mind: "But why do you need me?"

Iparhan leans forward. I lean back. She's suddenly too eager, too focused on me. I wish I hadn't kept asking my questions, perhaps I could have delayed the reply. "Now that the Emperor has taken Altishahr our traitorous cousins are preparing to travel to Beijing. There they will be given imperial honours for their part in the Emperor's victory." Her voice is shaking with rage. She pauses for a moment, then takes a deep breath. "There is a daughter. She is going to be given to the Emperor as a concubine. It is supposed to be a great honour and if she pleases the Emperor her family will receive many more gifts and privileges."

It's still not an answer. I don't see why she's even bothering to tell me about this girl. "He must have lots of women," I say, hoping to calm Iparhan. "I expect he'll barely notice her."

Suddenly her face is close to mine. I start back. "He *will* notice her," she breathes and her dark eyes are too dark, too fervent. "'She' will be you—and it will be your task to be noticed."

I don't even think. What she's suggesting is so impossible it's not even worth thinking about. "No."

She sits back, a half-smile on her lips. "Yes," she says simply. "We need an insider. We need a woman who is close to the Emperor, who can ask questions, who will hear of plans being made. You will take the place of my cousin. You will endear yourself to the Emperor. Then you will talk of your homeland. What could be more natural? He believes your family to be his loyal allies, so he will let slip information which will aid us."

"Aid you to do *what*?"

She answers without meeting my gaze. "Start a rebellion."

I'm sure my mouth falls open in shock. "How would you do that? Do you have an army you haven't told me about?"

"The people will rise up if they have a strong leader. We have a network of those who wish to reclaim our land."

I have my doubts about anyone raising an army that can withstand the Emperor's troops. Now he's made his conquest, after years of fighting, he surely won't let it go that easily. But I don't really care about her ridiculous plans of fighting the Emperor of China. I'm shaking at the very idea of what she's suggesting. "It can't be done. Everyone would know I'm not from a noble family."

Iparhan nods. "You will have a few months here first. You will learn how to behave like an imperial concubine. By the time our cousins set out for Beijing you will be able to pass yourself off as the girl. We will intercept them and you will take her place."

I clutch at this. "What happens to this girl, then? She's hardly going to step out of the bridal palanquin and say, 'Oh, by all means take my place,' is she?"

Nurmat looks at Iparhan. She says nothing, just looks back at him.

I shut my eyes for a moment. I can feel tears of fear welling up. I'm sorry I asked the question. "I don't want to know. Then what?"

Iparhan presses on. "Once you are at the palace you will be given a title, your own rooms and servants, clothes, money. You will be kept in splendour – this place will be a hovel compared to it."

I shake my head. I'm beginning to feel sick. "You're crazy. It's just not possible."

She's coaxing me now, her voice pitched low and soft. It doesn't sound natural coming from her. "All you need to do is live your life. There will be gardens to walk in, other ladies to keep you company, wonderful food to eat. You may keep a pet. There will be games, visits to the summer palace and the hunting lodge, boating on the lakes. Your life will be –"

I stop her. "Oh, yes. My life will be one long round of pleasure and happiness, I'm sure. Until my 'brother' comes to visit and he sees a complete stranger masquerading as his sister. Then what?"

She shakes her head. "We will arrange the timing of the changeover so that you are almost at the palace when it happens. The court will send out a palanquin for you to ride in. You will be wearing a wedding veil. Once you're in the palace your 'brother' may visit you only if you are ill or if there is a very special occasion. Even if he does, he will not see your face. He is a man; you will be an imperial concubine. He will wait outside your rooms and send in his compliments. Once you enter the Forbidden City he will never see your face again. You will live there for the rest of your days and be our spy."

The tears I was trying to hold back spill over. I stand up too fast. My heart's pounding and I think I might throw up. I need to get away from Iparhan's dark eyes and the madness coming out of her mouth. My legs feel weak beneath me and I have to lock my knees in place to stand upright. "I'm going to bed," I say and my words are an ugly distorted gulp.

Iparhan stands as I do. "We need an answer tomorrow morning."

I pause in the doorway and look back at her. I think of the endless grey desert outside, the way Iparhan talks of the hapless concubine-to-be who is her own cousin. No one knows or cares that I'm here. No one would know or care if a dagger stopped my heart. "Do I have a choice?"

Her silence follows me to bed.

I don't sleep. Instead I lie awake fully dressed and think. This could be my way out of life on the streets. Concubine to the Emperor of China! I would live in comfort for the rest of my life, would never again feel the pain of hunger cramping my belly. I'm quick and smart, I could learn what must be learnt to pass myself off as a lowly concubine, couldn't I? It's not as if I am trying to impersonate an Empress. I could find out whatever Iparhan wants to know and then she can raise her rebellion and succeed or fail – it will make no difference to me. My life will go on, secure within the gilded cocoon that is the Emperor's Forbidden City. What harm can come to me there?

But… but… their plan is a folly. For all their talk of the luxurious life I would lead, how can they possibly expect it to work? The women chosen to be concubines for the Emperor will have come from the best families. They will have spent their whole lives being prepared for their role in his court, in his bedchamber. And I? I have spent my life scraping – not even a living – only enough food to keep me from starving, enough warmth to keep me from freezing. Besides, they want me to be a spy, to ask questions that may raise suspicions. I will have to draw attention to myself, which will only risk my position further, exposing the deception. It can't be done. And I know enough to know that if it can't be done; someone will suffer for it when the deception is revealed – and that someone will be me.

By dawn I am decided. In the early light I slip out of the room and make my way to the outer door. I touch the thick sheepskin of Nurmat's jacket and slip it on. It engulfs me but it's warm. I think I might need it. I open the door and step out.

It's freezing. The desert is the unpleasant colour of dirty, peeling, dead skin, a grey undulating endlessness.

I look more closely at the old dead poplar tree. What few branches it has left poke into the sky, black stumps against almost-white. From the stumps flutter tiny shreds of cloth: red and green, yellow and blue. Each tiny scrap a prayer or a wish from some unknown person. Under the tree is a large dome of pale mud, hard baked by the sun. The scraps of cloth should be faded, unravelling from years of past-forgotten dreams. The mud-domed tomb should be better shaped and dusty with age. But the scraps are brightly coloured and the dome is misshapen and cracked as though it was made by unskilled hands and then dried out too fast. I move closer to it and look down at it, then rest my left hand on the poplar, looking out across the dunes. The bark crumbles and gives way under my touch.

I see a small shed tucked into the edge of a dune and hear a snort, telling me that the horses are stabled there. In the distance are the mountains I think would lead me back to Kashgar. I take a deep breath and prepare to move towards the shed when I hear a thud and find I cannot move my left arm.

I look down and see a dagger pinning the sheepskin jacket I am wearing to the tree. I look up and see Iparhan, standing in the doorway of the house, a second dagger in her hand. I turn slowly to face her, my left hand still pinned to the tree.

The wind changes direction and I get a mouthful of thin dry sand. I cough. I try to keep my eyes on her though. I'm afraid of where her second dagger might land if she lets it fly but I can't let her see my fear. "Whose tomb is this?"

She keeps the dagger lifted in her hand, ready to throw. "My father's."

"But you said—" I stop. "So when the Shah said he'd 'mislaid' the head of your father, he hadn't."

"No."

"Who did the body belong to, then?"

She shrugs.

"So he came with you? You, your father, Nurmat and Mei?"

"Yes."

"And what was the plan?"

She sounds proud. "He would have roused the people behind him and Altishahr would have rebelled against the Emperor."

"And your role in all of this?"

She is silent for a moment. "I was to be the Emperor's concubine."

"The spy, you mean."

"Yes."

"What went wrong?"

"My father died of a wound that rotted his flesh. We buried him here."

"And decided to do it all yourselves?"

"Yes."

"But something went wrong?"

She's silent. I look at her for a moment. In the cold her skin is bone white, the scar purple.

"You couldn't be the concubine because of the scar. You needed someone else to take that part."

She dips her head.

I sigh. "Why me?"

She doesn't answer.

"Because you thought no one would miss me?"

She moves away from the house and comes towards me. I'd like to step back but her dagger is keeping me firmly attached to the poplar. She hesitates, looking me over. That same searching look.

She pauses, then speaks quickly: "I look like my cousin, the one who is to be the concubine. And you look – enough – like me." She sees my puzzled face. "Your height, your build," she adds. "Don't you think you look like me?"

I shake my head, confused. I can't say I see myself in mirrors that often. The hat stall in the market has a mirror, but I've only glimpsed myself in passing. Certainly I don't think I look like Iparhan, who despite her scar is beautiful. I frown. "But the Emperor will never have seen this girl before anyway – oh, what does it matter? At least the silk in the palace will be better quality for my hands to rest on, I suppose."

Iparhan frowns. "The silk?"

"Nothing. Talking to myself."

We stand in silence. I'm thinking fast. I have two choices: defy her and die, or agree to her plan. I try to push back the conclusion I came to in the night's darkness: that the plan is impossible. Instead I look up and meet her gaze directly. "I'll do this for a warm bed and a full belly," I say, trying to sound unafraid. "And a quiet life in a forgotten part of the Forbidden City once your crazy plan is done with. Do you understand? I don't want to be your comrade in arms or a part of whatever glories you have in your mind. I want to be left alone when this is over. And you must keep me safe. You must teach me every trick I will need to stay alive. I have to know how to dress, how to move, how to do whatever it takes to stay alive."

"You agree to my plan?"

I spread my hands open, the left one pinned to the tree, the other shaking with cold and the realisation of what I am agreeing to. "If I ran away now, in front of you, what would you do?"

She looks down and then hardly moves. I hear a *thud* and my right arm jerks back. Now both my hands are pinned to the tree behind me, my arms pulled open in a gesture of submission, the second dagger's handle still trembling.

I nod and start to laugh. "I thought so."

She watches me as I laugh and laugh. I can't seem to stop. I struggle to breathe and my lungs hurt but the laughter carries on without air.

Eventually my laughter fades and there's only the hissing of the sand dunes.

She pulls out the daggers in swift movements, her eyes never leaving my face. I look away from her as soon as she's finished. Her eyes burn too brightly for my liking. Back in the house Nurmat and Mei are standing waiting for us.

"I'm alive," I say. "So that must mean I've agreed to her plan, don't you think?"

Nurmat leaves the room, Iparhan following behind him. Mei looks concerned.

"Well," I say to Mei with blustering confidence, "I must be able to survive in a palace if I can survive on the streets. At least they'll feed me and keep me warm. It can't be much harder than my life up until now, can it?"

Mei looks at me without answering.

"Don't bother to reassure me," I say.

"I will do all I can to help you," she says, although she doesn't sound confident. "But we don't have that much time, perhaps only a couple of months. First things first, you have to learn good table manners."

"If you had just one meal a day and only if you stole it or begged for it or worked hard for it, you'd eat in whatever way got the food into your belly fastest."

She nods. "But you'll be a court lady now. And court ladies have more food than they know what to do with. They've no idea what it is to be hungry. So they just pick at their food."

"What do you know about court ladies?"

She smiles, revealing her secret. "I was a maid in the Forbidden City."

I stare at her. "What are you doing here, then?"

"I had served my time. I was released to be married. I married a man from Yili and when he died I carried on living there."

I narrow my eyes and lower my voice. "Until they kidnapped you, too?"

She hesitates, looks behind her, then nods.

"To teach them about the Forbidden City?"

She nods again.

"Don't you mind?"

Mei answers cautiously, her voice low. "I had no children. My husband had died. Besides," and there is some pride in her voice, "I was always a good servant to my mistress."

I feel sorry for the little bit of pride left which leads her to make the best of her imprisonment. "And who was your mistress in the Forbidden City?"

"I was maid to the Lady Wan. One of the Emperor's concubines."

"Did you live there a long time?"

"They were such *happy* years. My mistress was so *kind*."

We both jump. Iparhan is standing in the doorway and she has just mimicked Mei's voice. We stare at her, for she does it perfectly. It sounds like Mei speaking.

She uses her own voice again and it's cold. "This is not the time for reliving your past. Get on with teaching Hidligh some manners."

Mei obediently starts hurrying in and out of the room, setting down all manner of little dishes on the table, each filled with local delicacies. Roasted lamb with herbs, kebabs spiced with ground cumin and chilli, various vegetables and noodles, as well as *polo* – a dish of rice with mutton and vegetables. It's usually served at banquets and the only time I've eaten it was when I managed to get my hands on the scraps from a wedding.

I gaze at the food and shake my head in disbelief. "So," I manage. "How *does* a court lady eat?"

"Don't reach for anything, just nod towards it," Mei says. "I will pass it to you."

I nod in an exaggerated way towards the *polo*. Mei passes it to me. It's glistening with fat and the smell makes my mouth water. It's a dish eaten with the fingers, and I try to eat in a way that suggests I am only picking at it, but greed overtakes me and I take a heaping scoop, which allows grains to fall from my mouth and fingers.

"Peasant." Iparhan is watching me and mutters it quietly, but it annoys me. I let my mouth hang open as I chew as noisily as possible, slurp the hot tea placed by me, then exaggeratedly suck each of my fingers clean even though there's not that much food on them. Mei shakes her head but I wipe my mouth with the back of my clean shirtsleeve, then belch loudly when I'm finished. I look over my shoulder at Iparhan, eyebrows raised, daring her to make another comment.

She's looking away, out of the door towards the desert. From where I'm sitting all I can see is the scar on the curve of her cheekbone.

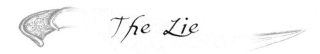

The Lie

WHAT ELSE COULD SHE SAY *but yes? What other choice does she have? Nurmat watched her standing in the women's lane, shifting from one foot to the other, nervous, desperate, one step away from selling her body for a filling meal. She scraped her food up from the dirt by the traders' stalls or caught it mid-air as it was thrown to her, like a mangy dog.*

"She has spirit, though," says Nurmat. "She can ride," he adds.

"Spirit is nothing without food in your belly," I tell him.

"She tried to escape," he says. "Several times."

"She failed," I remind him. "Several times."

He doesn't answer.

"She has accepted my proposal," I say. 'She had no other choices and besides, what street girl wouldn't do anything for a life of ease and luxury like the one I am offering her?"

My own life of ease and luxury, the noble daughter of a noble house, was swept away when the Emperor's men beat on the great doors and demanded the heads of my father and uncle. As the heavy doors swung open and the hideous bloodstained bundles were passed from the defeated to the victorious, there was a great wail from the high walls.

Each of us turned our faces to the sound, only to see the silent fall of my mother through the air, her multi-hued skirts rippling against the grey sky. Hidden away for her own safety she had not been told of our subterfuge, only seen what she believed was her husband's dead and mutilated body being given to our enemies. Her despair so great she chose to leave me, her only daughter, to an unknown fate. I was left with a mortally wounded father and no guidance from my mother. I stood alone.

Except for Nurmat.

"It is dangerous," Nurmat says. "She may forget how to behave. She may be found out."

I shrug. "If she is found out she will be executed and no harm will come to us," I say, although my heart beats faster.

Nurmat turns to me so that our faces come very close together. His voice is low. "Iparhan. You still swear it?"

I keep my eyes on his while my heart beats faster still. I can see before me so plainly what really intend to do that I cannot believe he does not see it himself, that the bloodied image does not rise up before him. "I swear," I say. "She is to be a spy. She will gather information and I will use it – we will use it – to further our plans for rebellion."

"Nothing more?"

I lift my free hand and cup his cheek, stroke his warm skin. His eyes close at my rare touch. His breath is on my lips. "Nothing more," I say.

The House in the Dunes

"I'M NOT BATHING WITH HIM in the room!"

Iparhan's face is white. Her scar stands out, a red streak of fury. "Take off your clothes and get in the bath, you stupid girl."

I turn away from her. "No!"

Iparhan's voice drops to a hissing whisper as she comes close to me. Her teeth are so tightly clenched I think one of them might crack. "Your bath will be filled by men. You will be soaped and rinsed by men. They will wash your hair. They will touch every part of you. They will pat your legs dry while they kneel before you." She's so close to me now I can feel her breath on my lips. "Which part of your body do you think their faces will be next to when they do that?"

I step back, trying to avoid her fury. "They'll be *eunuchs*!"

Mei is busily filling the tub, taking no notice of either of us, nudging past with each new pail of water.

Iparhan picks up a handful of dried rose petals and scatters them into the bath. Their scent warms the room more than the clouds of steam. Her hands are shaking. "Take. Your. Clothes. Off. Get. In. The. Bath."

I turn to Nurmat. "Shut your eyes."

He holds out his hand, which has a scented soap in it. His face is serious. "I am supposed to bathe you. I have to be able to see."

"You're a man, not a eunuch! This is ridiculous. Can't I just act ignorant when I get there and insist on bathing alone?"

Iparhan leans over the bath and tests the water. "Get in."

I'm so angry I rip my skirt as I try to undo it. Mei comes to my rescue and I pull off everything as fast as I can so I can get into the tub and have something, even if it's just water, covering my naked body. Mei leaves the three of us alone then, taking my clothes with her to mend. Iparhan stands by the small window as Nurmat kneels by the side of the tub and rubs the scented soap between his hands onto a small soft cloth.

The autumn moon has long since died away and a bitter cold surrounds us. Because of her past, Mei is designated my tutor for most things, and I'm glad of it, for I can't bring myself to willingly spend much time in a room with Iparhan. Mei serves me with care and kindness, as though I were her beloved mistress, not a fellow prisoner.

My only interest in Iparhan's scheme lies in learning enough to protect myself. Mei rebukes me for looking at her when she talks to me, for paying her any attention at all.

"You must not laugh at what I do. You must not even notice me. I am a servant. I am invisible to you."

I make a great show of ignoring her as I eat but this is not enough. "You are not supposed to *act* ignoring me," she chastises me. "You have to be oblivious to me. Forget about me. I am a maid. I am nobody."

I sigh and keep eating, trying to manage chopsticks with grace. Mealtimes come sooner for me than for Nurmat and Iparhan. They eat at normal times but I'm fed several more times a day. They were right. You can't eat as I've been accustomed to when you're not really hungry. So I begin to pick at my food, with Mei having to coax me. I'm aware that my starved angles are filling out into the slender curves of a rich woman and I'm glad of it. A bit of extra fat on me may be my saviour if this plan goes awry. I attempt to get some noodles into my mouth in an elegant manner but several fall out of my mouth. I catch them but my white cuffs get sauce on them. Behind me I hear an impatient sigh. I don't bother turning round. Iparhan's perfume follows her everywhere. If I can smell it, then she is in the room.

"What do you want?" I ask. I'm afraid of her daggers and her eyes that are too dark, too certain. I compensate for my fear of her by speaking rudely to her, by showing a bravado I don't feel.

"You need to learn poetry."

I roll my eyes. "Poetry? Why would I want to do that?"

"All cultured women at court can recite poetry."

I give up on the noodles. I look pointedly towards some vegetables and Mei passes them. At least eating them is a bit easier. "Well," I say through a mouthful. "You'd better teach me some poems then, hadn't you?"

Iparhan looks away from my half-filled, fast-chewing mouth and addresses the cushions.

"Blossoms fall
Mist rises
She arrives in darkness
And fades in the light
How long will this spring dream stay?"

She looks back at me.

I grimace. It sounds like the merchants from Beijing but I never understood them, even when they shouted. This just sounds like a whining child, all ups and downs. "I don't speak that language."

Her lips tighten. "It is Mandarin and it is what the court speaks. You had better learn or you will understand nothing of what goes on."

I shake my head and help myself to more vegetables. "I can't learn a whole new language in a few months. Besides, he knows I'm from Kashgar, doesn't he? He surely doesn't expect me to speak his language?"

"You need to know what is being said around you – or possibly about you."

She's right. I can't get by anywhere if I don't know what is being said. I shake my head in despair at what I have to learn. A whole new language. This is madness. I sit for a moment in silence, my confidence sapped.

She looks at me and waits.

I lean back against the cushions and repeat the sounds back to her. My version sounds like a child talking garbled nonsense, whining to its mother for sweetmeats. Mei stifles a laugh.

When Iparhan leaves the room, glowering at my incompetence, I turn to Mei. "I need to know," I say. "What happened to Iparhan's face?"

Mei sits back and sighs. This makes her cough, something she does regularly. She takes a drink of water. "Iparhan's father and uncle ordered Iparhan to leave their side although she was unwilling. She wanted to stay and fight but they insisted that she escape from the siege and come here. It's a safe place and the family had many taels of silver to hide away for as long as necessary. Nurmat is a distant cousin, they have been promised to each other since they were children. He too had intended to stay and fight but was ordered to make his way here and protect Iparhan. Her family was afraid that if they lost the battle against the Emperor and were killed there would be no one left of their family line, so they wanted to save the two of them. Nurmat has never cared for war. He wanted to marry her many years ago, take her away from all of the fighting and rebellions and family feuds. He said they could live quietly somewhere out of the way and be happy together. But Iparhan got it into her head that she must stand by her family until they had defeated the Emperor. When her uncle died her father made his way here. But his wounds began to rot and when he died she vowed she would not marry until she had avenged them. You've seen how she can hide herself, how well she can use weapons. She trains every day."

I know this. Iparhan spends most days outside. She trains in the dunes of the desert. The cold, the heat, the wind and blowing sand never seem to affect her. Her daggers fly straight and embed themselves in the blackened poplar trees, which are scarred and shredded all over with her rage.

"And the scar?"

Mei looks down into her lap. "Nurmat hated the idea of her marrying the Emperor, even for show. He did not want her to be a concubine to the Emperor before Nurmat had taken her as his wife, if indeed at all. They argued. He begged her to marry him first, to live together as husband and wife and that then she could go and be a concubine. She refused. She had to be a virgin for her first night with the Emperor. Nurmat was enraged at the idea. He attempted to take her maidenhood before it was taken by the Emperor."

I frown. I can't imagine this of Nurmat, who worships Iparhan. "He forced her?"

Mei slowly shakes her head. "He didn't try very hard. He was drunk that night and was a little rough perhaps in trying to persuade her. And she refused, she said she would not come to his bed until she had raised a rebellion against the Emperor. She threatened him with her dagger, said if he took her virginity she would kill herself out of shame at not being able to carry out her revenge on the Emperor. Nurmat took the dagger out of her hand." She stops.

"And?"

Mei speaks fast. "And he cut her face. He said if she was disfigured the Emperor would never take her into his court, but he, Nurmat, would still love her."

I gape at her. "It wasn't an accident?"

She shakes her head. "No."

"And she still refused to lie with him?"

"Yes. Nurmat thought that would be an end to her plans but she saw you in the marketplace and chose you as her replacement. You will allow Iparhan to take her revenge."

"And then they will marry? Not before?"

"She is a warrior at heart, not a maiden. She took a solemn vow not to marry before she has her revenge. She is stubborn. She will not change her mind now. She wants to see the Emperor dead – probably at her own hand – and these lands returned to their people."

I sigh. "She's hardly going to come face to face with the Emperor in battle. I believe he has generals and foot soldiers to do the fighting. So long as she leaves me alone once she's finished. I'm doing this for a warm bed and good food. I don't want her causing trouble for me for years and years to come."

Mei is silent. She opens her mouth, then closes it again. Then she starts again but ends up having a coughing fit. I fetch her some water. When she's breathing properly again I get up. "We'd better carry on, then. Wasn't I supposed to be learning how to eat noodles without them falling down my waistcoat?"

Clothes are worse than table manners. Although my new clothes are warm and clean, I'm clumsy in them. A long wide skirt, after being used to trousers, is difficult to manage. I regularly trip over it or catch it on everything from protruding hooks to, memorably, Mei's head, sitting on cushions near a door I come through. Nurmat laughs so hard he cries.

"It's that sort of accident that will give me away at court," I spit at him, and he shakes his head at my sudden temper.

I pull on yet another long skirt, this time in a vivid pattern of green and blues, then stand while Mei fastens my green waistcoat's little buttons, which I always fumble over. "Shouldn't I be wearing court clothes?"

Iparhan, watching me, shakes her head. "We know that our cousins have decided the girl must wear clothes that show where she is from. They wish to flaunt their allegiance to the Emperor. She is to be a daily reminder of his conquest of our lands." She looks enraged.

I shrug. I've got enough to cope with without wearing entirely unfamiliar clothes. At least I know how these ones should look – if I wore court clothes I might put the wrong things on or wear some item in the wrong way and give myself away. Besides, I've seen drawings of the headdresses the court ladies wear and I don't know how they balance them all on their heads, what with flowers and dangling hairpins. My plaits are easier. But the billowing sleeves of my shirts are a problem.

"Get them out of your soup," admonishes Mei.

I curse and Iparhan frowns at me.

Nurmat laughs out loud. When he's not arguing with Iparhan he can be funny, with a lop-sided smile and a laugh that makes me laugh too. "I want to be there when you do that in front of the Emperor," he says. He mimics my trailing sleeve, dripping with soup at the elbow while uttering a string of such coarse words that I get a helpless fit of giggles. For the rest of the meal the two of us hold up our sleeves at intervals and mouth obscenities at each other. Mei shakes her head and laughs at us, although even she is tiring of our game by the end of the meal. Iparhan ignores us.

The shoes are worse. They have a small elegantly raised heel and I am used to walking in men's boots. I stumble and fall regularly. Nurmat gets used to catching me in time after the first bad sprain.

Iparhan is displeased with my clumsiness. "You still have the same feet—you're not foot-bound," she admonishes. "What's the matter with you?"

Exasperated, I kick them off. They strike against the door, making a clatter that brings Mei to see what the noise is about.

"I have the same feet but wobbling about on stilts!" I yell at her.

Nurmat fetches the shoes, grinning at my temper, then kneels in front of me holding them. They're made of finely tooled leather, with little flowers etched into them. I put a hand on his shoulder and feel the warmth of his cheek against my thighs as he slips them back on. I blush and step backwards from him and in doing so very nearly fall over again.

Nurmat laughs. "The day will come when it will all seem natural."

I sit down, slumping forwards, my face resting in my hands, my feet, encased in the foolish shoes, tucked under me. I'm too tired and worried to reply with any spirit. "I'm not sure it ever will, you know."

Perched high on a stack of cushions, Nurmat focuses his attention on Iparhan. By his side Mei, also on a stack of cushions, looks down benevolently. A fit of coughing mars her regal performance as the Empress Dowager but she recovers and nods graciously to Iparhan to continue her demonstration of the perfect kowtow.

Iparhan advances very slowly, head high, hands by her sides. As she nears Nurmat and Mei, her knees bend without seeming to affect her upper body at all, for it remains upright until she is fully kneeling before them. Then she folds herself in two, her forehead touching the ground. Lifting her head she calls out in a clear voice: "I wish your Majesties ten thousand years!"

She touches her forehead to the ground twice more and then rises in one smooth movement, as though lifted by invisible arms.

"Ten thousand years?" I say from behind her in my place in the corner of the room. "Who wants to live that long? Wouldn't a hundred do?"

Iparhan ignores me. She is kneeling down again.

"Yes, yes," I say. "I got it the first time. Walk forward. Kneel down, touch your forehead to the ground three times, ten thousand years, get up again."

Mei lays a finger on her lips. "You must do it three times," she says.

"The whole thing? Three times?"

"Yes."

I sigh and sit down on a cushion with a bump. "This is going to take all day. Doesn't the Emperor get bored of it?"

Iparhan has finished her set of nine reverences. "Your turn."

I stand and step forward to take my turn.

Iparhan sighs behind me. "I wonder how long it will be before you fall over."

I turn and make a face at her. "Watch me."

She does, and I fall over as I try to stand up. Nurmat tries to help me but we end up in a tangled mess on the floor.

"Much use you are," I scold him.

"Much good *you* are," he retorts, straightening my skirts as we stand. "I've never seen such a clumsy girl."

I swipe at him but he ducks too fast for me and I nearly slap Iparhan, who's standing behind him, her face cold.

Iparhan and Nurmat are praying. I sit and watch them, then suddenly interrupt.

"Praying!"

Iparhan pauses, then turns to face me. "What?"

I speak fast, excited. "You have to teach me to pray!"

She is disbelieving. "You don't know how to pray?"

I shrug. "Who do you think was going to teach me that? No, I can't pray. But I need to. It will help me fool them – it's a very good distraction."

Iparhan's face freezes. "A what?"

I sigh. "Don't get all upset. I just mean, when I am in the Forbidden City, they'll know I am a Muslim, won't they?"

Iparhan is unforgiving. "I'm not sure you are, if you don't even pray."

I ignore her. "They will be expecting a Muslim woman. So of course I must be – I must pray, and only eat certain foods, and make a big fuss about it all, so that they'll be so busy trying to accommodate my requests they won't spend time wondering whether I really am who I'm supposed to be. You see?"

Iparhan barely speaks to me for the rest of the day, but Nurmat agrees that I must be educated in the fundamental aspects of our religion, in which I am sadly lacking.

And so I have to listen to long passages from the Qu'ran, then practice my prayers so that I don't stumble over the words or actions.

"You will have to fast as well," points out Iparhan.

I laugh at her. "You want me, who used to be near to starving, to fast?"

"You must," she says simply.

I walk out of the room, but we both know she's won the next day, when I pay more attention to the rules governing the food I may or may not eat, although privately I think that when I reach the court I may play the part of a good Muslim girl but I will not mention any need to fast.

"Enough!" I shriek. "Enough!"

Mei tuts. "What a fuss. What a baby," she scolds.

"It hurts!"

She shakes her head, focusing on my second earlobe. "You must have pierced ears. Even a peasant girl has pierced ears," she says.

I moan as the second lobe is pierced and pull away as she finishes.

"I thought it would never end," I say.

"It hasn't," she says sternly.

"There's one in each ear! What am I, a pin cushion?"

Mei wipes a drop of blood from the first earlobe. "The Emperor's ladies dress in the Manchu fashion. That means three earrings in each earlobe. You'll have pearl earrings, little strands of them, one strand hanging from each hole. You must look like a court lady," she adds, her voice lowering to a warning. "You cannot raise their suspicions. If they find out - "

I back away. "No."

"You have to."

I hold out my hands to stop her advancing on me and stand my ground. "No. I'm doing enough. I'm learning a ridiculous amount of new things every day. I'm being made to learn a religion backwards. I am *not* having triple piercings. I'm a Kashgarlik girl, not a Manchu. If the Emperor doesn't like it, that's just too bad. He should have picked another Manchu girl to add to the rest of them."

Mei lets her hands drop and shrugs. "Suit yourself," she says. "At least you've got enough piercings for these parts."

My shoulders slump with relief. "I've got a headache," I say. "I can't remember all the things I'm supposed to be learning."

"It will come," says Mei soothingly.

"I doubt it." I sit down on the cushions in a huff. "I want some noodles."

"I'm busy," says Mei.

I sit up straight and give her a withering stare. "I am an imperial concubine," I say with as much grandeur as I can muster. "Bring me my noodles the moment I ask for them or I'll tell the Emperor and he'll have you beaten for being a disobedient wretch."

Mei chuckles and goes to the kitchen.

Now it seems I must learn how to flirt.

"You can place your hand on a man's arm," suggests Mei. "Or pull gently at his sleeve, to draw his attention to something you wish him to see, to share with him."

"Such as?"

Mei sighs at my lack of imagination. "A beautiful landscape. A flower. Yourself."

I can't imagine such a moment between myself and a man.

Nurmat holds out his arm and I tug at his sleeve. He pretends to be pulled to the ground by my strength. I make a face at him and he laughs.

"Stop your foolishness," Mei chastises us. "You must learn to draw the Emperor's attention, his interest."

I roll my eyes but I learn to pull gently at a sleeve, to smile coyly, to glance up from under shy lashes. I feel like an idiot and my smiles feel like grimaces. I cannot imagine how they would attract anyone.

The moon grows and wanes again and again. Slowly, so slowly, the days begin to come.

"I wish your Majesties ten thousand years," I say, and rise to my feet.

Nurmat laughs out loud. "You didn't fall over! For once, you didn't stumble!"

He jumps off the pile of cushions and picks me up, swings me round till I shriek with dizziness. Mei comes to see what all the fuss is about.

"She did it!" yells Nurmat. "She did the whole kowtow and she didn't stumble. She got up in one move and kept her back straight, like Iparhan does."

Mei smiles, but Iparhan, silent on the cushions where she had played at being Empress next to Nurmat's Emperor, continues to read the Qu'ran and ignores our laughter.

The dice are thrown and it's my turn to recite a poem. I don't pause. The words flow from me with something approaching rhythm. Iparhan's eyebrows go up.

"The poet's name?"

I'm smug. "Li Shangyin, Tang dynasty."

She nods. It's the first time she hasn't had to correct me. I struggle to hold a coherent conversation in this strange new tongue, but I can recite an awful lot of poems. I hope the Emperor's happy to talk in riddles.

I reach out for a bowl of tea that's not there and Mei places it in my hand. I don't thank her. I don't even acknowledge her.

She claps her hands in delight. "You are a lady!" she says.

We grin at each other before I remember my training and gesture to her to leave me. She goes and I sit alone for a few minutes. I've been here for several months now. The Emperor has already sent for Iparhan's traitorous cousins and they will be planning their journey. Soon they will leave, and when they do, we will be in their shadows until they reach Beijing. Somewhere outside the Forbidden City, as an unknown girl steps from her own carrying litter into the imperial palanquin… I think of her for a moment, this faceless girl. Each of us chosen for a destiny not of our own making. The path I have been forced on to will collide with hers and at that moment the girl…

I stop thinking about her. I am about to be cast alone into a new world and my own fear is growing so great I cannot summon up any more fear for another girl's destiny. She must remain faceless to me. My eyes fill unexpectedly with tears and I dash them away. I've always been alone, I tell myself angrily. At least this time I will be well fed and dressed with a warm bed at night, for the rest of my life, even if I do have to share the Emperor's bed from time to time. *How bad can it be?* I think to myself. I say it over and over again in my head, *how bad can it be, how bad can it be* and I do not let myself listen to the reply. I have tried to escape and I have been caught every time. Now I can only step forward blindly and hope I never have to find out how badly it might end for me.

I spend the rest of the day sat in silence, turning my new skills over and over in my mind. Are they enough? Yes, I can dress well and walk well. I can perform a kowtow smoothly. I can recite meaningless poems and converse – poorly and only for a few moments – in Mandarin. I can flirt very badly and I can eat without noodles falling down my clothes. I am not sure any of this is enough. I may have prided myself on being quick-witted but will that be enough when there are quick blades waiting if I am found out?

The next day I wait but it seems no one is going to teach me anything new nor test me on what I have learnt so far. Iparhan is in a foul mood. She snaps at Mei, she turns away from Nurmat. She acts as though she cannot bear to be in the same room as me. We eat in silence, everyone's eyes lowered, our attention supposedly on the food although none of us seems to be eating much.

At last Mei stands. "It is time to begin," she says.

"We'll begin tomorrow," says Iparhan, without looking up.

"There is much to be done," says Mei.

"Tomorrow," says Iparhan.

Her tone makes my fingers clench and twist with fear. I daren't ask what we will be beginning tomorrow, but I don't sleep well.

I eat my breakfast in silence, in an empty room, my tired eyes aching. Only when I have finished and Mei has cleared away the food do Iparhan and Nurmat enter. Iparhan is holding something, which she drops into my lap as though it burns her fingers. "You will acquaint yourself with this," she says and heads immediately for the door, Nurmat following her.

When the door closes behind them I pick up the object. It is an album of paintings on silk. The first shows a maid, peeping through a crack in a door leading to a bedchamber. Inside the bedchamber, only their feet visible, are a man and a woman engaged in lovemaking. I hastily turn the leaf over to the next painting although as soon as I do so I begin to blush. In this painting two lovers embrace outdoors, surrounded by blossoms. Their robes are pulled up so that the woman may grasp the man and guide him inside her.

Painting follows painting. They grow more and more explicit, the couples entwined in every possible way, their most intimate parts clearly shown. There are kisses, embraces, all manner of positions. There is a man who is coupling with two women, one older and one younger. There is a man with four women in a garden, all in various states of undress. There are couples on beds, in boats, in gardens, in baths. In one a man kneels before a woman, his lips on her, while her head is thrown back in pleasure. When Mei brings me some tea I nearly drop the album, flustered.

"It came from the Forbidden City," says Mei. "The Emperor will have many such albums for his pleasure. She takes the album and shows me a picture of a couple that is engaged in looking at just such an album of drawings together. "It is possible you will be shown such paintings. You will also be expected to know how to assume some of the positions. A woman destined for the palace would have been taught such things."

I can feel myself grow hotter. "How will I know what to do?" I ask.

"You will practice."

Iparhan's voice is so close I nearly scream. I manage to gasp instead. She is standing in the doorway, with Nurmat behind her. Her voice is too loud.

Nurmat looks uncomfortable. "She could just look at the pictures," he suggests. "She is not a fool, she can imagine for herself…"

"We will not discuss this," says Iparhan. "It will be done and that is all. She cannot appear uneducated in this. She must please the Emperor. Otherwise all this is for nothing. We will begin now."

Nurmat comes closer to me and reaches out his hand for the album. I hand it to him at arm's length. He opens it and discards the first painting, the one where only the couple's feet show. Instead he turns to the next picture, where the couple sit entwined at the moment of penetration. He examines it for a moment and then sits himself on a chair, his feet flat on the floor. He gestures to me to come to him. I look at him in silence, uncertain of what he means to do. He surely does not intend to enact these scenes? I can already feel Iparhan's anger, her unhappiness. It is filling the room. Nurmat gestures again.

"Come, Hidligh," he says. "You must sit on my knee as the woman does in this painting."

I don't move.

I can see that Nurmat is almost more uncomfortable than I am. His voice is curt, unlike his usual manner. "Come," he says.

I get up very slowly and move a little closer to him.

"You need to try each of these positions," says Nurmat. "You must know how to assume them should the Emperor wish you to do so. Some are more difficult to attain than others, so you must have practiced."

I move within his arm's reach and he stretches out and takes my arm, pulling me towards him. "So," he says, his voice tense. "You will sit with one leg between mine. The other is raised up and you will rest your foot on my knee. Then you turn your upper body so that you can embrace me."

I stumble my way into the position, my face hot and red, my movements awkward. I am too close to Nurmat. His breath is on my cheek. His arms are wrapped around me.

My right leg is trapped between his thighs, my left foot is resting too close to his most intimate parts. At other moments when we have touched we have been in motion – when I have fallen and he has caught me, for example – a brief touch and then we have come apart again, not sat like this, in an embrace which is watched over by Iparhan. Her face is perfectly still, her hands, which are by her side, are shaking.

"And the next one," says Nurmat.

I want to cry. There are dozens of paintings. The idea of enacting each one, under Iparhan's barely controlled gaze, is horrible. The silence in the room, broken only by Nurmat's terse orders and the rustling sounds of our clothing and bodies fumbling to execute them, is excruciating.

But I have no choice. Day after day we enact the positions from the album, over and over again. Some are difficult or even painful to maintain. All, with Iparhan watching over us in silence, are uncomfortable.

One morning Iparhan does not appear. It seems she has a fever, so while Mei takes her foods and medicines, Nurmat and I sit together and eat breakfast, before taking up the album. Many of the positions we can now perform from memory, so we begin without discussion or referring to the paintings. At least our daily repetition means that some of the positions have become physically easier. My muscles no longer ache. I sit on a chair, padded with cushions, and lift my legs so that my ankles rest on Nurmat's shoulders, my knees pressed back against my breasts as he kneels between my thighs. There is a pause.

"I don't remember the next position," I admit. It feels easier to speak without Iparhan in the room.

Nurmat nods. "I think you sit more forward and wrap your legs around me," he says.

I adjust my position. Our faces are closer and our bodies more tightly pressed together. "It's difficult to hold," I say.

"Cross your ankles behind me," he says.

I try, although he has a broad chest and my legs only just reach far enough. The relief of not having Iparhan here, watching over us, makes me giggle a little, and Nurmat also lets out his breath in a little laugh, the tension easing despite the intimacy of the position.

"On to the next position, then," says Nurmat. He consults the album, then lies down on the floor, holding out his hands to me to help me as I lower myself over him, sitting astride him on my knees. Once I am settled he places his hands on my waist and helps me to raise myself up and lower down again, over and over again. I struggle to do it gracefully, but Nurmat does not smile at my efforts. His grip on my waist tightens a little and he speaks to me softly. "Slowly," he says. "Slowly. Hold my arms so that you keep your balance." His face has grown flushed. I lean forward so that I am holding his upper arms, his muscles bunched beneath my hesitant grasp. I slow my movements, trying to follow his guidance. Below me, he closes his eyes. As I lower myself onto him I feel him grow hard beneath me and see his lips part, his breathing grow faster.

I rise up, pull away from him as quickly as I can.

His eyes fly open. "I am sorry," he says, his voice hoarse. "I did not – I was not…"

I manage to step over his legs, although I almost stumble. I head towards my room, but find my way blocked by Iparhan. Her eyes are bright with fever, her face is flushed. Beads of sweat are on her forehead. She leans against the doorframe, unable to hold herself upright without its support.

"What are you doing?" she asks.

I don't answer, only push past her, the only time I have ever deliberately touched her since I came here. I go to my room and lie on the bed, my eyes closed as Nurmat's were when he grew aroused. My thoughts spin. Does Nurmat desire me? It's not possible. He has Iparhan. Except… except he does not, of course. She refuses to consummate their betrothal. She will not marry him. She will not share her body with him. And so… and so now he has become aroused whilst enacting these scenes with me. I twist on the bed, turning one way and another as I try to think my way out of the situation. What if he forces himself on me? I turn away from the thought. It is not in Nurmat's nature, I believe. The greater danger for me is Iparhan, who would surely kill me from jealousy if she even suspected such an interest in me from Nurmat. Does he care for me? Does he love me? I do not know what to think. I lie awake for hours while the day slowly passes and still my thoughts whirl and I cannot see the way ahead.

I awake in darkness to perfume all around me and Iparhan's dagger against my throat. I lie very still. My voice is hoarse with sleep and fear.

"What do you want, Iparhan?"

Below the scent of her perfume is the smell of hot fever: sour, dried-up sickness. "You are trying to seduce him, to draw him away from me"

"He wants you," I whisper. "His eyes were closed. He was thinking of you." I only hope it is true. I sit up in bed and feel the dagger move away. I breathe more deeply. She's a dark shape in the night. My eyes ache with tiredness. I can think of nothing that would placate her. "Marry him, Iparhan," I say, weariness bringing truth to my lips. "You can't keep a man waiting for ever."

"I cannot marry—" she begins.

"He's yours, Iparhan," I say, into the darkness that holds all her sorrow. "Forget your obsession with raising an army against the Emperor and marry Nurmat while he's still yours. Before he grows weary of waiting. Before he begins to look elsewhere. But he is still yours."

"I am his," she says. "I do not know if he is mine."

She gets up and stands over me. I know she could kill me, that one quick movement could end my life, remove me as any threat to the love between Nurmat and herself. If she does so, though, she will lose her chance to know the thoughts of the Emperor and use them to feed her plans for rebellion. If she cannot exact her revenge then she cannot marry, according to her own vow. My breath stops and I listen in the darkness for the movement of her arm that will end my life.

She hesitates and then leaves the room.

I touch my breast and feel my heart trembling. I lie awake for a long time in the dark, my skin cold under the blankets and my eyes full of tears, which slowly trickle down my cheeks. My life is hers to take at any moment. My only protection is her desire for revenge and the part I can play in achieving it. If I fail to carry out her dreams then I am worthless to her and to be worthless to Iparhan is to be dead.

"This afternoon, you will take a bath," says Iparhan.

I glance at her to see if she's thinking of last night. I wonder briefly if she means to drown me rather than stab me, but she's already speaking to Mei.

"She has to learn to be bathed by other people," she says. "She will be bathed by eunuchs there. She cannot be shy about it."

I shrug. "I don't care if the two of you bathe me," I say.

Iparhan turns to me and her eyes are very dark. "Nurmat will bathe you," she says, and her voice trembles. She stops, as though she does not want to continue. She looks towards Mei who nods, although she looks a little wary at this turn of events.

Iparhan goes on. "In the bath water will be my perfume."

I look up. "Why?"

"When you smell that perfume what do you think of?" she asks.

"You," I say. "No one smells like that but you."

She nods. "You must have something that is special," she says. "Something the Emperor remembers. You must stand out. He must think of you first when he thinks of his ladies. He must spend time with you alone, not with all the others. You need to spend time with him if you are to know his mind."

I nod eagerly. This is a clever trick. I will need all the help I can get to stand out for the right reasons rather than for any errors I may make. The perfume will be a valuable tool in what I'm coming to think of as my armoury.

Iparhan isn't smiling. I think about the little vial that carries her scent, a tiny golden-yellow thing, held with silver clasps.

"Who gave you the perfume?" I ask, but I know the answer already even as I ask the question.

She gets up and leaves the room. I look to Mei.

"Nurmat," says Mei. "An engagement gift."

Iparhan pauses in the doorway. Outside I can hear the horses' bridles jingle. Recently Nurmat brought a third horse back to the stable. Later today I will be bathed by him. I'm anxious. Iparhan's face is dark. I think the poplar trees had better brace themselves for her daggers. Today she will show no mercy. Her scar is turning an ugly purple as it heals, with little puckers where the scabs have dried and flaked away.

Since yesterday I have kept my distance from Nurmat and he has not looked me in the eye. I don't know what will happen now. How much longer will we be here? How much longer can this situation be held in stillness? Nurmat and I cannot be together in the same room, yet now he must bathe me. Iparhan hates me, yet she cannot kill me.

Iparhan leaves and I slump down onto a cushion with relief. The house seems lighter when she is not here. I look up at Mei.

"Come and tell me more of your outlandish stories about the Forbidden City."

Mei chuckles. She likes to tell me of daily life in the palaces and for my part I ask her endless questions. The more I know about the Forbidden City the better prepared I will be.

She offers me a tea and settles herself next to me. "There is a great moat around the Forbidden City," she begins, her voice as dramatic as any storyteller. "It is three times deeper than a man's full height and wider than fifty paces across. The walls surrounding the City are red and so smooth no-one could climb them without falling. There are four gates: the great gate of the South, called the Meridian Gate, the North gate, called the Gate of Divine Might, and the smaller gates called the East Glorious Gate and the West Glorious Gate. There are four watchtowers, one at each corner."

I'm not that interested in the walls and gates. "Tell me about daily life. What do I eat for breakfast?"

"You will be served up to one hundred dishes at every meal."

"One hundred dishes? At one meal? For one person? Don't be silly."

"Truly."

"Even I can't manage a hundred dishes."

She laughs so much her cough gets worse and I have to pass her tea to sooth her.

"You don't eat them all. You eat whatever you have a fancy for. Then your servants will eat the leftovers."

"So they'll all be watching me thinking 'Oh, don't eat that dish, that's my favourite.'"

"Probably."

"Tell me about the rooms."

"You must look up. In the throne rooms especially. The ceilings are a wonder of carving, painted in gold and red, with dragons writhing round them."

"And the private rooms?"

"Beautiful as well."

"All of them?"

"All of them."

"Was your room beautiful?"

Mei laughs at me. "I was a maid, not a concubine. Our rooms are hidden away at the back of the palaces. They were no better than soldiers' barracks – half of them were falling down. They leaked and the wind blew in during the winter months."

"Why don't they mend them?"

"We were servants. They thought they were good enough for us."

I think about the strange world I am to be sent to. Magnificent palaces with crumbling barracks hidden behind them. "What else?"

Mei thinks. "There are no men allowed in the Forbidden City at night except the Emperor and the Court Physician who is on duty."

"Apart from the eunuchs."

"They don't count."

"How many are there?"

"Perhaps three thousand."

"Three *thousand*? All eunuchs?"

Mei nods.

"Iparhan says it's a disgusting practice," I say.

Mei nods. "It is a great sacrifice. But many of the boys and men who choose that path do so because they can then feed their families. They are poor people, with few choices in life. Iparhan is a nobleman's daughter, she has never known such hardships."

"And I'm to be bathed by eunuchs? Or is Iparhan just teasing?"

Mei raises her eyebrows.

"All right," I concede, "Iparhan doesn't know how to tease. So that's true?"

Mei nods. "You won't be left alone for an instant. You'll have a eunuch sleeping on the floor beside you, for protection. You'll have them all around you, whatever you do."

"How annoying," I say, though in truth, secretly, it sounds comforting. There were nights in Kashgar when I would have been grateful to have someone sleeping nearby for my protection or even just to know I was not alone.

"What will I see when I first go there?" I ask.

"The Outer Court," she says promptly. "The City is made up of two parts. First the Outer Court, with great temples and throne rooms. Behind those is the Inner Court, which is made up of gardens and all the palaces of the Emperor and his family. That's where you will live."

"And is there a marriage ceremony?" I ask.

Mei shakes her head. "Iparhan says that the rank chosen for her cousin as concubine will be below the four highest-ranked concubines, so there will not be a full ceremony for you. There will be a ceremony before you enter the palace and then you will be presented to the Emperor. Once that has been done, you will be a concubine of the court."

"So I'm not really married to him?"

"You will be married as such," says Mei. "The Qing dynasty allows all children of the Emperor to be equal. Your own child could be chosen as the next Emperor above the Empress' children. So in that regard you are as much a wife as she is. But of course at court your rank is very important. And because you are from a newly conquered land they may celebrate your arrival more lavishly than a concubine of your rank would normally receive. The Emperor has chosen a concubine from Iparhan's cousins' family to reward their services to him and to emphasise the conquest of Xinjiang."

"What's he like?" I ask.

"The Emperor?"

"Yes."

Mei pauses. She looks down. "You will probably not see a great deal of him. He is a busy man."

"I'm supposed to spend as much time with him as I can," I point out. "If I'm to spy for Iparhan."

"He likes poetry."

I sigh. "I do *try* to learn the poems," I say. "There's just so many of them."

"He writes them too."

"Heavens. Does that mean I'll have to learn his as well?"

"Probably."

"Wonderful."

Mei smiles. "He has other interests. The Emperor loves to ride."

"Really?"

"Of course. He's a Manchu. They've very proud of their heritage. They're supposed to be able to fire an arrow whilst riding at full gallop."

"And can they?"

"They practise a lot, so they probably can."

"What are they firing arrows at?"

"Animals when there isn't a war. He has a hunting lodge set in huge grounds and forests. He goes there as often as he can. You'll go with him."

"Hunting?"

"Probably just watching. But the whole court goes."

I snort with laughter at the vision of dainty concubines tiptoeing about in a forest, ruining their nice clothes, tripping over fallen trees.

"Will I be the only lady without bound feet?"

Mei shakes her head. "None of the Emperor's ladies has bound feet. He is a Manchu, remember. Their women do not have bound feet and the practice has been banned. It still goes on of course. Every time new concubines arrive to be chosen there will be some sent home in disgrace because their feet are bound. You will not see a lady with bound feet amongst the women of the court."

"Why am I learning Mandarin if he's a Manchu?"

"They speak Mandarin at court. Manchu is only used for a few words. It is an old tongue now, no one uses it for everyday speech."

"Is the Emperor a nice man?"

Mei shrugs.

"Come, Mei. Iparhan never speaks kindly of him. She spits his name. She says he is a greedy man, that all he wants is endless new conquests."

Mei nods but doesn't speak.

"But she's never met him. And you have, Mei. So what's he like?"

Mei looks sad. "He loved the Lady Fuca."

"The first Empress?"

"Yes. She made him a little carrying purse once, a plain thing such as the Manchu warriors used to have before they became emperors. He was so proud of it, he wore it on his belt."

"So?"

Mei tries to make me understand. "He wears robes covered in gold embroidery," she explains. "His belt is covered in jewels. He shines. And then on this magnificent belt, hanging by other purses woven in gold and bright colours he hung this little purse, like something a peasant would wear. Because he loved her and because she had remembered and honoured his ancestors and their way of life, which he reveres."

"He can't be all bad, then, is that what you're saying?"

Mei pats my hands, which are growing softer by the day, mostly thanks to her creams that she insists I use almost hourly. "You do not need to love him," she says. "To love him can bring jealousy from other women, even poisons to your table. Do what you must do, but make your own life at court. Make friends. Enjoy a soft life. Do not seek out the Emperor too closely."

"I'm supposed to seek him out," I protest. "If I don't then I can't get information for Iparhan and if I don't do that…" I trail off.

Mei leans towards me and lowers her voice. 'When you get to the court," she all but whispers, "You must seek out Lady Wan."

"Your old mistress?"

"Yes. She is a kind woman and if you tell her that I sent you to her, that I think of her still, she will help you however she can. Perhaps she is not a great favourite but she has lived happily at the court for many years now in peace and contentment."

I like the sound of this. "And how can she help me?"

Mei is serious. "You need to be warned about the factions."

"The what?"

"The factions amongst the Emperor's women. There are many women in the Emperor's court and they fall into different factions. They change often. One woman might form an alliance with another and then turn against her, for jealousy. You must know which women are in favour and which are embittered by their lowly status in the Emperor's eyes. You must know who is trustworthy and who might work against you."

"Work against me? What would they do to me?"

Mei becomes aware she is frightening me. She pats my hands again. "Do not fret about it now. We cannot know which women you must be wary of until you are at court. Got to Lady Wan and beg for her help. Tell her I served you as I once served her. I am certain that she will be kind to you."

"But…" I begin.

Mei shakes her head at my questions. "You will be taken good care of no matter what happens, whether you are a favourite or not. Your hands will rest only on silk."

I feel cold and pull my hands away from her.

The room is filling with steam. Through the clouds of it I watch Mei pour in the last bucket of water. She takes the tiny vial from Iparhan and opens it, allows a few drops to fall into the bathtub. Iparhan's perfume fills my nostrils as though she were standing with her skin touching mine. Mei nods and leaves.

Now the three of us are alone and although the water is warm I am shivering.

Nurmat's hand, large, warm and brown, touches me and I flinch. He draws back for a moment but then seems to make up his mind. One hand lifts my hair and holds it up, the other, holding the cloth which is wet and scented with rose soap, slips over my shoulders and the nape of my neck in a smooth movement, rubbing my skin with soap and water.

By the window Iparhan shudders, then swiftly steps to my side and grabs my hair from Nurmat's grasp. With two bone pins she savagely twists and fastens my hair so that it will stay up on its own. I wince as the sharp ends scrape against my scalp. "You need both hands or you'll be there all day," she snaps at Nurmat.

She returns to her place but then as his hands slip beneath the surface of the water and the scent of the roses and her own perfume grows stronger she gasps something under her breath and leaves the room. Nurmat and I are alone. The heat of the water is bringing a pink flush to my skin exceeded only by the heat in my face turning my cheeks a darker rose. I try to imagine myself to be in the Forbidden City, a concubine to the Emperor, bathed by eunuchs as a matter of course. I close my eyes, the better to believe that Nurmat is a eunuch, not a man.

With my eyes closed I can hear his breathing, which is faster than it is even when he's been riding. I feel its warmth on my cheek and then on my shoulder, on my arms and knees, which are not covered by the water. His hands have lost their hesitation and now he lifts my limbs to better reach behind my knees, between my toes, under my armpits. The little cloth is dipped again and again in the water, rubbed with the soap, then stroked over my back, my thighs, my belly. It follows the curve of my breast and to my shame I can feel my nipples harden under his hand. The heat in my cheeks is unbearable and I open my eyes, thinking somehow to make him stop, to form words which might bring an end to this moment. But he takes my face in his hands, turning me towards him. I look at him, bracing myself for his gaze, but I see he's taken my instructions to heart. His eyes are closed. He is washing me by touch alone, his nostrils filled with the scent from the tiny vial. In this moment I know that he is washing Iparhan, not me, and I begin to tremble as he lifts the little cloth to my face and wipes each part of it, across my forehead, down my nose and then a little circle over my lips, which part under the pressure. He lets his hand slip down and in the warmth and wetness of the scented water he uses only his fingers to clean between my thighs. I close my eyes for a moment and then I can take no more.

I spring from the tub, splashing water everywhere, leaving Nurmat soaked. I grab at a cloth to dry myself and wrap it round me but Nurmat has risen to his feet. He takes my hand and leads me to a seat by the window, pushing me gently so that I sit down while he kneels by my side. From his pocket he takes the vial and opens it, releasing Iparhan's heady scent once more. I shake my head but he ignores me and with one finger dips into the little pot. He dabs the perfume onto my skin, down the nape of my neck, then across each collarbone and then, reaching down, he slips a hand under the cloth I am wrapped in and puts a little on each of my thighs. The room is filled with her perfume again, that smell of delicate spring blossom and rich summer fruit. Nurmat, kneeling by my side, has closed his eyes and now he inhales deeply.

I reach out and put one hand on his shoulder, where his shirt is open, and my fingers can brush his bare skin. He opens his eyes and my hand shakes at the love in his eyes. I push him away from me, hard, and he loses his balance and topples backwards to the floor.

"I'm not her," I hiss, and rise to leave the room. I don't get very far.

Iparhan is in the doorway. She's as upright as ever, poised as ever, but tears are running down her face. Nurmat is unaware of her; he sits with his eyes still closed, breathing deeply, perhaps imagining a compliant Iparhan bathed in his love. I stand facing her, she in her long skirts with her little plaits under a red cap, me wrapped in a damp cloth.

"He looks at me and sees you, Iparhan," I say, afraid of what she might do, but I see the rage build up in her eyes and her lips tighten.

"You still believe he is mine?" she says, her fists clenched by her side.

I want to reassure her but I hesitate. I know that Nurmat sees Iparhan instead of me, but the longer he looks, the more likely it is that he will eventually see me.

I open my mouth to say something to calm her, whether it's true or not, but Iparhan shakes her head.

"It doesn't matter," she says, her voice too loud. She addresses Nurmat. "It's time to leave."

"Leave for where?" I ask stupidly.

"Beijing."

I gape at her but she ignores me and continues to speak to Nurmat. "I have received word. Turdan's sister has begun her journey to the Emperor and we must intercept her before she reaches the Forbidden City. We leave in the morning."

I look over my shoulder at Nurmat. Slowly, he gets to his feet. He and Iparhan gaze at each other for a moment and I know that in their minds her plans, so long discussed, are being made a reality. They know everything that is about to come and I know nothing. I feel a deep terror. All this play-acting, this transformation, this pretence is about to come true. I've almost treated the past few months as a game, with food and a warm bed as my prizes. I've grown used to Mei's pampering and her wrinkled smiles, believed that the tricks I was learning would help me to win against the odds. But the truth that I have always known is now here in front of me: if I lose this game I will forfeit my life.

I think of the moment when I chose, laughing without air in my lungs, of Iparhan's daggers trembling in the tree trunk, pinning my arms open, rendering me helpless. I had no real choice then and now it is too late to turn back.

Nurmat clears his throat but his voice is still husky when he speaks. "I'll prepare the horses," he says and walks towards the door and Iparhan.

As he passes he inhales the scent I wear.

Mei

M EI IS STANDING BY THE *doorway, a dripping pail in one hand. I make sure to shove her as I pass, my shoulder hitting her squarely so that she has to drop the pail and grab at the doorframe to avoid falling. I have so much anger inside me, so much pain that I must let it out and she can say nothing to me, cannot stop nor reprimand me.*

But she does.

"Iparhan," she says, and I pause, my back still turned to her, facing out into the cold blackness. She does not often address me, preferring to keep her distance, wary of my temper.

I wait but she does not continue. "What do you want?" I ask over my shoulder. My teeth are ground tight together, it costs me an effort to unclench my jaw enough to speak.

"Beware of the path you tread," says Mei, and her soft voice has an edge to it I have not heard before.

Nurmat's plan is simple.

"We will go away from here," he says to me, his warm hand holding my cold one. "We will be married. We will have children. We will put all of this behind us. The Emperor has what he wants. Let him have it. You have suffered too much loss. I will not let you suffer again. I will love you always and keep you safe."

I stand before my father's grave, the desert wind whipping at my mother's skirts, the only clothes I brought with me. Slowly I draw my hand out of Nurmat's and place it on my father's misshapen tomb. "I will not rest until Altisharh is returned to our people," I say, and see Nurmat's face grow pale. "I will carry out my father's plan. When the Emperor sends for his concubine I will make my way to the Forbidden City."

Nurmat grabs for my hand, pulling it away from the hard clay but I speak before my hand has left its rough surface. "This I swear."

He faces me and there are tears in his eyes. "You will break my heart," he says.

I do not answer, only reach for my horse's reins and pull myself into the saddle, my muscles stiff with shivering.

Mei's wrinkled face peers up from her hunched shoulders. She is afraid of me, I can tell it by her shaking hands. But she stands her ground. "You have a plan," she says. "I see it because it is there to be seen. Nurmat does not see it because he does not want to see it. The girl does not see it because she has no notion of herself. She has only ever thought about survival. But your plan will destroy you all."

"My plans are none of your business, old woman," I say. "You do not understand. I must reclaim my country."

Mei shakes her head. "Your plans are shaped by grief and pain," she says. "You claim to seek restitution."

"Yes," I say. "Of my country. For my people."

"No," she says. "You seek revenge. And it will destroy you and Nurmat, the only other person you care about in this world."

I step closer to her, look down into her narrow eyes. "You are a nobody," I say. "You will keep your mouth shut."

"Or else?" she asks. "Do you plan to look after me in my old age, Iparhan? Do you plan to take me with you when you leave this place?" My eyes blink before I can stop them and she nods. "And when the food and fuel for the fire is gone, will you send more? I do not think so."

"Finish making the bread," I say, turning away from her. The cold air strikes my face and I have to force myself to step out of the house's warmth into the darkness.

Journey to Beijing

I'S DARK.

I stand, shivering, in the doorway. I can't see much beyond a few steps. I can hear the horses nearby, stamping and huffing in the cold air. Iparhan's with them, she left the house before I did. My teeth chatter together so hard that even when I clench my jaw they don't stop, only start to grind back and forth instead.

Nurmat appears out of the darkness. "Are you cold?"

I shake my head.

Nurmat tuts at my shaking and pulls my sheepskin coat tighter round me. When our skins brush against one another his hand lingers.

I grab his arm hard, pulling him close to me. "Stop it," I hiss, my fear sinking my nails into the skin of his wrist so that he winces. "Stop thinking I am Iparhan. I need you to be my friend now, not some half-wit whose head is turned by a perfume and his imagination."

He turns his face away to where Iparhan's appeared, standing in the doorway. The two of us stand silent as though we had been caught kissing.

She doesn't move any closer. "Ready?"

I stay silent and Nurmat nods.

"Then mount."

I turn back to the doorway where Mei has joined Iparhan. She looks small in the flickering light from the house, her face hidden in shadows. I ignore Nurmat and make my way back to the door. I embrace Mei, feeling the bent bones of her back. "Thank you," I say.

She returns my embrace and murmurs something I don't catch in my ear.

"What?" I ask but Iparhan has taken my arm and is leading me to the horse. Nurmat throws me into the saddle and busies himself with the straps but all my attention is on Mei. "I didn't hear you," I call out to her but she stands silent. The horse shifts beneath me while Nurmat and Iparhan mount their own horses.

I can't see Iparhan's face well enough to read her expression but her voice is cold. "Ride," she commands.

"Mei," I call again. "I didn't hear you."

Her old voice reaches me through a sudden wind that whirls sand around us. "A mirror," she calls out. "Look in a mirror."

I hear a whistling sound and a dull thud. By my side Iparhan is holding a whip. She leans over now and brings it down – crack – on my mare's rump. Startled, she leaps forward. I grab at where the reins should be to try and stop her but then realise that

Iparhan has secured my horse to hers and left my horse without reins. I have no control over my own mount. I clutch at the horse's mane and twist in the saddle to look back as we build up speed. To my horror I see Mei slowly crumple to the ground, her small outline framed in the light of the doorway.

"Mei!" I scream. The sand whirls up from the horses' hooves and into my open mouth, making me choke. I cough and spit, the hard grit in my throat immovable. I almost fall, unable to keep to the horse's rhythm for all the coughing.

"Cover your mouth," yells Nurmat, riding just behind me.

I pull my jacket collar up with one hand while clinging on to my galloping horse. If I throw myself from the saddle I will end up under the hooves of Nurmat's horse.

We gallop for a long time. The horses are fresh, the early morning is cold. But at last we have to slow down. At once, I throw myself to one side, landing hard in the grey sand. I stagger to my feet and look up at Iparhan, who has stopped her horse and wheeled it round so that she can look down at me.

"Mount your horse, Hidligh," she says. Her voice is calm.

My voice comes out in a hoarse wail. "You killed her!" I scream up at her.

Her face stays expressionless. "Mount," she repeats.

I back away from her. "I will not," I say. I find tears rolling down my face and sob, the tears trickling into my mouth when I open it. "Why did you kill her?"

"She was no longer useful," says Iparhan, unmoved.

My legs are trembling too hard to stand. I fall forwards, on my knees with my hands sinking into the cold sand. "You could have sent her home to her family," I say.

"She had no family," says Iparhan from above me.

"I have no family," I say.

"Get her up," says Iparhan to Nurmat. I hear him leap down from his horse and then his arms are about me, lifting me into the saddle. I sit slumped, hands loose by my side.

Iparhan moves her horse a little closer to me. "Look about you, Hidligh," she says quietly.

I keep my head down.

"Look about you," she repeats.

Slowly, I raise my head. I avoid her eyes and look about. Sand. Tall dunes. The odd scrap of a bush, struggling to survive.

"I can leave you here," says Iparhan. "Or you can hold on to your horse's mane and ride."

I look down at the dead grey sand beneath my horse's feet. Slowly I move my arms and take my horse's mane into my clenched hands.

We sleep, ride, sleep, ride. The first night we dismount I sit in silence. When Nurmat gets the fire going he brings me hot flat bread filled with chunks of lamb, like the first meal he ever gave me. I chew the lamb without tasting it, then sit and hold the empty bread until it grows cold, knowing that Mei's crooked old hands kneaded and baked it yesterday. Then I lie down and sleep, the shrivelled bread clutched by my side.

As we ride the next day and for many days after, tears trickle down my face while I think of Mei's wrinkled tortoise face and her hunched back. I hear that shrill whistling and see her bent back crumple to the ground. I turn over her last words to me. A mirror. Look in a mirror. Why?

Each night I dismount and walk a few paces in agony before I fall asleep. My body, grown used to bathing and scented soaps, reeks of sweat and horses. My thighs are red with drips of piss and the rubbing of the saddle. I smell unwashed. I don't care. I don't speak. I only obey orders I am given. I am numb.

I have no idea where we are but many many days go by before I care enough to ask. "Where are we?"

Iparhan seems surprised at hearing my voice after so long. She twists in her saddle to look me over. "We are very close."

"To Beijing?"

She snorts in disbelief at my ignorance. "To Turpan. Now we will join the trading caravans on their way to Beijing. There is safety in numbers and we can follow behind my cousins."

The caravans are immense. Camels, horses, mules and donkeys, all are weighed down with burdens. Some carry medicinal rhubarb, fine teas and brick teas, hazelnuts and other foods. There are silks and velvets. Others carry pearls, jade, tourmaline or amber as well as fierce looking guards. Occasionally the trade routes are interrupted by yaks bearing huge quantities of jade from the local rivers. Guards stand on the riverbanks and wait for jade to be lifted from the waters, while clerks note down weights and colours - white, green, red, yellow, brown and black. The Emperor's court has an insatiable appetite for jade, and Altishahr has it in bountiful quantities.

Iparhan's expression grows bitter whenever she sees jade being taken in this way. "So it begins," she mutters. "All that we have is his. Our jade. Our women. Our taxes. Our crops. Our labour."

Up ahead of us, a party of armed riders surround a covered palanquin in which sits the Emperor's future bride. Its slow rocking must make for either an uncomfortable or a soporific journey. I wonder whether its occupant is excited or afraid. I wish I didn't know that she should be afraid of the dark-robed figure that rides by my side. I wish I did not have to watch the palanquin's slow rocking, day by day, as the paths of our fates converge. As we move onwards I wonder sometimes about whether I could attempt another escape or whether my path is now set, whether it has been carved into a jagged lump of jade, at the bottom of some river where no human hands can touch it nor erase the choice that has been made for my life. I wonder whether that choice has been made by divine hands in heaven or whether some darker hand has inscribed it.

Days pass and then one morning Iparhan begins to smile. I find even her smile frightening. I've hardly ever seen it and anything that makes her smile worries me.

"What?" I ask, wary of this change in her.

"They say," she says, her voice louder than usual, "that the lady in the palanquin ahead has an extraordinary fragrance. It is not a scent that can be bought. It comes from her very skin. The Emperor was so bewitched that he commanded she should be his bride."

I look at her, waiting to understand what she is doing.

Behind us a merchant leans forward on his horse. "Is that so?" he says. "I thought as much. I smelt a very fine perfume when we passed their party at the inn the other night. I said at the time it was not a perfume I had ever smelt before."

I gape at him but Iparhan turns on her horse and smiles radiantly. "You were right, then!" she says with admiration. "You must know your perfumes. Of course, a man so well-travelled…" She stops, shrugging charmingly, as though to imply that such a man would be an expert on any manner of topics.

The man beams and straightens his shoulders. By the next night the whole of the caravan knows for sure that the unseen lady in the palanquin is destined for the Emperor himself and that her body emits a natural fragrance so heavenly that she cannot be seen in public for fear that men might not control their carnal desires. I turn to Nurmat when I hear this and he looks away.

Every night Iparhan slips away from us. One night I follow her and watch her approach the tent that holds her cousin. I want to call out a warning as she slips a hand into the folds of her skirt, but hold my tongue. I see her hand emerge holding the tiny vial with which Nurmat anointed me. One quick motion and it is applied, her hand slipping over the threshold of the tent's folds. I turn away as she comes back towards my hiding place.

"Goodnight, Hidligh," she says without pausing as she passes me.

The rumours surrounding the girl grow in magnitude. Now we hear that her family anoints her daily with camel's butter, anxious to enhance and maintain her newly developed natural fragrance. Iparhan rolls her eyes when she hears this. "Idiots," she says. "It'll go rancid and she'll stink of the stuff."

We travel for so long I begin to think we will never arrive anywhere, just keep riding and riding forever. But at last there's a change in our surroundings. Up ahead are the walls of a great city and around us are ever-growing crowds heaving towards them. The faraway traders of fine goods in great quantities are now surrounded by locals, peasants carrying loads of firewood, vegetables, camellia flowers, fruits and other fresh goods on their backs, in little hand-carts or occasionally on the backs of reluctant mules. I look at Nurmat.

He nods. "Beijing."

My throat grows tight as I look at the walls again. Somewhere within them lies another, hidden, city. And my future, whatever it may be. My hands tighten and I keep my head down.

Up ahead, the family's caravan of horses and camels breaks off and heads in a new direction.

I tug at Nurmat's sleeve. "Where are they going?"

"There's a senior official at the palace. He has invited them to his house for the night, so that the bride can be prepared in comfort before she enters the Forbidden City. The house sits within the walls of Beijing but outside of the Forbidden City. They are making their way there."

"Are we following them?"

By way of an answer he jerks his chin forwards at Iparhan, already riding ahead, her horse following the family at a discreet distance. Nurmat and I turn our horses towards her.

It's dawn and barely light. A sharp wind blows our skin to chilly paleness, marred by goosebumps. We're in the gardens of a fine house, hung all about with red lanterns and long strips of red silk tied to trees and columns, embroidered with gold characters, which I can't read.

"Happiness," whispers Nurmat, when I point to them.

I shake my head. Happiness is not what I am anticipating. How can we possibly enter such a house without being seen? We've already had to dodge servants bustling about everywhere. The house is in an uproar, even though it's so early.

"What are they all *doing*?" I ask Nurmat. Iparhan has left our side and slipped round the corner of the house. I can't help wishing that they'd find her, that one footfall in the wrong place will alert someone to her presence.

"Getting ready for the imperial ladies," Nurmat replies.

"What imperial ladies?"

"They come from the Forbidden City to bathe and dress the bride ready to be taken to the palace. They're important women in the court, wives of senior officials and military men."

"Does that mean I have to dress the same way as her so we can swap later on?"

He looks at me as though I have said something stupid and doesn't reply.

We wait. My legs are cramped from the half-squat we've been in for hours, the cold dew is making my clothes damp and I'm afraid. I try to focus on the cramp and the dampness, as well as on my urgent need for a piss. The discomfort stops me from thinking about what lies ahead.

When it comes, it happens so fast I hardly understand. I catch a glimpse of Iparhan's figure in the garden and am about to turn to Nurmat when his hand is clasped firmly round my mouth. With his other arm he lifts me. My legs, freed from their long-held position, shriek in pain as they unfold. I kick but his grip is too strong. In a moment he has moved from our hiding place in the bushes to the wall at the back of the house where Iparhan is waiting. As we reach her she turns her back on us and begins to climb an ancient wisteria, its barely budding branches giving her easy places to place her hands and feet. She's above our heads and then disappears into a window. I struggle against Nurmat.

"Keep still," he says, and there's no gentleness in his voice.

From above I see Iparhan's hand throw out a rope, which falls down the wall to our head height.

Now I think Nurmat might release me and urge me to climb. He doesn't. He takes a cloth from his pocket and binds it about my mouth, so that I can't speak but he now has two free hands. With one he hoists me over his shoulder, with the other he grabs hold of the rope. I struggle.

"Don't," he says. "I mean it."

I hang over his shoulder like a sack of rice while he climbs. I had never realised how strong he is, not even when we used to mock-wrestle. Then, he would let me win. Now, I know there's nothing I can do to escape.

I'm tipped over the windowsill, Iparhan grabbing at my clothes to help pull me into the room. I land mostly on my right thigh with a bruising thump. Nurmat climbs in behind me and I hear them fasten the window. Still winded, I sit up and look about me, trying to understand where I am.

The room is large and well appointed. A *kang* marks it as a bedroom. There are artfully arranged flowers in a little niche, various silk hangings with unfamiliar characters on the walls. Several large chests are open, fine clothes spilling out of them. The room is rich with the scent of Iparhan's perfume.

There's been a struggle. One of the wall hangings is askew. The covers on the *kang* are dishevelled and most have fallen to the floor. There's a broken lamp. I'm afraid to look further. I know now that when Iparhan left us in the garden she came here, and the girl whose room it is does not seem to be here. Where is she?

Iparhan catches me looking about and jerks her head.

My eyes follow the direction she's indicating before I quickly turn my face away. I caught a glimpse of a coverlet, wrapped about a shape that is partly hidden behind a clothes chest.

Iparhan turns to Nurmat. "Help me," she says.

I stare at the floor and feel the shape pass by me as they lift it to the window. My skin shrinks from the silken brush of the coverlet as it passes me and I feel a trickle of piss down my legs. I sit in the spreading puddle, not moving. They're not gone long. I wait as they rearrange the room, restoring order. When Iparhan comes over to me and begins to undress me I don't stop her, sitting limp and unresisting as she strips me. She sops up the wetness around me and wipes me down. The last thing she removes is the gag around my mouth. She looks into my face to see if I'll suddenly scream but I know we've gone too far now. To be found in this house now, as we are, would mean certain death. I've thought of escape before but even I know that it is too late for escapes. I gaze back at her and when she takes my hand and pulls me to my feet I walk naked across the room with her to the *kang*. Nurmat gazes out of the window as we pass.

Iparhan tucks me up into the *kang* and then sits on the edge of it. She speaks fast. "The ladies from the palace will arrive shortly and they will wash and dress you. They do not expect you to speak much Mandarin. The clothes laid out for you will be unusual to them. They are red, as befits a wedding to the Emperor, but they are made in our style. You may need to show them how they should be worn. Your brothers and father," and she does not even pause over this falsehood, "will not see you until you descend to the palanquin which will be brought for you. By then you will be veiled for your wedding day, so they will not see your face. Follow the ladies to the palanquin. Climb inside. Sit still. When you arrive at the palace within the Forbidden City you will be taken to meet the Emperor and his court. From then on, I cannot guide you. You must make your own way."

I shake my head and my voice is small and hoarse. "I can't do it, Iparhan," I say. "I can't."

"You have trained for this," she says.

"I can't do it," I say, my voice beginning to rise above a whisper. "It'll go wrong. They'll know I'm an imposter as soon as they look at me."

Iparhan unsheathes her dagger and very slowly, with care, lays its tip against the hollow of my throat. "Remember who you are supposed to be," she says. "Endear yourself to the Emperor so that you will be of use to me later."

I look up at her in silence.

Nurmat turns from the window. "The Imperial Guard is arriving, along with the eunuchs and ladies," he says. "I just saw them turning the corner of the road outside. They will be here shortly."

Iparhan rises, sheaths her dagger and pulls out the little vial. She tips it onto her finger, then dabs the contents on my neck. Her perfume fills the air. She turns to go and I grab at her hand. It is cool to my touch. She looks down at me, almost in surprise.

My voice deserts me. "Please," I mouth.

She pulls her hand out of my grasp. "Remember who you are supposed to be," she says and turns away. A quick movement and both she and Nurmat disappear through the window.

I am alone.

I lie still. I try to think, try to imagine what is about to happen, but I can't marshall my thoughts. They're made up of blurred, unformed pictures in my mind, which don't come together to provide me with answers. I have to think, I have to remember how to behave. One thought only is clear in my mind. I am not brave enough for this. I did not understand the risks. Yes, yes, I told Iparhan and the others I would be risking my life but it was a figure of speech to me. I thought I could trick and turn my way out of any danger if it happened. I was arrogant from years of fighting for survival on the streets. Now I have seen two innocent women die – Mei and the unnamed girl, the wrapped body that passed me. And the danger has not even truly begun. How many more lives will be lost to maintain this illusion I am engaged in? And when will my own life fall forfeit to this dangerous game?

There's a whisper at the door. I lie still. I don't know how to answer or even whether I should answer. My mind whirrs.

My silence is taken for assent. The door opens. Slowly I turn my head towards the sound.

The doorway is filled with colour and pattern. I blink, trying to understand the many-headed creature standing before me.

A gaggle of women peer in at me. In front, filling most of the doorframe, stands a larger, older woman. Behind her and to both sides are more faces.

The woman falls to the floor and kowtows. She does it with ostentation and the others, taking up most of the landing behind her, quickly follow suit, taking direction from their leader. When they've finished they stand and crowd into the room. There are eight of them. Behind them, still on the landing, stands a group of men, who look very young. Beardless and with soft plump faces, chattering in high voices, I take them for the young sons of the ladies, until I realise I'm seeing eunuchs for the first time.

I'm still lying in the bed, face turned towards them, motionless except for my eyes.

The older lady steps towards me with a commanding smile. "Your ladyship," she says. "This is a wonderful day. And an honour for us all to prepare you for your union with the Son of Heaven."

I gaze at her. I understand most of what she's saying but I don't know what to say in reply.

Her smile falters for a moment. She must think there is something wrong for me to just lie like this, expressionless, motionless. But she's not a senior lady for nothing. "Your ladyship must be overwhelmed with the joy of the occasion," she presses on.

One of the ladies behind her whispers. "Does she speak any Mandarin at all?"

The older lady beams at this reminder. Of course. I am not a simpleton. I am foreign. What a relief. She raises her voice and speaks very clearly. "Your ladyship is *very happy* today," she affirms.

I blink at her. I feel as though my body will not obey me. I make a small movement as though to sit up, though I'm not sure I can go through with the whole motion without simply tumbling off the *kang*.

The ladies dart forwards and the most senior pulls me upright, completing the motion I've started. They smile. I'm showing signs of life. This is better. Now that they are close to me I hear them whispering to one another.

"She really does smell of perfume."

"Probably something they wear in those parts."

"No, I heard it said she smells of it *naturally*. That it comes from her own *skin*."

I see each of them discretely sniffing the air.

"Your ladyship will have a *bath*, now. Then we will *dress* you," enunciates one loudly. They have obviously decided that they must only use loud simple words and gestures with me. It's just as well. I speak very little Mandarin and there's not much I can manage to take in at this moment. I have to give them something and so I manage to nod. This sets off a wave of smiles and nods. They are on firm ground now. They begin giving directions and orders at high speed. I see eunuchs hurrying away and servants bustling about. A large wooden lacquered tub is wrestled into the room and an endless procession of maids begins to traipse back and forth with pails of hot water. The room fills with steam. The ladies begin to sweat. Their robes are made of heavy silks and seem to consist of multiple layers – long skirts that peep out under calf-length heavy robes with wide sleeves. On top are long waistcoat-like strips of fabric with a great deal of decoration. Looped over these clothes are many long strands of colourful beads, which swing back and forth as they rush about the room, threatening to entangle the ladies with each other's corals, ambers and jades. Their carefully made-up faces shine with perspiration under heavy headdresses.

The tub is full. The ladies advance on me. I'm almost lifted into the tub by their many eager hands. I slip into the hot water and sit there, my vision still blurred by steam and the many colours surrounding me.

The ladies vie with each other to be part of the bathing process. Soap is passed from one to another. Impatient hands reach out for little scoops with which to pour water over me. I am being washed by a sixteen-armed spider. There is soap everywhere, water everywhere. Rubbing, stroking, pulling, scrubbing. I go limp and close my eyes, allow them to do whatever they want with me. The heat stops my limbs from shaking. I think, *breathe. Smile. Be helpful.* People are reassured by small gestures, by meaningless pleasantries.

More water is used for rinsing and I'm pulled from the tub a vivid scarlet colour. Again the hands descend to smooth me with many creams and unguents. As my skin fades to bright pink they mull over my hair. They have been given instructions to dress me according to our traditions, not theirs, and this is confusing them. I make vague motions of plaiting and when they try to make one large plait I shake my head and indicate many with my fingers. They are mystified but tentatively begin many smaller plaits. When I nod and encourage them with a smile, they proceed at speed, murmuring in confusion at the unusual style, which seems too plain to them. They consider decorative options and finally bind gold and scarlet ribbons at the end of each plait and weave in tiny red flowers and strands of gold. My own dark hair has all but disappeared beneath a river of red and gold by the time they are satisfied.

The clothes provided to dress me are once again a surprise to them. They're a surprise to me too. Although the clothes are the same as I've worn before in structure, these are made in a rich red silk and then covered in intricate gold embroidery. Formalised waves, flowers and birds adorn them so thickly that their weight makes my knees weak and knocks me off balance. The long skirt is stiff with gold, the shirt, which would normally be white, is also red and the scarlet waistcoat is lavishly adorned with more embroidery and studded with pearls. On top of all this I'm helped into a heavy jacket of red silk with wide sleeves. A cap of red and gold is perched on my head. Long looped strands of pearls are layered round my neck and dangle from my – strangely only single pierced – ears. They apply makeup, which feels heavy on my skin.

As one, the ladies step back to look me over. I can see that the lavish use of red silk and gold embroidery is pleasing to them, as are the pearls. The style of the clothes they're still finding it difficult to reconcile themselves to. They try to adjust the way the clothes sit, perhaps thinking that by a tweak here or there they will magically become like their own. Their heads tip to one side as they consider the overall effect. Reluctantly they agree amongst themselves that certainly, if not traditional, I look *exotic*. This will have to do. I am, after all, foreign, and so looking odd is to be expected. Time is slipping by and the Emperor can't be kept waiting for his bride. They lift a red gauze veil over my head and the senior lady takes my hand to guide me. I'm not certain that my face is fully hidden but we're already out of the door. At the last minute I think of Mei's words but there has been too much going on and I forgot to look for a mirror in the room.

I stumble down the stairs. Ladies, maids, eunuchs and guards are everywhere, trying to keep out of the way and managing to do the opposite. I feel slow and heavy, weighed down with gold and pearls, with layer upon layer of thick silk. My hair pulls my neck backwards; my skirt pulls me forwards. The heels I'm wearing are higher than I'm used to. Were it not for the firm grip of the many ladies I would surely fall.

An older eunuch, wearing an elaborate hat with a peacock feather stuck in it, meets us at the foot of the stairs. He motions us into a large room in which are laid out tables bearing various large documents covered with writing I can't read, stone tablets, and other items. I look about me and freeze.

There are a number of men and women here dressed in the Altishahr style. The family of the bride. I wait for one of them to cry out, to say that I am not their daughter or sister, that I'm an imposter. I feel one of the ladies push me slightly and the trembling in my legs makes me fall to my knees. As I do so the whole room follows suit and I realise we are all kowtowing to the tables – or rather, to the items on them, which I assume are in some way important, probably sacred. Perhaps this is my marriage ceremony.

The bowing loosens my veil and I clutch at it, the only thing keeping me from being found out, but other hands have already taken hold of it and are adjusting it as I rise. My face remains covered. Slowly I'm turned around and led outside, the family following behind me.

Outside the house the courtyard has been transformed. The silence of the pre-dawn has been replaced with chaos. There are guards everywhere, hundreds of them. There are eunuchs. There are the members of the household, their own servants as well as what appear to be many animals whose coats and feathers are dyed bright red. I want to lift the veil to see if it's just the fabric making them appear red, but the ladies are holding my hands too tightly. Ahead of me is a huge palanquin, like a carved version of my own clothes, shining gold and red. The roof is topped with gold birds and bearers await my arrival.

I step out of the house and jerk back from a crashing and wailing sound. Trumpets, gongs and drums greet me. Firecrackers are let off all around me. Bright streamers are thrown under my feet. I hesitate but the ladies are unperturbed and half push, half pull me onwards. I'm helped into the palanquin, which rocks alarmingly.

Once in, the ladies hold open the curtains and one after another the members of my 'family' kneel in the dust of the courtyard and kowtow to me. I sit silent and rigidly motionless, waiting for their eyes to see what's really in front of them, but they're too swept up in the festivities. This wedding is their reward for loyalty to the Emperor, payment for the treachery to their own family, and they know more favours and riches will come their way if I please my future husband. Their faces beam with pleasure at the sight of the rich clothes, my many jewels, at the noise and pomp surrounding me. My actual face, hidden beneath the crimson gauze, is of little interest at this moment.

The last bows are made and the ladies drop the curtains. I'm left alone inside my new tiny world.

I feel something uncomfortable under me and shift position, thinking of the layers of thick gold making up flowers on my skirt. But the discomfort remains. I reach under myself with my left hand and find a familiar vial. I unstopper it and once again Iparhan's perfume fills the space. I apply the perfume, then hide the vial in a small pocket of my skirt.

Sitting in the palanquin, I'm bathed in a strange dim red light as the sun shines through the scarlet walls and roof. I can hear chattering and people milling about. I sit and wait, my eyes strained by the strange light and the blurring effect of my veil. I look down at the clothes I'm wearing, the gold embroidery stiff on the silken skirt. I fiddle with the sleeves of my jacket and feel something wet. I look down at my hand and see blood. It takes me a moment to understand that my right sleeve, silken red, is soaked in red blood, that the colours match one another so well it can't be seen, only felt. I squeeze my arm, trying to feel pain, seeking a wound that isn't there and then become very still. This blood is not mine but has come from the girl I've replaced. Carefully I wipe off the blood onto the red seat of the palanquin and then hold the sleeve away from me with cold fingers, hoping that it will dry quickly, that I will never again have to feel that wetness on my skin. I try to breathe.

There are loud shouts outside and running feet. I feel my body tremble, from my tapping feet up to my chattering jaw. At any moment I expect to be discovered. They must have found the dead girl's body, or seen a smear of blood from where my sleeve brushed through a doorframe and understood that something terrible has happened. I clench my hands and wait for the curtains to be ripped aside, for a hand to reach in and grab me, pull me out. I get ready to run, but curse myself for my stupidity. I can barely move, I don't know where I am and dressed like this it would be impossible to hide. I will have to rely on new skills here – my old street tricks will not save me now.

The palanquin tips and I gasp as it's lifted and begins to move forward. I lift one shaking hand and pull aside the curtain just a little. The bright clear daylight blinds me after the dim redness inside but I see hazy rows of people kowtowing as the palanquin passes them and then the gates of the house as we leave them behind and enter a street. I let go of the curtain and as I do so I catch one brief glimpse of two dark-robed riders traveling away from us. Iparhan and Nurmat are gone.

I feel sick. The palanquin tilts and sways as I'm carried along, there are shouts as we pass through the streets, one phrase repeated over and over again, the only words I can make out in all the noise.

"Make way! Make way! Make way for the Imperial Phoenix! Make *way*!" The call is sometimes interrupted by a thud and a shriek as some too curious or too slow passer-by impedes the progress of our procession and receives a blow with a staff for their impudence.

I try to breathe slowly and deeply but the rich scent of the perfume and the iron tang of the still-wet sleeve, the sway of the palanquin and the shouts of the street make my head spin and my stomach dip. I feel the sharp rise of vomit in my throat and swallow again and again to force it back.

The swaying goes on for an eternity. I lose count of how many times I swallow.

From inside my scarlet cocoon I can hear the streets grow ever busier. I hear beggars asking for alms, street vendors calling out their wares, enticing housewives by enumerating the many fine quality of their goods or cooking up meats so that a thick smell of roasting seeps through my red and golden walls. It makes me gag. I can hear children and singers and once I even hear a snatch of a storyteller beginning his tales, as fanciful as any back in Kashgar. I shut my eyes and imagine I am back in my home town, that in a moment I'll leap out from this carrier as its rightful occupant, some fine lady, boxes my ears for the cheekiness of having sat my ragged arse where her silk-clad backside should be. I'm comforted for a moment until a shift makes me tip a little and I feel the heavy silk slide against my own skin and know that I'm no longer clothed in rags and that the rightful occupant of this chair is lying dead somewhere, her corpse denied mourning while my own body takes her place and her destiny.

The palanquin stops suddenly. I wait for it to move again, to hear curses and more shrieks as the staff is wielded against whatever obstruction is in our path. But we stay still, and then I hear a loud creak. I tilt my head to line up my eye with a tiny gap at the side of the curtain and see the hinges of a huge red gate slowly open.

The Red Wall

WE RIDE TO THE HOUSE *that our silver has bought. I leave Nurmat with the horses and make my way to the bedchamber I have chosen for myself. I stand at the window and look out. The view from here is as I was promised – this house abuts the outer wall of the moat. Across the dark water rise the red walls of the Forbidden City. This area is to be the newly appointed Muslim quarter, in honour of the Emperor's new bride. Here I will be close to my own people, those who may support our cause, as well as close to those who come and go from the red walls – the servants, messengers, supplicants and emissaries. I rest my hands on the windowsill and look at the wall. It rises more than four times the height of a tall man and is pierced four times: the gates of the South, North, East and West. Behind that wall lies the Forbidden City. The palaces, the great halls, the Emperor and his women. Today Hidligh will take her place amongst them.*

My hands grip the sill more tightly. Tonight as dusk comes Hidligh will no doubt be called on. She will be taken from her own palace and ushered into the bedchamber of the Emperor. She will be undressed and given to him to do with as he wills. By the morning she will no longer be a virgin.

I let go of the windowsill, bring my stiff hands up to the fastenings of my travelling clothes. Slowly, I unfasten each one, letting my clothes fall to the ground until I am stripped bare.

Nurmat's fingertips caress me. "Iparhan," he whispers. "I cannot lose you to another man. I cannot bear it. Lie with me. Lie with me now."

I pull back from him. "I cannot," I say, my voice made harsh with my desire for him. "I must be a virgin for the Emperor's bed, or I will be discovered. I am sworn to this path, Nurmat."

He moves so fast I do not feel the pain, only see the glint of his knife come close to my eye and pull back for fear it will touch me. Only when I see his face grow pale and feel a wet heat trickle down my cheek do I realise the knife has already touched me. I begin to raise my hand but stop before I touch my own skin, afraid of what I will find there.

Nurmat is shaking but he reaches out for me. "Forgive me," he says. "Forgive what I have taken from you. You can no longer go to the Emperor but you will stay in my arms forever and you will be as beautiful to me as you were the day I first saw you."

"What have you done?" I ask, my voice a whisper. "What have you done, Nurmat?"

There are footsteps on the stairs and Nurmat enters the room shoulder first, carrying the weight of our bags. As he puts them down and straightens up he sees me. Naked, framed by the dark windowsill and the sun's pale winter rays. He stands still, a hunter confronted by his prey, afraid to believe what he sees before him.

I try to keep my voice steady. "We cannot marry yet," I say. "I have not taken my revenge." Nurmat nods, uncertain of what is happening.

"But we are so close to our goals now," I say. "So close that I thought perhaps…" I allow my voice to grow soft. "I thought perhaps we, too, might be close. For one night," I add, mindful that I cannot risk my offer being misinterpreted by a too-eager Nurmat.

He does not speak, only steps forwards and takes me in his arms. There is nothing gentle about his embrace. He crushes me to him, his breath fast, his face buried in my neck. "I have dreamed of this moment, Iparhan," he says.

I am about to reply but he all but throws me onto the bed, half his clothes already removed. His lips are on mine, hot and hard, his arms about me, every part of my body caressed, kissed and grasped. His hands are everywhere upon me. I cannot help being aroused, even though I had promised myself I would not give way to passion, that I would stay cool and calm inside myself, no matter what he did to me. I find myself reaching for him, pulling him to me, my lips on his lips, my teeth on his skin.

But when he kneels between my thighs he checks himself. "I will be gentle," he promises me, his voice shaken with desire, and I can see the effort it costs him to hold back, to enter me with care.

It hurts, of course, but it is that gentleness, the moment's pause he takes, which allows me to cool the heat rising within me. So at the moment when ecstasy overwhelms him and he cries out my name I push away the desire that threatens to pull me towards him. Instead I turn my face away and look out of the window at the red wall. I close my eyes and see blood, trickling.

The Forbidden City

A LL I CAN HEAR IS the sound of running feet. The bearers move more freely now we have left the overcrowded streets behind us. The guards, running alongside, add their own noise – their shoes heavier, their armour and weapons rattling.

I reach out a tentative finger and touch my sleeve. It's dry, hard with the invisible blood shed by its former wearer. I let it go, then pull aside the curtain a crack, barely enough to see out.

We're crossing a paved courtyard, although I've never seen a courtyard this size. I blink and pull back the curtain a little more. It stretches into the distance. At the edges of my vision are high red walls. Here and there we pass huge buildings with swooping rooftops, topped with golden-glazed tiles and beyond them the tops of trees. A guard, trotting alongside, catches a glimpse of movement from my curtain and turns his head. I let the silken folds fall back into place.

My breathing grows faster remembering Iparhan's last words of advice – *remember who you are supposed to be.* Her warning. *Endear yourself to the Emperor.*

She didn't need to say, *or else.* That, I can say to myself.

We come to an abrupt halt. Hands pull aside the curtains and are then offered to me. Tentatively I reach out and take them, am helped out into bright daylight, where I stand, in the shadow of a huge building. There are many steps falling away behind us, explaining the additional jolting I felt before we stopped. In front of us is a massive doorway.

I stand uncertain, wondering whether I should step through it. I look back at the guards and bearers but they all stand immobile, their faces empty of any expression. I look back at the doorway. Only now do I notice a small doubled-up figure prostrate before me, completing a series of bows. I step back a little as the person unfolds. A soft face and meek expression. A eunuch. He's only a little taller than me, although older, perhaps thirty years old or more. His well-made robes are a deep blue, decorated with delicate embroidery.

"Your ladyship," he murmurs. He speaks my language, but in a voice so soft I have to lean forward to catch his words. I smile. The relief of hearing my own tongue is so great that I forget what's about to happen until he reminds me.

"I am your humble interpreter, madam," he says.

I nod.

"My name is Jiang and I will accompany you as you meet the Emperor," he says. His eyes pass over my clothes and the veil, which hides my face from him.

I try to nod again but my neck feels stiff.

Shadows move in the doorway and what appears to be a very senior eunuch comes forward. His robes are magnificent and he looks stern. Jiang virtually fades away into a very low bow. His murmur to me is almost silent. "The Chief Eunuch."

I wonder whether I should kowtow and start to bend my knees. I'm wrong. The Chief Eunuch is already on his knees, kowtowing to me while I hastily straighten my legs. He begins to speak and my interpreter's lips move at the same time, without pause, without hesitation. I wonder how many times he's repeated the same greeting, perhaps to every woman brought here to be the Emperor's new bride. "Your ladyship," he says. "On this most auspicious day, it is my honour to welcome you to the Forbidden City. I beg of you to accompany me into the presence of the Son of Heaven, his Imperial Majesty, the Emperor."

I nod uncertainly and start forward towards the doorway. The Chief Eunuch looks startled and holds up a hand to stop me.

"Shouldn't I enter?" I ask.

The Chief Eunuch blinks at me. "There is a correct moment," he explains. I look at him, confused, and he elaborates as though to a child, "An *auspicious* moment."

We stand like idiots for a few moments and then the Chief Eunuch, based on a signal I fail to see, waves me forwards.

We enter the darkness. I can barely make out my surroundings, only that I'm in a cavernous room and that it's full of people.

The Chief Eunuch turns to me. "Allow me to assist your ladyship," he says, and with one quick gesture he pulls away the veil covering my face. I blink and tighten my hands into fists to stop from grabbing at it. Without it I feel naked. Slowly I raise my eyes to see my future.

The room is enormous. With the haze of the veil torn from my eyes, even its darker recesses can be seen. The floor is simple enough, but I remember Mei talking of the decorated ceilings and my eyes follow the lines of the great gold columns up to their tops. The ceiling is extraordinary. There's not a single part of it that isn't shining with gold and painted carvings. I try not to gape like some country bumpkin and instead look about me. All around the room are people in dazzling robes. Every hue of thick, quality silk is on show, every kind of motif that can be embroidered or picked out in jewels is here.

Standing apart is a group of women. One, who is slightly turned away from us, is wearing a bright yellow robe as well as a complex headdress, which makes her head look too big for her body. The headdress is blue and has a bird rising from the centre. All around it dangle pearls and other jewels.

"The Empress Ula Nara," whispers Jiang.

I nod.

"And some of His Majesty's other ladies."

Clustered around the Empress are more women, wearing similar robes, although they're in every possible colour – purples, blues, apricot orange, golden browns. Their huge hair is absurd. It's drawn up onto what looks like a small plank of black lacquered wood laid horizontally above their head, decorated all over with combs, flowers and hairpins. It's huge and looks like a balancing act just to keep it upright. I can't help wondering which one will tumble off first. These then, are the Emperor's other concubines, the women that I am about to join. I think of Mei's warning about their rivalries, the factions they may be part of, alliances made and lost through jealousies and success or failure.

The women stare at me. One, a wrinkled old thing, offers a timid smile. One looks me up and down, as though considering a beast at the market or a length of cloth. She purses her lips, and nods to herself, as though she has decided on a price for me. I'm not sure I've been valued very highly. Two watch me with their heads tilted to the same side, as though they were twin dolls, their faces curious, a little wary. I'd find it hard to tell them apart if I saw either again. One glowers at me under arched eyebrows, then turns her head and mutters something to the lady closest to her. They both smirk. I feel my palms grow damp. What if they can see at a glance, these women from illustrious families, that I am nothing but a street rat, whose fine clothes and gold-entwined hair do nothing to cover up my lack of breeding? My brief period of training is nothing compared to the years of preparation these women will have gone through to be chosen as brides to the Emperor.

The other women in the group glance briefly at me, then turn their faces away as though I am of no consequence, although the rigidity of their necks as they turn away tells me they want to look at me for longer, that they want to know more about me, to find out how my presence here will disturb their precarious equilibrium. Perhaps they are fearful of me – the newest and youngest recruit for the Emperor's bedchamber. *If they only knew how much more afraid I am of them*, I think. And which woman should I be most afraid of? Who has the greatest power here?

Slowly, the Empress' head turns towards me.

She hates me, I think. I look away and try to gather myself. *How can she hate me? She's never seen me before.* I glance back at her, thinking that my nerves are causing me to see what is not there, but her eyes, unwaveringly fixed upon me, leave me in no doubt. *She hates me.* My mouth feels numb. I can feel my hands tremble. I wish I could hide them.

All eyes are on me. Then all eyes turn to the other end of the room. I follow their gaze

The Emperor is seated on a large throne made of carved wood, lacquered in red. His head is bowed over some papers he is examining. To one side of him is a plump old woman with a square-faced jaw, seated on a similar throne. They are both wearing the same bright yellow robes as the Empress with intricate embroidery featuring dragons and other symbols. Their robes make those of the courtiers look insignificant. For a moment I see Nurmat and Mei, sitting on the heaps of cushions in the little house in the dunes, waiting for me to practice my kowtow.

The Emperor seems to finish whatever he was doing. He folds the papers neatly, passes them to a servant and looks up. I know he's almost fifty years old but he looks younger, not even forty. He sits very erect. His face is a long smooth oval with a very straight nose and full lips. The Chief Eunuch whispers something and the Emperor beckons me forward.

I look to Jiang who gives me a small but frantic nudge. "His Majesty should not be kept waiting."

I hiss back at him. "I can't speak Mandarin well enough. You need to come with me." He shakes his head. "*Go.*"

The room falls silent as I make my way towards the throne. I'm afraid I'll trip at any moment. I'm also afraid of what will happen next. No doubt he'll speak to me and I won't understand. This is the moment when I will give myself away in some foolish way, by some tiny slip. I look back at Jiang but he stays put and waves me on.

I reach the throne without falling. As I approach him the Emperor stands. He's taller than I expected and bends his head slightly to look down at me. I come to an uncertain stop. Should I kneel and wish him the ten thousand years of life I spent so many hours training for?

"Welcome to court," he says, and smiles.

I can't help it. I gape at him. He speaks my language!

He laughs at my expression. "I speak all the languages of my empire," he says. "I have been learning yours in preparation for meeting you."

I stand in front of him, not sure what to do next or how to reply. I feel like a dolt.

He looks me over thoughtfully. "Your clothes are not court dress," he remarks.

He sounds curious, not angry, but there's a sudden silence and I can feel the tension rise in the room. No doubt it's inappropriate to be incorrectly dressed in the presence of the Emperor. Will someone be in trouble for this? Is it a bad omen?

I curse Iparhan's traitorous cousins for their stubborn insistence on this clothing but I have to face it out. "They're – they are the traditional clothes of… " I stumble as I was about to say Altishahr and remember who I'm speaking to. "Xinjiang, Your Majesty. I thought it would please you to see them."

He smiles at once, a broad, happy smile and I feel the court relax around us. "Of course. Turn around."

I turn awkwardly on the spot.

"Charming," says the Emperor, looking at my hair. "All those little plaits."

I put a hand up to them. "There'll just be two tomorrow, Your Majesty," I say without thinking and immediately feel heat rising from my neck to my face.

He frowns. "Why?"

My cheeks are scarlet. "I will be m-married," I say, stumbling over the word, hoping that he will not think me presumptuous, as a concubine, to declare myself his wife. "Married women wear only two plaits."

He chuckles. "Then I will look forward to seeing you with only two plaits."

The court laughs.

I risk a sideways look and see the Chief Eunuch gesturing to me. I step back a little but the Emperor holds up his hand. "One more thing."

I stop.

"I have been told that you have a special attribute."

I look at him.

"I have heard that your body emits a natural fragrance."

I look down. Here comes the first of the illusions that have been created for this game – a move I can play to keep my pieces safe. Word of the perfume has already spread and now I can prove that yes indeed, I am perfumed.

"Is it true?"

I am afraid. What if this trick does not work? "I've been told so, Your Majesty." It comes out as little more than a whisper and he has to lean forward to catch it.

He smiles. "Come closer."

I step forward tentatively.

"Closer than that," he says. "I am not a hunting dog, to scent you from so far away!"

Everyone titters politely.

I step closer. He leans forward, so that our faces are only a hand's length apart. His eyes are bright and mischievous. I try not to shake. He inhales loudly, putting on an amusing show for the courtiers, but as he does so his eyes close. They reopen changed, his gaze on me softer and more wondering.

"It is your own scent? Not a perfume?"

I think of the tiny vial hidden in the folds of my skirt. *Endear yourself to the Emperor.* I take a deep breath. The perfume trick has worked. "Yes, Your Majesty."

He steps back and appraises me. "Remarkable. It reminds me of lotus flowers."

He sits down and gestures to the Chief Eunuch who hurries to him, and whispers in his ear. There's a pause and some consultation of documents and then the Chief Eunuch steps forward for my official presentation to the court. His voice is loud but what he says is too fast and complicated. It only sounds like a gargled song to me but there's a murmur of approval from the court as well as some laughter.

I turn to my translator, Jiang, who has crept up behind me and who now whispers to me. "You are to be known as *He Guiren* – Lady He."

The Emperor and Empress Dowager watch me from their thrones, waiting for my face to change in response to the announcement.

I shake my head. "What does that mean?"

"*Guiren* is your rank. You are sixth-ranked, which is an Honoured Lady, and *He* will be your new name."

I'm taken aback. "I have a new *name?*"

"Yes. It means Perfect Purity. So you are the Honoured Lady of Perfect Purity. A very auspicious name, especially as the Qing dynasty's name also means Purity."

"Why did they laugh, then?"

"The name He can also mean lotus flower, because it rises perfectly pure out of the mud. The Emperor has asked for your name to reflect your scent."

I look back at the Emperor, who smiles as he sees understanding dawn on my face. I give a tentative smile in return. The Chief Eunuch is gesturing at me, so I step forward and perform a kowtow. I stumble slightly as I stand but at least I don't fall over. The Emperor holds out an object like a sceptre to me and the Chief Eunuch indicates I should take it. It's as long as my arm and in parts almost as thick, made of a dark carved wood and inset with three panels in white jade. There are characters and flowers carved over every part of it. I've no idea what it is.

Seeing my puzzled face the Emperor leans forward from the throne to explain. "It is called a *ruyi*," he says. "It is a blessing, a symbol of good luck for our union."

I nod and try to look suitably impressed, although I can't read the writing on the jade panels.

The Emperor reaches out and traces the carved characters with his finger. "It says that all the world is now at peace," he says, smiling. He raises his voice a little so that everyone can hear. "Now that Xinjiang is part of our empire's family and Lady He has joined the ladies of the court, the world is at peace."

The court applauds.

I wonder what Iparhan would say but bite my tongue. I smile at him and he smiles back. I step away, holding the *ruyi*.

The Chief Eunuch calls out more announcements and I tilt my head towards Jiang for an explanation.

"Your father and brothers are to be given a fine house and many gifts," he murmurs. "They will live close by, in the newly created Muslim quarter of Beijing, just outside the walls of the Forbidden City."

I think of the men and women I saw for a few brief moments in the house on the outskirts of the city, who kowtowed to me believing me to be their sister, their daughter, their prize for the choice they made in turning away from their own family and lands, the allegiances of centuries. Their smiles, their pride. I think of the touch of the coverlet as it passed me, its wrapped burden made to disappear forever through an open window while hot piss ran down my thighs in fear.

I shudder.

The Chief Eunuch is by my side in an instant.

"We have not cared for your ladyship well enough," he says. "My humble apologies. You are tired and chilled from your journey here. You will be conducted to your rooms at once." He makes a tiny gesture and other eunuchs appear by his side. He instructs them at speed and bows very low to me as I'm guided from the room. I look over my shoulder and see him return to the Emperor, who is now examining a new document, oblivious to my departure. I look for the Empress, but she has disappeared.

My palanquin is waiting and I climb back in. I keep the window curtain open to cool my hot cheeks. I look down at the carved *ruyi* resting in my lap and revise the hurdles I have passed so far. My supposed family members are outside the walls of the Forbidden City, never to see my imposter's face again. I've not done anything terrible in the presence of the Emperor, have not yet given away my fraudulent identity. These thoughts should soothe me, but all they lead to is what may be coming next.

I'm whisked along stone-clad expanses, through endless gates and courtyards, past magnificent temples and palaces, their rooftops surmounted by strange little figurines. We pass golden-glazed roof tiles, red walls, monstrous golden guardian lions on pedestals, red columns, carved white stone, the colours and shapes repeated infinitely. It makes me dizzy.

We pass through a large red and gold gate and everything changes. Now we must be in the Inner Court that Mei told me about. There are more gardens with tall pines, smaller trees and bushes. A few are showing their first buds, creating, from a distance, the illusion of a gentle green haze. Here and there, nestling in the warmer nooks are early-blooming flowers. The cobbled pathways grow narrower and we pass close by many small palaces and shrines, their gates guarded by stone lanterns as high as my head. Carved wooden screens in red or dark wood shape the outlines of windows. Looking through the palace gates we pass I see little courtyards here and there with glimpses of flowers and trees within them. Once I hear a child laughing, but I don't see anybody, only a few other palanquins bobbing along in the distance.

The palanquin pauses briefly in front of a gate, which we pass through. We stop and I climb out. By my side, slightly out of breath, is interpreter Jiang, who must have trotted alongside us for the past few minutes.

We're in the courtyard of a small palace like the ones we passed coming here. The courtyard has three tall pine trees and many pots holding pink and white camellia bushes. The roof, its edges curved like a temple, reaches out over shining red columns. Blue and gold decorated outer walls are carved everywhere with wooden panels, forming balustrades, window and door frames in brilliantly bright colours as well as shaped ceilings over the walkways connecting the doors of the building. The carvings around the door are of many rich fruits and delicate flowers, piled high like the best market stalls of Kashgar.

Before me are gathered a group of men and women. One eunuch, who appears to be their leader, is about forty and very well dressed in brilliantly colourful robes. He's tall and thin, with a weathered face and a stately demeanour. Around him are other eunuchs, mostly dressed in simpler robes of sober blues and greys. The women all wear long pale green or blue robes with their hair in one long plait tied with a small red ribbon. They look to the senior eunuch as though for a signal. Sure enough, he drops to his knees, as does Jiang at my side, all of them performing a kowtow.

I wait for it to be completed and then the tall eunuch approaches me, his manner poised like an actor stepping onto a stage. His voice is high pitched, but louder and more certain than Jiang's soft murmuring. "My name is Huan, Lady He, and I am your first attendant. All that gives you pleasure is my desire. All that displeases you is my sorrow and disgrace."

I look to Jiang, who has spoken at the same time, repeating the words in my own tongue to be sure I will understand. "Thank you. Is this where I will live?"

"Yes, my lady. And we are your humble servants." He reels off a string of names, indicating various faces. I very quickly stop trying to take them all in. I will focus on just the two of them for now. Huan, because he is the most important servant, Jiang because he is my mouthpiece. I must stay alert, must stay focused on the people who will matter most in my new life.

"Who else lives here?"

"The other ladies."

"Do I have my own room?"

Huan looks shocked for a moment but hastily recomposes his face. "This is all your own palace. The other ladies have their own palaces, the ones you passed as you came here."

I've made an error but I'm truly taken aback. All this is mine? It's huge. Quickly, I recompose myself. "The Emperor is very generous," I say. "I had not expected to be given my own palace at once. I know I am not as highly ranked as other ladies here." I hope this sounds suitably humble and grateful. Sure enough, Huan's face clears. I heave a small sigh of relief.

He steps back. "Let me show you through the rooms of your palace, your ladyship."

Huan and I walk up a few steps onto a walkway and enter the palace. By my side, a constant shadow, is Jiang. When Huan speaks loudly to my left, his meaning comes to me from my right, in the soft murmur of Jiang's voice. Both have the same way of walking, toes turned out, bodies pushed forward, their legs close together. It gives them an odd, mincing pace. With one on each side I find myself falling into the same strange walk before I hastily correct myself and walk normally.

Inside we step into a sitting room. It is decorated in pale blue, with lavish use of gold and carvings. I hear birds singing and look about before I catch sight of two birdcages. The occupants flit about the cage and make a pleasant chirping sound. I approach them and then freeze.

Standing before me, in a shadowy corner of the room, is Iparhan.

I feel the room sway, hold out my hand, open my mouth to speak her name and then darkness falls.

I come to with a face very close to mine. The terrified eyes of Jiang are fixed on me. As I open my eyes he almost screams for Huan, who is by his side in an instant. I am half-lying on a couch, my shoes have been removed and a more junior eunuch is anxiously rubbing them. I feel very hot and then realise I've been heaped over with silk covers of every size and colour.

I try to speak and make a soft moaning noise, causing Jiang to whimper. Huan is firmer.

"You must drink this," he orders, and I sip some foul-tasting brew, which makes me gag. I wave it away but he persists.

"Iparhan," I say, when I can speak again.

"What is ipar-han?" asks Huan. Jiang shakes his head, mystified. I push them aside and sit up, looking into the corner of the room again where Iparhan stood. She is still there, although seated now. I rise, shaking. So does she.

A mirror. I am standing before a mirror. I make my way as close to it as I can and reach out, the very tips of my fingers brushing my cold hard reflection. Only now do I realise that I have never seen myself dressed as a lady. I never saw a mirror in the house in the dunes. I forgot Mei's instruction to look for a mirror in the room where I was dressed this morning. I think of the first time I ever saw Iparhan, when she stared at my face, searching over every part of it, touching my unblemished cheek, of Mei hastily hiding a mirror from me the first time she dressed me. How Nurmat checked my face when he first held me in the dark side street of Kashgar, how he stood frozen when he first saw me washed and dressed. His arousal when we enacted the images from the pillow books. How he saw me naked in the bath, his hands reaching out of their own accord. Now I understand. I look like Iparhan. With my rags taken away and clothed in rich colours, my hair swept back and powders enhancing my face, I am like her sister. Not twins, not so close, but if someone did not know us…

I stand in silence, my fingers still resting on the cold glass. Mei's last words echo in my mind. "Look in a mirror," she said. What did she need me to understand? Why does Iparhan need me to look so much like her? By the old poplar she had brushed over us having a 'similar' height and build. But this is much more than that.

As I gaze in the mirror, my mind full of questions, I suddenly realise that the two eunuchs are standing behind me. Their fearful faces reflect back at me through the mirror and I try to steady myself. I am behaving very strangely. I have to think of an explanation – and fast.

I turn to them. "I resemble a – a sister who died many years ago," I stumble, inventing as quickly as I can. "The heat – the journey – I thought of her. She would have been so proud of me today… of my great good fortune in being chosen by the Emperor himself."

They look hugely relieved but still think it important to check. "You thought of her. You did not – *see* her?" says Huan.

I shake my head, walking away from the mirror as though it is unimportant, although in truth I just want to stand in front of it and stare again at the reflection – at my face, which is no longer mine. "No, no, I was just… tired."

I can see they immediately thought of ghosts, that I have diverted them sufficiently. Now they can resume their fussing. I am made to rest, to drink more of their vile drinks, asked whether I wish to wear more comfortable clothes.

"May I see the rest of the palace?" I ask at last, hoping to escape the mirror in the corner.

Room after room unfolds. There's a bedroom with a huge *kang* piled high with silken covers and draped with long curtains, far larger than the one I thought so luxurious in the desert house.

A matching bedroom makes me turn to Huan. "I thought you said I wasn't to share with another lady?"

"If the Emperor should choose to visit you and wish to stay the night," says Huan, "then he will stay in a separate room."

"Why?"

Huan looks perplexed at this questioning of timeless protocol. I curse myself. I must stop asking questions that reveal my ignorance. "The Emperor never stays a full night in the same bed as one of his ladies. Once congress has taken place he will retire to another room."

I nod as though this makes sense. It doesn't. But I make a note of the word 'congress' as a reminder to myself. I might have forgotten and called it something coarser. I will have to watch my mouth.

We move on. Every room is luxurious and filled with beautiful things. There are flowers, paintings, scrolls with delicate calligraphy, decorative screens, carved furniture, mirrors, and cabinets. Everywhere there is a sweet smell of sandalwood, coming from the many items of furniture. Everywhere are gems, paint applied in brilliant hues, mosaics. On most surfaces pretty little items await my use or amusement – stone incense burners, implements for writing, fans, as well as little game boards, all their pieces tiny, exquisite carvings. It all begins to blur together – the scent, the brilliant colours, the endless new ornaments. I feel dizzy but I try to keep a suitable look on my face – somewhere between impressed at my good fortune and the natural acceptance of a noble lady surveying suitably adorned rooms, perhaps only one level more elaborate than those with which she would have been raised. It's a difficult expression to maintain.

There's a huge receiving hall, a miniature of the magnificent one in which I met the Emperor, which contains an altar and a throne.

"For His Majesty's visits," says Huan.

We pass again through the sitting room, where I avert my eyes from the mirror, then make our way to a dining room with enough space for a banquet should I choose to hold one and a bathroom with a gigantic lacquered wooden tub for bathing, so heavy it stays in its place always, unlike the one in the house where I was prepared to come here. Later I find that hidden away from my eyes are many more rooms, far plainer, which smell of food, sleep and bodies rather than incense, sandalwood and precious perfume. These are storage rooms, kitchens and my personal servants' sleeping and eating quarters. Such necessities are considered none of my concern, they exist to service my needs rather than to delight my senses and therefore must not be seen, heard or smelled.

We go back to the sitting room where I sit with my back to the mirror and Huan nods imperceptibly to a maid. In moments I'm brought tea. It's a tea beyond the imaginations of the common trading route tea merchants selling their so-called 'fine' teas. This is delicately perfumed and as I sip, a beautiful flower unfurls its scarlet petals within the depths of the bowl. I sip it gratefully while discreetly trying to shift my feet into a more comfortable position. My new high shoes hurt me but I daren't mention them, no doubt I ought to be used to them. Huan observes the slight grimace on my face and rises from his place opposite me, kneels, then gently removes the shoes and sets them aside, slipping a cushion under my feet.

I look down at him, surprised. "How did you know?" I blurt out.

He smiles. "It is my duty to know everything about you, my lady," he says, rising and going back to his place.

I hope he knows nothing at all about me. I wonder if he can tell that I'm not a noblewoman born and bred and shift uneasily in my seat. His eyes and Jiang's are on me at all times. Any error I make will be seen at once. I pray that they put down any slips to my being a foreigner. But now Huan seems to have other things on his mind. He clears his throat. "Because your ladyship is from the newest part of His Majesty's glorious empire, you must instruct us how to care for you. His Majesty has given orders that all must be done to ensure your happiness."

I wait for clarification.

"Your clothes, for example…" He pauses and both he and Jiang examine me with concerned expressions.

This is what I dreaded. Something is wrong. I curse Iparhan for having made some error, for not having noticed something that will give me away. "What about my clothes?"

The two eunuchs look awkward. Huan clears his throat again. "They are not in the Manchu style and yet we understand you are to continue wearing them. Your chests of clothes were sent to us ahead of your arrival so that we might prepare them to be worn and examine how they are made. As they are not…" He clears his throat for a third time.

I'm worried. "I desire only to please His Majesty," I say hesitantly. Their faces smooth out. I'm on the right track. "You must speak freely so that I may know how I may please him best," I finish, hoping it's the right thing to say.

Huan lowers his voice and Jiang does likewise. A mistake, because this means he is almost silent.

I lean forward, and Jiang hesitantly repeats Huan's words. "The clothes are not, er, *elegant* enough for your ladyship's new status," he breathes, blushing as he does so. "What you are wearing now is of course suitable for your wedding day but the rest of the items…"

"I know the style is different," I say, struggling to understand what he's saying.

"It is not the style," they hasten to reassure me. "We can of course replicate your ladyship's traditional costume. It is the fabrics, the embroidery…"

I think back to the Emperor's clothes and those of the court women, how they outshone the courtiers. "You think they should be more elaborate?" I ask tentatively, hoping I've guessed their delicate hints.

They beam at me. "*Yes*, your ladyship."

I could cry with relief. Is this all that's bothering them? "You must have them made however you think best," I say quickly.

They spring into action before I've even finished speaking. Maids are dispatched and return bearing huge chests of clothes, which are pulled out and spread on the floor to be examined. Huan and Jiang kneel on the floor and hover over them, trying to understand the strange new garments, glancing up at what I'm wearing for confirmation.

"So there is a skirt," they mutter. "With a shirt? And then the waistcoat?"

I stare at them. I've never met people like this. They're like two old women with their bustling and concern over minor details, or little girls with favoured dolls. I feel lost. I had thought that at least I knew how to talk my way round most people, but these men are unlike anything I've ever encountered. Is this how I'll be spending my days? Fussing and fretting over clothes? *Until Iparhan comes wanting information,* I think, *Iparhan and her face that matches mine...* and quickly push the thought away with a small shudder.

Huan catches the motion and looks up at me. "And an outer jacket?"

I nod. "If it's cold enough."

Huan sits back on his heels and looks up at me with concern. "Beijing winters are cold beyond your imagination, your ladyship. There is snow and ice everywhere. The streams that run through the Forbidden City freeze over. And the *wind...*" He shudders theatrically.

I think of the freezing desert wind and the snow-capped mountains of home and try to look suitably impressed. The Emperor may have learnt my language but clearly his people have no notion whatsoever of my homeland. I might as well have arrived from a made-up world, a fairytale.

Jiang joins in the inspection. "And then there is a little cap?"

I indicate the heaps strewn before us. "Yes. As you can see, there are plenty to choose from."

From their pursed lips I can see that none of the caps meet their standards. Huan is holding up a waistcoat and comparing it to what I am wearing. "They seem very..."

"Very?"

"... small?"

I frown. I don't understand what he means. I'm beginning to panic. Is this how I will fail? Not because of some big mistake but because I don't know some tiny sartorial detail? "They fit me," I say, feeling my hands begin to tremble again. Have they ever seen the girl whose place I have taken? Do I not fit her clothes well enough?

"Yes. Very – very *fitted.*"

"Is that wrong?"

The two of them look at one another. I wait. Huan tries to explain. "Did you see the other ladies? In the throne room?"

I nod. Where is this leading?

"Their robes are more... loose-fitting."

I did notice. Their exquisitely decorated robes hung shapelessly over their bodies. Fat or thin, shapely curves or flat-bottomed and mean-chested, you could hardly tell when they were all standing together. I think of the girls of Kashgar, who try to make their waistcoats just that little tighter at the waist, just that little more curved at the chest, to give them a waist and bust more shapely than those with which they might have been blessed by nature. The wide skirts which float outwards when a girl dances.

I try to explain. "They make a woman more shapely. More... womanly." I draw a shape in the air with my hands, trying to show them what I mean. The two of them ponder the imaginary shape in silence. "So that men will find them... attractive?"

They consider this in doubtful silence before Jiang ventures to Huan, "Perhaps His Majesty will appreciate something a little different? Like Lady Ling?"

Huan's eyebrows go up but then he nods, first slowly and then a little faster.

"Who is Lady Ling?" I ask.

"A favourite of the Emperor," says Huan thoughtfully. "Han Chinese, not Manchu. Different." He smiles. "Like you, my lady."

The rest of the day passes in chaos. A selection of my clothes are picked out to be ripped apart for patterns and taken away to an army of unseen dressmakers who are told to replicate them many times over, but in fabrics and with decorations befitting my new status.

Once the clothes have been dealt with Huan approaches me and slowly undoes a few of my plaits. I sit still and await his verdict. I'd rather he focused on my hair and clothes than investigating anything else. So far their attention to my clothes has stopped them asking any other questions about me.

"Your hair is very unusual, my lady."

Jiang, watching him, interjects. "She said it must change from many plaits to only two from now on, as she is married."

Huan frowns, rubbing the loose hair between his fingers to feel its texture. "Two plaits? Down your back?"

I nod.

He shakes his head. "Your ladyship will look like a maid." He gestures and a maid rushes forward. Huan indicates that she should turn her back so we can see her hair. One thick plait hangs down her back, tied with a small red cord. Huan points to it. "Two plaits, one plait – what difference will there be?"

I pull one of my tiny plaits over my shoulder. The red flowers and gold ribbons in it shine. "Can't you do things like this?"

He considers them. "Perhaps..."

I wait.

"Gemstones," he says at last. "Your plaits must shine like a treasure house."

Jiang smiles. "Huan is an excellent hairdresser," he says. "Our previous lady, who is now gone from us, would have no one but him do her hair."

"How did you come to both be given to me then?"

"We begged to serve together," says Huan.

Jiang adds shyly, "I was taught by Huan when I arrived here and he saved me from many beatings, being older than I."

"Beatings for what?"

Both of them blush and look away. Jiang's murmur drops so low I can barely make out his explanation.

"When a eunuch is very young, my lady, he... struggles to control... his... his urination. Due to the operation – to make him a eunuch."

I can't help it, I wince.

Huan nods gravely. "Often eunuchs are derided for this, madam, for the... smell."

Jiang continues alone. "So new eunuchs are severely beaten for such crimes. But Huan, being older than I, knew what fate might befall me and would wash my robes and hang them to dry in secret, so that I might not be punished for my odour."

I'm about to reply but a loud cry makes me jump. It's repeated over and over again, first far away and then drawing closer, before fading again like echoes. "Draw the bolts, lock up, careful with the lanterns. Draw the bolts, lock up, careful with the lanterns." I hear a voice reply from my own courtyard and turn to Huan. Jiang answers. "All those who had business in the Forbidden City today have left. The gates are to be locked up now; only the Emperor and his family and servants will remain."

I speak without thinking. "And the court physician on duty tonight."

Their eyebrows go up simultaneously. "How do you know about the physician?"

I think of a wrinkled tortoise face and bent back. "I knew a woman who was once a maid here." They wait for more but I stay silent. I don't trust my voice not to waver if I speak again.

Huan claps his hands. "It is time for your ladyship to eat. A meal has been prepared."

They lead me back to the dining room and the gigantic table. I sit down at one end. Perhaps ten servants are already in the room, gazing at me. Huan and Jiang hover behind me as dishes are brought in. Mei was right, I think. Soon almost the whole table is covered in tiny dishes, which are uncovered before me. Each has a tiny strip of metal stuck in them. I prod one cautiously.

"For your safety, my lady," says Jiang.

I twist round to look at him. "Safety?"

"They are strips of silver. If there is poison in your food, the silver will go black."

I've never heard of such a thing. "Are you sure?" *Poison?* I think to myself. No one mentioned the possibility of poison before I came here. How many more hidden dangers are there?

They nod, earnest.

I shrug and pick up the chopsticks laid out for me. Huan hurries to intercept me. "One moment, my lady." He gestures and a eunuch steps forward and begins tasting the dishes, a little bite of each.

My eyebrows go up. "What's he *doing*?"

Huan looks surprised again. I've asked another stupid question. I must keep quiet. "Your taster, my lady. An additional precaution against poisoning."

It takes some time but at last I'm allowed to start. I want to try everything but almost immediately run into difficulties. Huan offers me a dish.

"Pork dumplings, my lady."

My chopsticks are halfway to the plate. I stop. "I can't eat that."

Huan looks bemused. "Dumplings?"

I shake my head. "Pork."

He looks down at the offending items. "You don't like pork?"

I adopt a devout tone. "I'm a Muslim. I cannot eat it. It is forbidden."

He blinks and I see the servants' eyes move slowly the length of the table.

I sit back in my chair, relishing having put them on the back foot. I was right. Being a Muslim is going to be helpful to me. "How many of the dishes here are pork?" Huan begins to indicate them. I hold up a hand to stop him. "Take the pork dishes off the table."

The servants start readjusting the dishes. Many are taken away. I pick up my chopsticks again and then pause. "These ones remaining – do any contain pork fat?"

Several more are removed.

I can see Huan getting concerned. The bountiful table looks diminished. They can hardly doubt my religion, at least, the amount of fuss I'm making. "These other meats – have they been blessed?"

"Blessed?"

I make it as simple as possible. "As they are being killed – they must have prayers said over them, otherwise…"

I stop. Incomprehension on every face. I point with my chopsticks. "Pass me all the dishes that are vegetables only. No meat."

There are frantic changes. I now have ten dishes before me rather than close to a hundred. The endless table looks bare. Still, I have rice, noodles, vegetables, sweetmeats. I begin to eat. A thump to the floor and a blur of movement makes me stop. Huan and Jiang, along with the other servants, have fallen to the floor, on their knees, their faces hidden. I look down and then touch Huan. "What are you doing?"

His face, when he looks up, is streaked with real tears. I drop the chopsticks in alarm. Something has gone badly wrong. My heart is suddenly thudding. "What is it?"

"We have failed your ladyship. You go hungry because of our ignorance."

I snort with laughter and have to turn it into a cough. I want to tell him that hunger, real hunger, is not ten dishes of good hot food. That hunger isn't even one missed meal but many, one after another until the gnawing in your stomach almost disappears into a numb acceptance. I open my mouth and then shake my head. I can't tell him this. I'm supposed to be a noblewoman, a suitable consort for an Emperor. What would she have said? I frame the words carefully and try to keep a straight face. "You've a great deal to learn about how to serve in my household. Tomorrow a servant must go to the new Muslim quarter in Beijing and find a – a priest of my people who will direct them in how to buy meats for my table. For tonight…" I pause at the enormity of the lie. "…I will have to go hungry."

They all hide their faces again. I want to tell them not to be so ridiculous. Instead I ignore them and eat the bountiful food before me, enjoying such delicacies as sweet potatoes, chestnuts and peanuts. Then I stand, forcing them all to rise with me and begin clearing the table, their faces downcast.

Huan and Jiang, meek now, follow me back to the sitting room. I decide I can't live with the daily reminder of my similarity to Iparhan. Whatever it means, whatever is to come of it. "I am not fond of mirrors," I say. "Can that one be removed? It is…" I think about what might constitute a valid excuse. "It is a temptation to pride, which as a Muslim woman is sinful."

They look taken aback but within moments the mirror has been removed. I feel my shoulders slump with relief.

An edginess is creeping over me at what is about to happen next. I look about me and take a deep breath. It has to happen sometime, I can't put it off any longer. I knew what playing this part would entail and I will have to go through with it. "What time will he come?" I ask.

"Who, my lady?"

"The Emperor, of course."

Their heads both tilt to one side. "He may not come here."

Have I made another error? "Do I go to him, then?"

There is a pause. "His Majesty," says Jiang, choosing each word with care, "might not see you at all today."

I take this in. "Tomorrow, then?"

There's a pause.

"When *will* I see him, then?"

Jiang makes a gesture of helplessness. "His Majesty's desires are not ours to know."

I'm confused. "But he will want to see me?"

Huan hurries to reassure me. "Of course. Of course."

"When?"

"That, we cannot know."

I must be missing something. "Does the Emperor see one of his ladies every night?"

They consider this. "Usually."

I think of the small group of women I saw standing in the throne room. It can't take him that long to work his way through us. "How many ladies are there?"

"Several dozen."

"*What?*"

They hurry to explain. "Of course, not all are as exalted as yourself and the Emperor's most important ladies. You are part of a small, elite group. There is the Empress Ula Nara. Then there are the Imperial Noble Consorts, the Noble Consorts, the Consorts, the Imperial Concubines, the Honoured Ladies such as yourself. But after those there are many more ladies of far lesser rank and in far greater numbers. All are housed within the Forbidden City."

I might not see him for a long time. Iparhan wants information from me. What will Iparhan do if I don't give her what she wants? And the information she wants can come only from time spent with the Emperor.

Huan sees my face cloud over and he speaks gently. He must think I cherish some foolish notion of being one of the Emperor's favourites. "Be patient, my lady."

I try to smile but Iparhan's face – now too similar to mine – rises up before me and I turn away from him.

Night comes. I peep into the courtyard and see glowing lanterns everywhere. Inside the *kang* is warmed and the pink and gold hangings around my bed are loosened to prepare for the moment when I'll be cocooned inside them.

The maids help to undress me. I've already found a moment to hide my perfume vial in a little sandalwood box down the side of my bed. Now that I see the maids up close they are practically children; the oldest looks barely thirteen. I'm given a soft loose robe in which to sleep. I'm shown how to use crude salt on a finger to clean my teeth. Perhaps ladies don't care about spitting in front of their servants because they're used to having people watch them wash and dress. I don't care because I've spat in the street a thousand times, so I pass this trial easily. Even using a chamber pot in full view of the servants doesn't bother me; I've pissed in alleyways enough times. Huan keeps up a running commentary on the next day's plans. I barely hear him; I'm in such a daze of tiredness.

"The second lunar month brings us the festival of the Azure Dragon – we call this the Dragon Raising Its Head. All homes must be expressly cleaned to honour the occasion and special dishes of pancakes and noodles will be eaten. Should you wish to visit a temple, a sedan chair will come for you in the morning."

I try to show some interest. "The same one I had today?"

"No, my lady. That was a bridal chair, used for the day when a new lady enters the court. From now on your chair will be orange, like those of the other concubines. The Emperor, his mother and the Empress ride in yellow chairs. Everyone else rides in red chairs."

I try to shake away the ache in my head. I must concentrate. "Is everything colour-coded like this?"

He smiles. "Yes, my lady. It will all seem natural soon."

They finish preparing me for the night. I'm halfway into the bed when I suddenly remember. I turn to Huan. "Which way is North?"

He looks startled but points. I think about the right way to face and then kneel on the floor and ostentatiously begin my prayers, bowing and murmuring. A hush descends.

I'm grateful my face is mostly hidden from view and that none of them will know if I make a mistake. As I finish I keep my head bowed. How long will my tricks and illusions keep me safe here? A real, unbidden prayer comes to my mind. *Let me be safe here.* I stand and see twenty pairs of eyes fixed on me in amazement.

"It is how I pray," I say, trying to keep a straight face. "And you must find me a little mat on which I may kneel."

They continue to gape. I climb into the bed and pull the curtains closed. "Goodnight," I call through the thick folds.

I hear the thump as they all hit the floor to bow to me. "Goodnight, your ladyship."

I look up at the painted and gilded ceiling and listen to them leaving the room. When they've all gone I lie awake and think. I am shaking with exhaustion after less than a day here. The constant tiny errors I am making, the endless ritual and routine that all these people know backwards... I will need an escape plan. If this all goes wrong – and how can it not – I need to have food and simple clothes hidden away. I need to find a way to leave the Forbidden City. Tomorrow I will begin to put together my plan, for I can't believe this illusion won't shatter into a thousand pieces the first time true pressure is applied. My head aches from trying to keep my wits about me. I will have to remember to say the right things, to behave correctly, day after day after day. Perhaps for the rest of my life. And if I forget, for just one moment, it could lead to my life being a great deal shorter.

I look down at my hands, lying on the blossom-embroidered pink silk coverlet and think of the words of the old opium-riddled fortune-teller.

I see a great man, a man who will let your hands rest only on silk.

Fireworks

NIGHT COMES AND FIREWORKS RIP *the sky apart across the city, celebrating the marriage of the Emperor to his new bride. Nurmat is happier than I have ever seen him. He is all gentleness to me, all smiles to strangers we pass in the streets. We eat at a food stall and then walk about the Muslim quarter, learning the streets, greeting those from our homeland.*

Later in darkness I sit by the window looking out over the moat while Nurmat lies on my bed, his fingers lightly stroking my back.

"Of what are you thinking, Iparhan?" he asks softly. Perhaps he is hoping that I will reply that I am thinking of him, or of his caresses in this bed.

"Hidligh," I say. "I need someone to watch her, to report on whether she is playing her part well. I need to know how close she is to the Emperor so that I can judge what questions she should ask of him. I may have to bribe a maid."

Nurmat yawns. "You need a eunuch, not a maid," he says. "The maids are nobodies. The eunuchs are far closer to their mistresses."

As a child, the last offspring and much-desired daughter of an aging mother, I ran wild. I longed to play with the boys but my mother disapproved. "Weapons are not suitable playthings for a girl," she chided me gently. She made sure my horses were soft creatures, docile and trusting, not the warhorses I longed for.

The servants became my playmates. I rode on the menservants' backs, urging them on like racing steeds, laughing when they reared and snorted, attempting to throw me. I coaxed them to let me play with daggers and then swords, begged to mock-fight them when they had other tasks to perform. And so I grew: my aim more accurate, my seat in the saddle better than even my older brothers'. My ability to disappear from sight when my mother came looking for me was aided by willing servants, my sworn allies.

"A eunuch?" I repeat.

There is no reply. Nurmat's eyes are closed, his face half buried in the covers, his soft young skin flushed with sleep.

The Inner Court

T HE INNER COURT IS A strange place.

A whole day can be taken up with being bathed and dressed in ludicrous finery. Each day my plaits are variously interwoven with pearls, corals, jade, strands of multi-coloured silk, fresh flowers (which Huan changed three times that day just to keep them fresh and scented) and even, on one memorably dull day, with *zhe zhi*, tiny shapes intricately folded from paper to resemble animals and birds, then hung on red silk strands from my dark hair. They took hours to fasten and I had to sit still while it was done, stifling my yawns.

I'm fed dish after dish, sitting all alone at the great table for my meals, then I sit in the garden or one of my rooms. I might play a game with the eunuchs, learning new moves on the board while picking at sweet cakes or little snacks. I might look at paintings or talk to the caged birds, some of who talk back in creaking voices. I sip fine teas, their leaves and floral additions changed with the hours of the day or my mood. I go to bed. This is a day.

At first I'm expectant. I wait to be summoned by the Emperor. I'm jumpy, nervous. But there is no summons. No word. Not even a suggestion that I might be called on as his companion. The work that goes into my clothes, my hair, my grooming – what is it for, if not for this expected summons which is so long in coming? I want to ask questions but I daren't reveal my ignorance. Perhaps this is normal. Perhaps the Emperor never calls for his new ladies until… until what? What do I have to do to be noticed? I'm nervous of being called for, but if I'm not called for then how can I get the information Iparhan wants? What will she do to me if I fail her in this? When I think of this I finger the hollow of my throat, where Iparhan laid her dagger against my skin. It becomes a nervous habit with me, a quick flutter of my fingertips against the hollow of my throat.

I set about protecting myself. I've not lived on the streets for nothing. I need to know the Forbidden City and its people as I knew the streets of Kashgar, but first I need an escape plan. You should always have somewhere to hide if things go wrong.

I ask for some cakes. When no one is looking I hide a few in the pockets of my skirts, then squirrel them away under my bed, along with a sleeping robe that could serve as clothing should I need to run away. The robe may look plain compared to my other clothes but it is at least Manchu in style and I would stand out less wearing it than I would in my foreign-looking, elaborately embroidered clothes. This little parcel will serve as my security in case I should have to escape. Each day I hide new food away and throw the old food into the pond in my garden where the fish eagerly rise for the crumbs I throw them.

Then I ask Jiang to show me Beijing from one of the watchtowers. "I've never seen it," I say to him. He calls for my palanquin and takes me to the very back of the Forbidden City, to the North-West corner and the watchtower there.

I stand in the uppermost storey, only too aware of the armed guards standing close by. Jiang chatters away to me while I try not to let my true feelings show.

"You can see most of the Forbidden City from here," says Jiang. "The Inner Court, beginning at the far North of the City and stretching South. That is Empress's palace there, and that is the Emperor's. That one close by is the Palace of Motherly Tranquillity, it is where the Empress Dowager lives. The surrounding palaces are those of the other court ladies and yourself. Then further away you can see the Outer Court. His Majesty's officials and courtiers come there of course, on official business and for ceremonies. Then if you turn this way you can see the city of Beijing itself…"

I try to drown out the sound of his voice and focus on what I need to know. I keep an interested look on my face, I nod and turn my face where he points as though listening to him but inside I have a horrible sinking feeling.

From where we stand I can see, not Beijing, which I had little interest in seeing anyway, but instead the outer walls and defences of the Forbidden City. The moat that Mei told me about is huge. Where its dark waters meet the Forbidden City rise the red walls of my new home. They are too smooth to climb, too high to jump from even if I could scale them. I would risk a broken limb at best, at worse a cracked head. There are only four gates in and out of the huge palace complex, and each is heavily guarded. Escape will have to be a last resort.

I need to protect myself from any dangers of which I am as yet unaware. I think of the Empress' face when she first saw me and remember Mei's warnings of the 'factions' amongst the women of the palace. "I wish to visit Lady Wan," I announce to Huan.

He pauses in his work, wrapping thin strands of purple silk in my hair, from which dangle tiny white jade creatures. "Lady Wan?"

"Is she still here?" I ask, wondering if perhaps she has died since Mei left court.

"Oh yes," says Huan. "But why would you wish to meet her, my lady? She is quite old and lives a very quiet life. She is not much in favour."

"Does the Emperor dislike her?" I ask.

"No, no," says Huan. "He is quite fond of her, but he no longer calls on her as a companion."

"I had a maid who served her," I say. "And she spoke well of her. I would like to meet her. What does she look like?"

"She is fully four and forty years old," says Huan, as though suggesting that she is practically on her deathbed. "She was known for the beauty of her hair and the fineness of its arrangements, but now it is no longer black and much of it is – ahem – missing."

"Missing?"

He lowers his voice theatrically. I've already learned that Huan will seize any opportunity for dramatic pronouncements. "She is *bald*, my lady."

"How does she have her hair done, then?"

"She has one of the best hairdressers in the palace. He spends hours creating wigs for her. If you see the Lady Wan you will be astonished by her hair. It is perfection. Even the Empress appears not to have such fine hair nor so beautifully dressed. But they are all wigs."

Lady Wan's palace is not far from mine and with all due ceremony, involving a train of servants and much fussing beforehand over my hair and clothes, we make our way to her.

She greets me with fluttering kindness, her heavily painted face almost cracking as she speaks. Her hair is spectacular. It towers above her, stretched across a thin black board. From it are suspended crimson peonies made of silk and tinkling golden strands. Her hair is three times the size of her head.

"My dear," she says, her voice breathy, girlishly pitched. "What excitement!"

Having experienced just a few of these empty days I have to agree. Meeting a new face will be the highlight of my day for sure. If she's been here for many years I might even be the highlight of her year. She may remember this as The Year I Met Lady He.

We are settled in with tea, little cakes and fruits piled high in elegant platters. I gesture towards them thinking to start with something polite. "How pretty," I offer.

Lady Wan almost blushes. "The Son of Heaven is all kindness," she says. "The fruits were a gift from him."

I nod and smile.

"Do you miss your family?" she asks.

"I'm sure my family is very happy in the accommodation the Emperor has provided," I say, afraid she's about to suggest a visit to me from them, something I'm very keen to avoid.

"Of course," she says. "His Majesty is most generous." She pats my hand. "Visits are not allowed in the general way of course, but should you ever be gravely ill remember that he may grant permission for them to attend you should it serve to help your recovery. He is a kind and generous man." She smiles at the thought of him.

I make a mental note never to fall ill enough to warrant a visit. "Do you attend the court very much?" I ask, hoping to steer the conversation away from myself.

"Oh no," she says. "I lead a very quiet life. I was always a shy girl," she adds with an awkward little laugh. "I have lived here for many years now, very happily, with only the company of my maids and eunuchs."

This is my way in. "I had a maid back in Kashgar," I say. "She served you many years ago."

"Really?" says Lady Wan. "What was her name?"

"Mei."

She looks disappointed. "A common name," she says. "What did she look like?"

I speak without thinking. "A tortoise," I say. I feel stupid at once, for Lady Wan will not know what I am talking about.

But her eyes light up. "Mei!" she says. "She had a bent back."

I had thought Mei's bent back was due to her age. "Yes," I say.

Lady Wan is all smiles. "She was my favourite maid when I was very new here," she says. "I did not wish her to leave me but her time was up and she was free to marry. How did she end up in Xinjiang?"

"Her husband was from my homeland," I say.

"And is she happy?" asks Lady Wan. "Is she well? Does she have children?"

I can't bring myself to tell her the truth, to hurt her with the image I carry of Mei, her crumpled body lying in the half-lit doorway of a house soon to be swallowed up by the dunes of a fearsome desert. "She was a good wife and mother," I say. "Everyone who knew her loved her. She served me for a little while before I came here, so that I might be ready to join the Emperor's court. She was very good to me." I can feel my eyes glisten and try to look away.

Lady Wan reaches out and pats my hand. "We never forget those who are kind to us," she says. "Mei was my faithful servant. I am so happy to know she is well and surrounded by those who love her. And she must have told you so much about the Forbidden City!"

"She did," I say. "But she also told me that much would have changed and she told me that you... that you might help me by telling me... about the other ladies at court?"

Lady Wan sits back a little in her chair. "The ladies are all very kind, of course," she says. "We are honoured to be part of His Majesty's court."

I will have to tread softly. "It is an honour, of course," I say. "But Mei told me that I should be aware of the different... characters of the ladies? So as not to offend anyone? I am very young and she said that I should know something of their... history? Will you tell me about them?"

Lady Wan nods slowly. "There are various ladies of lesser rank," she starts. "You do not need to concern yourself with them." She thinks for a moment. "Except perhaps Lady Wang," she adds. "Lady Wang is of a lesser rank but she is very ambitious for a higher position. And..." she pauses.

"Please go on," I say.

Lady Wan's soft voice grows quieter. "She is known to have a temper," she says. "She slapped a maid – which is forbidden."

"Why?" I ask.

"A woman's face is her fortune, even if she is a maid," says Lady Wan. "You cannot damage a maid's face. The Emperor was very angry with Lady Wang and she had to pay many taels of silver to the maid's family."

I think of the way in which my own face has become my fortune and nod. I'll try to steer clear of this woman. She sounds unpleasant. "Are there any ladies whom you count as friends?" I ask.

She brightens. "Consorts Qing and Ying are my very dear friends," she says. "They too lead a quiet life here. Their palaces are adjacent and Consort Qing has the guardianship of Lady Ling's eldest son. They are almost a little family. You should seek them out," she adds. "They would be good friends to you."

I'm glad to hear there are some women here who may be friendly. "Doesn't Lady Ling look after her own children?"

"Oh no," says Lady Wan, looking shocked at the suggestion. "It would not be correct. Besides, she is with child at present and must be treated with all due care. This will be her fourth child and she has been assured that it will be another son."

"She must be in favour with the Emperor then?" I suggest.

"She is," says Lady Wan. "She has given the Emperor a son and two daughters. She is ranked as an Imperial Noble Consort, only one rank beneath the Empress. She is often called to the Emperor's rooms."

"She is his favourite, then?" I ask.

She nods.

"Why does the Emperor like her?"

"She is dedicated to his needs," she says. "She is pleasant in her demeanour to him and she has proven herself fertile. Her children are strong and healthy. She was a beauty in her day and even now is considered a woman of charm."

"Is she pleasant to anyone other than the Emperor?" I ask.

Lady Wan hesitates. "She is very ambitious for her children," she says. "No Emperor has ever been born to the ruling Empress. Every son chosen for the throne has been the offspring of a concubine. So if a concubine bears a son who pleases his father she could one day become mother to an Emperor. Lady Ling hopes to achieve this. She is kind to those who do not stand in her way but to those whom she sees as rivals…" she trails off.

"What do you mean, rivals?" I ask.

"Those who have borne sons for the Emperor," says Lady Wan. "Those women who have borne no children, or only daughters, count her as a friend – and they seek her protection, which she will give freely. But those who have borne sons are afraid of her, for she is a formidable woman at court and has the Emperor's ear."

I think this over. Certainly it's not my intention to bear sons for the Emperor but Lady Ling is likely to look at me and see a young woman new to court, who may well bear children in due course. I'll have to watch my step with her. I don't need enemies at court. I believe I've already made one but I don't know why.

"Can you tell me about the Empress?" I ask.

Lady Wan looks sad. "I have known the Empress Ula Nara since she was a young girl. We both entered the Forbidden City as concubines when the Emperor was still a prince," she says. "She was full of romantic notions and hoped for the Prince's favour. But the Prince was in love with his Primary Consort, the Lady Fuca. They were very well matched." She gives a small smile. "We concubines were hardly ever called for – he was so happy with Lady Fuca. When he became Emperor, he made her his Empress, as we all expected. But Ula Nara was beside herself with jealous grief. The years went by and still she hoped for the Emperor's favour. Having failed to attract the Emperor's attention, she tried to endear herself to his mother, the Empress Dowager, by being the very model of a dutiful daughter and becoming an expert in court etiquette. There is no-one as well versed in the rituals of the Forbidden City as she is. But despite her efforts, the Emperor was still uninterested in her."

"What happened when the Empress Fuca died?" I ask.

Lady Wan's voice drops to a whisper. "She took a fever and died so quickly that none of us were prepared. In his anguish at her death the Emperor went almost mad. He ordered mourning throughout the Empire and even had people executed for not showing proper grief for his Empress. We all of us feared for his health. He said he would not appoint another Empress, that he could not bear for another woman to take her place. But his mother, the Empress Dowager, insisted. She said it was not fitting for the court to be without an Empress, and she recommended Ula Nara as a worthy successor. Reluctantly, the Emperor agreed, although he waited until the full mourning period was complete before he allowed Ula Nara to be made Empress."

"Was she happy?" I ask.

Lady Wan slowly shakes her head. "The Empress was at first overjoyed. But soon it became clear that the Emperor did not really favour her. Of course she was the Empress and he accorded her all proper respect, but she was called frequently to his rooms for only a few years – during which she bore him three children – and then he began to call for her less and less. It is known that he no longer calls for her."

"Doesn't he like her?"

"She is a very jealous woman. She has often made her displeasure known to the Emperor when he has shown an interest in the other women of his court. She is known to hate Lady Ling because she has been shown much favour. The Emperor finds such jealousy tiresome but the less favour he shows to Ula Nara, the more she craves it."

I swallow. I was right. The Empress must find any new concubine arriving at court a galling sight and now I am that new concubine. "How do I stay out of trouble?" I blurt out.

Lady Wan pats my hand. "Oh my dear," she says. "I have scared you! I did not mean to. The court is not an easy place for a young woman. Those of us who have been here many years have found our own ways to be happy. For myself, I have always lived a quiet life. I am not ambitious and so perhaps I have not risen very high – but then I have lived a happy and comfortable enough life here, with my servants and my own pastimes. Consorts Qing and Ying – well, they have found their own happiness in their friendship together. If you are not ambitious, then those that are will not consider you worth troubling themselves with."

I nod, as though grateful for her advice. I'd take it, too, if I were on my own here.

A full belly, a warm bed, servants and whatever pastimes a lady here is allowed – boring, perhaps, but how bad could such a life be? But I'm not free to take a quiet path. Iparhan wants information and that means that I must choose a path that will take me straight to the Emperor – and incur the wrath of the ambitious women who surround him.

I let the talk pass on to other things and when we leave Lady Wan clasps my hands. "Visit me again!" she begs. I agree that I will. She's frightened me but what she's told me has put me on my guard and for that I'm grateful. Besides, I'm sorry for her, she seems lonely.

In my palanquin, being carried the short distance back to my own palace, I think over what I've been told. I feel as though I've been set down in a nest of snakes and told to tell them apart, the venomous from the harmless. It seems that I can count Lady Wan as a friendly face, and perhaps her friends Consorts Qing and Ying will prove friends to me too. But Lady Wang seems one to watch and I am certain Lady Ling is watching me. As for the Empress… I bury my face in my hands for a moment. How am I to survive with Iparhan outside the walls and the Empress within them? I seem to be trapped between two women, each of them half-crazed with their own obsessions.

"Poor Lady Wan," says Huan once we are home. "She is more than twice your age but she will never be promoted now. She was young when the Emperor was young. He has his pick of younger women now and she is old and wrinkled. But kind," he adds. "She has never been a schemer."

"It sounds like everyone else is," I say. "It's scheme or be forgotten. As it appears I have been," I can't help adding.

"The Emperor will not have forgotten you," Huan promises. "No other lady dresses or smells like you."

Huan and Jiang are intrigued by my perfume. At first they are curious. They beg to know my secret.

I plead innocence. "I was born this way," I say, lying for all I'm worth. "In my cradle, I smelt like this."

They gape at me. Then I notice that they've begun to take an immense pride in this 'wonder' that is my supposed natural fragrance. They tell all the servants of every other palace that, yes, indeed, their mistress is naturally perfumed.

"The perfume-maker has been called to every lady's palace," says Jiang, eyes sparkling. "He has been ordered, cajoled, bribed with many taels of silver and threatened with whippings. He must make new perfumes for every lady. Every perfume must be better than those requested by the other ladies. All of them must be better than yours."

This rivalry worries me. I don't want to draw unnecessary attention to myself, especially from the more ambitious or jealous women. But Huan and Jiang are happy. "Every lady must be known for something, madam," they assure me. "And your perfume is without equal, for it is not made by the hands of a man."

I think of the tiny vial hidden in my bed and nod gravely.

Wary of losing this unique gift they anxiously ask me what they must do to ensure the perfume does not depart from my body.

"Who knows?" I say. In truth, the perfume itself is causing me some concern. I am known for it – so what happens if it runs out? I use it sparingly, but use it I must, or its absence will be remarked on. What if Iparhan refuses to give me more until I have provided her with information? I try to plan for the day when I am without it. "No one has ever found a way to make it stronger nor weaker," I tell them. "It could leave my body at any time."

Worried, they put their heads together and ponder. It's imperative that I should keep my unique scent. They make lists of possible substances that will support and enhance my odour. Their latest agreement is that it must be something I eat. As the Emperor says I smell like a lotus flower, then it must surely be the lotus. With this in mind I'm served lotus seed cake (even though I prefer sweet sesame buns) and stir-fried lotus roots. The roots are also served pickled, in soups, stews and deep fried. I find them a bit stringy, but I eat them by the plateful while the two of them stand behind me, beaming. They fill my rooms with vases of lotus flowers and have planted so many in the garden pond it's a wonder the fish can still move. The petals and leaves are used to adorn dishes on my table. The dried seed cups are used for decoration and even added to the carvings around my doorways. They only make me worry even more – with all these reminders of my 'natural' perfume, what will happen if I no longer have access to it?

"I'd like *something* other than lotus flowers embroidered on my clothes," I say, when the first batch of them arrives back from the dressmakers. Lavish silks in every possible colour are spread out before me, made into skirts. Waistcoats in velvets and more silks are paired with them. All of them are covered in embroideries and gems picking out the shape of the lotus flower. Every shade from purest white through to deepest pink illustrates the petals. Green stems and wide-open pad-like leaves twine about them, growing up from rippled blue waters. Dragonflies and songbirds twirl about their petals, skimming the water below. Silver threads trace the delicate shape of the seed-pods. They are extraordinary.

The palest, most see-through gauze imaginable makes up my new shirts. Most of them are indecent without a waistcoat on top.

"I can't breathe!" I complain as the buttons are done up.

Huan stands his ground, adhering doggedly to the new principles of dress to which he's now sworn. "Your ladyship said they should be *fitted*," he remonstrates. "To enhance your ladyship's exquisite figure."

"I still have to be able to breathe and eat!"

Along with my new clothes arrives a gift. Gifts have been arriving since I got here, from various courtiers, anxious to ingratiate themselves, from new officials posted to my homeland, from lesser ladies of the court. Most of them are small, delicate gifts of precious stones, or perhaps platters of towering fruits and flowers.

The new gift is a large parcel, which, unwrapped, reveals a length of exquisite green silk. It is decorated with fine embroidery but Huan tuts as soon as he sees it.

"What's wrong with it?" I ask.

"The Emperor hates the colour green," says Huan. "The lady sending you this is hoping that you will not know this, that you will perhaps wear it in His Majesty's presence and so displease him. Fortunately you are surrounded by good servants to protect you from such trickery," he adds, snatching the offending fabric away.

"Who sent it?" I ask.

Huan inspects the accompanying seal. His lips set firm. "Lady Wang," he says. "We will know not to trust her from now on," he adds.

"You could have it made into a skirt that I only wear when I don't see him," I suggest. "It's not as though I've seen him since I got here," I add.

Huan mutters something uncomplimentary under his breath about Lady Wang and has the fabric made into a skirt, which he rarely allows me to wear.

Huan and Jiang are excited.

"There is to be a great celebration," they tell me.

"Celebrating what?"

"The conquest of Xinjiang."

I'm puzzled. "Hasn't that been done already? The Emperor claimed it months and months ago."

"Such celebrations must be planned," they explain. "It requires much time. However, the celebrations will begin in a few days. There will be a procession of soldiers, who will display their prisoners of war. The Emperor and the court will watch them from the Meridian Gate, celebrating the peace which will now come to his empire, both through his army's victory and his marriage to you."

I don't like the thought of the attention this will draw to me but at least it's a chance to remind the Emperor of my existence. Meanwhile Huan and Jiang flutter away to consider my clothes and hair.

The orange silk allowed by my rank shimmers in the pale spring sunlight, making it high summer. Blue silk waves are embroidered at the hem. Across my skirts and waistcoat fly phoenixes. My cap is blue and gold, my plaits woven in the same colours with silken cream lotus flowers placed here and there. I'm shown what I look like in a mirror but I inspect myself only briefly. The face looking back at me reminds me too much of Iparhan.

We leave the Inner Court behind, heading for the huge public spaces, and finally arrive at the Meridian Gate, the tallest building, where I'm guided to a seat looking out across the vast complex. I bow towards the Emperor, who seems to barely acknowledge me, to his mother, who looks me over and then turns away and to the Empress.

Her eyes slide over my clothes, my hair, my face. Her own face does not change. It is like a mask, her eyes still, her neck turning where she wishes to look. Her expression is blank, as though I am not there, although she is looking straight into my eyes. I lower my gaze. She is frightening me. First hate, then nothing. What is she thinking?

I feel lost in a sea of dazzling robes and unknown faces, most of them turned towards me. My clothes mark me out here, I am the only person dressed in this style. Courtiers bow to me and I try to acknowledge them, though I'm unsure of which rank requires what sort of response. In the end I fix my eyes firmly ahead of me on the spectacle below us, hoping to avoid any further errors of etiquette. I can hear whispers amongst the crowd and make some of them out.

"Did you note the casket by the Emperor? It contains the left ears of the two rebellious Khodjas, a trophy."

It contains one of their ears, I think. *I don't know who the other one belongs to. The second left ear that should be there lies beneath a scarred poplar tree in the desert to the far west of here, under a dome shaped inexpertly by Iparhan's grieving hands.*

Below us a parade begins, with countless troops declaring their spoils and victories, while the Emperor looks on, smiling benevolently. Still I can hear the whispers from the courtiers.

"Oh, the prisoners of war. Are those the troops or some of the nobles? Is that their general who…"

"Who knows. They all look the same to me."

"Even the new concubine?"

"They're all the same. Dog-Muslims, my husband calls them."

I was wrong. There are people here dressed like me, in the style of Altisharh. They are the prisoners of war, dragged here to be displayed and gloated over. My eyes suddenly fill with tears of fear. If anything should go wrong with this plan, if anyone should find out who I really am, I too would be displayed below – and executed afterwards. My little escape bundle seems ludicrous. I wipe the tears away discreetly, hoping no one notices, and bite my lip as hard as I can to distract myself.

The Emperor has composed a poem commemorating the celebration and now it is read aloud:

"The casketed Khodja's heads are brought from desert caves;

The devoted Sultan knocks at the palace gates…

By Western lakes, the might of Qing Eternal is decided,

At the Meridian Gate our triumph is thrice proclaimed.

From this day forth, we no longer stay this military course.

My people, sharing joyful plenitude, now shall take their rest."

I think of Iparhan, somewhere in Beijing, hearing this poem immortalising her father and uncle's deaths as nothing but the crushed and fallen enemies of the victorious Emperor. Her rage brings my fingers fluttering to my neck over and over again and by the time the procession is over the hollow of my throat is red with rubbing.

At last we can leave. Huan strides ahead, clearing the way for me to get back to the safety of my palanquin and palace. I'm almost shaking with relief. It's clear many courtiers think little of my people and I've no desire to be anywhere near the Empress.

But Jiang catches at my sleeve. "The Empress Dowager," he hisses. "She has summoned you to her."

I bite my lip again and taste blood. Slowly, I turn and make my way back to the three thrones. The Emperor is speaking with one of his generals, oblivious to me. The Empress Dowager is waiting for me to kneel to her. Barely an arm's length from me is Empress Ula Nara, who watches me as I approach.

I stumble as I rise from my kowtow and feel my face grow hot and red under their gaze.

The Empress Dowager is a tall woman, made larger by the grandeur of her robes and the squareness of her jaw. She dispenses with the niceties of greetings. "You cried," she says. "When the prisoners of war were displayed."

Her eyes must be as sharp as a hawk's. "Yes, Your Majesty."

"Why?"

The truth would be impossible. "I – I am a little homesick, Your Majesty," I stutter. It's a poor excuse but it's all I have.

She nods. "All the ladies are at first," she says. "You will grow accustomed to your new life and the world within these walls. Each lady finds her own way to be happy." She considers me for a moment. "Or not."

"Yes, Your Majesty," I say, keeping my voice soft so she won't hear it trembling.

She doesn't speak again, only looks closely at me, her eyes travelling over my clothes and hair. Then she makes a dismissive gesture, a quick jerk of the chin. I step backwards with care, afraid of stumbling again. As I move away I risk a glance over my shoulder. The two women, Empress and Empress Dowager, are watching me leave. I trip as I get into my chair and only Huan's steady hand saves me from falling.

I'm not sure what to do. Staying away from court will not allow me to fulfil Iparhan's wishes. Being in the gaze of the court is terrifying. I find myself seeking out distractions, ways to forget why I am here and avoid having to make a move.

Yapping brings me to the window. Two tiny dogs are frisking about under Jiang's delighted gaze.

"Whose are they?" I ask.

He jumps up, flustered. "My lady! They are my pets. They are bothering you. Naughty. *Naughty!*" he shrieks at them.

I laugh and sit down on the steps, holding out my hands to be sniffed. "Can I play with them?"

I hold them down while he brushes their silken coats. "Are cats allowed here?" I ask.

"Would you like a cat?"

"A kitten?"

The next day Jiang comes to me with a half-wild black kitten, enraged at his capture, who hisses and backs away when I hold out my hand. When I seize him by the scruff of the neck and lift him up to look at me he flattens his ears and spits. It takes only a few hours and a small dish of egg yolk to tame him. I call him Fury and he lives up to the name, attacking lizards in the garden. When he swiftly graduates to snakes I stand and look on in horror while the eunuchs shriek and poke ineffectually with brooms. Fury wrestles the snakes to their death, risking their gaping mouths and slashing fangs while his still-tiny body whirls through the air. He always wins and his smugness in victory is palpable.

Slowly my palace becomes a menagerie. There are caged birds everywhere, hanging above the walkways, in the garden, even in my sitting room. Some are set free every day, to whirr about in the evening sky before returning to their familiar roosts. Others are taken for a 'walk' in the courtyards and gardens each day, sitting inside cages that swing back and forth from the end of long poles.

I have fish brought to the pond in my garden. A greedy heron lives there and can eat a pail of the wriggling, glinting, bodies a week.

The beloved little dogs of the various eunuchs are allowed free rein. The courtyard and palace fill up with chattering and barking, mewls and squawks, as well as the shrieks of maids and eunuchs either playing with the creatures or running about keeping the place tidy, following small trails of destruction. It's a vast improvement on the endlessly refined silence of days passing. I like to sit in my garden, stroking the ears of a panting dog and watching Fury stalk shadows. It lets me forget why I am really here. Perhaps, I think, I could just live here quietly, like Lady Wan. But the little rough patch on the hollow of my throat tells me otherwise.

Huan is in the doorway with news although he seems reluctant to divulge it.

"Well?"

"The Empress has summoned you."

I can feel my heart speed up. "Summoned me for what?"

"She wishes you to visit her in her palace."

"Why?"

Huan looks uncomfortable. "She has been known to request visits from His Majesty's other ladies," he admits.

"For what purpose?"

Huan twists a little under my worried gaze. "She rarely calls for one of the ladies. When she has done so in the past... it has been to ascertain..."

"Ascertain *what*?" I ask.

"She calls for those ladies of whom she is jealous," says Huan in a rush, trying to get it over with quickly. "She will try to frighten you away from His Majesty, to dissuade you from any ambitions you may have in his regard."

"I've not even spoken to him since my first day here!"

"Even so. The Empress disliked the attention given to the celebrations for the conquest of Xinjiang. She sees you as part of that."

"I attended because I was told to and I left as soon as I could," I protest.

Huan is already busy planning. I could have done with him in Kashgar, he's born for survival in difficult situations. "You will dress humbly," he says. "Perhaps in the green silk Lady Wang sent so that the Empress will not think you are dressing to please the Emperor. You will show her every respect and you will agree with whatever she says. Spend as little time there as possible."

He's making me nervous. "What do I say to her?" I ask.

"Nothing, if you can help it," says Huan. "She will twist your words against you."

I'm shaking by the time Huan is finished with me. My hair would shame him under any other circumstances. I have two plain braids, adorned only with green ribbons. I wear the ill-wished green silk skirt with a plain white shirt and a hastily-made green waistcoat. I'm dressed as humbly as is possible without borrowing a robe from a maid. Huan bites his lip at the sight of me but calls for my chair and watches me from the palace courtyard as I am carried away.

We travel down the narrow lanes linking one palace to another. The day is overcast and the little paths are gloomy. Spent lanterns hang everywhere awaiting nightfall. I wish they were lit now, to bring some warmth and light to this unwelcome journey.

At last we turn through a gateway into a large courtyard. The Empress' palace is far larger than mine. The courtyard is full of fragrant white flowers and should be a delightful sight, but the eunuch waiting to greet me is unnervingly silent. He bows and gesture to me to follow him into the palace. I do so, feeling more and more nervous as I enter.

I'm show into what must be the sitting room. If I thought my rooms were lavish, I was wrong. This room is more elaborate than anything I could have dreamed of. There is a huge screen at one end of the room, decorated in gold and black silk with a pattern of flying cranes over a mountaintop. It stands taller than a man and gives a heavy air to the room. Indeed, the whole room feels heavy and silent, too full of precious objects, as though they are clustered here to bring comfort or show status rather than for beauty or because their owner liked them. I stand uncomfortably in the room until the eunuch indicates a chair by the window. I sit and a maid brings a little bowl of steaming tea and a small dish of sweets. The two servants withdraw and I am left alone, with no indication of where the Empress is or when she might arrive.

I glance at the refreshment I've been left with but I don't touch it. There is no second bowl of tea – am I going to wait here alone for a long time? Or does the Empress not want to eat and drink with me? A small voice inside me tells me I don't even trust the food and drink in this palace.

I look out of the window. Her courtyard garden is silent and still. My own garden is full of animals and bright flowers, but here all is quiet, there are not even any birds. Her flowers are all white, set against artfully piled-up dark rocks in strange formations. It's a cold, hard space.

I shift in my seat. How long will I be kept waiting? Is this some sort of obscure punishment by the Empress, to summon her rivals into her palace and then have them sit in silence, alone and nervous? If so, it's a very effective way to display her authority over a woman of lesser rank.

I stand. Sitting is making me uncomfortable. If I'm to be kept waiting here for a long time without being free to leave – and I don't believe that I am free to leave – then I may as well look about me.

A niche in the wall provides a frame for what is probably a poem, although I can't read it. On a golden table are displayed four *ruyi*, the first a simple though beautifully carved rosewood, the second made of almost-black sandalwood inlaid with rubies. The third is an ornate green jade. The fourth is magnificent, with intricate gold filigree studded with precious gems and characters. These four pieces must be those given to Ula Nara as she was promoted through the ranks of the Emperor's women, the fourth one being when she was made Empress. They are her talismans of success in the Forbidden City and displayed here as though on a shrine. What promises did she make to her gods to be rewarded with the dizzying climb from concubine to a golden throne at the Emperor's side?

I sit down again and sigh. I've been waiting a long time now. The tea has stopped steaming. I dip a finger in it. It's grown cold. I sniff my finger to see if I can smell anything untoward but I can only smell tea. I tap my feet on the ground for a while and then without thinking I do something I haven't done for a long time. I blow a spit bubble. I look cross-eyed down my nose at it as it shimmers and grows. It bursts and I wipe my chin and try again.

"Is this how they raise the daughters of Xinjiang's noble families? Or just you?"

I jump to my feet as the spit dribbles down my chin. The room is empty but the Empress' voice was clear enough. I wipe my chin with a shaking hand and look about me. There's no one here. Her voice came from the far end of the room and there is a door there. I wonder if perhaps she's in an adjacent room. Cautiously, my breath fast and shallow in my chest, I make my way towards the door. But it's firmly closed.

"Behind you."

I whirl round. There's no one. My breath is loud now, it fills the room with my fear. The tall dark screen looms over me, black and gold. Flying cranes and snow-topped mountains.

Eyes.

The Empress is watching me through the gap in the panels of the screen.

I step back, a little scream in my throat and suddenly she is here in front of me, stepping from her hiding place, her robes dark purple, her face a hand's breadth from mine.

"Answer me."

I want to step backwards but there's nowhere I can move to but the closed door behind me. "W-what?"

"Are all the daughters of the noble houses of Xinjiang allowed to blow bubbles from spittle or just you? Or are there no nobles in your cur-ridden land? Have we been sent nothing but a street rat, a flea-infested stray from the back alleys, a prisoner of war masquerading as a woman fit for an Emperor's court?"

I'm trembling and my lips move without noise. I'm struggling to hold her gaze. Does she know everything about me or is she just spitting out every insult she can think of?

"Your – Your Majesty – I – I didn't know you were…"

"Clearly not," she says. Without moving her head she allows her eyes to slide to one side, taking in my untouched tea and sweets. "You have not partaken of the refreshments I offered you."

"N–no," I manage.

"Why not?" She moves slightly to one side of me, giving me an opportunity to back away from her, towards the tray bearing the cold bowl of tea. I nearly back straight into it and stop myself just in time. She has followed me across the room, matching me step for step. She looks down at the offending refreshments. "Drink. Eat."

"I – I would rather…" My voice trails off. Refusing is not an option. I move my fingers down by my side without taking my eyes off her face and feel about until I touch the small bowl. I lift it with trembling fingers and feel a little tea slosh over the side, wetting my hand. I don't dare react to it. I bring the bowl to my mouth and take a sip. It tastes only of tea. Cold, slightly bitter, tea. I drain the bowl as fast as I can, my throat clenching with every swallow, then set the bowl back down, my hand still wet.

"Eat," she commands. Her voice is steady, her face is blank. Her eyes stay fixed on mine.

The sticky sweets feel as though they are gluing my teeth together. There are too many to be eaten at one sitting but I eat them all, my jaw aching, my throat too dry. I choke a little under her fixed gaze and put my hand over my mouth, afraid of spraying her purple silk with half-chewed food. Finally it is over. I wait. I daren't speak.

Her face moves forward. She is so close her breath is on my lips and her eyes are blurring into one all-seeing eye, the eye of some monster from a storyteller's dark mind. "Welcome to the Forbidden City, concubine," she says.

I don't reply. I stand still and wait for more – for her nails on my cheek, for her fingers round my throat.

She doesn't move. "Return to your rooms," she says at last.

I back away, expecting her to follow me but she doesn't. She stands where I left her, staring at the wall behind where my head was as though seeing something else there.

I run. I forget any pretence at dignity, at graciousness, at elegance. I run through her rooms, afraid I will lose my way and somehow find myself faced with the Empress again. I see the door leading to her garden and run at it, slamming both hands into it so that it opens too fast and I almost fall down the steps. My bearers look up, startled.

"Run!" I cry at them and almost throw myself into the chair. It lurches upwards, one of my legs still dangling out of it. They run, the chair shuddering at the pace, my body jolted.

I feel sick. I'm afraid of why. Am I scared? Or poisoned? At last we come through the gate to my own garden and I am out of the chair before it's even fully stopped and running to one of the great metal urns that is filled with plants and a small tree. My fingers press against the back of my tongue and I heave again and again, a horrible flow of tea and sweets pouring over my hand and into the earth.

Jiang is at my side and screaming for Huan. Huan takes one look at me and calls for water, which he makes me drink, then thrusts his own fingers into my throat so that I retch again and bring up dirty water. Huan half-drags me back into the palace and to my bedroom. He dismisses everyone but Jiang.

"Were you poisoned?" he asks, all but ripping my green silk clothes from me and lifting me into the bed.

"I don't know," I say. My voice is hoarse from crying and gagging. "She made me eat and drink even though I didn't want to. Then I felt sick. I didn't know if it was poison but I was afraid."

Huan finishes covering me. "The water will have cleaned your stomach," he says. "It may not have been poison."

"She made me eat," I repeat, starting to cry. I can't think how to describe to Huan the fear I felt. Saying that the Empress kept me waiting and then made me drink tea and eat sweets… how does that describe what I felt, the fear that surrounded me?

Huan waves away my explanation. "The Empress has frightened many women," he says. "You will stay away from her."

"If she calls for me again…" I begin, shaking at the thought.

"She will not," says Huan. "She tries to frighten the new women, she tries to make sure they will not be rivals to her. She will have finished with you now."

I begin to sleep badly. Night after night I dream of the imperial women. I see the Empress' dark eyes watching me through a screen of green silk, ripped as though by unseen claws. I see Lady Wan's wig tumble, leaving her bald. I see Lady Ling with an endless parade of children who surround me and yank at my clothes, pulling me down to the ground with their little hands while their mother watches, smiling. I wake sweating and ask myself what I was thinking of, to agree to Iparhan's plan. When I sleep again I feel once more the thud as her dagger pinned my sleeve to the blackened poplar tree and I have my answer: I had no choice.

The weather turns warm and one morning when I wake the maids are rushing about. Piles of clothes, blankets and coverlets, kitchen utensils and more make their way from the palace in armfuls, chestfuls, cartfuls.

I watch from my sitting room. "Where are they going?"

Jiang answers from under a heap of silk clothes. "The imperial gardens – the summer palace, my lady. We leave tomorrow."

"We?"

"The whole court, your ladyship. To escape the heat."

"Heat? It's not even mid-spring. It's just started getting warmer!"

He's serious. "The summer brings many illnesses – miasmas, plagues. The hot winds are very injurious to health. The Emperor always leaves as the warm weather arrives."

"Where is the summer palace?"

He draws me a map. I study it and frown. "It's barely any distance. We could walk there. The weather can't be that different."

He shakes his head. "The summer palace is built on the lakes. They draw the cool breezes."

"And where do we live there?"

"You will have another palace. Just as lovely as this one, but far more suited to the summer heat."

The procession my household joins is endless. Palanquins. Guards everywhere. Maids and eunuchs in a blur of blues and greens.

Inside my chair I'm nervous. I keep my curtains closed at first, peeking through them only occasionally. I'm afraid that somehow one of my 'family' might seek to see their 'daughter' ride by. But I peek out at the moat as we cross over it. The waters are a dark murky green. As we cross the bridge from the Forbidden City's gate into Beijing itself I see that the streets are lined with bamboo screens standing higher than a man's head. We're making our way through this strange bamboo-coloured tunnel, behind which I can hear the noises of everyday street life. I pull the curtain fully aside and call for Huan. He hurries to me.

"Why are there all these bamboo screens?"

"The Emperor must not be seen by commoners, madam."

I shake my head and let him go back to his place in the procession. I feel safer now, and I leave the curtains open for the cool air they bring and watch my guards and servants as they march alongside me. Then I doze for a little while.

A familiar voice brings me wide-awake and sweating in an instant.

"Find out how a eunuch is made. Every detail."

I look out, startled, straight into the eyes of Iparhan. She's wearing a guard's uniform, her hair pulled back tight simulating a queue beneath her helmet. Her scar suits her soldiers' garb.

I gape at her.

"Find out," she says. "I will come for the answer."

She is gone. I clutch at the window, look both ways. My maids and eunuchs, my guards, look back at me. One eunuch hurries to my side.

"Do you desire something, my lady?"

"I – I am unwell," I choke. My chest feels tight and I struggle to bring air into my lungs.

My palanquin stops. Huan is sent for. He gives me ginger sweets and exchanges the fan I was holding for another, as though it might better provide me with fresh air. "We will be leaving the city soon," he promises. "Your ladyship can see now, the kind of foul airs that beset the city at this time of year."

I nod, as though a warm spring wind could have made my skin pale and clammy, my throat retch.

Reassured, he fans me for a little while and then gives the signal for us to continue.

As we lurch on our way I think over what I saw and heard. Was it a dream? I was dozing. Perhaps I dreamed of Iparhan, who is never far from my thoughts. Maybe I thought up a demand from her for information I couldn't possibly have. *Find out how a eunuch is made.* Why? What need could she have for such information? I wipe the sweat that has risen under my eyes and on my upper lip. I try to fan myself. I hear the streets grow quieter and pull back the curtain, half-afraid I will see her again. Only my own familiar household figures are nearby. Beyond them, now, are open fields and a cool breeze lifts towards me. I gulp it in and try to assure myself I was only dreaming.

But I know I wasn't. Iparhan has made herself known to me at last. And she wants information. Why she wants it I can't begin to imagine. But if she needs it, then I need it. Thankfully it doesn't involve the Emperor. Yet.

I should be amazed by the summer palace. It is a place of exquisite, unending gardens, encompassing hills and valleys, lakes and buildings. Some of the buildings are Chinese in style and seem familiar to me now. But my own chair is carried to a newer part of the gardens, where very different buildings await me. They are huge and made of carved stone, unlike anything I have seen before.

Huan is proud of their strangeness. "European, my lady," he tells me. "Built by the Jesuits at His Majesty's express command. The other ladies will be staying in the Chinese buildings but you have been given this palace for yourself. It is called the Immense Ocean Observatory."

The servants are already rushing inside, carrying all my belongings, preparing to make everything inside perfect for me. I try to look about me. The stone rises above us, shining white in the bright sunlight. Nearby are huge, fantastical fountains, each spout of water emerging from the mouth of a bronze creature – the twelve animals of the Chinese zodiac. Some of the spray, carried on a soft breeze, reaches my face and I startle.

"Your ocean," says Huan, smiling.

I try to force a smile on my face although I cannot take any of it in.

I ignore offers of food and bathing, rest and entertainment. I ask for Huan and Jiang to bring me tea and to sit with me, alone.

They comply, still concerned for my wellbeing. I wave away sweets and herbal teas, offers of a physician.

"I want to know how you came here," I begin, addressing the floor, unable to meet their eyes. I feel nauseous at what I have to do and it makes me abrupt. "How you were – made."

They look shocked. Huan frowns. "Why, my lady?"

I haven't thought of a reason. There is no good reason to ask them to tell me about the pain and shame of their early lives. "I – I want to know more about your lives. You – you have been so kind to me and looked after me so well…" I stumble to a halt but their faces have softened a little, soothed by my praise.

Huan takes the lead. "I suppose such things are strange to your ladyship," he says. "Do you not have eunuchs in your land?"

I shake my head.

He nods, serious, then begins. He sounds as though he is telling a story of a far-off place, not his own painful experiences. Perhaps this is how he bears it, by telling his own life as though it were a legend. "Just outside the gates of the Forbidden City in a tumbled-down building dwell the 'knifers'. They have done their work for generations. Boys are sold into service as eunuchs, but any man who wishes can go to them and for six taels of silver they will be castrated, their manhoods lost forever."

I can't help leaning forward. "What happens to them?"

"The man lies on a low bed, and the knifer will ask him if he is certain he will not regret his choice. When he answers that he will not he is given a tea to drink that stuns his nerves. Then tight bandages are wound about his legs and stomach, before three men enter to hold him down. His private parts are bathed in hot pepper water to numb them."

I brace myself for what is to come. Huan takes a deep breath and goes on. "The knifer has a small curved knife. Using quick cuts he removes the – the-"

He comes to an uncertain halt, fearful of damaging my ladylike ears.

I try to imagine what he is trying to say. "Both – parts?" I ask tentatively. "The – and also the…?"

Huan nods.

I wince but gesture to him to continue.

"He takes a metal plug to fit into the man's – hole, that he may not lose the ability to urinate. They cover the wound with water-soaked paper and the man must walk about the room for three hours, supported by the knifers. Then he must lie in that same room for three days. He may not drink nor urinate. Some men become delirious. At the end of those days they pull out the metal plug so that he can urinate. If he fails to do so because the passageway has sealed itself, then he will die in agony.

The three of us sit in silence for a moment, thinking of those men who sacrificed everything in the hope of a better life and in doing so lost the poor life they had. Huan seems drained, his face a little pale.

Jiang picks up from Huan. "After two or three months the eunuch is fully recovered and he may join the household of a prince, where he will be trained for perhaps a year. Every prince of the dynasty owes the palace eight eunuchs every year, who must be trained, inspected and confirmed free from disease and uncleanliness."

I nod. "And the – the parts?" I ask. "Are they – disposed of?'

The two of them look appalled. "Oh, no, your ladyship," says Jiang. "We keep them for ever – if we are buried without them we will not be whole in the afterlife."

Huan has recovered a little. "And they are necessary for our promotions," he adds.

Jiang leaps to his feet and rushes away. I sit in silence for a few moments with Huan, both of us staring into bowls of tea, now grown cold. When Jiang returns he is carrying a small jar, wrapped in a delicate piece of pale blue silk. He hands it to me and I hold it as though the little container might break.

Jiang looks at me holding it and his eyes glisten briefly with tears. I gently pass it back to him and he holds it for a moment and then leaves the room again, this time more slowly. I watch him go and when I look back at Huan he is watching me.

"I am sorry," I say, and I mean it. "I did not wish to cause you both pain."

He looks at me a moment longer, then nods. "I know," he says, his voice gentle. "But you are very young, my ladyship. You are only a child. And a child does not always know that there are some questions that should not be asked."

I turn my face away a little so he won't see the tears rise up at being chastised. His gentleness is a greater punishment than his words. But he touches my shoulder as he stands and later on, as our household goes about its day both of them are kind to me, as they have always been.

Now I have what Iparhan needs. When will she come for the information? Will she wait until we return to Beijing, for that single moment when we are travelling, when she can impersonate a guard, a maid? Or can she find me even here, even within the palace grounds? I wonder whether I could escape before she comes for me. Here, with none of the high red walls or the moat of the Forbidden City, might I be able to slip away more easily?

I sit, with no appetite, in front of the dishes laid out before me. The sweets and vegetables are good. The cooks have been trying, with very little success, to cook traditional foods from my homeland. Today, the *polo* rice dish is a disaster. It drips with grease. I tried to explain how to make it but having never made it myself before had to describe the end result rather than the recipe. I told them it should be generously fatty but this coats my throat and I have to ask for a sharp plum juice to cut through the layer of oiliness.

Huan's eyes fill with tears of despair. "Beat me, my lady. I have failed you."

"Oh, stop that!" I snap at him. "It's just too oily. Tell the cooks to try again another day."

There's the now-familiar thump as everyone hits the floor in a miserable bow. I feel like bursting into tears myself. It would be easier just to eat the food they make here; it's probably delicious. Their attempts at my food are laughable. I feel like a fool for insisting on it – I'd have eaten anything when I was on the streets, while these poor wretches think I'm a high-minded noblewoman who can't soil her dainty Muslim mouth with the food of infidels. I get up from the table and walk away, the dishes half-tasted, the knock of heads on the floor echoing behind me as I walk into my bedroom and climb onto the bed, pulling the curtains about me, wrapping myself in the tumble of silk coverlets, tears welling up.

Underneath me is something hard. I reach down and find a tiny flat tablet of wood. On it are painted the first rays of a rising sun over a lake. Nothing else. I turn it over in my hands but I understand it well enough. And I also understand that I cannot hope to escape this place. Iparhan will find me anywhere.

Dawn comes. I slip from my bed, placing my bare feet with infinite care as I tiptoe past the sleeping eunuch whose turn it is to watch over me at night. My bed curtains close behind me, masking my absence from view. The eunuch stirs but doesn't wake and I push the doors open. Thankfully they're kept oiled so no creaks give me away. I wish I'd brought a thicker robe with me, but that would have made more noise. It may be early summer but it still feels cold at this time of day.

I make my way past the fountains and then follow a small path down to the lakeshore. My back is cold on the white stone balustrade. I shiver and look about me but I'm alone. I peer into the water and the fish rise to the surface, hoping for crumbs that I have not brought.

"At least you understand pictures even if you can't read."

I don't turn to greet Iparhan, just wait in silence. She sits by my side. I look at her feet, spread out in front of her. She's dressed like a maid today, the pale blue robe skimming her ankles. Her feet are bare, perhaps to walk more quietly. They're wet with dew. I never heard her coming.

She grows impatient, snaps her fingers in front of my face. "I can't stay all day," she says curtly. "Stop staring like an idiot. Tell me what I need to know."

I turn. Her face is so close I can see how the scar, now fading to a pale pinked-violet, almost enters her eye. It makes my own blink in sympathy. I try not to stare at it, to keep my gaze fixed on hers, but it's unnerving.

"Do you want to know anything about the palace?" I ask tentatively. "About my life here?" I want to blurt out what happened with the Empress, my fears of the scheming women surrounding me but I am afraid she will be angry that I have unwittingly turned people against me.

"I don't care how you fill your pampered days," she says. "I asked you for information. Do you have it?"

I nod.

"Well?"

"How much do you need to know?"

"I told you. Everything. Every detail."

I take a breath and begin Huan and Jiang's story, the tale repeated over and over again throughout the palace walls and centuries. I keep my face turned away from her and I tell her only what is true of any eunuch. I hold back what I know of Jiang, the beatings received for wetting himself and how Huan helped him, hiding the evidence of his disgrace and washing his robes so the smell wouldn't give him away. Their closeness now. I refuse to let her steal the pain of my kindly servants and use it somehow for her own plans. I'm aware that I almost gabble the details, that I rush them so that I will not have to think of the suffering of the thousands of eunuchs all around us, of the many more thousands that were here before and will come later. Finally I finish. I look at Iparhan but she is unaffected.

"What happens to their private parts?"

"They keep them forever in a jar," I say, omitting the description of Jiang's soft trembling hands on mine as he passed me his little silk-wrapped treasure. "They can never be promoted without them. They need to be buried with them so that the gods of the underworld will believe them to be whole men."

Iparhan snorts. "Infidels."

I want to slap her. Want to make her see Huan and Jiang's eyes, downcast before me. My hand itches.

She presses on. "Do they really stink? I've heard the saying 'he stinks like a eunuch'."

I shake my head. "They have difficulty containing their urination at first and are beaten for it. But once they've been trained they master the flow and smell no different to you or me."

"You had better smell finer than a eunuch," she says. "Do you still have the perfume?"

"Can't you smell it?"

"Yes. Do you need more of it?"

I nod and she passes me a new vial. I take it and drop it in my pocket without looking at it. I don't want her to see the relief in my eyes, I don't want her to know that I was afraid of running out of it.

"How do you discipline the eunuchs?"

I sit back. "Why do you need to know so much about their lives, Iparhan? Didn't Mei tell you about them?"

"I did not need the information then."

"Why do you need it now?"

"That is not your concern."

I wait but I can see she'll say nothing else. The rules governing the eunuch's lives are known to all here. Huan instructed me in them shortly after I arrived, so that I could govern my household. "If they run away they're caught and imprisoned for two months, beaten and sent back. If they do it again they're put in a *cangue* for two months. It's a wooden frame. It stops them lying down or feeding themselves. Some of them die in it. If it happens a third time they're banished to Manchuria for two and a half years, or if they stole something precious they're executed away from the walls of Beijing."

"And for minor matters?"

"For laziness they're whipped one hundred times and then have the wounds dressed.

Three days later the dressings are removed and the same place is beaten again to 'raise the scabs'."

Her interrogation doesn't stop. I have to get up to demonstrate the way they walk, imitate their high-pitched voices. Describe their daily duties, from the highest to the most menial. Their careful protection of any hedgehogs found in the gardens, believing them to bring great good luck. Their gambling and the silly little dogs over which they fawn as young mothers with their first child. Their sorrow at not being able to ascend the altars of the main deity in the temples – being deformed they are considered not clean enough to do so. Their sensitivity to taunts about being a 'spoutless teapot' or a 'tailless dog'. The petty squabbles between them. Their tender care towards the women and children who are their only reason for being.

"I've told you everything," I say finally. "There is no more."

"Good," she says. "Now, the Emperor."

I stiffen.

"Have you been called to his bed?"

"No."

Something flickers across her face and is hidden. "Why not?"

"I don't know."

Her voice is cold. "I need you in his bed. You're no good to me if you do not lie with him."

I'm angry. "I'm not a whore."

"Yes you are," she says. "You agreed to become a concubine so you would be fed and housed. What else is that but a whore?"

The anger leaves me in a rush. My dreams of living here peacefully were the dreams of a fool. Of course Iparhan has found me. I must play my part or she will follow me for the rest of my days, wherever I might hide. I lean forward, resting my hot forehead on the cool stone of the wall and listen to the sound of the fountains splashing. I let my eyes close. "Don't do this to me again, Iparhan," I say softly. "It was cruel to ask them so many questions. And for what? Why would you care? How could it possibly aid your plans for rebellion? Don't make me hurt the only people I know here."

She doesn't answer. I keep my eyes closed a moment longer, waiting for her to speak, then raise my head.

She's gone.

I'm afraid of the information I've given to Iparhan. I think back to my days in the little house set among the Taklakaman dunes, how I seized on any scrap of information about the Forbidden City, ready to use it to my own advantage once I got here, to be used as a trick, an illusion, a distraction. How will Iparhan use what I have told her? All I know is that she is planning something and that my only protection is to play the part she has given me and give her what she wants. I need to get closer to the Emperor. I try not to think of the Empress.

Most days I walk by the lake. The weather has turned hot and my heavily embroidered silk skirts do nothing to keep me cool. Besides, I have a secret task that I need to perform alone – throwing the stale cakes, breads or fruits from my secret hoard to the fishes. Back at the palace I replenish my supply daily.

Across the lake rises the Emperor's own palace. I look across the waters and wonder whether I will ever be called to his rooms. I think of ways I might draw his attention but they seem foolish and unlikely to work. I find myself kicking loose pebbles into the water, frustrated by my lack of ideas.

One morning I find someone already at the water's edge, in a scholar's dark robe. His back is to me and I see he's a painter, for he's putting the final touches to a silk painting of a pink lotus flower. Two butterflies dart across the silk, one large and dark, one small and pale.

"Pretty," I venture.

He turns to face me and I step back. Although he's dressed as a courtier, he's not Chinese, nor even from my homeland. He's a foreigner, a European. Old, nearing seventy, with a full white beard and a stooped back.

"Lady He."

"How do you know who I am?"

He chuckles. "I have been here many years," he says. "A new member of the court is worth learning about."

I hope he doesn't learn too much about me, but he seems friendly. "I don't know your name."

"My name is Lang Shining."

"You don't look as though that's your name."

He chuckles. "My original name, then, for you who have such sharp eyes, is Giuseppe Castiglione. I came here many years ago from Italy."

I try to pronounce his name and he has to correct me. "You're a court painter?"

"I am whatever His Majesty requires me to be." He smiles, rueful. "Except, perhaps, that which I would most like to be – a spiritual advisor."

"Are you a priest?"

He nods. "A Jesuit. I followed Our Lord's work to this country many, many years ago but I think perhaps He has in mind for me other lessons. Patience, perhaps."

"I might need to learn that too," I say and he nods. His wry smile tells me he already knows that I've not yet been called for.

"I gather your new name was meant to reflect the lotus," he says. "May I be so bold as to offer you this painting?"

I'm pleased. The palaces I have been given are luxurious beyond words but nothing in them really feels like it belongs to me except the animals. I take the painting and have it hung in my bedroom.

I wake with a start. Loud bangs echo across the lakes. I clutch at my nightclothes. Has Iparhan come? Has she somehow stormed the palace at the head of an army? I pull aside the bed curtains and almost walk into Jiang, who is standing in the darkness just outside, his back to me.

"What's happening?" I whisper.

Jiang turns, lifting up a small lantern. He forces a smile onto his face. "Imperial Noble Consort Ling has been safely delivered of a son, your ladyship. Tonight there are celebrations throughout the Summer Palace."

My thudding heart slows. I make my way to the window. Firecrackers leap into the air, turning the sky many colours. I can hear music from the palaces and chanting inside the temples. The sounds all carry well here, floating across the waters.

I sit in a chair by the window, looking out onto the fireworks reflecting in the lake. The fireworks and celebrations seem far away, in another part of the world, from which I'm separated by the lake before me. The court is celebrating Lady Ling's success while my failure keeps me here alone. I get up and Jiang springs to his feet. "Bring me something to tap my ears," I say. "I want to sleep."

I see the distant figure of Giuseppe and hurry down to the lake to speak with him. I think he might be a useful ally to me. A man who's been at court so many years and is friendly may be able to help me.

"Painting again?"

He opens his arms to demonstrate the lack of painting tools. "Today I only think about painting. Another day I will paint. I am not as busy as the Emperor is in his daily life."

I try to make my voice sound careless. "Do you know how he passes his days?"

He nods.

I was right to seek him out. Giuseppe can help me to understand more about this place and how I can get closer to the Emperor. "Tell me."

"On an ordinary day there are a great many demands on his time. He wakes very early, with the sun. He washes and dresses, then eats breakfast. He enjoys reading history but cannot do so for long, for his ministers and officials await his presence to discuss matters of state."

"Such as?" I wonder whether this is a time when he hears reports from Xinjiang.

"Reports of weather conditions and harvests, passing judgement in serious legal cases, progress on special projects such as the building of temples. And of course there are many, many petitions from his subjects."

I think of the papers he was reading before and after our first meeting. "Doesn't he get bored?"

"He is very conscientious. But after the work of the day is complete he eats his main meal in the mid afternoon."

"Does he have ridiculous amounts of food too?"

He chuckles. "I am sure that however many dishes are brought to your table, far more are brought to his."

I shake my head. "Can't he just order his favourites?"

"He likes bird's nest soup and duck, but mostly he favours game, for he is a keen hunter. But you have seen for yourself how meals are prepared here. Abundance is all."

"And afterwards?"

"He is at liberty to read or write poetry, to paint, attend the theatre or view his art collections. Or to practise his calligraphy, which is very fine."

We walk a little further in silence. Finally I work up the courage to ask what I really want to know. "And his – his evenings?"

"He eats only a light meal at sunset."

"What's a light meal in these parts?"

He chuckles to acknowledge the truth of my question. "Then he prays. He is a Buddhist, sadly for me."

"Neither of us is successful with him, then."

He chuckles. "You still have many years ahead of you, Lady He. I am sure you will be more successful than I."

I shrug. "So – his evenings?"

He smiles, understanding what I'm really asking. "Part of his evening is spent with a companion, who I believe is usually chosen in the morning. A tray is proffered with the names of the palace ladies written on little tablets. He chooses one and she is then informed. This gives her the opportunity to prepare herself – I understand it may take some time," he adds, with a hint of mischief.

"I was told he would not stay the night," I say, wondering if this was just nonsense, stories put about by the servants to make more of a mystery of the event.

"He does not, if he is visiting you. He will stay in the other bedroom."

"And if I visit him?"

"Then you will be escorted back to your own palace."

"Why?"

"The Emperor must get a good night's sleep so that he can be rested for his duties in the morning."

"So he thinks we ladies might snore, or kick him in the night?"

He laughs out loud, startling a heron by the water's edge. "I think it is a protection against assassination. Or perhaps against infatuation." He grows a little more serious. "Either of which are grave dangers to a ruler."

"Well, he needn't fear either from me. I've only been near him twice and I'm not sure he even remembers me."

Giuseppe stops and looks at me. "I am sure he does," he says with kindness. "It is only a matter of time."

"Everyone says that," I say, kicking a large pebble into the lake.

"Then they are right," he says. "And may I offer some humble advice, Lady He?"

"Go on," I say.

"I can tell that you wish to know more about the court. But be careful what questions you ask, and of whom."

"Why?"

"There are many secrets at court, Lady He."

"Are there?" I ask.

He stops walking and turns to face me. "We all have secrets, Lady He," he says. "I am sure you have your own, do you not?"

I can feel my mouth turn dry. I force a smile and quickly swallow, trying to bring back my voice. "I suppose everyone does, " I say. "I'll be sure not to ask the wrong questions."

Giuseppe regards me for too long a moment, as my smile struggles to stay on my lips. "A wise choice," he says at last and although his voice is kind, his eyes are searching and I find it hard to hold his gaze.

The hem of my skirt, the green silk from Lady Wang, is soaked in dripping mud. The dogs followed me on a walk and now they rush in and out of the water, full of excitement, wetting me and ruining the silk. I suppose Huan will not mind, I think. He never liked this skirt anyway and I'm not that fond of it myself after my encounter with the Empress. Above the yapping I hear another high-pitched sound and turning, find Huan and Jiang running through the gardens towards me, shrieking.

"What is it?" I ask as they reach me.

They're panting from their headlong rush and rosy-cheeked. "My lady, he is here!"

I've waited so long I don't even know what they mean. "Who?"

"The Emperor. We received no prior warning! He is making his way to your palace. You must be ready to receive him!"

I gape at them. This moment, so long awaited, has come too soon.

Huan is almost wailing at the sight of me. "Green! Why did you have to be wearing the green?" he moans, indicating my skirt. "And mud everywhere. How did that *happen*?" He doesn't wait for an answer, just stretches out his hands beseechingly towards me.

I take a step in the direction of the palace. Heedless of protocol they each grab one of my arms and begin to run back towards the palace, forcing me to run between them, my wet skirts clinging to my legs. Within a few strides I'm out of breath. It's a long time since I've done any running.

Inside is chaos. Maids and eunuchs run in all directions, some ensuring the palace itself is prepared, others with animals in their arms, hiding them away. The muddy dogs cause even more horror than my clothes. When we arrive a wave of servants come towards me, sweeping me towards the bathroom. Hands engulf me, tearing off my clothes as we go, so that I reach the room entirely naked. Behind us, maids on their knees clean the floor of the mud I have dripped through the rooms. Water splashes everywhere, I narrowly avoid soap in my eyes and already I'm out and dried, being hurried back to my room, where clothes are thrown this way and that. Huan is combing my hair, his usually gentle hands ripping through it so hard that I cry out.

"Hush," he begs me, almost weeping. "You must be ready for His Majesty. This is your moment!"

I bite my tongue hard to stop myself swearing at the pain.

Normally I dress myself, with maids helping here and there with fastenings and passing items to me. The dressing and hairdressing is a leisurely pastime, designed as much to kill time as to prepare me for an empty day. Now I'm being dressed like a child, my limbs not my own. In a few brief moments I'm resplendent in shimmering silk, velvet and gauze. Pink and white lotus flowers rise up from the pristine waves of my blue silk skirt, reaching towards the magnificent golden waistcoat as though it were the sun. My sleeves bear the outlines of wheeling birds. My still-damp plaits are interwoven with gold threads and interspersed with tiny pink lotus flowers carved from tourmaline, glinting against the gold.

Jiang is almost hopping in the doorway. "I can hear his approach," he whimpers.

Huan pulls me to my feet. I nearly fall flat on my face. The heels on my shoes are higher than I've ever worn before. I'm almost his height.

"You are ready," he pants. I'm about to reply when he turns on the other servants. "Get out, get *out*," he cries. "Get ready or I'll have you all whipped!"

There is a rush for the doors, as each servant tidies their own appearance and hurries to their stations.

Huan turns back to me. "You should be in the receiving hall," he hisses. "Come."

But I stand still. "I need to be alone." I say. "Just for a moment."

Huan and Jiang's looks of horror would make me laugh if I wasn't so scared. "Alone? *Now*?"

I nod vigorously. "You must leave me. Now!"

I've never raised my voice to them and they both take a step back, then reluctantly leave the room. I almost throw myself at the bed, slipping my hand down the side of it to find the tiny gap where the vial of perfume is hidden. The hot water splashed all over me will have washed off the scent. Hastily I dab more of it on, then hide the vial again before running to the door of the bedroom and making my way through to the receiving hall. I arrive panting and turn immediately towards the windows, looking for the Emperor's palanquin. Sure enough there is the imperial yellow chair in my courtyard. I put a hand to my throat and then take a deep breath, waiting for him to step out of it. This, then, is the moment I become a whore and a spy.

"You were expecting me, Lady He?" A deep voice, amused, behind me.

I turn to face the Emperor, already seated on the throne, surrounded by his own servants and mine.

Dream

B ELIEVING HIMSELF USEFUL NURMAT HAS *been making enquiries in the Muslim quarter and beyond for the past month and more. Now he has gathered together allies to our cause. Those of our own country, who, like my own family, have been crushed beneath the Emperor's armies and seen their leaders fall. Who have lost wealth and power. And those from further afield, the countries bordering our own, fearful for the future should the Emperor look beyond his New Dominion and see further conquests to be had. They too, come to us and swear loyalty to our cause. They talk late into the night, making and remaking plans.*

We rode fast, away from the fortress. The darkness of the night concealed our escape and by morning we were far away from the Emperor's banners.

My tears fell as we rode. My mother gone, my uncle gone. Our position lost. My father wounded. He said, through gritted teeth, that he would recover and we would carry out our plan for rebellion, but I knew already that he would not survive. The pain on his face as we rode told me he had not long to live. Nurmat rode with his mouth in a grim line and behind him, her old face frightened, rode Mei. She knew that our power was waning, that we were clutching at the last vestiges of our status, and she feared for her life.

The little house in the dunes waited for us, our hideaway, prepared many years before and now newly stocked with food and goods. Nurmat helped my father inside while Mei, her old body stiff, hobbled along behind, ready to cook and clean for us.

I sat on my horse, the incessant desert wind blowing my plaits. Hot tears turned cold on my cheeks. Slowly I slipped down from the saddle, lifted my head, wiped my eyes and went to my father, my face showing none of my growing fear.

The men talk on and I listen with only one ear. Perhaps I should be planning uprisings, but in my mind is only one image, an image I see every night when I go to sleep. A battle rages around me. The Emperor's face, close to mine, blood tricking from his mouth, as I plunge a dagger deep into his chest and twist the blade. To others it might be a violent image, to me it is soothing. I fall asleep when I have this image in my mind, the relief of his life draining away so great that my muscles can at last relax and allow me peace in the darkness.

The Hunt

I FALL TO MY KNEES AND perform the elaborate kowtow I've practised so often. Where I once cursed the never-ending bows and the discomfort of the position, now I'm grateful. I have a chance to slow my breathing although as I stand for the final time I'm well aware that my face is flushed.

The Emperor is smiling. "Lady He."

"Your Majesty. I'm – I am very honoured to receive you. May – may I offer you some refreshment?" My eyes slide towards Huan, who makes a quick gesture that has maids hurrying off in all directions, soon to return with teas and sweets.

He waves me over. "Come and sit with me," he invites, indicating a chair which is not yet there but is hastily provided by the ever-attentive Jiang. "I am sorry I have not visited you before. I have been very busy."

I sit down, my skin still damp from the bath, awkward under his gaze. He looks at me, curious. "Do you still have the lotus scent?" he asks.

I imagine the tiny vial and for a moment I think he knows about it. I feel my cheeks grow even redder but try to control myself. Of course he doesn't know, how could he? I think quickly and hold out my arm to him, newly anointed. "I believe so, Your Majesty."

He takes my hand in his and lifts it to his nose, smells and then smiles, letting go of my hand as he does so. His skin is very soft. "It is still there," he says, with some satisfaction. "Truly, like a lotus."

I wait for more questions, but he seems to take it for granted that one of his ladies should be naturally perfumed. Perhaps, I think, he's surrounded by such wondrous things all the time – works of art painted on silk, carved sandalwood furniture, the striking chiming clocks of which I've heard he's fond – that a woman whose very skin releases a scent beyond the skill of the court perfumer is not such a strange thought to him. Instead his mind has turned elsewhere. He looks about the room.

"I used to visit this palace as a child," he says. "It belonged to one of the ladies of my Honoured Grandfather. She was very fond of songbirds. Are you fond of birds?"

"Yes, Your Majesty." I indicate a couple of the hanging cages. "I have many birds myself." As I finish speaking I hear a sharp yap, immediately muffled.

But he has keen ears. "And a dog?" he asks.

I nod, ignoring Jiang's mortified face. "Yes. Several. I have quite a few animals here."

He frowns, looking about. "Where are they, then?"

I'm a little cautious. The court is so formal. He might object to the noisy chaos that is usual in my palace. "They have been taken to other rooms so as not to bother Your Majesty," I say.

He shrugs. "Have them all brought here."

It takes a while. The newly washed and still damp dogs, Fury, my birds, even the latest pail of fish for the garden are brought for his inspection. The room grows noisier with each addition. But he seems pleased rather than put out. When the last dog has joined us he looks about and then chuckles.

"I see you are fond of animals, as you say."

I nod. "They keep me company, Your Majesty."

He tilts his head. "As I do not visit you often enough, is that it?"

I shake my head hurriedly, thinking he's offended but he only laughs. "My mother says you are homesick. Perhaps I should come and see you more often, or next time I visit you will have elephants here."

I smile more broadly. At least he has a sense of humour. Perhaps spending time with him won't be as bad as I feared. If my being 'homesick' has drawn him here then I'll have to pretend to be homesick more often. I'm about to ask him what animals he favours but he's risen to his feet and I follow his lead.

"I must go now," he says.

I nod, although I'm disappointed. Given his past record, I probably won't see him for another few months. Before he reaches the door he turns back.

"Lang Shining told me he enjoys his walks with you. He said he gave you a painting. May I see it?"

A eunuch hurries to my sitting room and returns with the painting of the lotus and butterflies. He examines it, nods and then makes his way to his chair. I bid him farewell, standing on the steps surrounded by my servants and animals, then return indoors.

"I didn't know what to call him," I confess to Huan. *Of all the things not to know*, I curse Iparhan for not telling me this basic information.

"'Your Majesty', of course."

"Doesn't he have a name I can call him – like…" I stop, about to say "like Hidligh", and correct myself. "Like my childhood name?"

Huan shakes his head. "That is no longer your name. You are Lady He now."

"Does no one here have the name they were born with? Not even the Emperor?"

"Especially not the Emperor."

"What was he called as a child, then?"

Huan lowers his voice and looks about as though we might be overheard before answering. "Hongli."

I find myself whispering too. "Why are we whispering?"

"His childhood name is now taboo. As he became older he was given the name Prince Bao. That name is also taboo. Now he is the Qianlong Emperor of the Qing dynasty."

"Can I call him Qianlong?"

Huan shakes his head as though I've said something very stupid. "Qianlong is the name of his reign, not his own name."

I give up. "So I'll just call him *The Emperor*, shall I?"

Huan ignores my tone. "Yes."

I sit back in my chair. The visit has tired all of us; the strain of getting ready and then being in the Emperor's presence – we are too used to days of nothingness. And I can't help feeling disappointed. I was ready to play my part, to ask questions. I thought I would have to lie with him and although the thought frightens me it also somehow draws me. "He didn't stay the night."

Huan shakes his head. "If he had planned to do so we would have been warned this morning." He sighs. "I wish he had, then I could have arranged your hair more elaborately." He tuts, looking it over.

I wave him away, suddenly weary of his fussing. "Hair isn't everything in life, Huan. You sound like Lady Wan's hairdresser. *Why* didn't he want to stay the night?" I was dreading being called to his bed, but now I feel as though I've failed. Did I do something to displease him?

Huan, insulted by my disparagement of his favourite task, only shakes his head and repeats his mantra. "In due course, my lady. In due course."

I send an invitation to Giuseppe to come to my palace. He has helped me and I need to keep him as an ally. He joins me at dusk, as the birds set out on their 'walks' or are set free for their evening flights.

I offer him tea and little mooncakes. "Thank you."

"For what?" he asks, sipping tea.

"You mentioned me to the Emperor and he came to visit me."

"I am sure he was intending to visit you anyway," he says.

I shake my head. "I could have been here for years without seeing him."

He chuckles. "I am sure now you will see him more often. He was most taken with you."

I find myself leaning forward. "Really? What did he say?"

"That your palace was very noisy."

I make a face. "It is. Did it annoy him?"

"Not at all. I believe he found it refreshingly different."

"Did he say when he was coming again?"

"His Majesty does not share his plans with me," says Giuseppe. "But I am sure you will see him again soon."

I sit back in my chair. "Perhaps," I say doubtfully.

But the spell has been broken. The next time the Emperor visits he catches us unawares yet again. Barely a week has passed and the weather is growing ever hotter. Fortunately I'm better dressed this time but I'm sitting on the steps of the building with the dogs while Jiang tries to groom them, as ever with limited success. The birds, hearing the yapping of the over-excited dogs, respond with their own shrieks and cries. Meanwhile Fury begs for food, yowling more and more loudly as we ignore his greed to focus on the dogs.

"I can hear your palace from the other side of the lake," comes a voice.

We leap to our feet and then fall to our knees. The Emperor is standing by the fountains below us, having dismounted from his chair. Behind him stand his many servants, most looking appalled at the spectacle of us.

"Take them away," I hiss at Jiang, who begins to scramble about with a few other servants to try and collect up and hide the various animals.

"Oh, leave them," says the Emperor. "Bring chairs outside. It is a nice day. We will sit by the fountains and you shall continue whatever you were doing."

His commands supersede mine and the carved throne kept for him is brought outside, as are teas and sweetmeats. He ignores the sweets but drinks the tea, encouraging Jiang to continue the grooming. Jiang, aware of his own weaknesses in this respect, calls for other servants, who hold each dog still for him so that for once the grooming is undertaken with some decorum. Meanwhile Fury is given his favourite egg yolk and some of the birds are set free to hop about us. Fury watches them, tail twitching, egg yolk dripping from his eager whiskers.

"You really do like animals," observes the Emperor. "Did you have many as a child?"

Of all the questions I dread, it is questions about my childhood that worry me the most. My 'family' were the Emperor's allies – how much does he know about them? Would he know what kind of childhood I am supposed to have had? I improvise. "Only a small cat, Your Majesty," I say, thinking of the autumn sun in the marketplace of Kashgar and the filched raisins I enjoyed in the company of the small crooked kitten.

He nods. "You were not allowed any other pets?"

I shake my head and make a sorrowful grimace, somehow implying a strict family upbringing. I don't even know if this is right. What if he knows that 'I' had a spoilt childhood, denied nothing? He may seem friendly towards me, kindly in his manner, but I can only imagine what would happen if he were to find out that he has been duped, that sitting by his side is not a noblewoman from a family of his allies but a street rat, a girl who picked up food from the ground if it was tossed to her.

He smiles, benevolent. "You may have as many as you wish here," he says.

I indicate the chaos around us. "I believe I already have, Your Majesty."

But having seen how many animals I have he begins to send me all manner of creatures, even a hedgehog, which the eunuchs revere and which disappears into my garden, to be found only when it wants to be fed fragments of honey glazed buns.

"I like your palace," the Emperor tells me. "It is unlike the others here."

"It's as noisy as the market of Kashgar," I say in an unguarded moment.

"Tell me about Kashgar," he says at once, turning to face me.

I describe the market stalls and he listens, sometimes with his eyes closed to better take in my descriptions. I try to remember mentioning being carried in a palanquin, to describe my 'servants' buying raisins for me.

He continues to visit me often and soon only a few days pass between his visits.

Iparhan was right. He loves to talk of Altishahr – although I have to remember to call it Xinjiang. His new toy, his new conquest. He likes to hear how different it is; it makes him feel that he has taken a far-off land, a whole new country, not merely an adjoining region.

"You must miss it greatly," he says, and I see that he likes this thought, that he's beginning to think of me as a rare bird, longing for its home. I don't try to relieve him of this idea. If it pleases him, if it makes him visit me more often, then that's all to the good.

"I do miss it," I say.

He nods gravely, then reaches out and covers my hand with his. "I will try to make you happy here," he promises.

I smile and wait for him to let go, but he keeps his hand over mine for a little while and when he rises to leave my hand feels cold without his touch.

"Tell me what here is strange to you," he says one day.

"Your Majesty?"

He waves a hand. "In your daily life. What is different from your life before you came here?"

I think of carrying heavy pails of piss and shit alongside the stinking nightsoil men, of old Mut and his hot dumplings tossed to me if they broke up in the pan and were therefore unfit for his paying customers. Nights sleeping out by the tombs. Stealing food, having fake fortunes told to bring in the crowds. The women's lanes edging closer as my only option. I'm silent, but he's expecting an answer and I have to think quickly. The sound of the fountains brings an acceptable answer to mind.

"We have bathhouses. We call them *hammams*," I say.

"*Hammams*," he says, turning the unfamiliar word over in his mouth. "How are they different to being bathed here?"

"They are very dark," I say. "With domed ceilings. Full of steam. And little old women scrub you clean when your skin has been steamed like a hot dumpling. Then they throw buckets of cold water at you, to refresh the body and make you glow."

He listens intently. "Do you miss them?"

I keep a straight face. "The little old ladies? No, Your Majesty. They are very strong and they show no mercy."

He laughs.

Then a few weeks pass without his visits. I find myself looking out for him, going quickly to the window if I hear footsteps in the courtyard, even though I know that if he were arriving there would be more than a few footsteps outside. But in the end it's Jiang who comes to me, his face holding an exciting secret. Behind him hovers Huan, his usual upright bearing entirely spoilt by almost hopping from one foot to the other.

"What is it?" I ask.

"Your chair is waiting for you, my lady."

"I didn't order it," I say, wary of perhaps another unwanted summons from the Empress.

"His Majesty ordered it. He wishes you to meet him."

I'm already on my feet. "Where?"

"Close to the Hall of Martial Valour. In the Outer Court of the Forbidden City."

"Why are we going there?"

Jiang shakes his head, eyes shining. "I do not know, my lady."

I make my way towards the palanquin and pinch his arm as I pass. "You're lying, Jiang. You're a terrible liar."

His giggle tells me I'm right as the pair of them hurry out after me.

The ride is shorter than our journey here, since we are not caught up in a huge procession – just my own palanquin, with a plainer chair following me for Huan and Jiang and an escort of guards surrounding us. Our footsteps echo as we cross back over the moat's bridge and enter the Forbidden City's gate. The Outer Court feels very quiet, for everyone is in the Summer Palace. When we stop I find myself outside a small building, capped with a domed roof. The Emperor is already waiting. I step out of my chair and begin my bows.

"Never mind that," he says. "Look!"

I look, then turn back to him, unsure of what I'm supposed to be seeing.

"A bathhouse!" he says, grinning like a boy. "It was built in the Yuan days and no one uses it now but when you said the bathhouses in Xinjiang had domed roofs I remembered it. There is a well just there for water," he says, pointing, "and I have had it cleaned and prepared for you so that you may use it as a *hammam*." He pronounces the foreign word with care and pride.

I stand, speechless.

"Do you like it?" he asks. "Come and see it inside. Tell me if it is done well."

I step inside the dim room. The walls and floor are tiled and the ceiling reaches up in a perfect dome. It's already been filled with steam and my heavy silk clothes are rapidly becoming damp. By my side the Emperor stands rapt, gazing upwards through the steam. The heat makes our breathing faster and the tiles echo back our words in the darkness.

"Do you like it?" he asks again. His voice is a little anxious.

I reach out and touch him for the first time, placing a tentative finger on his arm. I'm glad the steam and dim light in here hides my face. "It is perfect, Your Majesty," I assure him. "I believe I am standing in a *hammam* in Xinjiang."

"Except for the little old ladies," he reminds me, chuckling. Without warning he puts an arm about my shoulders and pulls me towards him, resting his chin on my now-damp hair. "You will have your own eunuchs and maids to bathe you here. They are at your mercy, not you at theirs."

I stand very still, feeling his body pressed against mine, smelling his scent. I've never been so close to any man except Nurmat. This is not like being close to Nurmat. I feel stiff and awkward but as he continues to hold me to him I relax a little into his embrace. I cannot remember a time when someone embraced me for this long; I have no memory of being held like this.

"I must go now," he says, satisfied. "You may stay here and bathe, if you wish." He pats my shoulder, releases me and makes his way out.

I stand alone in the dark steam, unsettled by the feeling of loss I feel at no longer being held. Jiang and Huan, having seen off the Emperor, come to find me and hover uncertainly when they see me motionless in the darkness.

"Is something wrong, my lady?"

I shake my head and struggle to bring my words together. "I only mentioned the bathhouses in passing," I say. "To – to make conversation. But he…" My voice trembles and I stop.

Huan beams with pride. "The Emperor is a kind man," he says. "And he cares for you. He wants you to be happy here. I told you this day would come."

I nod and stumble my way towards the chair. I hadn't thought to be so moved by a gift, after all the Emperor has only to wave a hand and buildings can be built up or torn down again. But his good-hearted notion of soothing my supposed homesickness makes my eyes sting with tears. Since my mother died, no one has cared about how I might be feeling. I wonder whether Iparhan ever considers my happiness. I know she does not and for the first time I ask myself where my loyalties would lie, if I had to choose.

Now when the Emperor visits I laugh with him more readily, and I'm sorry to see him go, not only because I am failing to meet Iparhan's instructions in joining him in his bedchamber, but because I would like to spend longer in his company.

Soon it will be autumn and Huan begins to plan my winter clothes. He has little fur caps and waistcoats made, as well as heavy outer coats.

"I feel like a beast to be hunted," I tell him, as I try on a skirt and jacket, both thickly trimmed in fur.

He nods, pleased. "Hunting season is almost upon us. It will not be long now until we head for the hunting lodge."

"Is everyone going? The whole court?"

"Oh yes. There will be many thousands."

"Thousands?"

Huan shrugs. "All the court. All the servants – cooks, dressmakers, cleaners, maids, eunuchs. All the courtiers, the officials, their families. Then of course there are the beaters, the groundsmen, the woodsmen – they will all meet us there."

"How far is it?"

"Seven days' travel."

"That's very far!"

"Well," he concedes, "It can be done in three days. But there are staging posts along the way, where the court may rest for the night. The Emperor loves to hunt but he is mindful of his duty to his mother. The journey is in part to provide her with interest and entertainment, with fresh air in the hot months."

I make a disbelieving face. "The hot months are coming to an end."

Huan raises his eyebrows.

I make a gesture of surrender. "Very well," I agree. "We are going to the hunting grounds to please the Emperor's mother and protect her from the terrible heat of the autumn, when all the rest of us will be wearing furs against the cold. How filial of him. And in order to pass the time on this journey of his mother's the Emperor will hunt. When do we leave?"

"In the next few days. There will be a rite before we leave, when all of the Emperor's family will gather together and pray to the ancestors for their blessing, promising to honour their memories in a glorious hunt and prove themselves worthy of their Manchu heritage. You will enjoy it."

The night before our departure I make up my own little bundle of goods. I put in my simpler clothes and then pause. But then I add some fresh food. I cannot rest easy.

Our first glimpse of Chengde comes on the seventh day. Built into a hilltop, gleaming palaces and temples rise from the trees.

"Is that where we stay?" I ask Jiang. "Will I have my own palace?"

He grins. "You will have your own tent."

"*Tent?*"

"The Emperor prefers to stay closer to the hunting grounds. Everyone stays in tents. They are very grand of course, but tents nonetheless. The Emperor's grandfather was very fond of staying in a tent. He said he felt at one with nature, as though he was a Manchu warrior of old."

I shake my head. "You're teasing me. We're going to live in tents? All of us?"

But he's right. The tents are laid out like the Forbidden City, the same configuration of private palaces and great halls, with added rows of tents for the many people who would normally reside in Beijing but now live in the same city of tents as their emperor. The tents are luxurious, with hangings, screens, silk coverlets for our beds and scented chests for our clothes, but they're still tents, and it's not long before I hear that other ladies in the encampment are unhappy.

"The ladies are grumbling," reports back Jiang.

"Why?"

"They are not fond of the hunt. They find the tents draughty, not refreshingly cool, and they miss their gardens. It is fun for the men, of course; they go hunting. For the ladies there is little to do."

"There's not much to do back at the palace either," I retort. "Is the Empress complaining too?"

"The Empress never complains," says Jiang.

"Except about the Emperor's other ladies," I say.

On the first day that the hunting parties set off I stare after them in amazement. There are more than a thousand men taking part in today's hunt. It takes hours before they all disappear, and the duck whistles, hunting horns and dogs, the shouts of the men, can be heard all day.

"There can't be an animal from here to Beijing that won't hear them coming," I tell Huan. "How will they ever catch anything?"

"The animals are surrounded," he explains. "Beaters drive them towards the hunting party. There are little clearings here and there amongst the woods and when the animals reach them the hunters may shoot them easily."

"Easily sounds like the right word," I agree. "There can be no skill in it at all."

He shakes his head at me and places a finger to his lips, indicating that I shouldn't make such comments. I smile and say no more.

I find Giuseppe again, standing amongst the red-leaved trees.

"My Lady He," he greets me.

"Don't you hunt?" I ask. "The horn has already been sounded."

He shakes his head, smiling. "I'm a little too old for such pastimes now," he says.

He's painting and I stand behind him to watch. It's a huge piece, depicting the Emperor and his men hunting stags. The colours are rich and the size of it allows for some idea of how many men are engaged in the hunt, although the true number wouldn't fit in a painting ten times the size.

"How do you know how it all looks if you do not follow the hunt?" I ask.

"Oh, I have been on many hunts over my years at court," he says. "I remember them all too well. But painting and riding do not go hand in hand. Now that I no longer hunt, I am free to paint my memories."

"I thought the Emperor could draw his bow and let fly arrows whilst riding," I tease him. "Can you not paint whilst riding?"

He chuckles. "It would be a poor sort of painting." Suddenly his expression alters. "Your Majesty," he says and bows.

I turn to see the Empress standing behind us. I feel like hiding behind Giuseppe but I only bow to her and wait. I'm trying to think how I can avoid going anywhere with her, if she were to invite me to go with her to her own tent, for example.

She looks me over. "Are you enjoying the hunt, Lady He?"

"It's very interesting," I stammer. It's a stupid answer and I can feel myself flushing. I have to be more on my guard, I think. I should have noticed her approach and made my escape before she could even reach me.

"It's very dangerous," she corrects me, a little smile playing on her lips. "There are wild animals all around us and hunters have been known to let fly an arrow in the wrong direction."

I don't answer. If she wants to frighten me, she's doing it well enough alone, I don't need to help her.

She waits for an answer, then when she sees I have none to give she turns and walks away without saying goodbye. I let out a breath of relief and look at Giuseppe.

"It seems the Emperor's attentions to you have not gone unnoticed," he says. He looks serious.

I shake my head. "He's not even called me to him," I say. "What will she do to me if he does?"

It's late afternoon and the encampment is drowsy. Many ladies sleep in the afternoons so as to be fresh for the banquets often held in the evenings. Their servants take advantage of the peace to rest from their labours or carry out less demanding tasks. Most of the men are out hunting. Only the elderly or the infirm, the women and the servants are about.

I'm restless. The encampment makes me more visible than I'd like. I'm not hidden away in a quiet part of the Forbidden City or protected from close scrutiny by the waters of the lake palace. Instead I'm watched wherever I go, for my clothes mark me out. The Empress' talk of arrows worries me. Is she planning for me to have an accident? I retire to my tent where I feel safer. But there's a strange noise just outside and at last I investigate, too curious about the soft huffs coming from directly outside the tent flaps.

It's a horse. Saddled but riderless. It's nosing at the walls of my tent, munching at some tasty grass that is growing at its edges. I stand and stare at it for a moment before I notice that it's trailing a broken cord, which must have been keeping it tied up, maybe to a tree during a pause in the hunting. It has perhaps snapped it by pulling and then, unnoticed in the tumult of the hunt, has wandered back to the camp. I wonder if there is some poor riderless courtier cursing it out in the woods. I stroke the horse, which snuffles into my hand, hoping for tidbits. I look about but there's no-one nearby to ask for food. The only food I have is in hidden in my little escape bundle thrust under my bed.

My breath stops. My bundle. The woods. A horse.

I could escape now. I could take my little bundle, slip it into the saddlebags. I could lead the horse to the edge of the woods and then mount it, ride away and change my clothes at the first opportunity. The gemstones in my hair alone would keep me fed for many years. No-one would notice I was gone until enough time had passed for me to ride a long way off. If I am questioned while I lead the horse away, I can pretend helplessness and say I was searching for its owner.

The bundle fits into the saddlebags. My hand shakes as I take the horse's cord and urge it softly forwards. I think it will not obey me, but it is placid enough. I try not to look about me, afraid if drawing attention, but for once no one is looking my way and I walk slowly, so slowly I think my heart will stop, towards the woods. There is a steep drop with a little path that leads into the woods and I find myself holding my breath as I make my way down it, gradually dropping out of sight of the main encampment. The only thing I allow in my mind are the words in Mandarin to explain (with wide eyes and a hesitant, girlish demeanour) that I thought I heard a man calling for help just down this path and since I saw this riderless horse…

The woods are empty. I can hear the hunting horns further away but I can't see anybody. I allow myself to turn and look behind me. There is no one there. I daren't change my clothes until I am further away from the encampment, so I bunch up my skirts and hoist myself into the saddle. The horse, now calmer, accepts me as its new owner, standing still as I mutter a few choice words that haven't passed my lips for months. My pink silk skirts are heavy with silver embroidery and do not sit well on a horse. My purple velvet waistcoat, as I told Huan, is too tight. It's suited to sitting about in a palace, not riding. I loosen a few of the buttons, although I can't undo them all. The fine gauze used to make the shirt underneath it is all but see-through. I undo as many as is still decent and take up the reins.

I'm uncertain of what direction to take, but I pick a path which I believe will take me back to the main road by which we came here from Beijing – but leading me through the woods first, so that I will have time to get my bearings and dress in simpler clothes. I can hear the beaters coming closer and I turn the horse away from them. Judging by the sun the hunt will be over soon and the men will return to camp with their spoils. We've seen all manner of game brought back in the past weeks. Deer, hare, ducks, boar. Even a tiger on one day. The Emperor rode past beaming with its body draped over a horse behind him. There was a celebratory banquet.

We come to the edge of a large sun-dappled clearing. The horse shies and will not enter it. I urge him onwards, first gently and then with a firm kick of my heels.

It's a mistake. As we enter the clearing there's a crashing from the undergrowth opposite and suddenly I'm facing five large, dark boars emerging from the golden leaves. They're frightened and their tusks are huge. The horse rears at the sudden apparition and it's all I can do to hold on. I wheel him about, thinking to turn back from where we've come but now there are shouts and the horse pulls away from my command and turns back to face the boars. They stand, irresolute, then charge towards us. As they do, one after another falls, arrows quivering in their flanks. They scream and my horse rears again. I shout and grip on to him with my knees, feeling myself beginning to slide off. Just in time his feet touch the ground again and I can scramble back into a better position on the saddle. I look about me and from all the sides of the clearing ride out the hunters.

At their head, the Emperor.

We stare at each other for a moment while several men run forward and finish off the thrashing boars, their squeals abruptly cut short with large knives. Blood spurts and the hunting dogs accompanying the party bark frantically, held back by their handlers.

My horse, now among other familiar horses, becomes calm. I let the reins go a little, my hands still hurting from the effort of keeping him under control.

I don't know what to say. I'm surrounded by men in their hunting coats and faced with the Emperor. I'm a concubine on horseback, my skirts rucked up, my waistcoat unbuttoned. My hair would no doubt make Huan weep. I am everything I should not be. In my saddlebags, should anyone think to look in them, are plain clothes and a parcel of food, all but announcing my plan to escape.

I bite my lip and then, glancing at the boars, I see that the lead one is stuck by an arrow that belongs to the Emperor – I recognise his feather colours, used by him alone.

I think of the storyteller of Kashgar and at once it comes to me, what will make this a triumph and not a disaster. I have to speak fast, I have to explain myself before questions are asked to which I have no answer.

"Thank you," I say, looking directly at the Emperor. "You saved my life."

He frowns but I press on. "I was walking and this horse came riderless from the trees. Then I heard the boars and I was afraid, so I tried to ride the horse away from danger. But I rode the wrong way and –" I gesture towards the lead boar "– had it not been for your skill with the bow he would surely have gored my horse and brought me to the ground."

I know it's the right thing to have said as soon as I finish saying it. The men's shoulders relax. I've shaped a story that offers glory to the Emperor and his men and casts me as a lady in need of rescue rather than a wild girl on horseback appearing where she has no right to be. I see a few of the men chuckle and slap each other on the back, see one of the men closest to the Emperor turn to him and say something jovial which I can't make out. The Emperor rides towards me. I wait for him, wishing I could rebutton my waistcoat, but that would be too obvious.

He brings up his horse close to mine, facing me. He's still frowning a little, but not angrily. "You can *ride*," he says, and I hear his surprise.

I think of the Manchu heritage to which he clings and decide to align myself to it. "The women of Xinjiang are fine riders," I say, thinking of the Mongols who are our neighbours and are known for their women warriors and hoping he will too. "I have ridden since I was a child," I add, with enthusiasm. I might as well tell at least a part-truth. "It is a wonderful pastime."

He sits back on the horse, still regarding me for a moment while I wait for his true feelings to emerge, then a broad smile grows on his face. "Are you a good rider?" he asks. "I mean, can you gallop?" he adds. "Or must you be led?"

He seems to have forgotten I reached this clearing by myself but I answer truthfully. "I love to gallop, Your Majesty."

He purses his lips and his eyes shine. Next thing I know he's slashed a whip across the back of my horse, which leaps forwards. I'm surprised but I keep my seat and urge the horse on, across the clearing, past the startled hunters and into the woods. I glance behind me and, sure enough, there is the Emperor, his horse also at a gallop, leaning forward in his determination to catch me up, laughing. Behind him is a chaotic muddle of hunters, beaters, dogs and hangers-on, all taken by surprise, all trying to turn themselves round to keep pace with us and failing miserably.

To ride fast through woods is hard work. I've never done it before and I have to duck my head repeatedly although one branch does catch my hair. I have to look ahead and guide the horse whilst keeping my body and head low on its back. It's not long before the Emperor has caught up with me – after all he's an accomplished rider and no doubt has the finest horse available – and for a little while we ride neck and neck, before I slow my pace and he matches me, until we gradually come to a halt. Close behind us comes the noise of the hunting crowd but for a moment we're alone.

He grins. "You told the truth. You are an excellent rider." His glance takes in my disheveled hair, which has been shaken loose of its plaits. My pink ribbons and purple gemstones must be scattered across the woodland floor. He suddenly laughs out loud and reaches out to stroke my cheek. "An excellent rider," he repeats with satisfaction, before gently pulling the last ribbon from my hair. He looks down at it and smiles, then tucks it into a little pouch at his waist.

By now the others have reached us and I sit up straight and try to tidy my hair, at least away from my hot face, and tug at my waistcoat, which I know must be revealing rather more than it should. The Emperor calls to two of the men and tells them to take me back to the camp. I nod and turn my horse to follow them but as I leave he calls out to me.

"Lady He!"

I look over my shoulder. The warm sun shines down on my face and suddenly I feel free, as though my escape plan had worked and I am far away from the court and all the fears it has held for me since I arrived. "Your Majesty?"

"You will ride with me again."

I grin, a huge, happy grin. "Yes, Your Majesty."

"Tomorrow!" he calls.

I nod eagerly and he laughs at my enthusiasm, then turns his horse away and leads the hunting party back into the woods, while my escorts guide me back towards the camp, where I insist on the saddlebags being taken directly to my tent.

Huan's face is a mask of horror. "My lady!" His shriek brings the other servants running. His eyes are wide and panic-stricken. "Have you been *attacked*?"

I look down at my loose hair, unbuttoned waistcoat and crumpled skirts and grin again. "I have been out riding with the Emperor." I say. "On horseback," I add, in case he's imagining this to be a euphemism for something else.

He hustles me inside, out of sight of any passers-by. "On horseback? On a *horse*?"

I giggle. "Yes."

I explain what happened while he has me undressed and washed, then redressed and my hair rearranged. The servants keep their mouths shut as they follow his orders but their eyes and ears are kept wide open. By the evening the whole camp knows that I can ride a horse, that the Emperor saved me from what is now described as a whole herd of wild boars and very possibly a tiger as well, and that we rode together for many, many hours. Meanwhile, now that he knows that the Emperor wishes me to ride out with him again, Huan has a dressmaker stay up all night to modify my clothes for riding, making some of my widest skirts into a kind of wide-legged trouser which allows me to sit better on a horse but still maintain some elegance, as well as hastily loosening some of my waistcoats. My hair still has to be dressed with due care, but he binds it more tightly and doesn't risk adorning it with precious gems, settling for more of his paper creations in the form of tiny woodland creatures, appropriate to our surroundings.

There are a lot of 'casual' passers-by about in the morning when the hunt sets out. Not the other ladies, who are conspicuous by their absence, but courtiers, both men and women, gather to watch us depart, while servants seem to dawdle at those tasks which keep them close by. The Emperor has ordered a horse for me today and we ride out together.

He seems at ease out here in the woods. He talks of past hunts, explains how hunting is seen as a way to develop one's skills for battles. He can let fly arrows whilst riding with ease, and indeed this is a skill that he insists all his soldiers should exhibit, ordering that they should practice it often and calling for demonstrations by archers on a frequent basis.

"Who taught you to hunt?" I ask.

"I was educated from a young age in such skills," he explains. "My days were very long, for I had to learn all the skills of war as well as the skills of peace. My grandfather, the Kangxi Emperor, took me hunting at this very place once when I was only eleven," he adds. "He wounded a great bear, and invited me to take its life. But as I drew near it reared up and charged towards me. He managed to shoot it in time so that it crumpled at my feet."

"Were you scared?" I ask, picturing a small boy in front of a wounded, raging bear.

He's proud to be asked the question. "I stood firm before it," he says. "I did not move. My grandfather said I was destined to live a charmed life."

I shake my head. "You were a brave child," I say.

"I am a Manchu," he says, as though this behaviour might be expected of any Manchu child.

When I next see Giuseppe he laughs at me. "I hear you outrode the Emperor himself," he teases.

I shake my head, smiling. "Hardly. But it was fun."

He continues to paint while he talks to me. "He has talked of you often. He was most impressed. I believe he thinks you are almost a Manchu yourself."

I make a dismissive gesture but my cheeks grow warm. "Only because none of the other ladies ride."

Giuseppe turns to me. "Indeed," he says, eyes twinkling. "That is what makes you memorable to him. I think you are fast becoming a favourite."

My cheeks are too hot and I shrug, then mutter some excuse and leave him. Back in my tent I take the food I had squirreled away and throw it out, then give the plain robe to one of the maids as a gift. Whatever comes now, I will not run away. The life here may be worth keeping my wits about me for after all.

The Emperor takes me riding with him several times after that. Not every day, but on days where the quarry is small or harmless, where the hunt rides close to the camp. He is solicitous of my wellbeing, arranges for servants to carry cooled teas and snacks for me and sends me back to camp once I have ridden with him for a few hours. For my part, I relish the outings. I love to ride and to have a horse that is not stolen and no particular destination in mind makes the excursions relaxed and pleasant. I enjoy the fresh air, the leaves, the animals we spot. And the Emperor's company becomes a deeper pleasure to me. Here he's talkative and light-hearted, freed from his duties. Messengers still arrive daily with official documents and work for him, but he brushes much of it aside and concentrates only on those actions that must be taken. For the rest, he revels in his freedom, the company of the hunting parties and his strongly held belief that in coming here, in carrying out these hunts, he is maintaining his duty to his Manchu heritage.

I watch him shoot a deer herded towards us, his horse still moving while he pulls the bow back easily and lets fly the arrow which kills it immediately.

"May I try?" I ask.

He turns to me at once. "Of course," he says, passing me his own bow. He watches, grinning, as I try to pull it back to let fly an arrow. It's impossible; I can't even pull it back by a hand's width. "I must be stronger than you think," he says and waves a servant forward with an easier bow, but I don't have his aim and my arrows fall pitifully wide of any target.

The nights begin to grow cold and the complaints of the ladies grow louder. I hope our time here will last a little longer but Huan tells me the farewell banquet for the hunt is being planned and before I know it I'm being seated with many hundreds of people. It is the first time I've attended a court event after that first one to celebrate the conquest of my homeland. Although I get a few stares there are other foreign dignitaries and with the diminished attention I am more at my ease. I know there are officials and courtiers here from Altishahr, but to my relief they are not seated near me. I was dreading awkward questions about my family but I'm spared.

"May I offer you some of this? It is delicious."

I look up and meet the eyes of Lady Wang. I've not been sat so close to her before and it's my first chance to observe her. She's young, perhaps my own age. Her eyes are very long and narrow, her eyebrows plucked to accentuate them, arched high on her forehead. She's pretty, but her calculating expression makes her seem older than she is. She's holding out a little dish that clearly holds five-spiced pork, a favourite dish here.

I glance at the dish and back up at her. "I don't eat pork, Lady Wang." I don't feel the need to be polite to her. She is a lesser rank than I am and this is the second time she has offered me something inappropriate, her outer semblance of friendship masking a deviousness I don't care for.

She keeps a steady smile on her face. "Ah yes," she says, loud enough for anyone nearby to hear. "Your religion forbids it. Does it also forbid sleeping with your husband?"

There's a titter from some of the younger, lower-ranking women who despite their lesser status have already been called to the Emperor's bed. I feel myself flush but am distracted by a eunuch who is bowing low by my side. I turn and see he is holding out a platter containing sliced melons. Hami melons.

"From His Majesty, direct from Xinjiang, for your ladyship," he announces, and I see Lady Wang's face stiffen.

I lift the nearest slice, dripping with juice, and take a bite. The memories it stirs are so strong that I put the slice down and stop chewing for a moment, before slowly beginning again and swallowing. I remember raiding the melon fields close to Kashgar or being thrown the odd slice by traders as the day's trading drew to a close. But the strongest memory is the last time I tasted these melons, the night Nurmat stole me away from Kashgar and wooed my shriveled belly with a whole melon to myself. I pass the melon on to other ladies and knowing the gift to come from the Emperor they are forced to comment on how fine the taste is and ask about other crops from Xinjiang. I answer them without thinking, my voice a monotone while I think of Iparhan fattening me up in the little house in the dunes, preparing me for this uncertain future.

Further up the table I see the melons being presented to the Empress and see her look at the platter, then down the table to where I am sitting. Her gaze meets mine for a moment but when I bow my head to her she does not respond, only waves away the slices of melon without tasting them.

Morning, and we begin our journey homeward. I send a message to the Emperor thanking him for the gift of the melon. The answer I receive puzzles me.

"The Emperor is pleased that you enjoyed his gift and believes that soon you will no longer miss the dishes of your homeland."

I feel a moment's panic. "Is he sending me home?" I ask Huan.

He shakes his head, confident. "Hardly, when he has been paying so much attention to you of late."

"What does he mean, then?"

He shrugs and turns away to cuff a maid for dawdling over the packing. "All will be revealed, I am sure," he says.

The seven days of travel are slow and tedious. I miss the riding and the fresh air, jolting about in my hot, dim palanquin. At last we reach Beijing and then the lakes of the Summer Palace. It feels like coming home.

We enter the complex as part of the procession of other ladies' chairs, but my chair comes to an unexpected halt and when I look out I see that the Emperor's chair is waiting for us. We join him while the other chairs set off along the lakesides towards their own palaces.

The Emperor leans out to speak to me. "I have a surprise for you," he says, beaming.

I can't help smiling back. "What is it?" I ask. Probably another pet, I think. Maybe even a horse.

"Follow me," he orders and his chair sets off, my own bobbing along behind.

We make our way through the gardens and bridges leading across the lakes to my own palace and I wonder what he has in mind. Has he had a new garden planted? Or given me some new furnishings? We reach the fountains and stop. I step out, blinking in the bright daylight after the dim interior of my chair. My servants are gathered on the steps. They fall to their knees, their faces pressed to the ground.

The Emperor steps out and waves me over. I join him and he points to one of the kneeling servants, dressed in a plain robe like the others.

"Your new cook," he announces.

"A cook?" I repeat stupidly.

He nods. He's proud of something. "I know you miss the foods from your homeland," he explains. "So I have had sent here a new eunuch, from your own lands, who can cook any traditional dish of Xinjiang that you desire."

I smile broadly. This is a welcome gift. At last Huan will no longer have to weep and berate himself or the other servants when they produce terrible renditions of foods I've described to them. "Then you will have to dine with me," I say, a little surprised at my own boldness. "So that you can taste the dishes from the West."

He's delighted at the notion. "Yes!" he says. "Rise," he adds, as an afterthought to the kneeling man. "Present yourself to your new mistress."

The man rises and I take a step backwards, fighting to keep from crying out.

The man is Nurmat.

Dressed as a eunuch, now bowing low to me and quietly speaking his name before meekly returning to a kneeling position before us. Nurmat.

The Emperor turns to me, so pleased with himself that he doesn't notice the stunned expression on my face. "He is from Kashgar," he says. "And he can cook all of the dishes of your homeland. He says he makes very fine noodles. I look forward to eating them." He gestures to his servants that he's about to leave.

I manage to wet my lips and speak to him, although my tongue feels big and clumsy in my mouth. "Th – thank you," I stutter. "You are too kind to me." I fall to my knees to kowtow, as much to hide my face as for correctness.

He nods and smiles, then climbs back into his chair and within a moment is gone, his chair making its way away from us along the lakeside.

I get up very slowly and stand looking after the Emperor's cortege as it leaves the grounds of my palace, my back turned to the servants, who are still kneeling. When someone touches my arm I jump and startle Huan, who has come to my side.

He's pleased – and proud. My status within the court is rising with each new mark of favour. "His Majesty must care greatly for you," he says with confidence. "He has thought of what new thing might please you and has ordered that it might be done. He is not so thoughtful to all his ladies."

I don't turn round. "Dismiss the servants," I say.

He blinks, but immediately does so. When I hear the last footstep falling away I turn to him. "Where did that man come from?"

"The cook? He is a eunuch. From your own homeland. Made a eunuch once he was already a man. Lucky for us. It was difficult to find a eunuch from your region, and only a eunuch could serve you, of course."

I nod slowly. "Of course," I repeat.

He smiles. "Tonight you will have a meal that will remind you of home," he promises. "Will you come inside now?"

"In a moment," I say.

"Is anything wrong?" he asks.

"No, no," I say quickly. "Nothing."

He bows, then makes his way indoors.

I stand alone by the fountains, hardly daring to enter the palace that I had begun, tentatively, to think of as home. Now it is filled with fear for me.

Fear

I AM AFRAID. NURMAT HAS ENTERED the red walls and I am left alone.

He was displeased at the role I gave him to play. No man wants to be a eunuch, nor even portray the illusion of one. But I coaxed him; I promised he would advance our cause.

"Guide her," I said. "She is a foolish girl who cannot even bed the Emperor. Do all you can to advance her at court. Impress the Emperor with good foods at her table. Make her seem special in his eyes, remind him of his conquest. No doubt it will make him lustful," I add with disgust. "Doubtless a man like that needs to feel powerful before he desires a woman."

Nurmat caresses my face, his fingers covering up the white outline of my scar. "I will miss you, Iparhan," he says gently. "I long for us to be together."

"We will be," I promise. "Soon. You need only guide her towards the Emperor and in what she must ask. We will find out his secrets and then we will strike. A rebellion will be raised. We will reclaim Altishahr and then…"

He smiled then and kissed me, left our home to go beyond the red walls.

Once within those walls he will spend much time by her side. I have disparaged her to him many times but in truth I know that she is doing well. The Emperor may not have come to her bed but he is wooing her as he has wooed no other woman. Her servants are fond of her. She has even managed to endear herself to another woman of the palace, a task beyond most concubines. She has not been found out. She carries herself with grace. And I know that when Nurmat sees her again he will be reminded that here is a woman who has not only my own appearance but the nature he wishes I had been born with – spirited but kind, longing for nothing more than affection and happiness, for a gentle life.

I am afraid.

The house in the dunes reeked with the smell of the rotten wound festering in my father's leg. I tried to clean it, my lips tightened against gagging, my hands steady although my legs trembled. When he began to see things that were not there and to babble nonsense I drew my own dagger and cut the flesh away although he screamed. But it was too late. The rotten smell had seeped into every part of his body and within a few days I was kneeling in the sands, shaping his tomb with my cold hands.

Nurmat believes he knows my plans but once the Emperor beds Hidligh he will find out their true nature. He will be trapped within the red walls and within the nightmare of my intentions. He will look back on every word I have said and know me for a liar. He will know the depth of my rage and the emptiness of our futures. I sit here staring up at those walls and ask myself unending questions.

Will he try to save Hidligh, if she has softened his heart?
Will he try to stop me when I take up my daggers?
Will he ever look upon me with love again?
I am afraid.

The Maze

ENTER THE DINING ROOM IN silence and smell familiar foods. The meal spread out before me could be served in any fine house in Kashgar. All the dishes look as they should, although they're served in the same ludicrously high numbers, on the same little plates with strips of silver that my other meals are brought on. Tentatively, I seat myself. The servants beam, certain of success and praise but my face is very still. Slowly I help myself to a few dishes and put them in my mouth. The noodles, served with a fiery sauce, are good. The *polo* rice is perfect. There is a steamed multilayered bread which I know requires a great deal of skill to make, lamb soup, little pies and meatballs and much else. I have to acknowledge that Nurmat is a good cook. The food is delicious and all of it tastes exactly as it should. No more strange flavours and textures, no more odd Chinese additions to the traditional recipes of Altishahr. I should be delighted.

I'm very frightened.

Why is Nurmat here? He can't really have become a eunuch? If he's not, he's risking his life, for to be discovered as a whole man here would mean death, instant and unforgiving. I don't believe he's become a eunuch — his love for Iparhan's cause might be great but his desire for her body is greater and to have that dream taken away — no. So he's in great danger, as am I. Before today, I was always at risk of discovery, but as the days and months passed I'd begun to feel that I might be safe, that no one suspected my subterfuge. But now Nurmat's here my risk has grown much greater. There can be no scandal attached to me. There can be no question of my purity — when the Emperor has not even touched me! Nurmat's presence is endangering us both and for what — for noodles?

My mind and stomach churn together. I eat more and more slowly, nauseous with my thoughts. Is Iparhan tired of my slow progress? Has she sent Nurmat here to poison me? I can almost believe it. I feel so sick I think I might vomit at any moment. I look at the strips of silver but none have darkened and the eunuch designated my taster seems well enough, although his smile is fading with the rest of the servants' happy expressions as they see my face grow ever more solemn. And how would it benefit Iparhan's plans to make me sick? Or to kill me? Surely she needs me alive?

I sip my tea, which has grown cold, I've taken so long over the meal. The tea is served black and strong, as it would be at any tea stall in Kashgar's market, but the familiar taste seems strange in these surroundings.

I rise to my feet. The servants look at me in dismay. I've eaten very little. I think about what to say. My behaviour is too strange to go unremarked. I think of the Emperor's conviction that I'm homesick. I feel sick enough now.

"His Majesty's wonderful gift has brought back so many memories," I say, putting a hand to my head. "I am overwhelmed with sickness for my home."

At once their faces lighten. Of course. I am homesick. The food is so good it has made me homesick. They are all smiles and sympathy. Huan and Jiang hurry the others away and flutter round me. Their cooing voices, which I'd begun to find comforting, now make me want to strike them. At last I beg for rest and am put to bed early. Once the curtains close about me I can be alone.

I lie still, hearing the servants go about their chores, although they do so on tiptoe in order not to disturb me and their voices are low. I hear the last echoing calls from the courtyards and palaces as the Forbidden City's gates are closed for the night. I see the faint glow of lanterns slowly extinguished and at last there is silence.

I wait. I know he will come.

Every night I wait. Huan frets over the dark circles under my eyes, convinced that the late autumn and coming winter will finish me off if I am so sickly now. I yawn constantly. At last the night comes when Nurmat takes his place in my room to guard me while I sleep, a task that the eunuchs take it in turns to perform.

We wait in silence for hours, until there are no more sounds anywhere. Then I hear rustling as Nurmat gets up from his place by the door and makes his way towards my bed. I hear water being poured before the bed curtains are pulled back and he stands over me, a dim lantern from the door in one hand, a little drinking bowl in the other. He places the lantern nearby and sits on the edge of my bed, still holding the water.

"An excuse," he murmurs, holding it up. "You were thirsty and called for water."

I nod but stay silent.

Nurmat's voice is gentle, careful. "Are you well, Hidligh?"

No one has called me by my own name for the better part of a year. I can't speak.

He waits for an answer, then speaks again. "No harm will come to you," he reassures me. "I am here to help you. To watch and listen as you do. You cannot speak with servants as I can. Between us, we will discover much more than you could alone. You have not yet been called to the Emperor's rooms. I am here to help you in that. Iparhan needs you to be closer to him and many months have passed since you came here. We thought you needed help."

At last I find my voice, though when I speak my whisper comes out as a croak. "You're posing as a eunuch with the information I gave Iparhan."

He chuckles. "Yes. I would have tried to enter as a eunuch for any one of the palaces but then we heard the Emperor wanted a cook from Altishahr. It was too good an opportunity to miss; we knew it had to be for you. I spent two weeks cooking every dish you can imagine with an old woman from Kashgar. We cooked day and night so that I could learn all the recipes. She'd never received so much silver in her life."

My voice is cold. "Is she still alive?"

He's silent.

I lean forward so my face is closer to him. "You're risking your life," I hiss. "And mine, too. If you're found out…"

He shakes his head. "I am very careful," he assures me.

I want to scream at him but instead I grab his arm, digging my nails in as hard as I can. He flinches. My voice is a barely-controlled whisper. "Careful? You're posing as a eunuch! If you were found out it will mean death. For both of us."

He lays his hand on mine and I snatch it back. "Don't touch me."

"All will be well, Hidligh," he soothes me. "You are playing your part well. In Beijing they say that you are homesick and the Emperor dotes on you, that he has given you many gifts and shown you much favour. It is said that he is relishing wooing you, that he finds this new conquest romantic. Carry on as you are and I will help you however I can. Or leave me to make my own investigations and forget I am even here."

"I'll know you're here every time I eat!"

He starts to say something else but I'm too angry to let him explain himself. "Where's Iparhan?" I ask, for this is what really frightens me.

"In Beijing. In the Muslim quarter. She lives there, gathers information, corresponds with those whose plans are similar to hers both here and in Altishahr. I will be able to communicate with her more easily than you can. I can read and write. She has homing pigeons that can fly between us with notes. You'll hear the little whistles tied to their legs sometimes."

"You're risking my life!" I say.

"Live your life here as you did before," he says, still calm. "Forget about Iparhan and myself. We will call on you only when we need you to tell us something. Your task is to endear yourself to the Emperor and I hear you have been doing just that." He pauses. "But it is strange that he has not yet called you to his rooms. Why is that?"

I'm cold with anger and fear. "Get out," I say. "Get away from me before I scream and wake up everyone here."

He acquiesces, pulling aside the curtains and setting down the glass of water, before he turns back to me. "Are you beginning to care for him, Hidligh?" he asks.

I pull the curtains shut against him and after a moment I hear him lie down on his sleeping roll by the door. Soon enough he sleeps, but I do not.

The Emperor sends word that he wishes to dine with me. Although it's an honour – and certainly one that I can't refuse – I curse myself for my rash invitation. In the days that follow my heart frightens me. Sometimes it beats so quickly it feels like a fluttering in my chest and I stand, breathing fast, trying to still it with my fingers pressed against my waistcoat. Sometimes it beats so slowly that I feel heavy and my feet refuse to move.

I'm convinced Nurmat will try to poison him.

I call Nurmat to me, under the pretext of discussing the menu. I choose a moment when Jiang is busy elsewhere, so that no one can understand us when we speak together.

"The Emperor's visit," I begin, and then stop, unsure of how to phrase my fears. If I'm wrong and there's no harmful intention towards the Emperor, then perhaps my speaking of such a fear will put the idea in Nurmat's mind. If I'm right, he may lie to me and I'll be none the wiser.

He bows to me, mindful of the servants that surround us, even though we speak in a tongue they don't comprehend. They will be wondering what we have to speak of, an Honoured Lady of the Emperor's court and her cook. "All will be magnificent, my lady," he promises me, in a meek voice, as though he were truly just my cook.

I bite my lip but try to keep my face calm, as though this conversation were of no more interest to me than that of a good wife, anxious that her husband should eat well at her table. "Tell me about the dishes you will make," I say, to give me a chance to think.

He lists them. The list goes on and on, dozens of names and variations. Some I've eaten, some have never crossed my lips – dishes only served at feasts and on special occasions. I let the sounds wash over me and I see the servants lose interest in our discussion, for it's clear even without knowing our language that a tedious list is being related, with no room for mystery. At last Nurmat finishes.

"Very good," I say, my mind elsewhere. Then I sit back, although I would like to lean forward. "You know, of course," I say, as though the matter were of no importance, "that there are strips of silver in every dish, to identify poisons? And that there are tasters at every meal, who will taste each dish before His Majesty eats?"

He bows again but when he straightens his eyes gleam with a suppressed smile and I know he's heard the fear in my voice. "I will ensure there is a bountiful supply," he promises, as though the taster might be expected to eat whole mouthfuls of every dish, leaving none for myself or the Emperor.

I want to scream in his face to leave the palace. But I only nod and say, "Thank you, I am sure all will be satisfactory." I turn my face away and he bows and leaves the room. My hands are shaking. I tell the servants that there has been too much to do today and that I must rest.

By dawn all is in a fuss. The palace has been cleaned as though it were a miserable hovel. Huan stalks from room to room, dissatisfied with all he sees. The dining room is filled with hundreds of tiny coloured lanterns, to be lit at the start of the meal. All day servants dash back and forth with dishes, ingredients, knives. I am very nearly abandoned until the day draws on when it becomes my turn to be prepared. Today I'm in purple, with adornments in palest orange and early autumn flowers in my hair. I sit, shaking, while Huan readies me.

He frowns when he sees my trembling hands. "Are you well, my lady?"

I nod, my lips so pale that he tuts and applies a deeper colour to them. He takes a brief moment to reassure me. "The Emperor visits you often," he reminds me. "He has never found fault with you yet."

Until he's poisoned at my table, before my very eyes, I think. *I will die for this treachery.*

It's too late to plead sickness or lack of ingredients for a special dish. The imperial yellow chair arrives and the Emperor is in a fine humour. "Amaze me," he says, beaming. "I wish to taste all the flavours of Xinjiang."

I force a smile and lead him to the dining room, now glowing with lanterns and scented with incense. We sit down. Although only the two of us are dining, the room is filled with servants, his and mine. Among mine, Nurmat stands, silently watching. My legs tremble out of sight below the heavy tabletop.

The number of dishes I'm customarily sent seems paltry compared to the food on offer today, most of the items only ever seen at banquets. There are hand-pulled *lagman* noodles, thick in the mouth but light to the stomach, served at weddings as a sign of love – promising that the love being celebrated will last as long as the noodles are long; *polo* rice – glossy with flavoursome mutton fat and studded with chunks of lamb, raisins, carrots, apricots and onions; a whole lamb baked in the oven and kebabs of all kinds – from chunks of roasted lamb to minced lamb which is mixed with onions and cumin before being grilled, and then variations made with livers and kidneys. A dish with chicken pieces, potatoes, red and green sweet and hot peppers arouses the Emperor's interest. I explain that its name means Big Pot Chicken, although of course here it has been served as a dainty little portion. Small dishes of vinegars and heat-filled chili pastes sit ready for dipping into. There are soft breads, some plain and others filled. Hot-spiced broths send steam up from their bowls, filling the room with good smells. There are cold salads made of many vegetables, chopped and shaped into multi-coloured flowers.

The tiny strips of silver are all present. I check them as each dish is brought in, my eyes searching for any hint of darkness, of blackness overtaking their shining surfaces.

The Emperor, though, is happy. He waits for our tasters to try each dish, but while I watch them with fear, he ignores them, too used to their presence to give them any thought. "What are these?" he asks, lifting up a basket of little steamed dumplings, filled with pumpkin.

"They are called *manty*, 'the food of brave men'," I say.

He helps himself to them and pronounces them good, enjoying the new flavour. He presses his new favourite dishes on me, choosing the choicest morsels for my own plate. He asks questions about each dish.

"The *polo* rice is eaten with the fingers", I explain.

He follows my instructions and holds out a mouthful to me. I have no choice but to open my mouth so that he can put the scoop of rice in my mouth. His fingertips brush my lips and tongue while Nurmat watches us.

The Emperor tries wine made of grapes, brought from Kashgar, which bring a flush to his cheeks and makes his laugh louder. I laugh too, although it costs me an effort to do so. My legs are shaking so hard that I expect him to hear the tapping of my shoes on the hard floor, but I manage to keep the heels from moving by bearing down on them with all my strength and he carries on, oblivious.

We finish with black tea and sweets, as well as dishes piled high with golden-hued dried melon strips and nuts. Fried *aiwowo* balls, made with glutinous rice, hold fillings of sugared seeds and have been topped with roasted sesame seeds.

When we have finished we sit a while and talk. I don't make very good conversation, for while we speak I'm watching his face – is he flushed? Sweating? Are his eyes steady? Does he breathe well?

"I heard you had a maid from the Forbidden City in your homeland," he says.

I blink, brought back to the conversation from my fears. "What?"

"Lady Wan told me," he says smiling at my confused face. "Here nothing is secret."

"Yes," I say carefully, conscious of Nurmat standing only a few paces away from me. "Her name was Mei."

"Does she still serve your family in Xinjiang?"

I shake my head. "She died," I say.

He pats my hand. "A shame," he says. " I would have had her brought to you if she was still living."

I blink back tears and offer him more tea, but once again I'm disappointed in his intentions towards me, for he rises, bids me farewell and returns to his own palace, leaving me alone. As soon as I can I undress, my clothes clammy with sweat. I call for a bath to be drawn of cool water and even though Huan shakes his head at the foolishness of a cool bath on a cold night, I insist and it is done.

The days are growing shorter and the nights colder. Soon we will return to the Forbidden City. Under Nurmat's tuition the other cooks and servants are learning to make the dishes of Altishahr, and so my table is loaded with good foods.

But I come to dread the nights when Nurmat is on guard. Even if I ignore him as silence falls across my palace I wake to his shadow leaning over me or to his soft voice speaking my name at the foot of my bed. In the darkness we talk, a little bowl of drinking water always held in his hand.

"Have you spoken with the Emperor recently?"

"Yes," I say reluctantly, knowing I can't lie. Every servant from my palace to the gates of the Forbidden City knows where the Emperor is every day. If he visits me I can't deny it to Nurmat.

"And?"

"And nothing."

"What did you talk about?"

"The weather. My animals."

"Did he ask for your company?" He is more interested in this than in any other information I might have about the Emperor. He wants to know when I receive gifts, if I'm shown favour.

I sigh. "Stop asking that. Don't you think everyone in the court would know by now if he had?"

"You should draw him to you," says Nurmat.

I blush. "I don't know how."

"Touch him," says Nurmat. "Reach out to him. Touch his hand. Pull at his sleeve to draw his attention to something. Smile at him more. Perhaps even touch his face."

I think of my time in training, how I was told to reach out to Nurmat, how I caught at his sleeve and told him jokes to make him laugh, how I drew him towards me with gestures and requests for his attention. How I had to perform over and over again until the gestures became meaningless and empty. I think of the brief moments when the Emperor and I have touched. My fingertips on his sleeve in the bathhouse; his embrace of me and how his scent was still on my clothes afterwards; how I caught myself smelling them. How he drew the last ribbon from my loose hair in the forest and kept it in the pouch at his belt. I feel hot. The thought of deliberately reaching out to touch his warm skin makes me shake. "I will try," I mumble, beneath Nurmat's searching gaze. I try to turn his thoughts elsewhere. "How is Iparhan?" I ask, although I am not sure if I want to hear the answer.

"Impatient," he says.

I believe him. I imagine her raging outside the high red walls of the Forbidden City, awaiting news that will aid her plans. The eerie drone of whistles on homing pigeons flying over Beijing, which used to be a pleasant enough sound, now makes me want to hurry indoors to block out the sound, afraid of what messages Iparhan might be sending with her own flock, of what plans she might be making. I wish I could give her whatever she wants and have her leave my life for good, but the only way to do that is to draw the Emperor closer and I do not like to think of Iparhan when I think of the Emperor. The warmth I feel when I think of him, the fluttering in my breast, turns to something cold and dark when I think of her.

I make the most of the last days in the Summer Palace and walk by the lakes. In the distance, on a small rowing boat, I spot Consorts Qing and Ying, accompanying a little prince. I think back to Lady Wan's description of them. I could do with kind friends, I think, and when they come closer I ask them if they would like to take refreshments with me.

The two ladies glance at each other first, something I find out later they always do – checking that each is satisfied with what is being proposed, before turning back to me and nodding.

I arrange for chairs, tea and sweets to be brought out to them. Cautiously, they step from the boat and we make our introductions, then sit, while the servants light a little fire so that they can boil our water for tea.

"This is Prince Yongyan," says Consort Qing. The little prince just about manages to make an obeisance to me before rushing off to play with my dogs.

I ask how many years they've been at court.

Consort Qing counts and then smiles. "More than twenty years," she says.

I gape at her. "But you are very young!"

She smiles more broadly, flattered. "Not so very young," she says politely. "I am seven and thirty years of age."

She doesn't look it and I tell her so, at which she beams. "I was very young when I first came here. But of course His Majesty was also very young, and his first brides were of a similar age."

Consort Ying is younger. "One and thirty," she says, when I ask. She also arrived young, although after Consort Qing. The two of them have formed a close friendship over the years they have been here.

"Are many of the ladies good friends?" I ask.

They glance at each other and then shake their heads. "Most of the ladies keep to themselves," they explain. "There is much rivalry and each lady wishes for the attention of the Emperor, not for that of the other ladies."

"You are different, then," I say.

They nod in unison. "We are not…" says Consort Qing, while Consort Ying says "We have not…" There's a pause and then Consort Qing says carefully, "We have not been the most… favoured."

"We *have* been promoted," says Consort Ying.

"Oh yes," says Consort Qing nodding with vigour. "We have been promoted, certainly. But…" she glances at Consort Ying and then adds in a rush, "there are always new ladies and the Emperor's attention… can… wane."

"And there are those whom the Emperor has favoured," adds Consort Ying. "The Empress Ula Nara."

They glance at each other.

"Well," amends Consort Ying, "The Empress Dowager favoured her."

"And Imperial Noble Consort Ling is shown much honour, of course," says Consort Qing. "She has borne many children." She straightens her back a little. "I have the care of her son," she adds with pride, pointing to the little boy who is growing increasingly muddy along with the dogs, despite the pleadings of the eunuchs following him.

We talk a little longer. They're friendly but also wary. The Emperor's interest in me is well known, and yet they're puzzled.

"His Majesty dines with you often?"

"Yes," I say. "It is a great honour."

"And he has made you a gift of the bathhouse – the – the *hammam*."

I know that every lady in the palace has secretly made a journey across the wide courtyards of the Forbidden City to peer inside the little domed building. I nod and smile.

"But," says Consort Qing very carefully, "He has not yet…"

They both look at me and wait.

I look down, a little ashamed, knowing that they are wondering what is wrong with me. "He has not yet requested my… company," I say.

Their heads are tilted towards one another. "You have been here the better part of a year," says Consort Ying.

I nod and feel my cheeks getting hotter under their enquiring gaze.

Consort Qing pats my hand. "All in good time," she says. Her voice is kind but her eyes remain curious.

They leave me then, but begin to visit me every few days when their boat takes them in my direction. Perhaps they think I am also abandoned by the Emperor as they have been and expect that one day I will join their quiet little world. They are fond of boating and sometimes I join them, to dip our hands in the cool water, pick floating lotus flowers and allow little Prince Yongyan to admire his reflection in the ripples.

Close to my own palace there's another, smaller one. It's called the Belvedere, and the Emperor decrees that a room within it should be refurbished in the Islamic style and that I may use it for praying. It seems an absurdly large room just for me to pray in, but it's another mark of his favour and Giuseppe himself designs the decorations. He tells me that the name of the palace means 'Beautiful View' in his own tongue. My prayers have changed since coming here. I performed them as a trick at first, an affectation to ensure my religion could not be doubted. But I have grown used to the rhythm of them and here, in this peaceful room, I find myself praying without thinking of how I look or whether I appear pious enough. My prayers are one of the few times when I feel unafraid and so I undertake them willingly.

Sometimes the Emperor comes to the gardens of the Belvedere and waits for me. Today we've been sitting in the gardens for some time while Giuseppe paints us. When the Emperor gets up to go he doesn't look at the painting, knowing that it will be brought to him later, when it's complete. He nods to Giuseppe and departs. I'm not so patient.

"Let me see," I plead, like a child.

He waves me over and I join him. I look at the painting over his shoulder and frown. Sure enough, there is the Belvedere and gardens. The Emperor looks as he always does, although his head seems to be painted rather large – I know from the eunuchs that he prefers himself to look this way and by now all the painters know better than to paint him in any other way. Perhaps the volume of his robes make his real head look small and he does not like the effect. I smile at the large head and then turn my attention to my own figure. I frown. I am dressed as a European woman, in a dress tight at the waist and then frilling out into great skirts, with a giant hat, which Giuseppe has told me is called a *bonnet*. I step back.

"I look ridiculous," I say. "Why am I not in my own clothes?"

Giuseppe smiles. "I was thinking how different you look from your surroundings," he says, "and I wondered how you might look if your surroundings and your clothes were of one mind."

"But you have painted the Emperor in his own clothes."

"The Emperor likes to collect the exotic," he says. "These palaces and gardens, for instance, are European. They are not Chinese."

"And nor am I?"

"Nor are you," he agrees.

I look again at the picture and then turn away. I don't like how out of place I look.

There is a banquet that all the ladies attend. As the meal comes to an end platters piled high with honeyed walnuts are brought out.

"The Emperor wishes you a happy birthday," says the Chief Eunuch, "And he wishes to honour your special day with your favourite sweets."

All eyes turn to me. I bow my head towards the Emperor and he nods back to me, smiling. He is the first to taste the sticky walnuts and everyone else follows suit. I had forgotten this was my official birthday and Nurmat must have prepared these nuts for today at the Emperor's request. It might as well be my birthday, for I don't know when my real one is.

Lady Wan, seated nearby, draws my attention to the Dowager Empress. "She's looking at you," she murmurs. "You should go to her and pay your respects."

I get up reluctantly and make my way to her. I perform a kowtow and she waits patiently for it to be completed.

"Are you less homesick now, Lady He?" she asks, direct as always.

I nod and bow again. "I am very happy here," I say meekly.

She tilts her head. "I hear you cry or seem sad when my son gives you gifts that remind you of your homeland," she says. "You cannot be entirely cured of your sickness."

I think of servants and how they love to gossip. How I wept after I saw the bathhouse and how I pleaded homesickness for my distress after Nurmat's arrival. All that I do is reported back to her, usually, it seems, with plenty of embroidery. "His gifts bring back memories," I say.

Her large dark eyes stay fixed on me. "Not pining for some past lover in Xinjiang?" she asks abruptly. "Your older sister, the Empress Ula Nara, has suggested that might be the case. She has… heard of such attachments."

I feel the blood drain from my face. This sort of idea, if embedded in her mind, could have me executed. "Of course not, Your Majesty. Only memories of my family and my childhood home, the customs there." I say quickly.

She gives me a slow smile. "I can see you still cling to your own customs," she says, indicating my clothes with a sweep of her long golden nail shields.

"Do they displease you?" I ask.

She tilts her head and takes her time, thinking. "No," she says at last. "They are a reminder of my son's conquest of Xinjiang. So they have their use at court; they remind visitors and courtiers of His Majesty's triumph. Your family was clever to think of it when they first sent you here. They must be good strategians." She pauses. "They chose where to place their allegiances, of course," she adds, evidently thinking of the treachery they showed their own family.

I bow my head and when I look up again she's dismissed me. I leave with my skin grown clammy. She's not a woman to cross. The Dowager Empress is Ula Nara's patron, having insisted that the Emperor should raise her to her high status, and since the Empress is clearly beginning to get angry about the amount of time the Emperor spends with me, even if he hasn't called me to his bed, perhaps I have unwittingly created another enemy here. If she knew of Nurmat's existence, of his being a man rather than a eunuch… I must get rid of him. I must make the Emperor call me to his bedchamber. Only then will I be enough in his confidence to find out whatever Iparhan wants. Once she has what she needs, perhaps both of them will leave me alone. I might still have the Empress' enmity but there could be a chance to be happy here if I didn't have Nurmat's shadowy nighttime visits to wake me, his constant requests for information, my fear of Iparhan's expectations. I need to be closer to the Emperor. I need to find a way.

Three days later Nurmat approaches me with news.

"It has been decreed that tomorrow will be the last day and night in the Summer Palace for this year. The day after, we will return to the Forbidden City." I nod, but Nurmat goes on. "The Emperor has asked for his ladies to come to the maze tomorrow evening." He pauses. "With their lanterns."

I look up at him. His eyes are shining. "What does that mean?"

"The Emperor enjoys seeing the ladies of his court make their way through the maze," he says. "Each lady carries a lantern and each enters the maze alone. The Emperor sits in his pavilion at the centre and awaits their arrival. The lights making their way through the maze charm him. He finds it romantic," he adds, meaningfully.

I think about what he's said. "Is there a prize for the lady who reaches him first?" I ask, and see that I've guessed right.

"The Emperor often leaves the pavilion with the lady who reaches him first," says Nurmat. "If her company is pleasing to him. This could be your chance, Hidligh."

I nod, then call for Jiang. "Does anyone here know the secrets of the maze?"

He smiles. "I do, my lady."

I narrow my eyes. "How do you know its secrets if no one else does?"

"I used to play there as a child," he confesses. "When I first came to the palace. I used to run away and play there. I was beaten for neglecting my duties many times. But I learned its secrets."

I know this is my best opportunity. For once I have some knowledge that will help me get closer to the Emperor. He may be enjoying his slow wooing of me but I can't wait forever with Iparhan waiting in the shadows.

"Bring me Huan," I say and Jiang hurries away to do my bidding. Nurmat bows and leaves us, his face excited.

When Huan reaches me, I'm surrounded by maids who are scurrying about with armfuls of silks. My clothes are scattered everywhere. He stands and stares.

"Tomorrow I will be joining the Emperor in the maze pavilion," I say. "You must make me lovelier than any other lady there."

Huan clears his throat, as though to soften the blow he is about to deliver. "The maze is hard to walk," he says gently. "Not every lady can hope to reach the Emperor's side. Most wander lost until they are rescued by their servants, long after His Majesty has made his way back to his palace."

"That is my concern, not yours," I say firmly. "Your task is to dress me appropriately."

He wants to test my resolve. "Appropriately for…"

"For a night with the Emperor," I say.

His gaze travels over the clothes laid out before us. He grabs a passing maid, pulls the bundle of exquisite clothes she's carrying out of her arms and drops them unceremoniously to the floor. "Fetch me the dressmaker," he commands.

I turn to Jiang who has been listening to all this. "Take me to the maze," I say. "You have to teach me its secrets so that I can reach the centre before any other lady. And we only have until tomorrow evening."

"It will grow dark soon," he protests.

"All the better," I tell him. "I will have to make my way through it in darkness tomorrow, so I should learn it in darkness."

The maze is made of carved grey stone and at its centre sits a pavilion, raised up so that whoever sits in it can see the shape of the maze and the lost steps of anyone in it. In the dusk, with no lanterns lit, it has a forbidding air.

"Show me quickly before it is fully dark," I say. "Then I can practice in the darkness."

Jiang shows me the main entrance and we begin. He walks quickly, assuredly, a child sure of his playground. I follow behind him trying to remember each step I take.

"Did we turn left or right? Before this corner?" I ask him.

Jiang turns to face me, his face serious in the half-light. "You cannot hope to memorise each step," he says. "You must remember it as a whole, as you do your own rooms in the palace. You do not remember each step you take from your bedchamber to your receiving hall, do you?"

I shake my head. "I don't understand. My palace isn't a maze. Every room is different. This – " I gesture at the narrow path in which we stand, identical carvings on all sides, grey stone as far as we can see, " – this is all the same."

Jiang smiles. "No, my lady," he says. "It is not." He moves so that he is standing close behind me and then rests his fingertips lightly on my shoulders and head, turning me as he speaks. "This path, facing this way. When you look up you can see the far branches of the willow tree on the opposite lake. And when you walk this same path the other way the pavilion will be on your right, not your left." He leads me round a corner. "Here, when you look up, you will see the mountains in the distance."

"It will be dark!" I protest.

"Then the stars will be your guides," says Jiang. "On this path where we are standing, if you look up, the four small stars will be clustered like this," he gestures, "and facing the other way you will see the great bright star to your right. Do you understand now? You must look in a new way. Not down at your feet but all around you."

I fumble and turn as the darkness falls. I struggle to remember the stars, I cannot make out where the pavilion is. I make one wrong turn after another. The moon is bright, which helps me a little as it rises. As it travels across the sky I travel through the maze, my feet growing surer. At last Jiang leads me back to the beginning of the maze and I walk it alone as the moon vanishes and the sky turns from black to grey, my footsteps echoing in the emptiness.

We stumble back to my palace at dawn. For once all is quiet. Inside is intense focus. Outside the animals, banished in no uncertain terms, sulk by the giant flowerpots.

The dressmaker has worked through the evening and on into the night, his own helpers stitching, stitching whilst my servants kept them supplied with teas to stimulate, to keep their eyes from drooping. Huan's eyes are heavy with dark circles. I nod to him without speaking and make my way to my bed, where I collapse, waving away the maids who want to help me undress. I pull a cover half over me and sleep.

When I wake I'm hustled into a bath and emerge, my skin scarlet with scrubbing, my hair still damp. Silently the maids and eunuchs gather around me as we look at the newly finished clothes.

The skirt is deepest crimson, so thickly embroidered in gold that barely any of the silk shows through. Imperial dragons roar through rising waves. The scarlet waistcoat uses tiny gold fastenings in the shape of the omnipresent lotus flowers whilst delicate clouds outline my curves. The sheer gauze shirt allows the viewer to see the shape of my arms, the fabric making no real attempt to cover my skin. My shoes are shaped and adorned as fishes, swimming below the waves of my skirt. My customary cap is set aside in favour of a gold and pearl diadem, while blood red autumn chrysanthemums and ribbons of finest beaten gold await my plaits.

Huan's eyes are bloodshot and his wrinkles are showing but his smile is heartfelt. "You will be as a new bride," he says. "As you were the first time the Emperor ever saw you."

I nod and seat myself for his work to begin. He takes a bowl of tea to fortify himself and embarks on his masterpiece.

When my chair arrives by the side of the maze twilight is already turning to dusk and the lakes, from their daily blue, are turning black. A cool wind blows against me as I step out.

The maze is transformed. There are lanterns hanging everywhere outside of it, in all different colours, shapes and sizes. Two giant red lanterns frame the entrance and tiny yellow lanterns await each lady who will enter the maze. From here we can see the pavilion rising above the dark corridors of the maze, lit with hundreds of lanterns, surrounding a golden throne in which, from here, I can just make out the Emperor's motionless figure, awaiting our arrival on his golden throne.

All around me are crowds of servants. Bearers for every chair that arrives, eunuchs making last-minute adjustments to their ladies, maids hoping to watch the spectacle and not be sent back to their duties, hiding themselves amidst the chaos.

In the centre of this hubbub stand the women of the court.

Not all have yet arrived, but each is dressed beautifully. Their hair towers above their heads and there are so many flowers, both silk and real, entwined within our locks that together we seem like a moving garden.

I'm the only one who has chosen to wear the bridal colour of red. All around me are purple, blue, orange, pink as well as less showy golden-browns and silvery grays and even the risky, ill-favoured green, perhaps a sign that Lady Yehenara, still grieving for her child who died young, does not even wish to meet the Emperor tonight. My own clothes, picked out in gold, shine in the flickering lights of the many lanterns held by servants all around us.

The Empress stands apart. She has chosen to wear imperial yellow, with matching silk flowers in her hair. She is the only one of us allowed the colour and thus it adorns her as a reminder to all of us of her superior status. I try to stay with the other ladies but she signals to me to come closer. I reach her, then make my reverences.

She stands, still and silent, looking over my clothes. I am dressed as a bride, a young woman destined for a night with an eager husband. Slowly her eyes travel over me while I wait for her to comment.

"Red, Lady He?"

I bow. "Yes, Your Majesty." There's nothing else I can say.

"Do you know your way through the maze?" she asks.

I lower my eyes and shake my head. I'm afraid she will see that I am lying, or that she has somehow found out that I have spent a whole night here, learning the maze. That she will know that I have chosen a path that will bring me into direct conflict with her.

When I raise my eyes she is looking down at the dragons embroidered on my skirts, symbolising the Emperor. "Have a care which path you choose tonight, Lady He," she says at last, still not meeting my gaze. "The maze is a dark place in which to be lost."

She moves away and I let out my breath.

"We have not yet spoken."

I try not to jump. I've been joined by Imperial Noble Consort Ling. Hastily, I bow to her. She looks me over for a moment without speaking. She's a rounded woman, not fat but with an easy plumpness to her which speaks not so much of ample food, which we all have, but of her knowledge of being ranked second only to the Empress, of being an imperial favourite. She doesn't have about her the fluttering lonesome failure of poor Lady Wan, nor the diffidence of Consorts Qing and Ying, who stand on the edges of the crowd, speaking only with one another, nervously licking their painted lips. Her own clothes are embroidered with bats and persimmons, peaches and cranes, all signs of fertility, all subtle reminders of her four imperial children, her many nights with the Emperor.

I try to think of something to break the silence. "How is your son?" I manage. "I remember the fireworks to celebrate his birth."

She smiles. "My children are all well," she says, reminding me that she has already given the Emperor not just one son but two, and also two daughters.

"You have been blessed," I say, seeking for a platitude that might make her leave me alone.

"I have chosen the path I wish to take," she says. I remember Lady Wan telling me that no Emperor has ever been born to an Empress, that a concubine with favoured sons can hope to become the mother to an emperor and thus the highest ranked woman at court. Lady Ling's eyes travel over my crimson clothes. "Have you chosen a path, Lady He?"

I bite my lip. "I think I am still seeking it," I say, which is true, although perhaps tonight I'm starting out along a path, although I can barely make out where it might take me.

"Be careful where your path leads," she says. "I have never sought the love of the Emperor, but my children are my chosen path and those who bar my way will find it hard to walk onwards."

I try to think of a response but we are interrupted by an announcement from the Chief Eunuch and the ladies make their way forwards, each being handed one of the yellow-glowing lanterns. I take mine and wait to see what to do next.

The Chief Eunuch makes a gesture and suddenly we are plunged into darkness. Every lantern, except the tiny ones we hold, has been extinguished. The only light now comes from the moon, our tiny flickering lanterns and the great glowing Emperor's pavilion at the centre of the maze.

The ladies form into their ranks, ready to enter the maze according to status. First the Empress, upright and elegant, her pace dignified. Then Imperial Noble Consort Ling, who strides off, her plump figure full of confidence. Consorts Qing and Ying take up their own lanterns. Holding hands they follow her into the darkness, before turning left, an immediate false step that will bar them from ever reaching the Emperor's pavilion. More ladies follow. I watch as Lady Daigiya and Lady Yehenara make their way in. Soon it is my turn and Lady Wan's, while behind us hover Lady Wang and Lady Chang as well as the lesser-ranked ladies, eager to outpace us if they could.

I wave Lady Wan forwards. "I will follow," I say, bowing. Lady Wan smiles back, pats her wig and straightens her shoulders, makes her way through the lengthening shadows towards the entrance and disappears into the maze.

I stand still for a moment and then begin my journey to the centre. I make my way through the towering gateway, turn right, then turn again and again before stopping. The stone walls rise above me and my first steps sound loud. Behind me I hear the tentative clatter of high-platformed shoes, as more ladies follow. I look behind me but I can't see them, they've already taken other turnings and are lost within the maze.

I stand still for a moment and then set down my lantern and walk into the darkness.

Behind the walls I hear little shrieks and the endless footsteps passing back and forth, seeking out paths that inevitably prove to be false friends. My own footsteps are few. I can see, shining above the intricate walls of the maze, the lanterns of the pavilion, where the Emperor sits, waiting. I take first one turn and then another, the darkness forcing me to check my pathway with my hands, running my fingers cautiously along the walls, mindful of my nail shields in lacquered scarlet, each painted with a tiny golden phoenix, the symbol of the palace's imperial women, the chosen ladies of the Emperor. I look up at the stars to choose my way and hope that I have not forgotten their constellations.

I hear footsteps close by and without thinking I flatten myself against a wall. A dim light comes into view and I see the fast-bobbing lantern that illuminates the eager face of Lady Wang. I wait for her to see me but she is too focused on choosing her path and she misses me as she hurries past. I let out the breath I've been holding and turn away from her chosen direction.

The light of the pavilion fades and I know I'm drawing close. From a distance it shines, but here, at only a few paces from its steps, it barely sheds its light over the tops of the walls.

I turn and turn again and suddenly I'm standing in front of the pavilion, bathed in the light of more than a hundred lanterns. The gold of my clothes leaps into glittering relief and the crimson fabrics glow. High on a golden throne, observing my approach, is the Emperor. I make my way up the steps of the pavilion. He looks me over and smiles.

"No lantern, Lady He?"

I shake my head. "I found the way by my fingertips," I say.

I stand in front of him for a moment while he looks at me before he rises, taking up a lantern of his own. He steps towards me and I do the same without thinking. I lift my face to his and close my eyes. His kiss, when it comes, is gentle, his lips resting on mine for too short a moment before he takes my hand in his and leads me down the steps. I glance back at the now-vacated pavilion, filled only with shimmering lanterns, illuminating the empty throne which is all that awaits any other ladies who succeed in making their way through the hidden pathways of the maze.

We enter the twisting stone walls. I may know some of the secrets of the maze but he knows more. We never meet any of the other ladies, even though once or twice we hear them close by. Once I hear a sob on the other side of the wall and turn my head towards the sound, but the Emperor does not hesitate, only walks on. When we emerge it's not from the main entrance, but from a smaller side entrance. We walk, still silent, through the gardens and then down to the lake close to my palace. Under a willow tree a small boat awaits us, its oars manned by a young eunuch. The Emperor helps me into the boat. We sit, his lantern casting a dim glow over us, as we glide across the dark waters.

"The lotuses have died away for this year," the Emperor remarks in a low voice, as though to speak loudly were to break the shadows surrounding us.

I don't think, only hold out my hand to him.

He lifts it to his lips and turns it palm up. He inhales my scent, then speaks. I can hear his smile even though I can barely make out his face. "I was wrong," he says. "Tonight the lotus flowers bloom as though it were still summer."

The Gift

"**C**OME FORWARD, GIRL," SAYS THE old woman.

I step forward, my right leg dragging a little in a shuffling limp. My plain cotton robe is barely warm enough for the weather outside, but this room is well heated. The old hag must have cold bones. I bow deeply and as I rise up I see her wrinkled eyes narrow to inspect me.

"You limp," she says.

"Yes, my lady," I say, my voice heavy with the accent of an Altishahri peasant girl, a servile whine. "I was crippled as a child."

"And you are scarred," she observes, disapproving. "It's an ugly cut. I doubt any man would want you for a wife. But I suppose a woman would want you for her maid. At least you would not draw her husband's eye, eh?"

"I am a good worker, my lady," I say.

"I can barely understand you," she says. "Your accent is very bad. I suppose it is to be expected, coming from the New Dominion. Still," she says with some satisfaction, "I am sure your future mistress will not object. She's from that part of the empire herself, so presumably she will understand you."

This is the rumour I followed, that a maid was wanted for a great lady from my own lands. There can be only one woman who could be so described. "Are you not to be my mistress, then, my lady?" I ask, full of innocent ignorance.

"I wouldn't have a scarred cripple serve me," she says. "You might bring bad luck to my household. But I am related, you know, to the Emperor himself."

She pauses for effect, to impress me. I widen my eyes to look suitably awed. In truth she is a puffed-up liar; her blood-link to the Emperor so distant as to be laughable. But she wishes to ingratiate herself with him and I am her means to that end.

I tied scraps of cloth to the dead poplar above my father's tomb. Each strip one of my prayers, an unfulfilled wish. I wished for time to roll back, so that I would not have lost my family, my house, my future. But I knew it would not do so and so I made my vow. And in doing so I lost both my beauty and my chance for revenge to Nurmat. Until I saw the girl.

"I wish to present the Emperor's new concubine with a maid from her own lands," the old woman says, pleased with her idea. "It is said she is homesick or some such nonsense and that the Emperor is so besotted with her that he offers her every favour to woo her from her sorrow." She snorts. "A stupid girl if she cannot appreciate her good luck. But that is beside the point. If *he wishes to indulge her foolishness then I will help him to do so. I daresay he will be grateful. It's a shame I could not find someone better formed," she adds, disappointed.*

I wait, a paragon of patience and meekness. She shrugs at last and nods. "You will be obedient," she specifies. "There are severe beatings for a girl who is not an obedient maid within the red walls. It will reflect badly on me if you are not all you should be. You will be trained within my household and I will present you to the Son of Heaven when you are ready."

I have been ready for a long time.

The Bazaar

I T TAKES ONLY ONE NIGHT with the Emperor to change my status.

My servants beam. They hold their heads a little higher, and speak with more assurance. When the Emperor calls me back to him again and then again my newfound status is assured and I see them grow confident in their future. I had not realised how many people's fate depended on my own. Now that their mistress is truly favoured, not with mere gifts but with access to the Emperor's bedchamber, they can rejoice, knowing that their work has been rewarded, that greater things might be in store for me – and them – one day. Their efforts redouble. The dressmaker labours longer over the embroidery on my clothes, knowing the work will be displayed before the Emperor himself. Huan's folded paper creatures for my hair grow ever more fantastical and are even painted or gilded, while more valuable gemstones glitter between the woven strands. Elaborate gifts from the more junior ladies are sent to me, each of them hoping for my favour as I rise in the Emperor's estimation. No-one dares to send ill-omened gifts, not even Lady Wang.

Only a few nights pass before Nurmat makes his way to me again. I am expecting him.

"You have done well," he says, excited. "Now you will find out more information and Iparhan's plans can take shape. We may finish this business yet, Hidligh!"

I nod. This is what I had planned, that I would hurry along the Emperor's wooing and that as a result I could find out more, find out whatever Iparhan needs to make her satisfied with me and leave me alone to live my life while she plans her rebellions and Nurmat pursues her for marriage.

Nurmat begins to list questions I might ask. I know I should be listening, should be remembering them all so that I can think how I might raise the topics with the Emperor, but instead I find myself thinking of our first night together, a night which fills my mind whenever we are apart.

The splash of water against the oars is all I can hear above the rushing in my ears and the hard beating of my heart. The Emperor still holds my hand in his, cradling it between his own two hands as though it were a kitten. His touch makes me tremble but his hands on mine stop them shaking. He does not look at me; his face is turned towards the lanterns on the shores, his demeanour peaceful and content. But I gaze at him, for once free to look at him without being observed by the court around me, without his eyes on mine. The lantern flickers with the rocking of the boat. His dark eyes are large and his skin very smooth, even on his hands, which I know are no strangers to weapons and reins. I raise my free hand and slowly stroke the back of his, tracing its contours in curiosity, as though he were a carving.

My touch makes him look down at my finger as it moves across his skin and he smiles, releasing my other hand. I look up at his face and tentatively raise both hands, slowly stroke his cheeks, cup his face in my palms. I forget that he is the Emperor and lean forward to kiss his lips.

"The borders are our hope," says Nurmat. "If he should threaten lands further than our own they will fight back and we can ally ourselves to them. Already they are discomforted by his endless quest for power. His empire has grown threefold in living memory and he is never satisfied. So ask about the borders, find out if he is greedy for more lands, his plans for the future."

His mouth opens under my lips and I almost draw back. But somehow I am drawn closer to him, so that I find myself held in his arms, my own arms about his neck, my hands stroking his long silken hair. I have never been held like this. I have never kissed like this, his tongue seeking mine, our mouths hot while our skin is chilled by the night air.

I can barely remember alighting from the boat, only that more lanterns, held by unseen figures, await our arrival and that the light around us grows and grows as we reach his rooms. His hands caress my shoulders and his fingers rest for a moment on the fastenings of my waistcoat. He half undoes it before he smiles and strokes my cheek instead, as though remembering something.

"My servants will help you undress," he says.

I want to cling to him. I want to say that I would rather he undressed me himself. When his fingers rested on my clothes I wanted him to go on, to undo each of the golden flowers holding my silken clothes together, to do it quickly so that I could feel his skin against mine. But my voice fails me and already he is making his way to another room.

Blinking, I find myself surrounded by unknown eunuchs and maids. I stand still, awkward again, my dark boldness lost in the light. At first I think they may be puzzled by my strange clothes but by the deftness of their ministrations I realise they have already prepared for this night, have already learned how to undo my fastenings, that they know all the elements of my traditional clothing, even though no other woman here wears such items. Perhaps they sent for my clothes, perhaps Huan taught them; who knows how long ago they all made ready for this night, so long in coming.

Stripped naked, I wait for a sleeping robe to be offered but none is forthcoming. Instead a senior eunuch gestures to me to follow him and I walk behind him through the warm rooms, my bare skin raised into gooseflesh, not by the fear of what is to come but by my sudden, desperate, desire for it.

"I have found us many allies," says Nurmat. "Iparhan has the names of those who will rise up when given the word, those who can offer silver, horses, weapons. We must know if he has any inkling of their identities, if he suspects any of them so that we can assure their safety."

We reach the bedchamber where the eunuch bows and leaves me. The Emperor is nowhere to be seen and I stand alone, feeling small in the large room. I look about, wondering where I should put myself. There is a large carved bed, hung with silken drapes. A strange wooden chair, with arms twice as long as usual, as well as a padded silk seat and a cushioned headrest. Where one's feet would go, if sitting on it, is a large padded silken base. I stare at it for a few moments wondering at its form… and function. I decide against it and climb awkwardly onto the bed. It is heated, of course, and the silk covers feel like warm skin against my own. I lie there on the bed for a moment but my nakedness and the emptiness of the room makes me feel too exposed. The positions I was obliged to learn… will I have to perform them now? How will I know how to begin? I lift the top cover, intending to climb under it, seeking its protection.

"Stay where you are," says a voice.

I look up to see the Emperor closing a door behind him. When it swings shut it disappears, becomes part of the painted wall, showing a summer garden full of delicate flowers and birds.

The Emperor stands still, watching me as I turn a deep shade of pink. I have never been alone in a room with a naked man before. His long dark hair, usually plaited in a queue, is now hanging loose down his back. His chest is broad and his legs are long and well-made. I find myself glancing away from any other detail, too conscious of our nakedness. I shift uneasily on the bed and at once he smiles and comes forwards.

"I should not stare at you so, is that it?" he says, his voice gentle. I try to smile but my lips will not curve as they should. I have lost all my bravery and indeed all my desire. I am a little afraid, now.

The Emperor kneels by the side of the bed. I have never looked down on him before and I feel strange doing so.

"Lie back," he says.

I do so, feeling awkward. My hands are clenched. Now, I think. Now he will climb on top of me and…

He rises from his kneeling position, then sits himself on the bed and lifts each of my feet so that they are in his lap. Slowly, he begins to stroke each foot, from the toes to the ankle, over and over again. He does it for so long, without seeming to want more, that I feel my fingers slowly begin to unclench. My head sinks a little deeper into the bed. His hands are warm and his touch is firm but gentle.

Suddenly I need to know. "Why didn't you call for me before?" I ask, my words blurted rather than chosen.

His smile deepens and now his hands are on my calves. "I thought there was no hurry," he says, his voice low, the stroking motion not changing but slowly reaching upwards towards my thighs. "You were new to court and you seemed afraid. I wanted you to become mistress of your own palace and gardens, to feel at home here. I wanted you to be happy." His hands caress my thighs and I tense again, believing that I know where they will move to next, wanting but afraid. But his hands move smoothly past the dark hair between my legs and upwards, beginning to follow the shape of my belly. Again I wait for him to touch me more intimately, to fondle my breasts, and again he proves me wrong and instead sweeps up my arms. I feel a wave of disappointment, of unsatisfied desire. He rests his fingers on the hollow of my throat for a brief moment, feeling my fast pulse before easily moving to lie beside me, face to face, and his hands cup my cheeks and trail through my hair. He does not even need to pull me towards him, for the lake's darkness is upon me again and I press myself to him, to his kiss, his body, his embrace.

"If he grows suspicious," says Nurmat, "then withdraw a little, or ask some foolish question that will show that you are only a young girl, curious about many things. Then when he is lulled into believing there is no danger, you can ask more questions."

The Emperor half laughs at me. I am clinging to him so tightly, kissing every part of him, that he can hardly move. "I enjoyed wooing you," he murmurs. "I enjoyed surprising you with gifts. I enjoyed riding with you. It made me delay the moment when I would call for you as my companion." Suddenly he is kneeling between my thighs. "It will hurt a little, my love," he says in a whisper and the endearment makes me long for him. "I am sorry for it. But afterwards there will be pleasure again."

I cling to him and he takes me in his arms, then guides himself into me. I whimper at the stinging pain, but his arms hold me in a gentle embrace and his lips on mine wash away the sensation and slowly, slowly, he moves within me and I begin to feel the pleasure he promised. I find myself trying to match his pace and when I feel the pleasure begin to grow I wrap my legs about him and hear him groan. "My lotus flower," he says, his words a harsh whisper in my ear. "I should have called you to me long before this."

Afterwards I expect to be dismissed, to be sent back to my own rooms as protocol demands, but instead he holds me to him.

"Are you sore?" he asks as I nestle into his arms.

"No," I say. It is not true, of course. I am sore, but the pain is so wrapped up in the pleasure I felt that it makes me happy.

He smiles, as though he knows what I am thinking and holds me closer to him. Only when his embrace grows soft do I realise that he has fallen asleep.

In the red-yellow glow of the lanterns I observe him. His face is peaceful, untroubled. His arms grow soft about me. Briefly he even snores a little and I have to stop myself from giggling. I want to stroke him but I do not want to wake him. Instead I slowly move my fingers a hair's breadth above his skin, following the outline of his face, his arms, his chest. Gently I let my hand rest on his warm skin and he stirs a little but does not wake. I lie still and gaze at him, his closed eyes, his dark lashes and the tendrils of loose hair fallen over his shoulders. This intimacy is so far removed from what I was obliged to practiced in the dunes.

Each position came naturally, I was not ordered to assume them. I was not embarrassed and uncomfortable. Most importantly, I was not watched over by Iparhan. She may be only on the other side of the red walls, but for now she feels far away. I feel his sleeping breath, slow and steady, on my temples until the easy warmth lulls me and I, too, sleep, a smile still on my face as I drift into darkness.

"There are even those who think like us here in Beijing, in the Muslim quarter," says Nurmat, "and they will have questions of their own, of course."

I wake to the sounds of bathing and dressing. His many servants, clustered about him, pay no attention to me but he turns and smiles.

"I must go," he says. "You will be taken back to your own palace."

I feel suddenly bereft but I nod. I wonder if he will want to see me again but I daren't ask. Standing before me, in his imperial robes, he is the Emperor once more, not the man who held me in his arms last night.

One of the eunuchs offers him a tray. His smile deepens and I recognise from Giuseppe's description the little tablets marked with the names of the palace ladies. I lower my eyes, not wishing to seem presumptuous but my hands grip the silk coverlet. He flicks through the tablets before holding one up.

"Will this one do, do you think?" he asks.

I can't read all the characters they use but these ones are familiar and I know it is my own name. I blush and nod and he laughs, then drops it back on the tray, face down to indicate his choice. "Tonight, then," he says, and he's gone. I hold the warm bedding to my nose and inhale his scent, then realise his scent is on every part of me, as mine is on him. I stroke my own hair, my own skin, as though it was his, my eyes closed for a few moments until I remember where I am and open my eyes to see the servants waiting to dress me.

When I return to my palace, my servants are gathered by the steps. They should be packing to take us back to the Forbidden City but instead they are kneeling, faces to the ground, like the day I first came here. My hair is unbound and my clothes are disheveled but Huan's smile, as he lifts his face to greet me, matches mine in happiness.

"Your ladyship," he says, and cannot speak further, his voice choked.

I rest a hand on his shoulder and look about me as though all were new to me. Another servant's head rises to look at me but I turn away from Nurmat's gaze and make my way into the palace.

"… and above all we need to know which nobles from our homeland are still his strong allies or if any seem to waver in their support," finishes Nurmat.

I nod slowly, still feeling the Emperor's warm skin against mine, against my breasts, my belly, my thighs.

"Do you understand?" presses Nurmat.

"Yes," I say, to make him go away.

"Then as a reward for your nights with the Emperor I have a gift for you," he says, smiling. From his pocket he pulls out a new vial of perfume. He holds it out and I take it, but along with it he drops a little wooden tablet into my palm. On it are carved some characters. I look at them but they mean nothing to me.

"What does it say?"

He grins. "The name of the perfumer who made that perfume. Have it sent to him and he will know you are its new owner and provide you with it for the rest of your life. He is sworn to secrecy. Once this is all over you will still be here and you will still need your supplies of it."

I frown. "Won't Iparhan want to keep wearing it?"

He shakes his head. "I will find her a new perfume for our new life together," he says, his face filled with hope.

I look doubtfully at the tablet. This may solve one of my fears, but it now seems such a small fear compared to the others that beset me at every turn. "If it ends peacefully for us all," I say.

But Nurmat's eyes are full of the happy future he is envisioning, a future he thinks is coming closer every day. He pats my hand. "Soon it will all be over," he promises me as he leaves. "Ask the questions and when Iparhan has the answers she needs this will all be over. We will be free of this, Hidligh.'"

I try. But I do not want to ask the Emperor questions when I am lying in his arms. Later, I think, later. When we eat, perhaps. But when he selects choice morsels from his own plate and offers them to me I am too hungry for the touch of his fingers on my mouth to remember what questions I should ask. When we walk in the gardens I am distracted by the touch of his hand and his laughter when my dogs shake their paws at the first hard frosts underfoot.

"You said you had a question for me," he reminds me as we watch the birds at their evening flights.

"Did I?"

"Yes," he says. "Something about Xinjiang's borders."

"It doesn't matter," I say.

I begin to ask for particular eunuchs to guard me, often Jiang or Huan, sometimes others, but I ask for them by name, rather than allow Nurmat to take his turn as my guard. Night after night different eunuchs guard me but it is never his turn and so I am left alone, free to enjoy the Emperor's attentions.

He doesn't call for me every night, for Imperial Noble Consort Ling and others are still favoured. Nor on those nights when I'm called may I always stay by his side till morning. Sometimes he will kiss me and send me away in the darkness. But I find myself smiling more often and sleeping more soundly. Huan tuts proudly as my waistcoats and waistbands have to be adjusted. I'm not grown plump yet but my curves are more shapely and I walk more freely, hold my head higher. The Emperor favours me and my place at court is assured.

His gifts are made yet more lavish by our caresses.

By the south-western red wall of the Forbidden City a new building is erected. The Tower for Gazing at the Precious Moon is two stories high. Inside its upper level the walls are lined with mirrors, which Giuseppe tells me is like a great hall in a famous European palace. When I first ascend the steps of the hall and find myself in the room I'm startled by the view.

Beyond the moat is Beijing. I've grown so unused to thinking of there being another city surrounding our own that I step backwards, which makes the Emperor laugh.

"A window on your homeland," he says. I step forward again and realise that the tower has been built so that we can look out at the Muslim quarter, which the Emperor has encouraged to flourish since my arrival.

"I had not realised there were so many…" I say.

"So many of your own countrymen?" He nods. "Your family, of course, amongst them. But many more people from Xinjiang are coming to the capital now."

I look across the waters to the bustling streets, a little wary that someone – Iparhan – might see me. But the figures are too far away to make out their features in any detail, although I can see by their styles of dress that they do indeed hail from my own land. There is a lot of building work going on.

"It is growing day by day," I say.

"It is," the Emperor agrees. "And there is one building that will truly remind you of home. But that is a secret for now."

It's not a secret for long. I hear a wailing cry one morning whilst entering the bathing house close to the Tower and afterwards, curious, I direct my chair to the Tower, for the sound was familiar and yet I can't quite believe I heard what I did.

In the Muslim quarter a mosque has risen, with its own minaret, echoing my own tower. The sound I heard earlier was the call to prayer, and it can be heard in much of the Forbidden City, although most clearly from the Precious Moon Tower. I go there often now, looking out at the bustle of the streets and bringing out my little prayer mat to join in with the prayers being said when the call sounds.

The Emperor however, is not satisfied with the tower, the calls to prayer, the viewing platform he has created for me. "You would like to be amongst them, would you not?" he asks.

Quickly I shake my head, although I keep a smile on my face. Not only do I know it to be an impossibility, but I'm afraid that Iparhan might reach me if I walked those streets. Or that my 'family' would see me. They are not allowed to come and see me here but if I were to go out they might catch a glimpse of me. I've no desire to walk amongst them, indeed, the thought horrifies me.

"You must!" he says. "I will arrange it."

I try to continue smiling, for I've no choice in the matter.

But I've underestimated his plans. "I will make you a bazaar," he promises. "Within these very walls."

"How?" I ask.

"You will see," he says, and is gone.

And so it's decided. There's to be a bazaar, modeled on all that I've told him of Kashgar and its marketplace. It will be created and made to disappear again in only a few short days; a gift of illusion.

All of the court is invited to attend and they're curious to see this, my latest gift and a taste of a far-off region of the empire.

It's Lady Wan, of course, who most enters into the spirit of this pretence. She calls for Huan to show her own hairdresser how to arrange her hair "in the Xinjiang style" and her interest sparks more of the ladies to take part. On the first day of the bazaar, a cold autumn morning, she arrives early, her wig in the form of two long plaits laden with gems.

"You look lovely," I tell her and she blushes as though I were the Emperor himself.

"What a wondrous spectacle," she says. "Do all the sights and sounds take away your homesickness?"

I want to tell her that this illusion, this multi-coloured lavish display of how the Emperor imagines Kashgar to be is hardly how my 'home' was. Here I am an Honoured Lady, chosen companion to the Emperor, dressed in my finery and walking amongst a perfect tiny world rather than dressed in ragged layers for warmth, begging or stealing food, worked too hard or going hungry. But innocent Lady Wan, who has lived within these sheltering walls for decades, would not understand and so I nod and smile. "His Majesty has been so kind," I say, which is true. "It is just like home." Which is a lie, but it pleases her and she darts forward and gives me a quick impetuous embrace before stepping back, as though she had done something very daring. I act without thinking, reaching out my arms to her so that she clasps me to her again. I breathe in her perfume, her warm smell of kindness and tighten my arms about her. Faint memories of my mother's hard life rise up in me and when I leave Lady Wan's embrace I have to draw her attention to my little dogs who are pawing at her skirts so that she will not see that my eyes are glistening.

Other ladies arrive with their hair arranged in variations of my own style and many have dressed in versions of the clothes I wear. I know that the dressmaker I use has been much in demand for they've learnt how to make my clothes and have been able to replicate them to suit the other ladies. The ladies walk oddly, conscious of their tight waistcoats outlining their figures. My high-heeled shoes, however, come easily to them. They are used, after all, to walking in shoes raised on platforms the height of a hand. Perhaps they hope that by dressing like his new favourite they will draw the Emperor's favourable attention to themselves, but in this they are mistaken, and I see Lady Wang's face grow dark when she is not even glanced at. Meanwhile Empress Ula Nara is notable by her absence. Word is given out that she is unwell and has asked for the Emperor to attend her. He does so, but briefly. She is not seen again until the festivities are ended, whether by her own choice or his command I am unsure. But something new in all our lives is to be welcomed, and soon there's a festive air, even among the most ambitious ladies.

The bazaar itself, starting at the base of the Precious Moon Tower and stretching across the courtyards of the Forbidden City, is extraordinary. It is huge, once in it one can walk for many minutes before catching a glimpse of its boundaries. There are stalls everywhere, tightly packed to create small walkways between them. Fruits, vegetables and eggs are stacked so high one fears a single item plucked from the towering heaps would bring all crashing to the ground. Sweet raisins and round melons tempt the tongue. Cones of coloured spices and sugars can be cut or scooped to measure. There are stalls with food that can be eaten there and then – hot noodles, stuffed breads, dried melon strips, roasted meats and piles of sweets made with nuts, sugars and honeys. Much of the food has been made under Nurmat's command using an army of cooks and he is here, overseeing the stalls, ensuring foods are offered to all the visitors while he explains what they are and how best to enjoy them. There is a stall of knives with elaborate handles and one of jade. Hats, scarves and shawls made from every kind of fabric and in every colour imaginable flutter in the breeze. The younger women try them on in endless combinations, giggling at themselves as servants hold up mirrors for them to admire the effect.

The stallholders are all eunuchs, those who usually give performances for festivals or in the Emperor's own theatre. They are dressed in traditional clothing, although far too lavishly. It makes me laugh to see stallholders dressed in fine velvet waistcoats, sporting fancifully embroidered felt caps on their heads.

There are animals, too. Camels have been brought here. Goats, sheep, geese, mules. We might be at the trading fairs where the men barter, except here even the animals must be luxurious and so they are brushed and gleaming, some dyed bright colors while others toss their heads at the fluttering of cheerful ribbons woven into their manes, tied about their horns.

Nothing has been overlooked. When the call to prayer sounds from outside the stallholder-eunuchs pull out newly made prayer mats and say prayers they learnt only two days ago. I join in, although I am the only one who understands the words being recited. The ladies and courtiers stand and stare. My praying is usually done behind closed doors and although they have seen many altars and temples, many forms of prayer in their time, this is something new to most of them. I rise a little flustered, but there are so many sights that soon their attention is diverted elsewhere. Performers have been brought in from the Muslim quarter outside. Singers croon the traditional song cycles of the twelve *muqams,* wrestlers and acrobats vie with one another for ever-more daring feats of physical prowess and dancers swirl, the rhythms of their feet growing faster with the clapping of the spectators.

The bazaar lasts for several days, enough time for all those who wish to try their hand at bartering (although the goods on the stalls are theirs for the asking), to ride on camels, to clumsily learn the secretive trading codes of the men. Even some of the little princes and princesses join us and squeal at the unfamiliar sights and sounds. Consorts Qing and Ying are hard-pressed to keep Yongyan in sight as he darts about the stalls. The street foods are popular, though I see to my amusement that even these are protected with the omnipresent silver strips, which look odd amongst sizzling kebabs and stuffed breads laid out on rough platters and grills rather than the dainty porcelain dishes more generally used in the palaces. The Emperor visits every day, striding about greeting his ladies and children, well pleased with the success of his plans. We walk the length of the bazaar together, his arm tight about my waist. He stops to kiss me sometimes and I wrap my arms about his neck and return his kisses under the gaze of his courtiers, insatiable for his touch, the taste of his mouth. I laugh at his antics as he eats from the stalls, tries on hats and plays with the younger children. He feeds me sweetmeats from his favourite stands, so that I have only to see his outstretched fingers to think of honey in my mouth.

Winter comes to the Forbidden City and the winds are unforgiving even within our high red walls. Sparkling icicles dangle down from the edges of the golden roof tiles, adding to their splendour. I'm wrapped in furs and thick velvets, double and even triple layers of silks make up my skirts. The *kangs* of the palace are heated day and night and even Fury doesn't venture out into the snowy gardens.

Sometimes I invite Lady Wan to my rooms and we play drinking games, although I don't drink alcohol and she cannot hold her drink at all – I stumble over the words of poems in my poor Mandarin while she grows pink and flustered, giggling over innuendoes that don't even exist. But I enjoy her company.

Giuseppe asks me to pose for him and I accept willingly. Any indoor pastime is welcome in the cold. After many days of sitting, a servant arrives, with the picture wrapped in silk. I step back, surprised. The face is my own, for Giuseppe is a fine painter. But once again he has disregarded the clothes I wore whilst sitting. Instead, he's painted me in a dark red Manchu dress, my hair in the Manchu style, like a court lady rather than the way I've always been dressed here, in my Altishahr style.

"Why am I dressed as a Manchu?" I ask Jiang, who is peering over my shoulder.

He is unsure and I am puzzled. But I find as the days go by that I'm beginning to like the portrait. I imagine wearing court robes at the big banquets and court events, being a part of the Emperor's entourage rather than the odd one out in any crowd, unable to take part in court life without being noticed and commented on, even after all this time.

When I do meet Giuseppe again he asks if I like the picture.

"Yes," I say. "It is a lovely likeness."

He tilts his head. "And the clothes?" he asks, with mischief in his eyes.

I mimic his tilt of the head. "What about them?" I ask, and he smiles.

I awake in the darkness, a figure standing over me. I wait, silent, trying to keep my breathing steady as though I were still asleep. But Nurmat is not so easily fooled.

"You are in his chambers often now," he begins without preamble.

I sigh. I have escaped Nurmat's questioning for a long time and now I can tell he will not be pleased with me. His hopes of a happy life with Iparhan rest on my ability to provide whatever information she needs. I try to avoid the chastisement I am about to receive. "Where is Jiang? It is his turn to guard me."

"He swapped with me willingly enough. He would rather sleep elsewhere."

"Go away. If they find you…"

He holds out the drinking bowl and lets a few cold drops fall on me. "Water. Your ladyship was thirsty."

I push him away. "Go."

"I have questions for you. I need answers."

I sigh and sit up in bed. "Go back to her, Nurmat. Tell her I am a clot and a useless girl who can't even ask simple questions of the Emperor. Tell her she should give up and go away with you to be married. Or find some other way of raising a rebellion."

He ignores me and sits heavily on my bed, head and shoulders slumped.

"Do you have questions for me, then?" I ask impatiently.

"Is he gentle to you?"

"What?"

"You heard me."

"What do you care?"

"She wants to know."

"Why would she want to know that?"

"Just tell me," he mutters, his face turned away from me.

I frown. "Yes."

"And his rooms – do you stay in them all night?"

I don't understand this line of questioning. "Not always."

"Does he favour darkness or light when you are in his company?"

I blink. "There are lanterns," I say. "But they are only a soft light. Why?"

He shakes his head but doesn't answer.

I wonder if he enjoys thinking of the Emperor and I together in his chambers and shift my feet away from his perch at the foot of my bed. "I am tired now, Nurmat," I say, my voice cool. "You should leave."

He gets up and stumbles, catching himself on the edge of the bed close to me. When he breathes out I catch a strong smell of alcohol. "Are you *drunk*?"

"Mind your own business," he mutters.

I catch hold of his arm and put my face close to his, sniffing. He reeks of drink. "You idiot," I hiss.

He keeps his face close to mine, inhaling my scent and slurs his words. "Kiss me, Iparhan."

I push him away, hard. "I'm not Iparhan, as you know all too well," I snap.

"I wish you were."

"What do you mean?"

He sighs. "Look at you, Hidligh," he says. "Full of love for the Emperor. Making friends even with the other ladies. Playing with your pet animals. You have a gentleness that I would wish for in Iparhan. If she were more like you she would have turned away from all of this, she would have come to me when I begged her to, rather than chasing this dream."

"It's not a dream, it's a nightmare," I say.

We sit for a moment in silence before he sighs again. "I have questions," he says. "Questions that have to be answered."

"What are they, then?"

"When you are with the Emperor, does he like to fondle your breasts – or does he prefer your buttocks?"

I gape at him in the darkness, then feel rage boil up in me. "Go and drool over that album of paintings I was forced to enact with you if you want to know what a man and a woman do together. It's not seemly to ask me."

He laughs. "The street girl is growing modest," he says with a jeer in his voice that I don't care for.

"I was always modest, even when I was on the streets, Nurmat," I spit back. "I was penniless, not a whore. Leave, now."

"Show me what you do with the Emperor," he says, coming closer to me.

The slap I give him is loud enough to make him back away. "Get *out*," I say as loudly as I dare. "And take your filthy suggestions with you. What would your precious Iparhan have to say if she heard you propositioning me?"

He stands, swaying, above me. "She asked," he says. He sounds sad, but there is anger underneath. "She asked."

"Asked what?"

"What you do with him."

I frown, afraid now rather than angry. Why would Iparhan ask such a question? "I don't believe you."

He shrugs, sets the water bowl down unsteadily and shuffles towards the door. "She asked," he mutters.

"Wait!" I hiss at him, wary of making too much noise. "Why would she want to know such things?"

He pauses in the doorway without turning to me and takes a breath as though about to speak, but instead he exhales and shakes his head. "Better you not know," he says wearily. "Go back to sleep, Hidligh."

I lie awake throughout the rest of the night although my eyes ache with tiredness. Something has changed. Nurmat knows something about Iparhan's plans, something that has taken away his hope of a happy future, something that has made him full of despair. I reach out for the answer but it will not come to me and by dawn I give up. No doubt Nurmat will come to me again and I will ask him then.

But he does not come at night and he avoids me during the day. If I try to catch his eye he looks away. I think of calling him to me and demanding an explanation but I cannot bring myself to do it. I want to enjoy this freedom from his questions and so I pretend all is well, although I know I am lying to myself.

We celebrate the Emperor's birthday. It's an occasion of lavish gifts, good wishes, elaborate clothing and rituals carried out to perfection. In the evening we make our way to the palace theatre, where giant floats are paraded by hundreds of costumed officials and actors, waving banners while loud music is played. Twisting imperial dragons dance while giant peaches – symbols of longevity – split open to reveal colourful carved flowers, Buddhas and gods hidden within. Princes and nobles make their obeisances and all is joyfulness. The servants chosen to accompany me include Nurmat and he presents sweetmeats made to my orders, which are offered by the Emperor to those closest to him. Nurmat carries the dishes of sweets from one lady to another while I keep a wary eye on him.

The Empress arrives, causing a flurry of bows in her direction. She looks about her and her eyes alight on me. I bow and send Nurmat to her with the sweets. She looks down at the platter and I think she is going to refuse but then she chooses one and lifts it to her mouth. Nurmat bows again but she holds up a hand to keep him by her side.

"Are you happy here?" I hear her ask. "So far away from your homeland?"

Nurmat blinks a little at being addressed directly. "Yes, Your Majesty," he answers.

She gazes at him in silence before selecting another sweet, her golden nail tips holding it as though in a bird's beak. "These are good," she tells him. "You will stay by my side while I eat."

I frown as I watch her eat one after another without any apparent enjoyment. Her mouth opens to speak but a new float arrives and the gongs and cymbals accompanying its shower of sparkling fireworks prevent me hearing what else she says. I see her mouth move and Nurmat's mouth responding but I cannot make out what they are saying. I watch them, wondering at her interest in him, until the Emperor waves me over to him. He offers me a slender pole from which dangles a giant pearl carved from white jade. He points to a writhing dragon and shows me how to offer the pearl, his hands on mine, our bodies pressed close together. I forget about the Empress and enjoy the warmth of his touch and his laughter in my ear while below us the dragon roars and bites at the pearl.

"Come to my rooms," murmurs the Emperor in my ear and I nod, feeling a sudden heat rush through me.

I stand impatiently as I am undressed, my feet twitching, ready to walk behind the eunuch to the bedchamber. Once there, instead of making my way to the bed I stand before the strange chair, my feet on its padded base, my hands resting lightly on its absurdly long arms. I cast my mind back to the dunes. Was there a painting with such a chair depicted?

"Kneel," says the Emperor's low voice behind me.

I don't turn to face him. Instead I lift up one leg and then the other, kneeling on the silken seat, my knees spread apart. From behind me the Emperor lifts up each of my hands and places them on the high, upholstered headrest. The position tilts me forwards, my own weight pinning down my hands, my backside lifted towards the Emperor. I find my breath growing short as I feel him caress me, hear his own breath growing quicker. His fingers slip between my parted thighs and when he finds me wet to his touch he groans my name. In a moment he is inside me and I cry out with the suddenness of it, with the urgency of his desire.

On my return to my palace I find the servants waiting anxiously.

"The Empress has sent for you," says Huan, and seeing my face turn white he pats my hand to comfort me, but he cannot countermand her order and so I am forced to step back into my chair and feel the lurch in my stomach as I am lifted.

I'm shown into her palace and taken once again to the room with the black screen, but this time she is standing by the golden table, staring at her four *ruyi*.

I perform my kowtow to her and she waits until I rise, then dismisses the servants from the suddenly empty room.

I shift from one foot to the other, too aware of the wetness between my thighs. I did not have time to wash before I came here. Can she smell the Emperor on me?

"The Emperor shows you favour," she says.

I feel my heart sink. "Yes, Your Majesty," I say. "He has been gracious to me – as he is to all his ladies," I add, hoping to divert her attention to those other women whom he also favours, such as Imperial Noble Consort Ling.

She ignores my ploy. "I am concerned."

I bow my head, waiting.

"I have heard rumours," she says.

I look up, frowning. "Rumours?"

"I have heard that the cook that His Majesty gave you is of your own country and that you speak often with him."

"He comes to me for his orders," I say, too quickly. "To agree on the dishes he should serve at my table." *Does she know?* I think to myself. *Does she know somehow that he is not a eunuch?*

Her smooth calm face does not change. Her steady eyes meet mine. "At night?"

I feel my skin grow cold. I try to keep my eyes on hers but can feel myself fail under her gaze. "He is a eunuch," I say and then curse myself for bringing attention to something over which there should be no doubt. "There can be no harm in his attending me."

She tilts her head slightly. "There are many ways in which a eunuch may please his mistress," she says quietly. "It has been known before."

I gape at her. Such a thought had never even occurred to me. "I – such things – how?" I stutter at last.

Her lip curls. "Perhaps when you are older you will understand more of what can be between a woman and a man – or even a eunuch," she says. "You are still a child who believes the storytellers' lies of true love."

I wait. She could have me demoted, stripped of my title, even, perhaps, executed, if she can prove wrongdoing.

At last she turns away. "Thank you for your visit, Lady He," she says.

I kowtow to her back and when I am done I back nervously away, expecting her to turn on me at any moment. She keeps her face turned away but speaks softly just as I reach the safety of the doorway. "Lady He?"

I hold onto the doorway for courage and turn back. "Your Majesty?"

"I will not fail to undo you if I find you are betraying the Emperor."

Back at my palace I call for Huan. I'm shaking with fear and anger. "I have a spy amongst my servants," I tell him. "Someone who reports on me to the Empress. I will not have such disloyalty."

Huan is devastated. He orders a search of the servant's quarters and when a maid is found with a jade hairpin and a eunuch is found with several large coins, more than most servants might have, they are dragged before me, each protesting their innocence.

"Whip them," I say, my fear overriding their tearful faces and protestations.

I've never ordered a punishment before, but then I've never been so afraid either. But I can't watch for long. The eunuch gets only a few lashes before I put my hand on Huan's sleeve and beg him to stop. The sight of the red wheals rising on his back make me feel sick. Huan tuts at my softness.

"A spy in your household is a dangerous thing," he says. "They must be punished."

I shake my head. "How do we even know they are the right people?" I say.

Huan is stubborn. 'Well, the maid has not been whipped yet," he says, "But she will kneel in the courtyard throughout the night tonight, in the cold, as a warning to any of your servants who might be disloyal."

I let her begin the punishment but that night, when all the servants are asleep, I make my way outside and pull the weeping girl up by her arm. She staggers, for she's already been kneeling for some time, but follows me back to the palace, sobbing her thanks for my kindness to her.

"Be quiet," I tell her. "You will wake Huan and he will send you back out to the courtyard."

She manages to stifle her sobs but the next morning she is brought to me by Huan. She is carrying a stick.

"Don't beat her, Huan," I say, weary from a night spent unable to sleep. "I will not have her beaten when I do not even know she is a spy."

The girl falls to her knees before me, her face pressed to the ground. "I *am* a spy," she sobs. "But not for the Empress."

Huan pulls her to her knees. "Tell her ladyship what you just told me," he demands.

"I was sent to work for you by Lady Ling," sobs the girl.

I rub my eyes, which are aching. Nothing makes sense. "Lady Ling? Why would she want to spy on me?"

The girl holds out the stick to me. "For this."

I take the stick. It's nothing special, a plain piece of wood, shaped into a long flat stick. It has notches on it, roughly etched on its surface. I turn it over in my hands. "What is it?"

The maid points to the notches. "Lady Ling wanted to know when you bled and for how many days, how much blood. Which days the Emperor summoned you. If you were to fail to bleed, if you were to fall with child, I was to tell her at once."

I look down at the notches, which tell me what I know anyway, that my courses are erratic and short. Perhaps the years of poor food and cold as a child and young girl damaged me inside, but certainly I do not expect to bear children. I shake my head. Huan's fists are clenched; he will beat the girl himself if I do not stop him.

"Why did you confess to me?" I ask.

The girl looks up at me, tears still flowing. "You stopped my punishment," she says.

I sigh. "You will stay here and serve me," I say and Huan tuts under his breath. "You will be loyal only to me."

"Yes, your ladyship," breathes the girl. "But Lady Ling? I am afraid of her."

I turn the stick over in my hands. "Wrap this in silk and take it to Lady Ling," I say to Huan. "Give it to her and tell her that her children have little to fear from me. Tell her to keep to her own path and that I will keep to mine. Our paths will not cross."

Huan is reluctant but he does as he's told and the maid is sent back to the servants' quarters, her eyes shining with new-found devotion to me.

The bitter cold continues and now the Kitchen God must be sacrificed to. This year, being in favour with the Emperor, I see many of the rituals in person. The altar is loaded with fat sheep, cakes, tea, soups as well as fruit and vegetables. I pour sugar on when it's my turn to make an offering. There are firecrackers everywhere and I clutch at my furred skirts to make sure none might set me on fire, so wildly are they thrown about. But in all of the chaos it is the Emperor himself who holds my attention. He enters into the celebrations with gusto, banging on a little drum and singing a song that sets the courtiers laughing, called 'The Emperor in Search of Honest Officials'. His face grows flushed with the performance and I find myself laughing. He laughs back and carries on with his song, his drumming growing ever louder to compete with the din of fireworks. Afterwards he takes my hand and leads me to the main gates, where mighty fireworks rise over the walls into Beijing itself.

"Happy?" he asks and I only nod, my cheeks pink from the cold and excitement, my hand warm in his. He chuckles and then leaves me to make his way to yet more altars, for the New Year celebrations require him to undertake many rituals and ceremonies.

I watch him go before turning back to my chair to be carried home. I wish I could go with him.

Mid-afternoon and Huan almost runs into the room. "My lady! My lady!"

I look up from a board game, my piece still held in my hand. "Yes?"

"You are to be promoted!"

I feel my heart swoop. "Promoted?"

He kneels before me, his face flushed with happiness. "Yes! You are to be made *Pin*!"

"Pin?"

"An Imperial Concubine, not just an Honoured Lady. Only six of that rank are allowed within the palace at any one time. Whereas there can be any number of Honoured Ladies! Your rank rises to fifth."

His pride in me is touching. "And this is because the Emperor has…" I blush.

He shakes his head, beaming. "It is because the Emperor is *pleased* with you," he is keen to clarify. "Not all the ladies who are called to his rooms are promoted."

I blush more deeply, but I'm happy. My only fear is the Empress. Will she use this as an opportunity to expose me, to humiliate me? Or has her unknown spy told her that Nurmat no longer comes to me at night?

My clothes, as ever, are magnificent, rich pinks and golds, silk flowers pinned in my hair and gold earrings that drip with pearls.

"The Lady He is promoted: she is made *Pin*, Imperial Concubine!"

Lists of my new privileges are read out. New allocations of taels of silver, bolts of cloth, servants and more will be given to me. I am also presented with a new *ruyi*, this one of delicate white jade inlaid with many coloured gems which take the shape of a garden of flowers.

I look about me and see the ladies of the court watching me just as they did on my arrival here. Now I see the friendly faces of Lady Wan, Consorts Qing and Ying and I smile at them, but I am also aware of the less friendly gazes fixed on me. The Empress, Lady Ling, Lady Wang. Their eyes travel over my face and the precious *ruyi* clasped in my hands, symbol of my promotion. Lady Wang's scowl is quite terrifying, although I don't believe she holds enough power to be a real threat to me. Lady Ling is only interested in her children and as the months pass and still I am not pregnant I must surely become less of an enemy to her. But the Empress…

I move to leave the room, hoping that my absence will mollify her but the Emperor holds up a hand. "I have another gift for you," he says, smiling. "Something to mark the anniversary of you joining my court."

All heads turn towards him. His lavishness in my regard sometimes creates jealousy amongst his ladies, but the nature of his gifts is intriguing to the courtiers, for they're often unusual.

I smile and bow. "I am honoured, Your Majesty. You have done more than enough."

He's pleased, but his eyes still twinkle with the thought of his new gift. "I believe your cook has been satisfactory," he says. "I have enjoyed good meals at your palace and

I even hear your clothes have been altered to ensure you can continue to eat your fill."
He chuckles.

My eyes slide to the Empress, whose face is motionless, then back to him. I try
to smile as though amused and a little embarrassed by his reference to my new-found
curves. "Yes, Your Majesty. He is a most excellent cook."

"Very good," he says. "Now I have brought you a new servant. A maid."

My eyebrows twitch towards a frown although I try to keep a pleasant expression on
my face as he watches me, beaming. *A maid?* I think, *I have many maids. Why another?*

"A maid," he clarifies, "from your own lands. One who will remind you of Xinjiang
and help you to feel more at home here."

I feel my legs begin to shake beneath the heavy folds of my skirt. *No,* I think. *It's
not possible. Please.* I feel Jiang by my side, discreetly placing a hand against the small of
my back for support, for he's seen my colour fade and can sense my distress, although he
must be unsure as to what's causing it.

But the Emperor has already waved his hand towards someone behind me. I turn
very slowly and there on the floor, prostrate in a bow, her hair tied back into a plait with
a small red ribbon, her robe a humble blue cotton, is Iparhan.

I know it's her, before she even lifts her head. I know her too well to be fooled. She
kowtows to me, her face, as it lifts up towards me, a picture of submission, then stands
and makes her way into the shadows by the door to await me. She is limping, her right
leg drags a little behind her.

I look back at the Emperor and lock my knees so that my legs can no longer shake.
I wait for the truth to appear on his face, for him to have seen what I know is there to be
seen: how Iparhan and I are so alike. I wait for his face to grow puzzled at our similarity,
for the whispers around the court to begin, for the Emperor to command us both to
stand before him so that he can see our faces more clearly and then... and then demand
to know what is going on here, how it can be that a humble maid should look like her
mistress, how...

He is waiting for my thanks. His smile is beginning to fade, for I am standing staring
up at him as though mute. I wait a moment longer. Can he not see us, I think? I glance
over my shoulder and see Iparhan's outline in the shadows. I would know her for a palace
maid anywhere, I think. The pale blue robe, the little red hair ribbon holding her single
plait...

And now I see that it is our clothes that have saved me. How could anyone look at
this maid, in her humble cotton robe in the Manchu style, and then at my glorious pink
and golden silks in the Altishahr style and think us alike? I may be safe if I can keep her
as hidden away as possible.

I swallow and wet my lips. "Your Majesty's generosity knows no bounds," I say.
"Thank you."

His smile returns. He enjoys giving gifts and in me he has found a supposed reason
to give even more of them. My 'homesickness' allows him to be inventive, to give gifts

which are not just tokens or commonplace priceless items. He is enjoying this chance to woo me in a different way. "You should go back to your palace now," he says cheerfully. "Your maid can tell you of life at home. You will enjoy her company and forget your longings for Xinjiang."

I kowtow to him and then stand, making my way to the door. At the door Iparhan steps to my side. She is all demureness and respect.

"Are you mad?" I hiss to her, moving away from Jiang who might overhear and understand us. "What are you doing here?"

She smiles and dips her head to me in a parody of obedience, which from a distance must look convincing. "I am here to take your place," she says as she helps me into my chair, her voice so soft I cannot be sure I heard her correctly.

Blossoms

I DON'T ENTER THROUGH THE IMMENSE red doors, of course. I am led into the Forbidden City by means of the side gate on the western wall, surrounded by the crowds of beggars and street vendors who are unceremoniously kicked out of the way by the guard who leads me here. I keep my head down and my limp heavy. Past the endless walls we walk, across the bridges where the water lies frozen beneath us and at last up the many many steps to the huge receiving hall.

There was once a great orchard estate outside the walls of Kashgar. In spring we children ate mulberries, the first sweet taste of sunshine yet to come. In summer we ate cherries and apricots, crammed our greedy mouths with juicy figs before autumn's sunshine brought us sweet new almonds and pistachios, fresh pears and crunchy apples, icy pressed grape juice and bejeweled pomegranates. We ate until we were full, refused the meals our servants had prepared, ruined our clothes with the dark juices of fresh fruits and climbed the trees, standing swaying in their tops to allow the breeze to caress our flushed skin.

Then the newly-appointed officials of the Emperor decreed that Kashgar was too congested for their liking. The blossoming trees were felled to make way for the barracks, the armoury, the granaries, treasuries, the Imperial Hall and Temple. Where once fruits and leaves reached out to the sun, now there are only soldiers and officials and scribes, the Emperor's men, doing his business, securing his conquest.

At first I barely recognise her. She is dressed more magnificently than we were ever able to clothe her, her dark hair shining with silk flowers, her whole body richly adorned with pink and gold silks. Strings of pearls fall from every part of her – her hair, her ears, her throat.

But it is happiness that has truly changed her. She stands taller; she is more graceful. As she rises from her kowtow she looks into the Emperor's face and the smile she gives him is for him alone, as though they were in their bedchamber together.

Standing in the shadows of the cavernous receiving hall I too look at the Emperor's face, for the first time. This is the man who has taken my country, my family, my home. He took my family's power and crushed it; his men have taken the blossoms of our orchard and trampled on them. Because of him I have lost everything. I want nothing more than to see him dead.

He holds out a hand, indicating me with a smile. I strip my face of my true feelings and fall to my knees, ready to be presented to Hidligh.

Five Hundred Oleaster Trees

I SIT IN THE GLOWING ORANGE-TINTED interior of the chair as it rocks back to my palace. I can think of nothing except pulling air into my lungs and releasing it. Each breath is a struggle. I pull aside the curtain at the window hoping that cooler air will help me but by the side of my chair trots Iparhan, her eyes looking ahead, one foot dragging a little. I close the window again and gulp the air although it does not seem to reach my lungs.

Once we reach the courtyard Iparhan's hand appears in the doorway of the chair to help me out. I ignore her and step out alone, then walk swiftly into the palace, making my way to the bedroom. I call for Huan, who is all happiness at my promotion and is busy instructing my new servants in their duties.

"I need tea," I say, "and rest."

"Of course," he says. "It has been a busy day. I will send your new maid to you."

I open my mouth but it is too late to refuse, he has already left the room. I sit on the edge of my bed, my shoulders hunched until she arrives. "Why did you come?" I ask.

"I have come to do what must be done," Iparhan says. She keeps her voice light and pleasant, so that anyone hearing her and not understanding our language would think her a well-spoken serving girl with a cheerful demeanour. While she talks she busies herself tidying the room, as though dusting the playing pieces of my board games were her only concern in life.

I try to keep my voice from trembling so that anyone listening will not know that I am in distress. I have to lie back on my bed as though at rest, although I'm finding it hard to lie still. "You are putting me at great risk. You said all I had to do was live a life of luxury and tell you what you wanted to know. I told you all about the eunuchs and you sent a fake eunuch to live within my palace, risking his life and mine. I was encouraged to become the Emperor's favourite which I have done and now you are here to carry out some plan of which I know nothing and which is probably risking my life even further. We look like each other! Someone will notice. I can't believe they have not seen it already."

"They all look the same to me," she says. "No doubt we all look the same to them."

I think of Huan's worried wrinkles, Jiang's gentle smile. My maids, the one with the round plump face and the one with the surprised eyes. "They don't look the same to me," I say.

She shrugs. There is no one to see her but me. "There's no need for you to fret about what your maids look like," she says brightly. "Carry on living your life of luxury.

Meanwhile your people are oppressed by a greedy Emperor who drains our country of its goods and its pride."

"You think he is a monster," I say. "He is a kind man."

"A kind man when he gets what he wants," she says, still with a smile on her face.

"Stop pretending to be pleasant, Iparhan," I say. "There's no one here to see you except me and I know better."

"I will speak with you tonight," she says, her voice still light, her smile still fixed. "Appoint Nurmat as your guard in the bedchamber and ask for me to wait upon you. You can tell Huan that you wish me to talk to you of your homeland." She snorts. "I am sure he will believe you, the fool dotes on you."

I don't answer her. I think for a moment of asking for someone else to guard me, of telling Huan that Iparhan is not to attend me at all, but I know this will only seem odd. A heavy weight settles in my stomach as I carry out Iparhan's orders.

The lights are dim in my bedchamber. Huan checks that all has been done according to my stated wishes – that Nurmat is ready to lie on his bedroll just inside my door, that Iparhan is standing, the very model of duty and good behaviour by my bed – then he wishes me good night. I want to ask him to stay by my side but I cannot and instead I force a smile onto my lips. "Good night Huan," I say, and he leaves the room, satisfied.

I pull my legs up tight to my chest and sit huddled among my silk covers. "Well?" I ask. "Are you going to tell me now what your plan is?"

Iparhan is already busy. She has collected my discarded clothes, as a good maid should, and now she lays them on a small table and begins to undress.

"What are you doing?" I ask.

"Be quiet," she says, her movements quick. Nurmat sits on the bedroll by the door. He does not watch her. He seems to know what she is doing already. He keeps his eyes lowered, fixed on her blue cotton robe, now lying crumpled on the floor. She pulls on my clothes, and busies herself with the buttons. She is now dressed in a magnificent skirt in a vibrant blue, embroidered in gold vines and pale pink blossoms with a waistcoat in rose, a shirt in sheerest cream.

I swallow at the sight of her, at the fear rising in my gorge. "Why are you here?"

"To take your place, as I told you."

"I don't understand."

She speaks as though to an idiot. "I will play your part. You will play mine. You will be the maid. I will be the concubine."

I blink. "That's not possible. The people here at court know my face."

"Don't be a fool, Hidligh," she says, stepping into my shoes. "You must have known the first time you saw yourself all dressed up in a mirror that we look alike. Didn't you ever wonder why you of all people should have been chosen? A dirty little street girl with the manners of a peasant? To be made into a concubine fit for an emperor? An ignorant child, who knows nothing of my plans, nor understands the troubles of our homeland, to be made into a spy? Come, you are not so dim-witted as all that."

And then I know. And I know how stupid I have been from the very beginning. Iparhan wanted to enter the Forbidden City but her scar stopped her from doing so. A concubine must be perfect. But when she saw me in the market and the resemblance I bore to her, she knew that her plan was not ruined on the day Nurmat scarred her. By having me enter the Forbidden City in her stead and endear myself to the Emperor, she could then take my place in the palace and in the Emperor's bed. She could find out whatever she needed to know. Her stories about how I should spy for her were only stories. All she needed was for me to arrive at court, to be known to my servants and favoured by the Emperor. I think of Mei's instruction to look in a mirror. I curse myself for being a fool, for pushing away my fears and believing in the possibility of a happy life here. But still I find myself groping for a reprieve. "Your scar…"

She finishes the buttons and nods as though I have been helpful in reminding her. Seating herself at the table where Huan does my hair and makeup she unfastens the small red ribbon holding her hair in its humble plait. Unbound, her hair is a river of black silk, still rippled from its former bindings. From Huan's small bags she extracts various little pots and boxes, before carefully applying creams and powders, slowly covering her scar, now grown white with time. I watch as her face changes to how it must once have been, her skin smooth and even. Once her scar fades away her eyes shine out, large and dark. She paints her lips a dusky pink and outlines her eyes. Once or twice she glances at me, then looks back into the mirror, making changes to her face. She adds a deeper blush to her pale cheeks, darkens her chin to give the appearance of a dimple, which she does not have. I do. She adds paler powder to the sides of her slender nose, making it seem a little wider, like mine. She is making herself look as much like me as possible.

I feel myself beginning to breathe faster, although each breath is too shallow to give me enough air. I try to think about how I look. Does she look enough like me? The dim light in the room is aiding her disguise.

"Light more lanterns," I say to Nurmat.

He looks up at me and I stare back at him. "Do it," I say, and my voice is hoarse.

He looks to Iparhan for confirmation and she shrugs as though my request is of little consequence. She is busy rebraiding her hair into my customary two plaits, entwining them with ribbons and gems. She is quick and certain. She must have practised this many times. "Do it," she echoes.

Nurmat stands and slowly lights another lantern.

"And another," I say. "Light them all."

It takes some time and while he lights the lanterns Iparhan examines herself in the mirror. Satisfied, she stoops briefly, then stands. In her hand are the blue cotton robe and the small red ribbon that bound her hair. She throws them towards me. The faded blue and red drift lightly through the room, landing on the edge of my bed.

"Put them on," she says.

I shake my head although I know already that I will do as she says. But I feel as though I must oppose her, if only briefly, if only so that she knows that I am unwilling. It seems so important that she should know that I am unwilling.

"Put them on," says Iparhan.

Slowly I reach out my hand and pick up the cotton robe. I let the silk sleeping robe I am wearing slip from my shoulders and pull the rough cotton over my head. I swing my feet to the floor and stand, unsteady as though I have been drinking. The robe falls nearly to my feet, its colour dimmed with many years of washing. The red ribbon slips from the bed and falls to the floor. I bend over automatically to pick it up. As I stand I find Iparhan behind me, her hands already in my hair.

"Keep still," she says. She braids my hair, her hands moving at speed while I stand motionless, one hand clutching the red ribbon. She pulls it from my grasp and ties the end of my single plait. "Now come here," she says.

I stumble as she leads me to the table, then sit, eyes lowered, unable to look in the mirror. Beside me, Iparhan rummages in the bags and begins to apply makeup to my face. The room grows brighter as Nurmat lights lantern after lantern.

"Look," says Iparhan. Her hands are still at last.

I stay still.

"You said it was not possible," she says. "Now judge."

The room is now so bright with light, it might almost be daytime. I lift my head and look into the depths of the mirror. Behind me, in the far part of the room, still holding a darkened lantern, stands Nurmat. At my side, Iparhan.

In the mirror are reflected two women. One richly adorned in fine clothes, her hair bound with gemstones. The skin of her face is smooth and pale, with flushed cheeks and pink lips. Her eyes are large and dark. By her side, shoulders slumped, sits a maid. Her dark hair is pulled back in a simple plait, tied with a worn red ribbon. Her skin is pale, although its smoothness is interrupted by a scar, which runs from the tip of her eye down across the whole of her cheek, marring any good looks a girl of her lowly stature might have been blessed with. Her rough cotton robe is a pale blue, the dye worn away by many years of service.

I reach up a hand to the scar painted onto my face and try to wipe it away but Iparhan's hand is already on mine, her grip so hard her nails dig into my skin.

"You can have it painted on or carved on with a knife, Hidligh," she says. "You know I will do it. Which is it to be?"

I let my hand go limp in hers and she releases me. I sit with my hands in my lap. Iparhan nods her approval.

My voice comes out as a whisper. "The servants may be fooled," I say. "But I have lain with the Emperor. He…"

Abruptly Iparhan holds out her hand. I flinch, expecting a dagger, but she places one hand over my eyes and the other close to my face. "Breathe in," she commands.

I breathe in and the perfume we are both wearing washes over me.

"In the darkness there are only two senses," says Iparhan. "Touch. And smell."

I sit, silent and blinded, the scent filling my nostrils. The perfume I've worn with such care and growing pride since I came here, the perfume that was first Iparhan's and then mine, is being turned against me. The whole world by now knows that the Emperor's concubine from Xinjiang is scented with a magical fragrance emitted from her very own skin. The court perfumer has been unable to replicate it. In the darkness, that fragrance *is* Lady He. Any suspicions would fall away in the shadows of the Emperor's bedchamber, once he smelled that scent. Besides, there is only one woman in all of the palaces who dresses in these foreign clothes, whose hair is arranged like this. I am unique at court and this uniqueness is Iparhan's greatest weapon.

Hot unbidden tears trickle down my cheeks and neck.

Iparhan pulls away her hand and wipes my tears off on her silk skirt. "You are beginning to care for him," she says. "You fool. You are nothing to him, just another woman at his beck and call. You are favoured now because you are still new and every time he sees you he thinks of his conquests and he feels desire rise up in him. But in time another girl would come along, another pretty face from some other conquered land. And then you would be a nobody. Waiting, like bald, wrinkled Lady Wan, for a call that never comes. Playing with your little animals in your gilded world. Theirs would be the only caresses you would ever receive."

I turn my face away from her.

Iparhan looks back into the mirror. "So," she says. "You believe me now. You have seen that it can be done."

I sit in silence.

"I will not take your place all of the time," says Iparhan. "Only when it suits my purpose. It does not suit me to spend my days being fawned over by those mincing eunuchs. And it would be difficult for me to hide my scar all the time when I must be bathed by others. For the most part, you will continue your life as it was before I arrived here. But when you are due to meet with the Emperor, or any other person whom I deem to be of use to myself, I will take your place and you will take mine. You will not argue with me when I order you to your room so that we can effect this change. If you do, I will see to it that you lose your life."

"Then you would lose your place here," I say quickly.

She shakes her head and stands. She begins to strip off my clothes and I feel myself slumping with relief that she is about to give me back my place. "I would take your place once you were dead, Hidligh," she says, the clothes slipping to the floor. "It would be difficult to hide my scar, but not impossible." Suddenly she raises her voice. "Huan!" she calls loudly. "Huan! Nurmat – go and fetch Huan for me."

Nurmat leaves the room and I turn to her. "Iparhan," I begin, but she waves me into silence as footsteps return. Huan has come at a trot, anxious to know why his mistress should be calling for him in the middle of the night. I stand up, uncertain of what will happen now, whether I should be preparing to run or plead my case. I find myself holding my breath, waiting. Huan knows me too well to be fooled by some makeup.

Iparhan has already darted across the room, grabbed my sleeping robe and thrown herself on the bed. She lies with the covers strewn about her. As soon as Huan enters the room she reaches out her hand to him. "I do not feel well," she says, and the voice that emerges from her mouth is so like mine that I blink. I think back to the dunes, how she mimicked Mei's voice. Now she has taken mine.

Huan is all attentiveness. "What ails you, my lady?" he asks.

"I have a stomach ache," complains Iparhan and I see Huan's eyes widen with fear that she has been poisoned. She reassures him. "A... a *woman's* ache," she modifies, lowering her eyes as though embarrassed at revealing such an intimacy.

Huan's anxious demeanour changes. I wait for him to say something, to realise the deception, but he is all comfort. He arranges the covers about her, settles her back on the pillows. Then his eye falls on me. "Don't just stand there, girl," he admonishes me. "Pour her ladyship some water."

I stand and stare at him. I cannot believe that he has been fooled, that he looks at me and does not see me, sees only the blue robe of a maid, any maid, but he is already searching through a box for some medicine from the physician. "Here," he says with tenderness to Iparhan. "It will help you sleep better."

Iparhan takes the proffered remedy.

Huan turns back to me. "Girl!" he says, annoyed. "Water! Now!"

I fumble with the water jug, slopping water over the table as the little bowl overfills. Huan strides over to me and cuffs me sharply round the head, the blow stinging my ear. He fills a new bowl and takes it to Iparhan. "Drink this, my lady," he says. Over his shoulder he snaps at me. "Clean up the mess you have made."

Iparhan pats his hand. "You are very good to me, Huan," she says, all but simpering. "Don't mind the girl. She has a good deal to learn. I am sure you will make her into an excellent maid. And I feel better now. I shall get some sleep."

Mollified, Huan arranges the covers one more time and nods to Nurmat to put out the lanterns. "Good night, your ladyship," he says, then turns to me. "Come along girl, back to your sleeping quarters."

Iparhan intervenes. "I will keep her with me until I am asleep," she says. "Then she will return to her bed."

Huan nods with satisfaction, bows to her and leaves the room.

I stand in silence while Iparhan slowly climbs out of my bed. She is smiling. "Your chief attendant is not very perceptive, is he, Hidligh? The room so bright, his face a mere hand's breadth from mine, and still he cares for me like a child while he cuffs you for being a lazy maid." She stands, removes the silk robe and holds out her hand. "Take off that robe," she says. "And wipe your face. You don't want to wake up with a scar, now, do you?"

I stand naked and watch her braid her hair. When she is done she heads for the door, her bare feet silent.

"When will you take my place?" I ask her.

She pauses for a moment by the door and answers without facing me. "Whenever I so choose," she says. "Goodnight, Hidligh."

I wait, dreading Iparhan's next move, but she plays her part to perfection for days. She does not speak much, she limps, her scar is clearly visible. Huan grows to like her.

"She is so helpful and reliable," he says to me. "So compliant. I believe she has learnt our ways more quickly than I expected after her first clumsiness."

I find even talking about Iparhan difficult. My hands ball into fists and I struggle to keep a smile on my face.

"Are you pleased to have her here?" asks Huan. "Does she talk to you of your homeland?"

I shake my head. I don't want to encourage Huan to send her to me more often. Just the sight of her makes my heart beat faster, my breath grow shallow in my throat. "She is a good enough girl," I say. "But her memories of home are different from mine."

"Of course," agrees Huan. "She is only a poor girl, not from a well-to-do family like your own. She would know little of the life you led before coming here."

I nod, thinking of how even her hideaway was luxurious whilst my own life was lived in the streets and stables of fine houses like those her family would have owned.

"I believe there may also be a little romance blooming," says Huan coyly.

"Romance?"

"Between your cook and the girl," says Huan, now happily gossiping. "I saw them talking together and he stroked her face. She turned away, of course, as a good girl should, but…"

I think about the parts they're playing and frown. "He's a *eunuch*," I say.

Huan shrugs. "Sometimes the eunuchs are permitted to take a wife. And besides, the poor girl will not have many offers, with her face scarred and that limp. But she is a kind girl and no doubt she would make a loving wife."

I nod, distracted. If Iparhan and Nurmat are seen together perhaps it will take away suspicion from myself and Nurmat, which can only be a good thing.

"Well, they have my blessing," I say, hoping that by doing so I will lend credence to their play-acting. "Although it does not seem much of a marriage for a maid."

Huan nods. "It can be difficult," he agrees. "But there have been many such marriages and she would be cared for at least. She might even adopt a child."

I try to imagine Iparhan dandling a baby and fail. "Enough chatter about servants' matters," I say, forcing my hands to unclench. "Tell me some court gossip," I add, hoping it will turn Huan's mind away from Iparhan and Nurmat.

Huan leans in to me. "Lady Wang is in trouble," he whispers. "She beat a servant to death. She is in disgrace and has been demoted."

I find myself wondering whether it would be worth a demotion to have Iparhan beaten to death but I know I don't have it in me to order such a thing, whatever crime I could invent for her to have committed. My fingers creep to my throat and the little rough red mark I'd thought gone returns with my nervous habit.

I am sitting with Lady Wan, drinking tea and playing a board game, when a servant appears at the door. "His Majesty requests your company this evening," he says.

These words always lift our spirits but I am a little embarrassed, for Lady Wan has not been called to his rooms for many years. But she is smiling. "Huan," she calls. When he joins us she pulls from a little purse at her waist a golden-wrought lotus flower. "For her hair," she instructs him.

"Thank you," I say as she rises to leave us.

She pats my hair. "Such fine hair deserves fine jewels," she says. "I will see you soon."

As soon as she leaves us there are plans and preparations. Clothes are selected, Huan mulls over hairstyles to incorporate the new golden flower, servants rush about. It's mid-morning and I say that I will eat and then sleep, so as to be fresh for the Emperor this evening. I've found this to be a wise course of action, for aside from his bedchamber we spend many hours eating and talking, looking at works of art and playing board games together. Sometimes, too, I am sent back to my rooms after we have lain together, so that it's often very late before I can sleep.

I awake to find Iparhan seated at my mirror, already dressed in my clothes, painting her face with great care. Nurmat guards the door, his face sullen. I leap out of the bed.

"No," I say.

"Be quiet," says Iparhan, slipping on my shoes and standing. As I am in bare feet and she is in heels she looks down on me.

"Don't do this," I say, my voice breaking a little. "I beg you."

"I am here to spend time with the Emperor, to understand his plans," says Iparhan, implacable. "And how fortuitous that he should call for me so soon."

"He called for *me*," I say.

"I doubt he will know the difference," says Iparhan. "I'm sure all you women are alike to him anyway."

"Please," I say. "He will not talk of military strategy, Iparhan. He will only want to – to – "

I see Nurmat's jaw tighten, but Iparhan ignores us both. "Sit down, Hidligh. I need to do your face. Put on the robe," she adds, passing me her maid's robe and hair ribbon.

"No," I say.

Iparhan sighs. "Do not try my patience, Hidligh," she says. "Dress quickly and keep your mouth shut. I am taking your place because I must be certain that the Emperor will not notice the difference between us. If he does not, you can be certain that I will not take your place too often for such moments. Why would I want his hands on me? I wonder you can bear it at all."

I stand motionless.

"Dress," says Iparhan. "Or I will kill you now and go to the Emperor anyway."

Slowly I pull on the robe and braid my hair into a scruffy plait, unlike the smooth gem-laden plaits that Iparhan's hair is bound in.

"Good girl," says Iparhan. "I knew you would see sense." She addresses Nurmat. "Go and tell Huan that I have dressed myself but that he must put the finishing touches to my hair before I leave."

Nurmat does not meet her eye. His hands are clenched in tight fists. He turns and leaves the room. Iparhan watches him go and then straightens her back. "I will see you later," she tells me. "When I return you will be waiting for me. You will tell Huan I requested that you wait up for me and help me to undress."

I'm shaking. I reach for something that will hurt her as she is hurting me. I wait till she's almost gone before I ask, "And Nurmat?"

She pauses without turning. "What of him?" she asks and her voice is low.

"Does he know you are willing to give yourself to the Emperor when you won't give yourself to him?"

She keeps her face turned to the door so that it is hidden from me. "He has made his peace with it."

"Really?" I ask. "Is that why he has started to drink?"

She does not answer, only pushes the door open and leaves the room. As her footsteps die away I sink slowly to the floor and begin to weep.

Huan finds me. "Get up, girl," he says. "What are you sitting there whimpering for?"

I daren't speak, only shake my head.

"Well up you get, then," says Huan. "Tidy this room, then lay out her ladyship's bedclothes. You will wait up for her. Then get something to eat," he adds, more kindly. "You may have to wait up till late, we cannot know when she will return."

I nod. I have no choice. I carry out Huan's orders, then make my way through the rooms of the palace. I know where the entrance to the servants' quarters is, but I have never entered them. I hesitate outside the door, uncertain of what to do, how to conduct myself. Jiang, who is hurrying that way, finds me.

"Is there something wrong?" he asks, seeing me standing motionless before the door.

I shake my head. Jiang pushes the door open and I follow him, remembering as I do so that I must limp.

The room I enter is large, but its plainness, after so many months living in splendour, is startling. The muted paints used on the walls are faded and peeling, there is little furniture and what there is looks very plain to me. Over twenty people are in the room: maids who are mending and embroidering clothes, eunuchs polishing silverware. From the smells I can tell that food is being prepared in a room close by. Some of the youngest maids come and go with foodstuffs to be used, or carrying heavy buckets of water, their little frames bent over with the weight. I've barely stepped into the room when one of the maids hands me the shoes she is holding. "The soles need cleaning," she says. "Her ladyship has been walking in the gardens and they're dirty."

Slowly, stupidly, I manage to find a little pot of water and a small brush, which I use to clean my own dainty shoes, their pale cream silk marred by dirt that has soiled them during one of my many walks. I hold the little shoe and look at it as I have never done before, my efforts at cleaning it so useless that the same maid tuts and takes the pair back to do a better job herself. I excuse myself as quickly as I can and make my way back to the bedchamber, forgoing any food.

It is fully dark and the Forbidden City has been closed up for the night before Iparhan makes her way back. Her face, in the dim light of the flickering lanterns, is drawn. She does not meet Nurmat's eye, only walks past him with such care that no part of her even brushes against him. She undresses so fast I hear a ripping sound as she pulls off her shirt and she wipes a wet cloth over her face with a roughness that turns her skin a livid red. Seeing how anxious she is to take back her place I hurry to remove the painted scar and the cotton robe I am wearing. The cool touch of silk on my body again is like a retreat to a place of safety. I sit on the bed, watching her replait her hair and tie the red ribbon in it.

"Did he…" I begin, unsure of what question I want to ask and whether I want to know the answer.

"Oh he did not miss you, have no fear," she spits back at me. "He could barely keep his hands off me. It was disgusting."

I feel my throat grow tight and gulp back a sob. "Get out," I say.

Iparhan pauses, looking at me in surprise. "Do not tell me what to do."

"Get *out*!" I cry at her, unable to contain myself.

Too late I hear footsteps come running and Jiang's anxious voice on the other side of the door. "Is all well?" he calls.

"Yes, yes," I answer.

I hear him walk away and turn to Iparhan. "Get out," I say. "And do not speak to me again of what you do with the Emperor."

She looks at me, gives a mocking bow and leaves the room.

I look at Nurmat and see my own tears reflected in his eyes. "What is to become of us?" I ask him, but he does not answer, only lies down on his bedroll by the door and turns his back to me.

In the darkness, our muffled sobs continue for a long time.

When I see the Emperor again I cling to him and he smiles down at me. "So full of desire?" he asks. "When I last sent for you it seemed you were not so willing."

I leap at this sign that he saw a difference between Iparhan and I. "Was I not myself?" I ask, filled with hope.

"A little reluctant, perhaps," he says. "Not so eager as you seem now," he adds, laughingly picking me up and flinging me onto the bed.

I hold out my arms to him. "I am eager for you," I say, my voice choked. "Come to me."

He climbs onto the bed, crawling slowly up my body until I seize his arms and pull him to me, twisting and rolling until I am seated above him, my legs straddling his body. He looks up at me and his hands reach up to stroke my hair where it covers my breasts. "I prefer you like this," he smiles, and I fall onto him, my body pressed against his, trying to make our flesh one.

Spring is coming. Consorts Qing and Ying are visiting me. I'm playing a game with little Yongyan, herding his carved wooden animals, when Iparhan, making tea close to us, speaks in our tongue, her voice humble, as though asking for instructions.

"Ask the Emperor for a grove of oleaster trees, to be brought here from Kashgar," she says.

I freeze for a moment but then continue the game although my hands tremble. Ladies Qing and Ying continue their chatter, talking of inconsequential matters, uninterested in whatever my maid is saying to me.

"No," I say. I don't know why she would want such a thing but all her requests make me suspicious.

"Ask for them," she says. "Or I will take your place again and do the asking myself when I am in his arms."

I turn my face away and don't answer her, but I cannot bear for her to take my place if I can prevent it. Reluctantly, I make the request, spouting some garbled nonsense about how they remind me of home.

A few days later the Emperor calls me to his gardens and we walk together. He slips his arm about my waist and I lean against him, feeling the heat of his body through the silk of his robes. "I am thinking of planting the trees here," he says. "And in your garden as well, of course."

"Trees?"

He frowns. "The oleasters. From Xinjiang. You asked me for them the other night."

I nod. "Of course," I say, trying to sound excited. "How many of them will there be?"

"Five hundred saplings," he replies, reassured. He walks a little ahead of me and points to a few places where he thinks oleaster trees will look well. "I liked your description of them," he calls over his shoulder. "Silver leaves and golden fruit. Very poetic."

I stand and watch him. Through me Iparhan is making demands of him but I don't understand their meaning. Why would she want oleaster trees?

I lose my appetite and barely touch my food. It grows cold before I finish. Fat congeals on plates, broths cease to steam, breads lose their fresh-baked softness.

Huan frets. "Why will you not eat?" he asks.

I shake my head and mutter something about being too hot, or too cold, or whatever other poor excuse comes to mind.

I lose my pampered curves and grow a little thin. The spot at the hollow of my throat grows coarse with my touching of it and Huan tuts and has my clothes altered, applies unguents to my neck.

Then news comes from Altishahr.

"There has been a rebellion," says the Emperor. His face is stern.

"What set it off?" I ask, wondering if Iparhan has had any hand in it.

"Your trees, it seems," he says.

"My trees?"

"The oleasters you asked for. It seems the porters rebelled against transporting them here. Two hundred and forty men were requisitioned to carry them here. They rebelled and used the trunks as clubs to attack their escorts, then went on to kill local officials and install their own leaders."

"I am sorry," I say, horrified, cursing Iparhan in my head. "I would not have asked for them if I had known they would cause so much trouble."

He shakes his head, stubborn. "You shall have whatever you desire," he insists. "It is not for porters to tell their Emperor what he may or may not command of them."

Sure enough more oleasters are sent for.

"All you have done is make him angry," I say to Iparhan when no one is nearby. "You are a fool. Now he will not withdraw troops from Altishahr for many more years."

"I have shown our people what can be done when men rise up together," says Iparhan, her head bowed while she brushes my dogs. "They are sick of his demands. Now they know what they can do they will rise again and again."

"And cause more bloodshed?"

She shrugs. "Whatever blood is shed is shed for the glory of Altishahr and its future," she says and I stop talking to her, knowing that my words go unheard.

The oleaster trees arrive, their silvery leaves rustling, yellow flower buds shining. Hundreds of saplings fill the courtyard while they wait to be transplanted into their new homes, each housed in its own crate filled with soil from Altishahr. I touch a little handful of it, let the dark earth trickle through my fingers. I stroke the leaves and smell the buds. This autumn there will be fruits, if the trees recover well from their journey. I wonder if I will be here to see them.

I know that their presence here is a triumph for Iparhan. She has created unrest in Altishahr through a simple request of the Emperor. There are many more such requests she might command me to make. I must make them or Iparhan will take my place to do so and the Emperor will fulfill them because he believes he is assuaging my homesickness. If they lead to greater unrest, so much the better for Iparhan's plans. She could ask for many things from our homeland – jade, cloth, fruits. She can stir up unrest through the petty demands of a favoured bedmate. Such power she can wield through me.

Jiang, always seeking to learn new things, inspects the trees, following one step behind me. "Is it true that their blossoms can be eaten? They are saying that you ate the blossoms as a child and their scent was transferred to you."

"You listen to too many stories, Jiang," I say. "Where do you hear such nonsense?"

"Everyone has stories about you, Lady He," he says with a happy smile. "About your perfume and the Emperor's many gifts to you."

I shake my head and walk away from the trees. "Stories, Jiang. All stories."

"He gave you the bathhouse," he says. "And the Moon Tower. The bazaar. Your prayer room. The melons, the sweets for your birthday. The cook and…"

I stop him before he can mention Iparhan. "Enough, Jiang. My life is not a fairytale."

He is delighted with the notion. "But it *is*," he says.

The Emperor walks with me in the gardens, through the groves of oleasters, now planted and rustling in the breeze. "You've grown thin," he says, disappointed that I'm not more impressed with his latest gift. "Are the trees not pleasing to you?"

"They are beautiful," I say quickly.

"But?"

"But nothing," I say. "I am happy, Your Majesty."

"You are thin and pale," he says. "And I know why."

I wait, my heart beating too fast. If he ever knew why I am thin and pale my life would be forfeit.

"You are missing your riding and travels," he says, smiling. "The hunt seems long ago. But that can be cured. We are going on tour."

"On tour?"

"It is part of my duty to travel around the empire," he explains. "And my mother much enjoys such travels."

I know by now that his filial duty is an excellent excuse to fulfil his own restless desire to travel. "Your mother is lucky to have such a caring son," I say, anxious to lift his spirits.

He smiles. "So! We will go on tour. You can ride, see the countryside. Get some colour in your cheeks and eat good food."

I can only smile and agree with his plans, but I'm wondering what new opportunities our travels will give Iparhan.

"A Southern Tour!" says Jiang excitedly. "I have never been on one."

"Where will we go?"

Jiang is all too keen to recite our route. "We will begin our journey overland through

Zhili and Shandong to Qingkou in Jiangsu. There we will cross the Yellow River and continue our journey on the Grand Canal. There are many cities that we will visit in this way: Yangzhou, Zhenjiang, Danyang, Changzhou and then Suzhou. After entering Zhenjiang, we will also go on to Jiaxing and Shimen to Hangzhou, our last stop, on the Yellow Sea. On our return the Emperor will inspect the troops at Jiangning. All in all we will be away from court for four or more months."

I gape at him. "So long? And so *far*?" I have grown used to the Emperor's constant desire for a change of scenery but so far all our travels have been short. I try to think in Chinese distances. "More than five thousand *li*?"

Jiang nods. "The Emperor is keen to ensure that the Yellow River is well maintained so as not to cause floods. I believe he wishes more barrages and ocean levees to be built to avoid such disasters. He will inspect the works."

"It sounds like a building project rather than a tour," I say.

"Oh, there will be processions and so on, of course," says Jiang. "There is special permission granted that the people may look upon the Emperor's face as he passes by, unlike here where we travel with the bamboo screens. There will be thousands who come to gaze upon him – and all of the court."

Iparhan, of course, has other views on the Emperor's tour. "How good of him," she mutters. "To allow his subjects to catch a glimpse of his luxury. The only reason he goes to the south is that it is one of the richest parts of his empire and he must keep it loyal to him. All the grain and silk comes through those parts. And every city that he visits will have its taxes cancelled out of his generosity but they will pay far more than taxes to ensure his comfort – and yours, of course," she adds. "They will have to refurbish palaces and lay on entertainment. It will drain them. He was only there three years ago, they will barely have recovered since then."

"Be quiet," I say, for Jiang is entering the room and she risks a beating to be heard speaking so of the Emperor.

"I could leave Nurmat and Iparhan here," I tell Huan, waiting to see his reaction. "There is no need to take many servants."

He looks shocked and my heart sinks before he even speaks. "His Majesty might be offended," he says. "He may think you are disparaging his gifts to you. Besides," he adds, "we need Nurmat to manage your kitchen while we travel and Iparhan is a most helpful and reliable maid."

I curse Iparhan for having made herself indispensable to Huan. "Very well," I say. "They will accompany us." Before we leave I give orders that the servants' quarters of my palace are to be repainted and put into good repair for our return. New robes are to be made up and issued to them all. My own shoes are to be modified, adding a thin layer of bamboo wood to their soles, making them easier to clean. And only the older maids or eunuchs are to carry the water buckets, not the newly arrived child-maids who reminded me too much of myself, struggling to earn a living in the streets of Kashgar.

As ever the court on the move is an extraordinary sight and one I'm not yet used to. Not all the court will come with us, however. Those in favour are taken along. The Empress, of course, as well as myself and other ladies. Others are not so fortunate. Lady Wan remains at home and bids me farewell with tears in her eyes.

"It is a little lonely here when the court is away," she admits and I wish I could ask for her to accompany us, but I know that many ladies are being left behind. Instead I embrace her and beg her to look after my dogs while we are away. She looks doubtful at first, but once they've greeted her, tails wagging and eager tongues licking her proffered hands, she gives way and I can see that they'll be spoilt in my absence.

"Be careful," she whispers, as I take my leave of her.

"Of what?" I ask.

"The Empress."

"Why?"

"She asked the Emperor not to take you on the Southern Tour," murmurs Lady Wan. "He refused her request and she is known to have wept in her rooms for many days. Now she is angry. You must know that she is jealous of you," she adds.

"I am only an Imperial Concubine," I protest. "She is the Empress, and nothing will ever change that."

Lady Wan smiles. "You are a beloved concubine," she says. "And she is not a beloved Empress, although she craves the Emperor's favour."

"Why doesn't she turn her jealousy onto Imperial Noble Consort Ling? She more highly ranked than I am and has many children by the Emperor. She is often in his chambers."

Lady Wan looks at me for a moment. "Lady Ling is favoured," she says. "But her love is all for her children and their future. She does not crave the Emperor's love."

I look at her. "And I do?"

She pats my hand. "I believe Ula Nara looks at your eyes when you behold the Emperor and she sees something she recognises," she says. She tilts her head. "Is it so?"

I shrug and look away, unable to meet her steady gaze. "He is a kind man," I say. I try to form more words but stop, unsure of what they might be.

Lady Wan smiles and strokes my hair. "Enjoy the tour," she says. "But be careful. She may not be in favour but the Empress has great powers and she can command whomever she wishes to serve her."

I embrace her again and make my way back to my own palace, where the servants are hurrying about, for we must be ready to depart in the morning.

We're almost ready to set out and everywhere are chairs, servants, officials and courtiers, ladies of the palace, children. I stand stroking one of the horses, which the Emperor has promised I may ride sometimes. I would prefer horseback to the endless swaying of a palanquin.

Prince Yongyan runs across my path, having once again escaped the ministrations of Consort Qing. He is dressed in bright orange silk, with painted dark stripes that have convinced him he is a tiger. He roars at a younger sister, leaving her whimpering until a nursemaid rescues her from the terrible beast.

I laugh at him and he bares his teeth. I cower. "Have mercy on me, noble tiger," I plead.

He roars again but giggles halfway through at the sight of my pretended terror, spoiling his fierce demeanour. I pick him up and allow him to sit on my horse for a moment. He clutches at the reins, then, remembering his training, composes himself more proudly, back straight and chin up as though he were posing for a portrait.

"Very good, Your Highness," I tell him. "Your father will be proud of you."

He beams. "I am a true Manchu," he says grandly and as I let him down he rushes away to boast to his siblings.

The palanquins assemble by rank. There is much confusion as each lady and her retinue takes her proper place. Soldiers and courtiers mill about us. For once the giant open spaces of the Forbidden City's Outer Court are not large enough. In the chaos my palanquin comes close to a chair draped in yellow silk. A hand emerges from the silken folds, its golden nail shields flick in my direction and I hear the voice of the Empress Ula Nara. "The dogs should be at the back of the procession," she says. "Especially that mongrel cur." Her voice lacks her usual slow, elegant delivery, it trembles a little. Huan quickly gestures to my bearers and my palanquin moves out of her sight. Jiang leans through my drapes and fans me a little, as though to blow away her words.

The travelling is tedious and I soon grow heartily sick of it, as do most people in the court. No sooner do we reach one place, then we are on our way to the next, our resting places changing from one night to another. The servants grow harried with the constant packing and unpacking that must be done.

Anywhere that dykes, levees and barrages have been built there must be inspections. We soon tire of the endless discussions regarding stone versus earth banks and the Emperor's insistence on arguing over the finer details of their construction. Fewer and fewer of the ladies attend such sessions, pleading exhaustion or even the effects of the 'Southern heat', although we're still in the early part of the summer. But the Empress seizes the tour as her opportunity to prove her devotion to the Emperor.

In every city there are rituals to be performed at temples. There are those dedicated to particular deities, great sacrificial ceremonies at the mausoleums of ancestral emperors as well as commemorations at the graves of local historical personages and officials, to honour their deeds and memory. The Empress throws herself into these obligations, whether by the Emperor's side or on her own, carrying out one rite after another. Her days are an endless round of ascending and descending the steps of temples and memorials, kowtowing to the gods and ancestors, breathing in the overwhelming clouds of incense smoke. Once she stumbles on the steps and falls, a rush of monks and servants failing to catch her in time. Back on her feet she stands, shaken, for a moment, looking down at the soft palm of her right hand, which has been scraped and is bleeding. For that day, at least, she is hurried back to her rooms and tended to. But the next day she sets out again.

She begins to look tired, her face seems more lined and her movements become a little slower. She looks thinner, as though the constant movement is stripping away her former slender curves. But she does not rest.

I see little of Nurmat. He manages my kitchen as he has always done but when I catch sight of him he looks weary.

"Are you well?" I ask him directly, when I see him passing one day.

He turns to look at me and I see his eyes are bloodshot, either from too much drink or too little sleep. "Your ladyship is kind to ask," he says, although each word is heavy.

"There's no one here to understand us," I say. "Are you well?"

"Ah, Hidligh," he says and his eyes fill with tears for a moment. "Do not ask such questions. Keep to you own life and let what is to be, be."

I want to question him further but he is already making his way from the room, his steps slow.

I call for Iparhan and she comes and stands before me.

"What is wrong with Nurmat?" I ask her.

She bows. "Your ladyship?"

"Don't seek to fool me," I say. "If Nurmat is unhappy it is you that are the cause. What are you planning now?"

"Do not question me," she says, her face still holding its pleasant expression. "Enjoy your pastimes and forget about Nurmat. His woes are not yours."

I dismiss her and she leaves me, her steps quick and light despite her pretended limp. I sit for a while thinking of Nurmat's unexpected tears but I know neither of them will tell me the truth. All I can do is continue to ensure that Iparhan does not take my place when I am called to the Emperor's side.

In Yangzhou we ride down the Grand Canal in the imperial barges, flying banners and flags of bright colours. On either bank silk-draped makeshift theatres have been erected. As we pass one and then another performers compete to out-do their rivals on the opposite bank, so that opera songs intermingle and dancers' rhythms blend into one cacophonous sound, neither harmonious nor pleasing.

I wake to find Iparhan standing at the foot of my bed, already dressed in my clothes, her face painted as mine. She throws the cotton maid's robe at me. "Get up," she says. "Today I am taking your place."

I'm immediately wide-awake. "Why?" I ask.

"I want to speak with that painter of the Emperor's," says Iparhan.

I feel protective of Giuseppe. "Why?" I ask, putting on the maid's robe as slowly as I dare.

"He knows more than you have ever bothered finding out," she says. "He has been

Melissa Addey

at court throughout the reign of three Emperors. He knows every building, every palace. He was here when they planned the campaign against our country."

I watch her as she leaves the room but at the door she turns back to me. "Today you will accompany me," she says.

And so I find myself trotting alongside the orange palanquin that I am used to sitting in as Iparhan is carried through streets and courtyards to the house where Giuseppe is staying.

He comes to greet us and I have to stand still rather than advance to meet him. Iparhan emerges from the chair's depths and makes her way to him.

"You will paint my portrait," she begins without preamble, and I see Giuseppe's surprise at her tone, so abrupt compared with how I speak with him. I have never demanded a portrait. He has offered or it has been the Emperor who has commanded him.

He bows, matching her formality. "It will be an honour, Lady He," he says. "I have mostly been requested to paint the building works. It will be pleasant to paint something prettier." He offers a warm smile, but Iparhan does not return it and he looks a little sad, as though he expected better of her – of me.

I feel my hands clench into fists by my side, but I have no choice but to stand here, silent by her palanquin until I am commanded to do otherwise.

Giuseppe bows again. "I will request that my materials are brought to me," he says. "Perhaps you would care to pose out here, in the garden. It is a pleasant day."

Iparhan nods indifferently.

Giuseppe calls for a eunuch and gives his orders. He turns back to Iparhan. "May I offer you some refreshment?" he asks.

Iparhan shakes her head without bothering to answer, as though he were a servant. I want to speak out, want to tell her to be civil to this old man who has been nothing but kind to me, who has treated me like a granddaughter since I came here, even reminding the Emperor of my very existence when I thought he would ignore me forever.

Giuseppe seems to see that no further conversation is forthcoming and in the ensuing silence he arranges his materials, asks Iparhan to take a seat before him and begins his work. But after only a short time Iparhan leans forward.

"You were here when the Emperor planned the campaigns for the conquest of Altishahr, were you not?" she asks.

Giuseppe keeps his gaze on the stretched silk onto which he is painting. "I have been at court since I was a young man," he says.

"The formations of the army are very particular," says Iparhan. "Are the archers always at the front? Their armour does not seem very protective."

Giuseppe pauses in his work and looks up, his face puzzled. "An unusual question," he says. "Are you very fond of military strategy, Lady He?"

Iparhan does not draw back. "I saw many battlefields as a child," she says. "My homeland was conquered. Such images stay long in the memory."

Giuseppe nods, a slow nod. He looks at her face for a long moment and then back down at the silk. "And as an innocent child, who watched those she loved die in battle," he says, with great gentleness, his voice so low that I have to strain to hear it. "Did you swear vengeance on the man whom you now call husband?"

Iparhan's face grows still and she sits back in her chair. "Yes," she says, when the silence has grown too long. Her voice is very low. Suddenly she rises. "I have sat here long enough," she says. "You are well enough acquainted with my face, I believe. You can paint the rest from memory or from the portraits you have already made of me."

The guards and servants quickly arrange themselves about her as she makes her way back to the palanquin. I turn to look at Giuseppe as we depart. He stands alone, in his little garden, looking down at the silk painting, his eyes not seeing what is before him, but something else.

I lie awake at night worrying about what Iparhan might be planning. One night I slip from my bed, past the sleeping eunuch on guard and through my own lavish rooms to the small lodging that houses the servants. I want to know if she leaves the grounds at night.

In the half-light of a lantern carried from my room, I see the kitchen, a washhouse and at last the rooms where the servants sleep. The smells here are of soap and food, of sweat and sleeping breath rather than the rare woods and incense that scent my own rooms.

I stand at the threshold of a room where many bodies are stretched out, wrapped in rough blankets and lying on bedrolls. I look them over, naming them in my head, the maids, the eunuchs. I see Nurmat, who is snoring, probably drunk. Then I spot Iparhan and my heart, which had been racing, slows. She is here, and asleep. I take a deep breath and step away, then move towards the kitchens to find some water for my dry mouth.

The kitchen, when I find it, is dark. I hold the lantern higher but then stumble against something soft at my feet. I lower it and see two bodies. Jiang and Huan. Their bodies are intertwined, Jiang's head resting on Huan's shoulder. They stir in the light and then spring apart.

"My lady!" gasps Jiang. Huan is on his feet already.

I back away. "I only wanted water," I say in a whisper.

Jiang cowers on the floor while Huan, clutching a sleeping-robe about him, hurries past me, head lowered. He is back in moments with water, his bare feet soundless on the floor. He gives me the little bowl and then both of them crouch on the floor before me, heads bowed.

I stand, awkward. I drink a little water and then turn to go. "Thank you," I say. "I am sorry to have disturbed you."

Huan looks up and his face is white in the darkness. "Forgive us," he whispers.

I turn back. "What?"

"Forgive us," he says a little louder and I hear someone stir in the other room.

"What is there to forgive?" I ask.

Huan's head rises a little higher. "Our... we..."

I shake my head. "I'm glad you have found comfort," I say, miserably. "I wish I could." I turn and walk away, back to my own rooms. When I climb into my bed I realise Huan and Jiang have followed me back. Silently, they tuck me back into the bed and when I seem comfortable, they leave me alone in the darkness.

We do not speak of what I saw again but the next day I order that from now on Jiang and Huan, as senior servants, will have a room allocated apart from the others, both here and when we return home. For now, we travel onwards.

Nurmat

H E KNOWS NOW, EVEN IF she has not yet understood.
   I see it in his eyes when I sit at the mirror, painting my face into Hidligh's. I see it in the trembling of his hands as he reaches for more drink, something to drown out the sound of my footsteps leaving him. I hear it in his breath when I we take our places in the servant's sleeping quarters each night, how he lets it go in a sobbing rush when he thinks we are all asleep.

I try to speak with him, to draw him to me so that he can help me but he turns away from me when I approach and shakes his head when I speak with him. I have lost him. He has lost his love for me, I am sure of it. He no longer wants to be by my side.

He does not love Hidligh. I was wrong in that. He saw me in her and loved what he saw, but now he sees that she has changed. She is no longer merely my reflection. She has her own love growing inside her; it is plain to everyone except her. She wants to be free of us – of me. She is afraid of me not for herself but because of what I might do to her new-found happiness and the one she loves.

Our betrothal took place with much celebration. Music was played and all around us people danced. Nurmat's face was full of joy and I was impatient for the fifteen days to pass so that we would be married.

On the tenth day, we saw the Emperor's banners approaching. My father promised us that the delay to our wedding would be short. We would fight off the Emperor as we had done before and our wedding day would be a day to celebrate our victory.

He was wrong.

I have broken Nurmat. I see that now. He was mine, body and soul, heart and mind. Until my plans began to break him. That quick blade in his hand should have warned me that he was breaking, even then. But I pressed on. Hidligh confused him. That one night when I welcomed him into my arms and then turned from him once more broke him as surely as if I had never lain with him. I made him play the part of a eunuch and then when he had proven his loyalty over and over again I showed him my true plans and took away all he had longed for.

Now he is alone in his misery. He cannot turn to Hidligh, for she believes him still mine. He cannot turn to me, for I have broken him. My desire for blood has ripped him apart.

To whom can he turn in his misery? Perhaps only to drink and oblivion.

Ula Nara

THE CITY OF SUZHOU BRINGS us close to the end of our journey. Criss-crossed with waterways to be navigated on boats or over tiny bridges, it is a beautiful place. The Emperor is fond of its famous gardens.

"You must see them," he says to us all as we enter the city. "Although they have all sorts of fairytales to tell you about them – rocks split by swords and other nonsense. But they are certainly beautiful." He leans closer to me, so that he can whisper his next words in my ear. "There is even a maze in the Lion Grove Garden," he says, his warm breath against my throat. I laugh and blush, thinking of our first night together, and he leans back in his seat, smiling. "It winds through dark twisted rocks made of *taihu* stone which seem to take on every kind of shape," he adds.

"Like lions?"

"Lions," he agrees. "But many other forms too. You must see it for yourself."

We enter the city on our decorated boats, sailing down the Grand Canal, so that the people may see their Emperor. The canal is lined with his subjects and music is played on the banks. Singers compete to draw our attention and everywhere are hung lanterns in bright reds and oranges. The ladies of the court add their own decorative styles to the boats, each competing in her lavish robes to outdo the next. The onlookers gape at our hair, our jewels, our clothes. They throw themselves on their knees and kowtow to us as we pass by. Even in a city known for its fine cloth and embroideries, we stand out.

Sitting close to the Emperor is the Empress Ula Nara, today resplendent in her imperial yellow with a diadem of towering golden birds and dangling pearls. Her face, though, is set and pale. Despite the bulk of her robes she seems still thinner than when I last saw her. Her hands are growing bony and they twist in her lap as though in pain.

"Are you sick? Smile," commands the Empress Dowager. She's bad-tempered today, weary of the constant traveling which apparently is all for her benefit. She is more than seventy years old and would probably prefer to stay at home but her son has wandering feet and the constant journeys – to the Summer Palace, the hunting grounds, the Southern Tours – are beginning to put a strain on her, although according to him they are all done for her benefit. She indulges him by pretending it's so. She chastises him for his gifts to her, which are many and priceless, but he doesn't listen. It makes him happy to be generous.

Ula Nara bows her head and when she raises it her lips are curved in an unhappy mockery of a smile. She stretches out a trembling hand and places it on the Emperor's sleeve, as though to draw his attention, but at that moment he sees ahead a group of local high ranking officials waiting for us to arrive and stands, ready to step ashore, causing her small gesture to go unnoticed. As I step out I see her watching me, her eyes narrowed. I bow my head but she only continues to gaze at me as though I were doing something that requires all her attention. A bowing official indicates which way she should walk and at last she turns to follow him, her steps a little unsteady as though her mind is elsewhere. I watch her go and feel a shudder pass over me. There is something growing in her, an anger or a pain that needs to be appeased, and I am afraid that only my own destruction will bring her relief.

Two days after our arrival, as the lanterns are being lit, I make my way from the garden of my allotted palace to my bedchamber and come across Jiang in the walkway, who has just left the room. He stops and regards me with something approaching horror.

"What is it?" I ask, concerned.

"I – you," stammers Jiang. He looks back at the closed bedroom door. "I just left your ladyship in your room and yet – you are here."

I feel my stomach drop. Jiang turns back towards the door, his outstretched to open it. "Jiang!" I say, as loudly as possible. "What is the *matter* with you?"

The door swings open and reveals an empty room. I feel the air come back to my lungs. Jiang looks about the room, confused. My tone of hysteria is not forced. "Are you *drunk*, Jiang?"

"No, my lady! I swear!"

"I will have you beaten if you are," I say, unforgiving.

"I swear, my lady!"

"Huan!" I call, at the top of my voice. Jiang turns back to me and behind him, in the room, I see Iparhan, dressed as me, drop down from her hiding place – she had been pressed flat against the ceiling, as she once did in the house in the dunes. Now she slips behind the curtains of my bed and waits.

Huan comes at a run. "My lady?"

"Jiang is drunk or seeing things. Tell him, Jiang."

Haltingly, Jiang explains. "I – saw her ladyship in her bedroom, she was dressing. Then I left her room and then – and then I saw her again, in front of me, here on the walkway, but dressed differently."

Huan sounds concerned. "I recall when your ladyship first came to us," he says, "You mentioned a dead sister whom you resembled. Perhaps her spirit is unhappy."

Huan has given me a way out. "Perhaps," I say slowly.

Huan takes charge at once. "We must perform an exorcism," he declares.

"An exorcism?" I repeat – but I'm talking to the air. Huan has already left the room to arrange matters, Jiang trotting anxiously behind him.

I enter my bedchamber and close the door. Iparhan emerges from her hiding place.

"We were nearly found out!" I say. "Why would you take such a risk?"

"I was in a hurry," she says, calm. "Hurry up and change before they catch us again."

I'm aghast at her lack of care. "They shouldn't have been given the chance to catch us at all!"

"Nurmat should have been guarding the door," says Iparhan, helping me to change.

"Why wasn't he?" I ask. "Is he turning against your plans?"

She does not answer.

The exorcism lasts three days. Altars are constructed in the garden and are surrounded by representations of what appear to be hundreds of benevolent spirits. There are monks everywhere. There is so much incense I can barely breathe and the interminable chanting and ringing of gongs begins to grate on my nerves.

I find my own way to punish Iparhan by insisting that the exorcism is so frightening that I must have her by my side, to fan me and offer me sips of fortifying teas. She glowers at me. Her eyes are red from all the incense. They make her look exhausted.

"Look at what you are doing," I say to her under cover of the endless chanting around us. "You are drawing attention to me. You are risking being found out. Whatever you have planned I'm sure it doesn't involve being discovered?" I try to stop my voice sounding pleading. "You surely need to keep me alive?"

She looks at me but her eyes are unsteady, as though she can hardly see me, although our faces are only two hands apart. "What good is your life to me?" she says. "I should throw you out on the street where you belong." She fans me, her hands poorly coordinated so that the fan moves erratically.

"I've done nothing to you," I say. "Think of what you have done to me."

She pauses in her fanning. "Brought you to a place where you are well cared for," she says. Her words sound almost slurred, as though she has repeated them so often in her mind that the words all run into each other. "A place where you are fed, watered, dressed, served. Befriended. Loved, even."

"A place where I am controlled," I say to her. "Threatened, put at risk, kept in the dark."

The chanting rises to a crescendo and Iparhan lowers the fan. "Loved," she says very slowly. "What is it like to be loved, Hidligh? Not as your lover wishes you were, but as you are?"

"As *I* am?" I repeat. "An actor playing a part? A puppet controlled by a madwoman? I cannot be myself until you are gone from my life, Iparhan."

She looks away. "I hope it will not be long, then," she says. "I am ready to go."

I take a deep breath and nearly choke again. I feel sick enough, miserable and afraid enough to ask the question to which I do not really want to hear the answer. "Will I be alive when you do?"

She shrugs. "Who knows," she says, her eyes blinking against the clouds of incense, her voice unsteady. "Who cares?"

I call for Huan then and tell him that despite the warm summer evening I feel cold, that he must bring me a thicker jacket. And that Iparhan can go back to her quarters.

The Emperor is still caught up in endless tours of inspection and rituals to be performed.

The vermillion ink used only by him marks hundreds of documents presented to him by black-inked scribes, detailing local taxes, noble houses, military ranks and endless, endless petitions.

"He has the Empress with him, anyway," I say to Huan sadly. "He will not miss me."

Huan shakes his head. "The Empress has not accompanied him since the first day we arrived in Suzhou," he says. "She is pleading illness."

"Maybe she'll leave me alone then," I say.

I spot Giuseppe again in a crowd of courtiers. "How are you?" I ask.

He bows but does not smile. "I am well, your ladyship."

I want to beg his forgiveness for how Iparhan behaved – how it must appear to him that I was rude and vengeful, but there is nothing I can say. " I would like to see the portrait," I say, smiling.

He looks at me for a long moment. "There is still work to be done on it," he says. "My memory is not as good as it once was."

"Should - should I sit for you again?" I ask, hoping to spend time with him again so that I can erase his memories of Iparhan.

"It is not necessary, my lady," he says, "and if you will excuse me I must speak with that gentleman." He leaves me standing alone and makes his way over to a court official.

"You are destroying my friendships," I say to Iparhan. "Giuseppe barely speaks to me now."

"Why would you want to speak with him?" she asks. "He is a doddering old fool."

"He has been like a grandfather to me," I say, unguarded.

She turns on me. "You don't have a grandfather, Hidligh. You have no family at all. Your supposed family wants only the favours and riches that your position brings. No one cares whether you are dead or alive. Remember that."

I turn away from her and do not speak to her of Giuseppe again.

Remembering the Emperor's enthusiasm for the local sights I set out late one morning to see some of the better known ones. The Garden of Books proves beautiful, as promised, with scenes arranged around a central pond, designed to recreate fairy tales. My guide, a stout local official, is delighted to have a favourite of the Emperor's as his guest and he tells one tall tale after another as the sun reaches its peak.

"And Tiger Hill," he says. "Have you visited that yet?"

I shake my head.

"Oh, but your ladyship must go there!" he cries. "It is said that to visit our city and not to visit Tiger Hill is not to have visited at all."

Once at Tiger Hill my guide enthuses about the Sword-Testing Rock – the one the Emperor dismissed as nonsense; a huge, perilously leaning pagoda that I decline to climb, fearing for my safety; as well as the Pond of Swords.

"There is a great treasure buried beneath those waters," my guide assures me. "Three thousand swords, each of legendary sharpness and with jewel-encrusted handles."

I nod, as though impressed, although I can't help thinking they must surely be covered in moss and mud by now. The afternoon is warm and before we leave he dips a bowl of water for me from the Spring of Simplicity and Honesty whilst telling me of its appearance to a water-carrying monk.

"And now the maze of the Lion Grove Gardens, your ladyship," he says, as twilight approaches. "We can be there in only a short while."

"May I walk in it alone?" I ask. He's a good-natured man and means well but his constant chatter is beginning to weary me.

The official is disappointed but he can't disagree with me. Once we reach the gardens he positions himself at the entrance. "I will wait here for you," he promises.

The garden has been cleared so that I can have it to myself, and it seems very silent. Lanterns have already been lit, although dusk has not yet fallen. I enter the maze.

It's made up of nine paths, which twist and turn through twenty-one caves, set on three different levels. It's not like the flat, easy walkways of the maze at the Summer Palace. I have to keep a hand on the walls to ensure I don't slip, for the path itself is rough in places and its changing levels, together with my high-heeled shoes, threaten the wellbeing of my ankles. But the rocks seem alive, misshapen and molded like no other rocks I've ever seen. You don't need a fanciful imagination to see creatures, people, trees, both commonplace and those escaped from some twisted storyteller's mind or the realms of the Immortals. Tiny lanterns cast flickering shadows in the darker areas, making the shapes come to life.

The silence, which I'd thought would be a relief, becomes eerie when I've walked for some time. I can hear water from the various pools and waterfalls, occasional birdsong and the breeze in the trees above me but nothing else. I'm unused to being so alone now, and find it a little unsettling. I'm about to turn back when an unexpected sound startles me. A whistling followed by a thump, like no bird I have ever heard before, followed by another and then another. Once I listen to it closely, it's oddly familiar although I can't place it.

I step through an archway of crooked shapes and make my way down a new path, wondering whether I will, in fact, be able to find my way back out of here. I suppose if I called out loudly enough the eager official would come rushing to my aid. Meanwhile I follow the source of the sound through the maze until I step past a little curve in the rocks and see before me an open area, still filled with the twisted rocks, but looking out over a pond and trees. The sound comes again and suddenly I know what it is and have to stop myself from ducking.

"Missed you," says Iparhan. Another dagger flies close by and embeds itself in a tree in the middle of the pond, its trunk studded with daggers. She's wearing my clothes, hairstyle and makeup and to see myself, or what appears to be myself, throwing daggers with such accuracy is frightening. By her side is a small heap of daggers and a thick jacket, which she's taken off and thrown carelessly to the ground.

"Stop that," I say.

She lowers her hand and looks at me. "What's the matter, Hidligh?" she asks in a mocking tone.

"You did not tell me we were swapping places today."

She shrugs and another dagger goes flying. "I heard that the Emperor was on his way here. It seemed too good an opportunity to miss. You were nowhere to be found."

I look quickly over my shoulder but the garden is deserted except for us. "How do you know the Emperor is on his way here?"

"I make it my business to know," she says.

"Why don't you make it your business to be more careful?" I ask her. "You are growing careless, Iparhan. Jiang has already seen us together. Now you are wandering about the city, dressed as me when I do not know you are doing so – what if others see us? How many times do you think we can be so lucky?"

"Ah, Hidligh."

I look up to see Nurmat emerging from the rocks behind me. His eyes are bloodshot and his walk is slow.

I look at him and shake my head. "You're drunk again."

He shrugs and sits down on a sleeping lion rock a little way off, pulls out a bottle and drinks. Iparhan ignores him. She stops throwing daggers and begins to pace back and forth like a beast caged for too long, her face twitching and her mouth moving silently, perhaps reciting a long list of the Emperor's wrongdoings to her family and country.

"Stop that," I say. "Be quiet. I can hear something." I stand, then grab hold of a rock and pull myself up so that I can see across the gardens. My shoes slip and I break a nail shield in the process. An imperial yellow palanquin is making its way into the gardens, some way off. I slip back down.

"Is he here?" asks Iparhan, Her voice is too keen for my liking, her eagerness is making me nervous. I am afraid she is growing less and less cautious, throwing all of us into danger.

"No," I say, playing for time. "I was mistaken."

She turns back to her heap of daggers and throws another. The thud it makes when it hits the tree brings a cold shiver down my back. I sit down next to Nurmat. He reeks of alcohol, his breath is sour with it and his breathing comes heavily from his half-open mouth.

"Why does she want to see him so urgently?" I mutter to him.

"Probably wants to make love to him," he slurs. "Whore."

I want to slap him for saying what's in my mind. "Shut up," I spit. "Take that filthy bottle out of your mouth and dunk your head in the pond. You need to be sober."

"What for?" he asks. "She's going to be off there shortly, rubbing up against him, whispering sweet words – you know it as well as I do."

"Do you know what will happen if we are found out?" I hiss.

"She'll be killed," says Nurmat. He drinks again from the bottle. "She'll be dead, I'll be dead. You'll be dead. Inevitable, don't you think? Nothing left to do now but wait. And drink," he adds, lifting the bottle once more.

I knock the bottle out of his hand and press my face close to his, the stink of his breath hot on my cheek. "We need to get her away from him." I whisper urgently, while Iparhan throws another dagger. "Neither of us wants things to end this way; this was never the plan. You were supposed to be here to help me get whatever information she wanted. Then you and she were going to go away and leave me to a peaceful life. That's what you wanted, isn't it? A life with her? If we are found out..." I can't even finish the thought. "Help me, Nurmat," I beg, kneeling in front of him and shaking his shoulders. "Think of something we can do."

He tilts his head back to look at me, and laughs out loud. "Like what?" he asks. "Like what, Hidligh? Like what? You're still clinging to what you believe is the plan. You're a fool, girl, as big a fool as I am. Iparhan lied to me. She lied to you. She told us both a fairytale, that all of this would lead to glory for our country and love for me and her together. That you would be left with a full belly and a warm bed." His voice grows louder and more ragged. He is half sobbing. "The night you entered the Forbidden City she took me into her bed and gave me her maidenhood. And she whispered such lies, Hidligh. She said it would all be over soon." He puts his head in his hands and for a few moments he sobs. Iparhan, further down the path, does not turn towards us, though she cannot fail to hear him. She throws one dagger after another, faster and faster, as through to drown out the sound of his grief.

I watch him with pity. I can't help remembering him as he was when I first met him, full of hope for his future with Iparhan. I sigh and squat down beside him. "It can still be over," I say, although I'm not sure I believe my own words. "If we can just..."

Nurmat looks up at me. His eyes are filled with tears. "Do you know why she took me to her bed that night, Hidligh?"

"Because she loves you," I say.

He shakes his head. "You're still clinging to hope, Hidligh," he says. "She took me in her arms because she was still a virgin and she believed you were about to be deflowered by the Emperor. She knew she would take your place one day and she could not be a virgin if the Emperor took her to his bedchamber. She used my love for her, my desire for her, to make herself more like you. Do you know how angry she was when she found out he had not yet taken you to his bed? She could not take your place until you, too, had lost your virginity. That is the only reason why she arrived at court so late."

There's a sound nearby and both of us spring to our feet and look about for the source of it. Without our having noticed, a palanquin has made its way down our path. It's decked out in imperial yellow silks and I freeze, expecting the Emperor to have somehow arrived from a different direction. I try to dab my face with my sleeves while Nurmat kicks at the smashed bottle with his toe so that the broken shards enter the lake.

The bearers, faces blank as though our presence here were expected, set down the chair so that the occupant can climb out. A shoe entwined with pearls emerges and my heart sinks. This is the chair of the Empress Ula Nara.

Once out of the chair she stands blinking, as though she cannot see us, even though it is not yet fully dark and there are lanterns all around. She gestures to the bearers and they disappear behind the bend in the path, out of sight and hearing.

I try to think how to present myself to her but I know that I'm ruined. I'm in a deserted garden with my cook, who is drunk. By my feet lie daggers and a crumpled jacket that appears as though I've removed it and lain on it. I might as well have been in Nurmat's arms. A little way beyond us is Iparhan, who has slowly turned to face us, presenting the Empress with the extraordinary vision of my double, a woman alike to me in every way except that she is holding a dagger in her hand.

Suddenly Iparhan drops the dagger and runs. She moves fast and in a brief moment she is gone. I am alone with the Empress and Nurmat.

I fall to my knees in the dust and kowtow to her, as does Nurmat. While he remains kneeling respectfully on the path as befits a servant, I rise and face her.

Ula Nara is very pale and thin, the pink painted on her cheeks making her look fevered rather than flushed with health. Her robe hangs loose on her and her neck and hands are beginning to look skeletal. She looks at me and at Nurmat, at the crumpled jacket on the path, the daggers. She looks beyond me to where Iparhan has fled.

"How can there be so much treachery in one place?" she asks at last, and her voice is broken, hoarse.

I look down. I don't know where to begin to answer her – I cannot even think what plea would be strong enough. What am I to explain to her? Everything? Nothing? The truth? A lie? There can be no lie that would account for what she has seen.

When I look up the Empress is still standing there, swaying slightly as though she too were drunk. Then she speaks, slowly. "You have been loyal to me," she says. "I will not forget it."

I frown. "Your Majesty?"

But her eyes are on Nurmat and it's Nurmat who answers from his place on the dusty path. "I live only to serve you, Your Majesty," he says, his eyes bloodshot from the drink.

I stare at him. "Nurmat?"

He returns my shocked gaze with a righteous glare. "Now your ladyship will be punished for your transgressions," he says. "For attempting to seduce a eunuch servant of your household. For having treasonous intentions towards the Emperor, spurred on by traitorous rebels from Xinjiang with whom you secretly corresponded in Beijing. Her Majesty the Empress will see to it that you forfeit your life for these crimes."

I gape at him and then look to the Empress. "I—" I begin, but she holds up a hand to stop me.

"You traitorous, lust-ridden bitch," she says to me. She's angry but I can feel her pleasure and relief, too, at being able to accuse me at last. "I will have you killed for this and then the Emperor will see how wrong he was to care for you. He will reward those who are loyal to him."

"Your Majesty—" I begin.

"You can deny nothing," she says. "Your own servant has testified against you."

I put out a hand but she steps away in disgust and fear. "Don't touch me," she says. "Or I will scream."

I draw back and she makes her way, unsteadily, to her palanquin. Before she climbs into it she pauses, her thin hand clutching at the yellow silk curtain of her chair. "Your country is a treacherous pit of mongrel dogs," she says. "It does not surprise me that we have been sent two of its bitches to commit treason against the Emperor. You will all die for this."

She dips her head to enter the chair and then the bearers, still blank-faced, lift her and are gone.

I turn on Nurmat. "You two-faced bastard," I hiss. "*You* were her spy. You were supposed to help *me*, Nurmat. I trusted you. I thought you wanted what I wanted, for all of this to be over."

"I wanted the Empress to send you away," he says, his face still hidden from me, his forehead resting in the dirt. "If she sent you away Iparhan could not come into the palace in your stead, could not go and whore herself with the Emperor."

"Send me *away*? The Empress will have me killed!"

At last he looks up. His shoulders are slumped. He shrugs. "You're a dirty little street rat," he says. "If you hadn't been born she would have lived a happy life with me after I scarred her. You made her obsession rise again. If it wasn't for you we could have been happy. Who cares what happens to you?"

I slap him hard across the face. "You deceiving piece of filth," I say. "I hope the Empress finds Iparhan right now and has her executed."

He's on his feet in a moment although he stumbles. "I must get her away from here," he says.

I pull at his clothes. Despite everything I've just learned, after all that we've been through, I still can't help thinking of Nurmat as my ally, my friend. "What about me?"

He pushes me away so hard that I fall on the path. "Get out of my way," he spits. And he's gone, running down the path and then through a small entranceway in the rocks.

I lie in the dust and let my body go limp. Slowly I finger the silk of my skirt. I try to think. If I can remove some of the more elaborate items, will I pass as a rich young woman rather than a concubine? Could I escape into the streets again? I shake my head, my braids rolling in the dirt. Every item of clothing I now possess is too magnificent even for a rich woman. And everything I wear marks me out as a foreigner.

"Your ladyship!" A shadow falls over me and I look up into the eyes of the eager official, who is white with fear. "Your ladyship! Have you been taken ill?" He bends over me, half afraid of touching me, more afraid of leaving me there in the dirt of the rocky path. At last he tentatively holds out a hand to me, which I take, then carefully lifts me to my feet. I stand and wait for him to call for the guards, for the Emperor to appear. Instead he stands and stares at me, at a loss for words.

At last I speak. "The Emperor," I begin.

"His Majesty is waiting for you," says the official, relieved to have something to say to me. "He said he would like to see you, to walk with you in the gardens. I – I should have come sooner – is it the coldness of the evening after the warmth of the day that has affected you, or…?"

I frown. No mention of the Emperor's wrath, no mention of Iparhan. No mention, either, of Empress Ula Nara. "The heat, I mean cold, yes," I say. "I felt a little faint…"

Now the official is all action. Tenderly he makes me sit on a rock, rushes away to call for my bearers and in moments I'm seated in my chair and heading along the little paths to the main gardens, whether the Emperor awaits me. Along the way I'm passed water, fans, even tea by the poor man and I thank him with tears in my eyes. He may be the last person to treat me with such care. For his part, his relief in having found me is tempered only with fear that the Emperor will hear that he has failed in his duties towards me, that he will be punished for returning me in so poor a state. I should comfort him better but I do not have the strength for it.

We round a corner and my palanquin comes to a halt. I put out my hand through the curtain to the official but a larger hand takes mine.

"Were you lost?" asks the Emperor, smiling, as he helps me out.

I stand before him, my legs trembling. I lock my knees so that I will not fall. I try to smile. "A little," I say, unable to think what else to reply.

The Emperor chuckles. "I thought you were an expert at navigating mazes," he teases. He sees the official hovering and nods to him to leave, which he does with much bowing. "Let us walk," he says to me. "Have you enjoyed the gardens?"

"Yes," I say. I can't think of any more words.

We stroll through the gardens, past flowers of all colours and pools of water. The Emperor seems happy to be silent and my mind is in so much turmoil that I can think of nothing to speak of. I wonder, for a mad moment, whether I should confess all and beg him to protect me, but why should he believe me? Iparhan would no doubt claim that she was the 'real' concubine and perhaps the family would be brought in to verify my – our – identity, which can only lead to certain death for us all. We walk on in silence, the servants following along behind us at some distance.

At last we come to a little clearing, with a tall tree surrounded by banks of flowers. The path from here leads to the exit of the gardens. The Emperor pauses to admire the flowers, then looks up as a eunuch enters the clearing. "Yes?"

The eunuch bows. "Her Majesty the Empress is unwell. She requests your presence."

I freeze, feel my hand clutch the Emperor's. But he does not seem unduly worried.

"Tell Her Majesty that I will join her shortly," he says. He pulls me closer to him. "I must leave you," he says. "But I will call for you as soon as I can." He smiles down at me, then kisses me lightly and releases me.

But I am overcome with a desperate desire. I reach out and grab at his sleeve as he turns from me. Surprised, he turns back, and I press myself to his chest. "Kiss me again," I say. I cannot bear the thought that the last kiss he ever gives me might be one so lightly bestowed, a gentle kiss. I need a kiss that I can take with me when I die, a kiss to comfort me from the torment of being wrenched away from him.

He laughs at my ferocity and crushes me to him, his arms tight about me. He kisses me, at first gently and then with a growing desire. I allow my hands to move down his robe, below his jeweled belt and fumble with the folds of thick silk, lifting them so that my hands can slip beneath and touch his skin. He pauses in kissing me for a moment, his eyes grown dark. He makes a gesture with one hand behind me and I hear the shuffle of feet as the servants back away, rounding a corner where they cannot be seen nor see us. They will hear us, but I find I do not care. The Emperor has backed me against the tree and I push back against it as he lifts me up, so that my legs are wrapped about his waist while he holds me, his arms crushing me, my hair catching in the bark. I don't feel the pain, I am too caught up in the pleasure as he enters me, my skirts pulled up, my waistcoat ripped open so that he can see my breasts through the gauze of my shirt. He buries his face in them while I grip his shoulders and cry out.

It's over too fast. I want the moment to go on forever, to stay in this clearing, where we are alone and suspended for this moment in time where I have yet to be found out.

He laughs, a little breathless. "What are you doing to me?" he says. "I have never done such a thing."

"Never?" I ask. "

He looks down at me and brushes bits of bark out of my hair. His eyes are very dark. "I have never been so overwhelmed with desire for a woman," he says, his voice low. "You have bewitched me."

I press my face against his chest, hear his heart beating fast beneath the yellow silk. "Let us stay here forever," I say, my voice breaking a little.

He smiles as he pulls away from me. "I wish we could," he says. He is regretful. "I must go to Her Majesty and see that she is well taken care of," he says. "But I will call for you very soon."

I try to think of some way to keep him with me but there is nothing I can say. He walks away from me and I watch him go and have to bite my lip hard to stop from crying out to him.

Inside my palace the servants are gathered, expecting me. Among them stands Iparhan in her plain blue cotton robe, her face now scraped clean of makeup, her scar fully visible. I look at her but she looks away.

"The Emperor sent word that you are to join him this evening," says Jiang, looking worried at the state of my clothing and hair. "We must hurry, there is hardly any time to prepare you."

I begin to shake. The Empress has already spoken with him. I will be sentenced to death for adultery, impersonation, treason…

I eat nothing; drink nothing. I don't speak whilst I'm prepared. When I climb into my chair to be taken to the Emperor's palace, I clutch hold of Huan's hand for a moment.

"Goodbye," I say, struggling to keep my voice steady. I want to thank him, to tell Huan how much his care and kindness have mattered to me. I want to tell him that he has been a father to me, a shrieking, fussing, mother hen of a father that I have grown to love as a daughter. But I cannot say any of this even though it's likely that I will never see him again. "Goodbye," I repeat, holding his hand more tightly in both of mine.

He looks puzzled but pats my trembling hands with his free hand. "Good night, my lady. I hope your evening is enjoyable. I will wait up for you should you return to us this evening."

Tears well up in my eyes. I let go of his hand and turn my head away, gesturing for the drapes to be closed around me.

The journey across the city is too quick. I'm not yet ready to face the Emperor and I call to the bearers to take a longer route. They ignore me. I may be their mistress but the Emperor cannot be kept waiting.

I find him in the gardens of the palace in which he is staying, accompanied by Giuseppe. He's beaming. "I have been telling Lang Shining about our walk," he says, a mischievous smile on his lips suggesting that he has not told the old man the truth of our time together. "The gardens are pleasant, are they not? It is a shame the Empress was taken ill and we had to interrupt our time together, but here we are again."

"Is – is she better now?" I ask.

He nods, dismissing the topic. "The heat, I believe," he says. "She was weeping when I arrived and I ordered that she should be taken back to her own palace to rest before we speak together." He turns back to Giuseppe. "And Lang Shining has been painting you again," he says, full of interest. "You must be his favourite subject – with all the travels we have made he still finds time to paint you rather than the scenery. All these days whilst I have been busy he has been painting you. Come and see the finished work."

I make my way forwards, wondering if this is a trick. Will guards rush out to seize me? But he's still smiling and as I join them he holds out his arm to me.

I daren't look him in the eye and so I address Giuseppe as I reach the Emperor's side and try to keep my voice steady. "Are you well, Giuseppe?" I ask.

He looks up at me. "Yes, my lady," he says, although he does not sound as warm as he usually does. "The portrait you requested is complete."

The Emperor laughs. "Giuseppe says he has chosen another unusual costume for you," he says.

Giuseppe turns the large portrait so I can see it. I step back.

The portrait shows a woman in full armour, her face filled with military fervour. Her broad high cheekbones and full lips are encased within a helmet topped with plumes. Long dark hair peeps out from the back of the helmet. One hand rests on her sword, the other on her hip. It's a portrait of a warrior woman posing victorious after a conquest.

It's a portrait of Iparhan.

We may look alike to those who don't know us well, but there are differences, of course; we're not twins. Looking at the picture I see how the woman's nose and chin are shaped differently to mine, how her neck is a little longer. There's a dimple in the chin like mine but I have watched Iparhan recreate that dimple with powders. There's no scar, but this is Iparhan's face.

The Emperor is delighted. "Here you are as a warrior," he says, chuckling. "Like a Manchu of old! It is all the riding you like to do." He puts an arm about my waist and pulls me closer. I try to move into his embrace, to feel the warmth of it, but I'm too much afraid. I turn towards Giuseppe, who is looking at the portrait and then at me, as though something is bothering him.

"I have seen a new side to Lady He of late," he says slowly. "She spoke of many things with me while she sat for this portrait. Of battles, of the Emperor's armies and their tactics."

The Emperor is still contentedly examining the portrait, ignoring Giuseppe's words. "She is happy here," he declares with satisfaction. "It has made her look more confident. Why, I remember her arrival. She was barely a girl and trembling with fear. I thought she was nothing but a child the first time I saw her." He chuckles. "Now she is a warrior. I will have it hung in a place of prominence when we return to the Forbidden City."

I smile politely. There seems to be no trick. The Emperor is happy. The Empress has not yet spoken with him but she may do so at any moment and my life here – my life anywhere – will be over when she does. I take the Emperor's hand in mine and feel his warmth and strength. I squeeze it tighter, hoping somehow to keep that feeling with me for the future. He clasps my hand in return, smiling down at the portrait.

Giuseppe stands behind me. "Is all well with you, Lady He?" he asks. He looks at me and then turns back to the painting, then back to me, waiting for an answer.

There is nothing I can say to him that can be said. "Yes," I say. "It is a fine portrait. Thank you."

"Come, it is time to eat," says the Emperor and I go with him, leaving Giuseppe standing there with the portrait of Iparhan, looking from the image to my departing back, a confused old man.

Huan comes running into the sitting room. He's shaking and his face is white. "The Empress Ula Nara," he gasps.

Iparhan, squatting over a tea that she is brewing, rises to her feet.

Slowly, I set down my fan. "What about her?"

"She has gone mad."

"What?"

Jiang joins us, his usually neat robes crumpled, sweating from running. "The Empress has cut her hair."

I frown. "Her hair?"

They nod, their faces pale.

I fumble to understand the meaning of this news, thinking of all the times Huan has cut my hair, to keep it smooth and fine and its thickness even. I glance towards Iparhan but her face tells me nothing. "Is she… not allowed to cut her hair?"

Huan shakes his head. "She has cut it *all* off."

I try to imagine any lady of the court without their towering hair, shimmering with flowers and gems. Even bald Lady Wan is never seen without her magnificent wigs. "None of the ladies has short hair," I say at last. "Why would she want short hair?"

Huan is frantically waving his hands. "Your ladyship does not understand," he says. "It means the Emperor is dead."

I feel the air leave my body and find myself half-standing, my hands clutching the arms of my chair, my legs trembling. "The Emperor is *dead*?"

They realise their mistake and hurry to reassure me. "No, no!" says Jiang. "The Emperor is alive and well. But when an Empress cuts off all her hair it means the Emperor is dead. It is done only when a senior member of the imperial family dies, and senior to Ula Nara are only the Empress Dowager or the Emperor. She has gravely insulted either the Emperor or his mother."

"So you see," says Huan, "the Empress Ula Nara has gone mad. There is no other possible explanation."

I sink back down into my chair and try to think while I catch my breath. The Empress saw Iparhan and I in the Lion Maze, and became ill, fainted. She has not been seen until now.

"Perhaps she is still unwell," I say, wondering whether I can blame anything she may say against me on hallucinations brought on by a fever.

"*Yes*," agrees Huan, vigorously nodding, relieved that I have at last grasped the severity of the situation. "She has gone *mad.*"

Whispers fly through the city and our departure is delayed for days while the court awaits the Emperor's punishment. It comes sooner than expected. I've barely risen, the day is still cool and the sky still pale when Jiang comes to me, Huan hovering behind him, anxious. I'm pulling on a thick blue silk jacket with wide sleeves over my clothes.

"What is it?"

Jiang's voice barely rises above a whisper. "The Empress is to be sent home," he murmurs.

"Home?"

"Back to Beijing."

"Alone?"

"With a small retinue of guards."

"Did the Emperor order this?"

"Yes."

We're silent for a few moments. Such an action is unheard of – although so was her cutting off her long hair in defiance of every protocol.

"Has he said why?"

"He says she insulted his mother."

I frown. "Empress Ula Nara insulted the Empress Dowager? How? Ula Nara is her favourite."

"It is not known."

I shake my head. "You have to do better than that, Jiang. What is being said?"

His voice drops so low I have to lean forward so that he's almost whispering in my ear. "It is said that she was jealous of the Emperor's love for another woman. The Empress Dowager and she argued and Ula Nara struck her."

Despite the shock of the Empress striking the Empress Dowager all my focus is on the other thing he said. I try hard not to be jealous but… "What other woman?"

Jiang draws back a little and looks at me. He does not speak but makes a small gesture forwards with his chin towards me.

"Me?"

He nods.

I can't help it. My lips curve into a smile although it fades quickly. "And why would she cut off her hair?"

Jiang hesitates and my heart sinks. "Well? Tell me."

"It is only rumours."

"Talk, Jiang."

He is careful. "The Empress Ula Nara made… accusations."

"Of what?"

"That – that the Emperor's life was in danger from you. She cut her hair to warn him that he was about to die. She said she had seen ghosts and warriors with daggers and…" He makes a face. "She is mad."

Suddenly I am calm. This, then, is the moment I have been dreading. This is the moment when the Emperor will find out all there is to know about me, for who knows what Nurmat has told the Empress and what she in turn, after those moments in the Lion Maze, has said to the Emperor. This is the moment when I may lose my place here – lose my life, even. But I will not sit here, waiting to be summoned. I will fight to live; fight to stay here. I think of Lady Wan, Huan and Jiang, my animals, Giuseppe, Consorts Qing and Ying and the little prince. I may have come here to fill my belly, but time has passed. I want to stay here now, even if I were to starve. I think of the Emperor's face, think of his arms about me, the smell and warmth of him and stand up. "Where is she?"

Jiang and Huan step back, alarmed. "You cannot go near her!"

"I have to. Fetch my chair."

Iparhan, who has been listening in silence, approaches me "I will go," she says, low enough for Jiang not to hear her.

I don't pause. "No," I say loudly. "Stay here, Iparhan."

The three of them walk backwards before me, trying to change my mind but I make my way past them into the garden of my palace and wait until my chair is brought. Then I give directions and Huan and Jiang, unable to disobey, are forced to trot alongside me along with a few other servants. I look out of the window and see Iparhan standing at the gates of my palace, watching us depart. The speed of my departure has wrong-footed her. We make our way across little bridges and down tiny lanes towards the Empress' allotted palace.

I arrive to find three imperial yellow chairs set down amongst the blazing scarlet flowers of her courtyard. The Emperor and Empress Dowager are here. The courtyard is full of servants – mine, the Emperor's, the Empress Dowager's, Empress Ula Nara's. They stand about, awkward and desperate for orders. I step from my chair and hold up a hand to forbid anyone from following me then make my way, unannounced, into the palace. Inside a maid sees me and backs away, helpless. She's too young and lowly to know what to do about my approach, neither announcing me nor preventing me from entering. I follow her terrified eyeline and walk into the receiving hall.

The Emperor is seated on a carved throne and the Empress Dowager is standing by a window, her face turned away. They look strange before I realise I have never seen them alone before. Always, there are servants present. Now there are only the three of us in the room.

Four of us. A strange gasping sound comes from a corner of the room. I turn that way and see Ula Nara, half lying on the floor.

She's wearing imperial yellow but her robe is dusty and unwashed. It hangs badly on her, for she's lost weight even since I last saw her and her belt has been pulled too tight trying to correct the difference in size, making crumpled folds instead of smooth lines. Her feet are bare, with dirty soles. Her skinny hands protrude from the wide sleeves of her robe and her golden nail shields are broken to different jagged lengths. But for once protocol is correct, for more shocking than all of this is her hair.

It's been cut raggedly, by her own hand, so that one strand of shoulder-length hair falls lop-sided, behind her left ear. The rest is cut very short, but in clumps, with some parts of her skull now all but bald and others clad in thick chunks of dark hair, like a moulting black camel. The hair itself is dirty, lank where it's long and stiffly greasy at its shortest. Her white scalp shows through in patches, giving her a mangy appearance.

I stop when I see her but as soon as she spots me she lets out a wail and points towards me. Her voice is hoarse with crying and I step back.

"They want to kill you," she screeches at the Emperor. "I swear I am telling the truth! She has a twin, a sister! I saw them – first one with her lover the cook, both of them with daggers, embracing. And then the other one – walking with you. There are two of them and they mean to kill you!"

I look towards the Emperor and his eyes meet mine. His face is stern but his eyes are sad. "The Empress is unwell," he says slowly. "She has been making accusations which I cannot believe are true. She says you are two different people, she accuses you of wishing to kill me, of drawing me close to you so that you might use these… daggers… to assassinate me in the Lion Grove."

I stare at him and try to find my voice. "And you believe her?"

He shakes his head wearily. "She is unwell, as you can see," he says quietly. "I walked with you in the gardens and all was well between us, as you know. There is only one of you. She is hallucinating."

"She will have hidden daggers in her clothing. Make her show you!" screams Ula Nara and throws herself at me, grabbing at the sleeves of my jacket. Her face comes very close to mine. Her breath is rank and she smells of sweat. I can hardly stand upright against her fury. She pulls at my jacket and I step away from her as she rips it off me, then stumbles and falls to the floor at my feet with the heavy silk in her hands. She frantically turns it inside out, then, seeing no daggers embedded in the cloth, sets about the sleeves with her ripped nails and uncleaned teeth. She writhes on the floor as the silk rips and the wadding is revealed, but still no daggers. I stand above her, my breathing almost as fast as hers. What if Iparhan has indeed left daggers in my clothing? But there's nothing there and Ula Nara puts her head to the floor and weeps, rocking back and forth, still clutching at the torn silk with her bony hands. I turn, helpless, to the Emperor.

But he's changed. I'm used to seeing him in good humour, smiling and calm. I've even seen him laughing and joking – with his children, with me. At the most I've seen him looking important and officious as he works his way through documents of state or the daily rituals of sacrifice and prayer.

Now he is terrible. He stands at his full height, making him a head taller than all three of us women. His robes of state add splendour and breadth to his stature and his face is angry. This is the wrathful lord of an empire and suddenly I'm afraid of him. *If he ever knew my story*, I think, *this is how he would look at me.*

"You will be sent back to Beijing in disgrace," he tells Ula Nara. His voice is low but carries as though he were shouting.

Ula Nara doesn't raise her head. Instead she twists towards the sound of his voice and begins a terrible parody of a kowtow. Where I've always seen her perform the reverence with the grace and poise of many years' practice and breeding, now she stumbles and pitches her head forward too fast, knocking it hard on the stone floor. Her eyes are glazed when she raises her face and for a moment I think she's going to faint.

"Do not punish me, my lord," she begs, and her voice is so weak and broken that I lower my eyes. "Punish her and her twin. They are treacherous bitches. I am your Empress and she is a nobody, a prisoner of war from a land ridden with mongrel curs." Tears roll down her cheeks. "I have been loyal to you," she whispers. "I have bound myself to you since I was chosen and I have done everything in my power to deserve your favour. Do not punish me."

I look at the Empress Dowager but she seems to know what's coming, for she raises her head to meet my eyes. I see that her cheek is marked by a long red scratch, reminding me of Iparhan's scar. I can only guess that Ula Nara attacked her before I entered the room. She holds my gaze for a moment and then with a minute shake of her head turns away again, towards the Emperor but without meeting his eyes, which remain fixed on Ula Nara.

"You will return to Beijing under guard," he says.

My legs begin shake. His voice is terrible but what he's suggesting is worse. An Empress, under guard rather than guarded? But he's not finished.

"You will remain there until my return and then you will be taken to the Cold Palace where you will live until the end of your days. You will no longer live within my presence."

Ula Nara's bloodshot eyes roll up. "*I am the Empress*!" she shrieks. "You cannot do this to me!"

"You are no longer my Empress," says the Emperor. "From this moment you are stripped of your titles and privileges."

I wait for his mother to protest. She herself chose Ula Nara as his Empress. Surely there will be some more discreet punishment? Perhaps she could be sent away to become a Buddhist nun or kept under house arrest without being demoted, with some mysterious illness as an excuse? But the Empress Dowager stays silent and I realise that I've witnessed something unspeakable.

There's a long silence, broken only by Ula Nara, who is lying on the floor moaning as though in pain. I want to comfort her but I'm afraid of her anger towards me and I don't know how a demoted Empress should be treated. I look at the Emperor but he stands motionless, looking down at her. His face is still angry but his eyes are glistening and I can see he, too, is shaken. I want to find a way to get out of the room, to remove my having been here at all, but there's no easy way to do so. So I stand, waiting, until at last his eyes turn to me.

"Call the guards," he says. "And a maid."

I nod and back away. By the doorway to the courtyard I grab the arm of the terrified maid who is still lingering, unsure of whether to go outside. "Go to your mistress," I hiss at her. "At once." She nods and scurries towards the receiving hall. I look out into the courtyard and every face turns towards me. They will have heard Ula Nara's shrieks, but nobody has stirred, fearful of what they might find on entering.

I look about me and spot Huan. "I need guards," I say.

He nods, unquestioning. "How many?"

I don't know. "Several," I say and he hurries to where the guards stand. Soon eight of them are making their way into the palace behind me.

"Stay here," I whisper to Huan and he stays by the doorway, preventing any other people from entering.

Inside Ula Nara is still on the floor and her maid is holding an armful of clothes.

"Something plain," says the Empress Dowager, who is directing her, although she has half turned away so that her damaged face can't be seen.

The maid hovers, uncertain. The Empress of China has very few clothes that might be called plain. She holds up a few robes but even those that are not official court robes are exquisite in their use of fine materials and embroidery. I see the Emperor shift his feet in growing impatience. The Empress Dowager, aware of this, waves her hand without looking. "A maid's robe," she says.

The maid gapes at her.

"Fetch one!"

The maid hurries away and returns with a pale blue cotton robe, cleaned so many times that it's faded, still crumpled from its latest wash. The guards, standing behind me, are silent as the maid holds it up. The Empress Dowager nods and turns away.

"Dress her," she says over her shoulder, her scratched face hidden.

The maid tries, but Ula Nara's body has gone limp and I have to kneel beside her. Together we strip off her outer robe of imperial yellow silk and cover up her sweat-stained inner robes in the faded blue cotton. She doesn't protest, only lies like a rag doll as we finish dressing her. I look up at the Emperor. He has not turned away while his Empress, in a few short moments, has been transformed into a lowly maid.

"Take her back to Beijing," he says to the guards.

They daren't gape nor disobey but they hesitate before laying hands on her. Carefully, three of them lift her up and make their way to the door. I follow behind as they carry her down the steps towards her yellow palanquin, topped with golden phoenixes and shielded from curious eyes by silk drapes.

"Stop!"

At the Emperor's voice ringing out behind us, every servant falls to their knees, face down on the ground. I stand still, surrounded by prostate bodies.

"She is no longer permitted to ride in that palanquin," he orders. "Fetch a red chair."

There's a disbelieving pause before one quick-witted servant jumps up and dashes out of the courtyard, returning a few moments later with an intercepted orange chair and bearers, its bewildered owner unceremoniously evicted somewhere just outside the palace gates.

The whole courtyard watches from half-crouched positions as the once-Empress Ula Nara is led out in a faded blue cotton maid's robe, to a plain orange chair such as is used by any lowly courtier or even a high-ranking eunuch. Her own imperial yellow palanquin sits nearby, discarded.

I stand still for a moment and then run down the steps to where the guards are trying to manhandle Ula Nara into the chair. She is not fighting them but her body is limp, like a sack of rice and just as unwieldy.

I crouch in front of her, aware that behind me the Emperor is watching. "Give me your hand, Your Majesty," I say in a whisper, so that no one else can hear me address her by her former title. "Let me help you into the chair."

Ula Nara looks down at me. Her eyes have become glazed over. "There were two of you in the garden," she says in a croak.

My heart hurts for her. Her jealousy has led her partway to the truth but I cannot save her now. "There is only one of me here," I say. "Will you give me your hand?"

She gives it to me as a child might offer their hand. I take it and help her into the chair. The jagged edges of her broken nail shields dig into my skin. When she is safely inside I straighten up and gesture to the bearers to lift her. I look through the little window at her confused face, the tracks of tears on her cheeks and pull the gauze curtain across, shielding her from the view of onlookers, the only protection I can offer her without risking my own life.

We wait as the orange chair makes its unsteady way out of the courtyard and the Emperor steps over the bodies between him and his own yellow chair. Behind him comes the Empress Dowager. The bearers lift the two chairs and turn towards the gates of the courtyard. Slowly the servants get to their feet and trot uncertainly after their masters' chairs. Those left behind, surrounding the abandoned yellow chair and my own orange palanquin lift their faces cautiously from the ground and look towards me as I stand on the threshold of the Empress' palace.

"Go back to your quarters," I say and enter my own chair where the darkness of the drapes hides my trembling as I'm carried back to my own rooms. In my mind is only one thought, which fills up every part of me and circles round and round in my thoughts until I begin to sob. If the Empress has been banished for making accusations that the Emperor does not wish to hear, even though she had almost perceived the truth – what would happen to me – what would he do to me if he found out they were true? Would he turn his wrath towards me, would he look at me as though I were nothing to him?

When I arrive I run to my bedroom and only Huan is brave enough to follow me. He finds me rocking back and forth, tears rolling down my face.

"Your ladyship," he murmurs. "What is wrong?"

I try to wipe my nose with my silk skirt. Huan reaches out very gently and wipes my face with the sleeve of his own robe. "Tell me what is wrong," he says.

"I thought my time here was over," I sob. "The Empress – Ula Nara said – things. She wanted me – gone."

"And the Emperor?" Huan asks.

"He was so angry. He – he sent Ula Nara away – he said she is no longer the Empress." I look up at Huan. "Can he do that?"

"The Son of Heaven can do anything," Huan says. "All things are in his power." He is silent for a moment. "And now?" he asks. "Are you afraid of him? Or do you no longer wish to be here now that you see what punishments may befall a lady of the court if she falls from favour? Is that why you are crying?"

I look up at him and the tears fall even harder. "No," I say between sobs. "It's because now I know how easily any of us could leave this place if we are found – if we are found wanting. And I – I want to stay. I did not know how much until now."

Huan almost smiles, as though he has known this all along. "And why do you wish to stay, my ladyship?" he asks, as though what I feel must be said out loud, as though my next words are an incantation that will protect my future here.

"Because I love him," I say. "I love the Emperor."

Iparhan

I CANNOT SLEEP. MY EYES BURN *with exhaustion and yet I cannot sleep for more than a few moments at a time. I sleep and then wake and see it is still dark, over and over again. I lie awake and my fingers slip beneath my bed and seek out the daggers where they lie hidden. I caress them and feel their sharp blades. In the mornings I examine my hands and see on each fingertip the skin shredded, sometimes too pink where I have almost cut through to where the blood runs, despite my gentle touch on their blades. I have to hide my hands inside the cuffs of the robes I wear to avoid comment. My eyes are so tired during the day that the sunlight hurts them. I blink too often and objects before me blur and change their shapes.*

I cannot eat. I grow thinner, my bones slowly revealing themselves through my skin, one after another – my collarbones, my cheekbones, the gaunt shapes of my fingers, my hip bones jutting out beneath my clothes like the hilts of my daggers. I try to force down food although there is no taste when I chew. I must not grow too different from Hidligh. I must be her reflection.

I do not hear. Huan tuts because I do not heed his commands. I emerge from my dazed thoughts and try to understand him, although his voice seems far away. Nurmat watches me and when I refuse to speak of an uprising, when I tell him to send away possible allies his eyes grow wary.

Always in my nostrils is this smell. The perfume that once adorned me now adorns the Emperor's concubine and its scent chokes me. It has become a stench, pervading every part of me, released with every gesture. I have come to associate it with the Emperor himself and it makes me want to retch. But still I must smile, must carry myself with grace when I take on her form.

I must gaze upon him as though he were my beloved, when he is the reason for all my suffering. I must speak to him with a soft mouth when I can feel my hand reaching for a dagger that is not there. My life grows more painful with every hour of this pretence and I do not know how much longer I can bear it.

I no longer wish to lead my people against him. Even his defeat in battle would not assuage my need for revenge.

Rong Fei

SLOWLY WE MAKE OUR WAY back north. In our procession there are still three imperial yellow palanquins, but the third is empty. Its bearers carrying nothing but rumours and whispers in the air around them, the heavy weight of sadness and fear inside its yellow silken folds.

Now Iparhan stays away from me. She does not ask to take my place. She does not spend time with Nurmat. She is a maid, nothing more. This frightens me more than her shape-shifting. Why would Iparhan lose all hope, all her obsession with revenge now, when she is where she has planned to be all along? She is here at court, at the very heart of the Emperor's world. She can take on my shape to do her spying and yet she does nothing. I watch her when she is close to me and try to catch her eye but she keeps her gaze on the floor and slips away as soon as she can.

Her behaviour convinces me that my days here are numbered. There is an ending coming. I can feel it. I do not know what ending it will be – whether it will end a part of my life or my life itself – but meanwhile I cling to my time here. The Emperor laughs at me, for I beg to stay close to him, both in his bedchamber and on his tedious building expeditions and visits to temples.

"What is it you want of me?" he asks, chuckling. "Are you about to beg a great boon of me? There must be something you want very dearly to follow me about like a lost lamb."

"I only want your company, Majesty," I reply and he smiles and wraps me in his arms. I inhale the scent of him, warm and masculine, and let my fingers stroke the back of his neck, his cheekbones and his lips until he kisses me with ever-growing desire and leads me to his rooms. The endless temples and incense, the great building works, fall away from me as he strokes my skin until I pull him to me and he smiles at my eagerness.

Iparhan does not smile. Her hair is unwashed. It hangs limp and greasy in its single plait. Her clothes look crumpled and I hear Huan berate her more than once for not attending properly to her duties. Her mask of the consummate maid is beginning to slip, her anger too strong below the surface to be properly hidden. I keep her in my sight when I am in my own rooms. I tell Huan to watch over her when I go out, telling him in front of her that I am worried for her health, that she has not enjoyed the 'Southern climate'. She can say nothing but I know that she will not submit to such restrictions for long.

Nurmat's drinking is by now common knowledge. He rarely cooks any more, since my other servants have learned to make the dishes from my homeland and so he is often to be found asleep or slumped in a corner of the servants' quarters. Huan despairs of him. "But we cannot dismiss him," he says. "He was a gift from His Majesty. It would be an insult."

"Leave him be," I say. I know that whatever Nurmat's fate is, it rests in Iparhan's hands, not mine. I wish I could still believe in him as my ally in this folly but I know now that his loyalty will forever be with Iparhan. He is hers, as he always was. I am left to find my own path and fight my own battles.

We return to the Forbidden City in time for the Mid Autumn Moon festival. As soon as we're installed back in our palaces the servants busy themselves with preparations. The whole city is hung with lanterns – from trees, rooftops and down every alleyway. Tonight we gather in the Emperor's private garden to gaze at the fullness of the moon and celebrate the harvest that she brings.

My chair makes its way through the tiny passages between palaces on its way to the gardens. Each palace glows with lit lanterns and every courtyard is full of people preparing for the celebrations. Other ladies' chairs join mine along the way so that we begin to form a procession; one filled with laughter and accompanied by many servants carrying lanterns hung on bamboo poles which light up the way ahead. Even the little children will attend tonight's festival, and their high-pitched squeals of excitement make me laugh.

Just before the gardens come into sight we pass one more palace and our procession, so noisy and bright a few moments ago, stutters into silence and our festive pace becomes a shuffle.

The palace of the now-deposed Empress Ula Nara, a building that once sat majestic among our lesser dwellings, now hides in the flickering shadows of our chairs as we pass by. No lanterns shine out, there is no sound from her courtyard. As the Emperor threatened, on our return from the tour Ula Nara was sent away from Beijing with a handful of her servants. The rest were redistributed amongst the other palaces and women of the court. I myself received a eunuch and two maids from her palace. Humbled by their mistress' fall from grace, they obey Huan without question, go about their tasks in silence and creep away to their quarters when they are not needed.

Once past this silent reminder our procession increases its pace and gradually the sounds of revelry rise again as we reach the Emperor's gardens.

Trees rise up above delicately balanced rockeries and deep pools of water, reflecting the hundreds of lanterns hung on every available surface – perched on rockeries, hanging from trees, suspended from tall bamboo poles. An altar has been set up in the open air and each lady's chair makes its way towards it as she arrives. A flute is being played somewhere close by.

I climb out of my own chair and Huan places in my hands an open carved casket containing mooncakes, each the size of a small peach, their golden pastry marked with gilded characters, their soft insides filled with sweet lotus bean paste. I approach the altar, place my offering with care among the many other cakes, light sticks of incense and then bow. As I do so the Chief Eunuch announces my name.

"The Lady He's offering! May the Mistress of the Moon grant her honoured daughter eternal beauty!"

As I stand to make way for another lady's offering one hundred sky lanterns are released around me. Each one a delicate white orb, painted with the characters of my own name, they rise above us to join the hundreds more already floating towards the full moon. I make my way to join the Emperor and the rest of his family. He's surrounded by his children as well as by those ladies senior to myself.

"Tell the story!" pleads one of the princesses, tugging at his robes. Her cry is taken up by the other children. "Yes, tell the story, tell the story!"

The Emperor laughs. "There are still ladies who must join us," he remonstrates.

We wait and watch as more ladies arrive. Each makes an offering and for each more sky lanterns are released. The sky above us is full of them, our names shining high above us, the characters illuminated by the fires within. The air grows thick with incense as hundreds and hundreds of sticks are lit.

Servants pass us platters heaped with peeled segments of citrussy pomelo fruits and mooncakes – some sweet, others filled with salted egg yolks. Close by fires are lit to boil water for tea. We eat and drink while admiring the spectacle before us.

I notice the children of Ula Nara, sitting as proud as the others, but perhaps a little too upright, their positions now threatened by their mother's shame. They may have seen little enough of her, being cared for by other ladies of the court as well as their nursemaids and wet-nurses, but to be the children of the Empress was a position of privilege. Now their faces may remind their father of her disgrace and they are anxious to please.

I touch the Emperor's sleeve and he takes my hand in his and caresses it. "My Lady He," he says smiling. "My fragrant concubine."

I smile back but point towards the children. "They are longing for your favour, Your Majesty."

The Emperor follows my eyes and gestures to them to approach. They do so timidly and he strokes their hair. "I believe there are dragons out there," he says laughing as a clashing of gongs heralds the arrival of the Fire Dragon dancers. The children, reassured, run to join their siblings.

At last every lady and child has arrived and the children cluster around the Emperor again.

"The rabbit!" shrieks Yongyan. "Tell about the rabbit!"

"Rabbit?" asks the Emperor, bewildered. "What rabbit?"

"The *rabbit*!"

"*This* rabbit?" From his robes he pulls out a tiny jade carving of a rabbit.

"Yes, yes!"

The Emperor laughs and nods to a eunuch at his side, who hands out a tiny carved jade rabbit to each of the princes and princesses, each one carved from a different shade of the precious stone. The tiny ones grab for them, the older ones incline their heads and examine the carvings with studied poise and appreciation.

The Emperor begins a tale of a moon-dwelling rabbit, but a eunuch is hovering at my side. "The Empress Dowager wishes to speak with you," he murmurs.

I rise and follow the eunuch to where she sits. I kowtow and open my mouth to address her but she holds up a hand and I fall silent, waiting for her to begin.

She doesn't take her eyes off the glittering dragons as they writhe before us. "Lady He. I wish to thank you for your management of the unfortunate... moment... with Ula Nara."

I don't know what to say so I say nothing, only bow my head.

"It is good to see that you understand how to behave in moments of difficulty," she goes on. "Despite your – " her eyes flicker over my clothes " – *foreign* ways."

I bow my head again.

"I know that my son is fond of you," she says. "I have cautioned him against becoming too fond of a woman from a country whose loyalty to us is yet in doubt. However, it seems your personal loyalty is strong and we must hope this bodes well for your country's future. You will be rewarded."

I don't know what she means but I bow my head for the third time and make my way back to my seat without having spoken a single word. The children have dispersed, running about the gardens shrieking.

I hold out my hand to the Emperor. "Come to my bedchamber," I say.

He raises his eyebrows. It is for the Emperor to make the first move with his ladies. "Are you wooing me, Lady He?" he asks, amused at my boldness.

"Yes, Your Majesty," I say.

He chuckles and stands, taking my hand. "How novel," he says.

In my bedchamber I wait patiently for the servants to finish undressing us both. Once they are gone I indicate the bed. "Lie back," I say, and he grins at the reminder of our first night together. Obedient, he does as he is told and I sit as he did that night, holding his smooth feet in my bare lap, caressing them softly.

"Am I to ask why you did not call for me before?" he asks me and I smile at the knowledge that he remembers every word and gesture of that first time.

"Oh," I say, allowing my hands to slip further up his legs. "You seemed so shy, Majesty, when I first met you. I thought perhaps you should grow in confidence, feel at home, feel yourself the master of your own palace before I called for you." And we are giggling like children as I fling myself onto the bed beside him. He takes me in his arms and our kisses, sometimes so urgent, now are slow, sweet and gentle. I close my eyes as he caresses me and as we move together I shut out all my dark thoughts and focus only on his scent and our skins touching, the sounds of our lovemaking. But when we are spent and he falls asleep, I hold my body very still so that he will not feel my sobs and press my face against his chest so that the silk coverlet will soak up my tears of fear.

The next morning I wake to an unexpected clamour in the room outside my bed. Fumbling, I pull back the curtains and find that the eunuchs and maids are all crowded into my bedroom, accompanied by what appear to be all my animals. The servants are bursting with pride and their suppressed excitement has made the dogs go wild, yapping and jumping up and down, their tails wagging and tongues lolling. Huan pushes through, slapping this way and that impatiently to make them part before him.

He hurries to my side as I draw a robe about me and try to fully open my eyes. "You're to be promoted again, my lady. You will be a *Fei*! A Consort, not just a concubine. Fourth-ranked! And," he says, his voice dropping conspiratorially while all the servants lean forward to hear him better, "of course now that there is no Empress, and the Emperor has said he absolutely refuses to appoint another as long as he lives, *really*, you will be third-ranked." He beams.

I look to the back of the crowd where Iparhan and Nurmat stand. Nurmat's eyes are bloodshot from his drinking while Iparhan's suddenly shine too brightly in her drawn face. If any of us live long enough to see this promotion, I think. "The Emperor is too kind to me," I say out loud, although I'm thinking of the Empress Dowager and Ula Nara's disgrace, through which it seems I have earned this promotion. "I am not worthy of the honour he shows me. When is the ceremony?"

"Tomorrow afternoon," says Huan. The eunuchs shush the gasping maidservants.

I stare at him. "Tomorrow afternoon? But last time it took so long to prepare for it!"

Huan waves away my concerns. "I have already sent for the dressmakers," he assures me. "You will need new clothes for the ceremony of course." He thinks. "At your last promotion you wore a pink skirt, with gold embroidery on the waistcoat and your cap was—"

I hold up a hand, interrupting him. "I will wear court robes," I say.

He gapes at me. "Not your Xinjiang clothes?"

I shake my head. "Manchu style. Court robes in the orange silk. And my ears need piercing for the triple pearl earrings."

He wants to make sure of his orders. "Just for the ceremony?"

I look into Iparhan's eyes. Slowly I shake my head. I know that my choice will trigger her rage but I can no longer live my life waiting for her moves. It is time I played my own game. "No. After the ceremony I will always wear Manchu robes." I pull the bed drapes about me and lie down on the bed. Outside I can hear Huan and Jiang shrieking at the maidservants. They sound cross but really they're excited. So much to do. So many wondrous new clothes to prepare. Their status, like mine, will rise again as I become a Consort, and there will be whole new wardrobes to arrange for me. If I wear court robes in the Manchu style I will be competing directly against the other ladies, no longer set apart by my clothes. I hear them squabbling over how my hair should be dressed for the important day – in the Manchu style of course but which ornaments? What kind of nail shields should I have? One thing they are all agreed on and that is that I should retain the lotus as my signature flower, an echo of my first court name, a reminder of my precious scent.

"It has brought good luck to my lady," opines Huan, and the other servants murmur agreement and then shriek over new details to be considered. They can barely list all the things that must, simply *must*, be done at once, now, this *minute*.

I leave them to it and make my own plans. I send alms to the beggars by the gates of the Forbidden City and hair ornaments to Consorts Qing and Ying. I send a nest made of golden twigs filled with silk feathers to Yongyan for his favourite toy, the little jade duck. To Lady Wan I send a puppy, a longhaired, lolloping creature with floppy ears and an eager wet tongue to lick her hands and warm her heart. To Giuseppe I send a gift of costly paints and a message saying that I was unwell when we last spoke and that I beg his forgiveness for my rudeness. I tell him I was not myself. Formal gifts to celebrate my forthcoming promotion will be chosen by Huan and sent to other important members of the court and the more senior ladies, but these gifts I choose myself.

The Emperor sends word that he will dine with me tonight, ahead of tomorrow's ceremony. This news very nearly reduces Huan to tears. He already has a room set aside for the dressmakers, who are frantically preparing my court robes for tomorrow's ceremony. He had hoped for no further interruptions, but now has to ensure that a lavish dinner is prepared, as well as readying me to receive the Emperor.

"You," he addresses Iparhan. "You will bathe your mistress and then take her to the bedchamber and dress her. I will arrange her hair and makeup when she is ready. I cannot spare any maids to help you beyond bringing the water, you will have to manage by yourself. Can you do that? I am giving you this task because I believe you to be trustworthy," he adds. "Do not fail me."

Iparhan bows her head and makes a small gesture to me. "My lady," she says, "Please come with me."

I follow her with some reluctance. I don't wish to spend so much time alone with her and she seems too eager for this menial task. I wonder whether she will command me to switch places with her and I linger in the doorway, thinking to back out of the door and call Huan, ask for a different maid. But Iparhan is silent. She behaves as any senior maid would, testing the water, undressing me when I slowly step forward, then helping me into the large tub, shooing away the last of the other maids when they have finished bringing hot water. When we are alone again she turns away to place my clothes out of the way of any water. I have my back to her and cannot see her, only hear her humming tunelessly. It makes me uncomfortable but I try to ignore her. I concentrate on my promotion ceremony tomorrow. I hope that by switching to court robes I will wrong-foot Iparhan. If I am dressed the same as any other woman at court I will take away part of her disguise, for my 'foreign' clothes mark me out against the other women. If my hair and clothes look like the others, perhaps more attention will be drawn to my face – or Iparhan's. It is a small step, but for now it is all that I can think of. I rest my face in my hands for a moment as I try to think and feel something brush against my fingers. "I still have my earrings in," I say to Iparhan. "Huan does not like them to get wet."

Behind me, Iparhan unplaits my hair and sheds its gemstones and ribbons. "It won't harm them," she says. She begins to replait my hair into a single plait. "Your hair is clean," she says. "I will not need to wash it but I need to keep it out of the way of the cream for your face. Close your eyes."

Reluctantly I close them and feel her hands on my face, her movements quick and light, rubbing in a cream that Huan swears will keep me wrinkle-free until I am older than the Empress Dowager herself. I'm not sure I believe him but I've grown used to it and it has a pleasant enough smell. Iparhan's fingers move over my skin until she is done. She takes longer than Huan but then it is not usually her task to perform. I open my eyes and stare at the wall as she bustles about behind me. I am trying so hard to think that I feel almost dizzy in the heat and steam of the room.

"Stand up," she says, and I do so. She pats most of me dry with a towel. "Put your arms up," she says.

I raise my arms and a robe slips over me.

In the brief moment I feel it fall about me I know something is wrong. What I am feeling is rough cotton, not silk. I look down and see blue, then turn my head just as Iparhan screams.

"Huan! Huan! Help me!"

I almost fall into the tub as I try to climb out, clutch at the sides and hear feet come running. As my bare feet touch the floor I twist my head to see Iparhan, fully dressed and made up as myself. She has her back pressed to the wall in an attitude of fear, while her face, turned to me, wears a triumphant smile. I don't even need a mirror to know that she has painted the scar onto my face while she told me she was applying Huan's miraculous cream.

The door bursts open and Huan stands panting, two eunuchs by his side, three maids peering out from behind him. "My lady!" He looks from Iparhan, her face now a mask of alarm, to me, standing frozen and barefoot by the tub. His eyes shift back to Iparhan, who motions, wordless, at my feet. I look down as Huan does. A dagger lies by my right foot, as though dropped from my hand.

Slowly, Huan steps forward. While I stand, unable to move, he walks with care until he is standing in front of Iparhan. Then he kneels, still with infinite caution, and stretches out until he can reach the dagger, all the while looking up at my face, to see if I will attack. I look at him, keeping my eyes on his, praying that for once he will see the difference in us.

Huan reaches behind him with the dagger and carefully lets Iparhan take it. Then he advances on me, his hands ready to grab. Behind him, Iparhan whimpers. "Be careful, Huan. She stole my earrings and then she attacked me. She had this dagger concealed on her. What if she has another?"

Huan reaches me. In one swift moment he grasps my wrists and forces me to the floor. For all his usual elegance in bearing, he is a strong man and I sink down to my knees without any attempt to fight against him. Held in a tight grip, my face pressed to the floor, I begin to weep.

"I will beat you myself," says Huan. "And when I am done beating you the Emperor himself will hear of this and you will forfeit your life."

"No," says Iparhan above me. "I do not want him to know of this matter. He will feel affronted that this girl, his gift to me, should be such a disappointment. Better that we manage this between us, Huan."

Huan sounds uncertain. He shifts his grip on me. "You cannot keep her," he says. "She attacked you. She should be executed. She can never be trusted again."

"You are right," says Iparhan. "I want you to take her to the gates of the Forbidden City and cast her out."

"Out?"

"Into the streets of Beijing," says Iparhan. "There she can live or die. She will no longer be a threat to me."

I feel my neck muscles wrench as I twist my head against the floor to try and look up at her but Huan reinforces his hold on me and presses my cheek back to the floor. "It is not usual…" he begins.

"It is what I command," says Iparhan. "Do it now."

I feel another hand come down on me, holding me in place, as Huan loosens his grasp, pulls out each earring from my ears with ungentle hands, then stands. "As you wish, my lady," he says, then addresses the unseen eunuch holding me down. "You will take her to the gates and have her thrown out. Now."

Until this moment I had not believed what was happening. Now I reach out an arm and clutch Huan's ankle as he moves away from me. "Huan! Please don't do this to me. I did not harm her!"

The eunuch pulls my hand away from Huan so hard that for a moment I believe my arm has come out of its socket. I shriek with pain. Huan moves further away. I twist my head again so that I can look up at him. He has gone back to Iparhan's side. His arm is about her shoulder and he is guiding her out of the room. He does not even look down on me.

I scream. I have nothing left to lose. "Huan! Help me! I – she – she is not who she seems to be! Her name is Iparhan! She comes from a family who fought against the Emperor and lost! She means to lead a rebel army against him! She – she found me on the streets Huan! I was a beggar girl, nothing more. But she had a scar and – "

Huan has almost taken Iparhan from the room but now he pauses. I stop screaming, half-believing that he will ask questions, that he will ask me to repeat my claim. Instead he addresses the eunuch. "Get her to the gates quickly," he says. "And bind up her mouth. She cannot say such things while you take her there. Someone might hear her ravings."

The eunuch jerks me to my feet in one hard movement. I stagger and try to find my footing as Huan turns and leaves the room.

The voice I hear from my mouth is not my own. It is a terrifying shriek of fear and pain. "Huan! *Wipe her face!* Wipe her face and you will see her scar! I beg you. I beg you! Huan! *Huan!*"

But he is gone.

I struggle against the eunuch who is holding me. I hope that I might wipe the painted-on scar from my own face, that when I do so it might give him pause. But he is too strong for me and my hands are pinned so tightly I can do nothing. A maid gives him a cloth and he gags me. When I struggle harder he binds my feet and hands as well, limiting my movements. Then he picks me up and slings me over his shoulder, so that I am hanging upside-down. I can no longer speak clearly. I can only scream.

I scream. I scream and scream as he carries me down the steps of my palace. I scream as he carries me through the little streets of the Inner Court and as we pass into the Outer Court I scream. My voice echoes off the paved courtyards, the red walls, the golden rooftops. I grow hoarse long before we reach the Western Gate. Still I scream, although my voice grows quieter and quieter, its strength fading with every step the eunuch takes. I see guards, eunuchs and courtiers passing. Some glance my way, many ignore me altogether. A maid is of little interest. A maid who has committed some misdemeanour and is to be punished is of even less interest. Only the maids we pass turn their heads to watch me. Their fear of my unknown misdemeanour and punishment makes them walk faster, keen to avoid a similar fate. They scurry away. My screams will be in their nightmares for many days to come.

I am released, dropped abruptly to the ground, my ankles and wrists roughly unbound. The gag is pulled away. I struggle to my feet, dizzy from having been upside down for so long. I stagger, then straighten up and look about me just as the towering red doors of the West Glorious Gate slowly swing shut against me, the eunuch already making his way back to Huan.

I rush at the gate, my hands outstretched. The impact as I slam into the unyielding wood is so hard I feel the pain shoot up both arms. My torn throat releases a cry that is barely audible as I sink to my knees, holding my shaking arms against my chest. Through my tears I look up at the red door, patterned with row upon row of gilded brass studs. Quickly I move to the outside of the arch that contains the door. There is a low panel of white stone, carved. I try to climb onto it, my hands reaching up the perfectly smooth red wall, a mad thought of trying to climb over it in my confused mind. For one precarious moment I stand pressed against the red wall, my arms reaching up to its endless summit, before I fall, my knuckles scraping against the stone as I try to save myself. My fingernails are broken, my hands are bleeding where the cool stone has ripped the skin from my flesh. I rock back and forth, my bare feet pressed hard against the cold paving, my tears dripping slowly onto the stone. The moaning I can dimly hear is coming from my own mouth. There is no other sound for the gate remains closed and there are no other people nearby. The late autumn day is already turning to dusk.

Dusk. I struggle to my feet and begin to run. To my left, the endless red walls of the Forbidden City. To my right, the dark waters of the moat. I run and run. My feet, grown soft in my silken shoes, hurt with every step but I only run faster. Finally I see where the wall ends and I turn the corner to my left, heading for the Meridian Gate, the great southern gate that is the main entrance to my former home. Here there is no silence. Here there are crowds of people. Beggars, street vendors, petitioners, guards. Courtiers, their servants pushing the beggars out of their way as they leave the Forbidden City. The beggars push their hands into the palanquins, their grimy fingers reaching for alms and being slapped away. There is a hubbub of voices all about me as I press through the crowd, my ears filled with only one sound.

"Draw the bolts, lock up, careful with the lanterns. Draw the bolts, lock up, careful with the lanterns."

The call is coming from very close inside the main gates and already, as I fight my way through the oncoming crowd I see the guards move to grasp the great red doors and swing them close. I try to move faster, but I am heading towards the gates and everyone else is moving away. Again and again I am pushed back, and I hear Jiang's voice in my head, from the day I first came to the Forbidden City, was frightened by the call and asked its meaning. *All those who had business in the Forbidden City today have left. The gates are to be locked up now; only the Emperor and his family and servants will remain.*

The gates are to be locked up…

I shove a street vendor aside so hard he stumbles. "Watch yourself, you stupid girl," he shouts, his little cakes falling to the ground, but I am already closer to the gates and a dark dread makes me push harder. I hear curses from all sides as I finally reach the red gates, but they are already closed. I throw myself at the feet of one of the guards.

"Let me in," I half-sob.

"What?" asks the guard.

I've forgotten to speak Mandarin. I try again, my voice coming out tight and ragged from my throat. "I serve as a maid to Lady He," I say. "I – I was running an errand for her and I returned later than I expected. Please let me in. She will beat me if I do not return tonight."

"Tally," says the guard, his hand outstretched, his voice bored.

"Tally?"

"Where's your tally?" he demands more roughly. "No servant leaves the Forbidden City without a tally. Otherwise how would we know who is a real maid and who is just –" he looks at my dirty feet, damp crumpled robe and disheveled hair, "– some beggar girl from the streets?"

"I dropped it," I say quickly.

"Then you'll have to wait till morning," says the guard, bored again. "A senior eunuch of your mistress' household will be sent for, to identify you before you are allowed to enter. And I should imagine you'll get a sound beating for being so careless," he adds.

"Please," I say, my tears beginning to fall again. "Please let me in."

"No," says the guard, and it is clear from his tone that no amount of begging and pleading will make him reconsider.

I fall back and let myself be swept away by the crowds around me, all flowing in one direction: over the bridge that crosses the moat, into Beijing itself. I hardly think, hardly even feel myself walking, only let myself drift along amongst the voices and elbows. Only when we reach the other side of the bridge and the crowd disperses in all directions, freed from the bridge's constraints, am I released from the flow. I stop. Motionless, I stand at the corner of the bridge, looking back at the red walls of the Forbidden City, now more than fifty paces away from me, protected from intruders by its cold dark waters and high walls. I have not been without the protection of those waters and red walls for almost two years. The warmth of the bodies about me fades and the cold of the approaching night creeps up my bare feet and into my bones.

Only when my teeth begin to chatter together do I move again. I turn around on myself, dazed by the cold. It's growing darker now and slowly the reality of what has just happened seeps into me. I am alone. Outside of the Forbidden City, with no way to return inside its walls. I am cold and poorly dressed for a night or indeed a life on the streets. My past life as a quick-witted girl fending for herself on the streets seems a long way away – and besides, that was in a city that I had known since birth. I know nothing about Beijing – I have never even seen it except from the upper stories of my own tower or snatched glimpses through bamboo screens and the shimmering silk curtains of a palanquin.

I try to think through the cold fog that has crept up from the soles of my feet and filled my mind. I have two choices – to get back inside the Forbidden City or to accept a life back on the streets. I cannot think how to get back inside the Forbidden City, unless perhaps to steal one of the tallies carried by the servants – and how carefully they must guard them, wary of the fate that has befallen me tonight! The guards will not let me slip inside, their lives depend on not allowing such things to happen. I stand on one foot and then the other, pressing the lifted foot in turn against my cold legs, hoping for some residual warmth to take away the now-painful chill of the ground.

I will have to live on the streets again. I have done it before. Iparhan is now stuck inside the Forbidden City. Without me there to swap places with she will be forced to play the part of a concubine until she dies, so perhaps she will leave me alone. In a city the size of Beijing there will be more opportunities for work. But there will also be more dangers and I will not know where they are until they find me. I try to think about how to begin.

I need to be warm. The remnants of the old days come back to me. Above food, above hunger, comes the need for warmth. If I continue to stand here like this, shaking with cold, my teeth clenched to stop them from breaking one another, my feet growing numb, I will lose the ability to think, to move. I will die here, on the corner of the bridge leading to the Meridian Gate of the Forbidden City. I need to move and I need to seek out some warmth – through clothing or shelter and preferably both.

Then I will have to find food, although I know that I can go for many days without a full belly, no matter how much my stomach rumbles and begs for nourishment. I have been fattened up these past two years, my pampered curves will sustain me until I find a way to feed myself. My shoulders slump. If all else fails I know full well that there will be women's lanes here, whatever they may call them in Beijing. I am no virgin now and so what is to stop me? I would be fed and clothed, after all, and isn't that what all of this madness, this pretence, was for?

But my head rises up as I think of what a life on the streets will really mean. It is not the hunger or the hard work that I am afraid of, nor the dangers from unknown men in the darkened streets and back rooms that frightens me. It is not that I will never wear silks again, nor be served a hundred plates of food at every meal. I will not miss the luxuries I have risked my life for every day these past two years. A flood of images comes to me as I stand shaking on the bridge.

I will never again see little Prince Yongyan running away from his guardians, Consorts Qing and Ying in hot pursuit of him, promising sweetmeats if he will only obey them, just this once.

I will never again sit in my rooms, surrounded by dogs and cawing birds while Huan frets over my hair and Jiang peers worriedly out of the windows as Fury attacks another snake.

Giuseppe will not be by my side in these dark cold streets with his words of advice and his portraits that show me another side of myself.

Lady Wan will sit alone in her rooms with only her towering wigs for company and no one to play her silly drinking games.

And I will never be held in the Emperor's arms again.

I will not do it.

I will not turn and walk into the dark streets of Beijing and be swallowed up by my old life. I will find a way to make my way back to the life I have unwittingly made for myself, the home and friends I have created out of a crazed plan, the love I never expected to find while playing the part of a spy. I look about me. I have to think quickly and I have to move before I freeze to death. Who can I trust?

Giuseppe.

He is the only person I know in Beijing. If I can find Giuseppe and tell him my story he may believe me. He is a kindly man. More, he is a painter, he has stared at both my face and Iparhan's over and over again. He knew something was not right when she sat for him, when she spoke abruptly to him and asked too many questions about war. I saw in his face that he was confused, that he saw something in her face but could not give what he saw a name against the too-obvious clothes, hair, makeup, status. If I can find him now I can tell him everything and pray he believes me, that he can find a way to help me. I don't know whether he can, whether this has all gone too far to be made right again. But I have to try.

I move my numb feet eastwards. I know that each night, when he leaves the Forbidden City, Giuseppe makes his way to the Jesuit Church. He calls it St Joseph's, but the local people know it as Dong Tang, the East Church.

I have to ask over and over again for directions. Some people don't know what I am talking about. Some point vaguely this way or that, seeming to contradict one another. But finally I see it. A towering building, thick grey stone rising above me. In front of it, a great gate rises. I press my face against its bars and look through. Three domes top the building, three doors pierce its facade.

"What do you want?"

A lantern shines too brightly in my eyes and I draw back a little. A man, dressed as Giuseppe always is, in a long black scholar's robe, is scowling at me from the other side of the gate.

"I wish to see Giuseppe Castiglione," I say.

"Brother Giuseppe has retired for the night, to pray and sleep," says the man.

"I must see him," I say. "It is very urgent."

The man shakes his head, looking at my crumpled maid's robe and bare feet, no doubt wondering what possible business I could have with Giuseppe. "You can see him in the morning," he says.

"Please," I say. "Please. I can't wait till then. I will freeze to death."

"Then go home to your master," he says and turns to go.

"Please!" I cry after him but he ignores me and walks away, his lantern bobbing in the darkness until it disappears into the grey stone.

I have to get warm. Now that I know where Giuseppe is, I can return in the morning and waylay him before he reaches the Forbidden City. But I will not last till dawn without more clothes or some shelter. I look about me.

On the corner of a street is a cobbler's. A lit brazier gives off a dull red light from the embers, which are burning low. The cobbler will not work much longer, for the light is almost gone and he will not want to keep a costly lantern flame burning. The small lantern he does have casts a weak glow over his busy hands, finishing the last shoe of the day. Behind him sits a woman, probably his wife, cutting up scraps of leather, making little decorations out of those scraps that are too small to be useful in making shoes but might serve to make the petal of a flower. Both of them have their heads bowed low, straining to see in the poor light.

I'm drawn to the brazier's heat. I shuffle forwards, as close as I can get without drawing attention to myself. I cannot feel the full warmth of the fire, but even a faint whisper of it is worth edging a little closer for.

"Stop hanging about, girl," says the cobbler, frowning down at his work. "What do you want?"

"Please," I say. "I'm very cold. I just need to stand by the fire for a little while."

"And then what will you do?"

"I don't know," I say. "I need to find some shelter for the night but I have nowhere to go."

I stand in silence for a few minutes, hugging my body, trying to preserve what little heat I have. I edge a little closer to the fire, hoping the cobbler will not chase me off. I wonder how long it will be before he finishes work for the night and douses the fire, leaving me alone in the dark and cold. I try to think of where else I might shelter but I don't know any of these streets and I daren't go too far from the church in case I lose my way and miss Giuseppe in the morning.

"Here," the cobbler says, without looking at me.

Something hits my leg and I look down in the glowing red darkness to see two old worn slippers. They are scuffed and worn away at the toes, and far too big for me, but I seize them and slip them on. The difference is immediate. My teeth almost stop chattering in surprise at the release from the frosted earth against my bare soles. I approach the cobbler until I am stood right in front of him, my white hands gripping the edge of his workbench. "I will repay you for your kindness," I tell him, trying not to cry. "And I will thank you every day in my prayers."

He grunts, looking down at his work as though uninterested.

I shuffle away, back towards the little fire when his wife speaks to me. "Girl!"

I look back.

"Take this," she says, holding out something shapeless. "And save your prayers for yourself, you look as though you need them."

I reach out a hand for the shadowy item. It is a jacket, thick but full of holes and with a greasy feel to it, perhaps used as a rag for polishing the finer shoes. It feels better than any of the furs and silks Huan ever ordered for me. I wrap myself tightly in it, then wipe away the tears that have fallen. "Thank you," I say to the woman. "You have saved my life."

She shrugs, embarrassed at my tears. "If you're still on the streets tomorrow come here and I'll give you bread," she says, her voice gruff. "I don't want to find you dead on the street, you'll scare away my best customers. Now be off with you. We've finished work for the day and I must put out the fire. There may be somewhere to shelter near the church."

I nod and back away. "Thank you," I say. "I will never forget your kindness."

The church is surrounded by a wall. At least it will provide some protection from the wind and keep me out of sight of any passers-by with less than good intentions. I make my way along the side of it until it turns a corner and curl myself into a small ball, pulling my thin robe down as low as I can to cover my feet, then wrap the jacket tightly about me. I rest my head against the wall and hope to make it through the night. I am not sure I can sleep.

"You took some finding."

The figure standing over me is only a mass of shadows and his voice has lost the humour and confidence that it used to have.

I wriggle away from him and stand up, wary of being too close to him. "How did you find me?"

"I came looking for you."

"How did you know where I would go?"

"How many friends do you have in Beijing?" Nurmat asks. "Giuseppe would have been your only hope of help."

"How did you know your way round these streets?"

He laughs. It's not a happy sound. "I wander through the streets of Beijing every night, Hidligh," he tells me. "I walk and I drink. And I hope for enough strength not to return to the Forbidden City. To leave this place and these lies and Iparhan. But every dawn I find myself presenting my tally at the Meridian Gate and re-entering my nightmare."

We're both silent for a moment.

"What do you want, Nurmat?"

His voice is very low. "I think she is going to kill him, Hidligh."

I don't ask who. I know. "She said she wanted to raise a rebellion…" I say. I know I'm stupid for even clinging on to this old lie, but I believed it for so long it comes out, even now.

"That was before she even saw you," says Nurmat. "She wanted revenge. I believed, like you did, that a rebellion would give her that. But what greater revenge could she have than to press a dagger into the Emperor's flesh and watch him die before her very eyes? She cannot wait any longer. She cannot play a part. You've seen her. She wants to see him die and nothing else matters. I was a fool not to see it long ago, but I wanted to believe her. Just as you did."

"She will die for it," I say.

Nurmat begins to say something and then stops. There's a sound like a sob before he speaks again. "She does not care about dying."

"She cares about you," I say. "And you still love her. Aren't you still loyal to her? Aren't you going to help her?"

"She's gone, Hidligh," says Nurmat. "She is gone. The woman I knew and loved from when we were little more than children – she is gone. There is a ghost in her place. A hungry ghost who seeks her revenge, by whatever means."

I shiver.

"Stop her," says Nurmat. "Help me stop her."

"Why would you care if the Emperor dies?" I ask.

"Because it would break your heart," says Nurmat. He is standing very close to me now and I take a step backwards, still wary of his loyalties.

"Why do you care if my heart is broken?" I ask.

His arms come around me in the darkness. I try to struggle away, afraid that he will seize me, drag me back to Iparhan to carry out some new part of her plan, but he holds me gently, my face pressed against his shoulder, his head bowed to rest against my hair. I stand still and listen to his sobbing breath before he lets me go and steps away. When he speaks he almost sounds like the old Nurmat I used to know, the one who loved Iparhan and still believed she would one day love him enough to seek his embrace rather than her revenge.

"My own heart has been broken enough times," he says. "I thought I loved you once. You were Iparhan, but in a gentle form. You were the Iparhan I could have been happy with. I longed for you because I longed for her. But you have found your own love and now you are your own woman. And Iparhan is gone."

"And what will become of you?" I ask.

"I will die loving her," he says. "And that will be enough."

We stand in silence for a moment.

"They have already eaten," he says. "He was with her in the bedchamber and then he left her to sleep in the other room. She will try to kill him while he sleeps. We have to stop her now or it will be too late. Are you with me?"

I reach out in the darkness and slip my hand into his. He holds it tightly for a moment and then we walk through the dark streets. He walks quickly, certain of his way and I shuffle behind him in my slippers, my hand gripped in his.

The Eastern Gate looms above us. Nurmat lifts a fist and hammers at the door. It creaks open a chink and a guard's suspicious face peers out. At the sight of Nurmat he nods and motions him forward. As we step into the light of the lanterns Nurmat suddenly grasps me roughly by the shoulder and jerks me forward. It hurts and I let out a yelp. Nurmat ignores me and holds out a small flat rectangle of wood, the size of a man's palm, the precious tally allowing him to re-enter the Forbidden City. "This one tried to run away after her mistress caught her stealing," he says. "I knew where to find her and she'll be given a beating when I get her back to the palace."

The more senior guard approves the tally and one of the other men opens the gate. Nurmat all but drags me through, raising his other hand to the guards in thanks. For a moment I'm desperately afraid that he has lied to me, that he is still on Iparhan's side, but as soon as we are out of sight he lets me go and grasps my hand again.

Hand in hand we run through the courtyards. We keep to the shadows, to the bases of the walls, the edges of the great temples and halls, keeping away from the well-lit areas where the guards congregate. The distances have never seemed so great. I am out of breath in moments. I tug at Nurmat's hand and we pause for a moment while I kick off the worn slippers. They are too hard to run in and I am afraid of the noise they make. Barefoot, I run on with Nurmat pulling at me, trying to make me run faster.

The Inner Court is quiet. Lanterns lead from one palace to another, little paths marked out with softly glowing orbs of yellow and red light. We hurry past the gates of my own palace, too brightly lit with lanterns signalling the Emperor's presence. Instead we make our way to the covering darkness of Ula Nara's still-empty palace and use her gardens to get closer to my servants' quarters.

There is silence everywhere. We avoid the sleeping quarters, where the servants have now retired for the night and make our way through the living quarters and then into my own reception hall. The room is in darkness and through the windows we can see into my courtyard. There, lanterns are lit but the guards and Emperor's servants seem mostly to be asleep. The Emperor has made his way to his bedchamber, his concubine is in her own room. There are no more tasks until the morning and every servant knows better than to waste the chance to sleep.

We make our way quietly through the rooms until we come to my bedchamber. I stop outside the door. "There will be a eunuch on guard," I say.

Nurmat shakes his head. "I was on guard," he says. "But she had me sleep outside the door, not inside. I knew she was planning something and did not want me to see that she did not go to sleep. She will be awake," he adds. "Be careful. I will go first."

He eases the door open. The room is dimly lit, with only one lantern. It is not enough light to see the whole room. He edges into the room and I follow him, a pace behind. I can just see that the bed seems empty and I look back over my shoulder, fearing that we are too late. She may have already gone to the Emperor's room.

In the moment that I hesitate I hear a gasp. There is a heavy sound and then Nurmat groans. I don't think. I enter the room and feel the door swing shut behind me, a gust of air on my cheek as the lantern is blown out, leaving me in darkness. I stand motionless. From somewhere in the room I can hear Nurmat's ragged breathing. I want to call out for help, to light a lantern and look down at him to see if he can be saved, but I feel a presence close to me and then the sharp tip of a dagger against my throat.

"Give me the perfume. I need more of it."

I shake my head, feeling the dagger slip on my bared throat as I do so, scratching the skin.

The dagger presses tighter. If I shake my head again it will draw blood. "Give me the perfume."

"Ask Nurmat for it," I say.

"He stopped giving it to me," Iparhan says and I hear a tiny catch in her throat.

I take a deep breath. "I cannot let you kill the Emperor," I say. "Kill me, if you must. I will not give you the perfume. I cannot let you go to him."

"Fool," she spits at me. I feel the dagger shake in her hand and brace myself for its thrust. "You think because you are to be promoted that he loves you?"

"I love *him*," I say. I try to back away but she follows me in the dark, her dagger kept tight to my throat. I find myself against the edge of my bed and stop. *I am going to die*, I think, and find myself speaking again, as though clinging onto my life through words. "When I am in his arms I am happy and when I am not I long for him. When he sees me his eyes are bright and he reaches for me with such desire that I find myself running to him, however unseemly it may be."

She snorts. "You must be the only Emperor's concubine in history who is happy to sit in her golden rooms, being pampered until you die of boredom."

"You forget where I came from," I say.

"Ah yes," she says. "The street rat turned lady. Is it the warm bed and the food that brought you crawling back here?"

"No," I say. "It is the care of my closest servants. It is the friends I have made here, those who rise above scheming. It is being free to pray with an open heart rather than a starving stomach. It is playing with my animals and being held by a man whom I love and who cares for me."

"And the jewels, and the clothes – they mean nothing, I suppose?" she taunts me.

"Not really," I say and as I say it I know it is true. "They are beautiful but they are not what has made me happy here."

"How virtuous."

"Iparhan," I say. "Take Nurmat and go away from here. Think how it would be to lie in his arms – the man you love – instead simpering at the Emperor, whom you hate, in the hopes of being taken to his rooms so that you might kill him. Think what it would be not to pretend to love."

"Too late for that," she says and her voice is choked.

"Nurmat would take you to his heart," I tell her. "He is only angry because he sees you with the Emperor when he wants you in his own arms."

"Too late," she says. Behind her Nurmat's rasping breath continues in the darkness.

I put a finger on the dagger, trying to lift it away from my neck. She holds it steady. I let my eyes close for a moment, trying to find some strength to carry on. "Iparhan, stop your crazy notions of revenge. Xinjiang is part of the empire now. You are not going to change that alone. It would take generations of fighting to reclaim it from the empire."

The dagger pushes tighter and I feel it prick my skin. "*Xinjiang*? You call our homeland *Xinjiang*?"

I have made an error but now I am growing angry. "You should have spent more time convincing me of your plans if you wanted a comrade in arms. You took a girl who needed food and shelter, who was starving for kindness and love and that is what you got. You never asked yourself whether I agreed with your ideals. Or your plans."

She makes an impatient sound and pulls the dagger away from me. My fingers go to my neck at once and I feel a little wetness on my fingertips. I put my fingers to my mouth and taste blood. She has nicked my throat, just where the little rough patch was. Now she stands above me in the darkness. I slide away from the bed and make my way toward Nurmat. I move slowly, afraid a sudden movement will find me with a dagger embedded in my side.

"If I fail they will execute you for treason. You had better pray I succeed," she says, watching me, a dark shadow in a dark room. "If I get away and nobody knows who killed him you will still live here as a concubine of the dead Emperor. You will have a full belly and a warm bed till the end of your days. Isn't that what you wanted? Isn't that the reason you agreed to my plan?"

"I agreed because I had nothing else in my life," I say. "No choice. And now I do."

"He will die for what he has done to my family and my country," she says, her voice shaking.

I've reached Nurmat's side. I kneel by him but it's too dark to see him properly. "Nurmat," I whisper. "Speak to me." I run my fingers over him, wary of what I may find. I try to lift him a little although I'm wary of moving him too much. His breath is too hard and rasping to answer me, but he lifts a hand and places it on mine. Above us looms Iparhan's shadow. I am suddenly angry. I lay him down and stand to face her. Our features hidden by the darkness, I can feel the heat of her body, we are so close. "You loved him!"

"He loved *you*," she answers, lowering her head.

"He did not, Iparhan."

"He let you back into the Forbidden City."

"And you killed him for his last shred of decency?"

She turns away. I stand watching her, shaking. Now I am truly afraid of her. If Iparhan has killed Nurmat then she can kill anyone. The Emperor, me, herself. There was no one she loved more than Nurmat and she has not hesitated to take his life. Nothing I can say now will dissuade her.

She strides towards the doorway, stepping over Nurmat's body without pause. She is heading towards the courtyard, where a door on the walkway leads to the Emperor's bedroom.

At my feet Nurmat gasps and I want to comfort him but I cannot. I run, barefoot, after Iparhan.

In the courtyard all is silence and darkness. The lanterns are growing dim. Their faint lights play on the carvings and make every shadow a person. My feet are cold on the walkway and I shiver. The guards and eunuchs who accompanied the Emperor are now all asleep, my courtyard littered with bodies as though a battle has already been fought and lost here tonight.

There's a small sound near the door leading to the Emperor's bedchamber and suddenly I am running along the walkway and throwing myself at Iparhan. She turns at once to grapple with me.

She's strong. I knew it, of course, but I've never had to pit myself against her. Now we clutch at one another, her hands unforgiving as she reaches round my back and presses hard on my spine. She is wearing the perfume, but its scent has faded beneath a mixture of sweat and fear, rage and the cold damp night air. I clench my teeth in pain but she does not slacken her grip and at last I do the only thing I can – I jerk forwards and bite her cheek hard, my teeth coming down on the raised line of her scar. I feel flesh give way and taste blood. She makes a groaning sound and pulls away. I open my jaw and let her fall backwards with the effort she has made to escape me. I've only a moment before she is on me again but this time I'm quicker, expecting her. I run into the courtyard, out of the gates into the little lane outside my palace and as I do so stumble against a pillar. She follows me, her hand coming out to rest on the pillar as she grabs for me but the pillar is already rocking from my weight and suddenly from it a figure falls – a giant golden guardian lion – and crushes her from the waist down beneath its bulk.

Even in her agony she manages to remain silent, only a gasp tells me she should have screamed. I wriggle away from her flailing arms and stand over her. She is trapped – her pelvis and legs crushed beneath the golden weight. Her fingernails scrape on the cobbles as she tries to pull herself away from it but the weight is far too much for her. I come closer and she twists and tries to grab at my robe but I step away.

"Bitch," she curses under her breath. "Traitor."

I stand and watch her. Her efforts are causing her greater pain but she does not stop writhing.

"Keep still," I tell her. "I will help you if you keep still and promise not to attack me again."

She becomes a little more still and I approach her. I kneel by her side but as soon as I am close to her she grabs for me and brings my face close to hers, her arm around my neck. Her hot breath is on my cheek and her hand, wet with the blood from my bite, pulls at my hair. I struggle and she spits in my face. "You will die," she hisses. "You and your precious Emperor and all your pampered court."

"Half your body is crushed," I tell her, still struggling to escape from her. "You will die if I leave you here. You will not be able to kill anyone."

She lets go of me suddenly, her arms weakening with the pain filling her body. "You're wrong," she pants, wiping blood away from her eyes. "The poison will kill all of you – you, the other whores and the Emperor."

"Poison?"

She tries to sit up and then gasps with pain as something else in her legs gives way. "You won't find it. But all of the court will die."

I hear steps nearby and turn quickly. A shadowed figure stands between the gateposts a few paces away. I've been expecting someone to arrive; there's been too much noise to go unnoticed.

"Reveal yourself," I say, my voice shaking. If it's a guard I am dead.

The shadows change and Huan steps forwards. I stare at him for a long moment and he looks back at me, then down at Iparhan. He takes in the clothes she is wearing, which are mine, and her hair, dressed in sparkling stones. He looks back at me. I open my mouth to speak but he raises a hand to stop me.

"I was right," he says slowly. "She took your place."

I nod. "How did you know?"

He shakes his head. "I am not sure," he says, looking between the two of us. "I am not sure," he repeats as though in a daze. "I knew but did not know. Until now."

I let my body slide down so that I am squatting before him. My head lowers and I stay in silence for a while.

At last I look up at him. "Do what you must do, Huan," I say. "If you must raise the alarm, do so."

He's gone. I've grown used to the eunuchs' skill in walking quietly so as not to disturb their masters, but even so his footsteps are like air. I'm alone again in the darkness with Iparhan. Time passes in silence and my thighs ache, I'm unaccustomed to squatting now, though it used to be my natural resting pose. "He'll be back soon," I mutter. "With guards."

Iparhan tries to move again and then becomes still, looking over my shoulder. I twist to look up. Huan has returned. He must have been running, for his breath rises and falls quickly in his chest but still he made no noise approaching us. He keeps his mouth open to breathe more quietly.

"Are they coming?" I ask.

Huan looks behind him. "Who?"

I shrug. "The guards. Other servants. The Emperor. Whomever you called for."

"I called for no one," he says. "I brought this."

He passes me something that seems to glow softly in the darkness, something pure white and soft to the touch. I hold it. It seems to be a white silk scarf but I am stupid with tiredness. "I don't know what this is," I tell him.

"It is for an honourable death," he says, his voice still soft despite his quick breath.

I turn it over in my hands. "Suicide?"

He bows his head.

I twist it in my hands, look down and feel its strength. "Is that what I should do, then? Is that what is expected?"

He snatches it back from my hands. "For *her*," he hisses. Not for you."

I rock back on my heels to look up at him and almost topple over. I am too tired to balance. "She doesn't want to die," I say. "She wants to kill."

He lifts his chin to indicate Iparhan and I turn to look at her. Her hands are reaching out towards the scarf.

I throw the scarf through the air and it twists and turns before floating into her outstretched hands. She wraps it about her neck and tries to pull it but even I can see at once that she will not succeed. She tries harder but at last lets go, leaving it crumpled round her neck.

Huan steps forward. "It is a task I can perform," he says.

I grab at the base of his robe. "You don't know anything about this," I say to him. "How do you know you should still be loyal to me?"

He looks down at me and at Iparhan. His hand comes to rest gently on my tousled hair for a brief moment, before he steps forward again.

I tug at him harder, stopping him. "Can't she be taken away?" I ask in a whisper. "We could get her out of the Forbidden City. She could go away," I add, although I know that Iparhan would do no such thing.

Huan shakes his head. "She will die by dawn," he says. "She can die quickly or slowly." He steps forward again but I hold up my hand.

"It is mine to do," I say.

He is silent for a moment and then nods. "I will find the well," he says.

I frown at him. "Well?"

"She said she had poisoned the court," he says. "She must mean a well. There are many in the Forbidden City but only a few large enough to provide enough water to be sure of harming so many."

I'd forgotten her threats. I look at her face and see from the bitterness on it that Huan is right. "Go," I say and he's gone before I can take another breath.

I make my way over to her and when I'm close I wait for her to attack me again, watching her hands carefully, but she doesn't move, only looks at me.

"Are you happy?" she rasps. "Happy in your golden cage while our homeland is crushed by your lover?"

"It's over," I tell her. "Your plans for rebellion and unrest – your plans to kill the Emperor. All over."

"The people will rise again," she says.

I shake my head. "The Emperor will crush them if they rise against him."

"Then they will rise again. And again and again. Until there is no Emperor, nor empire, and they will be free."

I nod, take the ends of the silk scarf in my hands and look down at her. My hands shake.

Her face softens and she strokes the silk at her neck, her eyes closing. "I loved Nurmat," she says, her voice soft and gentle as I've never heard it before. "Tell him I always loved him."

It takes a long time for her to die. I hoped only a few moments would suffice and I begin to release my grip on her too early. She twists violently as soon as the pressure eases, trying to take the breath that will save her and I'm forced to grasp the scarf again more tightly although my hands ache and the white silk cuts into my knuckles until I can hardly feel them.

At last her body grows heavy and slowly falls against me instead of struggling away. I'm wary, thinking she is playing dead to fool me, knowing how strong she is. I let go of the white silk finger by finger but she doesn't move and when I unwind its coils I bring my ear close to her mouth and there is no warm breath on my cheek.

I sit in the darkness and hold her for a while. I try to cry for her but I'm too tired for tears. My whole body is weak with the fear of the past two years draining out of me. At last I get to my feet and place my hands under her arms, bracing myself against her limpness. I need one last burst of strength to protect myself and then I will be free.

I begin the journey back to my room, staggering under the weight. It's not far but she's heavier than I expected and by the time I reach the bedroom I'm dragging her body rather than carrying it, her shoes making a noise as they bump into hard objects and her clothes swishing against doorways. A few guards and servants mutter in their sleep or roll over as we pass them but no one wakes.

My bedchamber is dark. Only one small lantern is lit and everywhere are shadows. I stumble through the doorway and rip off the old jacket and the maid's robe, then use it to wipe my face, removing my painted scar. I feel about for my silken sleeping robe and pull it on, then kneel by Iparhan's body. In the dim flickering light I wipe away her makeup, revealing her scar, pull away all of her gemstones and ribbons, leaving her hair unbound. I replait it, my fingers clumsy, the little red maid's ribbon badly tied. Throughout this I can hear deep rasping breaths close at hand and I keep up a whispered comfort. "One moment, Nurmat," I beg. "One moment and I will come to you. I must finish this. I must." I tug at her clothing. Her limp corpse resists me and more than once I hear the fabrics tear. At last she is naked and I use the stained cotton robe to cover her again. Dressed, she lies in the middle of my chamber floor, a crumpled broken shell, her pale skin flickering with dark shadows.

Now I make my way to Nurmat's side, lifting the lantern onto the floor so that I can see him better. He is half draped on the bed and when I touch the coverlets they are wet with blood. I kneel by his side. "Nurmat," I whisper. "Nurmat. Speak to me."

His eyes open but when he tries to speak blood gurgles from his open mouth. I wipe it away with my silk sleeve and then lay a finger against his mouth so that he will not speak but he tries again. I can make out only one word. "Iparhan."

I hold him closer with one arm. With the other hand I reach for my vial of perfume and hold it open, close to him, so that the faint scent that always clings to me is magnified a thousandfold. He breathes, hard and fast, and the smell of delicate spring blossom and rich summer fruits enters his nostrils. He stills in my arms, breathing slower and more deeply.

Then I close his eyes. "I am Iparhan," I whisper to him. "And we are married now. I am your wife and we will leave this place today. We will journey back to Kashgar and there we will live, you and I. I will bear your children and you will love me always."

His eyes flutter, trying to open. He tries to focus on me. "Hidligh."

I place a hand across his eyes, blocking his sight and whisper again, while his breathing grows ragged. "I, Iparhan, will love you for ever, Nurmat. Forever."

His breath is gone and his body grows so heavy I can no longer hold him to me, even with both arms. I let him go and he slides to the floor, leaving his blood soaking into my pale silk coverlets, staining them from palest pink to deepest scarlet.

I stand, every part of my body aching. Slowly, as though in a trance, I conceal the vial of perfume and rip the bed curtains, use the water bowl to clean my feet before binding my own hands, then drape myself across my bed.

Only then do I scream for help and hear Huan come running, his footsteps suddenly grown loud and heavy, as he echoes my cries and forces the heavy-eyed servants out of their slumbers.

Dawn comes and as soon as the gates of the Forbidden City open Huan sends for a man who will release me at last of the weight hanging over me. He may not see my face, of course, so I sit on one side of a painted screen and he stands on the other. I hear him kowtow, his forehead touching the ground nine times while I gather up the strength to speak.

"The casket is currently in the care of my chief attendant, Huan," I explain. "It must be treated with great respect. I require the best carriers and there must be mourners sent to accompany the casket."

"Yes, my lady. May I ask – who is the deceased?"

Within the casket lie two bodies, Iparhan's and Nurmat's, intertwined at last. Huan has concocted a romantic story for the court, hailing Nurmat as a hero for having given his life to protect me from an unknown assassin and cherishing Iparhan as a lovestruck maid who took her own life rather than live without her eunuch husband-to-be. Huan and Jiang carried her body to the casket, her crushed body hidden beneath the faded blue of her cotton robe. The Emperor sent additional guards to my palace to ensure my future safety and was assured that my other servants had learnt to cook Nurmat's dishes. At my request he granted me many taels of silver to send my loyal servants westwards to rest in our homeland.

I stay silent, thinking of this and of Huan's search in the darkness of that night for the poisoned well. Without his knowledge of the Forbidden City many of the courtiers and women here would have died in drawn-out agony.

"Your relative," the man surmises after a long silence has elapsed. "All due care shall be taken."

"It is a long journey," I remind him. "Do not let me hear that once gone from Beijing your care of the casket fell by the wayside." I know I need to say this, to threaten him, even though the silver he will be paid is more than enough to make him care for the casket as though it were his own mother's. He will never have been paid so well, even though he has over one hundred people to accompany him – to carry the casket, to mourn, to guide the way through the trade routes and finally to lay the casket to rest.

"I shall be by its side until your relative is laid to rest," he promises.

"It must be laid in Kashgar," I clarify. "There must be a tomb of great beauty for the people of that land will wish to honour it."

He probably thinks I am attributing too much importance to my unknown relative but I have the silver and he wants the job. "The tomb will be a place of pilgrimage for ever," he says in tones of dutiful piety.

I insist on specifying the inscriptions, the colours of the tiles adorning the tomb, the route they must take which retraces our steps from Kashgar to here. I wish I could have them buried in the Taklamakan Desert by the side of Iparhan's father, but there would be too many explanations and, besides, the dunes will have shifted by now and no-one could find that old poplar tree. I would be lost trying to find it myself.

I leave my rooms, now filled with servants and guards, and make my way to the pond, where I kneel among the grasses and murmur prayers for the dead. The air is cold, very soon the winter months will be here. Tears fall then, but silently, and I stay still for such a long time that the greedy heron joins me and gobbles fish without casting me so much as a glance. When I rise he stalks away, indignant over my interruption of his repast. The ripples of Iparhan's daggers slipping into the water make him turn back to see if the glinting metal is in fact the scales of a fish, but by the time he has returned they are gone from sight and I am already walking away, leaving him to continue his investigation of the edible inhabitants in peace. Huan is already waiting for me. The ceremony to promote me to a higher rank will take place soon and everything must be ready. Jiang has just returned from his errand: he sought out the cobbler and his wife and gave them more silver than they have ever held in their lives. They gasped their gratitude to him but it is I who will give thanks for their kindness every day of my life.

The stiff golden-yellow silk cocoons me. I look down at the imperial dragons raging around my high collar and the swirling ocean waves decorating the robe's hem, feel my triple pearl earrings sway forward as I do so. The movement hurts a little, for the piercings are still fresh. The horseshoe-shaped sleeves trimmed in fur all but cover my hands, so that only the tips of my fingers emerge, showing my golden nail shields, studded with tiny pink rubies. They hide the scrapes across my knuckles and my own broken nails, the last remnants of my attempts to climb the red walls. I had thought the elaborate Manchu hairstyles of the other concubines would be hard to balance but golden combs and green jade pins hold lotus flowers firmly in place, the very last of the season, rising above my head like a tiny garden. Lady Wan sent her hairdresser to help Huan and their final choice is beautiful but simple, all the attention focused on the pale and vibrant pinks of the lotuses. Amongst the flowers sits a tiny green jade tortoise, my only request, cunningly wrought by a court jeweller. I reach up to touch its curved back and think of Mei. Huan tells me he picked the flowers for my hair himself. That is, he stood on the bank of the lake and screamed ever more irate instructions at two lesser eunuchs getting their sleeves wet stretching out from a boat, berating their incompetence and general inability to spot a suitable lotus flower when they saw one.

I stretch out a hand to him. "You have performed a marvel," I tell him and he bows, his face suffused with pleasure. When he straightens I see the shine of tears in his tired eyes.

"I am proud of you, my lady," he says. "Your honour is my honour."

I clasp his hand more tightly. "It is indeed, Huan," I say and make my way towards the waiting chair.

From his throne the Emperor smiles down at me as he turns a magnificent green jade *ruyi* in his hands, topped with gold lotus flowers. I know the jade was brought here from Xinjiang, that one of my countrymen, stooping in a riverbed, touched its smooth shape with his bare feet and knew it for a treasure before it was lifted above the water and made its way travelling the trade routes just as I did two years ago. I smile, step forward, balancing gracefully on the hand-height platforms of my golden shoes, then kneel and begin my kowtow to the Emperor and his mother. My voice is steady as I wish them ten thousand years and rise to my feet in one easy movement as the Chief Eunuch calls out my new name.

"Lady He is promoted to the order of *Fei*, Consort of the fourth rank. Her name will henceforth be Rong Fei - Consort of Harmonious Beauty!"

The scribes and officials hurry to update the records and put into motion all the new privileges that will now be mine – more servants, larger rooms, richer clothes. My new name will be Lady Rong, a name encompassing harmony, beauty, the lotus flowers in my hair and on the *ruyi* about to be presented to me. And perhaps, with only the slightest change of tone, the meaning of martial valour.

From his place at the back of the room Giuseppe nods to me. The Emperor has commissioned a new painting. A hunting scene: the Emperor at full gallop on a horse, an arrow loosed from his bow at a falling stag. By his side on a dappled horse, rides a woman who passes him another arrow while her plaits fly in the wind. It is a private portrait, for the Emperor's own pleasure and mine.

To my right, the ladies of the court watch me. Lady Wang's lips are pressed tightly together but she does not permit herself a scowl. It is dangerous to insult a higher-ranking concubine, especially a favourite. I smile at Lady Wan, who clasps her hands in happiness for me. Ladies Qing and Ying nod to me, their friendly smiles broadening as I return them. Imperial Noble Consort Ling, now the highest-ranked of us all, meets my gaze with steady eyes before each of us bows our heads to the other. Our two name chips are still those most often chosen on the silver tray in the Emperor's rooms. I know that her children will be chosen as his future heirs. She knows that I have a place in the Emperor's heart. Each of us is happy to walk the path laid out before us.

In the imperial records of this dynasty I am reborn for the third time. A new name, a new status, a new being. All that came before this moment is swept away into rumours and exaggeration, stories to be told behind closed doors or whispered one to another with much embroidery along the way.

I take the *ruyi* from the Emperor and smile up at him. He leans in a little to breathe in my perfume as he lightly caresses my cheek. His eyes soften as they did the first time he smelt my scent. He cups my face more firmly and kisses me, his lips warm on mine. It's a lingering kiss more suited to a bedchamber than here in front of the whole court and I feel myself grow flushed but when his lips leave mine I am still pressed against him, relaxing into his warmth. He chuckles into my neck.

"I have a surprise for you," he murmurs. "Someone from your homeland."

I thought I was free. I pull away from him and turn very slowly, my fists clenching, wondering who can be left from those days. I wonder if I have the strength to fight for my life again.

Kneeling on the floor, the old man makes his obeisance to us. His eyes were failing him even then and now they are milky-white. As he looks up towards where the Emperor and I stand he will see only two columns of yellow and gold, shining in the dim light of the throne room.

"A storyteller," says the Emperor. "I thought you would like to hear stories from Kashgar."

I look up at him. He is hopeful in his latest gift. "Do stories help with homesickness?" he asks.

My smile is wide and unforced. I place a delicate golden-tipped hand on his sleeve and feel a wave of tenderness overwhelm me. "My home is here, Your Majesty. By your side. I have no more homesickness. I am happy."

He nods, content in his benevolence. "Begin, storyteller," he commands, and settles himself back on the throne while the rest of us gather round and arrange ourselves comfortably for the performance, the eunuchs hurrying to provide thick cushions on which we may recline.

The storyteller is old and blind but he still knows his craft. He straightens himself and spreads his hands wide to bring all of us into his circle. His voice is strong and confident, honed over many trading days in the market of Kashgar. From my place close to the Emperor, cushioned by soft silks and wrapped in glittering colours, I watch the storyteller and wait to hear the words I heard so long ago.

"All legends are true, even the ones that never happened," he begins.

My scarlet-painted lips move soundlessly with his.

For in them we find ourselves.

Author's Note on History

Legends of the Fragrant Concubine

In China, approximately in the year 1760, the Emperor Qianlong conquered Turkestan, also known as Altishahr, an area to the west of China. He renamed the area Xinjiang, the New Dominion, and took a local woman into the Forbidden City as his concubine. From this union came the legends of the Fragrant Concubine, although the stories differ wildly depending on the storyteller.

In China they tell of a beautiful Muslim concubine sent from Altishahr to the Emperor's court in Beijing. Her body emitted an irresistible natural fragrance and the Emperor was besotted with her. But the woman, known as Xiang Fei – the Fragrant Concubine – was homesick. The Emperor tried many things to make her feel at home. He built her a mosque and a bazaar, but nothing would stem her tears. At last, at her request, he ordered the silver-leaved, golden-fruited oleaster tree to be brought from her homeland, and with this gift the lovely concubine was homesick no more and they were happy together.

But in Altishahr the local Uyghur people say that the beautiful Muslim concubine came from a family of rebels. She was named Iparhan – Fragrant Girl – and the Emperor seized her from her husband and family, bringing her to court by force. But Iparhan refused to allow the Emperor near her, keeping daggers hidden in her sleeves to protect her honour. At last the Empress Dowager, fearful for her son's peace of mind, offered Iparhan the honourable option of suicide while the Emperor was away hunting. Returning, he found Iparhan strangled by a white silk scarf, whether by her own hand or that of the palace eunuchs is unknown. The Emperor held her in his arms and cried bitter tears. Her body was sent in state back to her homeland, where she was buried in a tomb that is still a place of pilgrimage today.

Official court records from the time show that there was indeed a Muslim concubine brought to court at the time of the conquest. She was the sister of a local noble who had aided the Emperor in his conquest of the region. She was named Rong Fei – Consort Rong – and it seems she was a favourite of the Emperor, who arranged for a Muslim cook named Nurmat to serve in her household so that her dietary requirements would be met. The Emperor built an observatory tower in the palace that looked onto the newly created Muslim quarter within Beijing. He indulged the concubine with Hami melons brought from her homeland and sweetmeats on her birthdays. He had many portraits painted of her, including one showing her in full battle armour, an unusual image for a concubine. She was twice promoted within five years of her arrival at court, ending her life there as a highly-ranked consort. She began her life at court in her own traditional dress but on being promoted ordered court clothing to be made for her. On her death many years later she was buried with all due honours in the imperial tombs near Beijing. There is a private portrait, intended for the Emperor's eyes only, of the Emperor hunting with a woman riding alongside him, a very unusual image. He is shooting an arrow at a stag and she, mid-gallop, is passing him another arrow for his bow. She is dressed as a high-ranking concubine and her hair hangs in two plaits, a style not used by Manchu women but by the women from Xinjiang. It is surmised that this could well be a portrait of Rong Fei, out riding and hunting with the Emperor. I found this portrait only *after* I had written about their riding together in the hunting grounds, an activity that I thought I was taking quite a lot of poetic licence inventing, so it was a wonderful find for me!

Key characters

I have tried to be authentic to the period and setting, incorporating as much of the history as possible, however I have also allowed myself some freedoms to enable better storytelling – and in the spirit of all legends being true whether they happened or not.

The period covered in the novel is only two years, while the key historical events described actually took place over about five years (1760-1765), from the concubine arriving at court to Empress Ula Nara cutting off her hair and including the grand tour. The Emperor Qianlong was very fond of hunting, which was an annual event as well as travelling, going on a number of grand tours of his empire. There were two in the period covered, which I have conflated into one. The portraits of the Fragrant Concubine described in the novel all exist.

Lady Wan lived to over 90. She was promoted to honour her long service to the Emperor, whom she outlived.

Imperial Noble Consort Ling was the mother of the future Jiaqing Emperor, heir to the Qianlong Emperor. Because of this she was posthumously raised to the rank of Empress.

Consort Qing raised the Jiaqing Emperor (Prince Yongyan in this novel). He was fond of her and when she died he had her posthumously promoted to the rank of Imperial Noble Consort.

Consort Ying raised the Jiaqing Emperor's younger brother (Imperial Noble Consort Ling's second son) who was also very fond of his adoptive mother, presenting her with gifts on her birthdays.

Lady Wang managed to be promoted again following her disgrace and later bore the Emperor a daughter who became his favourite child.

The Jesuit painter and architect Giuseppe Castiglione lived in the Forbidden City from his youth until his death, serving three Emperors, the last of which was the Qianlong Emperor.

The Dowager Empress began life as a fairly low-ranking concubine to a prince, until the choice of her son as Emperor made her the most senior woman in the Forbidden City. The Qianlong Emperor was very devoted to her and when she grew too old to travel stopped all of his tours of China. She died aged eighty-four. Giuseppe Castiglione and the Dowager Empress are the main characters of *The Garden of Perfect Brightness,* set in their youth.

Empress Ula Nara did cut off her hair and was banished from court. She died a year later and was buried without the honours due to an Empress. There is still a debate on why she acted as she did. Rumours at the time suggested jealousy over another woman. The Emperor Qianlong refused to have another Empress appointed during his lifetime. Her story is told in *The Cold Palace.*

Thanks

Many thanks are due. First of all to my mother, who not only taught me to read and write but is also the best storyteller I know. To the members of www.YouWriteOn.com for their feedback and encouragement for chapter one. To Professor James Millward of Georgetown University for his fantastic article *'A Uyghur Muslim in Qianlong's Court: the meanings of the Fragrant Concubine,'* and his enormous kindness in reading my manuscript and giving me a real education in everything from noodles and accents to tea and mountains. All errors are of course mine. To the British Library and the School of Oriental and African Studies library – your resources are amazing. Thank you to my Bookclub Ladies as well as Bernie and Camilla for cheerleading, Helen for detailed feedback right at the start and Ryan for constant love, encouragement and precious writing time. To Seth for arriving late and to Isabelle for taking regular naps enabling me to keep writing. Thank you to my agent Lisa for being excited, my editor Sam for seeing what had been left out and the Streetlight Graphics team for making the book both real and beautiful. All of you made it a better story.

MELISSA ADDEY

The
Garden
of
Perfect
Brightness

The Garden of Perfect Brightness

For Paul and Rachel.
Thank you for such a wonderful experience.

This whole inclosure is called, Yuen-Ming-Yuen (the Garden of Perfect Brightness).

There is but one Man here; and that is the Emperor. All pleasures are made for him alone. This charming place is scarce ever seen by any body but himself, his Women, and his Eunuchs. The Princes, and other chief Men of the Country, are rarely admitted any farther than the Audience-Chambers. Of all the Europeans that are here, none ever enter'd this Inclosure, except the Clock-makers and Painters; whose Employments make it necessary that they should be admitted every where.

Letter from Jesuit painter Jean-Denis Attiret. Beijing, Nov 1ˢᵗ, 1743

Memory Palace, definition:

1: Originally and chiefly historical, an imaginary building thought of as comprising various rooms and areas, each containing mnemonic objects and features that symbolize particular ideas, which can be visualized mentally as a systematic method of remembering those ideas.

2: A building, place, or structure that holds or evokes memories.

The Oxford English Dictionary

Early 1700s

The Crow's Summons

THE EYES OF EVE, AT the very moment of her greatest sin, offering Adam the apple in her hand, gave me pause. I looked down at the designs and shook my head. There was something too knowing about her expression. The moment of mankind's downfall should not contain malevolence, except from the snake, already painted yesterday, which watched with glittering wickedness for its plan to come to fruition. My pencil moved and now Eve gazed at her mate with a loving innocence. Her hair, long and dark, fell to cover part of her naked breast. The Garden of Eden might have been a place without shame, but the priests would throw up their hands in horror if I were to deliver them a fresco of a naked Adam and Eve.

Around me the church echoed to curses and the loud noises of the fresh plaster being prepared – scraping, mixing, water pouring.

"God's bones! Do you have to make such a din?" I finally bellowed. "I can barely think!"

"Sorry master," said the foreman. "Won't happen again." He cuffed his young assistant round the head and there was something approaching a blessed silence for a few minutes until one of the other labourers muttered something about the master having a sore head from too much drinking and the whole group burst into laughter.

I considered threatening to dock their pay but my head ached enough to persuade me to wait a few more minutes until they were done and gone, when silence would be restored and I could work without interruption. I nodded to my own assistant, who had prepared my paints for the day and dismissed him with a wave. He would return at midday with my lunch, for once the fresh plaster was up I was working against Old Father Time himself to paint what I could of the fresco, which was very large. The quicker the work was done the better, for each day's work left telltale marks between one section and another, which offended my eye even after blending the paints between the two areas as much as possible.

"All done, master," said the foreman. "Smooth as you like."

I did not inspect his work. Vannozzo's plastering was without equal, he was in demand all over Milan by artists painting frescos. I was lucky to have secured his services early in the morning, allowing me a longer working day before the plaster set and I could no longer paint on it.

"I'll see you tomorrow," I said.

"As God is my witness, master." He waved goodbye and took his labourers and noise with him.

Time passed and my headache began to subside. The quiet around me, the focus on my work, these things calmed me. Fresco work made some painters anxious, for there was no room for error: when the paint touched the wet plaster the brushstrokes must be accurate. Oil on canvas could be layered and then layered again to cover any mistakes or create desired changes. The only way to undo fresco work was with a chisel. But I loved its delicacy, its speed as well as the need for certainty and found a sense of calm in the work.

The quiet of the church was broken by quick steps, followed by a lingering pause, which irritated me, for it meant that someone was hovering behind my back without having the courtesy to introduce themselves. I have never cared to be overlooked whilst painting, much less by a stranger. I spoke without turning.

"Who's there?"

Further quick steps brought a man before me. His tall black hat and long dark robes, combined with an inquisitive air, made me think of the loitering crows near my family's home. I half expected the Jesuit's voice to emerge as a caw.

He made an inelegant bow and having introduced himself in a thick Milanese accent he paused, as though waiting for my own name, although surely he knew who I was, having sought me out in my place of work.

"Giuseppe Castiglione," I said at last. "Son of Pietro Castiglione."

He nodded but seemed uncertain of his mission, gesturing awkwardly at the fresco as though to buy time. "May I?" he asked.

I waved him towards it without pointing out that as he had hovered behind me for a lengthy period he must surely have seen the image already.

He fluttered closer to it and stood regarding the image. On the wall, as though seeing through an open door, was a glimpse of the Garden of Eden, with Adam and Eve standing beneath the Tree of Knowledge, their hands touching as the fateful apple passed from one to the other. The use of a forced perspective meant that the image would appear real, as though one might step through the door and into the Garden, to warn against evil or perhaps to partake in it.

The crow held out his hand and let his fingertips brush against the cold surface of the wall. "A remarkable illusion," he said.

"It is called *trompe l'oeil*," I said.

"To deceive the eye," he said, nodding. "I have seen it done before but not, sir, as well as it has been done here."

I waited. If the crow was intent on flattering me then it was likely he wanted something from me. Whatever he wanted, he needed to hurry up and make his request. The plaster was drying even as we spoke.

"Do you enjoy your work?" he asked at last.

I nodded but this did not satisfy him.

"The subject matter?" he pressed. "Images of a religious nature?"

I nodded again. Much of my work was of a religious nature, for the Church paid handsomely and there was scope for the imagination.

"Are you inclined towards the Church yourself?" he asked.

I shook my head. He seemed disappointed. "My brother Giovanni is a priest," I offered, as though this might console him.

He brightened at once. "Indeed?" he asked. "And would you consider a similar path yourself – but one where your talents as a painter might be put to service for a higher purpose?"

I frowned. "A painter-priest?"

Now he was all smiles. "Exactly!"

"I am already a painter. Why would I have need to become a priest?"

The crow smiled at my confusion. "May we talk?" he asked.

I had thought we already were, but I allowed him to draw me to one side, to a pew at the back of the church where we both sat, turned awkwardly towards one another. I looked at him, waiting for him to speak, while thinking of my fast-drying plasterwork.

"The Jesuit Brotherhood has a Mission in China," he began. "We wish to convert as many souls as we may there, that they may know the love of God. But in order to do so, we hope first and foremost to engage with the Emperor of China, that he may allow our work to continue there, but also perhaps hear the word of our Lord for himself."

I had heard of their missionary work and in particular of one of their missionaries, now long dead, a certain Matteo Ricci. He had a notion that I myself have used to great effect throughout my life, the creation of a 'memory palace', a building created and held within one's own imagination, in whose rooms one can store memories such that they can be easily retrieved. I began to speak of this with enthusiasm, noting that for a painter, such a technique was of particular interest, allowing one to store details which might seem trivial to others but which gave paintings true verisimilitude – the broken twig, a particular pose or colour, the ways in which water moves when touched by the breeze and more. I would have gone on but the crow only nodded and smiled.

"Indeed, indeed," he said. "It is through such talents that we hope to make our mark with the Emperor. We have taken him gifts of telescopes and other marvels of our own world and he has been much pleased with them. But his greatest interest is reserved for the men of skill that we have brought to China to serve him. Botanists, clockmakers, astronomers, mathematicians and architects. They have been chosen to serve him personally and through seeing their talents serve his needs he has in turn shown much graciousness towards our mission."

"Has he converted?" I asked.

The crow shook his head sadly. "Not yet," he said. "But we hope that he may still do so, despite his advancing age – indeed, many men convert as they grow older and come to think of their own demise."

"Who is this emperor?" I asked.

"The Kangxi Emperor has ruled for over forty years, since he was a young child. He is now approaching fifty years old. He has brought about stability and wealth for his country, but he is also a great lover of new ideas." He paused, as though thinking how best to frame his next words. "He has requested a new painter," he said at last. "Our Mission had previously supplied him with such a man, by the name of Gherardini, from Bologna. He arrived in China in 1699 and served the Kangxi Emperor well enough, but he could not accept the missionary lifestyle and left the Mission of Beijing after less than ten years, against the will of the Brothers there. Before him, there was a painter by the name of Fiori, who also tired of the life there and returned home to his native city. At present, therefore, we are without a painter." He looked at me expectantly.

"You wish me to go to China as court painter to the Emperor?" I asked, my voice betraying my excitement. Already I was imagining the long sea voyage, the arrival in a foreign land, the many new sights I would see, the service (highly praised and rewarded, of course) to an Emperor, no less. I laughed out loud, all irritation with the crow suddenly gone. "Well, I believe I am your man – it will be a great adventure and a fine story to tell my friends and family on my return!"

The crow gave a half smile at my newly found enthusiasm but was already shaking his head. "I have not made myself clear," he said. "Fiori and Gherardini were not Jesuits and therefore they were free to leave our Mission, but their leaving was not looked upon kindly by the Emperor. It has therefore been decided that the next painter we send to China must be a Jesuit, so that he will be obliged to follow the directives of our Order. The painter whom we choose must undertake to remain in China and to serve the Emperor and his descendants for the term of his natural life. The man we choose must take the vows of our Brotherhood: Poverty, Chastity and Obedience, within two years of reaching Beijing. He will go to China and never return."

We talked a while longer, that I might know what would be required. Behind us, the plaster dried. I did not care. A voyage by sea, not without danger, of over a year, followed by a further shorter journey across China to reach the Emperor's capital, Beijing. Unquestioning service to be rendered to the Emperor and any future successors. Painting commissions to be carried out according to his orders and taste. Above all, that once committed to this mission I would never again see Milan, nor my friends and family. When he left I sat before the fresco on which I should have been working, my eyes unseeing, my hands still and tools untouched, my heart beating fast. At last, an outlet for my ambition! Adventure, new sights to capture, a whole new world opening up before me. In my naivety the price to pay seemed low enough. The company of women? Well, I had met a few who had charmed me, in their own way, but they could not, must not, stand in the way of my career as a great painter – for such I wished to become – and so I might as well forswear their companionship. Some of my friends told great tales of love, but I had yet to experience such devotion as they described and indeed, rather suspected them of exaggerating for effect. I would be clothed and fed and housed, whatever vows of poverty might be made. Above all, shining above all, was the promise of an imperial patron. For me, there was no decision to be made. My assistant brought me food, which I did not eat. I dismissed him for the rest of the day, much to his amazement, then left the church without finishing my work. Vannozzo would curse all the saints tomorrow when he had to chip away the plaster I had left to dry unpainted. I could not wait to tell my family and friends about the adventure before me.

My mother Anna Maria was aghast when I told her my plan. She wept. "I will never see you again! I have already given a son to the Church. Why is this sacrifice demanded of me? I will never see my son again, never have grandchildren."

My father patted her awkwardly on the back. He did not like crying women, they made him ill at ease. "I am sure Giuseppe will make our family proud," he said, with excessive cheerfulness. "There is no higher position for a painter than to have a monarch as his patron. Our son's talent is already reaping rewards."

I nodded, smiling. This was a position I had dreamt of. Most painters would have to become better known, older, with a studio of their own, before being summoned to receive royal or imperial patronage. I was about to make the leap while barely out of my apprenticeship. I made my excuses and left my mother to weep while I made my way to the local tavern. My friends, at least, would be impressed.

"No women?" Antonio cried. "None at all? Your dick will fall off through lack of use!" He leaned against me, simpering like a girl, tugging at the corner of his eyes to make them seem Oriental. "And what if you were to meet a Chinese beauty such as myself, young sir? Would your heart not melt? Would your rod not stiffen, eh? Eh?"

The others roared with laughter.

I shoved him away. "You have no ambition, Antonio," I told him. "You only think with your dick. Imagine being painter to an Emperor! You'll be lucky if you ever attend a court, let alone be attached to one."

"The Emperor of China can go hang," said Antonio. "Give me a pretty girl any day."

"Then that's all you'll get," I told him. "Whereas I shall be a renowned painter. My work will be admired across the world while you spend the rest of your life painting portraits for merchants."

Antonio shook his head and waved for another jug of wine. "So *proud*," he said. "So full of yourself. Always certain you are destined for great things."

"I am," I told him. And I believed it.

My master Filippo bid me a kind farewell. "I am sure I will hear your name again," he said. "You have been an apt pupil and your talent is real. In particular your skill in depicting textures and illusions. I shall miss watching you develop further."

I raised my chin. "I will honour your name," I assured him.

He nodded. "A word of advice."

I sighed a little to myself. I was growing somewhat weary of advice and warnings, from opinions on the vow of chastity to my mother's endless weeping. I knew my own mind and considered it made up. "Master?"

"You may find their painting methods very different. And perhaps worth learning from?"

I nodded politely, although I doubted his point. If they were happy enough with their own painting skills, why call on mine? Surely because they wished to learn from a more advanced style? I was certain that I had much to teach them. Now I can only smile at the thought of my master's advice and Antonio's warnings. I should have heeded them both. And bid my mother a gentler farewell, poor woman. It is hard to see a son come into his own and then leave your side for greater things, as I now know for myself.

Perhaps it was only on bidding my grandmother Maddalena farewell that I faltered. She did not weep, even though she was very old and knew full well she would never see me again. She only laid her hand on my head and blessed me, her kindly smile never wavering. I held her warm soft hand in mine and had to briefly bow my head to her, less out of the respect I owed her than from a young man's pride in hiding the sudden shining in his eyes that might suggest a weakness of resolve. Then I left her, walking through her sweet-smelling garden, the place where my brother and I had played together as children, my head held a little too high, hoping that pride would conquer sadness.

If I had thought that I would leave for China at once, I was sorely mistaken. First, I had to spend a great deal of time with the Brothers in the city of Genoa, to be educated in their ways. I, who had never been called to the church as my brother had, was now obliged to hear Mass a great many more times in a month than I had thought possible, to listen with a solemn face to holy readings and be lectured on my future obligations as a Brother. I was given the task of completing a series of religious paintings on the walls of the Jesuit refectory there, perhaps in part to further demonstrate my talents. I painted *Tobias and the Angel*, *Abraham and Sarah* as well as other works, each meant to provide instruction and a point of contemplation and reflection for the Brothers as they dined. These works done to their satisfaction, I took my initial vows, admitting me as a lay brother to the Order, although my binding vows of poverty, obedience and chastity would not be made until I had been with the Brothers a couple of years, to prove my worth.

"Better make the most of not having taken them yet, then," suggested Antonio, visiting me in Genoa. He remained staunchly appalled at my choice and made it his business to point out every good-looking woman who came within sight, reminding me that I would be forswearing their company forever.

"I had better do no such thing," I retorted. "I am to travel to Portugal to await a ship and while I am there I have not one but two commissions. I am to paint frescos for a chapel there but I will also paint portraits of the Queen of Portugal's children. So you see I am already painting royalty, while you are painting nothing but the fat wives of merchants."

"I like something to hold on to, myself," laughed Antonio. "The wives of merchants show a great deal of interest in the man painting their portrait."

"And you show too much interest in them," I said. "You'll get yourself punched in the face one of these days, or worse." But I was sorry to bid him farewell, he was a rogue but I had known him since childhood and the thought of never again hearing his raucous laugh saddened me.

And so I left for Coimbra in Portugal, excited and ambitious, only to find that the tides and the Queen of Portugal alike were capricious. One ship and then another was promised and then postponed, while I painted her noble wailing babes and unruly brats, and when at last ships were ready the Queen pronounced herself so happy with my work that she commanded I must miss more than one sailing in order to wait for her new pregnancy to be complete, so that I might paint the portrait of yet another royal offspring. Meanwhile I struggled to learn Mandarin with nothing but Portuguese echoing in my ears, puzzling over meaningless symbols, not the simple two dozen of our own but the many thousands I had been told I must acquire to read even the simplest of texts. Speaking it was worse, for every sound was to be pronounced up or down, flat or high, in a way that drove me to distraction. More than once I doubted the choice I had made and yet when I saw one ship and then another leave the shores, bound for adventure and glory, I chafed at being left behind. I wrote repeatedly to the Father General of the Jesuits in Rome, reminding him of my great desire to begin my service in China as soon as possible.

My hopes rose of an imminent departure when I was joined by two new recruits to the Order. A Brother Costa, by profession a surgeon, arrived from Naples, his medical skills needed in Beijing. He was a taciturn man, not much given to idle chatter but apparently highly skilled in his profession. Another painter, Biondecci, this time from Rome, younger by ten years than myself, was to join me as an assistant. I went to meet Biondecci and was startled to find a young woman, scarcely more than a girl, whose thrown-back hood revealed an unusual mass of thick blonde hair, suited to her name.

"Biondecci?" I asked, disbelieving.

"The same," she said. "Laura."

"Giuseppe," I said.

Her expression lightened. "Ah, you are my new painting master. I am pleased to meet you."

I gestured to her to follow me and gave a small coin to a man to carry her trunk. "I did not expect a woman," I told her. "The journey will be arduous and once we enter the Emperor's employ we cannot leave again unless he or the Mission dismiss us."

"I know," she said. "I have dreamed of China since I was a child. My father had maps in his study and I would pore over them. After he and my mother died, I joined the Order as an apprentice painter. I have begged to serve in China for years and when I heard that there was a painter leaving I asked to be made your apprentice."

I could not but have doubts about the prudence of sending a woman, especially one so young, on such a long voyage to a distant land, surrounded by men. One might suppose the Brothers would protect her, of course, but there would be sailors about, possibly pirates, during the voyage and once we reached our destination, who knew how the local men might treat a foreign woman?

Still, Laura had talent, this I quickly ascertained from examples of her work and she had applied herself diligently to learning Mandarin. It having been decided that being a woman she would not have need to read or write the language, she had worked the harder on her speech and put my own efforts to shame, the odd tones seeming to come to her more easily. Thus our last days before boarding the ship were spent together attempting to speak only in Mandarin, something that reduced our conversation to the level of small children and gave us occasion to laugh at our efforts. Brother Costa only shook his head at us and practiced his writing of the symbols, his surgeon's exactness perhaps standing him in good stead.

Enough. My time in Portugal seemed endless to a young man and yet seems so very long ago now. The heaving boards of the ship, Our Lady of Hope, thrilled me to my very core.

My memories of that voyage, long as it was, are not unpleasant. For all the wild tales the sailors told us, boasting of encounters with savages and pirates, we travelled peacefully to Madeira and on to Cape Verde before making brief stops in Senegal and the Gambia.

"Stay close to me," I warned Laura, after our first disembarking on the tiny island of Gorée near Senegal. Her golden hair drew more attention than was desirable, the local people even approaching her quite boldly to touch it, rubbing it between their dark fingers as though to ascertain its quality, like goods in a marketplace. "Be off with you," I added, to one woman. "Do not touch her."

The woman smiled without letting go.

"They are friendly enough," said Laura peaceably. "I am sure they mean well. They cannot have seen many women with hair this colour."

"They should show a little respect," I said, gesturing to the woman to move away, which she did, reluctantly, only for a man to take her place. "I shall have to carry a stick with me next time we come ashore," I said, exasperated, "or leave you on board until we reach China."

"Why, are the women of China blonde too?" Laura asked, laughing. "We must grow used to being objects of curiosity on our travels, Giuseppe."

We saw much that still remains in my mind. The dark shape of whales, rising up through the depths, the fish that leapt from the water as though they might sprout wings and fly. By night the stars seemed brighter than we had ever seen them before and although the heat made us long to swim, we were advised not to by the older sailors, who swore that more than one of their comrades had been dragged down by the sharks whose fins we glimpsed from time to time. The sailors claimed that the creatures were ever hungry for human flesh. We were lucky to brave only one bad storm, in which Brother Costa's skills were called on to save the life of a man struck by a falling broken mast and many Brothers of the Mission were kept busy hearing the confessions of those with troubled minds who believed they might be about to meet their Maker. By the time we reached the Portuguese colony of Goa many of us on board were suffering the swollen legs and peeling gums of scurvy, having run out of the oranges we had previously taken on board. We were glad to eat fresh fruits and vegetables again, albeit they were strange in taste and form to us and the whole company soon recovered. Altogether, we were at sea for almost a year by the time we knelt in gratitude to sing Te Deum when the shores of Macau were sighted and we knew that our journey was almost over.

Once disembarked we heard Mass in a tiny plaster chapel decorated with a red and blue glaze which we were told was common of the local style. My legs still felt strange on land and I felt as though I staggered. About us was all the usual noise of the docks. I had thought of course to hear Mandarin spoken, but the locals mainly spoke either a mangled sort of Portuguese or Cantonese, neither of which we understood and so we were entirely reliant on the Brothers to translate for us. It seemed strange to see Portuguese custard tarts for sale at street stands and we were served a dish named Portuguese Chicken which bore no resemblance whatsoever to food from Portugal, being served with a yellow curried sauce. But it was a great relief to stand once more on the firm earth and know that from now on we were done with our sea journey and all its privations.

As we made our way round the local streets in an attempt to get our bearings we were surprised to see small piles of food left by the sides of the road, often with sticks of incense burning before them.

"It is the Hungry Ghost festival," a Brother informed us. "The local people believe their ancestors return to visit the land of the living and must be fed. Ancestral veneration is of great importance here."

We were soon settled in the local Mission, there to be instructed by senior Brothers on the behaviours we must learn in order to be accepted into this new land and in particular its court. Our spoken Mandarin was pronounced atrocious and a local convert to the faith was appointed to give us daily instruction. Certainly hearing the language spoken by a native made it easier to improve our own efforts.

I was given long black robes to wear, with oddly baggy silken trousers underneath. I was told this was what the Chinese scholars wore and that the Jesuits had thought it prudent to wear the same, to indicate our standing as men of intellect and skill. The robes felt odd, my legs unprotected beneath rippling folds of silk more befitting to a woman. Besides, there seemed little difference, to my untrained eye, between the men and the women's clothes here: all of us wore these long robes, from simple cotton for the maids to highly decorated silk. All were shapeless. Gone were the half-glimpsed cleavages of women, their tight waists pulled tighter still by unseen corsets and their billowing skirts. Gone were the well-turned calves of men in their stockings below form-fitting britches and waistcoats, jackets cut tight to show off the width of manly chests. I found myself tugging at the robes or irritably rolling my shoulders in them, trying to become accustomed to the feel of them. The black hat I was given was also odd, round but rising to a square, with two long strips of cloth which hung past my ears and which I found myself pushing back when they dangled at the edges of my sight. Laura laughed at me when she saw me and I in turn told her that her blonde hair looked most odd pinned up on a thin black lacquered wooden board.

"You should have them lacquer you a board in yellow, it would suit your hair better," I told her. "I am certain the black is supposed to be hidden by your hair being the same colour."

She shrugged. "I am not bothered about my hair," she said. "Look at my shoes."

They were odd, certainly, for while the tops were made of a pretty enough embroidered silk, below the sole was a high wooden block, lifting Laura's short frame to a loftier height, something like the wooden pattens a woman might have worn at home to keep her good shoes out of the mud, though these were higher and Laura stumbled more than once while she grew accustomed to them.

We were shown how to behave in the presence of the Emperor. We were to stand with feet together and hands at our side, this being a modest and respectful pose, before, at a given signal, kneeling and prostrating ourselves, our heads to touch the floor three times. We were then to rise and repeat the whole salutation a further two times, our foreheads to touch the floor nine times in all. This, we were informed, was correct on our first meeting and at any further great occasions such as New Year or the Emperor's birthday. Once would be sufficient on less formal occasions. It proved a difficult act to perform with any grace, although Laura seemed to manage it better than Brother Costa and myself.

Brother Costa was warned against practicing medicine on the Emperor himself, for there had been tales of local physicians who had attempted to cure the Emperor of some minor malady and having failed had been lashed and then jailed in heavy chains. They had been released only on condition of treating another member of the imperial family and on doing so successfully had still borne the shame of being obliged to wear a small chain and clasp about their necks for the rest of their lives, as a warning and reminder of what might befall them.

We were also given some guidance as to the Mission's reputation at court.

"There have been difficulties," admitted our instructor, an elderly Father. "There has been controversy over the permitted religious rites."

Laura and I raised our eyebrows, while Brother Costa nodded. Clearly he had already heard word of this.

"To better encourage our Chinese converts to adopt our religion we have allowed them to include ancestor worship as part of the Christian rites. Ancestral worship is of great importance to the Chinese, it would be very difficult to persuade them to convert were this forbidden. And of course it is entirely appropriate to show respect towards one's ancestors. And our leniency in this matter encouraged the Kangxi Emperor to allow us great freedom in preaching the Word. He issued an edict many years ago protecting both our Mission and our churches throughout the empire." The Father sighed. "However His Holiness Pope Clement the Eleventh has, in his infinite wisdom, just issued a Papal Bull disallowing ancestral worship, which he views as irreligious since it might be seen as making icons or indeed venerating ancestors as divinities, which of course cannot be allowed."

"And does the Emperor accept this ruling?" I asked, already feeling that I knew the answer.

"He does not. It has irritated him beyond all measure. We have just received word here of his response." He took out a folded paper written in a rich red ink, which I was later to find out was a colour reserved exclusively for writings by the Emperor himself. Peering closely at it, he read out: "'Reading this proclamation, I have concluded that the Westerners are petty indeed. It is impossible to reason with them because they do not understand larger issues as we understand them in China. There is not a single Westerner versed in Chinese works, and their remarks are often incredible and ridiculous. To judge from this proclamation, their religion is no different from other small, bigoted sects of Buddhism or Taoism. I have never seen a document which contains so much nonsense. From now on, Westerners should not be allowed to preach in China, to avoid further trouble.'"

"Does His Holiness not understand that the Mission would be damaged by this ruling?" asked Laura.

"We cannot question His Holiness's ruling," said the Father, although his tone lacked much reproof. "It is, however, all the more important that your work and service to the Emperor be most excellent, to perhaps soften his feelings in this matter."

"We are still waiting to be summoned to court," pointed out Laura.

But word of our arrival had travelled swiftly, even at such a great distance. A summons soon reached us that the Emperor Kangxi was impatiently awaiting us at court. Our education would have to be continued in Beijing. Laura's eyes shone when she spoke of the Grand Canal on which part of our journey would be made, though I knew little of it and had grown weary of travel.

"I will be glad when we arrive," I told her. "For then my work can truly begin."

"Our work," she reminded me.

"You are my apprentice," I said, perhaps a little arrogantly. "The Emperor has requested my service and I am anxious to begin."

"You are only anxious to be praised," said Laura, a little mischievously. She should have been more respectful to her master, of course, but she was very young and we had struck up something of a friendship, given the long voyage.

"And I will be," I said with certainty. "I will be."

I had thought to see something of the country as we passed through it, to have the leisure to accustom ourselves to the look of it, the buildings, the inhabitants and their way of life. Instead we found ourselves seated within a carrying litter, cramped and in half-darkness, day after day. I said that I was well able to ride a horse and indeed would prefer to do so, but was told in no uncertain terms that this would not be fitting and that we would travel as had been arranged. Brother Costa suffered from nausea at the constant motion of our litter and Laura and I grew ill-tempered with one another, confined as we were to close company with little to vary the monotony of our daily travels. By night we would stop at inns. They were poor places often riddled with various small creatures in our beds, which disturbed our sleep. I was also concerned for Laura's safety. I bid her to keep her door closed and to push some item of furniture against it, if possible.

When we finally reached the Grand Canal we caught but a glimpse of the quayside before we were ushered into the boats in which we would continue our journey. Laura's disappointment in finding that there was no way of looking out of the boats brought on a fit of weeping, which I could not condemn, for I was as frustrated as she at our shuttered journey. Brother Costa seemed more phlegmatic about our confinement, being more concerned with the movement of the boat and its effect on his digestion, but then he was not a painter like Laura and me, yearning for some form of visual simulation.

"The Emperor himself is never seen by the common people," said one of the accompanying guards, when we complained.

"How can he not be seen? Does he never leave the Forbidden City?"

"Oh certainly. But screens of bamboo and cloth are erected on either side of the road, so that he may not be seen."

"How absurd," I muttered to Laura and Brother Costa.

Laura passed the time by making small sketches and I passed comments on her work, correcting her shading or encouraging her to improve her technique in certain respects regarding movement and texture.

"Think of a bird," I suggested. "How it flaps to the ground, not the slow swoop of its wings when it soars high up in the sky but the last moments before it lands, the tremble of its wings, the delicacy of each feather."

She obliged and I nodded when she drew for me a tiny sparrow, its wingtips aflutter as it sought out a fallen crumb.

The black crow-robed figure of the Jesuit still perches on the high outer wall of my memory palace, cawing to me daily when I pass his post, his call always the same. "China! China!"

Hundreds of Butterflies

IT'S HOT AND STICKY. MY robe feels heavy. I try to loosen the collar a little to let some air reach my skin, but there is no air. Just more heat. I've never worn this robe before. It is my mother's best, the finest in our house and the only thing appropriate for today. It's too short on me, although it lies baggily on my still-flat chest. My mother tutted over the fit and scolded me for being a beanpole. I shift my weight from one foot to the other. The girl on my left has stood perfectly still for over two hours. In fairness, she's balancing on the tiny curved blocks that support cloud-climbing shoes, so perhaps shifting her weight back and forth is not a good idea or she might overbalance and end up falling on her backside. I'm grateful I have nothing so elegant to wear, for at least in my simpler cloth shoes I can rest one foot at a time. The only sign that the girl is even alive is the damp cobblestone at her feet, wetted one tear at a time from her expressionless face. I don't know why she's crying. Half the girls here are crying. There could be any number of reasons.

Before the eunuch guards and officials arrived to bring us to the Inner Court of the Forbidden City we were allowed to mill about while we waited. At least two of the girls were already weeping and wringing their hands because they were in love and wished to marry their sweethearts. They were afraid of being chosen to marry the Emperor or one of his sons and never seeing their beloveds again.

One older girl was unhelpfully passing on gossip she'd heard. She claimed one of her aunts was a lady-in-waiting in the Palace and that a distant cousin served one of the princes in his palace in Beijing. More and more girls gathered about her, their heads bent close to hers. I joined them.

"… there's the Crown Prince, my aunt said he chooses very young concubines, even ones who aren't yet of marriageable age… she's heard crying from his palace and seen bruises…"

Some of the girls whimpered and I turned away. I didn't want to be frightened by some busybody's gossip. I turned to the nearest girl, whose eyelids were puffy from crying.

"I'm Niuhuru."

The girl nodded and tried to wipe her eyes. "My father says he'll beat me if I'm not chosen," she confided. "He says girls have been chosen for imperial marriage from our family for generations and I'll bring dishonour to our family name if I'm not. Will you get in trouble if you're not chosen?"

I shook my head. "No-one's expecting me to be chosen," I said. "We're not very important. And anyway," I added, "my mother said I'm too tall and clumsy and I've got funny-coloured eyes."

"Lucky you," sniffed the girl. I wanted to tell her that if she made herself ugly by sobbing she was even less likely to be chosen, but thought that the idea would probably only make her cry more, so I stayed quiet.

Now I try not to let my lips move and keep my eyes straight ahead. "How much longer do you think we'll be here?" I whisper to the girl.

"Silence!" yells the eunuch who's watching over us. Curse him, he has ears like an elephant. I could barely hear my own voice when I spoke. I roll my eyes and he glares at me. I don't care. I'm not that keen to be chosen, so if he dislikes me, so much the better. Perhaps he'll tell the more senior eunuch I'm not suitable and then I'll be free to go home. I yawn and don't bother to hide it. They have over two hundred of us standing here, they're not short of girls to choose from.

There's a small commotion somewhere in the courtyard as a girl faints. When the first one went down everyone stared, now we only glance at the girl as she's carried out, to be revived or maybe just sent home, who knows. Perhaps I could pretend to faint? I consider it but the cobbles under our feet are hard and I am fairly sure that my ungainly height and rough hands, my too-short robe and oddly pale-grey eyes will rule me out as a concubine anyway, so it's just a matter of waiting some more before I'm dismissed. Who'd want to live here, with this endless formality? I'd rather stay in Chengde and marry someone local one day, stay close to my family and familiar surroundings.

I glance at the girl to my right. She, too, is perfectly poised, with a superior lift to her chin, which is meant to let the rest of us know that she comes from a high-ranking family, that she has been born and bred for this moment, that she will settle for nothing less than becoming a concubine to the Emperor himself, no matter how old he is now. Not for her the lesser status of marriage to one of the sixteen grown princes, each of them a possible heir to the throne. The odds are stacked against any woman foolish enough to believe she'd be chosen by the right prince and become consort to a future, younger Emperor. Better pin your hopes on the old Emperor now than end up married to some nobody of a prince, living in a house no better than the one you came from, the only difference being the addition of more rules and protocols to your life.

I shift my feet again but now there are footsteps coming and suddenly every girl stands a little straighter. A whole crowd of eunuchs, officials, guards… and amongst them, the Emperor. I catch a quick glimpse of an old but upright man, a skinny frame bulked out with magnificent yellow robes before we all sink to our knees and I'm face down on the cobbles.

There's a lot of noise as everyone arranges themselves. I can't see anything except the cobbles, which are cold against my forehead. Slowly I twist my neck so that my left cheek lies against the hard stone and look up as far as I can. I can see yellow boots, surrounded by many other feet. I can see some of the girls. Now we can only wait.

We are not required to stand. The selection for the Emperor has clearly already taken place long before this moment. Girls are named, they raise their faces, there is perhaps – since we can hardly see anything – a nod from the Emperor, some sign that he finds them to his liking. Their names are called again more loudly, along with the rank they have been given. The girl to my right is quickly chosen as a mid-rank concubine to the Emperor and I catch a glimpse of the satisfaction on her face as she rises. She has fulfilled her destiny. She will be an imperial concubine to the Emperor of China. I can't help thinking that he is old, he may even die soon. If he does, she will live in the Forbidden City for the rest of her days as a dowager concubine. She will never see or be touched by another man, even if she lives to a ripe old age. She will never leave the embrace of the endless vermillion walls. She will live only through the past glory of this moment when, as a girl of only perhaps fifteen years old, she was chosen. I shudder at the thought.

More girls are picked out of the crowd. They are supposed to be pleased to be chosen quickly, for their beauty and grace to have been noted. Even the nervous ones smile when their names are called, although their lips tremble when they think of their new lives. All those chosen are led away. They will return to their parents for just a few short days before they enter the Forbidden City for the rest of their lives.

I am not chosen, of course. I don't feel relief, because I wasn't afraid of being selected. I only hope the next selection will also be quick and I will be free to leave, to pass back through the great red gates and be met by my mother and father who are waiting outside. I can tell them everything I saw today and when we get home I will regale my younger brothers with how I saw the Emperor himself. I doubt anyone will be disappointed that I am not to enter the Forbidden City, since none of us expected me to be chosen. The Imperial Daughters' Draft cannot be ignored of course, every girl from the Eight Banners must be presented at the court between the ages of thirteen and sixteen, before she can be married, so that the Emperor and his sons have the first choice of any woman in the country. But for families like ours, whose daughters are not blessed with extraordinary beauty or grace, whose fathers are only mid-ranking officials, the Draft is simply an excuse for a visit to the capital. The journey from our home in Chengde to Beijing has been an adventure, a chance to wander the bustling streets, so much bigger and noisier than our own town, to be impressed by the majesty of the Forbidden City and to partake in a ritual that acknowledges our rightful place in the Banners, however minor my father's official post is. To belong to the one of the Banners is to be part of the Manchu elite, the ruling class, setting us above the general Han Chinese population.

The yellow boots move as the Emperor stands and there's a great clatter as he leaves. Slowly, we rise to our feet, our knees stiff and cold. I look about me. There's the odd girl in a huff, annoyed at not having been chosen for the Emperor. The worried girl, I notice, has been led away, avoiding any dishonour to her family despite her red-rimmed eyes.

We recompose ourselves for the next selection. More noise. Eunuchs and guards accompany a small woman, perhaps in her late thirties. She too is magnificently dressed, but not in imperial yellow, rather a slightly darker shade akin to apricot. Her hair is dressed with pearls and flowers. On several of her fingers are nail shields almost as long as her digits, worn only by the very rich, made of finely beaten gold, studded with jewels. She has a long thin face and highly arched brows. The overall effect is rather like a horse that has stuck its head through a flower bush.

"Imperial Noble Consort Que Hui," announces the eunuch who is managing the proceedings. "As chief consort of the Emperor, her ladyship will now select the consorts and concubines for their Royal Highnesses, the sons of the Emperor."

We sink to our knees again and prostrate ourselves, but once this is done we are told to stand. Apparently the consort wants to view us for herself. I wonder briefly why she's not been made Empress but then remember that this Emperor is rather tardy about appointing his Empresses. After the first one died, he only seemed to bestow the honour too late, when each of the subsequent chief consorts was near to death, when he would offer the title. Perhaps he hoped it would cheer them sufficiently to recover from their illness, but it never worked. There have been three dead empresses so far in his long reign, so perhaps for the sake of one's health it's an honour best not hoped for.

Lady Que Hui settles herself on a throne and regards us all in silence. She tilts her head minutely and at once a eunuch is by her side, consulting various folded papers and whispering to her, presumably indicating the more superior girls: noting their families, their beauty, how well they did in the preliminary selections. He will have little to say about me. A few lucky others and I were spared the first rounds of selections since we had to travel from further afield. Late in arriving to the capital, we were sent straight to the Forbidden City for the final choice of girls. Those who arrived in good time or resided in Beijing will have undergone the full examinations of the Draft. Stripped naked so their bodies can clearly be seen, they have had their teeth examined, their tongues scraped and their breath smelt, their height and weight recorded, their toenails scrutinized and even (though I can hardly believe this and suspect other girls of telling tall tales) their armpits and even more intimate areas swabbed and smelt for bad odours which might offend an imperial nose. I'm glad the horse pulling our wagon went lame, delaying us so that I have been spared these humiliations.

At last the selection begins. The Kangxi Emperor has over thirty living sons. Sixteen are old enough to require consorts and concubines. The Crown Prince is of course the most desirable as a future husband. If all goes well, he will one day become Emperor himself. But we have already heard the whispers about his sexual propriety or lack thereof. The girls who are chosen for his household look doubtful rather than excited. The rest of us watch those who are chosen with pity rather than jealousy. Of course being chosen for a lesser prince is not as impressive, but then one will still be part of the imperial family and perhaps have less to fear when summoned to the imperial bedchamber.

The naming goes on and on. The First Prince seems to be very fond of women, for a great many are sent to his household. Women are chosen for the Third Prince, the Fifth

Prince, the Eighth Prince, the Ninth Prince. I stop listening and hope it will be over soon.

There's a silence. Lady Que Hui seems to have finished. She casts her eye over our depleted numbers and purses her lips. She seems about to rise, when the eunuch whispers to her again.

"Ah yes," she says. "The Fourth Prince. He has not requested a new concubine, but his household is small and a new lady would be appropriate." Her eyes flicker over us and when they rest on me she frowns. "Very tall," she comments.

I try not to move. It's unsettling to have her eyes rest on me. No one has glanced at me twice since I arrived here. I've been passed over so often during this process that I find it hard to meet her gaze. I lower my eyes. When I raise them again she is still looking at me. Suddenly I find my throat is very dry, even when I swallow.

I swallow again.

The eunuch bows, somehow managing to convey his dismissal of me. "The girl is named..." he has to check his document again to be certain, "... Niuhuru. From Chengde, near the hunting grounds. She was late in arriving, madam," he says. "She was admitted because she will be too old at the next Draft but she has not been through the preliminary rounds. Of the Manchu Niuhuru clan, of the Bordered Yellow Banner."

"Father?"

"Only a fourth-ranked *Dianyi* in the military, madam."

There's a pause. Lady Que Hui's mouth twists a little in something approaching a smile. "Fourth Prince Yong is known for his dislike of corruption in the higher ranks of officials, both in civilian life and the military. He believes that the lower ranked men are often unfairly overlooked," she says, as though repeating an amusing anecdote. "Perhaps he would like a concubine from a more lowly background so that he can be quite certain that it is not her family connections that have brought her here."

Her small smile reassures me that she is joking. This Prince Yong doesn't want another concubine. Besides, everyone knows that it's the girls from the well-to-do families that get chosen. I'm too tall, as she has already remarked, and she's not close enough to see that my eyes are a strange pale grey, which no-one finds attractive, just odd. No imperial prince would consider me a suitable bride when they can choose from the most beautiful women in the empire. No doubt the Emperor's chief consort enjoys making a little joke during this tedious process. I give a faint smile, to acknowledge that I understand that she is joking, that I am about to be sent home and that I am not expecting anything else – Prince Yong may or may not be given another concubine, but certainly it won't be me.

I'm right. She stands, brushes down her heavy robe, taps the paper with one glittering gold fingernail and nods her head, satisfied, to the eunuch, then turns and walks away as the eunuch calls out:

"Lady Niuhuru, chosen as *gege*, concubine, to the Fourth Prince, Yong!"

I spend the following days in shock. I have to repeat what happened over and over again

– first to my incredulous father and mother, standing outside the gates of the Forbidden City, then to our relations, with whom we are lodging during our stay in Beijing, then to more and more people – distant relatives I've never met before, the neighbours, local girls not yet of Draft age who want to hear all about what it is like to be chosen. By the time my brothers arrive, hastily summoned from our family home in Chengde, the words have been said so often that they come out of my mouth easily, although I still cannot believe what I am saying.

"Then she tapped the paper where my name was and walked away. I thought I would be sent home but the eunuch called out my name. I'm to be *gege* to the Fourth Prince. His birth name is Yinzhen but he is known as Prince Yong."

My brothers are impressed. Here's their older sister, a beanpole and a tomboy, whom no-one has ever praised for her looks, and she's going to marry a prince! "Is he very important?" they ask eagerly.

I shake my head. "Not really," I say. "He won't be Emperor, because there's already a Crown Prince. He's just a prince. The Emperor has more than thirty sons."

"But he's a *prince*," says my youngest brother. "So you will be a princess."

I shrug in agreement. Yes, I'll be a princess, but really I will just be a concubine, to a prince who is not very important. It's a strange match – full of honour and prestige and yet at the same time oddly lacklustre. I am not marrying the Emperor, only one of his many sons whom no-one has heard of.

When I am not reciting and re-reciting my story, I spend hours sitting in the garden or at the window in silence and stillness. I might as well be a monk meditating, for my mind is blank. Occasionally thoughts drift across my mind – relief that I have heard no strange rumours concerning Prince Yong – wondering what my days will be like – trying to recall my family home in Chengde which I will never see again and which already seems to have a mist drawn over it so that I struggle to recall anything about it even though I was there only a handful of days ago. But mostly my mind seems empty. I cannot imagine my future. I cannot go back to my past. There is only now.

Already the decision made by the horse-faced Lady Que Hui has changed what I can do. I am not to leave the house and grounds until I join Prince Yong's household. I protest. In Chengde I ran our family's errands, walked freely through the streets with my mother to buy food for our household, even went with my younger brothers to catch hares in the woods. Now I am told that I may not walk through Beijing's markets and down its alleyways. Already the red walls of the Forbidden City hold me prisoner. My protests mean nothing. So I sit and look out of the window or wander without purpose in the garden. There is nothing else to do.

The neighbouring house and gardens belong to an elderly scholar, who has a pet gibbon. Its fur is a snowy white, and when released into the garden it climbs up into a peach tree and grabs for the sweet fruit, munching it and dribbling sticky juice onto the servants below, who try to prevent it finishing the whole crop but despairingly admit to me that they are forbidden to administer any punishment, on the orders of its master. The gibbon, having understood this, takes pleasure in cramming each peach into its mouth, taking one or perhaps two bites only, then letting the spoiled fruit drop to the ground, sometimes hitting a servant on the head.

I lean against our garden wall looking up and call out to it, laughing. "Such naughtiness! You should finish each fruit, not spoil them. Or at least pass me one, why don't you, before they're all gone?" The gibbon grins at me, baring his teeth when I hold out my hand, holding the peach close to his chest before biting it and letting the rest drop to the ground. I tut at him but he only makes contented noises and climbs still higher in the tree.

"Why do you keep him when he's such a nuisance?" I ask the scholar, who has hobbled out to the garden and is standing beneath the tree.

"I like his mischief," he says, chuckling. "The gibbon is a symbol of growing wisdom throughout life, as well as good fortune and nobility."

I nod. I'd rather listen to this old man talk about the symbolic beauty of his wicked pet gibbon than the hubbub of the household in which I'm sitting. Today my dowry will arrive. My father will not be providing a dowry, as would be customary were I marrying a commoner. Instead the Palace will provide one for me, thus eliminating any need for gratitude to my family or opportunity for us to claim favours because of our generosity. From the moment when the Emperor's consort flicked a golden nail shield against my name on a scroll, I belonged to the Imperial Household. It is only a question of time before I am claimed. The passing days are taken up with rituals, with decisions made on my behalf, with symbolism and protocol. I would rather hear about the gibbon.

"I hear you have had good fortune yourself," smiles the old man, peering across at me. "And are to join the Imperial Family."

I sigh. Does the whole of Beijing know my fate? It seems so. "I shall have to hope for the growing wisdom of old age to understand why I was chosen," I say, trying to be polite.

He looks at me, my head probably all he can see appearing over the wall that separates us, his smile gone. He seems sad for me, the only person to have expressed anything other than congratulations and wonderment. "It must seem like a strange future," he says. "Although all futures seem strange to us until they become our past and then it is as though they had always been so and could not have been any other way."

I force a smile onto my face. He's being kind but his words are designed to soothe an anxious mind full of worries about the future. I don't have any worries. I have only a strange numbness, a mind filled with fog.

Through the fog comes more noise, a clattering of feet. "I have to go," I say. "I hope you manage to eat at least one peach this summer."

The old man nods and waves to me. Reluctantly, I make my way back into the house.

Bolts of silk, taels of silver, new robes, gifts for family members and all manner of household goods, from dishes to furniture, flood into the house. My family marvel at our good fortune, at my changed destiny. I am surrounded by compliments, by blessings. Suddenly my beanpole height is 'willowy', my odd grey eyes are 'jade-coloured', although that could encompass almost any shade from white to brown via green. If the Imperial Household has chosen me, then clearly I must be beautiful. I think back to Lady Que Hui's half smile and wonder what Prince Yong will say when he discovers I have been chosen to tease him for his beliefs. I step out of the way of more Palace eunuchs, struggling to carry heavy household furniture.

My attention is drawn by a palanquin, decorated in red and gold, which is being manoeuvred with difficulty into a place where it will be at least partly out of the way of the many people trying to enter and leave the house. I make my way to it and peer inside. It's a small space, a dark red cocoon in which I, a wriggling caterpillar, will be taken to the Palace, to emerge, one presumes, a glorious butterfly at the other end of my journey. I smooth down the flat front of my new robe, hurriedly made for me in a delicate pink silk, and wonder how such a transformation will occur. How do I become elegant and beautiful, like some of the girls I saw? How do I learn to walk and carry myself with grace? How do I know… what… well, what is – what is *expected* of me when I meet the Prince? My family seems far too caught up in celebrations and expectations for anyone to have thought of this. I try to catch my mother's sleeve as she hurries by.

"Not *now*, Niuhuru," she says, pointing a maid towards a pile of silk cloth ready for cutting and indicating where it ought to be taken.

I follow after her. "Aunty said that I might see you all again if the Imperial Household go to Chengde for the hunting season." I hope that my mother will agree that yes, of course I will see my family again, that she might even pause to embrace me. I have allowed myself to think of the future, to wonder what it will be like, to be without my family, in a strange place where I know no-one at all. There are probably girls who have prepared their whole lives for this opportunity, who have been schooled in what to expect and how to behave. I have not. No-one thought I would marry a prince. If my family had been asked about my marriage prospects there would probably been vague mutterings about a few local boys in my hometown, from good families, similar to our own; officials, industrious but not exalted.

But my mother has not heard the tremble in my voice, or if she has she is choosing to ignore it. "Niuhuru," she says, her tone one of slightly impatient reassurance, "you are going to be married. A woman does not go running back to her family at every moment. You will have your own home and you will be used to it soon enough."

"I didn't mean all the time," I say, still trailing after her like a lost puppy. "But once a year…" But it is too late. My mother has spotted a maid who seems to be less than overworked and is issuing a stream of orders.

I retreat to the garden and practice walking gracefully in my new silken cloud-climbing shoes. They oblige me to take odd, swaying steps and I cannot stop or start abruptly without holding out a hand to steady myself. They say that noble Manchu women wear these shoes to give their unbound feet the illusion of being bound, the same swaying walk and delicacy of a Chinese girl. I've never worn them before and I dislike them. After a while I take them off and lie on the grass, heedless of the pink silk that only a few days before I would have been terrified to get dirty. I listen to the gibbon's screeches and stare up at the sky. I watch the peach tree's leaves swaying in the breeze and wonder how my life will be in the Forbidden City. I cannot really imagine it. I have been used to some degree of freedom, running about the hunting ground forests with my brothers and cousins, with little thought of what my future might hold for me. I thought Chengde would be my whole world and now it seems I am to disappear from my family's life, closed up behind the vast red walls of the imperial palace, never heard from again. Everything I have been until now will be irrelevant, for the Imperial Family will mould me into their own shape.

When the day finally comes the fog surrounds me, wrapped more thickly about me than the red silk robes and veils chosen to adorn me. I eat breakfast without tasting what is in my mouth. I don't hear the shouts and clattering of the guards and officials. I don't see my family's faces for the last time. I totter out of the house on my too-high shoes and step into the red palanquin, clutching at its sides to stop myself stumbling. Once inside I don't feel the lurching lift as the bearers raise me up. I sit and wait to enter the high red walls of the Forbidden City.

But the swaying goes on and on. My stomach churns and at last I put up one hand to the curtains and pull them back to see how close we are to our final destination. I blink. I cannot see the Forbidden City at all. I pull the curtain back further, lean my head out and see it at last – to my right and almost behind me, its northernmost wall slowly receding.

"Wait!" I cry out and the palanquin comes to a shuddering stop. The most senior eunuch's anxious face appears at the window.

"My lady?"

"Where are we going?" My voice comes out too high, it trembles as though I am about to cry.

"To the Garden, my lady." The eunuch is puzzled.

"Garden?"

The eunuch frowns. "The Garden of Perfect Brightness, your ladyship. The Yuan Ming Yuan. Residence of Prince Yong."

The red walls of my expected future are crumbling. "Not – not the Forbidden City?"

"The only man who may reside in the Forbidden City is the Emperor," the eunuch reminds me. "Prince Yong has a household in Beijing but prefers his country estate. That is where his consorts live."

I try to nod as though I know this. "Of course," I mumble. "I only thought… it doesn't matter."

The eunuch bows. "Is that all, your ladyship?"

I nod and he disappears as I let the curtains fall. The palanquin lurches again and we continue on our way.

I sit back on the padded seat. I know nothing. I am thirteen years old and I know nothing. I do not even know where my own husband lives. I do not know what other wives he has, nor have I heard of this place, this Yuan Ming Yuan, this Garden of Perfect Brightness. I know nothing of what goes on between a man and his concubines.

The numbing fog that has protected me so far begins to lift. Fat tears slide slowly down my face. I feel like a child, and I am afraid.

The rocking palanquin finally draws to a halt. We left in the morning and it is now late in the day. When I step out of the chair my knees shake from lack of use as much as nerves. I try to steady myself on my high-soled shoes and look about me, breathing in the cooling air. Slowly the churning in my stomach, which has threatened to disgrace me for many hours, fades.

I am standing on the edge of a large lake, surrounded by small islets linked together by bridges. On each islet are one or more palaces. There are flowers everywhere. Planted in great profusion, they trail over and around every part of the scene before me. Wisteria hangs heavy while roses reach upward, twining through branches of trees and across windows. Peonies in every shade burst out of their green foliage. The lake is full of lotus flowers reaching up towards weeping willow trees. It is a private paradise, a hidden world far from the stone courtyards and high walls of the Forbidden City. I wonder what kind of man I have married, who chose this secret flowering place as his home.

"Your ladyship?" The eunuch hovering by my side has already tried and failed to get my attention.

"Yes?"

"Welcome to the Nine Continents Clear and Calm, your home within the Garden, my lady." He gestures forwards and I follow him, still unsteady on my little shoes, the pebbled mosaic path along the lakeside doing nothing to help my balance. I focus so hard on my feet and where I am placing them that I almost bump into the eunuch when he stops. I throw out an arm for balance, then hastily try to regain some poise as he turns to me.

"This will be your palace," he says.

The building before me is larger than any I have ever lived in, but I can see that it is small by the standards of the Imperial Household. There are larger palaces further along the lake path, but a smile spreads over my face when I see it. It is so heavily weighed down with clinging wisteria that it almost seems as though it is made out of it. It is a flower-palace, something from a fairytale.

"It is lovely," I say.

The eunuch looks a little surprised at my compliment, but then he smiles and his formal demeanour softens. "It is very beautiful, my lady," he agrees. "I wish you much happiness here."

His good wishes make me nervous again. I nod, my smile fading.

Inside, he shows me round the rooms. Although they are comfortable and large, there is no ostentation, rather a quiet restraint. Unlike the glimpses of the Forbidden City I saw, here there is no ornate gilding or lavish scattering of precious objects. All the extravagance seems to be in the flowers surrounding the palace and in the elaborate floral arrangements in multiple vases within the rooms. I'm so busy looking at them that I almost trip over a small figure in a pale blue robe, doubled up on the floor.

"Your personal maid," says the eunuch, without paying much attention to her. "There are of course household maids who will provide for your meals, clothing and so on. Yan is just for your own personal needs. Get up, girl," he adds, almost as an afterthought.

The little figure unfolds herself and stands. She is considerably shorter than I am, but probably my own age. She looks terrified. "My lady," she all but whispers. Her robe is stiff with newness.

I smile at her. I'm glad someone else is scared and that I have not been given some dragon of an older maid, someone who might judge me and find me lacking against other court ladies she has known. "What was your name again?"

"Yan, your ladyship."

My nerves make me want to giggle. Her name means Swallow, it seems very apt in this country retreat for my maid to be named after a bird. I smile and nod to her and she bows, then follows about behind me as I move, hovering like a shadow, as though worried that if she does not do so I will make some request of which she will fail to be aware.

"It is late," says the eunuch. "You will visit Lady Nara tomorrow to present your compliments."

I feel like an idiot. "Lady Nara?" I ask, wondering if this is perhaps my husband's mother.

"Prince Yong's Primary Consort," says the eunuch, bowing as he takes his leave of me. I stand in the doorway, watching him disappear, along with the guards and the bobbing red palanquin, now empty.

When I turn back into the room, Yan almost leaps out of my way, then stands trembling, waiting for an order like a terrified puppy who has been beaten too often.

"How long have you been here?" I ask.

"Only since this morning," she admits.

"Where were you before that?"

"The Forbidden City, your ladyship. For my training. Then I was told that a new lady was arriving in Prince Yong's household and that I would be sent here."

I nod. It is a mark of my low status, I suppose, that I have been given a newly-trained maid, and only one at that. But it's a relief to me not to have to manage some grand household and for my only servant to be a girl my own age. "We will have to explore our new home together then," I suggest and watch her eyes widen.

"Yes, your ladyship," she says uncertainly.

We make our way through all the rooms. I am not sure how I am expected to use them all, the size of this tiny palace is twice the size of my family home in Chengde. I daren't wander outside, for fear of losing my way or bumping into someone unexpected.

"Do you know when I will meet the Prince?" I ask Yan.

She shakes her head. "I was told he is very busy," she says. "They said at the palace that he was very hard-working and did not like to be disturbed."

I take this in. A hard-working husband should be a good thing, I suppose, better than a man who thinks of nothing but his own pleasures, like the Crown Prince. But it doesn't tell me when I'll be called for. I have to assume that it will not be tonight, since no instructions have been left for me.

We both startle at a loud knocking, but Yan hurries to answer the door. Two maids and a eunuch appear. They bow to me but don't speak, only scurry past towards the dining room, carrying several baskets. Yan rushes after them. A few moments later they emerge, bow again and depart.

Yan hovers in the doorway. "Your dinner is ready, your ladyship," she says.

I follow her.

The table is very large and there are a lot of dishes on it – Yan quickly uncovers the little lids, and good smells emerge, making my empty stomach rumble. I sit and Yan pours water for me to wash my hands. I eat. The food is good and very plentiful. There is plenty left when I leave the table. Yan serves me tea in a sitting room, then disappears. I hope that the leftovers from my meal will nourish her skinny little frame into something more substantial.

I wake early. The soft bed and silken covers lulled me into a quick sleep. I woke only once and was comforted by the small rasping snores of Yan, sleeping by the door. When I wake, though, she is already gone and when I call out for her she comes quickly, holding a little bowl of tea in which float rose petals.

"I have to meet Lady Nara today," I tell her and she nods, serious at the challenge. She has already chosen the clothes I will wear, green silk with delicately embroidered peonies. My cloud-climbing shoes today are lower than yesterday's, for which I'm grateful. My triple-pearl earrings are inserted. Gently, Yan brushes my hair, then pins it up into coils, topped with fresh peonies from the gardens outside and some little dangling golden tassels. The effect is very pretty and I tell her so. Her anxious face breaks into a beaming smile.

Now that I see the lake and the islets again I realise that the name of this area, Nine Continents Clear and Calm, refers to the number of the islets surrounding the lake. The streams separating each one are tiny, one could almost jump across them, although certainly not in the clothes and shoes I am currently wearing. Instead Yan and I make our way across one little bridge after another to reach the islet where Lady Nara lives, almost opposite to my own, close to Prince Yong's. I'm a little nervous in case I should accidentally meet my husband nearby and not know who he is, since I have never seen him.

Lady Nara's palace is far larger than my own. It is surrounded by pink roses in full bloom, the scent is overwhelming. Her household is of course also larger, with several eunuchs and many maids in attendance. I am shown into a sitting room, where I am offered a seat and tea while Yan waits in an adjoining room. A rustling announces Lady Nara. I hastily rise and when she arrives in the room I prostrate myself, murmuring respectful greetings due to a senior wife. When I've finished she waves me to a seat, turning to take her own bowl of tea from a maid. I take the opportunity to look at her without being caught staring.

Her face is pleasant and slightly plump. She must be thirty years old but she looks well for her age, only perhaps a little tired. Her clothes are sombre and her hair is arranged simply. I feel a little overdressed.

"You are welcome here," she says, looking me over. "You are very young," she adds.

"I am thirteen, your ladyship," I say.

She nods. "We have not had a new lady join our household for many years," she says. Later I'm to find this is true. All the other women in Prince Yong's household are in their late twenties. I am considerably younger than all of them. "We did not know the Prince had requested a new concubine," she adds, but her tone is not angry or jealous. She gives me a weary smile. "As I say, you are welcome here," she says. "You will find us very quiet. I hope you will not be bored."

I try to nod my head and shake it at the same time, uncertain of the right answer. She rises and I understand that my audience is over. "You may always come to me if there is something you need," she says.

I stammer my thanks before I am shown out.

Walking back through the heavy scent of roses Yan whispers to me that Lady Nara is in mourning. Her only child, eldest son of the Prince, died a year ago, aged seven. The maids have told her that since then their mistress, once a happy woman, is now slow and sad, that she takes little pleasure in her life. We return to my own palace in silence.

Lady Nara is right about it being quiet here. It's late morning and I venture out of the palace again, Yan following behind me, but we see few people. An official rides by, eunuchs go about their work here and there, the odd maid hurries past on an errand. We make our way towards a cluster of women inside a pavilion. With them are two small girls. I feel a sudden shyness and hover for a moment, then force myself to approach them.

There are three women. They are dressed well in good quality silks but their robes are everyday wear, not formal court dress. Their hair is pinned simply, with only fresh flowers, no jewels. They are sipping tea and playing mah-jong. The fourth player is one of the two young girls, but she keeps breaking off to play with her younger sister.

"Pay attention!" scolds one of the women and the older girl consults the board, makes a move and returns to the lakeside and her sister. The women sigh at her lack of skill and interest.

The two girls are dabbling their hands in the lake's edge and dangling improvised fishing rods made of branches into the water. But now the younger girl has noticed me.

"Hello!" she says. "Who are you?"

All heads turn towards me. I can feel myself flushing. "I – I am Niuhuru," I stammer.

There's a bewildered pause and then one of the women stands up. "Oh!" she says. "The new concubine?"

I nod.

She comes closer and pulls at my arm to make me join the women at the table. "I am Mao. The girls are my daughters," she adds, not bothering to name them. She gestures at the other two women. "Lady Ning, Lady Zhang," she says by way of introduction. They nod and smile while Lady Mao continues. "We are concubines to the Prince. We knew you were coming but were not told when to expect you."

I try to bow to them all but they wave my manners away, staring at me with frank curiosity.

"You're very *young*," says Lady Zhang and the others nod.

"I am thirteen," I say. They nod. It's a reasonable age to be married, but still I feel very young, standing in front of these women, so at ease in their surroundings, so much older than me that they have daughters who in a few short years will be marriageable themselves.

"Sit, sit!" urges Lady Mao. "Can you play mah-jong?" she adds hopefully.

"Badly," I confess. It's a game my mother and aunts were fond of. I was too busy running through the woods with my brothers.

"Oh, we'll teach you," says Lady Ning. "We play every day."

I take the place of the elder daughter, who seems pleased to be set free, disappearing off along the lakeside path with her sister. I do the best I can, but clearly the women do play every day, for all of them are far better than I am, even with their attention only partly on the game. I'm quizzed about my family, my background, my hometown.

"Oh, Chengde," says Lady Zhang. "The hunting grounds. The whole court goes there every autumn. Of course the Prince does not really like to hunt," she adds, "so he usually stays as little as possible." The other ladies make faces. "It's a shame," she adds. "It's the only time we get to see everyone. The Prince is not a very sociable person."

"Have you met him yet?" asks Lady Mao.

I shake my head.

"He'll call for you soon, I expect," says Lady Mao. "But don't expect to be called for very often."

I wait for some warning to know my place, some sign of jealousy, but her face is open. "Prince Yong is not really the sort of man to indulge much in the pleasures of the bedchamber," she says, a little despondently. "He works very hard and has little time for pastimes," she adds, suddenly laughing. "You're the first new concubine here in years!"

The others chuckle.

I feel a wave of relief. The stories I've always heard of households full of warring concubines appear not to be the case here. Lady Nara was pleasant if sad, these women seem friendly and I detect no warring feuds, no jealousies. It seems they've all resigned themselves to a husband who is not that interested in any of them, and perhaps his lack of interest has softened what rivalries might have arisen. I can feel my shoulders relax. "Are we the only concubines?" I ask.

"No," says Lady Ning. "There are three others. There's Lady Dunsu, a sweet woman – but she is in mourning. You may not see her for a while."

"Why is she in mourning?" I ask.

Lady Mao looks sad. "She has been unlucky," she says. "She has borne three sons and a daughter, but none of them have survived. She was the Prince's favourite, but lately she has grown withdrawn."

I'm a little unnerved by all these stories of dead children and their sad mothers. Is the Prince's house unlucky? "How many living children does the Prince have?" I ask.

"Two sons and two daughters," says Lady Mao.

I'm a little taken aback. Only four living children is very few. The Prince has a fair number of women in his household. Doesn't he have any interest in them at all?

"Who are the other concubines?"

"There's Lady Chunque – a lovely woman. And Lady Qi."

I wait for a comment to be made on Lady Qi's character but nothing is forthcoming, so I don't enquire further.

An hour or two passes in friendly conversation and playing mah-jong, before we break up and make our way back along the lakeside to our own palaces. At the door of my own palace stands a eunuch, waiting for me.

"His Highness requests your company this evening," he announces and leaves before I have a chance to ask any questions. I turn to look at Yan, standing wide-eyed behind me.

"Does he mean…?" I begin, but Yan is already pulling me inside.

"You are going to meet your husband!" she says excitedly. "Quick, I must prepare you."

Bathed and dressed in my finest robe, a shimmering blue decorated with flying cranes and drifting clouds, I sit and wait. Yan and I have been too anxious to be ready on time and despite eating and bathing, followed by dressing and having my hair done, there is still a while to go before the appointed hour. I take off my shoes and try to ease my aching neck, where Yan has pulled my hair too tight and weighed me down with so many decorations that my head is twice its usual size.

I follow the eunuch who has been sent to accompany me. As I reach the gate I look back at Yan, standing in the doorway, shoulders hunched, her little face pinched with worry. When she sees me looking back she forces a too-bright smile onto her face.

We make our way in silence along the lakeside path towards the Prince's islet, crossing two bridges, one a simple thing made of painted wood, the other from blocks of carved stone. Along the way we pass a few palaces. I wonder whether the other ladies can see me from their rooms, if they see my overdressed hair and smile to themselves or laugh at me. I can see the largest palace looming ahead of us, where the Prince resides. Just before it we pass a palace that sits right on the lake's edge. Standing on a little jetty by the water's edge is a woman, dressed in a floating green robe. Her hair is pinned with pink lotus flowers and she stands absolutely still, watching me as I pass by. She is only twenty paces from me, yet she does not acknowledge me when I nod to her, only watches me, her face blank of any expression. I feel a coldness settle on me. This must be one of the women whom I have not yet met and her manner towards me is very different to the mah-jong-playing friendly group I met earlier. As soon as we have safely passed out of earshot I whisper to the eunuch, "Who was that lady?"

He does not break stride nor ask to whom I am referring. "Lady Qi," he says.

I look over my shoulder. Lady Qi is still standing there, still watching me as I near the Prince's palace, its swooping rooftops towering above the other palaces on the islets.

The late summer day is slowly fading away. I am surrounded by unfamiliar faces: the eunuchs and maids of the Prince. They undress me, which I suppose I must get used to, although my whole body grows goose-fleshed with embarrassment. My heavy robes, which had given me courage, are stripped away. My hair is unbound and falls down my back, unadorned. I wonder what the purpose was in Yan's careful preparation of me, since the Prince will see none of my adornments. So far the only person of note who has seen me in my splendour is Lady Qi. If I had known she would be my only witness, I would have worn a maid's robe.

At last the servants step away and I am left alone in the Prince's bedchamber. I'm not sure where I should put myself. I sit on the very edge of the heavy carved wooden bed, which is set into a niche, as is usual, although it's far larger than any other bed I've ever seen. I try not to pull my sleeping robe around me for comfort. My feet are cold on the floor, although the bed itself is heated with a kang underneath it. I consider pulling my feet up onto the bed but I am too nervous to make myself comfortable.

At last I hear footsteps and spring to my feet. I forget about elegance and clutch the sleeping robe to me, although it is made of such sheer silk that it is hardly going to shield my modesty.

The door opens.

The man who enters is of a good height. His robes are surprisingly plain for a prince. They are woven in a pale green silk, fastened with a simple belt. His long hair is neatly plaited in a queue. I know because Yan has told me that he is twenty-seven years old.

He pauses in the doorway, regards me in silence and then closes the door behind him. I stand facing him, only a few paces away. I don't know what to do or say.

"Lady Niuhuru," he says at last. "Welcome. Have you been well cared for here? Do you have everything you need? Are your rooms to your satisfaction?"

He sounds as though he is checking off questions against a list, not solicitously enquiring after his new wife's comforts. I nod and then try to speak, although my voice cracks.

"Yes, Your Highness. Th-thank you."

He nods, satisfied. There is warm wine and two small bowls waiting on a table and he pours each of us some. He holds out my bowl and I take it with one hand, the other still clutching my robe. I have only tasted wine once or twice at great occasions and I did not much like it. I take only a tiny sip and then stand holding the bowl, uncertain of where to place it. The Prince drinks his own bowl dry, then turns back to me. He holds out his hand and I place the still-full bowl in his palm. His hands are warm. He puts it back on the table and then comes close to me. I swallow. I am a tall girl, but he stands a good head taller than me. I have never stood so close to a man for so long.

Gently, he pulls at my sleeping robe. I unclench my fingers so that he can remove it and he lets it fall to the floor, heedless of the fine silk. I try to stop my cold hands balling into fists by my side and lower my eyes so that I do not have to meet his gaze. I will follow his lead, I tell myself. Whatever he wishes me to do, I will try to do it and be a good wife, even though I know little of what is about to happen.

But he does not move again. I can see his hands hanging loosely by his side. At last I look up at him and find that he is looking over my body with a frown on his face.

Shame burns through me. I wish now that I had been through the preliminary selection rounds during the Draft. Whatever he is displeased with now, they would surely have noticed it then. They would have declared that I was unfit for the Draft and sent me home. Instead I slipped through the net and now I am humiliated before a Prince to whom I am already married. What will he do, I wonder. Will he send me home in disgrace? Will he keep me here but only as a maid or simply leave me to sit all alone in my palace, year after year, forgotten and humbled?

At last he speaks. "You are very young," he says.

I look down at my flat chest, the white goose-fleshed skin shrinking further under his gaze, my narrow hips cold, the tiny hairless place between my pale thighs. "I am thirteen," I say. "I am of marriageable age." My voice is very small.

He lifts his gaze from my trembling cold body to my eyes, which much to my shame are now brimming with tears. In one swift movement he kneels and lifts up my discarded sleeping robe, which he places with care about my shoulders, helping me to put my arms back into the sleeves. Then he speaks softly. "I did not mean to shame you. I simply meant that you are not yet…" he pauses and then goes on. "You are not yet a woman. I am not – I would not wish to lie with you when you are still so young."

I am mortified. The Prince finds me a child. He is dismissing me. A hot tear trickles down my cheek.

He shakes his head and wipes away the tear with the back of his hand. "You must stop crying," he says a little gruffly. "I am not sending you away. You are welcome in my household. But you are too young and I will not lie with you until you are older. You will live here and I hope you will be happy. Later, when you are..." he gestures awkwardly, "... older, I will send for you again. There is no need to cry."

I nod because I know he expects it.

His face clears at once, as though I had offered a dazzling smile rather than a small and miserable nod. "Very well," he says, more cheerfully. "I will call for the servants and they will return you to your rooms."

"Can't I – can't I stay here a little while?" I ask. The thought of walking back to my rooms, along the little pathways where every other woman will be able to see me, when I have barely been in this room long enough to be undressed and dressed again is humiliating. Everyone will know that I have been found wanting.

He seems puzzled by my request. "You would have nothing to do," he says. "I must attend to some papers." He turns away, satisfied that the matter has been dealt with.

The servants gather round me and I am dressed in my robes once more. They leave my hair unbound, so that as I walk back towards my rooms, the evening wind catches it. It whips across my face and I have to hold it back with one hand so that I will not be blinded. As I do so I look across to the lakeside palace and see Lady Qi still standing there, observing me as I make my way back to my rooms. Her face twists into something resembling a smile.

Castiglione: A greyhound at his toilet

"CAN YOU DRAW A BIRD?"

I was not expecting to be tested at once, although I had of course brought with me certain paintings I had already completed, so that the Emperor might see my work. I fumbled in my bag and extracted the tools of my trade. My hands shook a little. I tried not to notice as the courtiers and eunuchs drew closer while the Emperor leaned forward. Quickly I drew a bird, of the kind I had seen in the streets of Beijing on our hurried way to the Palace. It sat in its cage, dangling from a long pole slung over the hunched back of an elderly man. I had remarked on them as we passed and was told that pet birds were taken for 'walks' each day in their cages, so that they might benefit from the exercise. I am not entirely sure even now how they can be said to benefit from the exercise of their master's legs rather than their own wings. Perhaps a change of scenery sufficed them. I did not have my colours with me, so it was only a sketch, but when I turned it towards His Majesty he started back and smiled, then held out his hand, into which I placed the image.

"Astonishing," he said, examining it very closely. "It seems as though it is swaying on the end of its pole!" He looked at me with some kindliness, his wrinkled face cracking in a smile. "You can draw a bird, I see. What else can you draw?"

I hesitated. I did not wish to seem too humble and of insufficient prowess, nor to make a poor first impression which might damage my relationship with my new patron. I had, after all, been chosen for this task and sent across the wide seas for this very undertaking, to act as court painter to the Emperor of China. I was nervous of suggesting that I painted portraits, although of course I was able to do so, for fear that he would immediately ask me to portray his own physiognomy. As I did not yet know his likes and dislikes in this regard, and I had already found that all sitters had very particular desires when it came to their own portrayal, I cast about me for some other object that I could illustrate for him.

In a corner of the great receiving hall was a greyhound, fiercely engaged in removing himself of lice, by means of his teeth, drawn up in a grimace as he twisted his neck round to his own hind leg. A greyhound being a good shape for this kind of quick drawing, all long lines and movement, I did not reply to the Emperor, only began to sketch again. He leaned forwards and within a few strokes he had recognised the shape and looked about him, following my eyes. He chuckled at the sight of the greyhound's efforts and then waited while I completed his likeness.

"I can almost see his fleas," he said, looking down at the sketch and then back at the dog, surprised. Later I was to learn that it was rare for a painter here to show an animal as I had done, in movement and in such a bestial pose. Their horses and dogs are much portrayed but they are shown with nobility and grace, posed as their masters might be for a formal portrait, not grimacing to rid themselves of crawling pests. Perhaps the Emperor had never seen such a sketch, of an animal caught in the midst of its own toilet. At any rate he seemed pleased with my work and spoke with his Chief Eunuch, a most magnificently dressed fellow, who nodded at his sovereign's commands. With much bowing and scraping and the never-ending kowtow which I had already practiced more than once, we were dismissed from the imperial presence and waited in an antechamber along with Brother Matteo Ripa, our interpreter for the meeting. The Chief Eunuch followed us there and addressed me rapidly. I struggled to catch his meaning and he became irate, until Brother Ripa interceded. Pacified, the Chief Eunuch spoke with him for some time, issuing a stream of instructions. Ripa nodded as though all was clear, while I cursed my slow learning of the language. Despite the years of study since I had first agreed to come here my Mandarin was still poor and I made a note to myself that I must continue to engage a native speaker to improve my pronunciation skills, for I knew I would not advance in my career if my patron could not speak with me.

The Chief Eunuch indicated we might depart.

"He thought you were me and could not understand why your Mandarin was not better," explained Brother Ripa.

"How could he have mistaken us for one another?" I asked. "We bear no resemblance at all."

"They say they cannot tell most of us apart," he replied unperturbed. "They say our faces are too similar."

I pondered this.

"You have been given a new name," added Brother Ripa, as though it were a matter of no importance.

"A new *name*? Why?"

"The Emperor finds your name hard to pronounce. You will be known as Lang Shining. Shining is the first name, Lang is the family name. It is pronounced Shur-ning," he emphasised. "You had better practice it."

I muttered it to myself.

"You will work under the auspices of the Palace Board of Works in the two Imperial Painting Studios," he continued as we walked back through the noisy streets of Beijing to the church of St Joseph's, my new home. "One is called the Painting Academy Office and is based within the Forbidden City. The other is located in the Hall of Fulfilled Wishes. It is situated within a country estate close to Beijing."

I was distracted by both my new name and my surroundings and did not enquire further into my future place of work. All around me were new sights and I was elated by the Emperor's praise of my skills. I would surely amaze him once I could work with my oils and canvas, a large quantity of which had accompanied me on this long journey to my new destiny and which even now was following me to Beijing from Macau.

Amidst the curved rooftops and single-storey height of the local Chinese architecture my new home, St Joseph's, stood out, the classical style from home that ought to have been familiar to me looking oddly out of place here. It was built in a grey stone two storeys high, finished off with three dome-topped towers, one of which housed the bells to summon us to Mass. The interior of the chapel was fairly plain by the standards of home, with little in the way of gilding or stained glass, but otherwise pleasant enough. Behind it were located both the living quarters and refectory of the Brothers, as well as a small garden for contemplation, somewhat in the Chinese style, with decorative black rocks from the South, small areas of grass and some simple flowers.

The names of the various Brothers of the Mission rushed past me at that first meeting, with only a few making a firm first impression. An elderly Father Friedel was our Superior, Brother Matteo Ripa who had acted as our interpreter was an engraver of copper and an ardent missionary. He was much pleased to welcome Brother Costa, since they both hailed from Naples. Meanwhile a Brother Michele Arailza, a Venetian by birth, was a fellow painter, but he seemed ill-disposed towards me from the very beginning. I wondered if he disliked the idea of two new painters, of having competition in serving the Emperor. The Brothers might have been a little taken aback by Laura's presence, but most of them welcomed us warmly enough.

Our first few weeks as we settled into St Joseph's offered nothing but boredom, for the endless cycle of prayers that made up our days was of limited interest to me. I viewed Brother Arailza's paintings and privately felt that he would indeed have something to fear from my arrival at court, for his work was mediocre at best. I could see Laura felt the same, although neither of us made anything but polite comments on the subject matter. The food was not what I had expected, consisting mostly of plain fare such as steamed breads and stewed fruits or foods prepared to our own homelands' recipes. Brother Arailza screwed up his face when I asked about the local food and said that many of the Brothers did not care for it.

"They have good enough fruits, I suppose," he allowed. "Apples and pears, quinces, tolerably good plums. You will find the nuts here are similar to our own although the cherries are wild and therefore too sharp. And they do not make wine from grapes, but from rice: it is passable."

I tried the rice wine and found it very pleasant, certainly better than the poor quality sour grape-wine made by the Brothers to use at Mass. When certain dishes were sent to us from the Emperor's own table, which was, we were informed, to be seen as a gesture of benevolence, the Brothers ate from them only sparingly and somewhat unwillingly, although myself and Laura tasted meat-filled buns, an oddly sour soup and some honeyed sweetmeats and thought them all good.

I chafed a little under Father Friedel's constant worried reminders that I must eventually take my vows. Autumn was already upon us but he seemed unwilling to let me start work, as though he thought I might disappear into the Forbidden City and never come out again.

"Gherardini," he would repeat often, returning to my predecessor's time here as though it haunted him, "Gherardini never really took to the Mission life. He did not take his vows, you see, and grew too accustomed to the local way of life, eating their food and following some of their customs. Eventually he refused to live within the Mission at all and the Emperor gave him lodging with one of his trusted officials." The thought of this almost made him shudder. "Therefore you must understand how important it is that you yourself will take vows and live as we do. And your work must be pleasing to His Majesty, for as you know at this time he has forbidden us from even preaching and we must find a way to soften his heart in this matter."

I nodded and promised more than once that I had every intention of taking my vows in due course. I waited impatiently to begin my work and was relieved when I was finally taken to my new place of work in the Forbidden City, late in the autumn, with sharply cold days already predicting winter's arrival. I was informed that my working hours would henceforth be from seven in the morning until five in the afternoon and therefore I must present myself at my place of work at an appropriate hour to begin my painting for the day.

"You will find that some of the eunuchs are jealous of the praise and attention we receive," muttered Brother Arailza. "They often keep us waiting before allowing us entry, perhaps they think to cause trouble for us."

My first impression of the Imperial Studios was of both speed and silence. Large rooms led one into another, each with a different focus. Ceramics were worked on elsewhere, as well as enamel and glasswork studios. Here, where I was to work, were primarily paintings and calligraphy used for decorative purposes. The more senior artists worked in frowning silence, their assistants and apprentices scurried about them on cloth soles, which led to a constant soft pattering sound. Scrolls of paper were being made up, laid out, painted on, rolled up and despatched elsewhere. There were racks for drying and wide tables for works to be completed on. Saucers containing paints were kept warm on a tiny stove, to prevent them freezing on cold days. The eunuch showing me around whispered softly about all that we saw and finally led me to an area which had been set aside against my coming, where I was grateful to see many of my materials had already been transported and set out for my use. A variety of young men bowed deeply to me and I was told more names than I could remember. Many of my assistants and apprentices were eunuchs, I was to realise over time, for eunuchs performed most of the tasks within the Forbidden City, from the very lowliest even up to the great offices of state. Those who showed artistic talent might hope to work here, in the Studios. In other parts of the complex, I was informed, there were also dressmakers and perfumiers, jewellery-makers and designers of such small ornaments as might please the Emperor and his family: board games, vases, carvings of jade and wood, scented furniture and much more. Altogether there must have been many hundreds of artisans and artists at work, each of us dedicated only to the Emperor's pleasure and the beautification of his surroundings. The Brothers had seen fit to provide him not only with myself and other painters, but clock-makers, astronomers, medical men such as Brother Costa and even engineers. Our purpose here was daily made clear to us: to enchant the Emperor with the wonders of our Western skills, that he might, in time, consider our God also worthy of devotion.

That winter was a time of frustration for me, attempting to recall people's names and observing the work of those around me, mostly eunuchs trained as painters, who laboured over various imperial commissions, from portraits to landscapes and still lifes. Some were on scrolls of paper, others on stretched silk, a few were made into screens and other such ornaments. I admired their ability to paint with inks on silk, for it was fast work that must be perfect the first time, there was no room for error. It reminded me of fresco work, each stroke quick and light, the brush lifted away between each touch to avoid drips or inadvertent contamination. I tried using the inks myself and spent many hours experimenting with their colours and shades. They used rice paper which was stronger than I expected, as well as mulberry bark paper which came in vast sheets the size of blankets and which could not be torn by a man's bare hands. My tools had all been delivered and I spent time arranging them for my work: metal styluses, pencils and pens, inks, white and black chalks, pastels, watercolours and of course my oils.

"The Emperor prefers watercolours," said Brother Arailza gloomily. "I have tried to persuade him of the quality of oils but he has stubborn tastes."

I nodded, finding Arailza's constant complaints about his work here somewhat tiresome. I was eager for a commission of my own. But I was made to wait. Nian Xiyao, a court official, had been assigned to me as a tutor for my first few months, to explain my duties, guide me in the meanings of local symbols and suchlike. He seemed to consider learning by rote the best way to educate me, and so I was made to repeat back the symbolism of bats, hedgehogs, persimmons, dragons and other such things until I thought I would go mad with boredom.

"I will learn best if I am commissioned," I tried suggesting, but Xiyao only shook his head and continued unperturbed with his instruction until the first warmer days made their welcome reappearance.

"You are given the task of painting a view of the Garden," he informed me at last.

I thought of the so-called 'gardens' I had seen in the Forbidden City so far. They were not what I would have called a garden, myself, being primarily composed of stone: not only the cobbles beneath one's feet but also strange, twisted, dark rocks taller than a man. They were brought here from the South of the empire and apparently much admired for their natural beauty. There might be one or two trees, some pots of flowers, but they seemed almost out of place, surrounded by stone. Nevertheless I smiled, pleased at last to have work of my own to do. "Which garden is it?" I asked, hoping it might be the Emperor's own.

"The Garden of Perfect Brightness," said Xiyao.

I was beginning to grow accustomed to their lavish names for even the simplest of places. "Certainly," I said. "Where is it?"

"A day's travel to the northwest," he said.

I stared at him. "What?"

"It was once the Emperor's hunting ground," he explained. "It is now the residence of Prince Yong, one of the Emperor's sons."

"And I am to paint it?"

"The Emperor wishes to commission a particular view of the Garden," said Xiyao. "A view of the Prince's own palace, seen from across the lake."

Clearly the garden in question was not some little courtyard after all. I was given an escort and a mule-cart, which was loaded up with my materials. I was advised that once there I was to join the painting studio located within the estate and to familiarise myself with the surroundings before carrying out my commission. There was no hurry, the commission was seen as part of my training in this, my new world.

Laura was jealous. "I have not even met the Emperor, only one of his senior ladies and she knew nothing about painting, she only played with her lapdog," she complained when I told her. "And I have no commission."

"You are an apprentice," I reminded her.

"I am not," she retorted. "I have completed my apprenticeship."

"Well, you are still learning," I amended. "Sketch the people who come to Mass. It will be practice for you in their costumes and physiognomy, as well as their customs. "

"I want to come with you," she said.

I shook my head. "We are in the Emperor's employ," I reminded her. "It is not for us to countermand his orders. Sketch the parishioners and await my return."

She pouted but was there to wave me off when I departed Beijing for the country estate.

The roads were bumpy and I was glad towards the end of the day when we reached large gates set within a long wall of rose and cream-coloured rocks. Evidently the site was large, for I could not see the end of the wall as it stretched away into the distance. My mounted escort left me at the Eastern Gate, where a guard admitted me and guided me towards a cluster of studio buildings in a pleasingly green setting: a large area of grass with trees here and there in blossom. This, I was informed, was the studio where various artists were based when work was commissioned. In a small village named Hai-Tien some way distant from the estate was a house the Brothers had purchased where those of us working in the Garden were to sleep, for it would be impractical to return to Beijing every day. I was weary enough not to wish to explore that evening and instead viewed the studio and then retreated to the house, which had stables for the mules that we were to ride to the Garden each day. A serving girl gave me food. I ate and slept.

I woke early and rode a docile if slow mule back to the Eastern Gate to request entry. Once in, I determined to walk across the entire estate, to familiarise myself with it if I was to be based here for a while.

Making my way along the edge of a small lake I came across a gardener kneeling by a tree, adding new flowering primroses to those already in bud.

"My name is Lang Shining," I said, remembering just in time that I must offer my surname first, in the local fashion. "I am His Majesty's painter. What is your name?"

The gardener stood and bowed with a smile. "My name is Kun," he said.

I smiled back at him, he seemed a pleasant fellow. "I am seeking the Garden of Perfect Brightness," I told him.

He spread his hands. "This is the Yuan Ming Yuan, the Garden of Perfect Brightness," he said.

I frowned. "It is the name for the whole estate?"

"Yes."

"I am to paint a view of Prince Yong's palace," I clarified.

"Nine Continents Clear and Calm," he said, nodding. "It is a lake around which are set nine islets, on which the Prince and his ladies live."

"Ah, I see," I said. "And where is it?"

He gave me directions and I set off at a brisk walk.

But it was hard to walk swiftly for long. Kun's directions took me along a tiny winding path which worked its way around a larger lake where willow trees dipped down to the water and an early-morning light mist drifted at its far side. The pale blue sky was filled with scudding clouds and everywhere I looked were the first signs of spring: tiny buds of pastel colours, a haze of green from the newly-leafed trees. The very air smelt of spring, a fresh wet scent of the earth while the early sun lit up everything around me with a delicate glow. I wished that I had my paints with me here and now and thought that I must paint my commission in this early light, no matter how many dawn risings it would take.

After some time I realised that I had perhaps misremembered or misunderstood Kun's directions, for I had expected to see the lake he had mentioned, ringed with the palaces of the Prince and his ladies and yet still I found myself walking, beginning to see for myself just how large the estate must be. I reminded myself that after all there was no hurry and began to explore the tiny paths I found here and there, each temptingly hiding another view of the Garden. Unlike the formal gardens of a grand house at home or even the grounds of a monastery such as those where the Jesuits had offered me training for my mission, here I found it impossible to locate a standpoint offering a view of the entirety. Low hills surrounded me. Many of them I suspected to be manmade, deliberately restricting my view to the immediate surroundings, before a few steps would take me beyond them and into another small area. Tiny streams were everywhere, linking up one lake after another until I began to think of the visit I had made years before to Venice. Here was the same delicacy of a water-rich landscape surrounded with both natural and man-made beauty: temples, circular ponds filled with large multicoloured fish and artfully clustered trees that reached out their blossom-laden branches. Coming to a far larger lake than those I had seen so far I found jetties at which were moored little rowing boats awaiting use.

At one of these I paused and then unhooked a mooring rope to free a small craft. Awkwardly, I climbed aboard and took up the oars. It took me a few moments to coordinate my strokes, so that the little boat bobbed this way and that before it steadied. Slowly I rowed across the large lake, circling around a building set in its very centre, perhaps a temple or simply a viewing point. It was surrounded by lanterns, now spent, their golden hues reflected in the stillness of the lake's waters. Two black swans glided by, their crimson beaks dipping to one another.

I stopped rowing then and allowed the oars to rest within the boat. A slight breeze meant that the boat drifted slowly on the water but I paid it no mind. Something in me gave way. It seemed in that moment that all the tension of the past years: the waiting, the journey, making my way in a strange new world, the summons to court, the desire for a commission to prove my worth – that all of this was gone and instead I was simply here, in the place I had long dreamed of, fulfilling my ambitions. It was a strange place to have such a revelation, for in my ambitious daydreams I had imagined such a moment coming when I delivered to the Emperor a portrait or other commission that he would praise. And yet this place, this Garden of Perfect Brightness, seemed suddenly very aptly named to me, for I felt that I was surrounded by some strange clarity and happiness. I lay down in the boat and watched the clouds in the sky, their ever-changing nature suggesting first one form and then another, my mind content to watch as each shape came and went.

I must have lain there for some time, for the sun began to feel warm on my face. At last I sat up and looked about me. The boat had drifted close to the far shore and it was the work of only a few moments to row to a nearby jetty and fasten its moorings. I clambered to the top of one of the small hills and saw another, smaller lake, which might be the one I sought, though by now I was certain that I was thoroughly lost. No matter. I set off along the lakeside and passed one or two palaces, which made me believe that I might indeed be close to the Nine Islets, although the path I was on began to grow smaller and led away from the main lake. Ahead of me was a tiny path lined in bamboo, casting a dim green light over the way ahead, the dirt path leading somewhere further on. I turned back and paused for a moment, uncertain whether to return the way I had come back to the larger, cobbled path or press on. But the little pathway, framed in the delicate green of fresh bamboo towering above my head, was too tempting. I turned to face it again, ready to explore further.

In the brief moment while I had paused with my back to the bamboo, a figure in green silk had come into my view.

The Emperor's greyhound still guards the threshold of my memory palace. I am old enough to know better but still I pretend to myself that I pause here so that I may caress him. In truth I pause so that I may take a deep breath. Even now, I need to take a deep breath before I see her.

Forty Views of the Yuan Ming Yuan

I HAVE NO-ONE ELSE TO CONFIDE in so, stumblingly, I tell Yan of my disastrous first meeting with my new husband and she, already fiercely loyal to me as her sole charge in her first official post, is indignant. "You're taller than any of the ladies," she declares.

I look down at my body as she bathes me. "I am not womanly," I say sadly. I think of my mother and a few unbidden tears come.

Yan tuts. "I will feed you up."

I can't help but giggle but Yan takes her new task seriously. She begins by ordering larger portions of food to be served at every meal and plies me with sweet cakes at any opportunity between meals.

"He didn't say I should be *fatter*," I remonstrate.

"You're too skinny anyway," retorts Yan, certain of the path she is following. "You need to eat more and then your womanliness will come for sure."

She spends hours sitting re-stitching my robes so that they are just that little more fitted, giving the illusion of curves where I have none, and I am touched by her efforts. Her mission gives her a new-found confidence and the ample food I am unable to finish adds some much-needed flesh to her own undernourished frame although she is still a head shorter than me.

But I quickly grow tired of this new life. The unending bathing, the dressing, the elaborately arranged hair which is only dismantled again each evening, the too-much food and sitting about bores me. I see the other ladies from time to time and they are always pleasant but their own lives are as sedate as mine. I find daily mah-jong tiresome and sitting with them makes me feel older than I really am, yet I do not feel I can roam about with their daughters, for fear of being thought childish.

"Let's go out," I say to Yan one day, already bored when I have only just finished breakfast.

"To the ladies?" asks Yan, obediently setting down her sewing.

"No," I say.

"Where to, then?"

"I don't know," I confess. "Just out, before I go mad."

Yan follows me, confused. I stand outside my home, gazing one way and another, before setting off along a path I have never followed before. It leads away from the lake, through an avenue of tall bamboos and softly waving pink and white anemone flowers. I totter along in my high shoes, occasionally stumbling. Yan has to catch me twice and in the end I hold her hand as though we were friends and her sturdy clasp gives me better balance.

"Where are we going?" asks Yan after we have passed a tiny temple, its swooping golden roof and scarlet paint hidden amongst the tall bamboos.

"I want to see where we are," I say.

Yan is bewildered. "In the Yuan Ming Yuan," she says, as though I have lost my senses and need to be reminded of my new home's name. "The Garden of Perfect Brightness."

"I know that," I pant irritably. We are walking up a small hill now. It's a hill I would have run up a few months ago but it's hot, my shoes are impossible and it's been a long time since I did more than saunter fifty paces down to the lake's edge. "But how big is it? What other buildings does it have in it? Do we have neighbours?"

Yan shakes her head. "I don't know," she says.

"Didn't you walk through the whole estate when you arrived?" I ask.

"No," says Yan. "I came through a side gate and the eunuch who brought me here led me along a little path through a grove of trees to the large lake, to your palace."

I pause for breath. Yan waits while I gulp in air, her little face worried. She must be wondering what has possessed me, after months of barely setting foot outside my own rooms, to suddenly be wandering down hidden paths and panting up hills. I am beginning to wonder the same. What am I trying to find?

But a few moments later I have my answer, for we reach the top of the hill. We stand in silence, looking about us and then turn to stare at one another.

"It's *huge*," I breathe.

The Yuan Ming Yuan is no large garden or even multiple gardens. Instead it stretches as far as I can see in all directions. Yan and I turn about ourselves and gape at its size. The lake onto which my own palace faces, which I had considered large, is dwarfed by another, far off in the distance. There are rivers and canals entwined across the whole landscape. I can see a few buildings dotted about, some nestled delicately into the embrace of trees and flowers, almost hidden from view, others in clusters bigger than any of the palaces by our lake, almost tiny towns. I look at Yan and she looks back at me, open-mouthed.

"I thought the lake and our palaces was all there was," I say.

Yan nods, dumbstruck. It is as though we have lived in one tiny room for the past few months and suddenly opened a door to find that we live in a city.

"Can we go anywhere?" I ask.

Yan is looking about. "There's a wall," she says, pointing. I peer at where she is indicating, a cream and rose stone wall higher than a man, which stretches out into the distance. Slowly we make out that there is a grand entrance to the Garden, sitting at the southernmost wall. After that there are a number of official looking buildings, which follow on to the lake and our palaces. But this makes up only a third of the first part of the estate, somewhat square-shaped. To the east of this part sits another, far larger square of land, the centre of which is a huge lake. Even further along, we can just make out another square, perhaps the size of our own plot. And finally, sitting below that, a smaller, less neatly-shaped area. We assume from what we can see that there is a perimeter wall surrounding the entirety of the Garden.

"We should explore all of it," I say, excited. "We can go to a new part every day!"

"Off again?" calls Lady Mao.

I nod and she waves, laughing. I think she finds my explorations amusing. I am sure she thinks I am turning back into the country girl from the hunting grounds I was before marriage rather than the overly-daintily-dressed concubine she first met by the lakeside. We spend most of our days outdoors. My cloud-climbing shoes are left back at the palace and instead I wear sturdy boots and fur-lined coats as the autumn descends on us. Behind me tramps Yan, bundled up against the cold. The brisk wind turns our cheeks pink even as the leaves turn red. We stride through waving golden chrysanthemums as big as our outstretched hands and scramble up the small but steep man-made hills surrounding us. Our hair blows every which way, pins falling as quickly as the leaves from the trees. When we are worn out we descend to the level of the lakes and follow canals and rivers to find our way home, where Yan pours cup after cup of hot tea and stokes up the kangs to warm us. Every day we find new sights. We pass temples and offices, the kitchens and even a vegetable garden, immaculately hoed and ready for the new sowing season to come. We find orchards of fruit trees, scattered with artful care across sloping fields as though each tree had planted its own children.

"What will it be like in spring?" murmurs Yan.

"Beautiful," I say, imagining clouds of blossom.

Snow falls like petals and we look out of the windows at the frozen lake. Yan hums lullabies and I drink hot tea until the drifts are deep enough, then I drag her outside and throw snowballs at her. At first she does not retaliate but then, quick fingered, she shapes a small ball and knocks off my little fur cap. After that, the snowballs fly fast between us and I know that my once-shy maid has become a friend.

My first year passes. The wisps of hair between my legs turn into a soft down. My hips, once so narrow, become curved. My breasts ache and then grow from tiny buds to rounded cups, causing Yan to beam each time she bathes me.

"Prince Yong will call for you now," she promises me, when my first bleeding comes. She is proud of her work, as though she had moulded my new body herself.

I blush. "Don't be silly, Yan," I say. "He will have forgotten all about me." But secretly I hope that he will remember me and that when I am summoned he will note with approval that I am no longer a child. I lift my chin as I think of being a real woman, desired by her husband, perhaps even favoured above the older ladies. I don't want to be part of a jealous war but still, it would be nice to be singled out. Perhaps I could be noticed for my beauty or elegance or some such trait, like the women in the romantic stories my mother and aunts were fond of. I might be known as the Prince's favourite. I cannot help making up little daydreams in which I am such a favourite, although my imagination fails at the thought of what would actually happen between the Prince and myself behind closed doors.

But he does not call for me. We hear that he is sent by the Emperor to manage a flooding along the Yellow River and does well, is praised for his hard work and diligence. More papers arrive for him to work on, he is often gone from the Yuan Ming Yuan. When he does reside there, the women of his household are not called for very often. Those that are do not even boast, only tell me with a resigned shrug that he does not linger with them. He is known for his kindness and gentleness towards us all, but shows little interest in our lives. He sends gifts to all of us without favouring one or another, and the nature of his gifts are such that I suspect that he appoints this task to one of the eunuchs and that our names are simply ticked off a list – conventional gifts of fruits, of flowers, perhaps hairpins or other delicate jewellery for our birthdays, a fan, game or other trinket for important occasions. Sometimes I wonder if he has forgotten me entirely, although when I see him at the celebrations for the New Year, which come just after my own birthday he at least seems to be aware of when I was born.

"Happy birthday," he says politely.

"Thank you for your gift," I reply, as though to a kindly aunt.

He smiles and nods without replying.

In the summer of my fourteenth year I take up archery. I used to play with my brothers' bows and thinking of them now I have my own bow made and arrows tipped with colourful feathers. Yan sets my targets and retrieves my arrows, and in return I teach her to shoot as well as I do. We become accomplished, but there is no one to praise our efforts excepting ourselves. I wonder whether my brothers would still beat me or whether I would shame them with my accuracy. In the heat of the summer I request a boat and we row – at first badly, then with greater confidence – on the lakes and explore every part of the Garden, from the great lake in the centre, which I now know is called the Sea of Blessings, across ever smaller lakes and down canals and tiny rivers which sometimes end up as minor streams or springs and from which we have to drift backwards to return to a place where our boat can turn round. No-one knows this place as well as we do. The servants only hurry from one designated spot to another. The Prince's other women prefer to follow well-worn paths – from one palace to another, from the boating lake to the shrines, from their mah-jong tiles to their own quarters: they do not venture further afield. The Garden is a quiet place, Yan and I can wander a whole day and see only the odd servant pass by or a guard in the distance if we venture close to the perimeter walls.

New Year comes round again. The Prince wishes me a happy fifteenth birthday, I thank him for his gift. He nods and smiles.

I grow bolder. The Garden is my home now. I may ask for anything and it will be done. I may dress how I please, for no-one of note will see me. Who is to care how I behave or how I appear? The autumn rains fall and after days of staying indoors I take an old robe of Yan's and we venture outside, where we make little streams and dams out of mud and twigs, stones and flowers.

"You're not five!" Yan yelps.

I laugh and reach out a filthy finger to paint her nose with mud. She slaps her hand in a puddle to splash my face and by the time we return home it is almost dark and our clothes will probably make the laundry maids weep.

It is New Year and there are fireworks. I pass Prince Yong who wishes me a happy sixteenth birthday. I thank him for his gift. I have almost forgotten that he is my husband. It is more like being a younger daughter to an often-absent father.

"Happy birthday, my dear," says Lady Mao a few days later. The other ladies join in wishing me long life and happiness. Today I have dressed elegantly and joined them in Lady Mao's palace. I make an effort to play mah-jong and listen to their conversation. They give me little trinkets – a string of prayer beads, silk flowers for my hair. Only Lady Qi is absent. She does not join the other women when we sit. I take the opportunity of perhaps being considered old enough for gossip to ask about her and at once their voices drop lower.

"She is ambitious," says Lady Mao.

"Ambitious for what?" I ask.

"She has two living sons. She wants one of them to be the Prince's heir."

It seems a small ambition. There are no other living sons, so her ambition would appear to be already achieved. I shrug. "If she has the only living sons…" I say.

Lady Mao makes a face. "She would also like Prince Yong to be made Crown Prince."

"But there is already a Crown Prince."

Lady Mao nods and lowers her voice. "Of course. But there are rumours that the Emperor is displeased with his conduct. The Kangxi Emperor has more than thirty sons and at least twelve could be considered for the position of heir. He could demote the Crown Prince and appoint another son in his place, should he so wish. This is what Lady Qi dreams of."

I grimace. "She has a lot of dreams."

The others giggle and we play on. Only as I return to my own place do I catch a rare glimpse of Lady Qi outside her own home. Even after three years here I have only seen her a handful of times. I change my course a little to avoid her, for I do not like her cold eyes and her fixed stare. But she seems uneasy to see me herself and disappears promptly into her own rooms. I wonder about her behaviour but later I see a male figure leaving her palace as dusk falls. I wonder who it is and where Lady Qi's loyalties lie. I tell Yan and she, curious after the gossip I passed on to her, makes it her mission to spy on Lady Qi. It does not take long before we realise that she often has visitors, men in sumptuous robes who, however, appear quietly and without an entourage, who visit with her for a short

Melissa Addey

period only before quickly making their way out of the Yuan Ming Yuan and heading back towards Beijing.

"Is she being unfaithful to Prince Yong, do you think?" asks Yan.

I shake my head. "I don't know, but surely if she is ambitious for her sons she would not want to be discovered being unfaithful? She would be dishonoured, maybe even sentenced to death and they might be set aside rather than being heirs."

"There's no-one to take their place," points out Yan. "Unless one of you ladies has a child."

"Not much chance of that," I tell her and she makes a face that shows what she thinks of Prince Yong for ignoring me all this time, something she takes as a personal affront.

"Perhaps we could plant blossoming trees on the island in the Sea of Blessings," I say. "Think how pretty it would be."

Yan nods.

"I need one of the gardeners," I say. "Can you arrange for one?"

Yan makes enquiries and on a bright late winter's day a young eunuch presents himself at my palace. He is my own height, with a pleasant face burnt brown by the sun and a ready smile. He bows before pointing to a boat by the water's edge, which is filled with young saplings, ready to be planted.

"Cherries," he says, when I ask.

Yan and I row ahead of him to our favourite place, the tiny island on the Sea of Blessings lake and I tell him where I want him to place the trees. Yan busies herself with making hot tea and I indicate that she should offer him some as well.

"Rose petals," says Yan, passing him the tea with a superior air. "I dried them myself."

He bows to me and takes the tea, smiling at Yan. He has done a good day's work and I wave him goodbye when we part. But the next time we visit the island to check on the trees he is there again, although I have not summoned him. We are used to having the island to ourselves.

"What are you doing here?" asks Yan, none too politely.

"Planting roses for you," he says, looking directly at her as though it was the most natural thing in the world. I have to stifle a laugh at Yan's expression.

"What is your name?" I ask, for I know she will not ask and something tells me she will want to know.

"Kun," he says.

I think perhaps they are well suited, this man of the earth who has dreamt up an island of roses for an insignificant little maid and my swallow Yan who is so practical and hardworking but inside has a soft little heart. I sigh as we leave the island.

"What's wrong?" asks Yan.

"It's a shame he is a eunuch," I say, unable to keep my thoughts to myself.

"What do I care what he is?" splutters Yan and I know her thoughts matched mine.

But now that we have met him Kun seems to be everywhere. We go rowing and he is on the lake, clearing away dead lotus leaves. We walk along secluded paths and there he is, sweeping away old leaves or planting new bulbs for springtime. He does not speak to us unless I speak first, for that would be presumptuous, but he bows to me and smiles at Yan and I smile back, while she looks this way and that and does not know how to respond at all. So she scowls.

Yan has a headache and is being grumpy, so I set out alone, along a tiny path thickly planted with primroses. The early spring day is marked with strange cloud formations that keep my eyes on the sky rather than what is in front of me. I startle when a dark shape appears on the path ahead of me.

"I beg your pardon," says a man's voice in stumbling Mandarin. I step back, alarmed.

The man before me is dressed in a scholar's dark robes but he is not Manchu, nor Chinese. He is a Westerner. His eyes and hair are a dark brown and his skin is coloured by the sun. I have only ever seen two such before, at the hunting grounds. They were elderly Jesuit priests, in service to the Emperor. This man is young. Their beards were long and grey whereas his is short. The old men I saw years ago were stooped and pale, their skin sheltered but their backs warped by years of study in cloistered rooms. I saw them only briefly and at some distance, for we were not permitted to approach the imperial party. This man is tall and is standing only ten paces away from me. He is staring at me as though I were a ghost. I am probably doing the same. I close my mouth and try to regain my composure.

"Who are you?" I ask and it comes out too haughty.

He makes a bow that must be how they bow in his country, one foot behind the other, both legs bent, one arm out to his side. He does it smoothly, but it looks strange in the robes he is wearing and as he finishes it I see him recall that this is not how to present himself here. He tries instead to bow as we do and does it badly, unsure of how low he should go and where his hands should be.

His double bow makes me bow in return, although I am not quite sure whether I should be bowing at all.

"My name is Giuseppe Castiglione, I am here to serve with the Jesuits as a painter," he says and at the frown on my face he amends what he has said. "You may wish to call me Lang Shining," he says, pronouncing it with excessive care, the 'Shining' emerging almost correctly as 'shur-ning'. "The Emperor has been so kind as to bestow a new name on me, for he says that my name is hard for people here to speak."

"Cast-eel…" I begin, but see that he wants to laugh. Something stubborn in me makes me shake my head. "I do not need you to have a new name," I say. "Say your real name again."

He says it more slowly. "Joo-se-pe," he says. "Castiglione is my family name."

I struggle but finally I say his name and he nods, smiling as though relieved that he is able to converse with someone here, even in his poor Mandarin.

"And your name?" he asks.

"Niuhuru," I say. I do not say who I am. I am not even sure why. Surely I should have told him that I am Prince Yong's concubine? But it is too late. He is already trying to pronounce my name, which he manages better. I smile. But now I am unsure of what to do next. We stand on the path in silence and at last I gesture awkwardly at the path beyond him. "I… go that way," I manage, wondering why I am simplifying my speech as though to a child.

He moves out of my way at once, stepping aside and bowing again as I pass, this time remembering to bow as we do.

I walk away. I don't look back, because that would be to show an unseemly amount of interest in a strange man, but when I come to a little hill I climb it more quickly than usual and scan the landscape below me to see where the Jesuit was headed. But he is gone. When I reach my own home I am about to tell Yan about my strange encounter with the Jesuit but find myself remaining silent, as though I am unable to summon up the right words to describe him, although the image of him is bright before my eyes when I close them.

The next day and the day after that I am up early and fretting to be out and about, striding through the Yuan Ming Yuan's vast expanse as though searching for something lost. Yan mutters something about household chores but she is willing to follow me on my explorations, although she does insist on at least having something to eat and some hot tea first. "It's still winter," she chides.

I laugh. "It's springtime," I tell her, standing in my doorway and looking out across the lake, turning my head this way and that. There is a pale green haze spreading across the trees as their new leaves emerge and everywhere I smell wet earth. There is a freshness in the air that makes me fidget.

"What's the hurry?" asks Yan, after we have rushed along the little path I took the day before, climbed the highest hill I can find, hurried back down and gone to find a boat. "Where are you trying to go? What are you looking for?"

Who, I think. *Who am I looking for?*

We row down one canal and then another. Yan is getting annoyed by my distracted air. "Go to the little island," she commands at last, as though I were her maid and she my mistress. "Let's see if any of the trees have blossomed or whether that eunuch has killed them all."

"His name is Kun," I remind her, although I know she needs no reminding.

She shrugs as though his name is of no interest but her cheeks are already pink. I can see her leaning forward a little as we approach the island and look over my shoulder to see that the first cherry trees are indeed flowering, some white, some pink. And there is a figure on the island already, a man in a blue robe. I smile to myself. Kun must be looking after the saplings, he has an uncanny knack for being wherever we are. I would almost say he was spying on our movements. My back to the island, I pull harder on the oars and smile as I watch Yan pretend not to look at our destination. It is only when she gets out of the boat that I hear her gasp as though she has stubbed her toe. I finish tying up the boat and turn, to find her folded up on the rough gravel of the shore. Standing over her is Prince Yong. My husband.

My mouth opens but nothing comes out. I am suddenly, horribly, conscious of the informality of my robes and hair, of having ordered the planting of these trees without my husband's permission, of having rowed here as though I were a servant rowing my maid, of... of... most dreadfully of secretly having been looking for a man, a stranger, a Jesuit Westerner that I have met only once, whom I have been seeking without even knowing why. I am sure it is written all over my face. I am very aware of my husband standing closer to me than he has done since the first time I met him in his bedchamber, of being almost alone with him rather than in a crowd.

"Highness," I half-whisper.

Yan quickly rises to her feet and creeps a little way off, pretending she is out of earshot.

I manage something like a bow, possibly the worst and most inelegant bow ever performed by a concubine to her lord. When I straighten I find I have grown more than I realised since coming here. I am almost as tall as the Prince.

Yong looks at me with his head on one side. "Niuhuru," he says. He says it as though he has dredged my name up out of some far-off memory.

I nod, unsure whether he is simply naming me or whether he is asking a question, possibly 'what on earth are you doing here, looking like that?'.

He is silent for a moment. Then he turns and gestures at the trees. "You ordered them planted?"

"Yes," I mutter. I wonder whether I should apologise at once, to save being reprimanded.

His face is still turned away from me. "Why?"

"I – I thought it would look beautiful in the springtime with flowering trees. I thought the falling petals would look like snow." What a stupid thing to say, I think. *Why* did I not ask for his permission? I swallow, feeling cold and small. I wish Yan was closer to me, so that I could clasp her hand for courage.

He turns back and looks at me in silence. I wait. Then he smiles. A full, warm smile, such as I have never seen from him before. Suddenly he looks younger. His usual expression, of serious attention to duty, is lightened. He actually looks happy. "They are perfect," he says.

I don't know how to respond, so I only smile back. It is hard not to respond to this new smile of his.

"Plant whatever you wish," he says. "It seems we are of one mind, you and I. You see this place as I see it. It is a refuge, a taste of the gardens of the Immortals. A place to have one's worries taken away. A place to fortify the soul. A place to be happy and free, unshackled by the expectations of others. It is unlike anywhere else in the empire."

I almost say that I don't know what he's talking about. The Yuan Ming Yuan is just a large country estate, however pretty it is. It is simply my home, now that I have lived here for some time. But I catch myself before I speak. Here we are, I in a violet robe that, although made of silk, is about as simple a robe as one could have made, especially when paired with my sturdy, muddied boots. He is so plainly dressed that I mistook him for a eunuch from a distance. And this is the first real conversation together we have had in three years and he is speaking to me as though I were a friend, someone who understands his thoughts and feelings. Slowly, I nod.

He nods back as though we have settled on something. "I must return to my work," he says. He looks about him at the trees and then turns back to me. "Beautiful," he says and smiles again, before walking briskly away, towards the eastern shore where his boat must be moored.

Yan hurries back to my side. I give her a surprised smile at what has just occurred. "He said the trees were beautiful!" I say, pleased with his praise and hugely relieved at how well this unexpected meeting has gone.

Yan is grinning a mischievous grin, her eyes alight with pride. "He was looking at you when he said 'beautiful'," she points out. "He wasn't looking at the trees."

The Screen of Twelve Beauties

HER EYES WERE GREY.

I clung to this certainty, for everything else in my life had changed.

Even at mass, which I had to attend more frequently than was my natural inclination, the music and liturgy that should have been comfortingly familiar was strange to my ears. They had their own instruments here unlike those to which I had been used and the brothers, wishing to make their devotions seem more familiar to their new converts, allowed their use in the church, as well as some songs to be sung in Mandarin. The unmelodic wailing combined with the sudden crashing of gongs and strange cymbals in the full midst of the service startled me the first time I heard it, turning sounds known to me from childhood into something strange and unknown, my own faith, such as it was, into a strange ritual devoid of meaning.

Most of all I struggled with the very thing that should have been my saving grace, my anchor in this strange sea: my skills and talent as a painter. After my initial success with the Kangxi Emperor, I had expected that my skills would be much admired and rewarded, that I would be master to grateful apprentices. Instead I received a rude awakening when my work arrived and I unpacked some of it to show the painters here, intending to instruct them in the techniques used by Western masters.

Xiyao, my assistants and the other painters stood around me, curious. But despite showing them numerous sketches and paintings, I was met only with puzzlement regarding the correct use of perspective, for they had only the most rudimentary grasp of how we Western artists used it, their own work using an oddly different approach.

Xiyao intervened, interrupting an explanation. "Shining, you must learn to use our own watercolours and inks rather than your oils. And also to paint onto rice paper or silk."

"Why?"

"Supplies of your own materials will be harder to obtain here. And also, the Emperor and the court prefer local materials to be used."

In vain I tried to explain that oils might bring a greater depth of texture, that the canvasses seemed to my mind more robust than rice paper. I was met only with stubborn silence followed by an insistence on their own ways. Silently, I determined that I would paint a full portrait in my own style, so that they might see once and for all how superior the technique was.

Her eyes were grey.

The very straight black hair and pale ivory skin of the women I had seen here I had already grown used to in only a few months here. The shape of the eyes, also. All brown of course, but that was hardly a novelty to me, since most of my countrymen also had dark eyes, myself included.

But her eyes were grey. Startled as I wandered, I had almost thought her a spirit of the Garden: the pale skin and eyes, the long loose hair whipped about her face, a lone woman in the deserted landscape. I tried to recollect the colour of her robe, what exactly she had said to me, how she had moved, the faint scent of her as she passed by me. All of it gone, details that I would usually notice and commit to memory to enable me to reproduce them faithfully with my paints. Gone. I was left with a confused feeling, something like desperation but I did not know what for. I had only her name, which I mouthed silently to myself, afraid of forgetting it amidst the too-many new things surrounding me daily. And her eyes. Strange, yet compelling in their difference. I could not stop thinking of them.

I picked up my brush and mixed a colour, which was wrong. Too blue. The next, too brown. The third, too dark. My trusted skills, dismissed and failing me in this cursed place.

"I need to see her again," I muttered.

"Master?"

An assistant, standing by too eagerly, noticing my mutterings and failed attempts too closely. "Do you need something?"

I shook my head, hoping he would leave me be, then closed my eyes and tried to see the colour once more.

"You are summoned."

I turned. Xiyao. "What?"

"You are summoned."

"The Emperor?" I asked, already moving towards the door, knowing that such a summons required an immediate response.

"His son."

"Son?"

"Prince Yong. Fourth prince."

"Are there many?" I asked, following dutifully. I had been briefed on the Emperor's family but could not recall all the details. A fourth prince did not sound very high-ranking and I knew he had not been named the Crown Prince. So he would not be his father's heir, only a lesser prince, bound to serve a future emperor-brother. Then again, he had been given this estate, the Yuan Ming Yuan, by his father the Emperor and so perhaps had been somehow singled out for praise and honours.

"More than thirty," said Xiyao. He walked swiftly, across a small bridge and onwards, as I hurried to keep pace, shaking my head at the thought of thirty princes, all vying for one throne, for I had been informed that they did not follow primogeniture as we would have done at home. Surely, I found myself reflecting, making the first son heir would prove the simplest solution when faced with such a multitude of offspring? Did these people not wish to learn anything from us?

We followed the curve of a lake's edge. Ancient willows dipped the tips of their tumbling branches into the shore-ripples of the water, while further into the lake the buds and first flowers of lotuses rose up from their fresh green pads. Winding paths led away from the water's edge and up towards small palaces, which ringed the lake. One was entwined with an ancient wisteria, its bare branches encasing the palace like a bird's nest. I thought that soon it would create a glorious frame of tumbling purple flowers. Still I looked about me, conscious that the path I had followed had led here, that the woman I had met must have passed by this place before she met me. I wondered if she was a maid, although I had been told that all the maids wore blue robes with red hair ribbons to tie their neat plaits. The woman – *Niuhuru* – she was not dressed as a maid, but neither did she wear the elaborate hair of a court lady or concubine. Perhaps she really was a spirit?

"Prince Yong's residence," announced Xiyao and I found myself ushered into the receiving hall of a lakeside palace far larger than those we had passed until now.

"Shining." A clear voice, quiet but purposeful.

I found myself before the Prince, a man perhaps my own age, of a similar stature. He was dressed less ostentatiously than two of the other princes whom I had met so far in my time here but there was something in the way he carried himself that reminded me of his father the Emperor: a regal bearing.

"Highness." I bowed.

He gestured to me to follow him. "How is your Mandarin? Do you still have need of an interpreter?"

I shook my head. "I manage better, Your Highness. I have daily lessons and hope I am improving. Although I am sure there is still much to learn."

"There is always something to learn," the Prince said, almost wearily. We had reached a room that appeared to be his study. There were so very many papers on and about his desk that most people would have allowed them to become a jumble of confusion, but it was clear even from a distance that they were laid out in a strict order. The prince took a chair and indicated that I should be seated.

"You have a most beautiful estate," I said. "It is a pleasure to be based here, in the studio."

He gave a brief smile and nodded. His serious face was much lightened by the smile and I thought that this was a man who should smile more and take his duties a little less seriously.

"I wish to commission an artwork," he said.

I made a small bow in my seat. "I would be most honoured," I said. I found myself hoping it would be a large piece of work including the portrait I had in mind, for until now I felt that I had only made small sketches here and there and mostly been instructed on how *not* to paint. I longed to show something of the skills I believed I possessed, the skills for which, after all, I had been selected by the Brothers. I believed that if I could show what I was capable of and the prince were to be pleased, I might yet change the painting conventions used and find my place here.

"A decorative screen," specified the Prince. "It will be used to adorn this room and it should be titled *The Screen of Twelve Beauties*."

I found myself wondering whether this seemingly severe and dutiful man was asking me to paint for him the kind of images of a woman that in my own country might be concealed within snuff boxes and other trinkets, for a man's personal viewing pleasures. Surely the Prince was not asking me to paint such images on a large screen to decorate his study?

"I would like each lady to be viewed within a setting of nature," the Prince continued. "And to show her perhaps undertaking a task to indicate her breeding and cultured mind. Reading, or perhaps studying a work of art… You can bring me the first preparatory sketch to approve within a month, along with your ideas for the others."

I nodded, still uncertain of what exactly the Prince was asking of me. I did not dare to ask for clarification, even as I bowed on leaving his presence.

"A classical idea," said Xiyao, when I recounted the commission. "Each lady should symbolise an ideal of beauty. I can show you some examples."

"Please do," I said. I felt my shoulders drop with relief as he showed me various examples, all of them fully-clothed. "Of course," I said, with enthusiasm. "I shall begin at once."

I wandered through the Garden, noting particular settings or plants that would provide suitable backdrops. I thought that with their being twelve beauties, it would be suitable to have them posed in the twelve months of the year and asked whether a gardener could be assigned to me for a day to describe the plants of each season, as I had not yet been here long enough to observe them all. Xiyao sent me the pleasant young eunuch Kun, whom I had encountered on my first day in the Garden. He walked alongside me and described what would be in flower or fruit in different seasons. He also pointed out structures that might be suitable, owing to their being covered with flowers: a lotus-framed palace, one wrapped in climbing roses.

"That one is the most beautiful," he said, pointing to the wisteria-entwined palace I had already noted. I could see the first buds of the purple flowers beginning to emerge. Seeing their first haze of growth I closed my eyes and in a rush saw the woman again, standing before me as I had first seen her. I dismissed Kun and all but ran back to the studio, to paint her before she disappeared again.

A frame of endless tumbling wisteria flowers, their rich purple almost like the dark bunches of grapes from home. Standing within it, the shape of a woman. Her robe a pale green, almost as though she herself was the stem holding up the multitude of flowers. Her hands should have been reaching up to touch the petals in a classical pose but were instead held up in a startled gasp. Long and black, set loose about her shoulders, her hair was unkempt from the wind's strength. Her eyes were grey and open wide as she met an unseen man, a stranger. I ignored the warnings I had been given and instead painted her as I would have painted her at home, oil on canvas, the shade falling across her face.

I called for Xiyao, wanting to show him the painting. I was confident that he would acknowledge, now that he could see a completed painting, the impact of the techniques I used.

His eyes lit up with recognition when he saw the image before him. "Lady Niuhuru," he said at once and I felt something in me turn over. I looked at him without speaking and he frowned and pointed more clearly at the painting, as though speaking to a fool.

"Lady Niuhuru," he said again. "Her eyes are like that. And the wisteria palace is her home," he added.

There was a sudden moment when I wanted to strike him for having noticed her strange grey eyes. A madness gone in an instant, since anyone not half-blind would observe her eyes at once. And then a sense of falling as I heard, after they were spoken, his other words. "Her home?"

Xiyao nodded. "Lady Niuhuru lives there," he said.

"Who is Lady Niuhuru?" I asked and even as I asked him the question I wanted to stop up his mouth, to unask the question because something told me that her title meant something I did not wish to hear.

"She is *Gege* to the fourth Prince," said Xiyao.

"*Gege*?" I asked, still hoping for some other word, some reprieve. My Mandarin was not good enough for this specific title and yet I knew the meaning of the word he had proffered before I had to ask him to translate it.

"Concubine."

I wanted to ask something else but my mind was a confusion of thoughts that I could not even name.

Xiyao, meanwhile, was shaking his head. "Lady Niuhuru is not a suitable subject for the screen," he told me briskly, as a housewife might discard a bruised fruit.

"Why not?"

"Images of Beauties should be idealised examples of beauty. They are not intended to portray real people." He paused. "And Lady Niuhuru... is anyway not really a true beauty," he added, lowering his voice as though to avoid causing offence to an absent Prince Yong. "Her eyes are rather odd and she is extremely tall. They say she was chosen as something of a joke by Lady Que Hui, because her father was a lowly official and Prince Yong likes to think that any man may rise through diligence and hard work. So Lady Que Hui thought he should have a concubine from a modest background. Usually the concubines are chosen from more high-ranking families."

I did not want to hear more about her, to hear details of how she was seen by others.

"But you can see what I mean about the technique," I said, almost curtly. "It is far superior to that used here."

Xiyao was still shaking his head. "This..." he began, indicating the heavy shading, "this... it looks like dirt."

I smiled, feeling myself on safer ground. "It is shading," I explained, adopting the kindly tone my master had used with me when I was still a boy. "We call it *chiaroscuro*. It means 'light and dark' and through its use in a painting, especially of a person as you can see here, can be used to give depth and the illusion of the body's contours being present, rather than flattened onto canvas." I paused, waiting for him to acknowledge that I was right, but he was already shaking his head again. I almost wanted to slap him to make him stop.

"The effect is inauspicious. It appears as dirt and would be entirely unsuitable for painting most subjects and particularly portraits." He almost shuddered as a thought crossed his mind. "Most *certainly* not of the Emperor or his family." He nodded at my bemused expression. "Your predecessors here also had to learn to paint without using this method, in our own style. Did the Brothers not tell you? Allow me to show you some examples." He hurried away.

I stood alone, feeling like a fool. I tried to imagine painting without the techniques that I had used ever since I was apprenticed to my master's studio. Now approaching my thirtieth year, I had spent close to two decades painting in this way. I could not help feeling irritated. What had I been brought here for? What had I promised my life to? Had the brothers lied to me, promised me that I might share my skills with devoted disciples whilst knowing full well that I would be obliged to become the student, rather than the master I had envisioned?

Xiyao returned. "Coronation portraits of previous Emperors," he said, gesturing to two minor eunuchs to help him roll out a variety of scrolls. On each appeared a past monarch, glorious in imperial yellow, bedecked with precious stones, magnificent on their carved thrones.

They looked like a child's paper dolls, flat and lifeless, gaudy but inert. No painter worthy of the name in Europe would consider painting like this. I nodded, wordlessly, as portrait after portrait was displayed before me. Emperors, lesser nobility, even animals: all lifeless. I felt my excitement for this post drain away and with it came the weight of knowing I was trapped here.

Time passed and still I struggled. The screen was completed with input from the other painters of the imperial studios, so much so that I barely recognised it as my own work, despite a half-hearted attempt to introduce a linear Western perspective, which they found unusual, although Xiyao seemed to have at least some interest in it. I found little pride in the finished screen when it was delivered to the prince, who nevertheless seemed pleased with it. I was not allowed the use of *chiaroscuro* and without it the non-existent women portrayed seemed devoid of life to me. The unusual symbols used around them, which I had dutifully tried to memorise (*bats mean fertility, mushrooms promise good luck, a calabash augers many sons*), seemed only a meaningless jumble of objects.

Laura, meanwhile, pestered me endlessly to look at her work.

"Very well," I said at last, exasperated at the failure of my own attempts. "Show me what you have been working on, then."

She put a sheaf of papers in front of me and I began to leaf through them. She was accomplished at sketching, she caught the quick small details that made an image come alive: a design on a sleeve, the turn of a head, the weight of a heavy burden being carried past.

"You will have to learn to do without *chiaroscuro*," I said, explaining what I had been told.

"How?" she asked, echoing my own thoughts.

"I don't know," I said honestly, for once unable to play the part of all-knowing master to her apprentice. "We will have to find a new way. Perhaps lighter shading, but I have tried it and it does not work: they will still see it as 'inauspicious dirt' – I snorted at the idea – and we will see it as inadequate to convey the depth that we must strive for. Show me the parishioners you have sketched."

She hesitated, but brought me another sheaf of papers. I looked at the first image, a woman caught looking over her shoulder as she entered the church, her gaze direct at the viewer, curious and yet bold. Even in a rough sketch Laura had caught the sunlight touching her hair, the flowers in it, the expression on her face.

"Very nice," I said without looking up. "Who is she, do you know?"

"A Madam Guo," said Laura. She did not elaborate.

I turned to the next image. The same woman, this time at prayer, her hands clasped in front of her, her head bowed.

The next, her gaze uplifted towards the altar.

Then her mouth open, the rest of her face only hinted at, as she sang a hymn.

Another, as she stood, one hand on the pew for balance, her fingertips spread out.

And again, this time passing Laura again as she left the church, her face closer, lips half-parted, eyes fully wide, fixed on the viewer, on Laura.

I looked up from the images at Laura. Her cheeks were flushed, a delicate stain of pink on her collarbones.

"They are very good," I said slowly.

She said nothing.

"We are in such a different place," I said to her gently. "We find ourselves enchanted by what is new to us, do we not? How strange it all is here, how we long to pin down what it is that makes it so. We think our skills must be able to do this for us, for they have never failed us yet, and yet they fail us. We try again and again and yet we cannot grasp what it is that we see. But perhaps it is ourselves who must change, who must grow used to what we see. Perhaps the magic will fade a little, perhaps it will become commonplace and then we will depict what we see with our accustomed ease."

She nodded quickly, her cheeks still pink and did not reply, only took back the sheaf of papers and hurried away. I let her go, thinking that this was a lesson to myself as much as Laura. I must learn to see this place as it really was. It was different, no more nor less.

The portrait of Niuhuru I rolled up and put away in a corner of the studio, telling myself that I had learned many valuable lessons in undertaking the screen commission, not least that I must set to and learn the many different symbols of my new home and that I had to find a way to share my own skills in a way that would be acceptable. I did not look at it again.

Once inside my memory palace there is a hidden winding path lined with bamboo. Within it she stands, surrounded by flowers. Her hands raised as I startle her in her wanderings, her grey eyes wide. It was the last time I painted the way I had been taught. I never saw the portrait again and perhaps after many years it was destroyed, yet as I walk in my mind along the lake's edge of the Yuan Ming Yuan she is always there, her image bright as the first moment I saw her, when a madness took hold of me.

It has not left me yet.

Lilies Tangled by Peonies

THE WISTERIA BLOOMS, INDICATING THE fourth anniversary of my arrival here. My palace is covered in the purple flowers and the Yuan Ming Yuan bursts into late spring: no longer a delicate blossom in a high-up branch or a hidden primrose here and there but great swathes of every-coloured petals rising up from fresh green growth and all around the sounds of ducks and songbirds returning from their winter homes. The lakes and streams come alive with butterflies and kingfishers. Tiny turtles crawl out from their winter sleep and sit on the sun-warmed rocks.

I tell Yan that since I am now seventeen I really should take more care in my appearance, even though I do still want to continue my walks across the Garden's vistas. Yan smiles a secret smile and shakes out robes decorated with skimming dragonflies and rising reeds, then binds up my hair with fresh flowers. So that I can walk easily she orders flat-soled shoes, decorated with tiny gemstones and embroidered crickets.

"Now if you should happen to meet the Prince on your wanderings you will not have to worry that you are not elegant enough," she says, as though the thought has only just occurred to her. I know that she takes it as a personal slight that I have still not been summoned as a companion, despite being a grown woman, not the half-child I was when I first came here. I have heard her muttering about it sometimes, how Prince Yong must be an idiot not to want me as a companion, where are his eyes?

The early summer heat begins to rise and the gardens of the Yuan Ming Yuan become busier. Eunuchs and maids trot back and forth along the tiny paths, each busy with their workloads. It takes a lot of work to keep such an estate in good order and I know that my husband has requested more gardeners: to plant over a thousand peonies, his favourite flowers, across a terraced field on one of the islets; to create new tiny streams linking up rivers already criss-crossing the meadows. He asks for ponds to be filled with carp. Yan and I follow the eunuchs carrying buckets full of slippery burdens and watch as the golden bodies are poured into the water. They soon learn to rise to the surface and beg for crumbs of cake that we throw in. Tiny fawns peep at us from behind trees, wide-eyed and curious.

The other ladies become more active in the summer, we see them boating and gossiping, collecting fruits and flowers, their maids wandering behind them with baskets, glad to have a pleasant task to fulfil rather than anything more onerous. I join them on a day when their gossiping seems to have taken on an ominous tone.

"They said he bought children from the South," says Lady Nara, lowering her voice.

"Who?" I ask.

Her voice lowers even more until she's barely speaking above a whisper. The others don't bother craning their necks, they know full well who she is talking about. "The Crown Prince."

I frown. "What did he buy children for?"

She looks at me.

"And then he had that man killed for questioning him."

The other ladies shake their heads. "Such a violent man," murmurs Lady Mao. "What will the empire be, in his hands?"

Lady Zhang looks about her. "They say that there are factions developing," she says, and all the ladies drift towards her, as though by accident. She nods at their interest. "They say that the Emperor may change his heir and that there are those who support the Eighth Prince Lian, those who support the Fourteenth Prince Xun and…" she pauses as though unsure of how far to go with this information. "Those who support Prince Yong," she ends in a rush.

We are silent for a moment. The notion of our own husband being appointed Crown Prince is a little overwhelming. Lady Nara looks thoughtful. As Primary Consort to Yong, such a move would one day see her crowned Empress.

"And Third Prince Cheng and First Prince Zhi?" asks Lady Mao, who clearly has a better grasp than I do of which princes are most likely to be considered for such an honour.

Lady Zhang shrugs. "Prince Cheng is wrapped up in his studies," she says. "He has no interest in becoming Emperor. Prince Zhi…"

"The Immortals protect us from Prince Zhi becoming the Crown Prince," shudders Lady Nara. "The man is a sorcerer. And seeks only after his own pleasures. *How* many concubines does he have now?"

Walking back with Yan I tell her I don't much care for the ladies' gossip. "It all sounds a little frightening," I confess. "I'm glad we live here and not closer to the Forbidden City."

The heat rises until even our woodland walks are too hot. I sleep badly, plagued either by heat or the hum of mosquitoes who enter my rooms at once if the windows are left open to cool me. I can only hope autumn will come quickly but the heat drags on.

One particularly bad night I don't fall asleep until several hours after going to bed. I'm woken what feels like moments later by Yan's face barely a hand's breadth from my own and yelp. "What?!"

Yan keeps her face where it is, her voice low and scared. "The Prince is ill."

I am still half asleep despite the rude awakening. "What Prince?"

"The Prince. *Your* Prince. Prince Yong."

I struggle to a sitting position. "Ill?"

Yan nods.

"What with?"

Yan shakes her head. "No-one knows. A fever. The physicians came in the night and now they have all gone away, they say it is sorcery and they can do nothing for him."

I look blearily about me. "Is it still night?"

Yan shakes her head. "Dawn."

"What are his servants doing?"

Yan whispers. "They have run away."

"They can't do that," I tell her. I have never heard of such a thing.

"They have," says Yan. Her little face is scared. "The ladies have all locked themselves in their own palaces and the servants of His Highness' personal household have run away even though they will be beaten for it. Everyone is scared."

"But who is looking after him?"

"No-one."

I think back to the times I have had fevers, the restless tossing, heat burning through me and all that kept me from fear was the soothing hand of my mother or the anxious ministrations of Yan. To be all alone and ill... "Help me get dressed," I tell Yan.

"Are we running away?"

"We are going to look after the Prince."

Yan shakes her head violently. "You can't go to his palace! You might be struck down by the sorcerer."

"I can't leave him on his own," I tell her.

"He's barely looked at you!" snaps Yan. "He hasn't even called for you! What do you owe him?"

I am getting dressed as fast as I can, without much help from Yan. I don't have a proper answer to give her, only that I still remember the warmth of his smile on the Sea of Blessings' island. He cannot be left alone with no-one to care for him. "Are you with me?" I ask her.

The Garden is silent. There are no maids or eunuchs to be seen, no officials. No gardeners. The little paths along the lakeside are empty in the grey light of dawn. It makes me nervous. At first I keep looking around for other people but eventually I fix my eyes on Yong's palace so that I will not be entirely unnerved by the quiet around me.

Once in his courtyard I call out, for I still cannot believe that Yan is right. For all she knows, the servants ran for help, not away. "Hello? Hello?" But no-one answers. I stand before the doors to his apartments and hesitate. What if the sorcerer-brother really is here, what if, as I enter, he calls on his powers and causes me to fall ill? Beside me, Yan makes a small whimpering sound of dissent.

In a fit of courage I push open the doors more violently than I meant to, so that they bang against the walls and Yan lets out a tiny scream.

"Stop that," I hiss at her. "You have to be brave. You have to help me."

"We shouldn't be here at all," she hisses back. "All the other ladies have stayed in their palaces where they are safe. So should you."

Standing in the empty receiving hall, I ignore her. I think back to the dim memory of being brought here four years ago. Tentatively, I make my way to the Prince's bedchamber.

The room is quite dark. The windows have not been opened and I hesitate on the threshold, one hand still on the door. In the silence around me I can now hear ragged breathing. I am almost ready to turn back, to run along the lakeside path and lock myself into my own rooms, safe with Yan by my side until someone tells me what to do. A touch on my hand makes me jump but it is only Yan, her small hand gripping mine. Together we step into the darkness.

"Highness?" I whisper. There is no reply, only the breathing, which seems to grow faster as I listen. I try again, raising my voice to something approaching my usual speaking voice. "Highness?" I am horribly afraid that the breathing will stop, even as I stand here, helpless in the dark.

Yan lets go of my hand and I nearly call her back to me but in a fit of boldness, she is already wrestling with a window shutter. At last the weak light of early morning filters through and I can see the room.

I have correctly recalled that this was my husband's bedchamber. It has not changed much. At the far end is his bed and a figure lies across it, coverlets crumpled to the floor in disarray. I make my way towards him as tentatively as though playing a game, hoping he may suddenly sit up and laugh at me, call his unseen servants and tell me he is well and that I am a foolish girl. I would rather be laughed at than find what I have been told is true: my husband is very sick and it seems everyone but Yan and I has run away.

But when I reach the edge of the bed and see my husband it is clear that he is not about to laugh at me. His skin is flushed and his eyes closed, each breath is closer to a pant and when I reach out a tentative finger his skin nearly burns me.

I turn to Yan, truly afraid. "What do I do?" I ask and I am ashamed of the tears trembling in my voice. "I have never looked after someone so ill," I add, although I know that this is not why I am so fearful. My own destiny is hanging in the balance with my husband's, for his fortunes are inevitably mine. If he dies, what will I be? A widow when I have barely even been a wife?

Yan looks as though she would rather be elsewhere, but being asked for advice seems to make her practical side come out. "Take off all the coverlets," she says.

"He will be cold," I say without thinking and then realise that this is a stupid thing to say about a man whose skin is on fire. I take one corner of the topmost coverlet and pull at it with very little effect. Beside me Yan tuts at my tentative effort and gives it a firm yank. The coverlet slips to the floor and my husband's body, entirely naked, is revealed to us both. I gasp and try to look elsewhere.

Yan glares at me. "He's your husband," she says. "It's not your fault if you've never seen him naked, you ought to have done by now. He needs something cooler over him." She busies herself removing all the heavy covers and then stalks away, muttering. I can hear her rifling through chests, presumably in search of something lighter to cover him with.

I look down on Yong. I have never seen him like this. Always, he has been in command of the situation during our brief meetings. It has been his place to speak, to command, to decide. It has been my place to listen and to obey, to reply when spoken to and to hope throughout that I do not displease him. I feel a sudden rush of tenderness for him, of pity. I sit on the edge of his bed and take out a little fan from my robe. I fan his face. He does not respond, but I think perhaps the deep crease in his forehead lessens a little, as though he senses that someone is at least trying to care for him, that he is not alone.

Yan takes charge. She orders me to grip my husband's ankles so that she can place fresh sheets under him and covers him with a light silk cover, which redresses his dignity. She has me bathe his face with a wet cloth while she cleans the room.

"How could the servants have left him?" I ask her. "When they know they will be whipped and dismissed for this?"

Yan struggles to open more windows, letting out the sour air of illness. The room is filled with a fresh morning breeze carrying the scent of blossom on it. She utters various choice words on what she thinks of Prince Yong's servants and what she thinks will happen to them. "Has he even been fed or given a drink?" she demands.

I look at him. He was a thin man anyway, but even under the cover I can see his ribs. Now that I can see better, his lips are cracked and his skin seems dried out, stretched across his cheekbones. "I don't think so," I say. "He must be thirsty."

Yan finds and brings fresh water. I try to hold a little bowl to his lips but he does not swallow properly and water dribbles down his chin. I look to Yan and she dips a clean cloth in the water and shows me how to drip water into his mouth drop by drop.

"I will find a kitchen maid and make her bring food," she says, stamping away.

"Find Kun," I say. "He will not run away, Yan. We need more help." I am not sure what I mean by help. I think I am just afraid to be here, alone and unsure of what to do. I need people around me whom I trust. Kun's cheerful face would be a blessing right now.

Yan hesitates, then she nods her head and hurries away.

The water drip drips into Yong's mouth and does not come back out again. Pleased, I try talking to him. Perhaps this is all it will take? A spring breeze scented with blossom, some water and he will be well again?

"Do – do you feel better, Highness?"

He does not reply.

"The flowers are out," I say, not knowing what else to speak of. I think for a moment how strange it is to be married to this man and to know nothing about him, nor even to have ever seen his naked body. All I know is that he loves the Garden. I do not know if he can hear me. But if he can, surely he would be pleased to hear of the Garden. "I went down to the river and the turtles have woken from their winter sleep. They lie on the logs and rocks and bask in the sun. If you were there, the cool water would take away the heat you feel." I can hear the pleading in my voice. "If you recover a little, Highness, I will take you there to watch the dragonflies."

"How romantic."

I leap to my feet, upsetting the bowl of drinking water balanced on the bedclothes, which falls to the floor and breaks into shards. In the doorway stands a man. Broader in the chest and waist than Yong, he is dressed magnificently in robes only a tone darker than imperial yellow. I stand, unsure of what to do. By his clothing, he must be one of the imperial princes. But which one?

"You should kowtow," he informs me. "Don't you know what the Crown Prince looks like?"

Slowly, I kneel. A shard of broken bowl sticks into my knee and cuts me through my silken robe, but I bow forward without flinching into a kowtow. I only raise my head a little for each of the three obeisances and when I raise my head fully I find the man has crossed the room and is standing in front of me. My face is now too close to his groin. I lean back on my heels and turn my face a little away as I rise to my feet. I have always been told I am too tall for a girl but at this moment I wish I were taller still, for the Crown Prince towers over me.

"Ah, the young concubine," he says, looking me over. "I was annoyed they did not send you to me. I heard you were barely *formed* enough to be wed." The tip of his tongue comes out of his mouth and wets his lips. "And I also heard that my brother wasted the chance to bed you at once. Fool."

I back away, half-sitting on the edge of the bed and taking up Yong's limp hand in mine, as though seeking his protection. The Crown Prince only laughs.

"You can't expect him to come to your aid, girl. He's as good as dead. Anyone can see it. He was a little too dutiful, you know. A little *too* helpful to our father. All that efficiently done paperwork. All those trips to ensure works were being done to the correct quality: roads, dams, canals. A little too much praise was spoken of him. It made the rest of us look bad. And we can't have that, can we?"

"He will be well again soon," I say, my voice cracking mid-sentence.

The Crown Prince looks at me and smiles. It is a slow smile, a pitying smile. "Afraid of him dying?" he asks. "Afraid of being a dowager concubine, an untouched widow for the rest of your days?"

I don't answer but my eyes blink without my will. He knows only too well the true source of the fear I feel at Yong being ill. I barely know my husband. He is almost a stranger. What should it matter to me if a stranger dies? And yet. And yet if he dies the Yuan Ming Yuan will be given to some other prince, whilst we, the little-used (or in my case not used at all) concubines will be packed off to some discreet but lowly household to live out our days. We will not have a palace each. We will not be free to wander through the Garden. We will all live together, perhaps on a quiet side street in Beijing, with just enough servants to satisfy imperial protocol. Our names will be forgotten on some dusty old bit of paper that once named us as consorts to an imperial prince, now long dead. I swallow.

"I would not wish you to go to your grave untouched," says the Crown Prince.

I hold Yong's hand tighter and press his fingers. *Wake up*, I think. *Wake up.*

"Come here," says the Crown Prince.

I don't move.

"Do as you're told," he says.

My grip on Yong's hand is so tight that he should be in pain, should open his eyes and speak, should send his brother away, heir or no heir. Slowly I release my grip and his hand falls back on the covers, as though lifeless. I stand. I wonder whether I can run, whether if I move fast, without warning, I can make my way out of this room. In my mind I see the receiving hall, the doorway, the courtyard garden, the tiny lakeside path, my own palace and the wisteria flowers that cover it. I stand before the Crown Prince, keeping my eyes on the floor.

His hands are large and suddenly all over me. One hand grips my behind, one hand roughly fondles my breast through my robe. "Undress," he says and his voice is hoarse.

"My lady," says Yan's voice, loud and clear, no hint of a tremble. "I have found the servants. His Highness' head eunuch will also be here in a moment."

His hands leave my body as he turns to see Yan and Kun at the far end of the room. Without a word he leaves, pushing past them as though they do not exist. Behind him, Kun quickly shuts the door and drops a bar across it, so that no-one else can enter. Yan crosses to me and looks at my face before kneeling to collect the broken shards. I sit back down on the bed and try to still my trembling hands.

"Have you really found the servants?" I ask.

Yan shakes her head.

A hot tear makes its way down my face. "What will we do?" I ask Kun, as though he were able to do something.

Kun's voice is soft. "I will remain with you night and day," he says. "We found the kitchen staff. They will bring food to the gates. Yan and I will collect it. They will not come to the palace. They are afraid of sorcery."

"He is ill, not ill-wished!" I say, although I know no such thing.

Kun is serious. "The servants are afraid either way," he says. "If it is illness then they have never seen such a strong fever. He has been ill for days, with no sign of recovery. He is likely to die if it continues. If it is ill-wishing then they are still scared, for who knows on whom a sorcerer may cast his eye next."

"Who is this sorcerer they are talking about?" I ask.

"Prince Zhi," says Kun, and as he says it I remember the gossip of the other women.

"Where are the Prince's other ladies?" I ask. "Shouldn't they be here too?"

Yan snorts. "They are afraid," she says. "There's loyalty for you."

The sun sets and food is brought to the door. I make Yan and Kun eat with me. I do not care if it is improper, I am too afraid of being left alone again. I try to feed Yong with broth, but I am not sure that he takes in much. When we have left the dishes back outside the gates I have Kun bar the door and Yan close the window shutters. We spread silk coverlets on the floor and Yan sleeps by me, with Kun by the door.

All night I wake, then sleep and wake again. Yan and Kun sleep, but Yong mutters and turns. I rise and go to him, hoping he may be waking, but his eyes are shut. I hold his hand again and think perhaps he returns my clasp. At last, my eyes aching with tiredness, I lie down on the bed by his side and sleep.

Morning comes. The three of us stand together, looking down on Yong.

"He isn't getting better," I say to Yan. My eyes ache from tiredness, I'm so weary I could sleep on my feet and my shoulders are slumped in defeat. He will surely die. What chance do we have of curing him if his doctors have deserted him?

Kun ignores our pale faces. He goes to the kitchens and returns with food and fresh water, he takes a broom to sweep the courtyard garden and then the rooms of the palace, one after another, methodical, calm, as though nothing at all is wrong. His practicality is the only thing stopping me from crying.

I sit, still dripping water into Yong's mouth, while Yan searches for stores of medicine, though none of us would know what to do with them.

"Enough," I say suddenly. "I am going to the other ladies' palaces. We cannot do this alone. They have as much to lose as I do."

But the palaces are all closed up, doors and shutters barred. I cannot tell if there is anyone is inside each one, I hammer on the doors with my fists and call out the names of each lady but no-one replies. I half-run from one islet to the next across the tiny bridges, only one thought in my mind. I am afraid the Crown Prince will return and find that we fooled him, that we are alone. He will not care for a maid and a eunuch, he will dismiss them and do whatever he wishes with me. I shudder at the thought.

I try Lady Qi's palace last, although it is one of the closest. I have never spoken to her directly but I no longer care for niceties. My fists already feel bruised from the other doors but I pound harder than ever and when the door suddenly opens I am so surprised I nearly fall onto Lady Qi.

She stands framed in the doorway, dressed in dark plum, her hair pinned up with green jade pins and decorated with dangling golden threads as though it were an ordinary day. I am well aware my own hair is a mess and that my clothes are crumpled. I have never seen her this close before, she always stood apart at events. Not tall, not short, of average build and beauty, there is nothing much to set her apart except her eyes, which are large but hooded, giving her a secretive look, as though she knows something precious and guards it with her life. I feel my heart sink, remembering the smile she gave when she saw me dismissed from Yong's bedchamber too quickly, knowing I had been found wanting in some way. But I have no choice.

"The Prince – please help me," I blurt. "No-one will help me." I can hear my voice shaking, can feel the tears building up.

She doesn't answer, only steps out of her palace and follows me. I am so out of breath that I do not even try to speak with her, only walk as quickly as possible.

When we arrive Yan and Kun look shocked to see Lady Qi. They do not know I had no choice. She walks past them as though they do not exist. Crossing the room, she looks down at Yong. She takes his pulse as though she were a doctor, feeling at different points, before inserting a golden nail shield between his lips and pulling his mouth open to inspect his tongue.

"Poison," she says.

I hear Yan make a hissing sound behind me, know that she will be making signs to warn off evil.

"How do you know?" I ask.

"His tongue is discoloured," she says, as though everyone knows the signs of poisoning. "And the twelve pulses are very weak. The poison may have damaged his vital forces beyond repair. Has he been like this all the time you have been here?"

I nod.

"Why are *you* here?" she asks, her dark eyes fixed on me.

"I felt sorry for him," I say.

Her eyes bore into me.

"And I… do not want him to die," I say. "If he dies, I…" I stop. It sounds selfish.

"All of us," she says, finishing my thought. "Some dreary back palace, squabbling amongst ourselves, our destinies warped and broken and no chance of changing them."

I drop my eyes. She knows full well what we have to lose.

"We will do our best," she says, her tone more practical than I expected. "My own servants will help us."

"Aren't they afraid?" I ask.

"They are more afraid of me," she says. I believe her.

The days that follow blur into one another. Lady Qi sends two serving girls whom Yan takes to commanding.

"Don't you know how to make a bed?" she chastises them. "Hurry up and serve tea for their ladyships."

In this way the palace is kept clean and everyone is fed. Between them they wash Yong's body and change his sheets, make up a bed for me on the floor in his bedchamber while Kun, quiet as ever, tends to the gardens and the indoor flowers. He lies by the door at night and I am grateful for his presence. There is no sign of the Crown Prince and after her first visit Lady Qi does not spend much time in the palace.

"I am going to Beijing," she tells me after a few days.

"Why?"

"I must speak with someone," she says.

"Who?"

"No-one for you to worry about," she replies.

"I need to know what you are doing," I say, more boldly that I thought I was capable of. I am so tired from broken nights that my mouth speaks the words I think out loud rather than holding back.

"The court is gathering around the princes," she says. "There are factions growing in favour for one or another, this is why someone will have struck out at Yong, he was growing to be a favourite to replace the Crown Prince. They have written him off as dead already. It is my job to ensure he is remembered, that his supporters do not give way to fear of Prince Zhi's poisons nor the Crown Prince's position. They must stand by him or the Crown Prince will be left as heir."

"Don't leave me here alone," I say. I have not told her of the Crown Prince and his everywhere-grasping hands.

"There is no use in him being kept alive if he is not remembered," she says and leaves without a backward glance.

I am alone with Yong and after days of caring for him with no response, I want to cry. I look down on him. He has not once opened his eyes, not once spoken. Sometimes he groans, or pants, as though the pain inside him or the heat burning up his skin is too much to bear, but mostly he lies still and quiet, a corpse in all but name. I put a hand on his shoulder and shake him a little, raise my voice. "Wake up, Highness."

He does not move, of course, he does not respond and suddenly I am angry, beating first my hands and then my fists against his bare skin, screaming at him. "Wake up! Wake up! How dare you lie here like this? How dare you leave me alone without protection? How dare you – how dare you – " and I am sobbing as I fall to my knees by his bedside, burying my face in the coverlet.

"Ladyship?"

I stand quickly, wiping my eyes with the back of my hand, trying to pat my hair into place although I cannot see what it looks like. I know that my eyes are red, that my skin is blotched.

"Enter," I say, turning. "Oh."

It is the Jesuit painter. He steps forwards and his eyes glance behind me to Yong. "It is true, then? The Prince is ill?"

"Yes," I say, wishing that I did not look so dishevelled.

"Will he recover?"

"Yes," I say. "Yes, he will."

His dark eyes meet mine and I know he sees the fear in my red-rimmed eyes that are now brimming with tears again.

"How can I be of service to you?" he asks. "To the Prince," he amends too quickly.

I am about to shake my head. What can he do that is useful to me? But if I shake my head he will go away and I know that I want him nearby, that I need people I can trust about me and that without even knowing this man, I trust him, for his level gaze and because he asked what he could do for me before he remembered that he serves the Emperor and Yong, not me. "You may paint a picture for him," I say, naming the only thing I know for sure he can do. "The Prince loves paintings and he loves the Garden. You must paint some flowers to please him when he wakes."

He bows his head. "I will do so and return to you as soon as possible," he says, turning to go.

"No!" I say, too loudly. He turns back to me. "You misunderstand me," I say. "You must paint here."

"Here?"

"In this room," I say. "I wish you to work in this room." I struggle to meet his gaze but I force myself to do so, to tell him what I cannot say. *I am afraid. Stay with me. Keep me safe.*

He looks at me for a long moment, then nods. "Kun will fetch my materials," he says. "And my subject matter."

Kun brings flowers and a vase and Giuseppe spends time arranging them. I sit by Yong's side and watch as first one stem and then another is placed and then re-placed. For the first time in many days I feel safe. There is something calming about him, he is so focused on his work that it leaves no space for other worries.

"Are you happy with the composition?" he asks me.

I nod. I do not care what he paints. I only care that if he is here I am not left alone. Watching him work soothes me, I can feel my shoulders lose their tightness and my face lose its worried frown. I feel my eyelids droop and I do not try to fight my tiredness. I can sleep while he works and I will be safe. I have such need of sleep.

Lady Qi returns from Beijing and frowns when she sees Giuseppe, ignoring his bow to her. "The Crown Prince is all but unseated," she tells me. "He went too far. First his proclivities, the scandals. Now his name has been linked to Yong's illness. His father is more than displeased, he is angry. It requires only a reminder that there are better princes to choose from for him to change his heir. But Yong needs to awaken or it will all have been for nothing. Has he stirred?"

I shake my head.

"I found a doctor who will treat him," she says.

"I thought the doctors said it was sorcery," I say.

"Silver changes minds," she says.

The doctor she has brought back with her is a wizened little man who mutters and shakes his head and spends an age looking over Yong, before beginning to grind up who-knows-what to give to him.

"He could be a sorcerer himself, for all I know," I say to Giuseppe.

He pauses in his work to watch the physician. "Lady Qi has much to lose if he is," he points out. "If your husband is made heir then one of her sons may be an Emperor one day. She would be the Empress Dowager, a great and powerful lady."

"I cannot think why she would want any such thing," I sigh.

He looks me over. "You do not wish to be…" he stumbles over the word concubine, "…married to an Emperor?"

"I want to stay here where it is peaceful," I tell him. "Or it was."

He smiles. "You like the Garden more than the Forbidden City?"

"I've barely seen the Forbidden City," I tell him. "I know it is grander. But the Garden is so lovely. And I do not like all this fighting over who is to be heir. Look at what it has done to – to the Prince." I am not sure why I do not just call him my husband.

He looks back at his painting, where bold orange-hued lilies stretch out their dark stamens above delicate white-pink peonies. "I hope the choice of heir falls on someone who can bear such a burden," he says quietly.

Night falls. Lady Qi and her doctor leave us. I see Giuseppe packing up his things and badly want to ask him to stay within the palace so that he will be close by, but that is an unthinkable request, so instead I try to engage him in conversation to keep him with me as long as possible.

"Have you spent much time in the Garden?" I ask. "Or is most of your work in the Forbidden City?"

"A little of both," he says.

"Which do you prefer?"

"The Garden," he says smiling. "It is so beautiful. Although I am frequently lost here. It is so large and each little part invites you to explore further rather than sticking to your own path."

I can't help but laugh, acknowledging the number of times Yan and I got lost when I first came here. "You need Kun with you," I tell him. "Kun knows every tiny part of the Garden. You should ask him to show you the fireflies one evening, they are magical."

"They sound enchanting," he says.

I have to let him go, with Kun accompanying him to carry his tools. After Yan and I have eaten I stand looking down on Yong. I sigh at the thought of another night of heat and worry.

"You should go and see the fireflies yourself," Yan says.

"I have to stay here," I say.

Yan shakes her head. "You need to get out," she says. "You've been indoors for days, you'll fall ill yourself. Go and watch the fireflies, dip your toes in the water. Breathe some cool air. He'll still be here when you get back," she adds gloomily.

I chew my lip. But Yan is right. I crave cool air and to be free of this sickroom. It's making me feel ill myself. "I will be back soon," I promise her and she waves me away.

The night air helps me breathe more deeply. I can feel my shoulders relax a little after days of anxious watching over Yong. I make my way towards one of the little streams that leads to the wider lake. Remembering that the riverbank is slippery, I take off my shoes and creep softly along its edge, disturbing the frogs who stop croaking for a few moments and then carry on with their usual night chorus, accompanied by crickets. I make my way along the twisting bank, knowing that there is a large rock further ahead on which I can sit and keep watch. The fireflies should emerge soon.

"Is that you, Kun?"

I gasp at the unexpected voice emerging from the darkness ahead and nearly lose my footing.

"Kun?"

"I am not Kun," I say. I recognised the voice at once. It is Giuseppe. No-one else speaks Mandarin with his odd accent, the tones in the wrong places, the vowels at the end of words where there are none.

He is silent. I am not even sure where he is, except that Kun has probably led him to the same rock that I was going to sit on.

"I have disturbed your evening, I will go," he says and I can hear that he has stood up.

"No, no," I say quickly. "If you are here to see the fireflies you should stay. They are beautiful. I will go."

"Please," he says. "Stay."

I think of what Yan would have to say about such a suggestion. "Where is Kun?" I ask, still hovering at the edge of the river, hoping that he might reappear. I try to peer about me but the darkness is made up of nothing but shadowy shapes which could be anything.

"Ladyship?"

I breathe out in relief at Kun's voice. All is well. I have a eunuch by my side. Decorum is preserved. "We are watching for fireflies," I inform him, as though this is a well-known pastime shared by foreign priests and concubines. "You will wait with me."

Faintly, I see his dark shape bow by my side. "Ladyship." His voice is calm, no surprise, no questioning. A good servant does not question.

I sit down on the grass. The ground is still warm from the day's sun. Kun squats down nearby. I hear a faint rustle, indicating that Giuseppe has also seated himself. We wait in silence.

They come so slowly that at first you cannot be sure you have seen them at all. A tiny spark. I twist my head and already it is gone. But there was another just there, but now it too is gone. And suddenly we are surrounded by tiny lights, as though the stars have come down to earth, twinkling all around us.

"Do you have fireflies where you come from?" I ask the darkness.

"I used to try and catch them when I was a little boy in my grandmother's garden," says his voice. "With my brother."

I hear something in his voice. "How long did it take you to travel here?" I ask.

"More than a year," he says.

I think of the distance, of how everyone he knows and holds dear is so far away that he cannot know how they are, what they are doing, even if they are alive. "When will you return to your home and family?" I ask.

There is a slight pause. Then, "I cannot return," he says. "The Emperor asked for a painter who would stay here. I accepted the post on this condition, that I will never return home." He is silent for a moment and then adds, "I will never see my family again." He almost sounds surprised, as though it has taken him this long to realise what he has agreed to.

"Are you homesick?" I ask.

He is silent and then, "Yes," he replies, and his voice is too steady, so calm that I know even in the darkness that my question caused pain, which he has covered up before replying. I am sorry for it. I think that I should stay silent, that I should think more carefully before I ask such stupid questions.

"Does your family live nearby?" he asks me, as though hoping to lighten the mood.

I hesitate. He does not know how my life is ruled. "I am a c-concubine," I say, stumbling over the word. "We do not see our families again once we marry into the Imperial Family."

He is surprised. "Ever?"

"Ever."

And then we are silent while the Garden twinkles and its night sounds surround us. The moon has risen very high by the time I tug at Kun's sleeve and tell him to escort me home. Giuseppe's voice is soft as he says goodbye.

"Thank you, Niuhuru," he says. "It was beautiful."

In the morning Yan looks me over. "You came back late but you look better than yesterday," she says.

"I needed to be outside in the Garden," I say.

"Did you see the fireflies?"

"Yes," I say. Now is the moment when I should tell her that I watched them with Giuseppe but I can't quite think how to frame the words.

Yan is anyway uninterested in me. "The Prince's skin seems cooler," she says.

I hurry to his side. "Is he awake?"

Yan shakes her head.

I look down on Yong. "Highness?" I say gently. But he does not stir.

"Perhaps the poison is leaving him," I suggest.

"Perhaps it was not poison, only an illness," says Yan, although she sounds doubtful. "Some of the servants have come creeping back," she adds disdainfully.

I see a few of them tentatively taking up their tasks again, although they all look afraid. The same thing must be going through all their minds: what is worse – to be infected or ill-wished, or beaten for desertion?

When Giuseppe arrives I am unsure whether I should refer to our evening together, but he surprises me by laying a small piece of paper on my table.

"What is this?" I ask, expecting perhaps a rough sketch for his floral composition.

"Something I painted last night when I could not sleep," he says.

I look down. A strangely-formed building made of stone clad with tumbling roses. A garden, neatly tended. Between the rows of vegetables, two little boys, their arms outstretched while tiny pinpoints in the air elude their grasp. I stare. The painting is not like any I have ever seen, it seems alive, as though it were a model rather than a flat painting.

"You and your brother catching fireflies in your grandmother's garden," I murmur and he smiles when he meets my gaze, although his eyes glisten for a moment.

"I think I have found a way to paint which may be accepted here," he says, and I can hear excitement in his voice. "Instead of dark shading I am using tonal shading: you see, here, the darker green against the lighter green which gives the depth. It is a question of the light source being more diffused and coming more from the front than the side, so that the shading is not as dark. Do you think it will be accepted?"

"It looks as though it is real," I say. "It is beautiful." I am about to ask him more, to ask him to draw me another such building, another moment from his unknown life before here, when Yan exclaims behind me and I turn to see Yong's eyes opening, his gaze fixed on me.

"Niuhuru," he croaks and I run to his side.

Atlas of Blossoms in an Everlasting Spring

I CONFESS IT: THERE WAS SOME part of me that hoped the Prince might die. There: I am not a good man, not a holy man who would never have allowed his mind to wander where it should not. There was some part of my mind filled with fireflies, where a woman's voice spoke to me of home in the darkness and she was mine, not another's.

I confessed it, of course. Kneeling in the stifling confessional beneath the high arches of St Joseph's criss-crossed ceiling I whispered my baser thoughts and received absolution, in return for who knows how many Hail Marys and Our Fathers, as well as a well-meaning reminder that I must set my thoughts to higher things, that I would find the years of service ahead less onerous were I truly dedicated to the missionary cause that had brought me here rather than continuing to think of myself as a free man.

I confess it: I even tried on a hair shirt beneath my robes, feeling foolish as I did so, as though I were self-aggrandising my thoughts, for what man has not had such thoughts after all? They were only thoughts with no possible conclusion, no possibility of a reality. What, the Prince would die and his concubine would run away with me to Milan? Of course not. I wore the shirt for a few days before I chastised myself for my own pride in imagining myself a holy man beset with doubt. Instead I lit candles and knelt to give thanks for the recovery of Prince Yong and, safely ensconced within the painting studio, hurried to complete my floral commission using the tonal shading I had at last found as a means of bridging the two styles of East and West together. First the eunuchs in the studio and then Prince Yong declared themselves delighted with the work. Yong set me to work on a portfolio of images, which he wished to name *Atlas of Blossoms in an Everlasting Spring*.

"Roam wherever you wish in the Garden," he told me, smiling, his skin still pale. He gestured across the view of the lake from his study window. "You must capture its beauty for me. I wish it to be a gift for one of my concubines, Lady Niuhuru."

Her name must have changed my expression for he nodded. "You know her, of course. She commissioned your painting for me."

I bowed, unsure of how to reply but the Prince was already speaking again.

"She is very young, but she has an eye for beauty in nature," he said. "She spoke to me of the Garden and I heard her, only for a moment. It is all I recall from my illness. She spoke of the river, the lakes. Of turtles and kingfishers. The Atlas will be a gift for her, in recognition of her loyalty to me."

I bowed again. "As you command, Your Highness. I shall ensure the Garden's beauty is captured."

Laura had heard gossip. "They say many of Prince Yong's ladies are in disgrace for hiding away."

"The servants were beaten and some turned out for their cowardice in the face of his illness," I said. "Although I cannot entirely fault them."

"You have met Lady Niuhuru?" asked Laura.

"Yes," I said. I was pleased that my voice remained steady.

"It seems the Prince is quite taken with her. He says she was the only lady truly loyal to him."

"I am to paint her a portfolio of images of the Garden as a gift," I said.

"And I thought he was such a stern and dutiful man," said Laura laughing. "Perhaps he has romantic side to him after all."

"Perhaps," I said, and turned away.

I was true to my word, spending my days roaming about every part of the Garden. The Atlas grew under my brushes, sixteen images to capture the unending landscape around us. Peonies in every shade opened their fat buds while poppies unfurled their fragile petals and then disappeared within days. Fresh green bamboo stalks soared heavenwards while morning glories wrapped their delicate stems about them and turned their faces to the morning sun. I recalled the pure white magnolias of early spring and captured the ripening cherries of summer. Every part of the Atlas celebrated the beauty of the Garden.

Frequently I came across Kun while I worked and he would greet me. Sometimes from afar, adrift in a small boat as he cleared the lakes of weeds, one hand raised in wordless salute. Sometimes close to, when I would settle down to paint a particular detail and he worked close by. I had never liked to have people watching me while I worked, but strangely I found Kun's presence soothing, for he did not speak overmuch, only continued his work, his rough hands tender with the flowers and shoots in his care. We often spent much of the day working side by side in silence. He would nod when he saw the fruits of my labour, not with admiration but in simple recognition, which somehow pleased me more, for to Kun each plant was an individual, not merely *a* peony but *this* peony, no other like it in the Garden.

"I am to be married," he told me one day.

I looked up, startled as much by his voice as by his news. "Married?"

He nodded and I saw from the happiness in his face that this was something much-longed for.

"I – " I paused. I did not want to hurt his feelings but then again I felt that there was honesty between us and so I spoke again, but carefully, choosing my words one by one. "I did not know eunuchs were permitted to marry," I said.

He nodded, acknowledging the question I had not asked. "Not all eunuchs marry," he said. "But it is permitted, if their masters allow it. And Lady Niuhuru is very good to Yan."

Yan, of course. I smiled. "Did Yan ask for permission then?"

His smile was so wide that it made my eyes fill up a little. "She asked her mistress before I asked her myself," he said.

I had to laugh out loud at the thought of fierce little Yan, always scowling, going to Niuhuru and then all but telling Kun he was to marry her, like it or not. Kun joined me in laughter, acknowledging that my thoughts were true.

"But will Yan have to leave Niuhuru?" I asked. "I was told the maids had to work a certain number of years before they were set free to be married."

"Lady Niuhuru permitted her to marry me only if she continues to serve," said Kun. "All will be as before."

For a few days afterward I avoided Kun. When I sought him out it was with a gift.

"For your marriage," I said, holding out a scroll.

I had painted tumbling climbing pale pink flowers, wrapped about a tree. He held the gift and did not speak, only nodded, recognising with his gentle smile the roses he had planted for Yan after the first time he had met her, on the island of cherry trees.

"Show me what you have been working on," I said to Laura and she brought me new sketches and some initial paintings using the refined version of the *chiaroscuro* technique I had developed, using the new direction of light and tones of colours rather than the darker shading we were both trained in.

"These are very good," I told her. If anything she had understood the new refinement required quicker than I, she had applied herself diligently to practising it and now she executed it perfectly, bringing her Chinese subjects to life with a delicacy that I admired. Secretly I was also relieved that I could not see any more sketches of Madam Guo and supposed that Laura had taken my words to heart and was striving to be less enchanted by the new world in which we found ourselves. I praised her for her work and she was pleased. I saw her set to such commissions as we now began to receive with greater confidence and enthusiasm and I congratulated myself on having managed her still-young emotions well. She had proven herself first as a worthy apprentice and then assistant and I was glad to have her working by my side.

But my own feelings neither left me nor could be hidden within my work, for over and over again amongst the flowers pairs of songbirds appeared, their tiny wings and flashes of colour fluttering within the branches of my trees and the petals of my flowers. They gazed at one another, sat so close together their feathers touched, sang for each other's pleasure. I was helpless in the face of their devotion.

I sought out Father Friedel, hoping that his customary fretting over my time here would remind me of my chosen path. I submitted to his lengthy reminders of my obligations to the Mission and his reminders of my as yet untaken vows.

"You will find spiritual guidance in the chapel, my son," he said kindly. "I have seen you little at prayers, of late."

At his urging I retreated from the imperial studios to the church, hoping to commit myself to a greater cause. As the final words of Mass were spoken and the final 'amens' resounded from the congregation, I raised my eyes and caught, for only a brief moment, Laura ahead of me as she rose and left. Before she reached the outer door, however, she turned and her eyes sought out Madam Guo, who in turn gazed after Laura with an expression of such love that I caught my breath at what was so obviously laid before me.

Afterwards I stood alone in the church, wondering what to do. Should I speak with Laura again or even take my concerns to one of the senior Brothers and ask for his advice in guiding Laura's soul away from this temptation? Yet the longer I stood there, trying to feel concern, the more I realised that all I felt was jealousy. Not for Laura's sake, for I had never regarded her as anything but my pupil, but for the gaze between her and Guo. It came to me suddenly that what I most desired but could not have was that same gaze between Niuhuru and me, the same certainty that what I desired was desired also by her.

Within my palace of memories, in a sheltered corner of the Garden, there is a peach tree where pink blossom bursts into flower while two swallows regard one another, their bodies entwined. Only in the moment of knowing I could not have Niuhuru did I come to know I loved her.

Flying Bats Filling the Sky

As Yong recovers, the Garden returns to life. The beaten servants hurry back to their neglected tasks. Gardeners pull up weeds, sweep the pathways, skim the lakes for algae. Maids see to the laundry that has built up, clean rooms with extra diligence. The kitchen staff send out elegantly presented dishes, anxious to make up for their failings. The disgraced ladies slowly re-emerge from their homes and sit quietly together by the lakeside, chastised but relieved. Lady Qi nods to me when she sees me now; I am an ally in her quest and she takes to updating me on the political machinations of the court, of which I understand little and wish to know less.

"The Crown Prince has been demoted," she tells me. "A new heir has not yet been announced. It's possible the Emperor will delay choosing a new heir for some time. He was not impressed with all the rivalry between his sons, the factions that developed. But he could well choose Yong. He is everything the Crown Prince was not. He is devoted, filial, accomplished in his work and mindful of the people of the empire."

I think of the Crown Prince, of his hands on me. I shudder.

Qi mistakes my reaction. "You would be consort to an Emperor," she reminds me. "A greater destiny by far than our current path. We are still young and could be promoted many times. Our children would be princes of the first rank."

Or made Emperor, I think, knowing this is her ultimate goal for her own sons. "I am not as ambitious as you, Qi," I tell her. "But I am glad the Prince is well again."

She smiles at me and pats me, as though I am an amiable daughter, one content to allow her mother to lead the way. I know that my lack of ambition must endear me to her, since no woman seeking power is likely to want a rival. "One step at a time," she says. "The first step is taken. Others will follow."

I am called to Yong's palace only a few days after his recovery and formally escorted to his bedchamber as though I do not know where it is. He is lying in bed but he sits up when he sees me. His face is deathly pale.

I kowtow. "I wish you all health and happiness," I say. I sit back on my knees and look up at him. "Are you well, Highness?"

His voice is hoarse. "I am not dead," he says. "Because of you."

I shake my head. "Lady Qi," I begin.

"You were the first to come to my aid?" he asks.

"Yes," I say.

"And I have been told you stayed with me until I awoke, night and day?"

"Yes," I say.

"Then I am in your debt," he says.

"No," I say. "I am grateful you were spared."

Yong gestures and his head eunuch comes forwards.

"Lady Niuhuru is granted an additional maid and her own personal gardener in recognition of her service to the Prince," he announces formally.

I kowtow, but the eunuch continues to read out additional gifts. My household allowance is increased by many bolts of silk, taels of silver and I am to receive gifts of jade and other precious gems. I am not sure when to stop kowtowing. When the announcement is over Yong smiles at me, but he looks exhausted by even this brief meeting and I am quickly led away. I do not see him for another month.

Yan is shining. "You are summoned."

"Summoned where?"

She is too busy to answer me. Kun is now attached to my palace as my own personal gardener and I have a second maid, as promised. Yan is making the poor girl traipse back and forth with armfuls of clothing. Every robe I have is on display, silk in every colour draped all over the room. Yan is examining each with the air of a general inspecting troops.

"Yan? Summoned where?"

"To the Prince."

"What does he want?"

Yan looks at me in disbelief. "You," she says. "He wants you. At last."

Something in my stomach turns over. I feel heat rise up my neck and into my cheeks. I swallow. "Tonight?"

"Tonight."

I sit down. Yan continues her inspections. I try to think. All those foolish daydreams I made up, where I was summoned by the Prince and he... he... he what? What? I never got beyond the summons; beyond knowing I was desired at last. All my imaginings ended somewhere out on the lakeside path, as an image of me – a more beautiful, infinitely glamorous and elegant version of me, of course, in my mind – tottered along the tiny pathways in my highest shoes, my most elegant robes, on my way to... to what? To being important, to being beautiful and a favourite, whatever that might mean. That was enough for me when I was thirteen, fourteen. I nod wordlessly at Yan's final choice: palest rose silk, jade pins to hold tiny rosebuds mixed with giant peonies in my hair. Shoes so high I have forgotten how to walk in them, sewn all over with gems. I stand in the doorway of my home and have to wait for Yan's small hand in mine to step forwards. She keeps me steady along the pebbled lake pathway, each tiny stone making up mosaic images of birds, flowers, even fish. We make our way over one bridge and then another, onwards towards the wide curved rooftops of Yong's palace, set amongst trees. At the gateway, Yan pulls her hand away and I must take the last tremulous steps alone. When I reach the doorway, where a eunuch stands waiting to receive me, I look back, but she is already gone.

His bedchamber should be familiar enough to me by now. I have slept by Yong's side for many nights, have given orders in this room. But now it feels different. It is no longer a sick room. Fresh flowers adorn niches in the walls, lanterns glow softly. The large wooden alcove of the bed has been adorned with fresh hangings in a deep red silk, something like a bridal chamber. I stand alone and try to keep my head erect, my hands from trembling. I wonder when the servants will arrive to undress me and unpin my hair. I wonder if the sleeping robe they will give me will be as sheer as the one I remember from the first time I was summoned, aged only thirteen.

"Niuhuru."

I turn to face Yong. He looks a great deal better than the last time I saw him. In my highest shoes I am now the same height as he is, our eyes level with one another. His eyes are bright, his skin has resumed its normal colour, his voice is clear.

"Your Highness is so well recovered," I say.

"Thanks to you," he replies.

I bob my head in some sort of acknowledgement. He steps to a small table and picks up the two small bowls of warmed wine and passes me one, as he did before. This time I sip it, thinking that its warmth will give me courage. When I pass it back to him I hope he does not notice my hand tremble.

He smiles and indicates the bed. "Come."

I follow him and perch on the edge of it, unsure of what to do about my shoes. Noticing my glance downwards he reaches out and indicates I should lift my feet onto the silken coverlet. I do so and he takes each bejewelled shoe and removes them, dropping them uncaring to the floor, their carved wooden soles clattering as they hit the stone.

"You don't look comfortable," he observes. He himself is cross-legged on the bed, at ease, while I am sat so close to the edge I am in danger of falling to the floor myself. "Sit beside me. I have a gift for you."

Awkwardly, I half-crawl to his side, my robes hampering my movements. I settle next to him, my back against the carved wood, unsure whether or not our bodies should touch.

He has picked up a package wrapped in silk. It is large but light and I unwrap it with care. It lands upside down on my lap and I see it is an album of paintings. I wonder for a brief moment if it is a pillow book and feel my cheeks flush, but as I turn it over I see its subject matter is not what I expected.

"It is called *Atlas of Blossoms in an Everlasting Spring*," says Yong. "I had it made for you by the Jesuit painter."

I had already recognised Giuseppe's work. His way of painting is not like the paintings I have seen all my life. There is something about it that is alive, that lifts each petal from the paper as though it might be touched, as though, plucked, it might fall from the page to the silken coverlet on which I am sitting. Entranced, I turn the sheets and see parts of the Garden held within delicate brushstrokes. The flowers, the trees, the butterflies and birds that I see every day around me are captured here, beneath my fingertips. I touch the petals and feathers, where his brushes have been before me. Beside me, I slowly become aware that Yong is watching, not the pages, but my face. His hand lifts to caress my cheek and I, unsure of how to respond, keep my eyes on the pictures and feel his caresses on my skin even as a breeze blows through the branches of a peach tree and two swallows incline their necks so that each caresses the other, their feathers intertwined.

He is very gentle with me. My silken robes are taken from me one by one and he does not hurry his task. My hair he leaves bound. He lifts my hands and guides them, he holds me in a tender embrace and even when there is pain I am not afraid, for he murmurs to me that I am his flower, his songbird, his Garden of Perfect Brightness.

When he opens his eyes he observes the petals loosened from my hair, now strewn across the bed and chuckles. "You are indeed a garden," he says. "See, you leave petals wherever you go."

I blush at receiving endearments with his eyes on me, unsure of what to say in return.

"You will come to me again," he says.

"Yes, Highness," I whisper.

Yan is delighted. "About time," she says.

"He said I must go to him again," I tell her.

"Of course," agrees Yan confidently and I cannot help but laugh at her conviction.

Her faith in me is rewarded. Yong calls for me nightly unless Yan informs his household that it is my time of bleeding. Each evening I walk the lakeside path to his palace. The moon grows round over and again. Each night I am welcomed with a warm smile. Sometimes he reads me poems, sometimes he will show me paintings he admires. A few times we stand by the lakeside and admire tiny lanterns he orders to have floated across the dark waters. I catch a glimpse of his study and see it piled high with unread papers. Each night I am taken into the scarlet hangings of his bed and gradually I learn for myself where my hands might be placed, to give as well as to receive tenderness.

"Where shall I put this?" asks Yan, holding up the silk-wrapped package containing the *Atlas*.

I shrug, holding first one autumn chrysanthemum and then another to my hair, smiling in the mirror. "Somewhere safe, Yan. Do you prefer the red or the orange?"

"The Prince doesn't care what flowers you wear, you should know that by now. You could go to him wrapped in a sack and he would be happy. You lovesick pair."

I giggle and tuck a golden-orange flower into my dark hair.

"Yan," I ask, almost in a whisper.

"Yes?"

"When you… with Kun… how…?" I stop, uncertain of how to continue.

Yan does not answer, only walks away and then returns with a box, lacquered in black. With the air of one confiding a secret, she offers it to me and I open it, then start back in surprise, for I have never seen such an object. Under a red silk cloth lies a porcelain model of a man's member, painted with tumbling roses.

"Kun had it made for us," she murmurs.

I think of Yan, how the frightened child I first met when I came here is now a fierce little woman, whose face shines with love when she sees Kun, who sings to herself when no-one is listening. I place the red silk cloth back over the piece and close the lid with a smile.

"We are both happy, Yan," I say. "We have been blessed."

She takes back the box with a little laugh, her cheeks flushed pink. "So happy," she echoes.

I bask in Yong's attentions throughout that autumn and winter. The first almond blossoms come into bloom, heralding spring.

"Wine?" he offers.

I nod, smiling, and take the little bowl from him, making sure to brush his fingertips with mine, for the simple pleasure of touching his skin. He stands by the window, looking out over the lake and I stand beside him, leaning my head on his shoulder and closing my eyes.

"My flower," he murmurs.

I am about to speak, to say his name when suddenly my stomach roils and I clutch at his arm, the little bowl falling to the floor.

He lifts me before I can even speak, carrying me swiftly to a chair and kneeling before me. "Niuhuru? What is it?"

"I feel sick," I gasp.

A servant manages to hold a bowl before me just before my stomach voids itself. I retch over and over again until, as swiftly as it came upon me, the sickness ends. Yong holds a cloth dipped in perfumed water to my face. I try to gasp my apologies but his face has lost its initial fear.

"I believe you need to rest," he says, a wry smile twisting his mouth. "I will send the physician to you."

"Highness?"

He strokes my cheek. "Farewell, my flower. I will miss you. But all will be well."

Yan might as well be with child herself, she is so pleased. "A son," she tells me. "You must have a son."

I make a face. "I'll have anything you like if you'll stop giving me disgusting drinks."

"The physician prescribed them."

"I don't care. They've vile. And I want to see Yong."

"You won't be seeing him till this child is born," says Yan cheerfully.

"Why not?"

"Oh, you'll see him at festivals or suchlike," says the uncaring Yan. "But not as a companion. It might harm the baby. Besides, now you are with child he has done his duty by you."

"I was not a duty!" I say angrily.

Yan rolls her eyes. "He has given you a child. What more did you want? A great romance?"

"He said he loved me," I protest. "He said... lots of things."

"I'm sure he did," says Yan, unbothered by my tone, which is growing tearful. "But there are other ladies to call on while you are otherwise occupied."

I throw a hairbrush at her but she only dodges it and tuts at my outburst.

Spring comes and I hear that other ladies are called on. I set my jaw and mope. I make Yan's life difficult, asking for first one dish that I claim to have cravings for and then another, before turning them away uneaten. I refuse to go out. I sit in the palace until Yan is tired of my sulking face and petulant tone. She drops Giuseppe's *Atlas* in my lap.

"If you won't go into the Garden, it will have to come to you."

Once again the petals rise up as though I might touch them. Butterflies hover above lotus flowers and I can almost hear the songbirds. I place the album on my chair and leave my rooms.

I had forgotten the joy of springtime in the Garden. Pale primroses and violets nestle in the shade of great trees, the first blossoms open their petals and everywhere tiny green tips emerge from the bare branches. I find a sunny ledge of rock by the lake's edge and sit myself down on it. I stay still long enough that a frog emerges from the water and sits on a fallen log, basking in the warm sunlight.

"I saw you from a distance."

The frog dives into the water with a splash. I look up at Giuseppe's dark form standing over me. "You walk quietly."

"I did not want to disturb you, only to know if you are well."

"Well enough." It comes out ungracious and I try to make amends. "The *Atlas* you painted of the Garden is beautiful."

He smiles an odd smile, as though I have said something sad but which must be smiled at. "I am glad it brought you pleasure."

I gesture at the rocky ledge. "Sit."

He hesitates, but then settles himself on a rock some little way off from me. He gestures awkwardly towards my hair. "An unusual motif."

I reach up to touch the hairpin I am wearing. A flying bat, its form shaped in kingfisher feathers, a gift from Yong. I grimace. "It symbolises fertility."

He nods. I can tell, from his face, that he has heard the gossip already.

"A reward for my loyalty," I add and hear the bitter note in my own voice. I know I should stop, but the bitterness will not be contained. "He has given me a child and now he ignores me." My voice shakes. "I thought he loved me."

"No-one could not – " says Giuseppe and suddenly he is on his feet. "Forgive me." He turns and strides away, his feet hard on the pebble path.

But he returns. As spring wears on and summer comes, I spend each day in the garden and he finds me again and again. I come to look out for him. I ask him to paint what surrounds me: the golden carp in the pools, the chirping crickets, the plum-red peonies. He does not speak much, unless I engage him in conversation.

"You still use your own paints," I remark. "But on our paper?"

He looks up at me. "I thought the rice paper would wrinkle or curl up when I first used it, as our paper at home would do. But it does not. It surprised me. And canvas is not as easy to find here."

"But you don't use inks and watercolours?"

"I prefer my oils," he admits. "They seem to work well with the rice paper. They seem to have an affinity – the finished texture has something silken to it."

"They always seem alive," I say. "The things you paint. As if they were real." I look down at the carp, who are begging for crumbs, their pursed lips mouthing at the surface of the water and then at his image of them, their bodies swirling through watery depths. "Can you paint people the same way?"

He smiles. "I am practicing with plants and animals first," he admits. "If I can achieve the effect I want I may go on to people."

My rooms fill up with his works. Some are only scraps, sketches or quick swirls of the brush that I beg from him when I see them, for there is something lovely even about his half-finished works, a glimpse of the Garden as it is in motion – a petal falling, grass swaying, the ripples of a turtle's dive. Some are larger works that he gifts to me. He does not give them into my hand, only leaves them where I may find them, on the outer windowsill of my room held in place by a stone, on a smooth rock where I like to sit. He will not let me thank him for them. When I speak of them he shakes his head and says they are nothing, only something half done. But I know better, for each blade of grass is finished and often the scene is something I have remarked on.

My belly grows and grows, a pumpkin swelling in the summer sun. I do not walk as far and find the heat too much. I stay within the sheltering shade of a giant willow and dabble my toes in the water, much to Yan's annoyance.

"You will chill your womb," she admonishes in doomed tones.

"Since when were you appointed Court Physician?" I ask, ungraciously removing my hot feet from the cooling lake. I lie back on the covers Yan has laid out for me but stretch my arms so that I can feel the grass at the edges, tickling my palms.

I am lonely. Yong's sudden withdrawal pained me. I had basked in the glow of his affection and now find myself left in a cold solitude, no matter how bright the summer sun shines on me. He sends me the same dutiful gifts I used to receive and has returned to court business, to long journeys away and hurried returns to the Garden and his study, to his piles of paper and a furrowed brow. I have only Yan, who worries incessantly about my health. So I turn to Giuseppe.

"Tell me about your home town," I ask him.

He describes the daily lives of his family, he draws little sketches for me to show me their strange clothes, their homes. I see his world in miniature, spread across scraps of paper, while in my mind it comes to life. Smoke curls from tall chimneys, beggars hold out their hands for alms, ladies lift heavy skirts out of the dirt of the streets. The summer leaves us and the first cool winds of autumn come. I sit in the Garden and walk the streets of Milan.

The pain is so bad that I cling to Yan and beg her to make it stop. But the midwife only rolls her eyes and tells Yan that I will be better at this next time, that all the ladies make such a fuss the first time, why, we have barely started.

"There will never be another time!" I scream at her, baring my teeth in rage and pain. "Never, you hear me?"

Yan, emboldened by the midwife's calm, shakes her head as though she has seen a hundred births. "Not pining for the Prince anymore then?" she asks cheerily and then yelps when I bite her. "You beast!"

"Beast yourself!" I shriek. "You are supposed to comfort me. Make it *stop*!"

Even Yan is sorry for me soon, as the warm autumn night drags on and I weep and writhe, covered in sweat and tears, sobbing that I will die for sure. She holds me in her arms and allows me to clutch desperately at her while the midwife only hums to herself and waits as though she has all the time in the world. I hate her.

"A boy!" Yan crows as a wriggling, mewling, blue-toned creature struggles in the midwife's expert hands. "A son for the Prince."

He is given the name Hongli and when they place him in my arms his eyes open wide and fix me in a commanding stare. I stroke his silken cheek and wonder what destiny holds for him and for me, his mother.

Long-haired Dog Beneath Blossoms

"**A** FROG! I FOUND A FROG!"

The boy came running towards me, his hands cupped. I held my breath for a moment, thinking he might fall, so intent was he on looking at his treasure, heedless of where his feet might be placed on the uneven lakeside path. But he reached my side safely, arms outstretched to reveal a terrified baby frog, crouching in his muddied palms.

"It is a very nice frog," I said, nodding at it before I dipped the brush back in my paints.

"Paint him for me!"

"I am supposed to be working on a commission for your grandfather," I reminded him. "And as he is the Emperor, I believe his command outranks that of a prince?"

"But you are my *friend*," said Hongli, smiling persuasively.

His room was filled with my paintings. Frogs, dragonflies, fish, turtles, painted on little scraps of paper. A recent and more formal painting, given for his tenth birthday, showed a small, brown, long-haired dog panting beneath a gnarled but blossoming tree: his own pet, now lying lazy in the spring sunshine, already worn out with its young master's endless quests for adventure by the lakeside. Hongli might be confined on a daily basis to a study by his tutors and by all accounts he was an excellent scholar, but as soon as he was let loose each day he roamed the Garden and sought me out to paint images for him.

Ten years had passed since Niuhuru had given Yong a son. I had seen him grow from a wrapped-up bundle in her arms to a waddling infant, enchanted by the waving willows overhead. He had grown fleet of foot as the years went by, racing about the Garden, now become his personal playground. Kun's skilled hands had woven for him a great water-dragon made from reeds, placed so that it rose from the waters of a small lake near Yong's palace, its tongue a bright swatch of red silk begged from Niuhuru's chests of clothes. He poked with sticks in the reeds, startling frogs and herons alike, ignoring Yan's wringing hands and pleas to take care, in part directed at her own daughter, Chu. Adopted by Yan and Kun shortly after their marriage, Chu was the same age as Hongli. She spent her mornings embroidering under Yan's supervision, her afternoons following Hongli about the Garden. She was as tiny as Yan must have been as a girl, quick on her feet and fearless, scrambling up rocks and leaning over the sides of walkways to gaze into the lakes, side by side with Hongli. He had now passed his tenth birthday but he was still a child and full of playfulness. The two children brought me gingko leaves and I painted them so that they looked like butterflies, which they tied to silken threads and ran with, the leaves fluttering like wings. Niuhuru drifted in their wake, carrying her son's many new-found treasures – a golden leaf, a fallen petal, a pebble. These she kept on a tiny altar in her rooms, changing them as he saw fit to gift her with them.

I saw them once when I had visited her to offer up a small sketch of a cricket for Hongli. The boy hopped excitedly about us, before suddenly diving outside, having glimpsed a timid cat peering at the window. Left alone, I moved away from Niuhuru. She had a scent about her, which I had identified as the blossoms of linden trees, a beguiling mix of fresh cut grass and honey. I found it easier to speak to her when I could not smell it.

"Is the Prince well? I have not seen him recently."

She gave a half-shrugged smile. "He is always so busy. Shall we follow the children? I am afraid the poor cat does not much enjoy their company, they frighten it with all their jumping about."

I followed. She never liked to speak of Yong. I remembered the old gossip, that said his short-lived passion for her had been partly his relief in coming back to this world after being so ill, that for once he had forgotten duty and work and obligations and given himself over entirely to love. There was certainly something of the romantic about the Prince: his flowering Garden bore testimony to it but once she had fallen with child he had remembered his duties and thrown himself back into work. His father the Emperor favoured him for it and I could not but reluctantly acknowledge him a brave man in continuing to stand out from his brothers and risking their jealousy, since years had passed and a new Crown Prince had still not been chosen. But his return to duty and his neglect of the romance he had once allowed to flourish must have hurt Niuhuru and now her attention seemed focused only on Hongli, as though she had closed up some part of herself, something I tried and failed to do myself. I had hoped, in giving time and attention to her son, to perhaps have created more of a brotherly kindness towards Niuhuru, but I knew full well that my continuing feelings towards her could not be dismissed as such.

I was not free to spend all my time in the Yuan Ming Yuan, much as it drew me. When Hongli was only five years' old an earthquake had rocked Beijing and while the local wooden buildings had weathered the shaking of the earth, St Joseph's had been irreparably damaged. It had been pulled down and was still being rebuilt, even five years' later. Its outer structure was in the hands of a newly-arrived Brother Moggi, a Florentine architect of a similar age to myself, a cheerfully enthusiastic man who had begged my time to help create the necessary decorations to the ceiling and walls of the building, now nearing completion.

"I have had flowers carved into the outer walls," he said, showing me round. "But of course it is the interiors for which I will need your help, Giuseppe."

I nodded. "I will do my best to aid you," I said. "Although I have little time these days. The Emperor keeps me busy."

"Whatever time you can spare me I would be grateful for," he replied. "I have in mind that the pillars might be painted to suggest a marble finish. And then there is the ceiling. I have heard you can create painted illusions, would it be possible to paint a false domed roof?"

I looked up the flat ceiling. "A cupola? Yes, it is possible," I said. "And the walls?"

"I leave them to you," he said confidently.

"I am concerned, my son."

I sighed inwardly. This was a topic I was growing tired of and yet I could not fault Father Friedel for raising it again.

"You have been here for many years now and yet you have not yet taken your final vows."

I nodded but did not answer. I applied the paint in tiny brushstrokes, going over the same area again as though there were some fault in it.

"I must remind you that you were chosen not only for your skills, which we acknowledge we are well pleased with – as has His Majesty grown to be – but because you agreed to our requirement: that you must take the vows of the Jesuit priesthood. It would be normal for these to have been taken within two years of you reaching these shores. And yet it is more than ten years that you have been with us now."

I opened my mouth to speak but he held up a hand.

"I know of course that you have told me many times that you have struggled with maintaining pure thoughts, that you have doubts and that you wish to allay such thoughts before you take such serious vows – and they are, of course, very serious. But to be a Jesuit does not mean you have no doubts at all. We all have doubts or we would not be human, vows or no vows. I have heard that you have used hair shirts, even flagellation, in your attempts to be worthy of the priesthood. I believe perhaps you are too harsh on yourself. And so, my son, I urge you now to take this final step. And soon."

I looked at the hand I was even now engaged in painting within the Church of St Joseph while he spoke with me, a rare commission of a Biblical scene which seemed almost strange to me now that I was used only to court commissions. Even this hand was Niuhuru's. I wanted to tell Father Friedel, wanted to turn his face to it and tell him that because I could not paint her face in this scene I painted her hand, because her hands were known to me so intimately that they came first to my mind, because my brush knew how to paint each line of her fingers as though I had held them in my own.

Instead I nodded. "I will pray for guidance, Father," I said.

He nodded. "When we pray for guidance we must also listen for it when it comes from the mouths of those about us," he said and walked away.

Laura was singing, a rare sound, for usually she worked in silence with her eyebrows fiercely drawn together.

"You are happy today," I said.

She looked up from her work. "The Brothers have allowed me to begin work on an altarpiece for the church," she said.

I smiled. An altarpiece was a rare piece of work and given only to those whose skill could withstand the constant scrutiny of the congregation. "Have you chosen your topic?"

"The Madonna and Child," she said.

I nodded. A fitting piece for an altar and also for a woman to paint. "Have you completed the preliminary sketches?"

She hesitated. "Yes."

"May I see them?"

She hesitated again and when she brought me the work I knew already what I would see: Guo's face, lit up with joy, a baby in her arms, the outline of a halo above her head. Laura hovered over me, one hand clenched as though to stop herself from taking back the sketch before I could examine it.

"I am sure it will be important to the congregation to have a local woman depicted as Our Lady," I said.

Laura nodded.

"Has she been delivered of a child?" I asked.

"He is so good-natured," she said. "They have sat for me again and again and he does not cry, not at all."

"Is her husband pleased with the idea of the commission?" I asked.

She took back the sketch. "He does not complain," she said. She returned to her usual, frowning silence and I was sorry to have taken away some of her joy.

"Can I accompany you to Mass on Sunday?" I asked her and she nodded in silence.

When we arrived at the church I watched as Guo arrived with her husband and baby. I saw Laura stand apart as though she could not see them and watched her as she closed her eyes in prayer.

After the service I intercepted Guo and asked to see her child, still tiny, with a growing dark shock of hair above sleepy eyes. I held him awkwardly and thought of Hongli when I had first seen him, the same dark hair but bold eyes, dark and commanding. As Laura passed us, her eyes looking only ahead I caught at her sleeve. "You will have to hold the subject of your painting," I said. "He must grow used to your company for his sittings if your altarpiece is to be a success."

She took him from me and for a moment held him stiffly, her own face held rigidly in a polite smile. But his small hand reached out and touched her face and she could not help herself. A smile spread over her face and she stroked his cheek with her finger, murmuring to him in our own tongue an old lullaby. Guo's husband had wandered away to speak with a friend and for a moment Laura and Guo stood together, their faces lit up with love for the boy until I had to look away as though I had seen something not meant for my eyes.

We walked together through the noisy streets of Beijing, saying nothing until we reached the gates of the Forbidden City.

"Do you regret the life you might have lived?" I asked her, as the guards examined our wooden passes and let us enter.

"What life would that be?" she asked.

"Remaining in your home city. Marriage. Children."

"Do you?" she asked.

I sighed. "Sometimes. I thought my painting would be my life, that I needed nothing else."

"And were you right?"

"Some of the time," I said.

"Do you regret leaving Milan?" she asked.

"No," I said, certain.

"Marriage?"

"I would not have made a good husband, leaving for China," I tried to joke. "And anyway, I was asking you."

"I have found everything I need," she said quietly.

"Everything?"

We paused outside the studios. "It is not how I might wish things to be," she said. "But what I have found here is everything to me."

We were silent for a while as we settled to our work, but after a time Laura lifted her head. "And have you found what you need here, Giuseppe?" she asked, and there was something in her tone that told me that she already knew the answer, that where others might have seen only a courtier's care for a young prince over these past years, she had looked beyond Hongli and seen his mother, just as I looked beyond the baby Christ she had painted and saw the face of Guo.

"I could not be elsewhere," I said.

Our eyes met for a moment and she nodded. "I hope that you find happiness," she said. "Even if it is hard, sometimes."

I thought of the moments when I undertook to run races with Hongli and heard Niuhuru's laughter behind us, of her smile each time we met, the scent of her perfume when we passed one another. "I take joy in the small things," I said.

We did not speak often nor directly of such matters, but there was a shared truth between us that no-one else could understand, and it gave me comfort.

The tiny stones I had asked Kun for were hard to work with but when I brushed the dirt off my hands I had to smile. Sheltered close to a rock, by the lakeside there now sat a tiny house, barely a hand's height, something like a fisherman's hut. I waited for Hongli's return from his studies and was rewarded with a beaming smile when he saw what I had made.

"Is this like the houses from your home?" he asked me.

I nodded. "A simple house, not a palace like yours," I told him.

"You could build me a palace from your own country! A big one, that I could live in!"

I let out a laugh. "It would take me years, Hongli. I would need a team of workmen."

"You shall have them," he told me grandly. "When I am a man, I shall give them to you. Then you can build me a palace."

I see him running towards me as a boy, his hands muddied, his eyes bright with the wonders of the Garden that now holds all my memories. By the lake of the Yuan Ming Yuan there runs a child I loved as though he were my own.

Engraved Moon and Unfolding Clouds

THE IMPERIAL HUNT IS THE favourite time of year of the Kangxi Emperor. Yong has never been a great hunting enthusiast, but even he has been unable to resist Hongli's begging to attend. Ever a dutiful father, he has held Hongli to excel at his studies, promising in return that he will be taken to the hunting grounds at Chengde, near my family home, when the Emperor decrees the start of the hunt.

"And I will shoot from horseback, like a real Manchu, while galloping!"

"You will do no such thing," I tell him. "You will stay at the back where it is safe and you will observe the hunt. No more."

"I am very nearly twelve," he tells me, his bottom lip already beginning to pout.

"And I am your mother," I say.

But he must have some freedom. He begins his day before the sun has even risen, he is taught not only Mandarin but Manchu and Mongolian scripts, he must study all aspects of Han culture. He has been studying since he was six, his little head bowed before his stern tutors for most of each day. His afternoons are given over to combat lessons using swords or improving his archery. He runs from his studies each day to target practice, even leaving Giuseppe alone for once. I cannot help but smile when I see his black-robed figure walking along a high ridge, seeking us out, wondering at Hongli's unexpected absence from his side.

"Ah, archery," he says when he sees us. "The hunt, of course, I had forgotten."

"Are you coming?" asks Hongli, eyes fiercely narrowed at his target.

"I go every year," he says.

"To paint the hunt?"

"Yes."

"You could paint me! On horseback! With my bow!"

Giuseppe laughs. "Of course."

"And you can paint me holding a tiger I have killed!"

Giuseppe's eyebrows go up and I see him try to hide a smile. "Of course," he says with great seriousness. "Will there be many tigers?"

"I am sure I will find one," says Hongli and his arrow flies true. "I hit it! I hit it!" he shrieks. Yan blocks her ears at Chu's squeals of excitement.

I exchange a smile with Giuseppe. Sometimes I feel as though he is Hongli's father, for he spends all his time with the boy and it is clear to anyone that he loves him. He paints at his command, he has made all manner of tiny buildings for him, hidden along the rocky edges of the lakeside, his eyes are warm when they rest on him. I remind myself that of course Yong is also proud, that he has chosen great scholars for Hongli's education and that the many hours he holds him to studying are a mark of his esteem. But still, sometimes I wish that Yong would leave behind his endless papers to crouch in the mud by the lake and hold Hongli's hand to steady him while he gathers tadpoles, or run hampered races with him, robes flapping in the wind while my boy easily outstrips him, giggling madly.

Chengde's rooftops seem strange to me now, half-familiar, half-forgotten. I have rarely attended the hunt, for Yong always has some excuse why we should not go, masking his own lack of interest. I think of my mother and father, my brothers. They are so close to me and yet they will not see my son or me. After all these years they seem distant even in my memory. I am almost thirty and I have not seen any of them since I was thirteen.

Our vast procession turns away from the path leading to the city. Instead we take up residence in the forest in a never-ending maze of luxurious tents erected by the thousand servants who have been sent ahead with the baggage carts. The tents are laid out to mimic the Forbidden City, with the various households of princes and other officials enclosing it in an outer ring. My own tent is comfortable enough and Yan is quartered close by.

Hongli is impossible to control. He wants to set off now, at once, at *once,* to catch a tiger or a bear or a deer or even a rabbit – anything to show his prowess with a bow.

"You have to wait," I tell him. "There will be a hunt tomorrow. Tonight your father will want to present you to your Grandfather the Emperor. You must be on your best behaviour."

He succumbs, fretfully, to being dressed in his finest robes and demonstrates, in the privacy of our tent, the correct way to kowtow. He has been well trained in his short life. His manners are flawless when he concentrates, he has a fine bearing and speaks well. I feel a welling-up of pride.

"Are you coming?"

I shake my head.

"Please come," he says, suddenly losing his confidence at the notion of meeting the Emperor alone, with only his quiet father by his side rather than my warm hand in his.

I embrace him. "You will like your grandfather," I say. "He is a great hunter. Talk to him of the hunt. Ask him questions."

Yong nods to me as I push Hongli forwards. "He looks well," he says formally.

I want to tell Yong that Hongli is nervous but I know this would bring a frown to his face, for he believes that his son should have been trained out of such childish thoughts. Instead I smile more broadly than I feel and say loudly that Hongli is very excited to be meeting his Grandfather and looking forward to the hunt.

Hongli is so far ahead of me that at first I can barely see him. He has been given a place of such honour that even Yong's face showed surprise. His still-short legs clasp his horse's sides with such keenness the poor stead is constantly trying to move forwards, mistaking his enthusiasm for a command to gallop. He looks up into his Grandfather's face with eager anticipation. By my side a guard helps me move forwards so that I can see the hunt better from my horse. It is a long time since I rode and I find myself nervous, although the horse has no doubt been chosen for its docility so that a woman may ride it. There are few women on the hunt today, the ladies of the court prefer to remain in the relative comfort of the encampment. I am conscious that just behind me, comfortable on his mount, is Giuseppe. I turn to smile at him.

"He is so excited," I say.

"The Emperor has taken a liking to him," says Giuseppe, smiling back at me.

"Now all he has need of is a tiger," I say and we both laugh. It makes me happy to know what joy this day brings to Hongli and to share that happiness with someone who knows him as well as I do.

Up ahead there are shouts as the beaters and dogs draw closer. The riders tense with anticipation for what will emerge from the dense thicket before us. Deer? Wild boar perhaps? Certainly from the crashing ahead it is a large animal or even several large animals. The men are eager for a first day of good hunting, to put the elderly Emperor in good humour and get the season off to an auspicious start.

It is a bear. Its dark coat pounds through the brush and now arrows fly towards it. The Emperor's bow is at full draw and his own arrows embed themselves in the bear's chest. I see the beast rise onto its legs, standing taller than a man, its great body riddled with sharp arrows, hear it roar in pain. I cannot help but wince. Quickly it is over, for what creature could withstand such an assault? The great body slumps to the ground and a cry of victory goes up. But now Hongli is being called forward by the Emperor, who indicates that he may finish the beast off with his own little bow. Hongli dismounts at speed and steps forwards, his face alight with pride, his arm draws back to let loose the final arrow that will allow him to say he took part in the hunt. I smile a little at his moment of childlike glory, not knowing the creature is already safely dead.

But the bear rears up again, its great claws reaching out to swipe at him, missing by less than a hand's breadth. There are shouts all around me. Men rush forwards while my child stands still, his face a mask of silent terror as a beast plucked from any babe's nightmare roars in his face, before it falls again at his feet and is still.

I open my mouth to call out to him but see my hands go slack on the reins as my body crumples in the saddle. I fall and am caught in a man's arms.

"Hongli," I say, my mouth trembling so that the word comes out badly formed. "Hongli."

"He is safe." Giuseppe's voice is close to my ear, so close his voice is a ragged whisper. "He is safe."

I feel my body go limp again in relief and turn my face towards his chest. My cheek now pressed against his warm body, I become aware that I can hear his heart beating, fast and strong. Unthinking, I put up a hand to press against his cheek before suddenly I recollect myself and struggle in his arms to draw away from him.

"Stay still," he says. "The guards are bringing a palanquin."

Slowly I begin to hear the noise about us, as though my ears had been unable to hear anything but his voice. I see the silk curtains drawn back and the bearers waiting for me. I turn in Giuseppe's arms as he lowers me to the ground and feel for one brief moment his arms grow tight about my waist when he should be releasing me. I look into his face and see all that he has never told me in all the years we have known one another, all he cannot ever tell me. Then his arms are gone and I am inside the darkness of the palanquin. Through the drapes I see the white face of my little son, brought to speak with me. Yong stands by his side, his face an equally pale mask of protocol.

"Hongli – " I say, tears starting in my eyes.

"I am unharmed, Mother," he says, his back too straight, his voice too loud.

I want to clasp him to me but I know he will cry if I do so, know that my embrace will prove his undoing. I look to Yong to help me, but he does not speak and so I look beyond him to Giuseppe.

"How brave you are. A true Manchu!" says Giuseppe loudly.

I smile a great smile, as though he has faced nothing worse than a rabbit. "A true Manchu," I echo, glad to have something I can say that will hold back Hongli's tears.

"He is indeed. I am very proud of him."

The Emperor. All around us, courtiers fall to their faces as he advances. I make to step out of the palanquin but he gestures that I should stay seated.

"Your Majesty," I murmur, bowing my head. He has grown older since the first time I saw him, he is more stooped than the upright old man I remember from the Imperial Daughters' Draft.

"I am impressed with your son, Lady Niuhuru," he says.

"He is honoured by your favour," I say, the meaningless response the only thing I can think to say.

"A brave boy," the Emperor says, patting Hongli's shoulder. He looks at Yong. "This boy is destined to lead a charmed life."

There is a murmur from the courtiers around us. Yong bows without replying.

"We will visit your family," announces the Emperor. "A formal Court visit will be arranged to the Yuan Ming Yuan."

And he is gone in a wave of courtiers and guards. I look out of the palanquin at Yong and he looks back at me.

"What does it mean?" I ask.

Yong shakes his head. "I do not know," he says and now he has finally spoken I hear his voice shake and know that despite his controlled formal manner he felt my own terror when he saw the bear rear up. "Hongli will return to the encampment with you," he orders.

I hold out my hand to Yong. "Return with us," I say. I cannot say more, cannot say that I am afraid of all the emotions I am feeling – the fear from Hongli's encounter with the bear still cold in my belly along with my heart which is beating too fast for a man I should not even think of. I want Yong to take his place by my side, to comfort Hongli, to erase the feelings I should not be feeling.

But he shakes his head. "I must attend my father," he says before walking stiffly away.

I offer my outstretched hand to Hongli and he climbs in beside me. Giuseppe steps forwards and closes the drapes about me and for a brief moment our eyes meet. Within the darkness of the palanquin, hidden from public view, my shaken son lies his head on my lap and sobs as he has not done since he was small. From outside, a hand reaches in and strokes Hongli's head. The bearers lift us but before the hand can be withdrawn I clasp it in my own.

The palanquin sways through the rustling woods while outside Giuseppe keeps pace with us. Exhausted, Hongli falls asleep while I stare down at our entwined hands and wonder how I will ever let go.

"Keep still," snaps Yan, exasperated with her task.

I twist under her hands, fretful. "They will be here soon. I must be there to welcome them."

"Not with your hair unfinished," says Yan.

More than one jade pin falls to the ground and Chu, standing by to help Yan, collects them and returns them to her mother, her little face serious at the gravity of the event.

The now-flourishing Peony Terrace is the location for the Emperor's visit. Set on a small island close to Yong's own palace, over ninety kinds of peonies are in flower, each bloom wider than the span of my hands. There will be seating so that we can admire the flowers, a throne for the Emperor. The peonies Yan has chosen for my hair are a deep pink, with contrasting petals of pure white at their centre. No fewer than six are pinned into my hair, now so full of flowers, tinkling golden strands and white jade pins that I can barely hold my head up. My robes are a delicate green embroidered with grasses and butterflies. I must look like a walking garden. I try to hurry along the path but my shoes are higher than I usually wear and I am forced to take smaller steps. I reach the pavilion on the Peony Terrace just in time to see the imperial party arriving. Beside me, Lady Qi glows with satisfaction.

"A formal visit from His Majesty can only mean favour for the Prince," she says quietly.

I nod, distracted by the sight of Hongli who is so excited he can barely keep still.

"Perhaps he has realised that it is time to choose a new heir at last," Lady Qi continues. "We must do all we can to ensure the Prince is seen to be worthy." She glances towards her eldest son, Hongshi, already an elegant young man. She indicates to him that he should stand further forward, where his grandfather will see him.

"Ladyship," says Hongshi, bowing his head politely to me.

I nod back to him, still half-distracted by Hongli. I am not overly fond of Hongshi, he has a touch of arrogance to him which makes me think of the demoted Crown Prince, an expectation that the world will shape itself to his desires. I am well aware that Lady Qi has high hopes for Hongshi. This meeting is crucial for her and Hongshi. If the Emperor takes to her son it may well move her one step closer to her ultimate goal.

The Emperor is surrounded by courtiers as well as his own ladies and it takes a while for everyone to find their correct positions around his throne. Hongshi, at a nod from his mother, steps forward and makes an elegant obeisance to his grandfather, who nods. I wait for Yong's glance towards me and then make a small gesture to Hongli, so that he may do the same. Hongli rushes forwards but entirely omits to kowtow, instead he perches on the arm of the Emperor's throne and thrusts a scroll into his hands. I see Yong's eyes widen in horror. Lady Qi's mouth twists in amusement.

"I wrote it myself!" Hongli declares. "A poem about the hunting grounds for you, Grandfather!"

"Wonderful," chuckles the Emperor, apparently delighted by my son's breach of protocol. "Read it to me."

Beside me I feel Lady Qi stiffen. Hongshi has lost his elegant composure. He shifts uneasily from one foot to the other, unsure of what to do, his face bewildered as his younger half-brother is embraced by the Emperor as he finishes reading his composition.

"A poet as well as a hunter, eh? The boy is a marvel! Now where is your mother, boy? We will not frighten her with bears this time, I think – peonies are safer!" He gives a hearty laugh and the courtiers hurry to join in.

Hongli looks about him and indicates me. I step forward, kneel and begin my kowtow.

"Enough of that," says the Emperor cheerfully. "Rise, rise."

I rise and stand before him.

"I believe your son will bring you great honour one day, Lady Niuhuru," he says, his tone more serious. He looks at Hongli and then at Yong, then nods, as though making a decision. "You are a lucky woman."

I hear the muted gasp from the crowd around us and see Lady Qi's face freeze over as she takes in the implication of his words.

The moon rises. Lanterns begin to glow throughout the Garden and we make our way to where a banquet has been laid out. Hongli is led to a position of honour at the Emperor's side, with Yong close by. I sit among the ladies and feel all their eyes on me but do not dare to meet their gaze. I cannot bear it if all of them are filled with the same sudden hatred as Qi's. I eat slowly, tasting nothing. I think back to the Imperial Daughters' Draft, the day I was chosen as a minor concubine to an unknown prince. Now the Emperor has implied before half the court that my husband will be made his heir with my own son to follow. There are whispers that he would have liked to skip Yong altogether and give the throne directly to Hongli, but that would not be the proper way of things. But everyone is certain that Yong has been preferred largely because of my own son to come after him. How has this happened?

"I never asked for this," I tell Yan, tugging at the peonies in my hair. They fall to the floor, crushed by my shaking fingers. "I never asked for this. I am happy here, in the Garden. I don't want to live in the Forbidden City, to have the other women hate me because my son is to be Emperor one day. I don't want to have scheming and whispers all around me. I don't want to be stuck inside those red walls and never be able to go out. I want my son safe by my side, I don't want his brothers trying to poison him like the Sorcerer Prince did to Yong. I don't want – "

"Stop pulling!" exclaims Yan. "Half your hair will come out with the flowers if you keep yanking at it like that."

I try to sit still while she dismantles my hair, my eyes brimming up with unshed tears.

"You should rest," she says, when she is done. My hair hangs loose and my high shoes are off. My green robe is still on but I wave her away.

"I will undress myself," I tell her.

"Rest," Yan repeats. "Tomorrow you can think about what the Emperor said. For now, be grateful your husband and son are shown such favour, instead of worrying about the other women. They would not be worrying about you, if they were in your position."

I sit alone for a few moments. I try to think of something else – the peonies, perhaps, the lanterns and how well they looked in the moonlight, but all I can think of is Qi's eyes locked onto mine as I stood with my son in front of the throne while she and her son went unnoticed on the sidelines.

At last I stand up. I cannot sleep like this. Instead I walk out of my room and stand in the entrance of my palace, the door wide open to the cool night air. Down by the lakeside I can see the outline of a man, standing motionless in the soft glow of the fading lanterns. My bare feet hurt as I walk down the rough path but I do not stop until I am standing in front of him, not quite touching and yet close enough to feel the heat of his body.

"I can't," I say and I am not sure what I am talking about. That I cannot bear the future that has suddenly opened up ahead of me or that I cannot reach out and touch him?

"No," he agrees.

We stand in silence and all I can hear is my own breathing and his.

"Why are you here?" I ask.

"Because I saw your face," he says and again I do not know if he means when we first set eyes on one another years ago or if he means the moment this evening when the Emperor spoke and I heard the muted gasp from those around me that meant I had interpreted his meaning correctly.

One of my feet hurts, it is resting on a too-sharp pebble. I shift. The tiny motion allows my robe to touch Giuseppe's and suddenly his lips are on mine, his arms wrapped so tightly about me that I can scarcely breathe. I return his embrace with such desperation that he draws back for a second to look at my face. It takes only that second for me to turn and run.

The summer heat rises and then falls. The months pass and for the first time in all the years I have lived in the Garden I do not venture outside the walls of my own palace during daylight hours. Instead I endure the stifling heat indoors, my fan in constant movement. Yan asks if I am well, frowns at me, even brings me disgusting concoctions from Yong's physician, which I leave untouched to grow cold. She tries to entice me out, makes Kun bring fresh flowers and water reeds to show me, talks of dragonflies and boating trips across the waterways of the Garden. I turn my face away and eventually she grows silent, hurt by my withdrawal from our friendship. I cannot find a way to tell her why I do not trust myself to walk in the Garden and not run to find Giuseppe.

Late each night I walk to the top of the path that leads to the lakeside and look into the shadows, where I can see him standing under the willow tree. Each night I see his outline turn towards me and each night I drop my head and return to my palace and my sleepless bed. The leaves fall from the willow and still his shadow waits for me among the bare branches while the wind turns cold and winter comes upon us.

The snow lies thick across the Garden, so bright it hurts my eyes, icicles sparkling from every rooftop. While my eyes are dazzled, my ears are left abandoned, the whiteness muffling any sound. My days are empty. As the leaves turned red, the high walls of the Forbidden City claimed my son. The Emperor decreed that Hongli's tutors were no longer good enough for such a talented child, that he must continue his schooling within the imperial city, alongside the Emperor's own youngest sons. I have been given an even more generous allowance along with my own eunuchs and additional maids, but my palace is quiet. Hongli is gone from me, Yan maintains her silence and I do not allow myself to speak with Giuseppe, for fear of what either of us may say.

It is the deepest day of winter and the sky is a darkening grey when my ears are assaulted with an unexpected sound of clattering armour and horses' hooves. From the window I see a senior eunuch surrounded by more than thirty imperial guards ride past, their sweating horses headed for Yong's palace. I have little time to wonder at their presence here when they pass my palace again, this time surrounding a mounted figure wrapped in thick furs. Yong.

The winter air almost makes me gasp, I have been indoors so long. I walk through the snow in high boots, a silk wrap clutched about me. I quickly wish I had chosen furs. When I hear footsteps behind me I turn to see Yan following me. I offer her a small smile and she nods at me without smiling, as though reserving judgement.

The eunuch who opens Qi's door regards me without speaking. He does not invite me in and I imagine he has been given orders to that effect. Instead he disappears and after a cold silence Qi herself appears. She looks at me with her eyebrows raised, ignoring any niceties due to a fellow concubine.

"Where is the Prince going?" I ask.

"*You* don't know?" she asks, mocking.

I shake my head.

"The Kangxi Emperor is dying," she says.

I gape at her. "Dying?"

"He has summoned seven of his sons to his bedside. What else do you think he is doing?" she asks me.

I swallow. "Who is the heir?" I ask.

"Yong," she says.

"You can't be sure of that," I say.

She looks at me as though I am an idiot.

"You should be pleased, then," I say, forcing a smile.

"Why would I be pleased?"

"You wanted Yong to be made heir."

"I wanted my son to be Emperor," she corrects me.

I don't want to ill-wish my own son but I do not want this future for him or for myself. "He still might," I say, but my voice trails away.

Qi half-snorts. "Yong has only been chosen for heir because of your son Hongli," she says bluntly. "He is too boring in his own right. Dutiful, yes. Filial, of course. A hard worker. No doubt capable of good things. But no spark of glory. Not a warrior. Not a poet. A conscientious official, a right-hand man, not an emperor."

I look down at the cold snow between us. "My son is very young," I say.

"The Emperor took the throne at eight years old," says Qi. "Your son is already twelve years old with a young enough father to go before him and pave his way."

I raise my eyes to her face. "I do not want this future," I tell her.

"You do not wish to be a consort to an Emperor? A mother to an Emperor? You do not wish to be the Empress Dowager, the greatest woman at court, one day?"

I shake my head.

"Then you're a fool," she says.

"I saw Yong poisoned," I tell her. "By his own brother. For the chance to take the throne. I do not want a life of ritual and grandeur. I want to live here, in the Garden and be happy with my son by my side, a princeling and nothing more."

"Too late for that," she says.

We stand in silence for a long time before I speak again. "I never wished you ill," I say to her. "You or your son."

"Too late for that," she repeats and steps backwards into the doorway, a eunuch appearing by her side to close the door in my face.

I turn and look at Yan.

"She'll still be consort to an emperor," says Yan, without much pity.

"That's not what she wanted," I say.

Yan shrugs.

"Is this what I will have to live with?" I ask her. "Hatred and fear? All the other women looking at me with loathing, hoping that Hongli will die so that a child of theirs can supersede him? The constant fear that Yong will be poisoned again?"

Yan sees my eyes fill up and steps forwards, slipping her small hard hand into mine, the way she used to when we were barely more than children. "One day at a time," she says. "Do not think of everything all at once."

Our hands still clasped, we trudge back through the snow together. I keep my eyes on the ground, for the path is slippery.

"The Jesuit is here," says Yan.

I look up quickly. Giuseppe is standing in his usual space, as the dusk grows around us. I hesitate, then let go of Yan's hand and walk over to him, her presence a safeguard.

"I saw the Prince leaving," he says. "Is it true?"

I nod. The wind is stronger now. I shiver and pull my too-thin wrap about me.

"Take mine," says Giuseppe.

I step backwards.

He holds his heavy outer coat out at arm's length. I take it, careful not to touch him, and drape it around me. The warmth is immediate. Without thinking I nuzzle into the heavily furred collar and at once the scent of him overwhelms me. With a jerk I let the coat fall to the ground and run back towards my palace. Behind me I hear Yan panting to keep up with me. I look back. Beyond her stands Giuseppe, the dark furs of his coat still lying in the white snow at his feet, mingled with the silken folds of my wrap.

I wait till Yan has crossed the threshold before pushing the door shut so hard it shakes in its frame. Two eunuchs and a maid come running to see what the matter is.

I turn to look at Yan. Her eyes are serious.

"You should have told me," she says.

Invitation to Reclusion

LAURA FOUND ME WITH AN old sketchbook in my hands, one finger tracing the lines of the greyhound I once drew for the Kangxi Emperor.

"He was a kindly man," I said. "Gruff. An old warrior, not a polished courtier. He loved a good feast, the hunting grounds, his ladies, all the pleasures of this world."

"Yong may be different," she said. "In all the years we have been here the Pope has never relented regarding the ancestral worship."

I nodded, still tracing the lines with my fingertip. Prince Yong was a man of duty, a hard worker, a man committed to equality and erasing corruption. I was not sure how much artistic pleasures would soften him towards Christianity now that he was about to be crowned Emperor, although I knew there was a part of him that responded to the beauty of nature.

"He may be more stern," she said. "Less lenient towards the Order."

I looked up at her.

"Time to choose, Giuseppe," she said. "Your vows or home."

I looked back down. "That is not the choice."

"There is no other choice," she said gently and for a moment her small hand covered mine, her touch at once comforting and a burden to me.

"I cannot leave you here alone," I said.

"I have already chosen my path," she said. "My vows are made. As should yours be after fifteen years here."

I looked up at her. "To whom did you make your vows?"

She looked away for a moment, her eyes on the half-finished Madonna and Child altarpiece, Guo's face now surmounted by a golden halo. "The Brotherhood, of course," she said very quietly. "Who else?"

I found myself walking the streets each night after my work was done. Beijing was familiar to me by now, its endless busyness always a strange contrast to the tranquillity of the Yuan Ming Yuan. Street vendors called out their wares as palanquins hurried past, their fortunate occupants hidden from view, while their bearers sweated, cursing at anything in their way. When I had first come here there were so many sights that were new to me that I would sometimes stop in the middle of a street and find a little place where I might crouch down and sketch something: a face, the blurred outline of motion, an attempt to capture the lives swirling around me. But I had whole sheaves of such sketches now and my surroundings were familiar to me. So I did not pause, only walked and walked until I was tired enough to sleep without thinking.

Perhaps Yong would have been content to leave matters as they were, the Brothers permitted to serve at court but not preach their gospel further abroad. But as the Kangxi Emperor lay dying a final rivalry broke out among the imperial sons. Even though Yong had clearly been indicated as the heir, an imperial cousin, Sunu, tried instead to have the eighth prince Yunsi crowned.

"This can only mean trouble for us," Father Friedel warned the Brothers when we were gathered together. "Sunu and his family are converts to our religion. It may go hard with us if Yong sees Christianity as the source of such disloyalty."

We awaited news and sure enough the Sunu family were exiled for their disloyalty to Yong. When members of the family were found to be preaching the Gospel in their place of exile Yong acted promptly. An edict was issued placing all members of the Order under house arrest. Our work for the Imperial Family was to cease at once. We were obliged to stay within the precinct of St Joseph's. My first thought was of Niuhuru, of being unable to see her. I found myself pacing in the tiny garden, thinking only of that other Garden, which Niuhuru would shortly leave as she entered the Forbidden City as a concubine to the new Emperor. Father Friedel counselled us all to have patience and to offer up our prayers, but the turn of events led to turmoil within the Order. There was nervous whispering everywhere, even during mass and the spacious refectory felt claustrophobic now that we knew there were few other places we could go except back to our own small and plainly furbished cells to sleep or pray. One of the astronomers who had served the Jesuits for some years now chose to return home rather than take his vows and be obliged to stay in a country he increasingly considered dangerous. Meanwhile the copper-engraver Brother Matteo Ripa had determined to leave also, although in his case he intended to take with him four young Chinese Christians, converts he was proud of. Removing them from the country would require some careful subterfuge in the current climate. Ripa had in mind to return to Naples where he would train the young men as priests and then send them back to China as missionaries.

Father Friedel, convinced of the necessity of patience and the belief that we might yet soften Yong's attitude through excellence of service, determined that the time was right to send Brother Arailza home.

"He has never really enjoyed his work here," he told me. "And has never yet won imperial preference. In all honesty, Giuseppe, Arailza's skill as a painter is not as great as yours and I believe that you have had some signs of imperial favour shown to you, which may yet stand us in good stead. You intend to stay, I hope?"

I watched the preparations for departure and saw the travellers' excitement grow, wondered what it would be like to travel to the South and back to Macau, to see a ship rocking on the waves and know that, God willing, I would see my home city and family again in a year's time. Even Brother Arailza seemed to brighten at the thought of returning home, even though my preferment over him must have hurt his professional pride. For some days I thought of my journey here and even found old sketches I had done on board the ship: the sailors at work, Laura half-dozing on deck, the far-off shore. And yet I knew that each step of the journey would take me further away from Niuhuru. If I stayed here there was some chance that Yong would eventually relent, that I would see her again.

"I cannot leave without bidding farewell to... to those I have known and cared for here," I said to Laura.

"And if we are never released from house arrest?" she asked softly.

"At least I will not be far away," I said, although my heart was heavy at the idea of spending the rest of my life within these narrow precincts.

It was Laura who took it upon herself to read me the two letters I received from my brother telling me of the death of my parents. They had been sent almost a year apart but had somehow arrived together and when I opened the first I found myself unable to read it. Laura's voice trembled when she read each one and I submitted to her embraces, her looks of concern, her reminders that I must care for myself. She did not allow me to forget to eat or drink in my sorrow. I nodded and thanked her and assured her that I was well enough. Strangely I did not think so much of the moment of our parting, instead small memories of my childhood would come to me at odd moments while I was working. The size of my father's hand wrapped around my own and his rough brown beard, which I would pull when sat upon his knee. My mother's scoldings, usually followed by some small sweetmeat, her tugging at my clothes to try and make me more presentable when visiting elderly relatives. Even while momentous events occur all around us, our lives are made up of such small details. When Matteo and his converts as well as Brother Arailza and the astronomer left us I bid them all farewell and put away my sketches of the sea.

That night I left my scholar's black clothing in my little room and instead donned the brighter robes of a well-to-do Manchu man, a man free of the burdens and expectations of the Brotherhood. I slipped out of the gates unseen, flouting the rules of our house arrest.

The streets of Beijing flickered with lanterns and the little fires of stallholders. I walked among the busy crowds and passed over a few coins for bread and meat, for a long stick of candied crab-apples, tart and sweet all at once. I walked first one way and then another, not aiming for any destination.

"A man should have company, so late at night."

I looked down at the hand on my arm and the set smile of the girl to whom it belonged. She watched me hesitate and her fixed smile grew a little broader.

"Come," she said and I followed.

Perhaps I thought that if I only saw her in the dim light of a lantern, her long black hair might convince me that I held Niuhuru in my arms and that I would be sated of this impossible desire. Perhaps I knew already that I would never leave this place and that therefore I must take the vows I had avoided for so long. Perhaps I thought I should be reminded of what I was giving up.

It no longer matters which of those is true. I returned to my room and when I awoke the next morning I wore my scholar's black and told the Brothers that I would take my vows whenever they so wished.

I knelt and heard my voice speak the words of the vows and yet they did not seem to come from my mouth.

Almighty and eternal God, I understand how unworthy I am in your divine sight. Yet I am strengthened by your infinite compassion and mercy, and I am moved by the desire to serve you.

I had knelt like this only a few days before, my forehead touching the ground as I heard Prince Yong proclaimed the Yongzheng Emperor, his former name now taboo even to those who had known him well. Now I knelt to repeat the words I had so long evaded, with Laura's serious eyes on me.

I vow to your divine majesty, before the most holy Virgin Mary and the entire court of heaven, perpetual chastity, poverty, and obedience in the Society of Jesus.

As I raised my eyes I saw the painting I myself had undertaken on the chapel wall, saw Niuhuru's hand. I thought of her standing on the bamboo path the first time I saw her, felt the weight of her body in my arms as she fell from her horse at the hunt, recalled the touch of her lips on mine under the willow tree. Last of all I thought of her standing with the other concubines by Yongzheng's golden throne as I raised my eyes from the ground and saw my foolish dreams turn to dirt.

I promise that I will enter the same Society to spend my life in it forever.

As the robes of imperial yellow were placed about Yongzheng's body, so the high vermillion walls of the Forbidden City claimed Niuhuru and immured her within its endless corridors.

I understand all these things according to the Constitutions of the Society of Jesus.

I did not need to hear the murmurings of the congregation behind me as the words came to an end, barely even saw their lips moving with good wishes or the beaming face of Father Friedel as I left the church.

Therefore, by your boundless goodness and mercy and through the blood of Jesus Christ, I humbly ask that you judge this total commitment of myself acceptable; and as you have freely given me the desire to make this offering, so also may you give me the abundant grace to fulfil it.

With the edict of house arrest still upon us I could only work on the chapel. I created the illusion of a cupola on the flat ceiling as Brother Moggi had asked, completed the pillars with the semblance of a marbled finish, then continued the work on the walls. One panel contained a *trompe l'oeil* showing a doorway leading to a room filled with beautiful objects, from scrolls and fine books to a cabinet of curios and a vase filled with peacock feathers on which a ray of sunshine shone. Brother Moggi invited a local scholar, Yao

Yuanzhi, to view it. The scholar reached out a hand, as though he might enter the room portrayed, then started back when he perceived that there was no doorway, only a wall, cold to the touch.

"It is like a fairytale," he exclaimed, much to Moggi's amusement and delight. I smiled at his pleasure, although I could not help feeling my spirit sink at the idea of henceforth painting only to amuse locals with pretty illusions or for the contemplation of the Brothers, my days spent more and more in prayer to be released from this prison-like existence.

"I have brought you a little gift," added Yuanzhi. He held out a little polished stone, a reddish colour with many stripes to it. "I gather you have a collection," he added approvingly. Collecting such stones to appreciate their natural beauty was a pastime amongst the literati here, I knew.

"Thank you," I said. "You are too kind." In truth, what he had taken for a scholarly pastime was only a further sign of my struggles here. My collection of little pebbles did not come from across the empire and beyond, rather each was a reminder of the Garden. It had become a habit with me to collect a little stone from there each time I saw Niuhuru, a concrete reminder of an illusory desire.

Among the silken-soft petals in the Garden of my memories there is one flower made of cold stone, a flower taken from the wall panels of St Joseph's. Where the other flowers are warmed by the sun, even now beneath my hand I feel as I did then the unforgiving chill of marble petals.

May God have mercy on my wretched soul.

The Endless Palace

PEERING OUT OF THE SWAYING palanquin I am reminded that most of Beijing appears grey from a distance, for the roof tiles give the mostly single-storey buildings a uniform appearance. But our destination shines at the centre of this grey city, its red walls and swooping golden tiles reminding all who see them that this is the residence of the Son of Heaven, the Forbidden City, which houses thousands of eunuchs and thousands more maids and other servants, hundreds of craftsmen and courtiers, hundreds of women and yet only one man. When night-time comes a call goes out across the palaces, a warning that all those who do not reside here must leave at once. At night only two men are allowed to be here: the on-duty court physician and the Emperor. Any other man found here at night will be executed.

The blood-red outer walls tower so high above us that I cannot see their tops without being blinded by the sun. Dazzled, I lower my gaze. The great red and gold gates swing open and our many palanquins and cartloads of goods pass through. We travel through endless vast courtyards until we reach the Inner Court, our new home. The palanquins separate, clatter away down one tiny pathway or another, delivering each of us to our new palaces. Here we ladies will be separated by hard stone and high red walls, not water and pebbled lakeside paths.

The sounds of imperial life are sharpened here, each footstep, voice and movement accentuated by the hardness of the materials around us. The golden roof tiles stamped with roaring dragons, the marble-carved clouds entwined about pillars, doors opening onto doors onto doors. The endless, endless hard cobbles where once there was soft grass beneath my feet. High walls are everywhere. When I touch them my fingertips come away stained red from the powdery pigment used to paint them.

"Your garden, my lady," announces the eunuch who first shows me my new home.

I look about me in silence. A courtyard. A solitary sombre pine. Pots of flowers, falsely bright against the hard stone. Dark pitted rocks, twisted as though by some giant malevolent hand.

"All the way from the south of the empire," the eunuch assures me, awaiting my praise, my pleasure.

I turn back into my rooms of my palace. No expense has been spared, every comfort has been arranged for me. I wonder briefly which still-living concubine of the Kangxi Emperor once called this palace home before being swiftly relegated to some distant part of the Forbidden City as his last breath left her unwanted and invisible for the rest of her life.

What freedom I had is gone. If I stand, squatting servants rise from their corners, ready for my command. If I sit, they crouch back down, waiting to be summoned.

Lady Nara, since she was already Yong's Primary Consort, is now made Empress Xiaojingxian. My own name and rank is changed to Consort Xi, a new name for each woman, our previous identities left behind as we take up our new positions. Lady Qi is also made a Consort. I wonder how often she counts the steps between Consort and Empress, how she intends to become a Noble Consort and then an Imperial Noble Consort.

It takes Yongzheng a while to soften his edict regarding the house arrest of the Jesuits. Only once members of Sunu's family have been executed does he relent and allow them to serve at court again. I ask to see the coronation portrait, believing Giuseppe may be tasked with showing it to me but he is not there. I stand before the portrait of my husband, the Son of Heaven on the imperial throne, his yellow robes of state draped in silken folds about him. I reach out a hand and touch the silk canvas, knowing that Giuseppe must have touched this very point, that it was his hand that held the brush to make this stroke, and this one and this one.

"Come away," says Yan softly. I follow her back to the walls within walls within walls that now make up my home. There is nowhere else for me to go.

I stand with Kun in the courtyard of my palace and spread my hands. "Whatever you can do, Kun," I say.

He turns on himself, looking around the space. When he meets my gaze I know that my sadness and sense of loss is reflected in his eyes. We have left something beautiful behind and this place, awe-inspiring as it is, is no substitute for the tranquillity and delicacy of the Garden.

I see Kun outside every day afterwards, as he tries to bring a softer touch to the space, filling it with multiple pots of flowers, adding ornamental grasses to the base of the pine. He brings a metal sculpture of a heron and adds a wide brass basin, which he fills with water and tiny water lilies. He makes as much of a garden as is possible in this hard space.

I eat and am watched. I sleep and am watched. Where Yan would turn her eyes away discreetly when I sat to empty my bowels, here there are many more servants and they watch me closely, the better, they think, to serve me. I try to dismiss them when I wish to be alone and a few, so few, will leave my presence and the rest will simply crouch in corners, waiting for my next command, ignoring my desperate need for solitude.

When I find that solitude is impossible, I try to lighten my days with familiar faces. I invite the other concubines to sit with me. They come, but something has changed. We were friendly nobodies, once, concubines to a distant prince, kept in a soft world of flowers and water. There was no need for jealousy or suspicion. Now we are concubines to an Emperor, in a hard world of imperial glory and opportunity. Daughters who were once indulged are now dismissed as useless, for what is needed is sons, many sons. And it is my son who has been shown favour. The gossips do not even bother to lower their voices when they say that Kangxi gave the throne to Yong so that Hongli might become Emperor one day, it is considered common knowledge. Where there was once sibling rivalry between the many brothers of Yongzheng, any courtier worth the name would now swear that the name concealed within a golden box and placed behind the throne is my son's. And so the women I invite, who once treated me as a pet, perhaps even daughter-like, certainly no threat, now look at me warily. How has this woman, considerably their junior, leap-frogged them to a path destined for imperial power? The conversation is stilted and they refuse my offers to play mah-jong, even though I know they still play amongst themselves. My own son, filial and good-natured though he is, visits me, bows, brings me gifts and is gone again, a young man eager to assist his father, to explore the empire that will one day almost certainly be his.

My son reaches manhood. I am promoted again, given the title of Noble Consort. With each change of rank my robes reflect my status, each rank a brighter shade of yellow, headed inexorably for the imperial yellow that is my destiny because it is my son's. And time passes, even within these unending walls.

The Empress, Lady Nara, dies. A dutiful woman, a kindly woman.

I wear white. I set aside jewels and I join with the visits to temples to honour her name as she is interred with all due ceremony in the Western Qing Tombs.

"Are you ready?"

I look to my left, where Lady Qi stands beside me, her long hair loose, her face set in a mask. "For what?"

"To be made Empress, of course."

I don't answer.

"Who else should he choose?" asks Qi. "You are already a Noble Consort. You are the mother of his favoured son."

I swallow at the bitterness in her voice. This is what I dreaded, what I wished to avoid. Women who have become awkward around me or worse, those who now actively hate me for straying into their path to greatness. "I have no wish to be Empress," I say.

"You will forgive me if I do not believe you," she says. "You say one thing but events prove you wrong, again and again."

I am summoned by Yongzheng and kneel before him.

"You are to be made Empress," he tells me. "I will have it announced." He waits for my smile, for my kowtow. Perhaps he hopes for some closeness to emerge between us again, as it once did so long ago in a different place to this.

I stay kneeling but I do not kowtow. I do not smile. "I do not wish to be made Empress," I tell him.

His smile fades. "Why not?"

I shake my head. "I do not wish for such an exalted position," I tell him. "I beg you to choose someone else. You could choose Lady Qi," I add, thinking that the honour might appease her.

Yongzheng frowns. "Nonsense," he says. "Why would I choose her?"

I don't reply. Does he know nothing of Lady Qi's desire for power? I can see that he is displeased with my stubborn silence.

"Very well," he says at last. "You will not be made Empress."

I feel my shoulders sag with relief and hurry to perform a kowtow. "Thank you," I murmur.

But he has not finished with me. "You will, however, be known as my Primary Consort," he rules. "You will oversee the conduct of the other ladies of my court and you will carry out such duties as must be undertaken in the temples and during festivities."

I sit back on my heels, aghast, as he stands and leaves the room. He has made me Empress in all but name. When the announcement is made I see Qi's eyes slide towards me. I know without her saying so that she thinks me a liar, a backstabbing liar who claims not to wish for power and yet inexorably rises towards the ultimate position of power.

Embarrassed at my superior role over women older than myself, instead I try to befriend the new concubines, who are now in my care. Fresh-faced, glowing at being chosen to wed a still-young emperor, I find quickly enough that they regard me with fear mixed with resentment. Having passed my thirtieth year, I am already old to girls more than ten years my junior. They fear me because I am highly ranked but they also dislike me for having already produced a son who is all but certain to reach both the throne and the imperial yellow which everyone here craves for themselves or their offspring. Where is the room for them, where is the space that they must claim if they wish to reach higher levels of glory? They are angry, too, that there is no way to become Empress because I have refused the position and so, without even taking the role, have blocked the path to it for those younger and more beautiful, more fertile, more ambitious, than I. They squirm in resentful silence in my presence and I do not know what to say to break the invisible barriers between us. Instead I let them go and do not invite them again, no doubt to their relief as much as mine.

I sit alone, watched in silence, until I begin to think I will go mad.

I take my place on a carved throne and watch as hundreds of girls kneel before me in a courtyard much like the one I knelt in many years ago. This time I am the one to choose, for it is time my son was married. He has been named Prince Bao of the First Rank. I tremble at the thought of choosing these girls' destinies but my face must stay still and calm, my choices must be firm.

I glance down at the paperwork containing their names while the Chief Eunuch, vastly more experienced in this task than I, whispers delicately in my ear.

"Lady Fuca. An excellent family. Well bred. Gracious in her manner, no sign of arrogance, a dutiful demeanour to her superiors and elders. Well versed in etiquette. Filial. An appropriate choice for the Prince's Primary Consort."

I look the girl over. I am choosing a future Empress, a woman who must carry a heavy weight and carry it without seeming burdened. Who will feel destiny creeping closer every day and who cannot hope to escape it. I am choosing my son's future happiness. I swallow and incline my head a fraction.

The Chief Eunuch's loud voice echoes around the courtyard. "Lady Fuca! Chosen as Prince Bao's Primary Consort!"

The girl sinks to her knees and performs a formal kowtow to me and when she rises I see her face is a little flushed, but she seems content. This is a girl whose family fully expected such an honour, who have moulded her for this life. I whisper a prayer that she may be happy, that I have chosen well, as she is led away to her new home within these walls.

Other girls are chosen. Few stand out for me. Lady Gao. Lady Zhemin, a relative of Lady Fuca. Lady Su, a girl from a lesser background like my own, looks startled to be chosen. A frightened slip of a girl I hesitate from choosing, but when her name is called out, Lady Wan's face lights up in a radiant smile and I can only surmise that she has romantic notions of marrying a prince. I hope she will not be disappointed.

I pause. My son is young. He has many years ahead of him to add to his ladies. There is no need to choose any more. I shake my head slightly but the Chief Eunuch bites his lip, considering.

"Perhaps one more?" he murmurs discreetly. "For an auspicious number?"

I sigh. The eunuchs are obsessed with everything being auspicious. Numbers, animals, flowers, days… the list is endless. I nod wearily and look about the courtyard. The girls stand motionless in their expectant ranks. One girl catches my eye. She is beautiful, as they all are of course but right now, among a sea of anxious faces, hers stands out. She has a dreamy expression, her eyes are lit up with some interior happiness. I think yes, here is a girl who can find the good in life and who may be content in this strange place. I indicate her with a golden nail and the Chief Eunuch nods, agreeable. She is a Manchu and from a good family.

"Lady Ula Nara! Chosen as Secondary Consort for the Prince!"

The girl's face drains white and her eyes meet mine in shock. Any happiness she had a moment ago is entirely gone. She drops to her knees but does not complete the elegant kowtow to me, her future mother-in-law, that she should. Instead she crawls forward a little and addresses me directly, breaching all protocol. Her voice shakes so badly I can barely make out what she is saying.

"I do not wish to marry the Prince, my Lady. I beg you to let me return to my – to my family."

There are gasps among the girls. Heads turn.

I feel my stomach turn over. I have never heard of such a reaction to being chosen. I don't know what to do. I glance for help towards the Chief Eunuch, who is both appalled and furious.

"How dare you question the Emperor's Primary Consort?" he screams at her, his face red. "How dare you refuse the honour that has been bestowed upon you? You have been chosen and you will take your place among the Prince's ladies!"

He makes a tiny gesture to me and I rise, causing all the girls to drop to their knees. I begin to leave the courtyard but cannot help looking over my shoulder to where the girl Ula Nara kneels on all fours on the cold cobbles, her head down and her body shaking with sobs. The other girls stare in helpless fascination.

"Ignore her, my lady," advises the Chief Eunuch. "Some of the girls behave very oddly when they are chosen. It is only nerves."

"But what if she was promised elsewhere?" I ask, the thought only now coming to me. The moment when she paused before saying she wanted to return to 'my family', as though she meant to say a name?

He is remorseless. "What marriage could possibly be as advantageous to her as one to your son, the Prince?" he asks.

If she was in love with someone, I think, but do not say it. *If there was someone whose name she barely dared whisper, whose scent overwhelmed her, whose touch she longed for.* But I know better than anyone that such a thought is irrelevant here, where a connection to the Imperial Family is all anyone could ever wish for.

I am called to Yongzheng from time to time but whatever connection we once had has long gone. He has become 'the Emperor,' his brow ever more furrowed with his workload and his concerns. He wishes the empire to be well-run and all he can talk about is how it might be managed better, how corruption must be driven out and more stringent laws and taxes passed to ensure good governance. I admire him for his dedication but I do not understand all of what he talks about, nor do I find intimacy in it. So I lie quietly in his arms and when I am dismissed I call for Yan and she administers the Cold Flower, so that I will not be taken with child. I cannot find it in myself to desire another baby, to bring a warm, living being into this chilled world.

I embolden myself and tell Yan that I wish to see Giuseppe. Here in the Inner Court of the Forbidden City, I know full well I may never see him again if he is not summoned to my presence. We do not have the freedom to find one another by accident among the streams and flowers of the Yuan Ming Yuan.

"Are you sure?" she asks me.

"Yes," I say, although my voice shakes a little.

When he arrives I am seated on a throne in my receiving hall, a formality that I thought would give me courage but instead makes me feel awkward, as I look down on him. He gives a small nod when he sees me, as though he can see the choice I have made and understands it, or at least I hope he does. His bow is deep and graceful, as formal as my choice of seating. I hear my voice crack as I begin speaking.

"You are well?"

"I am well, your ladyship," he says.

I struggle to think what I can say to him. Nothing I want to say to him is possible. "I saw the coronation portrait, it is very fine."

He gives a faint smile. "I seem to have refined my technique so that it has become acceptable rather than inauspicious."

I nod. The silence stretches out between us.

"You have seen the other portraits commissioned by His Majesty?" he asks at last.

"No," I say. "What portraits?"

"I call them *masquerades*," says Giuseppe, smiling a little more. "It is a word from my country meaning masks. The Emperor dresses as one thing or another and is painted."

"Dressed as what?" I ask.

"A travelling monk. A hermit. A poet or musician. Such things."

I frown, unable to imagine Yongzheng dressing up as any of these things. "Why?"

He thinks for a moment. "Perhaps he feels burdened by his role," he says. "For an emperor so dedicated to his empire, some respite must be necessary."

I think of the endless papers in Yongzheng's study and the endless notations in the vermillion script used only by Emperors on them, of his tired face. I nod. "He should not work so hard," I say. "He should enjoy some time without work, but he hardly ever does."

"Perhaps he has the portraits to make him think of other things he might be doing, other lives he might have led?"

I consider other lives I might have led. Of a life in which I would be free to take Giuseppe's hand and walk away from all of this. What other lives does my husband dream of? A life where he, the Son of Heaven, owns nothing? A life where he can retreat to gentle pastimes of music and poetry, rather than the endless unfolding papers of state? I shake my head a little to bring me back to the here and now. "And you are well? Your own life is happy?"

He does not answer me at once. His eyes do not meet mine and at last he says, with great gentleness, his eyes steady on the floor between us, "I try to be well. I took my vows when the Emperor was crowned."

"Vows?" I ask, although I know already from his tone that this is not something I should pursue.

"The vows required by the Brotherhood, the Jesuits," he says. "Poverty, obedience and chastity."

I knew before he said the word what it would be, the tiny pause before he spoke that final word told me. What else might a priest vow? "You took your vows when the Emperor was crowned?" I repeat.

"When you left the Garden," he says and his eyes meet mine.

I am summoned to one of the great receiving halls in the Outer Court. My palanquin bobs and sways while I consider for what reason I may be called upon. I am not aware that I have left undone any of my duties. I expect to see my husband but I am mistaken.

"A concubine has been found guilty of taking a lover," the Chief Eunuch tells me.

I can't help it, I feel a chill in my stomach and have to fight not to clear my throat before I speak. "A concubine?"

"One of the old ones," he says dismissively. "A minor concubine to the previous Emperor. She was selected from the Daughters' Draft the year before he died."

I think of a girl, somewhere between thirteen and sixteen years of age, chosen as a bride for an old man. She might have been selected as his companion once or twice or possibly not at all before he died and when his last breath left him she would have been hustled away into some dreary back palace, away from us new ladies, we who had the good fortune to be chosen for a living, breathing, emperor. One of us lives now in what used to be her palace and her days are so empty as to be desolate. She may live another fifty, sixty years or more and never be touched, never be loved, never have any hope at all of advancement, whether through children or through her own charms.

"With whom was she having an affair?" I ask. There are no men allowed within the Forbidden City overnight and who would she come into contact with anyway, in the Inner Court? The maker of perfumes, the robe makers, the shoemakers? Most of these within the Forbidden City are eunuchs, skilled in such tasks. The monks of the many temples? Surely not.

"A eunuch," says the Chief Eunuch, his face appalled at this breach. While he himself does in fact have a wife, the only reason for the eunuchs' very existence is to keep well away from the Emperor's women.

I think of Yan and Kun, of a love that made an impossible leap and found itself somehow safe, wrapped in a warm embrace, blessed by some unseen deity who took pity on the fate of mere mortals and their suffering here on earth. I picture for a brief moment this unknown girl and her loyal servant, clinging to one another in their need for love and I feel my heart grow heavy.

"It is a matter for the Emperor," I say, knowing this to be untrue. If it were, I would not have been summoned.

The Chief Eunuch shakes his head. "The eunuch was under my jurisdiction and he has already been beheaded at my command. The girl comes under your jurisdiction. Her fate is in your hands."

"The Emperor to whom she was married is dead," I say.

"She was unfaithful to his memory," he says.

I am silent. This is not an argument I can ever win. There are too many dynasties and centuries of such rules for me to overthrow them in one conversation with a eunuch.

From the folds of his robe appears a white silk scarf. "You may give her this," he says.

I do not touch the silk. I am aware of what he is implying. I try to imagine how I can stand, face to face with this girl, younger than myself, and suggest to her that she should take her own life for having been unfaithful to the memory of an old man she probably saw a handful of times in her short life here before he died. I can feel my eyes welling up with tears.

The Chief Eunuch has spent his life in service to this court. He has risen to this position of power because he knows what to do at every moment, on every occasion. He is not unprepared for my weakness. "Does your ladyship wish for me to take the matter into my own hands?" he asks.

I hold out my hand and he gives me the silk. It is so soft, so light that I wonder if it is capable of the task for which it has been made. "Which palace?" I ask and he steps outside the receiving hall, to speak with my bearers and direct them.

My own palace is sumptuous, of course. I am all but Empress. The courtyard palace where we stop, somewhere on the furthest boundaries of the Inner Court, is a sad affair by comparison. The bright paints adorning the walkways are faded and cracked, peeling here and there to show the weathered wood underneath, grey with years of neglect. A few half-hearted flowers struggle to grow in the shaded light but most are fading as autumn creeps closer. The walkway which winds its way around the entirety of the courtyard has loose boards.

I dismount from my palanquin and stand by it, uncertain. I am very conscious of the white silk of the scarf I carry, its soft folds now crumpled from being gripped in my damp palm.

"An Empress? Here?"

I turn quickly. On the opposite side of the courtyard a woman has appeared on the walkway. She is wearing a robe that might once have been grand but is now faded, like her surroundings. "I am here – " I begin.

"For the bad one?"

"For the Lady – "

"I know who you are here for." She spits. "The young one. The fool who got caught."

"Where is she?"

Slowly, the woman makes her way round the walkway until she is near to me. Up close, she is quite old. She must be one of the Kangxi Emperor's first brides, her face covered in fine wrinkles, her eyes hooded by drooping skin. Her voice grates, cracks. "What are you going to do with her?"

I try to regain some authority. "That is not your concern," I say. "Where is the girl?"

She grins at me, showing a missing tooth, the others yellowed with age. "Where is the silk scarf?"

I hold it closer to my body but she catches the small movement and suddenly her face is serious. "It's true, then?" she asks and her voice quavers. "She must die?"

"Where is the girl?" I ask more loudly.

"She is not so much to blame, you know," says the woman. "She was so young when they chose her. Perhaps they thought a young one would warm an old man's bones, but he barely saw her before he died and then she was all alone."

I look about me to see if I can find someone else to speak with. I do not want to hear what I already know, about the unfairness of what I am doing, about the rules which govern all of us and which some simple girl has fallen foul of. I want this to be over.

"We are all alone," adds the woman, her voice an unending sing-song, reminding me uneasily of childhood stories about witches and their curses. "Alone and forgotten here."

"You are cared for as honoured ladies of His Majesty's late father," I say.

"We are forgotten," she says. "As you well know. None of us leaves this place. Our walls were once the walls of the Forbidden City, with his death they have shrunk down to the walls of this courtyard."

"I need to see the girl," I say.

The woman raises her chin. I turn to see a girl standing on the walkway where the woman first stood.

"Come here," I say too loudly.

The girl makes her way towards me, avoiding the loose boards with an unthinking familiarity that saddens me. She edges past the older woman with a bowed head, coming to stand in front of me, looking down at me from her place on the walkway. She is quite short and her frame is delicate. Her face is very pale, as though she has not seen sunlight for many months, even though summer is now coming to a close.

"Ladyship."

"I need to speak with you alone," I say.

Her small hand extends, indicating a dark doorway into the palace. I step up onto the creaking walkway and enter, hearing her move behind me as she follows. I do not turn to see if the old woman has followed us. Instead I stand still and gesture that she should come round to face me, which she does, standing before me in the poor light, her eyes fixed on my face.

"You should know that your conduct leaves me no option," I say. "Do you have something to say?" I expect a denial or begging for my mercy but instead the girl continues to stare at me in silence. "You don't deny your misdoing?" I want her to deny everything, to suddenly prove, somehow, at this late moment, that she was innocent, that there has been some mistake.

"I loved him," she says. "And he loved me. No-one had ever loved either of us."

I want to speak but I cannot. I want to say something – perhaps to threaten her to beg for mercy although I know that no mercy will be shown – perhaps to beg her to lie. But my throat is closed. What she has spoken is probably nothing but the truth: that since either of them had come to the Forbidden City neither had been shown kindness, nor tenderness, nor love. That somehow they found such things in one another.

"You know he is dead?" I ask. I curse myself for the hard tone that struggles out of my cramped throat. I want my question to frighten her into lying to save her life but she only keeps her eyes fixed on me.

"Yes," she says simply. And then, "May I join him?"

And it is I, all-but-Empress, who am silenced by this nobody-concubine's grace and power. I hold out my hand and she draws from my sweating grip the silent white silk, turns and walks away into the dark recesses of the other rooms of this forgotten and damned palace.

I dream of the Yuan Ming Yuan. I walk through the bamboo-lined path where I first met Giuseppe and the bamboos turn from their delicate green to a dark red as I brush past them. I pause by the lake where Hongli used to play and the water turns muddy at my approach. I follow a tiny path and it leads me on and on, twisting and winding to nowhere. I try to change direction and the path is always the same. I wake sweating and have to sit on the side of my bed, my bare feet cold on the floor so that I can believe that it was only a dream. When morning comes I send a messenger to Yongzheng and ask for permission to go to the Yuan Ming Yuan. I have not seen it for so long that I am beginning to forget it and I want to be there and reassure myself that the bamboo leaves are still green, that the water is clear and the tiny path will take me back to my old home, the wisteria-covered palace.

But the messenger returns with my husband's refusal. He says that it is autumn, too cold to spend time in the imperial summer garden. He looks forward to a summer visit there with me, next year. I think of the snowball fights Yan and I had there when it was my home year-round and want to disobey him, but I know that protocol does not allow for me to leave the Forbidden City without his permission. I am stuck here, with my dreams and the consequences of my actions.

I ask to see Giuseppe again, send word that I wish to see whatever his latest work in progress is. When he arrives it is with two eunuch apprentices, who carry with them a huge hand scroll. Such a scroll would usually be viewed little by little, but I ask to see the entirety of it. It takes them a long time to unroll the whole length of and when they do it stretches the length of my receiving hall. It shows a landscape and trees on a plain filled with horses, with mountains rising behind it.

"*One Hundred Horses,*" says Giuseppe. "A commission from His Majesty."

The horses are beautiful and of many varied colours. Some play together, others eat grass, some even race one another. In the distance are two men on horseback, perhaps hunting or rounding up the herd. I admire the painting for some time.

"This horse seems different from the rest," I say at last. In the centre of the scroll, although set a little way back, under the shadow of a tree, stands a brown horse. Unlike the well-fed and healthy horses depicted with their companions elsewhere on the scroll, this one stands alone, its gaunt sides plainly showing its ribs, its head hanging dejectedly.

Giuseppe looks at the scroll for a moment in silence. "He is," he says.

"He seems unhappy," I say. "Lonely."

Giuseppe's eyes leave the scroll and come to settle on mine. "He is," he agrees.

I drop my gaze. "You may leave us," I say and he bows and leaves the room before his apprentices have even finished rolling up the scroll, scurrying after him even whilst trying to bow to me.

"There is no need for you to see the girl," rules the Chief Eunuch. "It is done and she will be disposed of. You have done your part, my lady." He is pleased with me perhaps, glad that I am revealed as a woman who will act as is right and proper, who will carry out even the harder parts of her position and do it without mewling to him that it is too much.

I shake my head. "I gave her the silk. I need to see her," I say and once again my palanquin makes its way towards the forgotten palaces.

I follow the Chief Eunuch's splendid robes into darkness and more darkness and then my eyes see what there is to see. Two little feet dangle helplessly from the ceiling, one faded blue silk cloud-climbing shoe still attached, the other fallen to the ground. And higher still there is something too horrible to be looked upon, perhaps I catch a quick glimpse of a mottled face or perhaps it is only my shamed imagination and I stumble into the dingy light of the courtyard and vomit spatters down onto my own silken shoes and I retch and retch until there is nothing left in me and retch again and all the while my falling tears mix with the stinking mess at my feet.

The Maze of Yellow Flowers

THE NORTH-EAST SECTION OF THE Garden became unrecognisable. Where once it had been a peaceful place of tiny paths set alongside lakes and wandering streams, with miniature hills and tall trees, now the ground was torn up for as far as the eye could see. Hongli had received permission from his father to do with the Garden as he wished.

"It will be the greatest garden the world has ever seen, Giuseppe," he told me. "It will be like a fairytale. My father has already ordered the famous Southern Gardens to be replicated here. And you, Giuseppe, you must create for me a Western Garden."

"A Western Garden?" I repeated, uncertain of his meaning.

"Yes!" he said, eyes bright with enthusiasm for his new plan. "You must build me mansions, a maze, spouting fountains. Like the ones you used to show me when I was a boy."

I thought back to the books I had shown him when he was a child, curious about my homeland: the copperplate engravings of grand palaces around Europe, of spraying waterworks. I shook my head a little. "They would look odd here, your highness. Out of place."

"You said that in the West they are building Chinese gardens."

"Yes."

"You said they had become fashionable and that all the great lords had one."

I sighed a little. He remembered everything I had ever mentioned, even in passing, it seemed. "Yes, Highness."

He laughed. "Then a Western Garden shall be fashionable here!"

"I am not an architect, Highness. I could have Brother Moggi assigned to the task?"

"No," he said decisively. "I want you, Shining. Besides, you will have the Lei family to help you," he added. "They have been architects to the imperial family for generations. They will take care of any details with which you need help."

"Should they not be in charge, then?" I asked him.

He shook his head, stubborn. "I have chosen you," he said and smiled his broad smile, the one I remembered from his childhood.

I thought of the little houses I had once built for him by the lakeside, made of scraps of wood, tiny pebbles and reeds, how as a child he had found them entrancing. Perhaps his excessive trust in my abilities as an architect sprang from that childish admiration in my ability.

I tried to warn him. "It will take years, Highness," I told him. "Possibly many years.

And there will be much disruption to the rest of the Garden. It will take many, many taels of silver as well as an army of workers."

But he was a young man with a young man's enthusiasm, and furthermore, a young man who knew that he was destined for greatness, that although the current work had required his father's blessing, one day it would require only his own orders for his desires to be made reality. "Ask for what you need, and it is yours," he told me and was gone.

He was not to be dissuaded. I let a little time go by in case he should change his mind, but again and again he would return to the topic until at last, sensing my reluctance to begin, he ordered me to bring him books on Western architecture. These I begged from Brother Moggi and from them Hongli chose a selection of buildings that seemed to please him.

"This one, I think Giuseppe, and this also. But perhaps with a wall more like this one and a roof more like that. And the fountains could be like a clock, like a sundial – a water dial!"

I wondered at the strange collection of buildings he was creating in his mind. Certainly they would look like nothing recognisable from my own city. Their component parts did not fit together into a whole, they were like buildings drawn by a child, who adds any element they see fit, regardless of its intended purpose. I comforted myself with the thought that, at any rate, the so-called Chinese buildings in the gardens of the nobility of Europe were probably equally incorrect in their dimensions, their details, and their proximity to one another.

"So you will begin at once, Giuseppe," he told me with an air of finality that I did not dare to disobey.

"Your father?"

"He is busy with reforming the administration of the empire," said Hongli. "You will see little of him, Giuseppe, he works so hard. But he has given me his blessing to turn the Yuan Ming Yuan into something truly magnificent. He says it will be a place for him to rest, when he has the time."

I thought of Yongzheng when he was only a prince, how his taste had been for the simple in nature; the delicate blossoms of early spring, the bold colours of summer, the gentle decline of autumn in all its fading colours, the soft snows of winter. Buildings had certainly sprung up under his instructions, but for the most part they were built for practical purposes. A full complement of administrative offices and receiving halls had been built at one of the entrances to the Yuan Ming Yuan, so that he might work there uninterrupted and to enable greater efficiency when receiving and sending dispatches to and from the Forbidden City. Otherwise his preference was for smaller buildings, perhaps a little pavilion perched by the side of a lake, a dock at which to moor a rowing boat. Even the temples he had ordered built had been small by imperial standards, gently set into their surroundings so that it seemed at times that they might have grown there like the plants which were allowed to creep up around them. What Hongli had in mind was building on an entirely different scale. I looked at the selection of images that he had chosen and tried to imagine them within the setting of the Yuan Ming Yuan. They seemed odd, like something imagined rather than real and I wondered whether my own eye had changed in the years I had served here, whether I had forgotten these buildings of my youth, which after all had once been as familiar to me as the sweeping golden rooftops of the Forbidden City were to Hongli himself.

When I did see Yongzheng it was fleetingly. He visited us only once or twice during many months of work and I was struck by his pallor, the dark marks under his eyes.

"There is little time for rest," he acknowledged when I remarked on his appearance. "I try to make do with two *shi*, if I can."

"Four hours is a very little amount of sleep, your majesty," I said.

"There is much to do," he said wearily. "The administration of the empire has been neglected. There is much corruption that must be weeded out. My father was a great man but he was not much interested in such things. But it is the small things that make a difference, that will give us important powers for the future. We need more arable land to feed our growing population. There are too many children without families and they must be provided for. I have ordered that there must be more orphanages built. They will be paid for from the pockets of wealthy officials. It is their duty to model how people should behave, to show charity. The imperial examinations have only been available to certain families, but they must be made available to all." He sighed. "And our borders are always under threat. They cost millions of taels of silver just to maintain."

I nodded. "But your father lived a long life, Majesty. I am sure you will have much time in which to complete all of these works. Perhaps you can proceed at a slower pace and have time to enjoy yourself as well, perhaps spending more time here in the Garden – or at any rate," I added with a smile, "the quieter parts of it."

He looked about him at the chaos of Hongli's plans being put into action and gave a small smile. "The Garden is in good hands, Giuseppe," he said. "And for myself, I will hope to equal my father's long reign. My physicians give me daily doses of an elixir of immortality. I am sure it will fortify me for the task ahead. And now I must go, there is still much that I must accomplish today."

I bid him farewell but something of his weariness stayed with me and I thought of him often after that, though I saw him infrequently. I was of the opinion that he drove himself too hard, but he had always been a dutiful man even when he was only a young prince and could have pleased only himself. I knew from court gossip that he rarely spent time with either his children or indeed his ladies, although I could not bring myself not to feel a silent gladness that Niuhuru saw little of him.

I told Brother Moggi of Hongli's plans and enlisted his assistance. He agreed readily enough but flung up his hands in despair when I showed him the odd mixture of styles and buildings Hongli had chosen.

"Madonna mia, none of it fits together!"

I sighed. "I know," I told him, "but it is what he wants. We have no choice in the matter. Can it be done, or not?"

"It can be done, but it is an absurdity," he said, his usual cheerful demeanour affronted by this approach to architectural planning.

"I do what I am told," I replied. "That, at least, I have learnt in my time here."

"There is a new Brother who has arrived recently," said Moggi, looking over the drawings. "A Brother Michel Benoist, French. He is a hydraulic engineer. You will need him for the fountains, I will send him to the site."

Brother Benoist was a serious young man, still overwhelmed with his new surroundings. He nodded at my description of the fountain I wished him to design, which would spout water at each of the twelve hours of the day, but he looked taken aback, as had Moggi, at the rest of the designs.

"Think of it as an Emperor's whimsy," I said. "You need only make it work."

I saw him from time to time for many days afterwards, sat out of the way amongst the chaos of the building works, his shoulders hunched while he attempted to sketch the interior workings such a fountain would need, his brow growing ever more furrowed.

The Lei family had served as architects to emperors for generations. They, at least, were neither surprised nor discomforted by imperial decrees, however unusual. My first meeting was with Jinyu, who had taken over from his father as the chief imperial architect. He carried with him sheaves of paper and a worried frown.

"Thank you for your help," I said. "I am not an architect myself, I am a painter. But Prince Bao has been kind enough to entrust the making of a Western Garden to me and I will need all the help I can get."

He nodded and gestured to an assistant, who sprang forwards with a large box, which he opened to reveal a beautiful little model of one of the lakeside pavilions, made in Yongzheng's time as prince. "This is how we work," he informed me. "First the sketches, then we create the models, made to scale so that the Son of Heaven or the Prince may see how the buildings will appear when completed and request any changes before work begins."

I nodded. "They are wonderful," I said. "How do you make them?"

Jinyu's worried frown smoothed a little. Perhaps he had been afraid that I would insist on strange foreign ways of working. "We use clay, wood and paper," he said and reached out to the small model. Gently, he lifted away the roof, to show beneath the walls and interior rooms that made up the building inside. "Everything can be altered according to his majesty's command," he said.

I smiled, thinking that the generations of service the Lei family had offered to more than one dynasty had taught them well. They knew that an emperor's command could easily be rescinded on a whim and were ready to respond. "I like your models," I said. "These are the first drawings of what the Prince has requested. His father has given him authority over this project."

Jinyu studied my drawings for many days, along with the original copperplate engravings that had inspired Hongli, trying to become accustomed to the very different style of architecture he and his family would be required to deliver. We walked across the landscape discussing materials, while various assistant scribes took down his muttered notes on costs, timings and the labour required. His knowledge relieved me, for even though the structures were foreign to him, he quickly understood what would be required. We even visited St Joseph's together, so that he could see a Western-style building. He drew many sketches and asked even more questions, not all of which I could answer, although I did my best and also read to him from such books on architecture as we had available to us, fumblingly translating technical words.

"I did not think to learn much in the way of architectural terms when I learnt your language," I confessed to him. "I am afraid I am a poor interpreter."

He managed a small smile. "Rather a poor interpreter than none at all," he said, issuing every greater streams of notes to his hard-working scribes, noting especially the heights of the buildings and the great weights of the materials we would expect to use, for stone usually made up only a small part of his usual range of construction supplies. I grew to like and trust Jinyu over time, for all his serious demeanour, for he was a hard worker and a superb craftsman and did not resent Hongli's having chosen me as the originator of his Western Garden. We built a friendship of sorts, immersed as we were in the same project, with no way of escaping the imperial demands made of us until it was complete.

Brother Benoist stood by my side in a state of disbelief. "How many labourers are there?"

I stood amidst swirling clouds of dust and looked about me. There were so many workmen I could not even count them all, I would have had to refer to the long lists of men, animals, silver, tools and more that we had been granted for the works to commence. Surveyors hurried to measure the land and mark it out. Tiny models of the Prince's future pleasure ground had been created by the Lei family for us to consider. Many of the workmen's heads were all but invisible to me, hidden as they were in the trenches they had dug for the foundations of the palaces I was creating.

I shrugged. "As many as are needed," I told him. "Whatever is needed, we have been granted."

He shook his head. "This is madness," he said.

"Have you found a way for the Fountain to spout water to mark the hours of the day?" I asked him, returning to the task in hand.

He nodded. "That is not the difficult part, the difficult part lies in building a reservoir which will feed it with water," he told me. "An ugly reservoir is unlikely to please the Prince. He will want everything to be pleasing on the eye, he has no idea of the practicalities involved."

I considered for a moment. "We can still create an attractive building around the reservoir," I told him. "Something like this, perhaps." I took out one of my books, showing engravings of Western palaces, those that had taken Hongli's eye.

Brother Benoist shook his head. "This is how we are choosing the buildings to be created?" he asked, disbelieving. "Choosing them from a book rather than designing something appropriate to their function?"

"They have no function," I reminded him. "Their function is to please the Prince's eye. No one will live here. No one will use the rooms within them. Perhaps they will wander through the maze. Perhaps they will admire the Clock Fountain. But these are not real buildings."

"They are illusions," he said, his practical engineering approach offended by the commission. "Fairytales. Absurd."

"They are his childhood dreams," I told him, my tone defensive.

"Father Friedel says the prince behaves as though he were your son," he said, a little curious.

"He is all the son I will ever have," I told him and had to turn away as my voice cracked.

Hongli made frequent visits to our works. He was active in his admiration, leaping into foundation trenches, the better to see the work up close. On one occasion he attempted to dig a trench himself, his silk robes growing muddied while his attendants looked on in horror. He wanted to know every detail, listening to complex explanations of how each building would be erected, how the waterworks would be arranged and the exact carvings to be made on the stone walls of the maze.

"And will people really get lost in it?" he asked me, laughing.

"For a little while," I told him.

"Make it harder!" he said, his eyes bright with mischief, looking back at Lady Fuca, his Primary Consort, who had accompanied him, along with his other ladies. They stood well back from the mess of our works, a huddled group of fluttering silks and bejewelled hair, but when Hongli waved them forwards they tiptoed towards us, their high shoes unsuited to the building works around us.

"Giuseppe is building a maze in which you will get utterly lost," he said to Lady Fuca. "I will have to come and rescue you. You will be wandering there until it is dark!"

"I know you would rescue me before dark fell," she said placing one delicate hand on his arm and smiling up at him. "You would not leave me to wander alone and afraid."

He covered her hand with his broader one and gave her a tender smile. "I would run to your side at once," he assured her and for a moment the two of them gazed at one another, oblivious to those around them. Behind them I saw the other ladies giggle together, although one looked away from their show of affection. I wondered whether Hongli was aware that his obvious love for Lady Fuca caused jealousy amongst the other young women who had perhaps hoped for a Prince's favour when they had married him.

"We will return soon," Hongli promised me. He broke off a yellow flower from a straggling bush that had survived the works so far and tucked it into Lady Fuca's already-laden hair. "The maze should have imperial yellow flowers planted all about it."

I bowed as they left and made a note to myself about the flowers, one of many hundreds on a never-ending list of tasks still to accomplish. Hongli had also asked for an illusion on a scale I had never yet created. Vast awnings on cloth, to be mounted on frames near one of the buildings, then painted to resemble, far off, a little village. I had suggested building a small village but Hongli still remembered a *trompe l'oeil* painting I had done for him as a child and insisted that one should be incorporated into the Western Garden. The outlines must be put in place to ensure the correct perspective required for the illusion to work and even then it would still require most of the imperial studios' many artists to complete the work in good time. And the entirety would have to somehow be sheltered from the elements. It made me sigh just thinking about the work and planning required.

I took to arriving onsite each day before dawn, in the hopes of a few moments' peace before the men arrived. In the early days I would catch a glimpse of the deer grazing by the lakeside or see the night creatures returning to their homes. Hedgehogs and badgers snuffled through the half-built foundations and over piles of earth while bats swooped past my ears, returning to their daylight perches. But as time wore on these animals made themselves scarce, moving their burrows to other parts of the Garden, away from our noise and destruction. From where we worked, I could see only mud or dust, as the rain decided, piles of materials and felled trees, deep holes appeared everywhere while the air was filled with shouts and the curses of hardworking labourers. The plants and even trees were trampled on, felled, ripped out or moved elsewhere until our location was nothing so much as a barren wasteland. I thought longingly of the soft blossom and waving willows, calm lakeshores and shy wildlife only a few minutes' walk away but never found the time to leave the works and find some peace. Besides, I found out soon enough that the peace that I longed for was hardly to be had within the Garden at all. The Western Garden was the most ambitious of Hongli's projects, but other works were taking place across the length and breadth of the Yuan Ming Yuan. Larger palaces, a Southern Garden replicating those in the South of the empire complete with huge dark twisted rocks. More administrative offices, grander temples. A vast field of pots filled with lotus plants and tended to daily by the gardeners, the better to create a glorious view of flowers come the summer. The Garden I had first encountered when I arrived here was changing, slowly but surely, into something else entirely. I missed the delicacy I recalled from twenty years ago. I remembered how I had first seen it, the sensation that I was the first to discover each little pathway, charmed by its air of secrecy, as though it were a garden forgotten by the world outside.

I returned to St Joseph's from time to time and for once found pleasure in the silence of the lengthy prayers.

"The exterior design is all yours," Brother Benoist told me as he delivered me the drawings indicating the interior workings of the fountains. "I am tired of it already. It has given me too many sleepless nights."

"I had in mind something classical," I told him. "Perhaps twelve women, each pouring water?"

But when the time came for me to create the design I found that each woman became Niuhuru. Again and again I cast my mind back to the Grecian and Roman ideals of womanhood and dutifully outlined their form and yet each had something of her. Their hair fell straight rather than in artful curls, their eyes took on her almond-shaped delineations until my sketches were blurred with lines drawn again and again, while little clumps of soiled bread gathered beneath my table, smudged with the charcoal they had erased.

My suffering was ended by Xiyao. He stood behind me to view my progress and visibly recoiled when I showed him my designs.

"Naked women are an unsuitable subject matter for an imperial building," he told me.

"They are not naked," I pointed out. "There will be drapes of fabric carved into the stone, to cover their modesty."

Xiyao was adamant. "It will not be approved."

"The Prince wants a Western Garden," I told him. "This is a very classical design for a fountain. I have seen scores of them in my home city and further afield, with far less clothing."

"Not in China," he told me firmly and I gave in, in part out of relief at no longer struggling with thoughts of Niuhuru.

Instead I thought back to the illustrations I had seen of the Gardens of Versailles, with their creatures from Aesop's Fables, each spouting water at a given time. I drew a design incorporating twelve seated figures, made up of enrobed human bodies with animal heads, each one a creature from the Chinese Zodiac. Brother Moggi raised his eyebrows when he saw them.

"Are you sure the Brothers will approve such a heathen theme?" he asked, his voice echoing slightly in the quiet of the chapel of St Joseph's where I had chosen to sit in a pew and contemplate the final design.

"I no longer care," I told him. "I am tired of the noise and dust and confusion of the works. They are never-ending. The Garden used to be a peaceful place."

I woke half-blinded by a bobbing lantern held too close to my face while one of the brothers shook my shoulders.

"Brother Castiglione! Wake up!"

I shielded my eyes from the lantern. "What is it?"

"You are summoned by the Emperor!"

"At night?" I knew full well that the Forbidden City was locked up at dusk, that no-one entered or left.

"The guard said it was urgent."

I stumbled into my clothes and followed the lantern outside, trying to judge the time. I had already completed the prayers of Matins before returning to my rest, marking the deepest point of night, or so it seemed to me. Yet there was no sign of dawn. Outside a palanquin stood ready, surrounded by guards and two lantern bearers. Their faces were pale in the darkness and I looked behind me to see if others of my brethren were to join me but it seemed I was summoned alone. I took my place inside the palanquin and it was lifted at once, its bearers breaking into a full run so that I clutched at the sides to steady myself. I had never been carried at such a pace before and I found myself afraid. Was I, a man, really to enter the Forbidden City at night? For what purpose? Had I in some way offended Yongzheng? I thought with a sudden shudder of the portrait I had painted years ago of Niuhuru, standing startled outside her home, her eyes fixed on me. Had it been found somewhere and hinted at something more than had ever taken place between us? And even as my mind protested, so something small and cold inside me thought of our lips together and acknowledged that I had certainly offended against the emperor and now I was about to be punished for it. Was this how executions were arranged? Was this how my life would end, summoned in the darkness to meet my maker in silence and secrecy? My knuckles grew tighter on the sides of the palanquin as I was carried closer to my destination. I heard the challenge by the guards on the gate and the muttered response from my escort, then the heavy sound of the gate to the Forbidden City opening.

The bearers ran on. I could not stop myself from looking out. I had never seen the Forbidden City at night and it was an eerie place, seeming larger even than it was by day now that it was empty of its usual bustle. Here and there lanterns burned and by their light I glimpsed silent guards standing immobile on their watch as my palanquin raced past them. We passed each of the great halls as we headed towards the Inner Court and suddenly we were out of the wide-open spaces and into the never-ending pathways between the palaces of the imperial family. I felt the cold settle into my stomach as I recognised Niuhuru's palace and believed my fears to be made real. I took a couple of slow steps from the palanquin, almost braced for a guard's heavy hand on my shoulder but the guards and bearers stood still, their faces devoid of expression. The small figure of Yan appeared in the doorway, urgently beckoning me in.

Inside the sudden brightness of many lanterns burning dazzled my eyes and for a moment I thought that time had somehow reversed, for Yan and Niuhuru stood before me, their faces white with fear and behind them in the alcove of the bed, panting for breath, lay a young prince. For a moment I believed I was seeing Prince Yong as he had been when his brother had sought to poison him to eliminate him from the rivalry for their father's throne but then I heard Yongzheng's voice behind me and fell to my knees. When I looked up the Emperor's face was pale and I could see the fear of the women reflected in his eyes.

"Shining. I am grateful to you for joining us."

I rose. "Majesty. I am at your service. What has happened?"

His voice shook before he mastered it. "My son is ill. His mother believes him poisoned and she begged me to summon you. She says you were of great use to her when I myself was poisoned."

I turned back to the bed, now seeing Hongli's face where I had mistakenly seen Yongzheng's. In a few strides I reached him, knelt by his side and saw to my horror that within his mouth his tongue was black. I looked up over my shoulder to the three faces hovering over me. "Lady Qi commanded the services of a physician when you were ill, Majesty, perhaps we can summon him now?"

The Emperor's face darkened. "I believe Lady Qi's son Hongshi to be behind this," he told me and even in my horror I noted that Yongzheng was already disowning his own offspring.

I glanced at Niuhuru and saw tears falling down her face. "Send for the imperial physician," I said, speaking as though I was confident in my orders. "There must be something that can be done."

"He is on his way," said Yan.

The physician's face drained of colour when he realised that he was tasked with saving the known heir from poisoning. But he set to, his eunuch assistants working smoothly at his side, brewing foul-smelling liquids and grinding strange concoctions.

"You will report to me on his progress," said Yongzheng to me. "I must speak with Hongshi."

I bowed as he left us and then turned, helpless, to Niuhuru. "I do not know what to do," I confessed to her.

"I am so afraid," she whispered. "If he dies…"

I held my hand up to stop her. "He will not die. Do not speak it."

"But…"

"Do not speak it!" I said and the physician turned to glance at me, a foreigner raising his voice to the Primary Consort of the Emperor. I ignored him. "Yong… the Emperor survived," I said, conscious of the taboo of having spoken his old name. "He was strong and Hongli is younger and certainly no less strong. He will fight this."

I did not know a night could be so long. The brightness of the lanterns inside the room stung my eyes and more than once I looked out into the darkness of the courtyard and hoped that I would see the dawn, something to give me hope and yet the darkness all around us seemed endless, our false light a mockery of Hongli's blackened tongue and closed eyes. I wished all of us could sleep, that we could escape this night and still it wore on.

When the dawn finally came I told Yan to open up the doors and windows.

"It will be cold," she objected.

"I cannot breathe," I told her. She flung open the doors and windows and the chilly autumn air rushed over us as Hongli let out a moan that had us all running to his side.

"He is awake," cried Niuhuru and it was true, his eyes flickered open and he blinked at us before closing them again. To my relief I saw his tongue seemed a more natural colour and he seemed to breathe more easily.

"Is he over the worst?" I asked the physician.

"I believe so," he replied. "The dose must have been small or he must have eaten less of the dish than his poisoner would have wanted."

I thought of the food tasters, the tiny strips of silver that were always included in every plate of food for the imperial household, how the eunuchs swore that poison would turn them black at once and reveal hidden dangers. "How could he have been poisoned?"

Niuhuru's voice was harder than I had ever heard it, her face hidden from me, buried in the silk coverlets covering her son. "He was practicing archery with Hongshi, who offered him water from his own water bag just before Hongli came in to eat. Perhaps he thought we would think it was the food at the meal and not the water that harmed him, but Hongli already felt sick before he began to eat."

I thought back to the elegant young man who had presented himself so correctly to his grandfather the Kangxi Emperor, hoping for favour, who had instead been passed over for his younger half-brother Hongli, the child prodigy who had broken all protocol to sit on his grandfather's lap and chatter to him of his passions. I remembered Lady Qi's desire to be Empress Dowager one day and thought that her son would surely have been raised with ambition burning in his heart.

"What will happen now?" I asked.

The physician began to list the curative and strengthening substances and treatments that Hongli must endure, how rest was imperative, how certain energy lines must be stimulated to return him to full health. But Niuhuru was not listening. She stood up and when she turned to face me I saw both terror and rage in her face.

"She tried to kill my son," she said. "She has gone too far."

Niuhuru rarely wore full court robes but in the great receiving hall of the Outer Court she took her place beside Yongzheng and I saw the might of an empire about to come crashing down on any individual foolish enough to believe they might shake its foundations. Lady Qi, her face white and her hands shaking, was made to stand before them. Her son was nowhere to be seen.

"The son of this miserable woman has been banished from the Forbidden City," began Yongzheng. For a usually quiet-voiced man, the echoes of his pronouncement filled the huge space without difficulty. Lady Qi fell to her knees, as though about to beg for mercy but the Emperor continued speaking as though he had not seen her.

"This unworthy son's name has been stricken from the *yudie*."

Lady Qi let out a wail of horror.

I turned my head to a courtier I knew and spoke under my breath. "*Yudie*? 'Jade plate'?" I had not come across the term before.

"The imperial genealogical record," he whispered back. "He is removed from the record of the Emperor's offspring."

"We can only hope," continued Yongzheng, "that this dishonour will lead him to take the only possible action expected of a man."

Lady Qi screamed.

I looked to the courtier, uncomprehending while around us the court stood in silent acceptance.

"He will be expected to take his own life," murmured the courtier.

I looked at Niuhuru's face, set in a mask. When she spoke her voice was controlled. "Lady Qi will be removed from her palace and will join previous ladies of the court in the back palaces."

Lady Qi crawled towards the throne, her voice a sobbing pant. "I ask for mercy. For my undeserving son and for myself, his unworthy mother."

"No mercy will be granted," said Yongzheng. He rose to his feet as Lady Qi was grabbed by guards and dragged from the room, her screams echoing around us. The room quickly emptied and I made my way towards Niuhuru. I did not speak, only looked at her.

"She found my lack of ambition suspicious," said Niuhuru and up close I saw that her voice had not trembled only because her jaw was clenched too tightly. "She thought I must be ambitious in secret, to have risen so far. But why would any woman wish to risk the life of her son by rising above others who crave power? To achieve what?"

I shook my head. "We cannot know what fate has in store for us."

Niuhuru let her hand touch my sleeve for a brief moment and I saw that she was shaking. "I cannot live like this," she said. "I cannot, Giuseppe."

"Come back to the Yuan Ming Yuan," I said in a low voice, knowing the offer was meaningless. "I am making a Western Garden for Hongli. He will get better and he will be happy again."

She tried to smile but her lips did not move as they should and her eyes filled with tears. "I was so afraid," she whispered. "I thought…"

"He will be well," I assured her and I allowed myself to lay my hand over hers for the briefest of moments before she nodded and hurried away, leaving me standing in the great hall. I tried to quieten my emotions, breathed deeply.

"You must be a great comfort to Lady Niuhuru," said a quiet voice.

I turned, startled, for I had thought the throne room had emptied entirely. Just behind me stood one of Hongli's consorts.

"Lady Ula Nara," I said, bowing. "You must be relieved that the Prince is making a recovery."

I thought she might smile, or nod in agreement but she met my gaze without expression. "Lady Fuca is by his side," she said.

"Of course," I agreed. "Although I am sure he would find the care of any of his ladies a comfort at this time."

She blinked slowly, as though my remark was foolish. "His Highness only has eyes for Lady Fuca," she said.

I smiled as kindly as I could, noting that there must be some rivalry between the young consorts. "Considering what has just happened, it is best to put aside rivalries if possible," I suggested. "We must take love where we find it and be content with what we find."

She looked down at my sleeve, where a few moments ago Niuhuru's hand had lain and my own hand had covered hers. "Take love where we find it," she repeated, her voice distant, her eyes glazed as though seeing something far away.

I felt a little shiver of fear. What inferences might an unhappy young girl make of what she saw between Niuhuru and I, what use of such glimpses might she make? "I will leave you now, your ladyship," I said and bowed. I walked away, fighting the desire to turn my head to see if she was still watching me, certain her eyes followed me as I left her.

Hongli was recovering, I heard, so that my heart lightened each day that I received the court reports on his health, although I was certain I would not see him for a while, as the imperial household closed ranks around their future emperor and the household physician would barely let him out of his sight for fear of a relapse of some kind. I sent him a little painting of an auspicious sleepy hedgehog in the Yuan Ming Yuan, the sort of thing he used to want me to paint as a child and in return was sent a message urging me on with the works in his new Garden. His father the Emperor could not come himself, I was told, for he was once again plunged into the endless paperwork and reform of the empire in which he had buried himself. I thought of how pale, and how much older he had seemed, despite having reigned only a short period so far. It seemed to me that his Elixir of Immortality was misnamed, if it could not even keep him in good health now, in the prime of life.

I had begged Kun's services as chief gardener for the Western Garden and Niuhuru had granted his release from her services. He frowned at the drawings I showed him.

"I know, it is not the kind of garden you are used to," I said. "But I want you to manage the garden elements around the buildings, Kun. I trust you."

He smiled. "I will do my best."

"I know you will. It must look odd to you," I added. "But the gardens of the West are very formal. They are mostly developed around circles and lines and the designs are to be followed to the letter."

"Where are they supposed to be viewed from?" he asked.

I nodded. I had expected this question. Kun was used to designing tiny scenes within the imperial gardens, each one to be viewed from a particular place, sometimes a section was to be framed with a moon-gate, a circular opening in a wall which forced the eye to see the garden as it had been created, a rock placed just so near a tree, a path winding out of sight, leading the gaze. The Yuan Ming Yuan was full of small artificial hills which restricted what could be seen, alongside tiny walkways which tempted the visitor to follow them to yet another elaborately created visual masterpiece disguised as only the work of nature when in fact it had taken much labour and sometimes whole seasons to achieve the desired effect.

"They are to be viewed from above," I told him. "That is the best effect of their shapes, their designs. And the viewer should be able to see for long distances, not one small scene but many, one after another, to show the grandeur of the Western Garden in its completeness. To impress them with the greatness of the Son of Heaven and all his dominion."

"It seems plain," said Kun. "Most of the plants are without flowers. Just bushes, cut into shapes?"

I thought of the great water dragon Kun had fashioned for Hongli when he was a child, the tiny painted gingko leaves made to look like fluttering butterflies. Cutting green bushes into balls and cubes was hardly making the best use of his talents. "He does want yellow flowers all around the maze," I said. "You will have to content yourself with those, Kun."

He nodded and collected up the drawings I had made. "I will need many men," he warned me.

I spread my hands. "The Prince will give you whatever you need, you know that," I told him. "Ask and it is yours."

I watched him walk away, a quiet figure amidst the chaos of the site and not for the first time I envied him. Kun always brought with him a sense of calm, of contentment, of joy in the small things. And somehow fate had smiled on him in bringing him Yan and making their love into something possible, no matter how unlikely it had seemed at first. Their daughter Chu was grown to a woman now, known by all of the ladies of the court for her exquisite embroidery, her nimble fingers recreating in silk the flowers her father coaxed from the earth. I wondered how one impossible love had been made possible while another was forever out of reach.

The men were almost finished for the day. I walked to the lake's edge to wash my face before returning to the site. I nodded to Jinyu, who was engaged in rolling up the scrolls depicting the buildings we were engaged in creating. Already the water reservoir was in place, now about to be hidden behind a cascade of stone carvings and flourishes to conceal its true function of providing the water for Brother Benoist's clockwork fountain. The stone statues waited, their bronze heads cast with mouths agape but as yet empty. Facing the fountain was an elaborate viewing platform, where the Emperor might sit in comfort to observe its workings. The workmen were packing up their tools for the night, for dusk was creeping in.

"You are not done, Shining?" asked Jinyu, seeing me pull a large ball of string out of my pocket.

I shook my head. "I am trying out a new layout for the maze," I told him, fixing one end of the string to a little wooden stake and pushing it into the earth.

He looked at the wide area of flattened earth surrounding the already-built central point of the maze, a small stone pavilion. "Do not get lost!" he chuckled and told his men and the workers to leave the site.

I smiled and waved him goodnight, then took up a little bundle of the wooden stakes. The design was already drawn up, but often, I had found, designs changed when they took up their place in their appointed locations, as though the place itself had plans of its own and the results were often better. I had already had lanterns placed around the pavilion so that I might work on it in the half-darkness. Hongli had said that he wanted to walk the maze by night, with flickering lanterns making the paths of the maze still less certain than in daylight. I thought that perhaps if the maze were to be used by night I would benefit from seeing how it might look at night. In truth I also knew that I wanted time alone, that the long noisy busy days tired me and that the Brothers' not unreasonable expectations that I should devote more of my time to prayers and theological conversation wearied me even more. With the workmen gone the Garden was at least quiet again even if my immediate surroundings were hardly in keeping with the rest of the Yuan Ming Yuan: here were no streams or lakes, no little pathways and delicate flowers. But as the men's voices faded into the distance I could at least begin to hear the croaking frogs from the nearest lake and the last songbirds' twitters before they regained their night's nesting spots.

For a while I walked steadily, my little bundle of stakes slowly diminishing while my string wound this way and that, creating imaginary pathways that only I could see in the dim light of the lanterns. At last I stood within the pavilion and looking down saw a woman's form standing outside the area I had marked out.

"May I walk with you?"

Her voice shocked me, it had been so long since I had heard it here. "Where is your palanquin?" I asked. We were some distance apart but the silence around us meant we could hear each other clearly.

"I told the men to leave me at the temple to pray. I said I would return to them when I was done and then I walked here."

"In the dark?"

She laughed a little. "I have walked the Yuan Ming Yuan enough times to walk it with my eyes closed."

"There might have been a new stream or lake dug since you were last here."

"Then I would have drowned."

"A risk."

"A risk worth taking."

"For what?"

She was silent.

I gestured in the dim light that I would join her. "May I guide you through the maze?"

She shook her head. "I thought those who walked in it were supposed to get lost. You should stay there and I will try to reach you."

I smiled. "You may try to walk it alone, if you wish."

"Where do I start?"

I gestured. "There will be a main entrance there. Then you enter and all of the pathways are designed to confuse you, to have you wander lost."

"And if I succeed?"

"Then you should reach the pavilion at the centre," I said. "Your son wishes to hold celebrations at night here. He thinks all his ladies should run along the paths holding little lanterns while he waits in the pavilion to reward the winner."

"Reward her how?" she asked and I heard her smile.

I did not answer. I did not trust my own voice.

"My son is a romantic," she said, walking forward to the starting point I had indicated to her. "Will he give Lady Fuca a guide to the maze, do you think? So that she may reach him first? He is besotted with her. I am happy for them both."

"Not all his ladies are so happy," I said.

She paused where she had reached what would one day be the gate to the maze. Her voice was sad. "I chose that girl," she said.

"Ula Nara?"

"Yes."

"I am sure it is seen as an honour for the girls to be chosen," I said.

"She begged me on her knees not to choose her," said Niuhuru. "I let the eunuch persuade me it was only nerves. But I knew it was more than that. I walked away from her while she knelt on the ground sobbing."

"I don't know her background," I said.

"She was promised to someone else," said Niuhuru. "She was in love with a young man and I chose her to marry Hongli."

I thought of Ula Nara's glazed expression, as though she was forever looking at something I could not see, how she had spotted something between Niuhuru and me that we had believed was hidden. "I am sorry for her," I said.

"I thought she would forget him," said Niuhuru. "But she has not."

We stood in silence for a moment and then Niuhuru began to walk through the strings I had laid out. I watched as she paused before choosing each new path to take, as she realised mistakes she had made and heard her chuckle softly to herself. I leaned my hands on the pavilion's carved ledge and knew that when she reached me I would be unable to resist taking her in my arms. I felt myself gripped with a strange sensation of mingled fear and desire.

She took her time. Once or twice I saw her hesitate before a path that would have led her to me and then turn away, as though she, too, was half-afraid of what would happen when she succeeded. At last, coming close, I saw her hesitate before she lifted up her face to look at me. I stood in the pavilion and looked down on her. It had grown fully dark and I was grateful for the many lanterns I had ordered lit, not because they had guided my work nor her steps but because now we could clearly see one another's faces. I am not sure how long we stood like that, each of us searching the other's face before she stepped forward, standing at the base of the pavilion, her pathway to me clear. I moved from my spot to the top of the stairs and held out my hand to her.

"Niuhuru," I said and heard her low answer, "Giuseppe," before a shout came from the darkness beyond the maze, a man's voice, desperate.

"Ladyship! Ladyship!"

I took her hand then, but not in the way I had intended, the two of us trampling over the string pathways to reach the voice and when I saw the guard I knew something terrible had happened.

"Hongli?" gasped Niuhuru.

The guard shook his head. He was a big man but he looked afraid and he had broken out in a sweat. "The Emperor is ill."

My mind was befuddled as though I had been drinking. "Ill?"

"On his deathbed," panted the man and then all three of us were running in the darkness.

My horse kept pace with her palanquin without difficulty, even though the bearers ran as though their lives depended on it. In the darkness all I could hear was their panting breath and the hooves of my mount. I wished that she could ride with me or I with her, anything so that I could be close to her and speak with her, to know what was going on in her mind. The distance to the Forbidden City had never seemed so great.

Yan was waiting, hovering anxiously on the walkway of Niuhuru's palace while behind her Hongli paced up and down. Kun, better at managing his emotions, squatted in the courtyard, rising to his feet as we entered. Too late I thought that we should not have arrived like this, side by side, in the pale dawn when I should have been in St Joseph's and Niuhuru should be within her own palace, since the gates of the Forbidden City had barely opened. But Hongli did not comment on this. Instead he knelt before Niuhuru and asked for her blessing. White-faced she gave it and at once Hongli was guiding her back to her palanquin while he took to his, calling to me over his shoulder.

"Wait here, Shining. I will have news sent to you at once. You must manage my mother's household until my return."

I nodded but he was already gone and I entered her rooms, uncertain of what to do. Certainly there was no need for me to manage anything, for Kun and Yan were in charge here and so I allowed Kun to hustle the servants away to their tasks while Yan motioned to me to sit, for I was pacing in front of the window. She stayed with me, fetching me a cup of hot tea before quietly retreating to her embroidery in a corner of the room. She faced away from me, towards a window, and did not speak to me, for which I was grateful, for I could not have formed words. My mind was only a jumbled mass of half-done thoughts. What did I hope for? That somehow things might change? The only change to come was one I could foretell well enough.

Time slipped by. I watched the sun slowly move across the sky until the growing darkness outside warned that I would soon have to leave the Forbidden City. I felt a great weariness come over me. At last the words that had been swirling inside of me all of the previous night in the Garden took shape. I spoke out loud, addressing myself to the soft glow surrounding Yan's work, a little lantern lighting only her hands. I thought that I must say the words within me, that if I did not speak them now, to someone, to anyone, that something in me would die.

"I dream of her," I said, and saw Yan's back stiffen at this sudden moment of truth. "I don't mean that I fantasise about a life together," I added. "I do not sit like some lovelorn boy and imagine that one day I will take her hand and walk away with her, that we will leave the Forbidden City with her son's blessing and that I will take her home with me, back to Milan, where my mother will embrace her as a daughter-in-law. I am not a fool."

Yan turned as I spoke and now her eyes were fixed on me. She had always been small, as though a little stunted in growth, but her eyes were very dark and there was a sharpness to them, as though she saw through the lies fools might try to tell her, as though she saw into what you said and understood something beyond mere words.

"I dream of her," I repeated. "I sleep and she is there. I can spend my day working and I would swear to you that she has not crossed my mind, that my thoughts were empty of her. And yet as my eyes close, so she is there. I do not summon her, I try not to be so weak. But she is there, Yan, she walks in my world. If I have painted the hunt, I see her through falling leaves in the forest. If I have painted some noble courtier's dog, she caresses its fur. If I walk by day in the Yuan Ming Yuan, where she no longer is, that night I will walk there again and she will be by my side. I dream of her, Yan."

In a quiet corner of my memory palace, there sits a stunted little figure, who sews and sews and whose dark eyes see all truths. I visit her often, kneel by her side to hear her speak, to remember again the fierce joy I felt on hearing her reply.

"If she has not visited the Emperor's bed willingly these many years it is for fear that he will hear her speak your name in the darkness. When she dreams of you."

I opened my mouth to ask her more, to beg her to sate my desire to hear Niuhuru's feelings but behind Yan the door opened and Kun's face left me in little doubt of his news.

"The Yongzheng Emperor is dead," he said. "Hongli is named the Qianlong Emperor."

The Palace of Motherly Tranquillity

SCARLET AND YELLOW LEAVES FALL into the black and white world of our mourning. Our robes are white, our hair hangs loose, seeming blacker now that it is bereft of jewels and flowers.

Everywhere we go there is chanting and incense. Rows upon rows of monks chant for the passing of the Yongzheng Emperor and to bring in the reign of the Qianlong Emperor. At first the chants are soothing, they block out unnecessary conversations and unwanted thoughts. But soon they begin to grate on me.

"Close the windows," I tell my servants and my rooms descend into deeper gloom as they try to shut out the noise. A useless effort, anyway, for I am required, as Primary Consort to Yongzheng and as the mother of his successor, to attend more ceremonies than I knew existed. I kneel and bow, light whole fistfuls of incense. I try not to choke in the swirling clouds of perfumed smoke that surround the court as we move from one ritual to another.

I watch as the women who were once my peers lose their palaces and status to make way for a new generation of court ladies. Lady Mao, who first welcomed me to the imperial family. Ning. Zhang. Chunque. I think of them all, playing mah-jong by the lakeside in the Yuan Ming Yuan, greeting me without jealousy. Qi will already be there, locked in a world of bitter grief after Hongshi killed himself. Even the younger ladies, who joined the court after Yongzheng took the throne, are not spared. Some of them are still in their twenties. All of them are taken away to the back palaces on the very edges of the Inner Court, where no-one ever visits, to join whichever crones of the Kangxi Emperor still live. I shudder in fear at the idea that one of them will be caught in an affair and that I will have to pass sentence again. I think to remonstrate with my son, but this is how it has always been, how it always will be. Only I am allowed to stay within the central complex of palaces, by virtue of having inadvertently birthed an emperor.

The most desirable palaces in the Inner Court do not sit empty for long. The Palace of Eternal Spring is given to Lady Fuca, my son's newly-enthroned Empress. She takes up her destined post without apparent fear, perhaps made confident by my son's evident love for her. Lady Ula Nara is located nearby to her, her face frozen in silent misery since the day I took away her smile. Little Lady Wan, a delicate girl, fills her palace garden and hair with flowers, apparently happy with her lot although Qianlong seems to treat her more like a sister than a concubine. One by one the palaces are filled with young women, the consorts of our new Emperor, each one ready for a lifetime of petty rivalries and struggles for promotion through the uncertain ranks of imperial favour.

I do not cry. My eyes water from the incense and yet the tears will not come. I sit and tell myself all of Yongzheng's virtues as a man and as an emperor and still there are no tears. My eyes are red from the smoke. No doubt the courtiers will think that I cry in my rooms and my servants must think that I cry when I am in the temples. But I do not cry. I try to remember the first time I met Yong, when he was only one prince among many princes and I was just a child. I remember his frown looking over my cold naked body and his covering my shame and still, I cannot cry.

My son comes to me. He, too, has bowed and burnt incense in vast quantities.

He kneels before me and I put my hand on his head. "Are you well?" I ask.

He looks up at me and I see tears well up in his dark eyes. He is still a young man and he has a warm heart. Given his grandfather's long reign, he might have expected to keep his father for longer. For a moment he is silent. But he manages his voice so that it emerges steady when he speaks. "I am well, Mother." He rises and sits in a carved chair by my side. "I have arranged for you to move palace," he tells me suddenly, as though to change the mood.

"Move palace? To where?" For one frightening moment I think I, too, am to join the women in the forgotten palaces, to be made invisible since my husband is dead. But of course I have forgotten. I am now the Empress Dowager, the greatest woman at court. Even the Emperor must kneel to me. There is no higher position.

"I have chosen a new palace for you. It is the largest amongst the ladies' palaces. I have renamed it the 'Palace of Motherly Tranquillity'. You may have it decorated however you wish. Spare no expense."

He waits for my admiration and gratitude, but I only look at him in silence.

"You must have the best," he tells me, earnestly. "You are my mother. It is my filial duty to see that you are happy."

"I am happy enough here," I tell him.

He shakes his head. "You must have the best," he says and then he is gone again, to attend some essential ceremony before his coronation.

He is crowned. My son is now the Qianlong Emperor. His own childhood name, Hongli, becomes taboo just as Yong's did and I must bite my tongue not to call him by it when I see him.

I am visited by the Chief Eunuch. "His Majesty will wish to call upon you in a few days' time, in your new palace. He will serve you breakfast."

"Breakfast?"

The Chief Eunuch is in a hurry, he has much to do and does not wish to be explaining what seems obvious to him, after his many years of service here. "Yes. You will be seated at a table outside the Palace of Motherly Tranquillity, so that the entire court can see you and he will kneel before you to present you with dishes from the table, thus demonstrating his love and filial devotion for you, his only living parent. It is most important that the Emperor should be seen to be filial."

"I have not even moved yet," I tell him.

"Well, the palace chosen by the Emperor as your abode is in need of renovation," he admits. "But it does not really matter. You will be outside it for the ceremony and the façade is being worked on as we speak."

Yan wakes me in darkness and helps me to dress. I swallow when I see the imperial yellow robes laid out for me. I feel the cold silk slip over my skin and look down at the hue worn only by three people: my son, his newly-promoted Empress Lady Fuca and myself. The colour envied, strived for, desired by so many men and women over the years here and worn by so few. Raging dragons mark out their territory across my thighs while at my hem a stylised sea ripples. I take a deep breath and step outside my palace, where a palanquin in the imperial yellow takes me to my official residence.

Some of the paint is still wet, I can smell it. The large façade is bright with gold and red, with every manner of decoration, pristine in the watery dawn light. The courtyard in front of it is huge, it could hold a few hundred people. Inside there has not been enough time to do any work and the dusty rooms are empty and faded. I step outside, where the servants are laying out a table. Maids with covered dishes of food wait nearby, ready to step forward. Courtiers and guards fill the courtyard in rows of multicoloured silks, our mourning now halted to celebrate a new ruler. Behind the bright colours I can see a figure in sombre dress. Giuseppe, ready to make a sketch of this ceremony, capturing Qianlong's filial devotion to his mother.

There is a stir and everyone readies themselves as two yellow palanquins arrive, followed by many more in bright colours. As my son emerges there is a ripple of silk and a clatter of weaponry as everyone present falls to their knees, their faces hidden. Only I remain seated and upright.

Qianlong steps slowly and gracefully up the stairs to where I am sitting. My son has always had a sense of occasion and at this moment he is all too aware of the eyes of the whole court upon him. He makes a tiny gesture and a maid hurries to put a little bowl into his hands. Kneeling carefully before me, he lifts up the dish so that I may take food from it.

I take a small bite and smile at him but his face is very serious. He offers me dish after dish and I taste a little of each before setting it aside. At last the charade is over and he kneels to receive my blessing before he returns to his palanquin and leaves, allowing the court to follow in his wake. Only Giuseppe remains. His assistants have hurried away his work for safe storage. He hesitates, then approaches me.

"At least I know I will be well fed by my son, now that he is Emperor," I say, trying to sound light-hearted.

Giuseppe's mouth smiles but his eyes remain serious. "I am sorry for your loss," he says.

I take refuge in formality. "He was a most devoted and hardworking emperor," I say. "His reforms have left a great empire for his son to inherit."

There is no-one in the courtyard. The courtiers have all gone and only Yan stands by, waiting for me to give the signal to summon my palanquin from the other side of the palace. Giuseppe steps a little closer to me, reaches out and takes my hand. I almost draw back but allow my cold fingers to be warmed by him for a moment.

"He was a good man," says Giuseppe. "I will never forget his love for the Garden and how happy he was there." He pauses. "As were we."

And the tears that should have come before come now. I put one hand to my mouth to stifle my sobs while Giuseppe watches me. He does not try to comfort me with words, nor does he step closer, he only holds my fingertips in his warm hand and keeps his steady gaze on me as I weep and weep for a serious man who once forgot his duties and loved me.

The Studio of Exhaustion from Diligent Service

"**A** NEW PAINTER IS TO JOIN US," said Laura.

I looked up. "New?"

"From France. But he studied in Rome, so we will be able to speak together in Italian."

"His name?"

"Jean-Denis Attiret."

"How old is he?"

"Thirty-six, I believe."

I nodded. "He will have a great deal to learn."

Laura smiled. "You will have to teach him," she said.

I sighed. "I am fifty this year," I told her. "And I begin to feel weary."

"Are you grown old all of a sudden?" she asked, laughing.

"I feel old," I said. "Especially at the thought of a young man who has much to learn and whom I must teach."

I was a little relieved when I met him, for Jean-Denis lacked neither enthusiasm nor talent. His works depicting animals were particularly fine and he was already accustomed to painting on a variety of surfaces, from silk to glass, which would stand him in good stead. He nodded seriously while I showed him examples of traditional Chinese paintings and explained how we had struggled to find new ways to modify our *chiaroscuro* techniques to create something pleasing to both our eyes and those of the Emperor and his people. I gave him various small commissions to carry out, that he might learn the style and he showed himself to be a quick and diligent pupil. I could not but wish I had had someone who could have shown me how to change my own ways when I had first come here, rather than struggling to find a path alone.

Jean-Denis was devout too, in a way that gave me pause for thought. His certainty of his purpose here as a missionary first and foremost, his undoubted skill as a painter wholly in the service of the Brotherhood, would protect him from the paths Laura and I had both found ourselves on.

"We would have found this work easier if we had had his piety, I think," I said to Laura.

"Easier?"

"We would not have looked beyond God for love," I said and we were silent then, together.

I knew that despite having taken my vows I continued to be a source of concern to Father Friedel, now an elderly man. The lavish gifts I received from Qianlong honouring my service worried the Father, for such honours made him think that I was less devoted to the Mission and more to the court and my imperial patrons. I saw his face when bolts of the finest silk were delivered to me, when food was regularly sent from the Emperor's table. Even a sculpture of Jesus on the cross caused him to frown, carved as it was in precious jade. The seemingly innocuous gift of a summer hat turned out to be regarded as an unheard-of honour and therefore even more worrying. My growing preferment at court could be counted in paintings, for where I had created only ten works for Kangxi and one hundred for Yongzheng, I had already surpassed two hundred works for Qianlong in a shorter space of time than either of his predecessors.

"Now that the new Emperor is enthroned," said Father Friedel, "I have in mind that you, Giuseppe, would approach him with a petition to undo the severity of the edicts of his father."

"We are forbidden from discussing matters of a political nature with the Emperor," I reminded him.

"He has a filial demeanour towards you," persisted Father Friedel. "It would be remiss of us not to attempt a reconciliation towards our religion through the relationship you have built up with him since he was a child."

"I will try," I said cautiously, although privately I thought Father Friedel could well be damaging my relationship with Qianlong past repair, which seemed a great risk. I was painting a portrait for Qianlong and had a sitting the next day, although I was obliged to hide the petition in my robes, for if the eunuchs admitting me had seen such a thing they would have removed it from me at once. Once in his presence, I knelt and pulled out the petition. The eunuch attendants looked on in horror.

"What is this, Shining?" asked Qianlong.

"It is a humble petition from the Order," I said. "They ask that you withdraw the condemnation of their religion."

"I do not condemn it," he said. "I simply forbid the Bannermen and their families to convert to it."

I prostrated myself, anxious that Qianlong might take offence at my request. "We mean no harm by our request, Majesty."

He nodded. "I will read your petition, Shining."

The eunuchs were not as forgiving. I was searched every morning from then on to avoid the possibility that I was carrying similar documents. Father Friedel was relieved when some small softenings of the edict were made following my meeting with Qianlong, but I refused to intercede any further.

"I am a painter first and foremost, not a missionary," I reminded him. I could see him struggling with the desire to insist, to force my vow of obedience to the Order, but in the end he let the matter go.

Despite his enthusiasm and willing effort, even Jean-Denis found his new life hard sometimes. He was reprimanded by Qianlong for not taking well to watercolours, having been at first reluctant to give up his oils. And he did not like the food, preferring, as did many of the other Brothers, more familiar tastes from home. Laura and I had long since adopted the diet of the Chinese, for the food that the Brothers preferred seemed plain to us now and besides there was always the risk of offending the Emperor if one did not eat the food at court, since dishes from his own table were seen as a sign of preferment.

It was a hot afternoon when I heard Jean-Denis throw down a brush with a vehement exclamation in his own tongue, which I took to be a string of oaths.

"Is all well?"

"I do not know how you have borne this life with such patience, Giuseppe! You must be a saint."

I shook my head. "Hardly, Jean-Denis. What troubles you?"

"To be attached to a chain from day to day, to have time to say one's prayers scarcely even on Sundays and feast days, to paint almost nothing according to one's own taste or aptitudes, to meet a thousand other difficulties. It would make me want to return home if I did not believe that my brush were useful for the good of religion, to make the Emperor more favourable to the missionaries who preach it. That is the only thing that keeps me here!"

I patted his shoulder. "All of us have such moments," I told him. "I think perhaps you have been working too hard and been cooped up too much in the Forbidden City. I will ask permission for us to visit the Yuan Ming Yuan, that you may see something different."

As I expected, Jean-Denis recovered much of his good humour when he saw the Garden.

"It is as big as Dijon!" he exclaimed, once I had shown him the extent of the grounds.

I nodded. "It is a vast place. I have been lost here many times," I confessed.

"Does the Emperor like your buildings?" he asked, when I showed him the Western Garden.

"He likes them well enough for play," I said. "But our different storeys piled one on top of the other are intolerable to the people here, they prefer buildings to be of one or at the most two levels only. They fear they will break their necks if they must ascend so high as to a fourth or fifth story!"

We spent a long time in the Garden and made many sketches. It was a peaceful day and one that brought both pleasure in the surroundings, which I had missed, as well as some sadness for days long passed and for my youth, which I saw reflected in Jean-Denis' vitality.

"I will write home describing this place," he said with enthusiasm. "No-one at home could imagine such a place, such beauty that seems as though made by nature yet is the fruit of man's artifice."

I nodded. I myself had written few letters, only the odd request for materials or books. Jean-Denis, by contrast, was an inveterate writer, always scribbling away, much like Laura with her diary. I saw her writing in it most evenings after we had finished eating, her blonde head bowed over the pages. I knew that she must have stored many volumes of her thoughts somewhere.

"You are cautious with your words, I hope," I said to her once.

"I cannot hide my thoughts from myself, Giuseppe," she said, smiling.

"No, but from the prying eyes of others," I said.

She was silent for a few moments. "If I die before you," she began.

"Unlikely," I said. "I am considerably older than you."

"You would protect my thoughts?" she said, ignoring my interjection.

"By destroying them?"

She shook her head. "Not if it can be helped."

I nodded. "I will protect them if I can," I said.

"Otherwise I may well vanish," she said, attempting a smile. "For there would be no-one left to remember me."

"I would not forget you." I said.

"And when you are gone? We have no children to speak our name after we depart this life."

"Enough of such talk," I said. "I have only just managed to make Jean-Denis smile again."

Our days settled back into a routine, now with three of us at work, our assistants and apprentices by our sides. The studio was always busy, there was always one new commission or another to add to the many already in progress: from enamels to paintings. We spoke little to one another except when a new commission was sent and then we would gather, the three of us, to consider how best to complete the work. More and more I tried to give Jean-Denis and Laura work that I might otherwise have undertaken myself. I told myself that I was being a good master, that it was my duty to encourage their works and that as they were highly experienced artists in their own right, it was only proper that we should share the work more evenly. But in truth I was growing tired. I had served three emperors now, over more than two decades. And there was something missing from my life, something I had dismissed as a young man full of ambition but which I recognised now as a lack. I had taken my vows knowing what it was I was giving up, for it already had a name, but as I grew older the yearning I felt did not diminish, as I had perhaps expected, rather it grew greater and I knew of no way in which it could be assuaged.

Father Friedel had another request for me.

"A Chinese novice has baptised abandoned children," he said. "And has now been beaten and accused as a criminal. Will you intercede for him with Qianlong?"

"You know that this may damage Qianlong's preferment for me," I told him, but he was adamant.

Qianlong shook his head, as I had expected. "Do not concern yourself with such matters, Shining," he told me and I did not see him for some time afterwards, a deliberate sign of his displeasure which only added to my weariness. It seemed to me that I had spent my life here torn between two lives, whilst longing for a third.

"Master?"

I opened my eyes and looked up at the young eunuch's worried face. I, his master, was lying on the floor of my painting studio, my eyes closed until he spoke to me. Perhaps he was afraid I had died. He can barely have been twenty and I was almost fifty. I probably seemed ancient to him.

"Yes?"

"His Majesty has a commission for you."

I stifled a sigh. "I will be with His Majesty directly," I said, waving a hand to dismiss him.

He hurried from the room and I sat up, wincing at a sudden twinge in my back. The hard floor sometimes soothed such pains but returning to my feet often undid the good work of lying still. In truth, the pain was not even so bad, but there was a growing weariness to my life that drew me to the floor and sometimes made me wish never to rise from it again. Slowly I regained my feet, gathered a few materials, stepped outside the studio and nodded to the bearers waiting with a palanquin.

The familiar rhythm of the ride brought familiar thoughts. A commission from the Emperor. Once, I would have been excited by such words. The Screen of Twelve Beauties, coronation paintings for Yongzheng and then his masquerade albums, the Western Garden, the inaugural formal portraits depicting Qianlong at the start of his reign alongside his Empress and eleven concubines: all of these had been both challenges and honours such as should have pleased any court painter of ambition. But in the past few years my enthusiasm had waned. I wondered how long my life would be and whether I would serve yet another Emperor one day. It was unlikely, I supposed. Qianlong was in the prime of life with a magnificent and wealthy empire at his command. He might well expect to live as long as his grandfather. For a moment I thought, *I will die serving him,* and despite my fondness for him it seemed as though someone had pronounced a prison sentence over me. To continue to be at the whim of a monarch who might demand anything of me, who was not to be gainsaid, whilst longing for something I could never be free to choose... but we had arrived.

Qianlong, as I had expected, was exuberant. "Shining!"

"Your Majesty."

"I have a commission for you. Something special."

I bowed.

"My rooms and gardens are to be entirely refurbished. Entirely." He was already unrolling a scroll to show me details of plans. I recognised the seal of the Lei family, newly released from their work on the now completed Western Garden and its palaces.

"*Studio of Exhaustion from Diligent Service*," I read out loud.

"Yes," he said. "I have renamed it. I think it suits me, don't you?"

"Yes, Majesty," I said, smiling a little. The idea of Qianlong being exhausted from anything seemed unlikely.

"There is a private theatre within the complex," he said. "I wish you to decorate it inside. You may use whatever design you think best. I trust your judgement entirely."

I bowed. Qianlong was fond of saying such things and no doubt meant them, although he could also suddenly change his mind and insist on some entirely different motif once work had already begun. "Your Majesty is kind."

He beamed. "Tomorrow I am taking my mother to the Yuan Ming Yuan," he said. "It is a long time since she saw it and so much work has been done to beautify it. She will scarcely recognise it!"

I thought of the first time I had seen Niuhuru, how I had been lost and wandering through the Garden, with few landmarks to guide me. How since Qianlong had taken the throne one building after another had appeared – not just the Western Garden and all the palaces he had commanded me to create but across the whole of the Yuan Ming Yuan: temples, walkways, pavilions, new offices, palaces, bridges, boathouses equipped with magnificent dragon-headed boats and more. "I hope the changes will be to her liking," I said.

"She will be delighted by them," said Qianlong.

The space I was shown into was large and had fine proportions. Set against the back wall and jutting out into the room was the stage itself, a miniature pavilion on which the actors could play out their stories. The rest of the room would be set out with comfortable seating – chairs or cushions according to the Emperor's command. It was unfinished; the delicately made bamboo flooring was still being fitted while the ceiling and walls were bare of any decoration: my commission. I stood for a few moments with my hand resting on the empty wall, my eyes drawn to the plain ceiling above me. I felt devoid of inspiration. I considered various scenes, various auspicious symbols. Remembering Qianlong's delight in my works of *trompe l'oeil* I sketched a bamboo fence, inset with a circular open gate, a moon-gate as they were called, through which further buildings and gardens could be glimpsed, leading the viewer to fancy themselves in a garden looking outwards rather than inside a building. A pretty enough idea, but it did not interest me much. I spoke with my apprentices, explained once again the concepts of forced perspective, had them mark out key points on the walls so that they might begin the work under my guidance. I thought back to my first efforts at introducing perspective, how much I had struggled. Since then Xiyao had written a treatise on the subject. I had worked with him on it and now its use was more and more widely accepted.

"And the ceiling, Master?"

I looked up at the empty expanse above our heads. Perhaps a blue sky, with soft clouds? But that would not be detailed enough, not of enough interest. I closed my eyes and of course she was there, as ever, the way I had first painted her, the wisteria of her little fairy-palace falling about her.

"Wisteria," I said. "Growing across a bamboo *pergola*." Without thinking I had used my own tongue for the word. "A gazebo," I clarified. "Made of criss-crossed bamboo with the wisteria trained to grow across it. It will add to the illusion of being seated in a garden."

The apprentices nodded eagerly and continued their work. I watched their bustle, their enthusiasm for the project and felt nothing. The work was not of interest to me. I had painted such illusions too often, the magic of them had gone, for I saw only the artifice behind them. I had come here wanting to do something magnificent and nothing I had done felt important enough.

Laura listened to my complaints about the Studio and shook her head. "You had better hope Qianlong does not decide you must refurbish all the rooms in the Forbidden City," she teased. "There are supposed to be nine thousand, nine hundred and ninety-nine of them in all. You are lucky you are only refurbishing the Studio."

"Why not just have ten thousand rooms?" I asked.

"Ah, they say that Heaven has ten thousand rooms," said Laura. "And that it would be presumptuous of the Emperor to have more rooms than there are in Heaven."

I shook my head. "All I need is a quiet place," I told her. "Even the painting studio is always full of apprentices. They make my head ache with their endless questions."

"You will need to find a secret quiet place," said Laura. "There must be one amongst the nine thousand, nine hundred and ninety-nine that will suit your needs."

"Where do you go when you need silence?" I asked her.

"There is a little garden behind the church," she said and I saw a blush rising on her cheeks.

"You go there alone?" I asked her, knowing the answer already.

"I go there because it is the place where I am happiest," she said and turned away, back to her own work.

I wanted to warn her, to tell her that what there was between her and Guo was forbidden, but I could not find it in me to remind her of what she already knew. The only happiness I could achieve was in my work and it wearied me.

"Nonsense," said old man Lei, patriarch of the Lei family, when I said as much. "Your scroll depicting the hundred horses is a treasured piece in His Majesty's collection. And many other examples of your work are highly praised. And I understand that Nian Xiyao has dedicated his book, *The Science of Vision*, to you, in admiration of your ideas on perspective."

I smiled. He was a kindly man and took a more practical approach to his own work than I perhaps did. His family had served the emperors of China for generations and he knew their work would outlive us all. But when he was gone I lay on the floor of my studio again. I could not think of the theatre with excitement. It bored me and my own boredom saddened me. I thought of Niuhuru, even now being taken to the Yuan Ming Yuan by her son and wondered if she, too, would feel that the place she had once known had somehow disappeared beneath too many layers of beauty, like a known acquaintance transformed into something otherworldly for a part in the opera, making one squint to recognise them under the costume and extraordinary makeup and somehow unable to see them at all.

"The illusion is wonderful," said Jean-Denis when he viewed the work in progress in Qianlong's theatre. "Will you instruct me further in its execution? I know the essentials, of course, but you are a master at it."

I nodded without replying. Jean-Denis' enthusiasm should have been pleasing to me, but it only added to my weariness, reminding me of myself at a younger age. I oversaw the work on the theatre each day and as each day waned I returned to my studio and lay alone on the floor, gazing at the colourful ceiling tiles, my mind so unwilling to think that I did nothing but count them, over and over until they seemed to swim before my eyes. Thirty of them, all the work of a craftsman who had cared about each and every one, or perhaps had not. Perhaps he had outlined every shape while his eyes saw something else, a life he had never been able to achieve.

"Qianlong has issued a death sentence on five Dominican missionaries," said Father Friedel, his wrinkled face pale. "We must stand by our Brothers in Christ. Will you intercede with His Majesty on their behalf?"

I shook my head. "He will refuse," I said simply. "You must know him better than this by now. My preferment as a painter, even his kindnesses in my regard, do not mean that he will listen to anything from me concerning the Order."

As I had expected, when I steeled myself to beg for mercy, Qianlong only shook his head. "You do not understand our customs, Shining," he said without rancour. "Continue your work. We will not speak of this again."

The missionaries were executed and I saw Father Friedel's disappointment, but I was used to the Order's disappointment in me as a missionary by now, it meant little enough.

"Shining!"

Fortunately when Qianlong came on an unexpected visit the studio I was not, in fact, lying on the floor. "Your Majesty. I am honoured."

Behind him were a group of his ladies, all looking about them with curiosity. I called for refreshments and had some of my apprentices unroll scrolls of works in progress. I watched them as they peered at the scrolls and pointed, commented on a painting showing the hunting season and smiled as they identified known faces.

"I believe you are enchanted by my ladies," said Qianlong, teasing. "Perhaps one of them has caught your eye?"

The women giggled.

I smiled. "They are all charming, Your Majesty, but I am quite sure they only have eyes for you. I am an old man and they are far too beautiful for me."

Qianlong was laughing. "But you must choose one!" he cried. "You, who have a painter's eye, must say who is the most perfect!"

I thought of Qianlong's own mother, her face now a little worn from when I had first seen her, strands of grey in her hair and yet to me more beautiful than any of the ladies present, exquisite as each one was. "I have not looked at them so closely, Majesty," I said. "I have been counting the tiles on the ceiling."

"Have you now? And how many are there?"

"Thirty, Majesty," I said.

Qianlong made a fuss about counting each and every one and laughed heartily when I was proven correct. "You are too good, Shining," he told me, clapping me on the back. "Surely even a priest may *look* at a woman?"

I smiled but did not answer and Qianlong grew serious again. "I am writing a new edict," he said. "You are to be made a Mandarin."

I shook my head. "That is too great an honour, Majesty," I said, thinking of the Brothers and their horror at the very idea of my being made a senior official. Such a change in my status at court would only remind them once again that I was not as dedicated to their missionary efforts as they would wish, that I was being rewarded as the painter I was, rather than the priest they still hoped I might be.

Qianlong shook his head at me. "You see, Shining," he said. "You are too good. Too modest. I will not force you to accept it now. But one day you must, you know. It is the post of Mandarin or marriage to a beautiful lady, you will have to choose!"

I endured more of his teasing for a while, but when he had gone I dismissed all of the apprentices. I thought of how relieved the Brothers would be that I had turned down such an honour. They would praise me for my devoutness, for my obedience to the Order.

"He treats you with great respect," said Jean-Denis, perhaps a little over-awed.

I nodded. "I have known him since he was a baby," I said. "They place great importance on respect for their elders here, even when they outrank them. He was taught to bow to his tutors as a boy, even though they all knew he would be Emperor one day."

"Do you think," began Jean-Denis but I waved him away.

"I am very tired," I said. "Perhaps we should finish for the day."

He nodded and cleared away his tools, then stood waiting.

"I will join you soon," I said. "Hurry or you will miss prayers."

He hesitated for a moment, before scurrying away. His devotion to Our Lord was true and honest and I knew that he found peace in prayer.

When he was gone I lowered myself to the floor, counted the tiles above me, and wept.

On a low stone wall of the Garden of Perfect Brightness where all my memories now reside there sit discarded, side by side, a crucifix and the bright red hat of a Mandarin. Either might have been my motive for decades of service in a land far away from my birth, yet neither are what held me here so long.

Vast Empty Clear Mirror

"YOU WILL BE ENCHANTED," PROMISES my son, riding alongside me. He has insisted that we should ride on horseback together to the Yuan Ming Yuan. I am nervous about seeing the Garden again. I wish I were his Empress, quiet and untroubled in a palanquin a little way behind us: she does not remember the Yuan Ming Yuan of the past, my son will not eagerly watch her face to see her every reaction to the changes he has wrought.

Yongzheng spent a little time there during his brief reign but rarely brought any of his ladies back there once we had arrived in the Forbidden City. Qianlong has deliberately kept me away, intent on completing the Western Garden and its palaces before I am to see them. He knows nothing of the evening I spent there with Giuseppe and anyway I saw little of the works: towering creations of carved stone in the half-light alongside still-open trenches, bundles of plants waiting to be planted. My eyes were fixed on Giuseppe and on the strings that might take me to him. I know that Qianlong has not just had works completed in that small area, either. He has incessantly told me of new buildings and bridges, of improvements to waterways and the enhancing of views: manmade hills focusing the eye on what should be seen rather than the eye being free to see what it wants. But my son is brimming with pride and I determine to like what he has done. It is still the same place, after all: there will be waterways and flowers, little paths and birdsong and I will go back to my own little palace to see the flowering wisteria. So I smile at him and nod my head as we ride away from the Forbidden City and towards the Garden, a vast procession of guards and courtiers and officials, Qianlong's own ladies, eunuchs and maids. We are to stay in the Yuan Ming Yuan for a few days, the better to enjoy all its new delights.

"There is even a surprise for you," says Qianlong, his eyes gleaming.

The roads have been improved, the earth pounded down and made hard, with straighter ways and well-managed planting to either side. The carts at the back of our procession will do well here. The Grand Palace Gate and its surroundings, have been enlarged and refurbished, the red doors freshly painted, studded with brass that gleams from polishing. As the doors swing open I see late blossoms, delicately planted terraces of flowers, a pathway turning to the left and one up ahead and my heart lifts a little. Yes, it is more managed and a little grander but it is much as I remember it. All will be well.

Qianlong calls for silence, he halts our procession and calls just a few of us forwards: myself, the Empress, his other ladies, a few courtiers of high standing. We are perhaps thirty people.

"The rest of you will enter by the Western Gate," he decrees. "I wish our party to enjoy a surprise I have arranged."

The vast procession moves away from the gate, trundling onwards to the where my old home lies. It takes a little while for the sound of them to die away. I hear birdsong and cannot help but smile. My son beams back at me.

"Now we must approach quietly," he says. "Come!"

I think that perhaps he has brought some animals here who are shy: swans and their cygnets, deer and their fawns. We walk quietly along the little path that turns to the left. There is a courtyard of low-built buildings which did not used to be here and although they are elegant enough I believe they are probably storage rooms for gardening implements and other such necessary but unbeautiful objects. On the other side of them will be one of the larger lakes, with a tiny winding path that one can follow throughout the Garden, a walk I often used to take Qianlong on as a child. He would play on the edge of the water, a stick in one hand, poking at the tadpoles and reeds while the gentle sunlight shone down on us and I looked this way and that for a glimpse of Giuseppe's robes. We step out of the courtyard and I turn right, onto the winding path.

Ahead, a cacophony of noise suddenly erupts. More than one of the ladies shrieks. I stand still, blinking.

The entirety of the road before us is lined with red stalls, each manned by a eunuch dressed as though he were a market trader. Up and down the road pace their customers: courtiers in their finest clothes, laughing amongst themselves at the role they are playing, mock-bargaining with the eunuchs, who offer their wares: grilled meats and bowls of hot noodles, caramelised fruits on long wooden skewers, pretty fans and table-games with intricately carved pieces, hairpins, cooling juices and warming teas. In a long winding row by the lakeside, blocking the view of the water, stand singers and musicians, performing a popular song. From the trees hang caged birds, perhaps to provide birdsong, although their inhabitants only flutter from one part of their cages to another, ruffled by the noise from below.

Qianlong is laughing. "You are surprised! I knew you would be. I know my ladies cannot enjoy the market streets of Beijing and so – I have created them here for your pleasure!"

Lady Fuca clings to his arm and smiles up at him. "It is astonishing! May I bargain with the stallholders?"

"Bargain all you wish," says Qianlong, waving her towards the endless red stalls, bright with streaming pennants. "But you know that all they have is yours to command."

The other ladies and the courtiers come forwards, exclaiming at the stalls, the music, the gaiety. They immerse themselves in my son's play-world as though they were children, sipping drinks and pretending to haggle over the non-existent prices of a fan or a silken scarf.

I try to look through the wall of musicians and glimpse a new raised wooden walkway that juts out onto the lake, culminating in a pavilion. I think to move towards it, to reach a quieter area but Qianlong is already at my side.

"Noodles?" he asks and I have to follow him, to express pretend outrage at the price the eunuch says the noodles cost and applaud Qianlong when he beats him down to a something more acceptable. I have to eat the hot noodles and drink the broth, I have to exclaim when a eunuch acts the part of a pickpocket and robs the Emperor himself and is taken away by eunuchs dressed as guards, I have to smile so that my son will be happy with his surprise.

At last I take his arm. "Your Western Garden!" I say, with great brightness. "I have not yet seen it! Take me there." I hope for a long quiet walk around the Sea of Blessings, to leave behind the noise and the madness, but Qianlong waves the courtiers and ladies along with us, nodding to the musicians to accompany us, so that I cannot escape at all.

The palaces of the Western Garden tower above us, immoveable and strange to me in their squat stone heaviness, incongruously topped with blue or green glazed roof tiles in our own style. The fountains spout gurgling water for us, the maze has the ladies giggling as they fail to reach Qianlong, laughing at them from his pavilion. I rest my hand on a small carved flower of the maze's walls and watch them.

Beyond the main palaces I see a tiny village, far off, the houses more modest in their appearance but still in keeping with the Western architecture I have seen so far.

"There is even a village?" I ask Qianlong.

He is delighted with my question. "Walk closer to it," he urges me.

I do so, only to suddenly realise that the village is an illusion, a painting on such a vast scale and using a trickery of sight such that it appears real and yet is only an image. "Did Shining do this?" I ask.

Qianlong is all smiles. "He did," he says. "I commanded it and he had more than a hundred painters brought here from the imperial studios to complete the work. He says it uses *forced perspective*," he adds, proud at knowing the technical terms Giuseppe uses. "It makes an illusion, to trick the eye and see what is not really there."

I nod. I wonder whether these buildings make Giuseppe homesick, whether these are the sights of his childhood. Has building them exhausted his last remaining memories of his homeland? Perhaps he considers the whole thing a playground for the child he once knew, a fairytale made real in stone but still an illusion.

I try to find some peace in the Garden but it is almost impossible. When I suggest boating a gigantic boat is summoned, lavishly painted and surmounted with a dragon's head, nothing like the little rowing boats we once paddled here and there. Naturally it is not made for just a few people, so a crowd climbs aboard. The musicians follow us in smaller but no less lavish boats, so that the singing goes on endlessly, adding to the chatter of the courtiers. At last I clasp Qianlong's arm and ask him if I may visit my old palace.

"Of course!" he agrees.

At once our party changes direction and we make our way back across the Garden, heading South-East. Tiny wooden bridges that I recalled walking over have been replaced with sturdy new covered bridges complete with marble steps grand enough for our entourage to sweep over. Buildings are everywhere, rising from little meadows, woodlands and even the middle of lakes. The emptiness and wildness of my memories is now gone, the little streams and secret hollows that Yan and I once explored are opened up, over-planted and no longer tucked away but boldly on show for all to see. I stay silent while the ladies and courtiers heap praise on everything that has been done here.

At last we reach the Nine Continents Calm and Clear, my old home. The palaces around the little lake have been refurbished, I am told, and there has been a lot of new planting but in comparison to other areas I am relieved to see that it is still recognisable: the islets still circling the lake, bridges linking each, the great willow trees.

"You will stay in the largest palace, of course," says my son. I look across the lake at the palace that used to be Lady Nara's, Yongzheng's Primary Consort when he was only a prince. I remember Yan dressing me to meet her, my anxiousness that she might be angry at my arrival and jealous and instead meeting a kindly, sad woman in mourning for the loss of her child.

"I would rather stay in my old palace," I say.

"Nonsense," says Qianlong. "It is tiny! It is hardly fitting for you now that you are the Empress Dowager. But we can go and look at it, if you would like to."

I nod.

Slowly we walk along the lakeside until we stand before it.

"The wisteria is charming," says my son. "We had to cut it back of course, it was threatening to envelop the whole palace! But I have given orders for it to be re-trained more delicately. As you can see."

I stand a little ahead of the crowd, so that no-one can see my face. I think of the little fairy-palace I was brought to when I was only a child and glad of a fairytale to soothe my fears. Then, the wisteria covered every part of the building, the hanging flowers a purple mist of loveliness. Now the vine has been cut back so that the palace can be clearly seen, the wisteria reduced to a thin snaking shape along the front, nothing more. My eyes fill with tears and I have to stand looking at the palace longer than is necessary to clear them and be ready to face my son.

"I have increased the number of gardeners three-fold," he tells me as I turn to him. "The Garden must be perfect in every way."

I nod.

"What do you think?" he asks.

"You have done so much," I say. "I do not know what to say."

He smiles broadly. "There is so much still to be done," he says.

Lady Nara's old palace is large and every comfort has been arranged for me. I am treated with too much care, as though I am an elderly lady. I have not yet reached my forty-fifth year, but tonight I feel old. I sip hot tea and allow myself to be wrapped in overly-thick furs against the possible chill of a warm spring night. At last I dismiss most of the servants so that I can hear the silence I have been denied all day. Yan kneels before me to remove my too-high shoes and when she catches my eye she makes a little face that shows what she thinks of the day we have passed.

"Do you remember when we first saw how big the Garden was?" I ask and she nods, silent. I go to sleep early and sleep badly, my mind a jumble of little red stalls and endless songs.

It is still half-dark when I leave my bed, leaving the unwanted furs behind. In bare feet I walk along the lakeside, feeling pebbles and grass, a sensation denied me for many years now. At last I find the shelter of a willow tree that will shield me from view. The ground is hard and cold but it feels familiar. I look out across the lake and see a duck escorting her ducklings between the reeds, hear her quack anxiously when one seems briefly lost. Above me in the tree I hear a crow caw and its mate answer. As the sun rises more birds sing and I close my eyes, the better to hear their sounds and the lap of the lake's water on the shore. Slow tears roll down from my closed eyelids as a great grief wells up in me and cannot be contained. I know, now, what the rest of my life will be like. It will be music everywhere and the illusion of simplicity while living a life absurd in its luxury. It will be always accompanied apart from perhaps a few brief moments, growing ever rarer, when I can slip away like this. I will have to accept lavishly unwelcome surprises from my well-meaning, generous-hearted son, for he will not listen to my desires, certain that he is right. The Garden will grow both ever grander and less precious to me. Those tiny moments in my life when Giuseppe has held my fingertips or stood close to me will grow fewer and fewer until I barely see him from one year to another. I will forget what it is to thrill to another's touch.

I am not permitted to indulge in either fading memories or growing fears. I see eunuchs and maids in the distance, hurrying on errands. The Garden is waking and I must return to my rooms, where Qianlong joins me for breakfast.

"There is so much we can do!" he tells me. "We must go on a Southern Tour, to view the empire. You must come with us to Chengde in the autumn, I know my father did not greatly care for the hunt but the fresh air will be good for your longevity and I will ensure the journey does not greatly tax you."

"You may travel without me if you wish," I tell him. "I do not wish to be a burden to you."

He kneels before me. "You are my mother," he reminds me reproachfully. "It is my filial duty to make you happy. You need only ask and it will be done."

I look down on his bright eyes and place my hand on his head in blessing.

What else can I do?

The Garden of Perfect Brightness

" **W**ILL YOU ENJOY THE HUNT?" asked Laura, watching the servants packing up my painting implements.

I nodded. I had accompanied the hunt many times during Kangxi's reign, since he was a keen hunter. It was a refreshing novelty to leave behind the formality of the Forbidden City and make our way into the woods of Chengde for the autumn hunting season. Yongzheng had shown little interest in its pleasures; he was not a man for outdoor pursuits despite his love for nature and perhaps he found it hard to forget the fear he must have felt in watching his son nearly die there. In any case it was some years since the court had departed in such pomp for the hunt. Qianlong, a keen hunter, was all-afire with anticipation.

"We may even kill a tiger," he said and I had to laugh at the same words coming from his older mouth, for they brought back an image of his child self, hopping from one leg to the other in excitement. "You will paint the hunt," he instructed me.

I bowed. "With pleasure." Certainly there was much scope for painting during the hunt, with animals as well as people set in a more untamed scene than could be found either within the walls of the Forbidden City or the ever-more-managed perfection of the Garden.

"My mother will accompany us," said Qianlong. "Indeed it is primarily for her benefit that we are going to Chengde. The fresh air and nature all around her will be most beneficial to her health."

I nodded, although everyone who knew Qianlong knew he loved to hunt and that his mother's health was nothing but an excuse to resurrect the old rhythm of attending the hunting grounds every year, as his grandfather used to do. But privately I thought that perhaps Niuhuru would enjoy the visit to Chengde, that being close to her childhood home and seeing familiar landscapes might bring her pleasure and that the natural world around her might offer a sense of the freedom that her ever more exalted positions had slowly eroded.

Jean-Denis looked me over. "Very grand," he said, smiling in genuine admiration tinged, perhaps, with a little jealousy.

I looked down at the brightly coloured, lavishly decorated blue silk robe I wore, marking me out as Mandarin of the Third Rank. "I could not refuse it again," I said. "The Emperor insisted." I did not say that this time the edict had come from Niuhuru, that for reasons of her own she had added her voice to Qianlong's to insist that I accept the honour. Qianlong I could refuse, claiming that my vows forbade ostentation or the seeking of worldly praise, but Niuhuru's distant command I found harder to ignore. Perhaps a part of me hoped that being granted such an honour, being known as a favourite of the Empress Dowager, would allow me more opportunities to see her, however briefly. I knew that this honour was a worry to the Brothers, that they saw in it confirmation of their fears that I was not truly one of them, that I was somehow apart, unmotivated by the religion they hoped to disseminate and therefore harder to control.

"And the hat," said Jean-Denis, eagerly. Perhaps in my new attire he saw the heights to which a man might aspire, if his work pleased the Emperor.

I turned the hat in my hands, its black upturned brim surmounted with a jewelled button and threads of red silk. Cautiously I placed it on my head. I had grown used to my severe black robes, their plainness.

"You are one of them now," laughed Jean-Denis. "You are become a Chinese after all your time here."

I nodded slowly, my own face serious. "I think I have been one of them for longer than I knew," I say.

Before we left I went to find Laura. She had always been annoyed at being left behind during the hunting seasons and had pored over my images from the hunts with a wistful expression.

"I am too much in the city," she told me. "I get tired of the noise of it, the busyness. I long for the clean air, the natural surroundings of the countryside. The silence."

"As do we all," I said, thinking of the Yuan Ming Yuan.

She was not to be found in any of the main church buildings and I had almost given up on finding her when I was reminded of the garden she had mentioned and went in search of it. It was situated to the rear of the building, a tiny plot of herbs with some of the vast southern rocks so much admired in the capital. I could not see Laura and was about to turn away when I saw two shadows on the ground ahead of me, the figures casting them hidden by the rocks. I opened my mouth to speak but then closed it as the two shadows touched, then became one embrace. I heard a low murmur and Laura's voice responding, too soft to hear what she said. Quietly I left the garden, thinking of the one moment when my own lips had touched Niuhuru's. I wondered if I would ever again have that experience, if my whole life would be marked by that one moment and the impossibility of it ever being repeated.

In Qianlong's theatre the works were progressing well. Above my head the wisteria now bloomed, twining delicately along bamboo supports, offering a glimpse of pale blue sky beyond. To my right, the wall was beginning to disappear into a formal moon gate shaped with curved bamboo and beyond it a garden scene was emerging, complete with buildings beyond and a pair of magpies who perched on its fence in the foreground. I nodded to my apprentices who, encouraged, continued their delicate outlines and preparations for flowering peonies and a crane caught tending to its plumage. I stood, considering the overall effect, when I became aware of Kun standing by my side.

"Is the Empress Dowager well?" I asked him. Any unexpected glimpse of Kun or Yan always made my heart beat a little faster in fear that Niuhuru might be unwell or in any danger, since they stayed so close to her side.

Kun nodded. "Her Majesty wishes you to know that she will be at the hunt," he said.

I smiled. "As will I, Kun. You can tell Her Majesty that I hope I will have the pleasure of seeing her there."

He nodded. His eyes travelled around the room, taking in the wisteria ceiling and the garden-illusion growing ever more real as its colours and shapes took shape. "It is like her old palace in the Garden," he said at last, raising his eyes to the ceiling.

I nodded. "Did Her Majesty enjoy her recent journey there?" I asked.

"She cried," he said bluntly. "She crept away at dawn to try and see it as it once was but there is little of it left as she recalls it. As we recall it," he added, looking directly at me and bowing before he took his leave.

The procession gathered in one of the vast outer courtyards of the Forbidden City. Palanquins, horses, guards, huge carts filled with tents, weaponry for the hunt, clothing, food and more, while endless courtiers joined the area with their own possessions. The Chief Eunuch looked exhausted and was no doubt quietly cursing Qianlong's enthusiasm for the hunt, thinking of his father Yongzheng who had been content to remain at home and not move thousands of people and everything needed to care for them to a place several days' distance from the usual facilities required to maintain a court in good order.

I waited patiently, sat astride my own horse, with two apprentices behind me in a covered cart, which held my painting materials. Jean-Denis, also on horseback, looked excited.

"I had not thought so many would be travelling."

I nodded. "It is something of an undertaking to move the court."

"There will be no-one left here!"

I smiled at his lack of knowledge. "These are just the favoured ones and everything needed to keep them happy. There will be many hundreds left here in the City."

"Make way for the Empress Dowager!"

An open yellow palanquin bobbed towards us and our cart was forced to one side. I looked towards it and saw Niuhuru. Her face was pale and she looked tired. I waited for her to see me but she was not looking about her, her eyes were fixed ahead.

"Make way for the Emperor!" came the call and Qianlong's own palanquin came bobbing along, empty, for he was on horseback, riding just before it, his smile open and happy. There was a jolting and jostling as everyone prepared to leave, for while all of us had been ready to depart since before the dawn, the Emperor himself could not be expected to wait for even a moment. Slowly the procession began to creep forward, the vast outer gates of the Forbidden City swung open and our journey had begun.

"It will be a great opportunity," said Jean-Denis, his face still beaming. "I will attempt to capture the motion of the horses, as you have shown me." He was always keen to be praised for his work, to carry out commissions that might earn imperial approval. I saw in him my own ambition from many years ago and wondered if he sometimes resented my own status above him, the fact that all the best opportunities were given to me before any other artist. The horses, in particular, were a favourite subject for Qianlong and he had praised my work in depicting them at full gallop, for lending the sense of movement which no doubt recalled for him the thrill of the hunt.

"Forward!" came the call from up ahead of us.

I watched Qianlong's palanquin follow him out of the main gate, saw the twin palanquins of Niuhuru and Lady Fuca bobbing behind it. I thought of Kun, describing Niuhuru's visit to the Garden. *She cried. She crept away at dawn to try and see it as it once was but there is little of it left as she recalls it. As we recall it.*

"I find I am unwell," I said suddenly. "I will leave you to paint the hunt on this occasion, Jean-Denis. Should the Emperor or anyone else ask for me, you can tell them that I am growing older and the cold air of the mountains would not do good things for my cough."

Jean-Denis looked bemused. "Your cough?"

I coughed loudly. "My cough. I would not wish to be unable to serve the Emperor through worsening it."

"But the cart, the apprentices…"

"I leave them all in your capable hands, Jean-Denis," I said. "You will do well, I am sure of it." We had barely made our way through the crimson gates but I turned my horse's head left and made my way along the wall of the Forbidden City, gaining entrance through the Eastern Gate.

I had perhaps thought Jean-Denis foolish for believing that all the inhabitants of the Forbidden City would be gone, but certainly the place was suddenly grown quiet, with only a few bored looking guards here and there, no doubt sulking at missing the adventure of the hunt. The odd official tasked with some boring errand scurried past. Inside, I knew from past experience, those residences now left empty would be cleaned or even refurbished in the absence of their owners. There was no let-up in work allowed for those maids and eunuchs who were left behind. And some palaces still held their unwanted occupants: older concubines from Yongzheng or even Kangxi's reign, all too aware of today's departure and their exclusion from it, their palaces full of silent resentment.

The Palace of Motherly Tranquillity was not silent. Its exterior had been painted and gilded to mark Niuhuru's official arrival, but I knew that the interior was still being refurbished and no doubt now, with its mistress away, the works could be done with greater speed and less discomfort to her, ready for her return. I noted two members of the

Lei family engaged in consideration of changes to be made and painters mixing pigments while maids brought out all manner of furnishings to be cleaned and freshened.

"Shining? I thought you were at the hunt?" Kun had arrived with his own apprentices, now busily uprooting withering summer flowers, which would be replaced with the autumnal colours of chrysanthemums, grown in a nursery elsewhere and now about to take pride of place as they burst into bloom.

"I thought of what you said about the Empress Dowager's visit to the Garden and found I could not leave," I said. "I need your help, Kun."

The refurbishment of her rooms took less time than I expected, leaving Kun and I perhaps ten days before the return of the court. Still, time was short and I was glad that I had been able to prepare in my deserted studio. When the works were done I dismissed her household servants, telling the Chief Eunuch's deputy to use them elsewhere while final touches to decorative panels were made. He did not ask questions.

In the cold dawn light Kun swung open the carved and painted doors to Niuhuru's palace. We were confronted with her receiving hall, an over-large room with a raised platform at one end. A screen stood behind it, painted with imperial dragons while auspicious objects surrounded the carved throne where she was supposed to sit. It was a rigidly formal space.

"She hates it," said Kun.

I nodded. It was everything Niuhuru had never wanted.

"What is it you would have me do?" asked Kun.

"I need you to make me a half room," I told him. "A hidden room." I had learnt from the Lei family and I showed him a tiny model I had created.

He looked at it in silence and then lifted his eyes to mine.

Kun was a fast worker. It took him only a day, with my help as his inept assistant, to create the wooden framed-walls of a room that sat behind the empty space of the receiving room's throne. The room was not large, it allowed a person to walk perhaps six or seven paces before they had to turn again in either direction, but cunningly its back wall stopped only a hand's breadth from a window of the palace, while its two side-walls enclosed the space entirely. In front of the window Kun and I pasted strips of white silk onto a light bamboo framework which created a new wall, its shimmering height reaching to the full extent of the high ceiling and meeting the floor below it. Light poured through the silk, creating a giant blank canvas of a wall.

"Now my work begins," I told Kun. "Your only remaining task is to disguise the outer walls so that no-one will know this room is here." I mixed simple paints and showed him how to use them to cover the walls and door of the hidden room, then despatched him to source hangings and scrolls to be used as decoration, masking the space we had created entirely. When he had done, I thanked him and told him that now

I would work alone. His only task was to warn me of the court's progress, should they for some reason return early.

I had seven days.

The white silk glowed with the hidden light of the window behind it. Alone in the little room, I cast my mind back to the first time I had seen the Garden. How the first vistas of flowers and carved bridges had given way to ever more beautiful sights as it revealed itself, the shimmering waters and delicate buildings hidden here and there, the quick fleeting life it harboured as all around me dragonflies glittered and frogs flashed their bright skins leaping to shelter as I passed. How, breathless and overawed, lost and dazed, I had come across an avenue of bamboo and within it caught my first glimpse of a face that had become, for me, something greater than I could put a name to.

I lifted up my hand. The brush touched the silk, giving it colour, taking from it light.

To paint with love is different, I found. In my lifetime I had painted to please a master, to prove myself, to complete a commission. To find a way to bridge two worlds, to please three emperors, whether young or old. I had painted, rarely, for my own pleasure, although usually when doing so I was trying to gain a new skill or solve a problem of perspective, colour or light. To paint without commission, without fear of a critical eye, to paint freely as you wish to paint and to do it as a gift of love… it is different. I painted what there had been between us over many years and what could not be said. I painted my memories and watched as the grey dawn light bloomed to sunrise through the silk, casting a golden light on a landscape now lost. As the day grew brighter the colours grew so vivid they seemed to ripple as the heat does in summer and when sunset came its pink-flushed hues touched the silk with a greater art than I would ever possess. In these moments the scene I was painting seemed to come alive and I would step back and cease my work, for it seemed to be creating itself without my intervention.

When it was done I stood alone and looked at the work in silence. A spring day blew wispy clouds across a deep blue sky and a light breeze rippled the surface of the lakeside, only a few steps away. Across the lake could be seen a small building, perhaps a little temple, a simple affair half-hidden by crooked pines. A haphazard path might lead there, although its outline was unpaved and faint among the rising willow trees and delicate pink blossoms that lined the water's edge, the grass a pale haze in the golden sunshine. In the closest shallows rushes came up between grey boulders and here, with his back to us, a little boy crouched, one hand gripping the boulder so that he might stretch out further with his other hand to touch the glistening green of a wary frog's back. By his feet was a tiny model of a fisherman's hut, something made with scraps of wood bound with rushes.

I thought of Niuhuru and how she would stand here, also alone, seeing her past come back to life before her eyes and knowing that I had offered her all that I could ever give: my art and my memories, bound up in love for her.

Exiting the room, I closed its small door behind me and ran my hand over it. Outside I found Kun, planting gnarled bulbs in the garden, ready for spring.

"Yan may need to change the servants," I told him. "Some of them will question where the space behind the receiving hall has gone. There may be gossip, whispers."

He nodded. "The household is in Yan's command," he said. "I will tell her as soon as they return." He stood, letting out a little groan as his back straightened. "I have a gift for you," he said, walking away from me. I followed.

We came to a little tucked-away building at the back of the palace and Kun gestured.

I stood in silence trying to take in what he had done. A small but complete weeping willow tree stood before me. Its sturdy trunk was artfully woven from new-cut willow branches, while as it rose to a height almost twice that of a man delicate branches fell downward as though trying to touch invisible water. But this was no bare winter tree. All along each branch trembled delicate willow leaves. Frowning, I approached the tree, squatted down and took one leaf between my fingers. It was a tiny scrap of green silk, cut to the shape of a willow leaf and embroidered with its delicate veins, its stem bound to the branch with a thread of green silk. I thought of Yan and Chu, their embroidery silks around them, delicate fingers adding the final touches to the work of Kun's calloused hands.

"It is for the room," said Kun. "As though it grew by the lakeside."

I looked up at him. "It is beautiful. A work of art, Kun."

His lined and sun-burnt face creased into a gentle smile.

"How did you know, though?" I asked, standing up. "What was in the room?"

His smile deepened as he hoisted the tree across his shoulders to bring it back to the palace. "What else would you paint for her?" he asked.

There is a tree in my palace of memories, a softly weeping willow set by the edge of the lake. Its rough trunk was woven by a man with a good heart, each tiny silk leaf embroidered with a silent kindness. A love that seems impossible can be made possible by such things.

Two Songbirds in a Cage

THE SERVANTS HAVE ALL BEEN changed, at Yan's strange command. I do not care, I am too weary to mind the new faces. I had barely had time to get accustomed to all the extra servants given to me when I moved into this palace. I cannot imagine what they find to do all day, but the Emperor's Mother must of course have more servants than anyone could know what to do with. I lie on my bed and try to rest, glad to be rid of the endless unsteady rocking of my palanquin on our journey here although Yan continues to bustle in and out, carrying cushions and silken coverlets.

"What are you *doing*?" I finally snap.

Yan only smiles. "Preparing a room."

"For what? Can't one of the maids do it? Come and sit by me Yan, fan me a little. It's stifling in here after the mountain air."

She shakes her head, stubborn as she has always been, determined on her chosen course. I sigh and rise, open a window hoping for some sense of the outdoors but there is only my walled courtyard garden, a few pots of flowers scattered about, which only serve as a reminder of how little nature is allowed here.

Yan is standing behind me when I turn back. "What?"

"Come with me," she says.

"Where?"

"The receiving hall."

I make a face. She knows what I think of sitting high on a carved throne in my own home. But she has already gone and I follow her, whining like a child. "Can't I just rest, Yan? What do you need me for? Arrange whatever it is however you want it."

The receiving hall is quiet, there seems to be no-one about. The walls appear to have been altered, enclosing the space behind the throne but then half the palace has been moved around and turned inside out in my absence so I do not even comment on it until Yan touches the wall with her fingertips as though she somehow expects it to move.

"What are you doing?"

But the wall does move, it opens up into a door that was not there a moment ago and Yan disappears into it. I step after her and gasp.

Beneath a weeping willow tree are piled silken cushions and beyond the cushions… I stand and stare while behind me I am faintly aware of Yan closing the hidden door, leaving me alone.

Slowly I sink down onto the cushions, taking my place where Giuseppe wanted me to sit and view his masterpiece. For it is his work, I know it at once. A dragonfly skims past my little son's crouched back. Further into the centre of the lake's rippling surface, beyond his reach or interest, a lotus flower opens up its heart to the sun.

I sit in the room all day and when sunset comes I call Yan and dispatch her to find Giuseppe before the Forbidden City is closed for the night.

"You wish him to come now?" she asks. Dusk is falling and no man must be found within the Forbidden City after darkness, on pain of death.

I meet her gaze. I have no secrets from Yan. "Tell him to come to the Garden," I say. "Tell him I will be waiting."

I know that if the door opens it will be Giuseppe himself who stands there and that he will be here because we have both made the same choice. I stand by the panel and rest my hand on it, waiting to feel his presence on the other side.

"Shining."

I rose up and followed Yan without challenging the summons, knowing who had sent her. We slipped into the Forbidden City's Inner Court just before darkness fell. As I entered Niuhuru's palace I heard the cry go out across the City to lock up for the night, the warning to any outsider, to any man, to leave this place or lose his life if he is found. In all my years serving here, I had obeyed that warning without question.

The throne was empty. I had not expected otherwise. I knew that I had not been sent for to receive her praise and bow, to murmur a courtier's thanks. The palace was quiet and Yan slipped silently away, leaving me alone in the red-gold light of new-lit lanterns.

I stood by the wall, adorned with a painting of two songbirds in a cage, their feathers almost touching. I allowed my palm to rest gently for a moment against the panel. I tried to quiet my breathing, to think upon the step I was about to take and yet all I could hear was my own heart's beat, or perhaps that of another.

They say that the Forbidden City has nine thousand, nine hundred and ninety-nine rooms, one room less than the Halls of Heaven.

But here within the walls of my memory palace, there is another, hidden, room, one half-step closer to Heaven.

Author's Note on History

The Yuan Ming Yuan (Garden of Perfect Brightness) was a pleasure garden over 800 acres in size (300 hectares). Originally a hunting ground for the Kangxi Emperor, he gave it to his son, Prince Yong, who began to develop it as a country estate and who lived there with his consorts and children until he was made Emperor.

When Prince Yong became the Yongzheng Emperor he used the Yuan Ming Yuan as his summer palace and as a retreat from the Forbidden City and his heavy workload as emperor. He took his duties very seriously and died quite young after a short reign, possibly from overwork (he slept only four hours a day) and possibly as a result of poisoning from taking an Elixir of Immortality.

The Qianlong Emperor, who had grown up in the Yuan Ming Yuan while his father was still a prince, went on to develop the Yuan Ming Yuan into an extraordinary pleasure garden. Full of exquisite buildings, miniaturised landscapes, scenes from fairytales, a 'shopping street', as well as a Western Garden which included a maze, various palaces and a fountain for which he commissioned Giuseppe Castiglione as architect, the Yuan Ming Yuan was written about by the Jesuits and other foreign visitors to China as being one of the most beautiful and extraordinary landscapes ever seen. The grounds were almost half water-based, including large and small lakes and streams, all connected together.

The Yuan Ming Yuan was burnt to the ground in 1860 during the Opium Wars. Today there are none of the original buildings left, only the stone ruins of the Western palaces (which were made of stone unlike the wooden Chinese buildings) remain within the grounds of the park, situated in the suburbs of north-west Beijing. It is still an exquisite place to visit and you can find a link to photos of my research trip there: just visit the book's page on my website.

Giuseppe Castiglione was born in Milan and trained as a painter from boyhood until nineteen, showing great talent. He was recruited by the Jesuit order, who insisted that he should take Jesuit vows and commit to living permanently in China, after various previous painters had returned home, annoying the Kangxi Emperor. He arrived aged 28, eventually took his vows very late (just after Yongzheng took the throne) and did indeed spend his whole life in China, serving three consecutive emperors. He died after fifty-one years in China and his tombstone bears an inscription extolling his virtues ordered by the Qianlong Emperor. The Kangxi Emperor named him Lang Shining, as his name was difficult for Chinese people to pronounce. He was an expert at *trompe l'oeil*, which the Chinese found an extraordinary effect. Through working with his own styles and Chinese approaches and using a combination of Western and Eastern materials, he managed to create a Western-Chinese form of painting that is now highly thought of artistically. *The Shining Inheritance*, by Dr Marco Musillo, covers his life and work as well as his artistic legacy.

It took several years between being recruited and Castiglione reaching China, due to some initial training with the Jesuits, followed by a prolonged stay in Portugal (to paint the Portuguese royal family) and then the long voyage to China, which I have mostly omitted so as to concentrate on his time in China.

The Emperor's mother's real name was recently found to be Zhen Huan, but Niuhuru was her clan name and I have used it here because I have used clan names for all the concubines in my stories, since many of their personal names are lost. She was the daughter of a fourth-ranked military official. Sources from the time remarked that she was very tall and the only surviving portrait of her as an older woman shows her with grey eyes. She was made concubine during the Imperial Daughters' Draft to Prince Yong, who at the time was a well-regarded son of the Kangxi Emperor but not the Crown Prince. The existing Crown Prince was eventually demoted by his father for dubious sexual practices and a lack of seriousness. With over thirty sons, there was a period of considerable rivalry, before Prince Yong was eventually made heir, in large part because the Kangxi Emperor had taken a liking to Yong's son, Hongli (later known as Prince Bao and then as the Qianlong Emperor). Niuhuru therefore went in her lifetime from being the minor concubine of a prince to being the mother of the Emperor, which made her the most important woman at court and the only person to whom even the Emperor had to bow. Niuhuru lived until she was eighty-four and her son Qianlong treated her with huge respect and care. She was known to chastise him for the overly-lavish celebrations he put on for her birthdays.

There is no mention of a romance between Niuhuru and Castiglione, although her son was described as 'filial' towards Castiglione (a serious obligation in China) and late in life she insisted Castiglione accept the honour of being made a Mandarin. They would have known each other for many years as both of them spent a great deal of their lives in the Yuan Ming Yuan. I wanted a personal reason for Castiglione being the first painter to really try to find a way of creating a bridge between Western and Chinese styles of painting.

The Qianlong Emperor went on to have the longest reign in the Qing dynasty and his era was probably the height of the dynasty, the last in China's imperial history.

Laura Biondecci was a real woman, the only woman we are currently aware of who joined the Jesuits to serve in China as a painter. Castiglione acted as her mentor and some of her works may have been attributed to him, including the painting of Guo Feiyan mentioned in the text. She kept a diary in Italian all her life, which was only found in the 1980s in the archives of the Southern Church in Beijing. She met Guo Feiyan in Beijing and it seems the two had a reciprocal romantic relationship. She painted Guo as a Madonna for an altarpiece in the Southern Church, possibly the first Chinese Madonna ever painted, although the image was destroyed in a fire.

Jean-Denis Attiret's frustrated outburst is taken directly from one of the many letters he wrote home (quoted in The Four Horsemen Ride Again: Portraits of China by J.F. Kearney). His description of the Yuan Ming Yuan, an extract of which is included at the start of this book, contributed to a craze for Chinese-style gardens in Europe.

The Kangxi Emperor's response to the Papal Bull is quoted verbatim from Dun Jen Li (1969), *China in Transition*, 1517-1911. Van Nostrand Reinhold.

Lady Fuca died quite young and Qianlong was devastated at her loss: this is covered in *The Consorts*.

Ula Nara eventually went mad and was banished from court. She died within a year. More of her story is told in *The Fragrant Concubine* and *The Cold Palace*.

There were actually more than one Jesuit Missions set up in Beijing and more than one church, but I wanted to focus on Giuseppe's experience and therefore I have only described St Joseph's Church (Dong Tang), which still exists in Beijing, as does Castiglione's gravestone in the Zhalan Cemetery, carved with an inscription written by Qianlong himself. The Qianlong Emperor gave the most money ever donated by an emperor for a European funeral for Castiglione's burial and had him posthumously raised to the rank of Vice Minister.

Maids and eunuchs sometimes married and adopted children.

The majority of the artwork referred to exists (with the exception of Castiglione's fresco of the Garden of Eden in chapter one, his first painting of Niuhuru and the final painting of the Yuan Ming Yuan for Niuhuru's 'hidden' room) and most of the chapter titles are taken from works of art, both Castiglione's and by other artists. I have altered the timing of when he completed some of the works to suit my own needs. The Studio of Exhaustion from Diligent Service was actually Qianlong's retirement complex within the Forbidden City but a lot of the decorative work in his theatre was in Castiglione's style, especially the *trompe l'oeil* work and the wisteria-covered ceiling.

There is a legend that Heaven has 10,000 rooms and that the Forbidden City has 9,999 *and a half* rooms. The half room intrigued me right from the start of planning this novel and so I gave Giuseppe the opportunity to create it for Niuhuru.

The text of Giuseppe's vows is taken from the www.JesuitVocations.org website.

I have occasionally adjusted the timings of real events to suit my fiction, for example Hongli's birth occurring after Giuseppe's arrival rather than before.

Thanks

My grateful thanks go to Dr Marco Musillo, an expert on Giuseppe Castiglione's life, author of *The Shining Inheritance*. His clearly-demonstrated point that Castiglione was a professional painter recruited by the Jesuits, rather than a Jesuit who could paint, showed me a very different person to the one I originally imagined. To Professor James Millward for his expertise on the Qing era and encouragement and to Elizabeth Scheuerman of Rochester University, NY for her wonderful article on Laura Biondecci, giving me insight into a fascinating woman and a whole new character, who no doubt deserves her own book. Professor Mark Elliott's book *Son of Heaven, Man of the World* on the Qianlong Emperor has continued to stand me in good stead. Their collective scholarship gave my imagination a wonderful basis to work from, although of course both errors and deliberate fictional choices are mine alone.

I am immensely grateful to the University of Surrey for funding my PhD: it has been a very precious gift of three years of creative freedom to explore not only this story and my craft, but many other creative outlets as well. This book is dedicated to my two supervisors, Paul and Rachel, with huge thanks for all their encouragement and interesting questions, their insights and knowledge generously shared for three years. It's been such a lot of fun: I would start the whole thing again tomorrow.

My beta readers, as ever: Camilla, Elisa, Etain, Helen: it's always fascinating to see a book through new eyes. Thank you to artist Kate Newington, my beta painter, who practiced painting on rice paper so I could see what it was like as a canvas.

Thank you to my family who accompanied me to Beijing and shared in my research there: especially Seth for demonstrating exactly what a little boy playing in the Yuan Ming Yuan would be like! My gratitude to Ryan for holding the fort in China on numerous occasions so that I could step back into the past unimpeded.

MELISSA ADDEY

The
Cold
Palace

❄

The Cold Palace

For Linda and Rick
With love and thanks for all your support and the joy you bring to my children.

The Cowherd and the Weaver Girl

One of China's Four Great Folktales

There was once a weaver girl named Zhinü (the star Vega), daughter of a Goddess, who fell in love with a mortal cowherd named Niu Lang (the star Altair), who loved her in return. They married and had two children. Alas, their love was forbidden, for a divinity may not marry a mortal. They were banished to the opposite sides of the Silver River (the Milky Way), where each was left to mourn the loss of their beloved: Zhinü sadly continuing her weaving, Niu Lang caring for their two children alone. But once a year, on the seventh day of the seventh moon (August), magpies all over the world took pity on the lovers and fluttered to Heaven to create a bridge between them, so that they could be reunited for one night. Because of this, a pair of magpies symbolise true conjugal love and faithfulness.

The Qixi Festival celebrates this story. On the seventh day of the seventh moon unmarried girls pray to Zhinü and Niu Lang for a loving husband and a happy marriage. They have competitions and create displays of their needle working skills. Newlyweds also worship the couple for the last time and bid them a fond farewell as they begin their own happy marriage.

China, 1730s

Snowfall

I WAKE TO THE PALE BLUE light that means snow has fallen. Outside I can hear excited shrieking, which can only be my younger sister, Shu Fang. Despite my thickly furred jacket and high boots, I shiver when I step outside.

"It's so deep! It is as high as my knees! Or even my waist in the snowdrifts!"

For once Shu Fang is not exaggerating, the snow really does come up as high as her knees, a little lower for me but still each step requires me to lift my feet very high. Our silly little dog Peach bounces around, leaping like a dolphin above the snow only to disappear beneath it again as she lands. Meanwhile her companion Star pushes with his nose, creating a tiny tunnel for himself through the drifts, his approach less enthusiastic but still determined.

Something hard and cold strikes the back of my head.

"Stop that, Shu Fang!" I yelp.

"It wasn't her," comes a laughing voice. I whirl round and look upwards, to the young man sitting on our rooftop, another snowball ready in his hand.

"How did you get up there?"

"Climbed."

"You'll fall off!"

"Will you catch me?"

"Why would I save a silly boy who has climbed somewhere dangerous?" I scold him.

"Out of love for a dear friend?" he teases back.

"What dear friend?" I ask, feeling my cheeks grow warm. "I can't see one. Can you see a dear friend, Shu Fang?"

Shu Fang is swinging under the old plum tree, its pink winter blossoms incongruous in the white snow. "Niu Lang! Isn't the snow beautiful!"

He laughs. "Your sister recognises me, at least."

"You'll break your neck," I say.

"Help me down and I'll be safe," he says, holding out a hand.

"I'm not sure young men are allowed to climb into our garden without permission," I say primly.

"Niu Lang, my dear boy, there you are." My mother, standing at the doorway, huddled in winter robes, smiles up at him. "Come inside and bring the girls. They haven't even eaten their breakfast. They'll freeze out there. I had the cook make honey buns, your favourite." She shuts the door to keep out the cold.

"It looks as though your mother knows who I am, too," says Niu Lang, edging forward on the rooftop. I hold my breath, watching him and gasp as he jumps down, rolling in the thick snow to soften the impact of his landing, then stands up gracefully, brushing snow off his robes. "Good morning, Ula Nara."

I let my breath out. "Are you alright?"

He grins. "So you do care what becomes of me. Here, I made this for you."

What I had taken for a large snowball in his hands is instead a tiny ice sculpture, beautifully carved. Two magpies, their bodies intertwined to form a spherical shape. I smile, turning it in my hands, not even feeling the cold from the packed ice. "Sparrows?"

"Magpies, as you well know," he says quietly and then raises his voice. "Shu Fang! If you don't come in at once your sister and I are going to eat all of the rice porridge between us. *And* the honey buns. There won't be a scrap of breakfast left for you!"

The snow lasts for days. Every time it begins to look as if it might be melting, growing dirty with footsteps and wet around the edges, a new snowfall returns it to its pristine beauty, unmarked and sparkling white. Every day Niu Lang creates an ice sculpture for me: some tiny, some huge. He has been building them since he was a little boy, taught by his father, who used to win competitions as a young man. He spends a whole day outside making the largest one; packing down snow with Shu Fang's eager help until it is ready to carve, then creating a full size man and woman, their robes fluttering, while all around their feet magpies fly.

"Isn't it beautiful?" says Shu Fang, clasping her hands in romantic wonder. "The Cowherd and the Weaver Girl, reunited for one night."

I stand silent. There is more than a touch of myself in the Weaver Girl that Niu Lang has carved. I recognise the style in which my hair is always pinned and her ice-white face has my nose.

"She is quiet for once, I think she must like it," says Niu Lang, winking at Shu Fang.

"It is lovely," I say softly and for once, I do not tease him or deliberately mistake what I am seeing.

Niu Lang waits for my tone to change and when I say nothing else he smiles. "Not as lovely as you, Ula Nara," he says and his voice grows a little thick. "Perhaps in a few years we will bid the Lovers farewell together, what do you think?"

I swallow and raise my eyes to his. "Perhaps," I say, my voice half a whisper while my lips curve to match his smile.

"Nothing against him," grunts my father when my mother broaches the subject. "Good family. Pleasant enough. Far too early though. Years to go until she needs to be married. Barely sixteen, even. Years. Ridiculous woman, chattering about such things so early."

"He is a lovely boy," enthuses my mother, encouraged by my father's dour comments, which, after years of experience, she rightly interprets as a glowing endorsement of Niu Lang as my future husband. She nods at me conspiratorially, delighted at her groundwork having been received so well. "All in good time of course, all in good time, but there can be an understanding between our families. There will be no need for matchmakers for Ula Nara, no need at all. I will ask an astrologer to consult their charts in private, just to be certain there can be no objection. I already have all his details, his mother and I have known each other so long, why, we are almost sisters."

My father sighs. "No need for that nonsense now. I told you, all in good time. Besides, you're getting ahead of yourself. There's still the Imperial Daughters' Draft. She will attend this summer and if she's not chosen then there's plenty of time to discuss her marriage."

I swallow and tug at my mother's sleeve in sudden fear. "What if I'm chosen? What if they choose me and I have to marry into the Imperial Family and… and… Niu Lang…" I can't even formulate my sentences properly.

My mother waves my fears away. "Stop panicking. There's hundreds of girls at each Draft. Hundreds. And that's *after* they've whittled out most of them for being unsuited in some way, which you are not. Nothing wrong with you, though they may make something up, they are so fussy. You would be a perfect Imperial bride," she adds with satisfaction, forgetting for a moment in her pride that this is not what I want to hear. Catching sight of my expression she reverts to soothing me. "*Hundreds* of girls. And our Yongzheng Emperor is known for having barely half the concubines his father had. *And* he only has one son old enough to need any concubines, not like the old Emperor with his thirty-five sons. So there's only two men needing concubines this year, why, there's barely a chance of being chosen at all, even if you wanted to be."

"*I* want to be chosen," says Shu Fang. "I want to be an Imperial bride."

"Oh, shush," says our mother. "You won't be going for another three years."

Shu Fang pouts. "I'd like to be chosen," she insists. "Think of living in the Forbidden City. The clothes and the jewels… and being married to a prince or even the Emperor…"

"Such a romantic," sighs my mother. "You've no idea what it means to be an Imperial bride. The rivalries, the gossip, the expectations. Never seeing your family again. Never leaving the Forbidden City again."

"They go to the Summer Palace," objects my sister. "And the hunting grounds."

"Just the three places then? For the rest of your life?"

"*And* Southern Tours of the Empire," insists my sister.

"Every few years, *if* you're invited," retorts my mother. "No, you marry a good man where I can still visit you, my girl."

I take no notice of either of them. Let Shu Fang dream of a prince if she wants to, I am comforted by my mother's certainty that the chances of my being chosen are slim.

"You might be chosen as a lady-in-waiting," she reminds me. "But if you are you only have to serve a few years and make sure not to catch the Emperor's eye, which can't be that difficult since he's so wrapped up in his paperwork, so they say. Then you'll be released from service and given a handsome sum to start your married life with Niu Lang."

Winter passes. Emboldened by our parents' approving smiles we hold hands as we ice skate with our friends and write one another poems inspired by our daily life: icicles and snowflakes giving way to the first buds of spring and nesting birds, certain that our love will be blessed. My mother returns beaming from the astrologer.

"'A great love,' he said," she announces. "'Undying faithfulness through all tribulations.'"

"What tribulations?" I ask, worried.

"All lives have tribulations," says my mother, unconcerned. "You'd rather face them with a great and faithful love by your side than on your own, wouldn't you? Besides, he also said that you were destined for a life of importance and that Niu Lang would be a man of wisdom. A famous scholar, perhaps," she adds, romanticising a different sort of man from her own husband's military career. "See, I told you that it was worth visiting the astrologer well before time."

My father only grunts.

Falling Blossoms

THE WOMAN SHAKES HER HEAD. "Malodorous," she snaps.

The rejected girl's face flushes crimson in shame as she is led away, back to her family. Apparently, the smell from her armpits would have been offensive to an Imperial nose. Beijing at the end of the sixth month is unbearably hot, I'm surprised all of the girls here have not been rejected for this reason.

The sturdy woman approaches and gestures impatiently for me to raise my arm. I, like all the other girls here, have already had to shed my fine outer robes, made of the best silk my family could afford. I asked my mother to send me in something plainer, still afraid of being chosen, but she refused.

"I won't be shamed," she said huffily. "I know you don't want to be chosen, Ula Nara, but you will be examined by the Palace officials. They will see your father's name and our Banner on the paperwork beside your own name. I won't have them look down their noses at us just because you wouldn't wear the best we can provide."

And so I arrived this morning at an administrative hall in Beijing, just outside the Forbidden City itself. It seems we will not be allowed into its hallowed precincts until we have been selected as the most superior candidates. I am dressed in a beautiful robe, the best I have ever owned. It is a delicate blue like a spring sky, covered with intricate embroidery featuring fluttering magpies and trees heavy with golden peaches, all symbols for love and happiness, for longevity, prosperity and future sons, highly auspicious and appropriate for today. It was removed in moments. Eunuchs gathered around each girl in turn to disrobe us and leave us in nothing but our under-robes. The room we are in is large and stifling, full of girls disrobing and re-robing as they are inspected by stout older women elaborately dressed to show off their status as senior ladies-in-waiting, perhaps wives to important court officials. Eunuchs bustle about: some assisting with the undressing and dressing, some noting down comments made by the ladies on each girl and reminding them of every candidate's status and family. Perhaps a smelly girl will be reassessed if her family is very important, perhaps a lowly girl from an out-of-favour family will be marked down as malodorous as a good way of removing her from the possibility of being chosen.

I lift my arm as instructed and the sturdy woman assigned to my row puts her face against my armpit and inhales loudly. I look away in embarrassment and when I look back she is nodding briskly to the eunuch at her side, who makes a note against my name. It seems I do not stink. I look hopefully about for my robe to be given back to me, but instead the woman kneels in front of me and lifts up my under-skirts. I step backwards.

"Keep still, you stupid girl," she says. I stop moving and gaze down at her in horror as she sticks her face under the skirts, close to my private parts and I hear her inhale again. She emerges and nods to the eunuch, ignoring my now scarlet face. Apparently, every part of me must be found to be acceptable to the sensitivities of a possible Imperial husband.

By the time I have regained my composure and my robe, my hair is being checked for lice and my teeth scrutinised. The Court Physician takes my twelve pulses and examines my tongue before he pronounces me to be of a cold and damp disposition, something the Imperial kitchens will take into account when cooking for me, should I end up residing here.

"Bound feet? You have *bound feet*?!"

Heads turn. A girl has been found with bound feet, despite being Manchu. She looks terrified. We all crane our heads to see under her skirts, catch a glimpse of tiny pointed stubs encased in embroidered slippers and then quickly look away again. The head eunuch is appalled.

"Bound feet are forbidden! As you and your family are well aware. What were they thinking, a noble Manchu family copying the disgusting habits of the common Han Chinese? Your family will be fined and you and all your sisters will be rejected for any possible union with the Imperial Family."

The weeping girl is led away while we try not to stare. I wonder whether bound feet are worth having to avoid marriage to the Imperial Family but it's too late now, they would have had to have been bound when I was a toddler and my family would never have done such a thing.

More and more girls are dismissed. I start to worry, thinking there are not, after all, hundreds of us to choose from, before recalling that today is merely one of multiple preliminary rounds, when any small reason will have us sent home again. I hope to be sent home for something trivial, perhaps poor posture or an inelegant kowtow but as the day progresses I am still not dismissed. I am from a good family and a military background, any minor faults I have are perhaps being overlooked or minimised, allowed to slip through. They can't get rid of too many girls, they want a good showing when we are selected, after all. In-between being tested for our suitability a few of the girls talk to one another. A tiny delicate girl, barely thirteen, sits next to me while we wait for our turn to be scrutinised again for some other fault.

"I am Ula Nara," I say.

"Wan," she replies, her voice as delicate as she is. I feel protective towards her, she can't be much older than Shu Fang, who, being only twelve, has missed this year's Draft. But where Shu Fang is full of chatter and silliness, this girl sits in silence.

"Do you want to be chosen?" I ask, thinking that such a girl must surely be terrified by the idea of both marriage and the expectations of joining the Imperial Family. But her face lights up.

"Yes," she says. "I have been praying to be chosen."

"For the honour to your family?" I guess.

She looks away. "To leave them," she all but whispers.

"Are you not happy at home?" I ask.

She shakes her head and a quick tear falls.

I wonder at what kind of family she has if she wants to leave them so desperately, but I don't enquire further. "I hope you are chosen," I say comfortingly.

"You too," she says. "I will include you in my prayers."

I shake my head violently. "I don't want to be chosen," I whisper, afraid that someone here will take offence at me even saying such a thing. "I have a – a sweetheart. We want to be married."

Wan's eyes shine with a romantic light only matched by Shu Fang's when such things are discussed. "Oh!" she breathes. "How exciting! Then I will pray that I am chosen and that you return to your true love."

I nod and smile at her before we are hurried on to the next test. I lose sight of her and at the end of the day when I don't see her in the crowd I hope she has not been sent home to an unloving family for some minor fault.

My mother is proud that I have made it through to the final round, but she remains comfortingly convinced that I will not be chosen.

"They'll pick two or three extra concubines for the Emperor, if that," she sniffs. "Then they'll already have chosen someone high-ranking for the young Prince's Primary Consort and give him an extra few ladies. If they have vacancies, some girls will be chosen as ladies-in-waiting. That's all. Keep quiet, stand where you're told and it will all be over soon enough. And then you can finish that embroidery you're supposed to be doing for the Qixi Festival, there's not long to go. And you need to pray to the Lovers for a happy marriage!" she says winking.

I can't help smiling. I have no need to pray for a happy marriage. If I am spared from the Daughters' Draft then I will marry Niu Lang and of course my marriage will be happy. We have known each other all our lives, we are best friends as well as sweethearts. He is the only man I could ever love.

On the day of selection I make my way through the side gates of the Forbidden City along with the other candidates. To my relief I see my mother is right. There are indeed hundreds of girls still left. I feel my heart lighten and look about me with interest. This is probably the only time I will ever see the Forbidden City unless Niu Lang becomes a court official or a very great scholar, as the astrologer suggested.

The spaces are vast. Even though we are hundreds of girls, surrounded by eunuchs and guards, we are dwarfed by the courtyards and gates we pass through, swallowed up as though we are ants. Everywhere I look I see the swooping golden-tiled rooftops indicating the presence of the Imperial Family. We pass gates and then more gates, temples and guard towers, huge courtyard after huge courtyard. I almost get the giggles wondering whether we will just keep walking forever, never reaching our destination in this unending complex. But eventually we find ourselves at a set of gates, which take us into a different part of the palace.

"The Inner Court," announces the eunuch accompanying us.

I have heard of the Inner Court. It is where the Emperor and his women actually reside, the Outer Court being reserved for public occasions and rituals, official, religious and administrative purposes. The space here is on a smaller scale, we pass multiple palaces and smaller courtyards filled with flowers or decorative trees. At last we reach a gateway and are ushered into a medium-sized courtyard with less decoration. We are left to our own devices for a short period, huddling in little groups or standing alone, lost and nervous, each of us perfect in our best robes, our hair pinned with fresh flowers and our mothers' best jewels, lent for the occasion. Now that we are all in one place I can already see that many daughters from lower-ranking families have been sent home, only the most beautiful remain, their looks elevating them above their less-than-noble or exalted backgrounds. My own family are middling ranked: important enough but not quite the very best. Then there are the girls from families who are only one step from the throne itself, who boast imperial connections throughout their generations, whose daughters are regularly chosen as brides and ladies-in-waiting. Among these it is easy to spot the very, very few who have been pre-selected, who will be astonished if they are not chosen. They have been groomed for the Imperial Family, everything about them speaks of a natural confidence in their destiny.

I spot Wan in the crowd and edge my way towards her. She beams when she sees me, as though we are already old friends.

"Ula Nara!"

"Hello Wan," I say. "You are still here."

"Yes," she says happily. "I am sorry you are, though."

"They have plenty to choose from," I say. "They don't need me."

She nods.

"Daughters of the Manchu Banners! Line up!" shouts a eunuch.

We form somewhat disorderly lines before several eunuchs hurry through our ranks, ensuring perfect composition and a precise geometrical layout. A few girls are shifted about so that a too-tall girl does not stand next to a very short one, spoiling the overall impression of uniform womanly perfection.

"That's Fuca, just behind us," murmurs Wan, standing next to me. "She's going to be Primary Consort for sure."

I look behind me. There's a very beautiful girl, her hair entirely jewel-free but filled with fresh flowers, her face serene and almost happy. I suppose she has been waiting for this moment for many years, certain of her future as an Imperial bride.

"Eyes front!" shouts the eunuch.

We stand still, an air of tension about us. The selection will come very soon, in only a few moments we will each know our fate.

Our fates seem to have been indefinitely postponed. We stand waiting for a ridiculously long time, until even the girls with the very best posture begin to slouch a little, their shoulders droop, while those of us with less composure shift from one foot to the other. Almost all of us are wearing cloud-climbing shoes, silken slippers precariously set upon high platforms, which require careful balance when walking. Standing still for a long time in them is uncomfortable. I risk another glance behind me to confirm what I expected: Fuca is still standing perfectly still, her head held high, her eyes looking only ahead. No wonder she's been pre-selected.

"Noble Consort Niuhuru, Primary Consort to His Imperial Majesty!" shouts the eunuch and we all straighten up.

The woman who enters the courtyard, surrounded by guards and attendants, must be about forty. She is very tall for a woman, she stands almost as tall as a few of her guards. She makes her way to a carved throne, which has been placed at one end of the courtyard, in front of our neatly-laid-out rows, then sits. Her attendants fuss about her for a few moments, adjusting the fall of her robes, angling an awning over her to keep the sun from touching her, offering fans, drinks and anything else she may be in need of before she irritably waves them away. Her face is set in a grimly determined expression and I wonder whether she dislikes the task of choosing exquisite young brides for her husband the Emperor, whether she is being eaten up with jealousy at this very moment.

By her side stands the Chief Eunuch, a very splendidly-dressed and imposing figure who arrived with her, currently consulting various folded papers so that he can give Lady Niuhuru advice on whom to select. These papers will give details of our families and fathers as well as any additional useful information: perhaps recent military prowess to be rewarded or noble connections to be taken account of. There is some discreet murmuring in Lady Niuhuru's ear before she nods and indicates three girls in rapid succession, each of whom falls to their knees and kowtows to her before the Chief Eunuch calls out their names and pronounces them concubines for the Emperor himself. There follows a few moments of murmured discussions, Lady Niuhuru shaking her head.

"There will be no further selection of ladies for the Emperor," announces the Chief Eunuch, looking a little disappointed, as do some of the girls who perhaps had their eyes on the Emperor.

A handful of girls are chosen as ladies-in-waiting. These look quite pleased: they will serve at court for a few years, catch the eye of a suitably high-placed husband if they can and be given a goodly sum of money with which to start married life.

"Her ladyship will now choose the Primary Consort and additional ladies for her son, Prince Bao of the First Rank."

Lady Niuhuru seems reluctant to begin the process of choosing her son's brides. She pauses and the Chief Eunuch leans to whisper in her ear. She looks up in my direction and for a horrible moment I think she is looking at me, before I realise that in fact she is looking at Fuca, standing in the row behind me. Lady Niuhuru nods.

"Lady Fuca! Chosen as Prince Bao's Primary Consort!"

I hear the rustle of silk from behind me as the newly-made Lady Fuca kowtows to her future mother-in-law. Wan gives a small nod, her prediction was correct.

There is another consultation. Another pause. Another nod.

"Lady Gao! Chosen as *gege*, concubine, to Prince Bao!"

"Lady Su! Chosen as *gege*, concubine, to Prince Bao!"

"She's not very high-ranking," murmurs Wan, who seems well-informed.

I watch the girl as she is led to one side. She is exquisitely beautiful. Whatever her family status, she has more than made up for it with her face and figure.

"Lady Zhemin! Chosen as *gege*, concubine, to Prince Bao!"

"She's related to Lady Fuca," whispers Wan.

I nod. It looks as though her family is being much favoured this year, being granted both a Primary Consort and a regular concubine.

A couple of other girls are chosen but they are standing right at the back and we cannot turn to see them.

Lady Niuhuru looks at our row and I hold my breath but her eyes rest on Wan instead. I can feel her whole body tense up next to me.

"Lady Wan! Chosen as *gege*, concubine, to Prince Bao!"

I want to turn and hug her but I cannot, so instead I stand very still and watch her as she is led away, beaming. I offer up a little prayer that she will be happier here than in her home if it made her so miserable, although I swallow when I think how young she is. How will she fare in such an exalted position, how will she cope with rivalries and petty jealousies?

I look back at Lady Niuhuru, who is shaking her head. I feel my shoulders relax. She has finished. The Emperor has a few new concubines, the court will welcome additional ladies-in-waiting and her son has not only a Primary Consort but a handful of additional concubines to begin his married life. The selection is over and in three years' time it will be Shu Fang's turn and goodness knows she wants to be chosen, the foolish girl. I smile a little at the thought of her. I might be married by then and she will be so excited at the thought of a wedding, it will be almost as good as being married herself, to be sister to a bride. I wait for Lady Niuhuru to leave so that we will all be dismissed, but the Chief Eunuch is whispering in her ear again. Lady Niuhuru looks over the rows and rows of girls still left over. I wonder whether the Chief Eunuch thinks there should be more ladies-in-waiting, for it is a great honour and a good opportunity for any girl and to choose so few might seem unfair for those families who hoped for advancement.

Lady Niuhuru's face suddenly brightens, as though she has had some good news. She lifts her hand and points a golden nail in my direction. I wait for a girl's name to be read out.

"Lady Ula Nara! Chosen as *gege*, concubine, to Prince Bao!"

For a moment I think another girl here must have the same name as me. I wait for her to move, to hear the rustle of her robes as she kneels. Then I see the expectant expression of the Chief Eunuch and realise that both he and Lady Niuhuru are looking directly at me. A great weight inside me drags me down. I feel my knees weakening, then the cold hard thud of cobblestones as I hit the floor without my will or knowledge. A huge pain spreads through me where my kneecaps have taken the blow of my body weight falling. I put out a hand to stop myself falling further. One hand on the cold cobbles, I look up in dawning horror at Lady Niuhuru and hear my voice, tiny in this large space, lost amongst the ranks of immobile girls towering over me.

"I do not wish to marry the Prince, my lady." Too late I see the Chief Eunuch begin to straighten up, his face shocked. But the words keep coming out of my mouth, I am unable to stop them. "I beg you to let me return to my – " and at least I do not say *my love* or even his name, *Niu Lang*, some last shred of self-preservation stops me but still I do not close my mouth " – to my family."

I hear muted gasps from the girls. Some cannot help themselves, they turn to gape at me, their mouths and eyes open, staring at me the better to tell this story when they return to their families, that there was a girl who was chosen, *chosen* and who refused, who told the Emperor's Primary Consort *to her face* that she did not wish to marry the Prince, her son.

Lady Niuhuru stares at me in the silence as though she can feel my fear, my dread of losing Niu Lang. She looks to the Chief Eunuch for help but his face is turning red with rage.

"How dare you question the Emperor's Primary Consort?" he screams at me, his voice echoing round the hard stone of the courtyard. "How dare you refuse the honour that has been bestowed upon you? You have been chosen and you will take your place among the Prince's ladies!" He makes a quick gesture and at once the guards snap to attention and Lady Niuhuru rises, still looking at me over her shoulder as she leaves, her face pale. The girls all sink to their knees as she departs. I hear myself moaning, a low sick sound as though I am an animal in pain, as if I am about to vomit. I place both hands on the floor and rock onto all fours, my head down, the moaning continuing, a thin dribble of saliva escaping my mouth and falling to the grey cobbles.

"Up," says a stern voice and my arm is gripped and yanked upright by a eunuch, only slightly less grandly dressed than the Chief Eunuch. "This way."

He has to drag me out of the courtyard. Behind me I hear the clatter of shoes and chattering voices breaking out as the dismissed girls are led back to the exit of the Forbidden City, no doubt only one topic of conversation between them. My name will be mud by the end of the day, my family will be shamed.

I stumble alongside the eunuch who is still gripping my arm tightly enough to hurt me, to a room where the chosen girls are waiting. No doubt they heard a commotion, but perhaps they did not understand what happened, for they look surprised to see me being forced into the room. At last the eunuch lets go of me, pushing me forward so that I totter towards the others. Wan hurries forward, her face full of pity.

"Ula Nara!" she whispers. "Are you a lady-in-waiting?"

I shake my head, unable to speak.

"Oh," she murmurs, embracing me and speaking into my ear. "Oh, I am so sorry."

"Silence!" shouts the eunuch, his demeanour evidently disturbed by the unexpected direction events have taken. He takes a moment to clear his throat and then bows, dignity restored.

"My ladies," he says. "You will be returned to your families to make your farewells, for all necessary preparations to be made and appropriate rituals carried out. You will return to the Forbidden City or the Prince's palace in Beijing in due course to take up your new roles within the Court. Officials will explain all protocols to your families. Please follow me, I will escort you to the gates where your parents will be waiting for you. They will be *honoured* by your appointments, I am sure," he finishes, looking hard at me.

The endless journey back through the Forbidden City seems like a dream to me. I manage to walk steadily only because Wan holds my hand in her tiny grasp, murmuring small sounds of comfort. I feel as though all my senses have been numbed, for I can barely hear her, can barely feel the heat of the sun on my skin. I walk because I do not know what else to do. I wonder why I am not crying, but when I put up a hand to my face I find it is wet.

Night Stars

THERE MUST BE CLOSE TO a thousand people waiting for the Imperial Daughters' Draft to be over and for the results to be announced. Most families are told their daughters have not been chosen and their responses vary from the shrugged resignation of those who did not expect such an honour, to those who look affronted at being overlooked. These daughters rejoin their families in short order and disperse swiftly from the gate, heading back across the empire, some facing long journeys home, which will take anything up to a month to complete.

Those chosen are greeted with smiles and amazement. Few girls have been chosen this year and so we are the elite among the mass of disappointment.

Wan squeezes my arm as she leaves me at the gate. "I will see you soon," she whispers. "We will strive for happiness, Ula Nara."

I nod at her kindness but I barely hear her well-meant sentiments. Instead I stand still, unable to walk forward without her little hand on my arm.

"Ula Nara!" Shu Fang is all but jumping up and down, trying to catch my attention. "We are here! Ula Nara!"

I do not move.

My mother makes her way through the crowd towards me, Shu Fang one step ahead of her, my father several steps behind. When Shu Fang reaches me and sees my face she steps back.

"Do you have to be a lady-in-waiting before you can be married? But lots of girls do, it won't be that long…" She tails off, uncertain of how to proceed, unnerved by my silence, my falling tears.

My mother does not make Shu Fang's innocent mistake. Her face is grim. "Chosen for whom?" she asks.

"Prince Bao," I say and my voice is a croak.

For a moment I see my mother's expression struggle. Her daughter has been chosen as a bride for the heir to the throne, a man who will one day become Emperor, should all go well. And yet she can see my misery and she is fond of Niu Lang, we are all but betrothed. She embraces me and at last my silent tears turn to sobs, my face buried in her shoulder, desperately seeking a comfort that she cannot offer. When I open my eyes I can see my father standing behind her, his face solemn. He reaches out a hand and places it on mine but does not say anything. There is nothing to say.

Eventually, we can leave. My family have been told about the lavish gifts that will arrive from the Palace, a kind of reverse dowry, for families are not permitted to give dowries to Imperial brides, for fear of the Imperial Family then being indebted to them in any way. Besides this there will be appropriate marriage rituals, although they will be minor: I will be a concubine, not a Primary Consort, and my husband-to-be is still a prince, not an emperor. An auspicious date will be set for my arrival at the Prince's palace. I can only assume they mean auspicious for him, it cannot be possible for even the best astrologer to find a date that will be auspicious for me.

We travel home in silence. My mother tries to entice me to look on my future with a little less grief by using up all her limited knowledge of Prince Bao.

"He is the Emperor Yongzheng's only eligible son," she says. "They say this Emperor was only chosen to succeed because of how accomplished Prince Bao is, that his grandfather already had him in mind for the throne. He is a superior warrior, a gifted poet and calligrapher, they say he has a brilliant mind. If all is well he will be the Emperor one day."

Shu Fang wipes away my tears. "Why did they have to pick Ula Nara?"

"They can choose any girl they want," says my mother. "If she has been deemed suitable, she can be selected. There is no knowing why they choose any girl on the day itself."

My shoulders heave with renewed sobs.

"He is devoted to his mother and filial to his father," says my mother, trying a new tack. "That speaks well for him, doesn't it? I am sure he will be a kind husband to you."

I do not reply. In the end she falls silent, unable to think of anything to say that will comfort me.

When we arrive at our home I stay seated in the covered wagon in which we have travelled. I do not know how to get out and face Niu Lang, who will be waiting anxiously to know that all is well. I do not know how to look him in the eye and tell him that I cannot marry him, that I will instead be marrying a prince, that this month will barely be over before I will leave my home for good and we will never see one another again. I sit in the half-darkness of the wagon and try to formulate the words that will break the news gently to him. At last I think of something to say, a formal and correct sentence and I step down from the wagon but as I do I see Niu Lang waiting by our house and Shu Fang throwing herself into his arms, weeping.

"Niu Lang! Oh Niu Lang! Ula Nara has been chosen to marry the Prince! Oh, how will you both bear it?"

Niu Lang's arms catch her but over her head he looks at me and sees from my face that what she says is true. Gently, he sets her aside, leaving her to weep alone and then clutch at my mother. His eyes stay fixed on mine as he reaches me. He does not ask questions, he does not exclaim outrage or anger or denial. Instead he kneels at my feet and takes my hands.

"I will always be yours, Ula Nara," he says with a seriousness and a calmness that belies his years. "Know this."

I try to say something of equal importance, to swear my love for him, but I cannot find anything to say and so I only let my tears flow and clasp his hands.

My mother allows this for some moments before she clears her throat awkwardly. "Inside, now, Ula Nara," she says. "Niu Lang, my dear, you must leave us to rest. It has been a very tiring journey."

Niu Lang stands and looks down on me for a moment before he lets go of my hands and turns away, back to his house. I stand watching him until Shu Fang obeys my mother's whispered command and comes to pull me towards our house.

"It is very late," says my mother, although in fact it is barely dusk. "I think we should all be in bed." She shushes the servants' curious questions and harries everyone through the evening tasks until we are all in our beds. I lie in the darkness and try to think about everything that has happened and what my future will be like, but my tears have drained me of any ability to think. I drift into the darkness, glad not to think.

When I wake I think for a moment that in my fear of being chosen I have imagined the whole thing, that I conjured up the moment of horror as part of a nightmare. I look about the room to see what has changed, but all is how it used to be. I feel a slow smile creep across my face. I was wrong then, I dreamt all of it and now my family will laugh at me when I tell them. Niu Lang will look at me with his head on one side, grinning at my foolish fears. Then he will grow serious and say that such a thing would be impossible: why, we are meant for each other, nothing can come between us. I will laugh at my night-time fears and at having escaped the Draft. I will play in our garden with Shu Fang, I will walk hand-in-hand with Niu Lang to pick peaches and all will be well.

But when I move to sit up my arm hurts. I look down and see a dark bruise has appeared on the skin of my upper arm, just below the shoulder. I frown for a moment and then I remember the eunuch who yanked me to my feet, who forced me to walk into the room where all the other girls who had been selected were waiting. I feel something wet on my legs and look down to see tears already dripping into my lap.

My tears fall continuously without my knowing it. After a few days I almost grow accustomed to their presence. At first I wipe them away again and again but at last I leave them to fall. I wake and my pillow is wet, the front of my robe is marked with the salt stains of previous days and new-fallen tears. At first Shu Fang wipes them away, her own eyes brimming with sympathy, but after a while she, too, leaves them to fall.

My mother tries to think of ways out of the situation. "Do something," she castigates my father. "The girl will die of unhappiness if she goes on like this. She is barely eating as it is, she will be nothing but bones by the time she returns to Beijing. Tell the Palace she is sickly or half-witted. Tell them they have made a mistake, that she is not fit for the Prince. If they want to honour our family, let them take Shu Fang at the next Draft, she'd be delighted to be chosen."

My father does not even bother to respond to this. The Imperial Family does not stoop to ask the Banners which of their daughters is suitable for service, it chooses through its own methods, honed over generations. I have been judged and found suitable. I have been chosen. There is no way out.

"Scar me," I say to Niu Lang.

"What?"

"Scar me," I say. "I cannot be a suitable bride for the Prince if I am scarred. Take a knife and cut my face."

He shakes his head.

"You would not love me if I was scarred?" I ask.

"I would love you anyway," he says. "But I will not scar you."

"I will do it myself," I say.

I try. I sit for most of a day holding a knife. I place the cold blade against my cheek and I press it hard so that I can feel its sharpness, but I am too much of a coward to draw the blade down and feel my flesh give way.

"We could run away," says Niu Lang.

Even I know this is not an option. "They will find us and execute us both," I say. "I have been chosen. I am as good as the Prince's wife now. I will be accused of adultery and you will have seduced the wife of a prince."

Niu Lang traces the lines of my palm. "I will not marry, Ula Nara," he says.

"You will have to," I say, and more tears fall at the thought.

He shakes his head, serious. "I will become a monk," he says.

I stare at him. "A monk? Your family will not allow it."

"They cannot stop me," he says.

I hear Niu Lang's mother weeping with my mother. "A monk! He cannot become a monk!"

My mother calls me into the room. "Ula Nara. You cannot let Niu Lang ruin his life and his family's plans in this way. You must speak with him. When you are… gone, he must come to his senses. Tell him he must live his life fully, he must give up this nonsense of being a monk."

I nod.

"It is not for you to decide," says Niu Lang, in the darkness of our garden as we sit side by side on the swing.

"But your family will be so unhappy," I say.

"Do you want me to be married to some other girl?"

I want to say *no*, but I think of his mother's tears and I stay silent.

Niu Lang strokes my cheek. "My family is not your concern, Ula Nara. I will become a monk when you leave your family for the Palace. And whatever happens to you there, you will know that for all of our lifetimes, I will think of you with love and will not marry another. It is all I can give you. I would have given you so much more but this, at least, I can do for you."

"I can do nothing in return," I say.

"You can think of me," he says. "Every year at the Qixi Festival you will look into the heavens and you will see Zhinü and Niu Lang reunited in the stars. And you will know that I will be watching those same stars and thinking of you. Every year, Ula Nara, until we take our own places in the heavens and are reunited for good."

"I will not know where you are," I say, my voice cracking at the thought.

"I will be watching the stars alongside you," he says. "It will not matter where I am."

With an absurd bitterness of timing, the Qixi Festival must be celebrated the night before I leave. I wonder whether there are other girls weeping across the empire tonight, selected for Imperial marriage against their will, forced to abandon any romantic secrets they held in their hearts. Already the Palace dowry has arrived, wagonloads of goods of every kind, from furniture to silver to bolts of silk. My mother is torn. She would like to boast of the good fortune and honour that I am bringing to the family, would like to show her friends all the beautiful items that are being delivered. Yet her heart is troubled by my white face and endless tears as well as by Niu Lang's insistence on becoming a monk. So I hear her showing her friends all the expensive goods in half-whispers before she returns to embrace me and murmur words of comfort. My father, unable to deal with this domestic crisis, spends more and more time at the nearby barracks, carrying out unnecessary paperwork and inspections of troops.

The local girls, friends and family alike, are uncertain whether to include me in the rituals and celebrations. They are praying for husbands and one has already been chosen for me – or I for him – and also they are praying for happy marriages, which it appears I have been denied before it even begins, implying that the two heavenly lovers have not looked on me with kindness. Besides, as a half-married girl I ought really to be bidding the couple farewell alongside my own husband, something which is impossible since my future groom is in Beijing and my sweetheart is about to be lost to me forever. Shu Fang hesitates in my doorway, clutching examples of her dainty needlework.

"It's alright, Shu Fang," I say, weary of everyone tiptoeing around me. "You can go without me."

"I will burn incense for you at the temple," she says awkwardly. "Perhaps the Lovers will find a way to... to..."

"Thank you," I say, to make her go away. When she has gone I sit in silence until I hear something strike the window. Looking out I see Niu Lang below, a lantern in one hand, a large bundle of incense sticks in the other. Quickly I make my way into the garden, where I find him kneeling by the pond, lighting the incense by the dim light of the lantern.

"What are you doing?" I ask.

"Bidding farewell to the Lovers," he says. "As we said we would one day."

"We are not going to be married," I remind him, my voice bitter.

"We are as much married as they were," he says. "And we will remain so, as they did. Here." He hands me half the sticks of incense. I take the bundle and together we bow in each of the four directions before kneeling and kowtowing before the pond in which we can see the two Lovers' stars clearly reflected above us. When we plant our incense sticks firmly in the earth where they can continue to burn Niu Lang holds out his hand to me. We lie on our backs in the grass, still warm from the sun. The moon rises above us while we lie, hands clasped. We do not speak, only watch the stars above us and the moon's path across the sky, our breath rising and falling as one.

I wake cold and stiff, my robe wet with dew, the sun barely over the horizon. Niu Lang is gone, the stubs of burnt-out incense are all that are left of our night together. I make my way back to the house, creeping up the stairs so as not be found out of bed and wait to hear my mother's footsteps.

She comes soon enough, holding a pile of shimmering red silk in her arms. Shu Fang follows her, eyes brimming.

"It is time to dress," my mother says gently. For once she does not chatter but instead helps me into my wedding clothes in silence, before spending time twisting my hair into an elaborate arrangement pinned with silk flowers.

I descend the stairs to my father and we stand in front of one another.

"You bring honour on our family, Ula Nara," he says at last and his voice is gruff.

I do not answer. I do not know what to say. I only know that I will never see him again, nor any member of my family, and I cannot think what to say in such circumstances. My father embraces me, followed by my weeping mother, who lifts my red wedding veil over my head, plunging me into a gauzy red-tinted world. I am led outside, to where a red and gold palanquin awaits, surrounded by bearers and Imperial guards. Neighbours crowd about to watch me go. I look this way and that for Niu Lang but I cannot see him anywhere.

Shu Fang throws herself at me so hard that I stagger backwards. "Oh, Ula Nara! I will miss you! I will be all on my own!" She buries her face in my red silk and sobs.

I wrap my arms around her. "Where is Niu Lang?" I whisper into her tousled hair.

She gulps back her tears. "Gone," she whispers.

My mother is tugging at my arm.

"Gone where?" I hiss.

"To be a monk. He took his father's best horse."

I am pulled away from Shu Fang. I look over my shoulder and realise none of Niu Lang's family members, our closest neighbours and friends, are there to wave me off. I look back at Shu Fang, my eyes wide. There was something in me that had not believed Niu Lang, that had thought he had said such things only to soothe me, that he would eventually bend to his family's will and marry some suitable girl.

"I will miss you," says Shu Fang again, her little face white and miserable. As I am hurried into the palanquin I realise I will never see nor touch her again, that our last embrace was taken up with Niu Lang's whereabouts.

"I will miss you too," I say and hold out my arms to her. She steps forward but the bearers have already lifted me and I am moving away. I struggle with the veil over my head and the curtain at the window, fighting to catch a last glimpse of my family and of Shu Fang, whose voice I can still hear, calling after me, high and full of tears.

"Ula Nara! Do not forget me! Ula Nara!"

Tangled in my wedding veil, I sit back. I can no longer see behind me, all I see out of the small window is the shape of the guards surrounding me.

It takes me several moments before I realise that the small palanquin contains an object: a dome-topped container covered over with a dark cloth. Unpinning my veil and setting it to one side I hesitantly touch the cloth, then pull it away to reveal a birdcage, whose inhabitants squawk in surprise at the light suddenly reaching them. A pair of young magpies, huddled together for comfort, stare up at me as my tears begin to fall again.

The journey is long and the palanquin is stifling in the heat of the day. I am offered food and a rest somewhere at a nobleman's home part-way to Beijing but I refuse and the bearers and guards shrug and continue our swaying journey, no doubt anxious to complete their day's work and deliver me to my new home.

It is close to dusk when we come to the outskirts of Beijing and dark by the time we reach Prince Bao's palace, somewhere close to the Forbidden City. I do not know the city well, but when I look out of my tiny window I see bright lanterns everywhere in still-busy streets, hear the street-food vendors calling their wares. We pass through smaller streets lit by lanterns behind which stand girls in cheap but gaudy robes, softly calling their own kind of wares. I pull back into the darkness of my palanquin.

At last the steady marching slows and then stops. Greetings are exchanged between a sentry and my own guards. I hear the creak of heavy gates being swung open as I try to re-pin my wedding veil in place, although in the darkness I cannot see what I am doing and drop more than one pin. Once again the palanquin sways forwards and I hear the gates thud together as they close behind me.

Now the bearers increase their pace, trotting at speed through courtyards dimly lit with large lanterns. Here and there I glimpse the odd guard, but otherwise everything is eerily empty, my own palanquin and its escort the only thing in motion, the only thing creating any noise.

We come to an abrupt stop and I am set down. I wait, uncertain whether I should emerge or whether we have still some way to go.

A plump wrinkled hand appears, pushing aside the curtain, extended to me. Hesitantly, I take it and step out of the palanquin, my limbs cramping painfully after their lengthy confinement. I reach back and lift out the magpies in their cage. They flap and squawk at the movement and I set them on the ground before looking at the owner of the hand, an old woman, round and with a pleasant face, which creases into a smile. "Lady Ula Nara," she says. "Welcome to His Highness' palace. I am Dan Dan, your maid."

I nod. I wait for someone more senior to appear, but Dan Dan only stoops to pick up the magpies' cage, then walks away from me towards a half-open door from which light spills out. I look back at the guards but they are already marching off, the bearers following them with the now-empty palanquin bobbing away from me. I follow Dan Dan towards the door.

Inside I find I am in a large and pleasantly appointed living room. There is a table set for a meal for one, as well as couches placed here and there, little tables with board games and other trinkets placed on them. Several vases of fresh flowers as well as paintings and examples of calligraphy and poetry are displayed around the room.

Dan Dan sets the magpies' cage on an empty side table near a closed window and turns to me smiling.

"Shall I remove your veil?" she asks.

I hesitate. "Won't there be a – a ritual?" I ask. I wonder where my future husband the Prince is. I expected to meet him on my arrival here, to carry out some kind of ceremony. Back at home I and my family knelt before our family's altar and ancestral portraits and before certain items of importance brought from the Imperial Family. But I expected something additional: for the Prince to raise my veil, to kneel before his own ancestral portraits, to – to no doubt be taken to his bedchamber where I would turn my face away in the darkness, to think of Niu Lang even while being made another's wife without my consent.

Dan Dan shakes her head. "I will take you to the ancestral tablets tomorrow morning," she says. "And to the temple to pray, if you wish."

"Where are the others?" I ask.

"The ladies have been arriving all day," says Dan Dan. "Except for Lady Fuca. She was brought here almost immediately after selection, she has resided here for almost a month now."

Of course, I think. She was pre-selected, her dowry and any other official matters would already have been taken care of. Besides, as the Primary Consort she and the Prince would have had a more elaborate marriage ceremony. I was forgetting that I and the other ladies here are only concubines, not deemed worthy of anything more than a perfunctory ritual, our husband's presence not even required, our assent assumed. Slowly I remove my wedding veil and place it, unwanted and unnecessary, on the back of a chair.

Dan Dan bustles about, while I sit in silence at the table. She brings plates of food and I try to eat. The food is good but I have eaten so little of late that my stomach has shrunk, a few mouthfuls and I am already full. Dan Dan shakes her head when I say I am finished.

"I will need to fatten you up," she says cheerily and clears the table.

I rise and walk to where the magpies are now sleeping, huddled against one another.

I stroke one of their silken wingtips through the bars of their cage, causing them to open their eyes in sudden consternation before returning to their loving embrace.

"You must be tired," says Dan Dan behind me. "I will make sure your birds are fed and watered."

I follow her to an equally well-appointed bedchamber. My bed at home was nothing as elaborate as this one, it is finer even than my parents'. Its heavy wooden frame is delicately carved, placed within an alcove and warmed by a *kang* stove beneath it. It is comfortably large enough for a couple, its heavy silken drapes embroidered with pomegranate trees and bats in a night sky, symbols of fertility, wishes for Imperial sons.

Dan Dan helps me to undress, my wedding finery gathered up to be taken away and stored, used only to journey here in solitude. She helps me into the bed as though I were a child and puts out the lanterns, leaving me in darkness.

I lie still and silent for a long time before I get out of the bed and make my way, hands outstretched, to where I recall the window was. I fumble with the shutters, struggling to open the unfamiliar catches, before sitting at the window seat and looking up at the stars. I wonder where Niu Lang is, whether his family have found him and brought him back or whether his father's best horse has taken him far enough away from home to evade their searches. I wonder whether he kissed my lips before he left me asleep in the garden and whether he is looking up at the Lovers' stars even now and thinking of me.

Rain on Water

"THE LADIES OF THE PALACE will take most meals together," Dan Dan advises me when I wake.

I shake my head. "I cannot," I say.

Dan Dan looks at me with a kindly pity. "It is normal to be nervous on your first day in your husband's household, my lady," she says. "But the Prince has given his orders and he cannot be disobeyed. Let me help you."

I wash and dress. Dan Dan opens one chest after another filled with robes that have been made for me. Dressed in a peach robe with delicate floral embroidery, my hair pinned with golden tassels and jade carved pins, I stand in the doorway of my rooms, uncertain and afraid.

Now that it is daylight I can see that the Prince's palace complex is large. It follows a fairly standard layout: Dan Dan indicates the direction of the main gates which give onto large courtyards and halls, housing temples and administrative rooms, receiving halls and other buildings relevant to the Prince's official and public life. Set back from this area, behind additional gates, mirroring the Inner Court of the Forbidden City, is a complex of small palaces and courtyards, each housing the Prince or one of his ladies, as well as some more communal buildings where we may eat, pray, or spend time together. These last are grouped around a large garden complete with a small lake filled with lotus flowers fed by a stream, as well as a little walkway through black twisted rocks.

"Brought here from the South," says Dan Dan as she leads me through them on our way to breakfast. "The Prince is very fond of gardens. He was brought up in the Yuan Ming Yuan."

"The Garden of Perfect Brightness? What is that?" I ask.

"It was the residence of his father the Emperor when he was just a boy," says Dan Dan as we walk around the perimeter of the water lily-filled pond. "Now it has been designated the Imperial Summer Palace. The Prince is having all manner of fine buildings and gardens developed within the grounds, some of them by the Jesuits in the Western style."

I have no idea what she is talking about and anyway my attention is focused on a hall straight ahead of us.

"The dining hall," says Dan Dan, seeing my eyes fixed on it. "Lady Fuca will be there already, she is an early riser. There may be some of the other ladies there too. You were the last to arrive, so this morning you will all be here."

I want to turn and run back to my own rooms, to hide there forever, but that is not a possibility. I take a deep breath and step through the doorway into the hall, Dan Dan following behind me.

"Ula Nara!"

"Wan," I say, sighing with relief when I see she is the only occupant aside from a few maids and eunuchs who are busy setting dishes on the table.

We embrace and she leads me to a place midway up the long table, to sit by her side. I see Dan Dan beam at us, no doubt pleased to see me smile for the first time since she has met me.

The table is lavishly full of dishes: not just the honeyed buns and rice porridge that my family would have served but steamed rolls, duck soup with yams, mushroom pastries, bamboo shoots, cooked lotus root and various other hot and cold dishes, as well as rice and pickles. There is watermelon juice to drink. The rest of the table is filled with beautifully presented dishes of fruits and nuts including walnuts and almonds, fresh peaches, dried dates and early pears. Wan gestures at the table.

"Enough for a banquet," she says, giggling.

Her demeanour here is different, it is as though a great weight has left her, turning her from a nervous child to a chattering smiling young girl. I cannot help smiling at her.

"Are you still unhappy?" she whispers.

"I will never be happy without Niu Lang," I say.

She nods and passes me a plate of pork and cabbage. "I pray you will find peace here, one day," she says.

I cannot speak of Niu Lang without crying and so I focus on Wan instead. "Have you met the Prince?" I ask.

She nods and smiles. "I arrived early yesterday," she says. "He walked with me in the garden. He is very kind, very gentle."

I nod. I am glad to hear good things of Prince Bao. I have enough unhappiness in my heart without hearing anything bad about him.

"Where are the other ladies?" I ask. "I was told Lady Fuca and the others would be here."

Wan nods. "My maid told me Lady Su is something of a late riser," she says. "But the others will be here soon." She frowns. "I am not sure where Lady Fuca is, I was told she was in the habit of rising early."

There is a slight commotion by the doorway and Lady Gao enters. I remember her from the Draft: not really a beauty, she has a calm, almost stolid demeanour about her. Behind her comes Lady Zhemin, a little flustered.

"I am sorry I am late," she begins. "I was feeding the ducks and lost track of time." Then she sees that only Wan and I are at the table. "Oh," she says. "I am Zhemin."

We all introduce ourselves and as we are doing so Lady Su arrives, her porcelain beauty untarnished by the journey here and the early hour. When I give my name I see the others' eyes flicker and know that they are remembering what happened when I was chosen, my name forever branded on their memory. I see them note my puffy eyes and am aware that they treat me gently, as though I may begin to cry at any moment. Since there is still no sign of Lady Fuca we settle round the table and eat. I cannot stomach much apart from fruit and nuts, but the watermelon juice is fresh and thirst-quenching.

"His Highness!" The eunuch making the announcement steps away from the door to allow first Prince Bao and then Lady Fuca to enter. Hastily, we all rise and step away from the table, then kneel to begin our kowtows to this man, our husband.

He waits until we have finished, then smiles radiantly. "Rise," he says. "I will join you at breakfast." He looks to his side at Lady Fuca. "Sit by me," he says.

They take their places side by side at the head of the table, although there is plenty of room for them to sit further apart. But I can see at once that there is already a closeness between the two of them. They allow their arms to touch and when he makes her laugh Fuca leans her head against his shoulder for a moment. He takes choice morsels from his plate and puts them into her mouth with his chopsticks, before remembering his manners and choosing select items for the rest of us, which however are passed to us on tiny plates by attentive servants, well-bred signs of favour but not of intimacy.

"I must leave you all," the Prince says after only a brief stay, during which he has eaten heartily, favouring dishes of game and noodles.

We rise and he nods his head to us all as we bow to him. "I will return soon," he promises, but his eyes are only on Fuca, who smiles and touches a late summer rose in her hair as though to acknowledge it as a gift from him.

"I suppose she has been here almost a month already, so they have had time to get to know each other," says Wan afterwards as we stroll around the little lake. "They look happy together," she adds a little wistfully.

I nod. It is clear to me already that the Prince is much taken with his Primary Consort. Nevertheless, he has other ladies and no doubt each of us will be called upon as a companion in due course. I feel my body tighten up at the thought of his hands on me, of his lips touching mine when mine have never even touched Niu Lang's. Part of me hopes he will be so besotted with Lady Fuca that he will simply forget about the rest of us altogether, perhaps forever.

We are called for, of course. First, to no-one's surprise, is beautiful Lady Su, who joins us at breakfast the next day blushing but all smiles when she sees the Prince. I don't feel that I know her well enough to ask any questions, but clearly both she and the Prince were pleased with the encounter. I wait for Lady Fuca to show signs of jealousy, but she does not, she seems happy enough and I think that probably she has been well-trained to expect this life, she will have been told that to show jealousy will not endear her to the Prince. And sure enough her gracefulness in this matter is rewarded, for several days go by before anyone else is called for, Lady Fuca returned to her place as favourite.

Lady Gao is called for and returns with her calm exterior unruffled. I cannot imagine that she is a very passionate bedfellow. Lady Zhemin looks a little flustered after her turn, but then she often does. When Wan is called I tremble for her but she returns more confident than before.

"He said I was very young," she confides. "He will not call for me until I am a little older. He says he will honour me in all other ways."

Reluctantly I give the Prince his dues. It was clear to most of us that Wan was very young to be married and he has not forced himself upon her still half-childish body. I have to concede that he is a kind husband. After that night he seems to treat Wan like a younger sister, bringing her the odd flower from the garden and teasing her a little when we eat together, showing her a friendly but passionless warmth.

Days go by and it is only Fuca who is called for. I know that the night she is not called for will be my own turn, for each lady has now been sent for except me.

The days pass so slowly I frequently think there must be some mistake and ask Dan Dan more than once if she is sure about the date. There is nothing to do here. At home there were visitors and we visited neighbours, went for walks, did errands, shopped, played in the garden. Here I feel I must act the part of a grown woman, for I am married now, and the Imperial Family, it seems, does not allow its women the kind of freedom most Manchu women enjoy. We do not leave the palace complex. Each day I wash and dress, then Dan Dan does my hair. I walk with Wan and the others in the garden, perhaps read or play a board game. I feed my magpies, whose wings have been clipped so that they cannot escape. They grow tame, eating from my hand and I have a larger enclosure built for them, an aviary in the garden courtyard outside my window, where I can see them flutter from perch to perch. I eat with the other ladies, sometimes the Prince attends as well, but mostly he does not.

I wonder whether he has been told something of my story, if he knows that I begged not to marry him or whether this information has been hidden from him. Either way, he has left me until last amongst his ladies and quite some time has passed since I arrived here, we are midway through autumn.

Outside there is a cold frost, the first of the year. I stand at the window watching the magpies, whose aviary has been moved to a more sheltered corner of the courtyard.

"The Prince has asked for you," says Dan Dan, bringing me a selection of robes, her round face beaming.

"Now?" I ask. "Isn't it breakfast time?"

"Not now," chuckles Dan Dan. "As a companion. Tonight. He sent a servant."

I feel a chill come over me. This, then, is the moment I have been dreading. It had to come some time.

It is the only day that has passed quickly here, breakfast seems to be over in moments. The Prince is there but I cannot bring myself to meet his eye and he leaves early, as usual.

I walk in the garden and feed the magpies, try and fail to read before asking Wan to join me in praying at the temple. Wan knows that I have been summoned and tries to take my mind off the fast-approaching nightfall. We pray at the Daoist temple, but all I can focus on are the monks. Does Niu Lang look like them now, I wonder? Is his head shaven and does he wear the dark blue tunic and leg wraps that they do? Does he spend his time at prayer and in practicing the martial arts he always loved? Wan takes me to her own rooms, offers me tea and sweets, plays a silly drinking game with me, hoping to lighten my mood and perhaps thinking that if I am a little tipsy I will not be so afraid or tense.

"I need to go now," I tell her, as dusk falls.

I am bathed and dressed, my hair filled with gold and jade, pulled so tightly onto a black lacquered board that I think I will get a headache. I cannot choose a robe, they all look the same to me in my jittery state, so Dan Dan selects one for me, a green that I think makes me look even paler than I already am. I do not care.

At the appointed hour she leads me to the Prince's own palace, larger than any of ours. It includes a receiving hall with a throne, adding to the formality of the place and reminding me of his supposed future. This man may be the Emperor one day: not just my husband but my ruler. A eunuch is waiting for me and Dan Dan leaves with an encouraging smile. I want to run after her but of course that is not possible. Instead I follow the eunuch.

We pass through a living room full of curious objects such as Western clocks, which make a ticking sound as I pass them: I have only ever seen one before but I count more than ten here. There are many delicate carvings on display, in everything from wood to jade. The walls are hung with scrolls of paintings and calligraphy, poetry. Clearly he is a man who admires beautiful things. I think of Lady Su and wonder whether she was chosen to add to his collection.

We reach the bedchamber, where the bed dominates most of the room. Even though it is set into an alcove as is usual it is, if possible, even larger than my own and hung with heavy drapes in a rich yellow, not quite the Imperial yellow reserved for the Emperor but certainly something which hints at it. There is little else in the room, focusing all my attention only on the bed. The Prince is nowhere to be seen.

"His Highness will be here shortly," says the eunuch, unfastening my robes. It feels awkward to stand alone in a room with a man, even if he is a eunuch, and allow him to undress me, but I stand still and let him dispose of all my clothes, leaving me entirely naked. I wonder whether he compares the Prince's ladies, since he has now seen each of us disrobed, whether he thinks that I am more womanly than Wan but less beautiful than Su, whether he feels any desire for us or whether all desire left him when he gave up his manhood to become a eunuch to the Imperial household. He does not seem very interested in me, once I am undressed he simply turns and leaves the room with no further instruction.

I shiver. I am not really cold, for the room is well heated, but I feel exposed, standing here naked and yet I am unsure whether I should climb into the bed or not. In the end I sit on the edge of it and pull one of the silken coverlets up a little to cover at least part of my body.

"Lady Ula Nara."

I stand up, still clutching the coverlet, to face the Prince. He smiles, apparently unbothered by the awkwardness of the setting: the two of us alone for the first time, he entirely clothed while I have been stripped naked. I try to offer a smile, although I doubt it looks convincing. I am trying so hard not to think of Niu Lang that he is all I can see before me. I wonder for a moment whether I should simply close my eyes and pretend he is here, accept the Prince's caresses as his and forget where I truly am.

"I hope you have been given everything you need," says the Prince.

"Yes," I say.

"Your magpies are delightful," he says. "A gift?"

"From my family," I lie.

He smiles. "A charming wedding gift," he says. "True love."

I nod. My lips are stretched out across my teeth but I am not sure I am smiling.

Finding me a poor conversationalist he begins to undress, his movements brisk and practical. I slowly return to my position on the edge of the bed.

"Be at ease," he says.

I make my way to the far side of the bed and cover myself entirely with the coverlets. The eunuch did not unbind my hair and the elaborate pinnings feel awkward if I lie on my side, so instead I lie on my back and look up at the ceiling. I hear the Prince reach the bedside and then the largest lantern goes dark, leaving the room in a dimmer light as he reaches out to touch me.

I try not to cry. But the tears start as soon as the Prince touches me and I cannot make them stop. It is not the pain, although there is a little pain. It is not his touch, for as far as I can tell he is gentle enough. He offers caresses and even a few words of tenderness, although since he barely knows me he might as well be speaking to any of his ladies, there is nothing meant only for my ears. He does not rush to take his pleasure but once he has done so, once it is all over, he strokes my cheek and finds the tears which he could not see in the dim light.

"Did I hurt you?" he asks.

I shake my head.

He rolls onto one arm, looking down at me where I lie, still and silent. I can just make out the shape of him in the darkness. "Is something wrong? Are you unhappy here?"

What answer could I give that would be acceptable? What can I say? There is nothing to say, so I say nothing. But this does not satisfy him.

"Speak to me, Ula Nara," he says. "Tell me what is wrong."

"There is nothing wrong," I whisper. "I am sorry, Highness."

"You may call me Bao," he says.

I nod.

"You must tell me what is wrong," he says. "I will make it right."

I want to laugh. Really? Will he send me away from here, back to Niu Lang, if I tell him that I have been taken away from my beloved, that I can never love anyone else?

"It is nothing, High – Bao," I say.

He tries again the next time I am summoned. My tears flow and he tries to find out what

is the matter. And again. After those three times, I am no longer summoned. He treats
me with every courtesy in public but he does not walk alone with me in the garden, as
he does daily with Lady Fuca and sometimes makes time for Su or Gao, or even, more
rarely, Zhemin and Wan. Each of us is called in dutiful turn to his bedchamber except
for myself and Wan, whose body has yet to develop a womanly form. The Prince is tired
of my tears, my silent refusal to name the source of my unhappiness. He does not wish
to lie with a woman who weeps and weeps and yet cannot be comforted.

Winter comes and buries our tiny world in an unending whiteness. Fuca, Wan, Zhemin
and Su throw snowballs and giggle together, while Gao wades through the thick drifts
in her high boots, her face solemn. I sometimes wonder if she, too, has a secret sorrow,
but I do not have the energy to ask her, to create enough of a friendship to allow for
such confessions. So we stand, the two of us, silent and apart from the others, watching
a world we should be a part of yet cannot seem to join.

Our husband proves his virility as first one lady and then another lets it be known
that she is with child. Zhemin almost disappears to her rooms, stricken with a constant
nausea that means the kitchen can only prepare the plainest of cold food for her, hardly
warming fare in the freezing late winter. I see her anxious face at the windows sometimes
and wave to her but she only waves back and disappears again from sight. Su spends most
of her time resting, for her pregnancy seems to weary her delicate beauty, she looks pale
and tired. I visit her occasionally with Wan and we play board games together, but her
rooms are kept at a temperature that I find stifling.

Only Fuca blooms. Her belly swells and her demeanour becomes ever more joyful.
Her child will be born first and the Prince sets aside more and more time to spend with
her, enchanted with her health and happiness. I see them sitting side by side on the
garden swing as the weather turns towards spring, heads together, hands clasped. I hear
their laughter and have to turn away. They remind me of what Niu Lang and I should
have been. Instead, I have been chosen for a life I never wanted and I am not even
successful at it: uncalled for, friendless except for Wan.

"You must try a little harder, my lady," says Dan Dan one day.

"What do you mean?" I ask her, stroking the male magpie who has come to eat from
my hand. The female is nesting, I offer them little twigs and scraps of cloth and they
diligently weave a home for their future eggs.

"You must try harder to be happy here," she says.

"How?" I ask.

"Make friends with the other ladies. Spend time with them. They will be your
companions in this life for many years to come, there is no use in petty jealousies."

"I am not jealous of them," I say, although this is not quite true. I am jealous of
them for finding some small happiness here. I am jealous of the love between Fuca and
the Prince, so open and easy, far away from what I may ever attain.

"Then make friends," insists Dan Dan. "I have served the Imperial Family for many years, my lady. The happiest women are those who find friends amongst their companions, who seek some joy in their husband's company."

"I am no longer called for," I say.

"Begin with the ladies," says Dan Dan. "Make friends and find some happiness in your daily life. When the Prince sees your changed demeanour he will call for you again. He is good to his ladies, he is a man of virtue. He seeks harmony. He will gladly call for you again if he sees that you desire his company."

I do not desire his company, I think, but I nod and Dan Dan goes about her business, satisfied.

I force myself to spend more time with the other ladies but Gao is too solemn and silent for my liking. Zhemin and Su are about to birth their children, they are wrapped up in their own little worlds. I see them sitting together, chattering of babies and mothering. I cannot bring myself to join them for long. They sense my boredom and politely try to speak of other things but I know that they would rather return to their most-beloved topic and so I leave them to it. Wan, as ever, is a good friend, but I cannot spend every day with her.

"You should walk with the Prince," she suggests, seeing my isolation. "He is very kind. And he talks of many interesting things. Have you seen his collection of clocks? He showed me how they work inside, all little cogs and wheels that turn. He let me wind one," she adds, like a child indulged by a loving father.

Dan Dan also encourages me, seeing how much time I spend alone. "The Prince might be a friend, at least?"

I tell myself that I do not need to love the Prince. I could be a pleasant companion to him. There is no need to be called to his bedchamber, he has enough women for that and more will be added over the years. I could simply be a woman with whom he can converse and share his interests. I have been well educated. I can read and write, recite poetry, I can play board games and paint a little. My calligraphy was praised by my tutors. Perhaps he would welcome such a friendship and I would not be untrue to Niu Lang, merely far away from him.

"Your collection of clocks is very fine," I begin, the next time I see him.

He looks my way and his face brightens for a moment but Fuca laughs.

"He is obsessed, Ula Nara! Do not talk to him of those clocks or you will never hear the end of it!"

At once his attention returns to her. "You do not understand their beauty," he says, teasingly. "Or perhaps you are simply jealous of the attention I give them?"

She giggles. "Are they more beautiful than I am?" she asks. "I think they must be, the amount of time you spend polishing them, dusting them, winding them. You are their servant!"

"I am your servant," he says, taking her hand and kissing it. "And none of them can match your beauty. You are without equal."

I look away from their faces, so bright with love and tenderness.

When Fuca retreats to her rooms and is delivered of a girl, I think that perhaps now Prince Bao will have more time for the rest of us while she is occupied elsewhere and besides, she has not given him a son. But he almost disappears entirely into her palace, visiting at all hours of the day and night to coo over his child. When both Zhemin and Su produce sons I set aside hope of a relationship of any kind with him. It is clear to me that I am superfluous to requirements. I cannot offer love, nor children, nor even hero worship as Wan seems to. I have been chosen for no reason, he would barely notice my absence were I to disappear or die, yet I have given up the man I love at the command of his mother, Lady Niuhuru.

I see his mother again for the first time since I was chosen, when we visit the court. Once more we enter the Forbidden City, this time not as candidates but as the chosen few, concubines to a man who will one day become an emperor. Everywhere we turn people bow to us, the eunuchs are excessively servile, maids scurry to do our bidding. We are dressed in our finest robes, our hair is bejewelled, we are the future of this court and the older concubines look at us with something approaching fear. The Emperor is still a man in the prime of life, of course, but on the day he dies, they will be banished to the back palaces, crumbling draughty places while we take their exquisite palaces and make them our own.

The Emperor sits in his carved throne, high above us. His Primary Consort, the Prince's mother Niuhuru, sits by his side.

"Why is she not the Empress?" I ask Wan, who always seems well-informed on court politics.

"She asked not to be named Empress," says Wan, her eyes wide at the very thought. "There was rivalry amongst the ladies and she did not wish to be the source of it."

"But she is still the Primary Consort," I say. "She is treated as an empress and she must carry out all the duties of the role. Why not take the title?"

Wan shrugs and shakes her head. It is an odd thing to do. Every lady of an emperor dreams of being made an empress, it is the pinnacle of achievement, superseded only by being a living dowager empress, mother to an emperor. The current Emperor's mother died within a short time of him taking the throne, so she did not even live long enough to fully enjoy the role.

We kowtow, the little group of us, Fuca at the front, leading the way, her every move perfectly formed, the epitome of grace. Prince Bao looks on, beaming, as his children's names are read out before the court, each lady who has birthed a child blushing with rightful pride. Those of us who have not yet produced a child lower our eyes, for no-one will care much for us until we have done so.

The Yongzheng Emperor looks weary, his face is pale and although he pauses in his work to celebrate his son's offspring and to greet each of us kindly, still a eunuch hovers by his side, holding a sheaf of papers.

"You must excuse me," says the Emperor. "I have much work to do."

We all kowtow again and he nods, distracted. I watch him as he takes up a writing brush dipped in the vermillion ink reserved for the Emperor alone and, frowning, looks through the folded papers he is being handed, writes a few notes here and there, passes them on to another eunuch and reaches out for yet more papers.

"He looks tired," I say quietly to Wan.

She nods. "He works very hard," she says. "They say he stays up late at night and then rises early again, he barely sleeps four hours each night. He drinks an elixir of longevity every day, for he says the empire will need much work for many years to come. He wishes to stamp out corruption, reform the taxes and ensure better provision for the very poor, such as orphans."

He sounds more like an diligent administrator than the Son of Heaven. "And his ladies?"

Wan shrugs. "He is not particularly interested. They are called for very seldom. He is a very dutiful man."

I look at the small gathering of older concubines and nod. Certainly he has very few ladies for an emperor. His father was known for having dozens of them. I wonder whether his taste does not lean that way, although from what Wan has told me of him it sounds as though he is simply too wrapped up in his work. Judging by the Prince's current behaviour I suspect he will be more like his grandfather than his father. I wonder what it will be like to have more and more ladies added to our numbers over the years. I shake my head a little. What do I care? It is not as if I will be jealous of them. I do not love the Prince. If there are plenty of concubines then I will continue not to be called for, which will be a relief to me.

"Lady Ula Nara."

I turn and find myself face to face with Niuhuru, the Prince's mother. I begin to kneel but she reaches out to stop me. Her face is very pale and up close her eyes are an odd grey colour that I have never seen before. As I recalled, she is considerably taller than I am, I have to look up to her.

"I hope that…" she begins and then clears her throat. "Are you well?" she begins again.

I know she is remembering the moment when she chose me, when I begged her to reconsider, her hesitation when she looked at the Chief Eunuch and was swayed to let her decision stand, when she looked over her shoulder to see me on all fours on the cobbles of the courtyard, my weeping as she chose my fate for me against my will. I look at her. I should assure her that I am well, that I have been much honoured by her choice of me for her son, that I am very happy here.

I cannot shape the words. I gaze into her grey eyes and say nothing. I watch as she waits for the reassurance she so badly wants and then the dawning realisation that I am not going to speak, that the damage she did to my life was greater than can be forgotten so lightly, so glibly.

At last she swallows. The silence between us is growing too long, it will be remarked upon. "I wish you happiness in your marriage to the Prince," she manages, as though she were some lowly courtier seeking to ingratiate herself. I only bow my head. I cannot find it in me to forgive this woman, who allowed protocol to override mercy and now wishes to be forgiven for it. There is a cold splinter trapped in my heart and she is the one who put it there.

Summer comes. The heat in Beijing is stifling. I think that it is almost a year since I was chosen and I wonder where Niu Lang is now. I wonder how he spends his days: whether in sadness or whether his life, of meditation and prayers, of constant and arduous physical training in martial arts, has brought a peacefulness to his life without me that I cannot seem to find without him.

"Tomorrow we will visit the Garden of Perfect Brightness," announces the Prince at breakfast. "We must leave very early to have time to walk around all of it, so that you can see how beautiful it is and how many great works are being undertaken there."

The sun has barely risen when we set off. I realise that, with the exception of the Forbidden City, only a short distance away, this is the first time I have left the Prince's palace since I was brought here. My world has grown smaller than I could ever have imagined.

To speed up our journey we are carried in mule-drawn wagons, something like merchants would travel in, but these have been equipped with as much luxury as possible, we are seated on thick cushions while silken drapes protect us from the gaze of any common passers-by, the wagon is surrounded by an escort of guards. The Prince rides ahead of us.

Fuca, as ever, is all bubbling happiness. "I am so excited to see the Garden," she says. "The Prince loves it so much. He has great plans for it."

I think that no doubt she knows all about his plans, for they spend so much time together, he shares all his thoughts with her. For all that she was chosen for her family's noble background, for her good breeding and elegance, somehow the heavens smiled on her match to the Prince, they genuinely love one another. I think with bitterness that I, too, could have had such a marriage if Lady Niuhuru had not chosen me for her son. I, too, could have listened to Niu Lang's plans for the future and shared in his enthusiasm for projects come to fruition. We would have planned our lives together, we would have been happy. I would have given him not one but many children and he would have cooed over them even as the Prince does, delighting in their every tiny gesture.

The other ladies babble together and I turn my face away, my excitement at being out now soured, looking through a tiny gap between the drapes into the world beyond, a world from which I am closed away.

The Yuan Ming Yuan, the Garden of Perfect Brightness, is more beautiful than I expected. My spirits lift a little as we walk along tiny pathways on the edges of large lakes filled with water lilies, over which iridescent dragonflies skim. The Garden is not some small country estate, it is a vast area, criss-crossed with water everywhere, from tiny streams one can step over, to canals and up to the largest lake of all, the Sea of Blessings.

"I grew up here," Prince Bao is saying, his face lit up with joy in his surroundings. "It was such a happy place to be a child. My own children must play here often."

I feel something in me soften towards him. I think of the Prince as a child, playing here by the lake's edge and can see why he loves this place. No doubt he is a good-hearted man. I do not love him, but that is hardly his fault, even as he does not care for me because I was meant for another and cannot help but show it. We should never have come together, each of us already had their own true love: he, Lady Fuca, I, Niu Lang. But he is happy because his true love is by his side, whilst mine has been lost to me forever.

"And now the Western Palaces," Bao announces. "You will be amazed."

I do not like the Western Palaces. The whole area designated for them is in turmoil. The tranquil beauty of the rest of the Garden is shattered here. Heavy squat buildings made of white stone tower over us, their facades over-carved with motifs that mean nothing to me and the whole lacking the delicacy of our own buildings. They are like hulking stone giants, lowering down on us puny mortals. Their whiteness reminds me of death and mourning robes. A few of the buildings are complete, others are half-built, sweating men toiling over their construction, dust everywhere. Piles of materials, felled trees and half-dug trenches threaten to harm us if we do not step carefully. Absurdly, Prince Bao leaps into a trench and tries his hand at the backbreaking work of digging, his silk robes growing stained with sweat and damp earth. Fuca and the others cheer him on, giggling at his efforts, but I stand back. He is like a child showing off to his mother, expecting applause for some foolish parody of a grown man's labour. At last he climbs out, grinning as though he has done something worthy of praise, then summons us to come closer and hear how the plans are progressing from his chosen architect, a Jesuit priest named Lang Shining, although the Prince addresses him as Giuseppe, apparently his original name. He is dressed as a scholar might be here, in long black robes and a tall black hat, all of which have become covered in dust and mud in a way that would be most unbecoming of any scholar. His face and forearms are sunburnt to a deep walnut, his eyes are a rich brown and he has a dark curly beard. He must be in his forties, a similar age to the Emperor and indeed the Prince talks to him as a child might a beloved father, with an eager expectation of being humoured mixed with respectful awe at his abilities.

"He is building a maze," he informs us, then turns back to Giuseppe with a laugh. "Will people really get lost in it?"

The Jesuit smiles, humouring him. "For a little while."

"Make it harder!" says the Prince and the other ladies all laugh. He turns to Fuca. "Giuseppe is building a maze in which you will get utterly lost," he says. "I will have to come and rescue you. You will be wandering there until it is dark!"

She smiles up at him and touches his arm. "I know you would rescue me before dark fell," she says confidently. "You would not leave me to wander alone and afraid."

He covers her hand with his and offers her a tender smile. "I would run to your side at once," he assures her and they gaze at one another. Some of the other ladies give forced giggles, no doubt each of them wishing the Prince would jest like this with them. I look away, wondering for how many years I will have to watch a loving relationship at close quarters whilst being barred from one myself.

At last we leave the works. The Prince promises that we will return soon, for another inspection. He plucks a spring of yellow flowers from a bush as we pass it and spends a few moments clumsily pinning it into Fuca's hair while she laughs at his efforts. "The maze should have Imperial yellow flowers planted all about it," he calls back to the Jesuit, who bows as we depart the Garden and return to our tiny world.

The Qixi Festival comes and goes. I see some of the unmarried maids giggling together, taking their little embroidery samples to the temple. As darkness falls I feel an eagerness grow in me. Tonight Niu Lang and I will gaze at the stars together and we will be united in spirit. I should not be celebrating this festival any more, for it is only for unmarried girls, but I cannot feel that I am truly married to the Prince. So in secret I have been stitching a little sample of my embroidery: two magpies entwined, like the ice carving Niu Lang made for me. I cannot take it to a temple of course, but I go early in the morning to the part of our lake that tapers off into a stream, which leaves the palace complex. I drop it into the slow-moving current, thinking that in this way I have made an offering and perhaps the Lovers will accept it as proof of my undying love for my own beloved.

The night is warm and as soon as the first stars can be seen I make my way into my own little courtyard garden. I look up at the vast dark sky and the tiny sparkles of each star. When I make out the Lovers' stars I wait a few moments but feel only emptiness. Niu Lang promised me that on this night we would be together in spirit but I feel nothing. What had I expected? That we would magically be together? That I would hear the fluttering of my magpies' wings, turn and see him standing by my side, come to his beloved, as his namesake the Cowherd once did in a land of fairytales? The stars glow in the dark night sky and I stand alone, whatever romantic notions I had for my life fading. The cold realisation sweeps over me that I will never see Niu Lang again, neither in spirit nor in body. I will live out my life in this enclosed world without love or friendship. I cannot even be a well-bred companion to the Prince, for he loves elsewhere and has already discarded me as a bedfellow. I will never be released from this place, from this marriage, except by Prince Bao's death or my own. I wonder which will come first.

"Are you well, Ula Nara?" It is Fuca.

"I am well," I reply stiffly, wondering why she has sought me out.

She is quiet for a moment, gazing at the stars before she speaks again. "I would like you to be happy here," she says at last.

"Why?" I ask, before I can stop myself. "You are happy here, why do you care if I am?"

She nods, as if what I am saying has confirmed something for her. "I care because I am Bao's Primary Consort," she says gently. "It is not my purpose simply to seek my own happiness in marriage. It is my purpose to care for all of His Highness' ladies, for the rest of my life. I am to choose his brides, to ensure they settle well into this life, strange as it may be. It is my role to set them a good example."

"You should have had a son then," I say spitefully. I cannot bear to hear Fuca, who has everything I could wish for, tell me that she wants me to be happy.

She is quiet again. "I pray one day I will be fortunate enough to bear a son," she says at last, with no hint of anger or hurt at my insult. "Meanwhile my daughter is a blessing to myself and the Prince." She does not remind me that I have not borne any children at all. "If you ever wish me to help you in any way, Ula Nara, I will willingly do so," she says, and then she walks away, towards her own palace.

I swallow. I have been unforgivably rude to the Prince's Primary Consort, a future Empress. I should be afraid. But there is a little bit of me that took pleasure in speaking hurtful words, in lashing out at Fuca's eternally sunny disposition. I find myself, sometimes, thinking of what else I could have said to hurt her, to make her as unhappy I am.

The Lovers' Festival has passed. Barely ten days later, the Festival of Hungry Ghosts is upon us. There is food laid out all over the palace complex for the ghosts who will walk among us when night falls, searching for food and worship to assuage their hunger. There are huge halls laid out with long tables covered with food and smoking incense, at which nobody sits, for these places are reserved for the dead. On this day the gates of the underworld open up and ghosts come wandering into our world. There are those who are our own ancestors, whom we honour by burning models of what they may be in need of in the other world: paper houses and money, horses and servants. There is food that they may eat. But there are other ghosts, unknown to us, unvenerated by their families, who are hungry and yet can never be filled. Afraid of the misfortune they might bring upon a family, food is also left for these wandering souls, hoping to appease their never-ending hunger. Every temple displays vast platters of food and even the maids and eunuchs place little offerings of food to add to the sacrifices. The temples' altars are heavy with offerings of food and incense, paper in vast quantities is burnt, folded and painted into the shapes of horses, money, food, houses, ploughs, palanquins and more, all of which will come to life in the afterworld and be at the service of those who came before us.

I wake that night to the clattering of guards running in our courtyard, a scream in the darkness from Fuca. I jump out of my bed and hurry to the window, where I see her form in lantern-lit shadows, hair loose and dishevelled, robes still being put on by servants who cluster around her before she is hurried into a palanquin, whose bearers run out of our courtyard at full tilt.

"They say the Prince is very ill and Fuca has been sent for," murmurs Dan Dan by my side.

I watch the palanquin as it rocks unsteadily away at top speed with Fuca inside it, the only one of us summoned, each of us reminded again of our worth to the Prince by this choice. Outside I can see Wan is already speaking with the guard. Everyone tells everything to Wan, her delicate features and wide eyes inviting confidences so that she is always the best informed of all of us. I make my way to her, as do my fellow concubines.

"They think Bao has been poisoned," Wan says, tears brimming in her eyes. "They say he was at a banquet in the Forbidden City and they believe his own brother Hongshi sat beside him and slipped poison into a dish that he ate from. They say his tongue has turned black. His mother and the Emperor are in attendance with the Court Physician."

The other girls gasp and chatter. I wonder what will happen to me if the Prince dies and I am widowed. Will I be handed a white silk scarf and encouraged to *follow-in-death*, as the Manchu women of old would have done? Probably not. These days it is more usual to become a 'chaste widow': to never remarry and instead live a life devoted to the memory of my deceased husband. But there is a part of me that wonders whether I might be permitted to remarry after all. I know that a few women are. I am childless, young. I am not an emperor's concubine. I am not even the Prince's Primary Consort. I might be sent back to my family. I might marry Niu Lang after all. My hands are shaking.

"Let us all sit together and comfort one another," says Wan, after Zhemin has had a fit of hysterical crying and it has taken three maids to calm her down again.

Reluctantly, I follow the others into the dining hall, where the maids light the lanterns, then bring hot tea and little dishes of sweets and nuts, of dried and fresh fruit, as though any of us would wish to eat in the middle of the night while our destinies hang in the balance.

We sit, mostly in silence, only broken by Zhemin still sniffling to herself. The lanterns burn on and on as the long dark night proceeds to a watery dawn and finally the arrival of a messenger who comes to tell us that all is well, the Prince will recover. Zhemin breaks into hysterical weeping again, unable to manage her emotions one way or another.

"I will go to the temple to give thanks," says Wan and Su follows her. Gao looks at me.

"I am going to bed," I say, although when I stand I feel my knees give way and have to clutch at the table to stop myself falling.

Fourteen days after the Festival of Hungry Ghosts, lanterns must be lit to guide the spirits home, for fear that any should stay here in our world. Each of us places tiny lanterns in the little stream that feeds our lake and then watch as they bob in the darkness. Each light that goes out is a spirit returning home. I sit by the lake long after all the flames have gone out, the darkness all around me a strange comfort. I cannot see my surroundings, can imagine that I am somewhere else, perhaps in a household of my own, with Niu Lang somewhere nearby.

The poisoning of the future heir cannot go unpunished and we are all summoned to the Forbidden City to watch the wrath of an empire fall on Hongshi, older brother but discarded heir. For once Yongzheng does not look like a weary scribe, he looks like an Emperor, his thin body encased in the heavy Imperial yellow silk that marks the Son of Heaven. Niuhuru, at his side, is white-faced and grim-mouthed. Hongshi is nowhere to be seen but his mother, Lady Qi, stands before the thrones, her hands clenching and unclenching.

"The son of this miserable woman is sent to the Cold Palace, he has been banished from the Forbidden City," begins Yongzheng and Lady Qi falls to her knees. "This unworthy son's name has been stricken from the *yudie,* jade plate."

Lady Qi wails.

I swallow. Hongshi's name has been erased from the Imperial Genealogical Record. He will no longer be listed as the Emperor's son. This is what a court can do to those who fail to comply with its rules and expectations, who dare to challenge it.

"We can only hope," continues Yongzheng, "that this dishonour will lead him to take the only possible action expected of a man."

Lady Qi screams and sinks to her knees.

I look at Wan, whose slight frame is shaking at the spectacle. I take her hand to try and comfort her. I wonder whether it would have been us, standing here, asked to take our lives, if the Prince had died.

Now Niuhuru speaks. "Lady Qi will be removed from her palace and will join previous ladies of the court in the back palaces."

Lady Qi crawls towards the throne, her voice ragged with sobs. "I ask for mercy. For my undeserving son and for myself, his unworthy mother."

"No mercy will be granted," says Yongzheng. He rises to his feet as Lady Qi's arms are grasped by the guards, who drag her screaming from the room.

The room empties quickly once the Emperor leaves but I linger by a large embroidered screen, half-hiding myself so that I will not be expected to visit the Prince in his sickroom, as the other ladies are about to do: what would he want to see me for? I do not want to cluster with the courtiers and hear more whispering gossip, I have seen and heard enough for one day. I feel sick to my stomach.

I trace the design of the screen for a few moments, feeling the silk beneath my fingertips, a pattern of delicate blossom against a mountain vista. At last I take a deep breath and compose myself. I will return to the Prince's household.

But there is a whispering going on in the huge empty room, the murmur of voices. I look out from the screen and see Niuhuru standing alone with the Jesuit Lang Shining, or Giuseppe as the Prince called him, although I cannot pronounce it.

I frown. Niuhuru's hand is on the Jesuit's sleeve as though they were close friends, their eyes are fixed on one another as she speaks.

"I cannot live like this," she says. "I cannot, Giuseppe."

"Come to the Garden of Perfect Brightness," he says, as though he has the right to invite her anywhere.

Behind me a maid appears, whom I wave away, losing track of what else the Jesuit has said to Niuhuru. When I look at them again her eyes are filled with tears and his hand is placed over hers, their bodies so close they could kiss with the slightest movement forwards. For one moment I think they will actually do so, before she steps back and hurries away, almost running, as though to stay one moment longer is to risk a terrible temptation. I stare. Have I just caught a glimpse of a forbidden relationship between the Emperor's Primary Consort and a Jesuit? It cannot be and yet the way they looked at each other was full of love and longing, full of fear of being seen. I cannot believe it.

The Jesuit is standing looking down at the floor, his face grave. I step out from behind the screen and approach him.

"You are a great comfort to Lady Niuhuru," I say.

He turns, startled. He had not seen me, believed himself to be alone. His eyes flicker towards the doorway where Niuhuru has just left, perhaps wondering what I have seen between them. My eyes widen. I am right. His eyes, his reaction, have told me everything, as though he had fallen on his knees and confessed it. But he is too good a courtier not to know how to smooth over this moment.

"Lady Ula Nara," he says, bowing. "You must be relieved that the Prince is making a recovery."

I want to laugh. Surely the gossiping maids have made half the court aware by now that the Prince has no interest in me. "Lady Fuca is by his side," I say.

"Of course," he agrees, a little flustered at my lack of courtly politeness. "Although I am sure he would find the care of any of his ladies a comfort at this time."

I will not allow this to go unchallenged, for him to keep repeating untrue statements while he tries to cover up what I have just witnessed. "His Highness only has eyes for Lady Fuca," I say bluntly.

He forces a smile. "Considering what has just happened, it is best to put aside rivalries if possible," he says. "We must take love where we find it and be content with what we find."

I look down at his sleeve, where a few moments ago Niuhuru's hand and his own were touching. "Take love where we find it," I echo. Does he think he can fool me, that he can take away what I have seen? Or is he confessing to me, allowing me to know some of the pain he feels in loving a woman who is absolutely forbidden to him? For a moment I think of Niu Lang and wonder, will I still feel this pain when I, too, am forty?

"I will leave you now, your ladyship," the Jesuit says and bows, then walks away swiftly, his body tense as though he can feel my gaze on him, can feel the knowledge in my eyes following him.

And so my life in the Prince's household continues. He makes a full recovery and life goes on as it did before, we women daily bejewelled and coiffed for the benefit of a man whom we do not even see each day, a man who loves only one and merely lusts for a few others, the rest of us already discarded before we have even reached our full maturity. Wan fills out a little and is summoned to the Prince's bedchamber once or twice but then seems to be as little desired as Gao and I, although she does not seem to care. Wan and the Prince seem to have achieved what I have failed at: they are friends. He sends her little gifts including a puppy, walks and talks with her, teases her as though she were a beloved younger sister while she makes fun of him in a way few of us would dare and this seems to content both of them.

"Don't you want more?" I ask her once, exasperated by her eternally sunny disposition.

"You left a happy family and a sweetheart to be here," she reminds me, her face solemn for once. "I left a home where I was beaten and worse. Here I am safe and cared for, with friends and a man who will protect me from any harm. I have been set free."

I nod, although I want to tell her that her notion of what life could offer has been stunted by her miserable beginnings. But I am unhappy enough, I do not wish to take away her contentment.

The early autumn arrives. My magpies are so tame I sometimes let them out of their aviary and they will go for brief flights before returning to me, to sit nearby and wait to be fed tidbits. I walk in the garden, watching golden gingko leaves twist in the air as they fall, the red swirling bodies of the fish rising for food in the pond at the sight of me. There is a beauty to the natural world that gives me comfort and I think of the Garden of Perfect Brightness, wondering whether we will be able to visit it again soon. Perhaps, when one day Bao is made Emperor, we will all live there every summer. The thought brings me some small happiness.

Up ahead I hear laughter and rounding the corner I catch sight of the Prince and Fuca. She is pressed up against the trunk of a red-leafed maple tree, its leaves entwined in her tumbling hair, which has escaped its gold and jade pins to fall down to her waist. The Prince's face is bowed to her neck, then lower to the top of one breast, half exposed through her unbuttoned silk robe. He is covering her with kisses and caresses, her face tilted up to the sky, eyes closed in delight.

I should turn away. I should hurry back through the twisting black rocks to another part of the garden or to my own rooms, should look away from their moment of intimacy and yet I cannot. I watch them, one hand on the cold black rock, the other clenched by my side. I watch their caresses and hear their whispers, I see their desire grow and in the end, shameless and choked with my own unmet desire, I watch their coupling, the wild intensity of it followed by the softness of their embrace, their secret murmurs as they leave the garden dishevelled and sated. I watch and know that this, what I have seen, has been taken from me without my knowledge, without my consent, that this happiness has been lost to me without even knowing it could exist.

The cold days draw closer. One night the heavy thud of running men in armour comes again to our quiet world and brings the announcement that we did not expect to hear for many years. The Yongzheng Emperor has died, overworked by his own diligence. The golden box hidden behind the throne in the Palace of Heavenly Purity is opened with much ceremony to reveal the name that all the world already knew would be there. Prince Bao is named the Qianlong Emperor and we, his women, are called to the Forbidden City.

Rain falls on the dark water of the lake in our garden as we leave, the Lovers' tears falling from Heaven.

Rosewood

THE FORBIDDEN CITY IS FOGGED with incense, the choking fragrant clouds billowing everywhere we turn as the weather grows colder. We wear white mourning robes for the Yongzheng Emperor, our pale faces disappearing into collars of thick white fur, our black hair unbound in grief and startling in contrast, whipped about our faces by the winter's winds.

If I thought I was lonely before, now I know the true meaning of the word. Where once we women all lived together and there was at least some company whether you wished for it or not, now we are isolated even from each other. Our palanquins clustered together one last time as we travelled through the vast stretches of the Outer Court on that first day when we entered the Forbidden City as the new Emperor's ladies, before one after another disappeared into a different gateway. Each of us has been assigned to a grand palace of our own, our meals will be taken alone unless we are called on to attend a formal banquet.

I walked from room to room inside my new palace, spaces which dwarfed my previous accommodation. The rooms were strangely empty, stripped bare of all but a few necessary items of furniture.

"The palace has only just been vacated and the furnishings returned to storage," the eunuch accompanying me said. "You must order whatever you wish in the way of decoration and furniture from the Imperial storerooms, it will be sent at once."

I wonder who the woman was that I dislodged. A previous concubine of the Yongzheng Emperor, now relegated to a back palace, her status gone in the dying breath of her husband. I noted, too, that whoever she was, her furnishings were not really her own, even if she chose them and lived with them for many years. They belong to the empire and they were taken away when she was no longer highly-ranked enough to have them about her.

Now I may choose furnishings to surround myself with, from the items befitting my rank as newly-made Consort to the Emperor, while Fuca chooses from the more exalted storage rooms and furnishings which only an empress may command the use of.

Alone in my hastily re-decorated palace I stand with a rosewood *ruyi* in my hands, the ceremonial sceptre I was given as each lady stepped forward to be acknowledged by the new Emperor, our husband, Qianlong. His old name is now taboo, we must not speak his childhood name nor his princely title. Each of us was given a new title, a *ruyi* to clasp, a list of entitlements read out: taels of silver, bolts of silk, servants. Our entitlements did not include friendship, love, nor even the sating of suppressed desire. Only material goods, with which I am now surrounded in abundance.

"Your ladyship?"

I lay down the *ruyi* and turn to the eunuch who is managing the arrangement of each new household. "Yes?"

"Your new chief attendants."

A wizened old maid, gnarled hands and a hunched bony frame, as old as Dan Dan but less pleasant in demeanour, bowing.

"My name is Ping, ladyship."

"Ping is a very experienced maid, ladyship. She has served in the Forbidden City all her life," the eunuch assures me.

I wonder why Ping did not take her freedom when it was granted, leave while she was still young, why a woman would choose to remain here as a maid, unmarried and childless, forever serving the whim of one pampered court lady after another. I nod to her and look to the man who is to become my senior eunuch, head of my household. A tall man, broad of shoulder, he has a masculine air about him, unlike the other eunuchs, most of whom are fairly short and tend towards a soft plumpness.

"Feng, ladyship," he says, bowing.

"Feng is not *perfectly pure*, your ladyship," says the other eunuch a little worriedly as he sees me looking Feng up and down. "If this concerns you, you have only to say."

Most eunuchs, I know, are castrated at a young age, before they are grown to men, making them *perfectly pure*. But some men choose to become eunuchs at a later age, once grown to their full manhood, and these, having known life as a man, cannot be classed as such.

I shrug. "He may stay."

The eunuch bows. "You will have other servants attached to your palace, of course," he assures me. "But Feng will be the head of your household and Ping will be your chief maid."

I nod. I do not much care who serves me.

The Forbidden City swallows us up, our small group vanished into the endless courtyards and palaces, pomp and ceremony. All of us have multiple court robes made ready, we are obliged to carry out endless rituals to promise prosperity and happiness, fertility and good harvests for the empire, now that a new Emperor has been crowned. My days seem endlessly to be spent in temples, praying for harvests or rain, sun or good crops. When I return to my rooms I hold the rosewood *ruyi* in my hands and wonder: is this what I gave up love for? For the title of Consort to an emperor and a carved rosewood sceptre? For the bowing of the courtiers as I pass them and heavy robes of silk in a yellow shade not *too* close to the Imperial yellow that Fuca may now wear as Empress?

We sit for the coronation portraits, each of us women dressed alike, our hair and make-up the same. As court painter, the Jesuit is commissioned for this most important work and he labours for many hours while we sit in perfect silence, our posture upright, our lower lips stained vermillion. When the portrait is complete, a long scroll featuring Qianlong and his ladies, it is hard to tell one of us apart from another: not so much an artistic failure on the Jesuit's part, but the result of our transformation into Imperial ladies: the same hair, the same robes, the same makeup. We are modelled on those who came before. Those who come after us will be modelled on our own image, one Imperial woman turning into another down the generations, all of us the same.

Ping knows her work, I cannot fault her service, but she has a taste for telling stories of the history of the Forbidden City that I find both frightening and compulsive listening. Once the night call has gone out, warning that all men must leave the Forbidden City on pain of death, Ping will begin her tales. She does not light enough lanterns in my rooms, even when I ask for more, so that the shadows are deeper than they need to be and her tales can creep about in them.

"Did you know how the Forbidden City was built?" she asks me on my first night.

"The Ming Dynasty's Emperor Yongle ordered it built," I say, thinking back to my history lessons.

"Yes," she says. "It took fifteen years and he press-ganged more than a million men to create it. It has over a thousand buildings and nine thousand, nine hundred and ninety-nine rooms, one less than the rooms of Heaven."

"It is very grand," I say. "Although it does not feel very homely, even here in the Inner Court."

"How could it?" she asks with relish. "Tens of thousands of labourers died building it. Their vengeful spirits must be locked into every room of the Forbidden City."

I shiver a little and her eyes gleam. "Oh, the labourers are nothing," she says. "Did you not know about the concubines?"

"What concubines?" I ask.

"Yongle had hundreds of Korean girls brought to the Forbidden City as his concubines, for he admired their beauty. But one of the concubines had an affair with a eunuch and when she was discovered she took her own life."

"How sad," I say, hoping Ping will stop talking.

"Oh, that was only the beginning," she says with satisfaction. "When the Yongle Emperor found out about the affair he had every Korean concubine slaughtered, their bodies sliced up into pieces."

"I am going to bed," I say.

But on the following night Ping is ready with the next part of the story. "Only one Korean concubine survived," she says. "A Lady Cui, who was a favourite and had been ill during the massacre. She returned to see the bodies of her fellow concubines lying in pools of blood, their limbs hacked off."

I swallow.

"And it seemed Heaven was displeased, for the Forbidden City was struck with lightning and set on fire. Many, many men and women burnt to death."

"And Lady Cui?"

"Ah, she survived. But the Emperor fell ill and died, cursed by the Immortals."

"He was justly punished," I say, a little relieved by the triumph of good over evil in this story.

"He was," says Ping, her wrinkled face shadowy in the darkness of the corner of my room. "But Lady Cui was still not safe. His will insisted that his remaining ladies should never lie with another man."

I think of the women and their relief at having outlived a cruel husband. "Perhaps they were willing to live a quiet life, after all they had seen," I say.

"They were not given the choice," says Ping. "Lady Cui and fifteen other concubines were taken to a quiet hall in the Inner Court and given white silk scarves."

I stare at her in horror.

"They were obliged to take their own lives," says Ping.

She will not stop, even when I ask her to talk of something else. Every night she tells me other stories: of ghostly dogs who run through the tiny paths between the palaces of the Inner Court, of a woman wearing white mourning clothes who weeps and walks but does not reply to those who approach her and fades away as the sun rises. She talks of concubines who loved one another and were discovered and punished, beheaded for daring to find some small measure of happiness here. She tells tales of maids beaten to death for trivial misdemeanours, of desperately poor men who sought to feed their families by entering Imperial service as eunuchs and whose castrations went wrong, leaving them to die in agony and their children to starve to death. It seems she has a different story for every dark night and even though I do not want to hear these stories, still they draw me, so that I listen every time she tells them and then startle at shadows, shiver in fear under my covers, dare not look out of the windows into the darkness of the night, afraid of what I may see there. The Forbidden City, already hard and cold, becomes a place of ghosts to me, of horrors lurking in every one of its nine thousand nine hundred and ninety-nine rooms, with otherworldly beings stalking both the tiny pathways of the Inner Court and the vast open courtyards beyond. I sleep badly and wake often from half-remembered dreams in which I take the place of all these past miserable people who once lived here and now are gone.

I cry out in the dark from a dream in which an unseen person hands me a white silk scarf and I know, from the deep sense of dread I feel, what is expected of me. Awake, I whimper to myself, wishing I had insisted on a lantern to be kept burning all night, too afraid to step out of my bed and light one myself, lest some shadowed half-being should reach out its ghostly hands and touch me.

"Ladyship?"

"Feng," I say, with relief, seeing him framed in the doorway, a lantern in his hand.

"Is anything wrong?"

"I had a bad dream," I say, trying to sound unafraid. "It was nothing."

"I will sleep by your door every night, if you command it," he says.

I want to say no, for I feel like a foolish child, but the dream was too full of dread for me to easily dismiss it and his voice is comforting. "Yes," I say at last. "If it does not disturb you," I add, my voice trailing away.

"It is my honour," he says.

I hear him pad away and then return shortly with a bedroll, which he lays out across the threshold of my closed door. He lies down and covers himself with a blanket before blowing out the lantern. I lie still and take comfort in the sound of his breathing, even when it slows and I know he is asleep, the thought of another living person in my room soothing me until I drift into sleep myself. True to his word, from then on Feng sleeps every night in my room and I am grateful for it. Ping's stories still make me afraid, but at least I know that I have only to cry out and Feng will be awake and at hand.

The Imperial Daughters' Draft comes around again and I wait to see the new faces who will join us. Qianlong is a different man to his father. There are plenty of women chosen this time: official concubines but also many young ladies-in-waiting, for Qianlong wants a bright and lively court, one full of beauty and splendour. An anxious-looking young girl named Qing arrives and tries to befriend me, asking me whether we ladies spend much time together, but I shrug her away. It is only when the ceremony is over and I find myself weeping in my rooms that night that I realise that somewhere in my heart I had hoped Shu Fang would be chosen. This was her year, her chance to be selected and she has not been: she has been returned to our family, to marry whomever she pleases. I think of what it would have been like if she had joined me here. She would have brought her foolish cheerful ways with her, her lightness and romantic notions. She would have made me laugh, would have been my ally in this world of rivalries and constant striving for greater power. Her heart would not have turned bitter here, it was too full of joy. I realise that I will never see her again, will never hear her laugh or shriek my name and I sob and sob as though I will never stop, curled up in my lonely bed in my too-large rooms.

"Ladyship? Is it another dream?"

I shake my head although Feng can barely see me. "I – I miss my sister," I gulp.

In the darkness I see his shadowy figure move towards me, he sits on the side of my bed and gently pats my heaving shoulders. "Tell me about her," he says.

I talk for a long time, an incoherent jumbled mix of our lives together as children and Shu Fang's character, her silly ways. The time we got lost and how cross our father was with us, the way she laughed, a kitten we had and somewhere in all of it there is Niu Lang too, the headstrong boy from next door who was always getting into trouble. How we followed his lead but then hid when trouble came and how he never told on us. The snowball fights and taunts and then the day when something changed, how we passed in a single moment from childish friends to something else which we could not even name, only felt it grow within us, taking form until we acknowledged it fully and by then it was already too late. I fall asleep still talking and when I wake Feng is asleep also, lying by my side, one hand still on my shoulder. At first I pull away, shocked, but then I watch him sleep for a few minutes, thinking of how he patted me throughout my garbled outpouring, never speaking but only listening. I lie back down beside him and pretend to awaken only after he quietly leaves the room and returns to open my shutters, accompanied by maids with hot water, ready to dress me for the day ahead. He does not speak of the night before and neither do I. But soon after that night I wake up with a start, afraid of a dark dream in which Ping's face is too close to me, her wrinkled face turning into something from one of her horror stories and at once Feng is close to me, his hand on my shoulder again, bringing me instant comfort. We do not speak that following day, no agreement is made, but when I retire that night Feng blows out all the lanterns as usual, but instead of retreating to his bedroll I feel his weight on my bed and his hand on my shoulder and that night I sleep better than I have ever done in the Forbidden City. From then on, he sleeps every night in my bed and I feel as though Ping's dark shadows have retreated one step further away.

My days are still lonely, though. Thinking back to Dan Dan I wonder whether she was not in fact right, that I will not survive this life without some friends in this place. So I seek out the women I first came here with, hoping for a friendship I did not cultivate at the time, but find I am too late. Zhemin died just before Qianlong was made Emperor. Su has grown jealous of the new women who have joined our ranks. Although she has given the Emperor two sons and a daughter I am known for not being a favourite and perhaps she feels a friendship with me would tarnish her in some way, so she does not welcome my half-hearted overtures. Gao has retreated from court life, she has taken up a liking for praying and her solemn demeanour now appears almost dour as she makes her way from one temple to another. I am not sure what she prays for, but I cannot find it in myself to become close enough to her to find out. There was a Lady Jin amongst our early numbers but she is busying herself being moved up the rankings as fast as she can and so does not wish anything to do with me. The new women who arrive hope for advancement, they hope to supersede those of us whom they see as already established, they hope the Emperor will want newer, younger women in his bedchamber.

But Qianlong still favours his Empress. Fuca is his true love, he smiles when he sees her, he always has a tender word for her. She has already borne him two sons and there is no doubt that he considers them his first choice as heirs, much to the disappointment of the other women here. Fuca is called often to his rooms, the rest of his ladies are always a second choice as bedfellows. I, of course, am not sent for at all and so cannot even hope for a child one day. The only person in the Forbidden City whom I might still consider a friend is Wan. I visit with her sometimes, although I find her ever-sunny demeanour more grating than anything else as time goes by. How can anyone, no matter what their family background was, find happiness in this place? Wan seems to have a knack for making friends, she is always with one lady or another, always smiling. She likes to fill her hair with flowers and jewels, she has a eunuch whose skills at hairdressing are beyond compare and she sports one elaborate style after another, outdoing even the Empress. Fuca prefers a simpler effect, using only fresh flowers or tiny creations woven from coloured straw, even though the jewellers of the Forbidden City are at her command.

"I don't know how you can spend your whole life just decorating your empty head with flowers and trinkets," I slur to Wan during a drinking game we have been playing too long. "Who is it for? Qianlong treats you like a baby sister. You'll never have a man's real love, you'll just sit here playing stupid games until you're old and wrinkled. You'll die without ever having been loved. Without ever feeling desire." I watch her cheeks flush. The ladies-in-waiting we are playing with look away in embarrassment and I know, even in my drunken state, that I have gone too far. "I am going now," I say and make my way back to my palace, where I vomit and then sleep, waking with a bitter taste in my mouth that has nothing to do with the contents of my stomach. I send flowers, fruits and a note of apology to Wan the next day, which she readily accepts, but after that I visit her less and less, preferring to avoid losing the one person who might feel some kindness towards me, even if that means barely seeing her.

The Western Palaces are complete. Qianlong is delighted. He insists on a special outing, accompanied by his mother and half the court. It is, apparently, a surprise for his mother, and for the rest of us. We make our way there in a never-ending procession of palanquins, surrounded by guards, and servants. When we reach the Garden of Perfect Brightness, he sends most of the group around to the Western Gate, whilst we enter through the Grand Palace Gate in the southern part of the complex. We almost tiptoe through a small passageway, before emerging onto the pathway by the lake. And suddenly a cacophony of noise explodes around us, and most of the ladies squeal with surprise. For the whole pathway is lined with tiny stalls, manned by eunuchs, who are dressed as common street vendors, pretending to sell their wares. There are singers and musicians, who have broken into song, which, combined with the shouts of the eunuchs, makes for an unbearable level of noise all around us. The Empress Dowager's face is a mask of barely concealed horror at what her old home has become. No longer is it a quiet retreat, full of flowers and lakes, wildlife and tranquillity. Now it is like a gigantic play, as though we are living inside a theatre. Eunuchs throw handfuls of gingko leaves from the trees above us, painted so that they look like butterflies. They flutter all around us as they fall to the ground and are trampled on. The real butterflies have been frightened away by the noise. All around is clamour and colour, little scenes which we are to observe or even take part in.

Fuca is ready to play her part. She goes from stall to stall, pretending to haggle for items that are hers for the asking.

"Husband!" she cries, giggling, drawing Qianlong's attention to her. "I am being disgracefully taken advantage of! This stallholder is charging me three times what I should pay for a bowl of noodles. You must help me!"

At once he is by her side, laughing, making an outraged face at the eunuch and demanding that he lower the price at once. The eunuch plays along, dropping the price only one tiny bit at a time, until at last, of course, the Emperor is successful and the delicate bowl of exquisitely presented noodles is offered to the Empress.

"They are delicious," she says smiling up at the Emperor. "And now, I must buy a fan."

"There is a stall with fans," he replies, delighted with her enthusiasm. "Let me show you."

The other women, seeing what is required of them, hurry to each stall and pretend to make little purchases, giggling and chattering amongst themselves, each glancing over her shoulder to see if she can draw the Emperor's attention to her. I stand still and watch them, unable to find in myself the spirit of the game being played. Besides, I can see the Empress Dowager's face and she is not happy. She forces a too-bright smile on her face every time her son looks at her, but she is not happy. At last she grasps Qianlong's arm and suggests that we make our way to the Western Palaces. Of course, the Emperor is delighted with this idea and we make our way along tiny paths over canals and streams, to the squat stone buildings from far away, Qianlong's pride and joy. Here we must admire the maze, now complete, and each of us is encouraged to enter it and become lost.

"We must have a festival here," the Emperor declares. His eyes shine with the idea he has in mind. "I will sit in the central pavilion and each of you ladies must try to find your way to me."

"Delightful," says Niuhuru, one hand on a carved flower in the grey stone that makes up the maze's walls. She does not sound delighted.

"And it must be by night, of course," he goes on. "Every lady will be given a little lantern. Think how charming it will look, in the darkness, to see little bobbing lights as they make their way through the maze."

"And is there to be a prize," asks Fuca, clasping his hand in hers. "Perhaps for the lady who reaches you first?" She looks up at him, suggestively, conspiratorially, and I have to look away.

"Of course," he says, his voice low and intended only for her hearing.

We are installed in our respective palaces within the Garden, according to our rank. I see that Niuhuru would prefer to stay in her old palace, a pretty little thing, surrounded by flowers, with an old wisteria trained across it. But apparently this is no longer good enough for her, and she is hustled away, to a larger and grander palace further down the lakeside, her face showing only loss beneath her smiles. I wonder if she knows that I alone can see what she truly feels, having spent enough time smiling to cover my own pain.

"Tell me how you came to serve here," I say to Feng in the darkness one night.

"I had – have a wife," he begins. "We had four children, more than I could feed working as a farmer, there were poor crops for three years and I could not stand by and see them starve. I thought I might find work in the city, so I came to Beijing but there are so many people wanting work here and I could not send back enough money to my wife. I heard of a man who had recently become a eunuch even though he had a family, he was able to enter service in the Forbidden City and his family were fed and clothed well because of it, his eldest son was even able to study a little, so that he might better himself."

I turn towards him and put my hand on his shoulder as he has done on mine all these past nights, and wait.

He draws a ragged breath, tight in his chest as though he has never spoken these words before. "I found the knifers who do the cutting, swore that I would go through with it and borrowed six taels of silver to pay for their work. I got drunk the night before, so drunk. I went to a whorehouse and lay with three women, one after the other and with every woman I cried out my wife's name. In the morning the knifer gave me more spirits to drink, I could barely walk by the time he told me to lie down. He tied me down, so that I could not fight him and bound me up – there – tightly so that I would not bleed away my life, then he gave me a tea to stun me and poured hot pepper tea on my member to numb the pain." He half-snorts at the idea. "The pain was like nothing I had ever felt. I screamed and screamed and cried out that I had changed my mind but it was too late by then, it was done."

His body shudders and when he speaks again it is in half sobs. "They fit a metal plug to ensure that the hole where one may urinate does not close up, then you must walk about the room for three hours, which they must support you to do, for your legs will not hold you up. Then I lay in that room for three days, neither drinking nor urinating. There were times when I did not know where I was and I was afraid that I would die, but on the third day they pulled out the metal plug and I urinated. After that they dismissed me and said I would survive."

I find myself with my arms about him, his arms about me, in a close embrace. I feel pity such as I have never felt before, even my own woes seem insignificant. Tears are running down my face. "And so you came here?"

"After a time. There are princes of the Imperial Family who must find, train and present eight eunuchs a year to the Imperial household and I was lucky to find one who treated me well enough. Once I was in service I could send back money to my village. Now I know that my children and wife are fed and clothed because of my sacrifice."

"What did your wife say?" I ask.

He is silent for a few moments. "She does not know," he says at last. "I could not tell her, could not find the words. She has letters written to me from time to time, asking when I will come and visit them and I cannot reply. She knows I found work but she does not know what I do, what I am now, it would break her heart. She loved me." He is silent again. "I loved her," he says, his voice very low. "I love her still."

And somehow in the darkness our embrace grows tighter and his lips touch the bare skin of my neck and instead of withdrawing I seek out his lips with mine and our bodies press tightly together, as a desperate heat grows between us and our mouths grow violent with the need to find tenderness. I do not know when I fall asleep but I wake bruised and with dark circles under my eyes and do not speak much that day, only wait till night descends again and Feng comes back to my bed.

The nights that follow do not bring love, nor release. They bring an endless hunger that cannot be sated, a bleak lust that neither of us can give up nor gain true pleasure from. Our coupling, if it can be called that, continues, unnamed, unspoken of, silent and sullen, brutal and addictive. We do not speak of it, we only turn to it because we have nothing else, because what we truly want and desire is so far away from us, so far beyond possibility, that this wretched shadow of it must suffice. I think of Niu Lang and wonder if this is a betrayal but it does not feel like it, it is so far from what I felt for him, what I still feel for him, that it does not seem to be wrong on my part. It feels like part of my sadness, part of my longing for him.

A bitterness begins to grow in me, not just the endless sadness that I had almost grown used to but something darker. I find myself watching Fuca more and more, following in her footsteps at court rituals as though by imitating her I might find happiness myself. I watch the way she walks and model my steps on hers, raise my hand as she does, turn my head with her same movement. Back in my rooms, I mimic how she moves before a mirror so that I can better mould myself into her likeness: the way she bows at the temples during rituals, how she takes her place on the throne at Qianlong's side. I bend to greet an imaginary beloved son, smile at an imaginary loving Emperor. Feng catches me at it but does not comment, only watches me in silence as I imitate the only woman I know who has everything her heart desires. I think that others will comment when I bow as she does, turn as she does, mimic her in every way but this court is too wrapped up in its own business, its own secrets and rivalries and whispers, it does not see an out of favour concubine who moves like the Empress.

I go further. I order great tomes of history from the Imperial libraries. I learn all the history of the Qing dynasty, the Ming before them and further back. I learn the histories of the Manchus, the Mongolians, the Han Chinese. I study Confucius and his sayings, I study the teachings of Buddha and the Dao Way. I make it my business to know the correct court etiquette for every occasion. I learn the rituals for every ceremony that the Empress must attend, I follow her to each ceremony and watch what she does, the words she must speak, the movements she must make. I commit hundreds of poems to memory. My days are spent in study more suited to a scholar, on secret observation more suited to a spy. There is nothing else to do here for a woman who is not in favour.

I stand before a mirror, light imaginary incense, bow to the four directions, kowtow. I stand, speak the words of the ceremony for praising the silkworms that are the Empress' sole preserve, it is her task to exalt them for everything they do for our empire.

Feng watches me. "She may die one day," he says, his voice low.

The words hang in the silence between us.

I hear through whispers and alleyways that a concubine has been found with the eunuch. Not one of us, but a concubine from the previous Emperor, one of Yongzheng's women. These past concubines live in the palaces at the back of the Forbidden City. Not that they are palaces in the way ours are. These buildings are battered by time, weathered by snow, sun and rain. The women who live in them share rooms, they do not have the luxury of space that we do. They huddle in these back palaces, forgotten by the court, made nobodies in the dying breaths of an emperor. Most are as old as the Emperor was, which is to say not very old. Some are very young. Chosen for service in the Imperial bedchamber only a year before his death, these girls have not yet reached their twentieth year, and yet their lives are already over. They have not had to *follow-in-death*, as they might have done in the past, but still, their lives are over. Now, it seems, one of the youngest has been found with a eunuch, their naked bodies intertwined, so that there could be no doubt, no dismissal of accusations. The eunuch has been beheaded at once, and now we wait to find out the fate of the concubine. It seems her punishment has been left in the hands of the Empress Dowager. Niuhuru. I think of her, her tall frame, her strange grey eyes, of the look on her face when she chose me for service and watched my life crumble. She showed no pity then, only guilt afterwards. Now she must rule over what will happen to a concubine who dared to dishonour the memory of a man she barely knew.

Word comes. The concubine has been visited by the Empress Dowager, and something passed between them. A white silk scarf. Now we wait. One day, two days, three days and it is done. The concubine, whatever her name was, is no more. I think of Ping's stories of the Korean concubine who lived through a massacre of her peers and then was forced to take her own life. I think of this concubine, following the women from long ago, taking one step and then another onto a wooden stool, her cloud-climbing shoes lifting her high enough for the white silk scarf to do its duty. The sudden moment when the scarf jerked and the concubine was no more. I had thought that Ping's stories were part myths, that perhaps the events she related were not as bad as she made out. Perhaps there were fewer girls, perhaps there were more reasons. Yet here is this concubine, in my lifetime, in this same palace as those who went before, and it is all true. This is what can happen to a woman of the court, to a concubine like myself, if we step out of line. If we offend the man whom we call husband, even though he barely knows us, as we barely know him, still we can be found guilty of dishonouring him. And if we do, this is the fate that awaits us.

"Her name was – " begins Feng.

"Be quiet!" I say quickly. "I do not wish to hear her name."

"You said you wanted to know about her," says Feng.

"I wanted to know what happened to her," I say. "I do not want to know her name." I cannot explain why to Feng. Perhaps it is that I wish for the girl, the concubine, to remain unknown to me, to remain only one of Ping's stories, told in the flickering half-light of darkness. I do not wish her to be a real person, a concubine like me, who turned to a eunuch, as I have turned to Feng. I do not want to think of Feng, beheaded, while I dangle from a white silk scarf. I do not say this. "She is not important," I say.

Feng nods and turns away. Perhaps he understands. Perhaps he, too, does not want to think of such things, knowing he stands too close to them for comfort.

I think of Niuhuru and wonder how she managed to give the order to the concubine. Did she tell her baldly to her face? Did she look down on her from a golden throne and ignore her request for mercy? Was there nothing in her, not one moment of doubt, of horror in what she was asking? If I hated her before, now I hate her more.

More women arrive that summer, including the rarity of a Mongolian girl, tall and pink-cheeked, with fierce eyes and a long-legged clumsy stride, a far cry from the elegant glide practiced by most court ladies. Named Ying, she takes an inexplicable liking to the hapless Qing, who has remained as little favoured as I. I see them walking together in the Garden of Perfect Brightness, hear them laugh and wonder how friendships seem so easily made when they have constantly eluded me. I stroke the silken feathers of my magpies, grateful for their friendliness, their loyalty in returning to my hand when they could leave this place forever, flutter into the bright blue sky and never be seen again.

The Qixi Festival comes round and once again I step out of my rooms when darkness falls and search the sky for the Lovers' stars. They shine bright above me while I strive to feel Niu Lang close to me and fail, as I have always failed. The bitterness that rises up inside me cannot be suppressed, it grows greater all the time as I feed it with my misery. The love I gave up is for nothing. I am one of many, one of so many that I cannot even be picked out from the crowd, a crowd which will only grow larger as the years go by, as the Imperial Daughters' Draft delivers ever more innocent girls into the dark splendour of the Forbidden City. I have lost a great love and received nothing in return.

I will be paid, I whisper to myself as I stand in the blackness of the night and feel my bare feet grow cold on the stone paving of my palace courtyard. *I will not be one of many. No matter what it takes, I will be chosen from the crowd, the sacrifice I made will be recognised. What I gave up is worth a great price, and it has not been paid.*

I will be paid.

Black Sandalwood

T HE FIRST TIME I HAVE a maid beaten it is for something serious: she has been caught stealing, a jade comb was found hidden in her sleeping roll. She will be dismissed, of course, but first she must be beaten.

"You do not need to watch," says Feng, but I do, I watch from a window as she is beaten in the courtyard, Feng's arm coming down again and again and her yelps give me some satisfaction, there is something in her sobs as she is led away that gives me peace, as though it were I sobbing, as though she has taken some of my own pain away.

When Ping tells me months later that another maid must be punished for something less important, some foolish slip which has led to a vase being broken, I tell her that I will beat the girl myself.

"No need," says Ping, looking surprised. "Feng or I will do it."

"No," I say too quickly. "I will do it."

I hesitate before my arm comes down for the first time but once I begin I feel again the strange release, a greater release than my nights with Feng. I bring my arm down over and over and in the end Ping has to pull me away, I have beaten the girl so hard her skin has broken and she is bleeding.

After that I seek out chances to punish. My maids and eunuchs grow fearful of me, for I become known for the severity of the beatings I give on the most minor of pretexts. When my own household grows so cautious, so well behaved that there can be no reason for beating them, I go further afield. I look out for misdemeanours wherever I go, sometimes I will loiter near another woman's palace and catch her maids gossiping or the eunuchs being lazy and report them, watch their beatings from a distance and find a twisted pleasure in them. I listen for secrets whispered in dark corners and find those who have transgressed: stealing, adultery, treasonous plans, all of these somehow fill a gnawing need in me. I draw away from Feng and our dark touches, I allow them now only when I have sated this other need and he learns this, seeks out misdemeanours that he can bring back to me to claim the reward of my skin against his.

He brings me word that Lady Wang, a young concubine, slapped a maid's face. This is forbidden. A woman's face is her fortune, even if she is a maid.

"Who knows about this?" I ask.

Feng shakes his head. "Nobody. Wang and the maid. They were alone in the room at the time."

"Who told you?"

"The maid came to me."

I nod. Feng has developed a reputation of his own, as a eunuch who will handsomely reward any rumours or secrets brought his way.

"Bring the maid here," I say.

I make the maid tell me every detail of what happened, every detail of Lady Wang's bedchamber, which I have never been in. Then I dismiss her and turn to Feng.

"Send for the Chief Eunuch," I say.

I tell the Chief Eunuch that I was present in Lady Wang's bedchamber ("we are great friends," I affirm) and that I was witness to the maid being slapped across the face. Lady Wang, called on to explain herself, stands aghast at my testimony against her. She says I am lying, but I am able to give details of her bedchamber and of the incident that tally perfectly with her maid's account. Lady Wang ends up demoted by a rank and that night Feng and I do not sleep until dawn.

I see other women and even courtiers begin to draw away from me. They fear my interest in them, the way my eyes gleam when I see something that should not be seen, hear something that should not have been said out loud nor even whispered. When I find out that a lady-in-waiting has grown too close to the court perfumier, when a little love note is found and he is whipped while she is dismissed in disgrace I watch it all, my heart beating hard. I know what would happen were Feng and I found out and even the thought of it brings me to a shuddering release greater than I have ever known. I search for greater and still greater misdemeanours, I watch every woman at court trying to find her at fault, trying to find a way in which I can bring her down, to taste a disgrace as bitter as my sadness. There are days when I stare in my mirror and wonder what I am doing, what I am becoming, but I cannot stop, I feel driven to continue.

Feng and I grow closer in our quest. He will whisper to me of what he has heard among the servants, I hiss to him of women who I believe have transgressed, what will happen to them if I can only find proof, he presses against me and describes whippings that have already taken place, those that are yet to come, of beheadings and exiles, of stocks and chains and death by a thousand cuts and in the darkness I dig my golden nail shields into his skin and feel the pain of his teeth on me and somehow in this pain there is a dark joy.

One morning I wake to deep snow. The Forbidden City has disappeared: the golden roof tiles turned to white as though I am no longer here but somewhere else, in another time and place. I think of Niu Lang's ice sculptures and wonder if I could make one, if I could form the snow into shapes from my past. The strange blue light that snow casts seems to change my surroundings and for once, just for once, I feel as though its light might penetrate this darkening life of mine, if it might turn me from the path I have begun to follow. I think that if I walk through the silent City, through the clean white snow, that I may return to my palace a different person, all my fears and bitterness swept away.

As I hurry to dress Feng presses his hands hard against the silk of my half-undone robe but I cannot be with him when my thoughts are filled with Niu Lang. "No," I say and he stands back, bound to obey. But his eyes are dark on me as I finish dressing and I know, can feel, that if he could, if I were not who I am, if he possessed his lost manhood, I would find myself forced to his pleasure against my will.

"My furs," I say to a maid and she brings them.

"Where are you going?" asks Feng.

"Out," I say.

He moves to accompany me but I shake my head. I cannot have him with me, cannot have our dark ways follow me into the clean whiteness.

The Inner Court is very quiet. The deep snow crunches under my boots, the bitter cold makes me shudder, but there is something exhilarating about the silence and cold. No servants and Imperial guards, no rivals, no Qianlong: it is as though everything that makes me miserable has been taken away, leaving behind only happy memories of long ago. I try to create a sculpture from the snow and it comes out badly, my memories of Shu Fang are fading into something generic and the sculpture before me could be any girl-child, but I smile as I stroke the little face I have shaped and for a moment I think I can hear my laughter and that of Niu Lang, Shu Fang's yelps as we played snowballs together in our garden.

But now I realise the laughter is not in my memory. Somewhere up ahead of me, through the gates into the Outer Court, come more yelps and laughter. I wonder whether some of the Imperial children have been allowed out to play, though it seems unlikely their guardians would allow the risk of any of them catching a chill. I walk more quickly, almost falling over a hidden step, then slow as I look through the gate into the courtyard beyond.

Concubines Qing and Ying are playing together in the snow. Ying is a good shot, almost every snowball she throws hits Qing, who is so overcome with giggles that she can barely stand up straight, let alone make and throw snowballs back.

In that moment I want to ask to play alongside them, to be part of their friendship, to forget all that has happened so far and only enjoy what is here and now. I think of making a snowball and throwing it at them, of laughing when they turn, preparing to duck when Ying – for it will surely be Ying – throws one back at me. She will probably hit me, her aim is excellent. And I will yelp and laugh and there will be something between us, a lightness that signals something that could be: a new start, a fresh beginning in this fresh snow, a way to change the direction my life is taking, to move away from a path that leads only into darkness.

But as I watch, Qing falls and Ying helps her up. Qing clings to her desperately, trying to steady her slipping feet on the icy paving and Ying's eyes are filled with such tenderness that the darkness wells up in me again. There is something between them, it would take a fool not to see it. All at once, I am the one outside again. They are nothing but another pair of hearts closed to me, open only to one another.

"What good friends you are," I say and my voice is so low, so bitter, that it frightens even me.

They turn, Qing still clinging to Ying for balance. Slowly they let go of one another and Qing speaks, her voice shaky.

"Lady Ula Nara," she says. "Are you well?"

I cannot help myself. I want to see their eyes when they know their secret is discovered, the fear I will make grow there. "I was told the two of you were friendly," I say. "I did not know you were *such* good friends."

Qing's eyes do not change in the way that I crave, she only looks scared and confused. But Ying's face changes. Her hand moves away from where she was still touching Qing's elbow, her eyes grow cold and sullen with recognition of what I am insinuating.

And the old game has its hooks in me again, the dirty pleasure of other people's secrets and fears fulfilling me for a moment. I feel a cruel smile grow on my face. Qing may be an innocent for now but Ying knows what I am thinking and she is fearful of my knowledge, of my power over her. "I'll take that silence as agreement, shall I?" I say and suddenly the pure whiteness of the snow everywhere is gone. I am back in the Forbidden City, the snow has hidden it from me only for a moment before revealing it again, its claws outstretched, ready to twist the hearts and minds of those who live here. I turn back, unable to meet Qing's wide-eyed gaze, Ying's protective anger. I walk fast through the snow, taking no pleasure in it. When I return to my rooms I am barely out of my furs before I press myself against Feng and he presses back against me, our hands frantic, each of us trying to get from the other something neither of us can give.

The promotion ceremonies are always boring, one stupid woman after another glowing at the thought of being moved one step closer to the Emperor without realising that his heart is already filled. They dream of success: of their name chip turned over and over on the silver tray, of ever grander titles and robes, of somehow securing Qianlong's favour. But today there is a stir of interest as the promotions are announced: a lady-in-waiting is made concubine, an uncommon event. Not chosen for the Imperial bedchamber during the Draft, somehow she has caught Qianlong's eye in the crowd and is now to join our ranks.

"Lady Ling is promoted from lady-in-waiting, she is made Concubine," announces the Chief Eunuch.

"Only so that the Emperor may lie with her and satisfy a passing lust," whispers Feng.

I nod. She is a nobody.

"Lady Ling is promoted from Concubine, she is made Imperial Concubine!"

"Twice in one year?" I hiss to Feng.

"Whore," he mutters. "She will have made herself useful in the bedchamber."

I look her over more carefully. No woman has been promoted so quickly in all the time I have been here. She is Han Chinese in origin, although honorary Manchu status has been bestowed on her family. She is only young, not even twenty, but she carries herself with an easy confidence, as though she knows herself valued. This second promotion has come as no surprise to her, it has been murmured to her already by Qianlong, whispered against her bare skin. She walks past me as the ceremony comes to an end. Her movements are languorous, she walks like a woman who knows the Emperor watches her. There is an easy plumpness to her body, not fat but a roundedness that comes from eating well and fearing no harm. She does not have about her the tight slenderness of many of the women here, whose nerves are shredded from fears and rivalries, from jealousy and pettiness. She has risen above such things, knowing the path she has chosen is successful, fearing no-one.

"Whore," I agree. It is an easy name to bestow, an easy dismissal. In the darkness that night we whisper to one another, is this what Ling does for the Emperor? This? She is a whore, she is clawing her way up the rankings of the concubines through filthy tricks, by doing *this* and *this* and *this*. We grow to hate her but there is nothing we can find that can be said against her in public, no way to wound the Emperor's second most favourite woman.

I follow Ling. I know that I follow her with a frown on my face, that my brow furrows every time I see her. I watch the way she walks, so different from Fuca, who glides elegantly, as an empress should. Ling does not glide. She sways. Even in the long shapeless robes we wear, an observer can be left in no doubt as to where Ling's hips are, as they sway back and forth, back and forth. She walks like a woman who is being watched and who knows that it is her walk, her body, that will have her called, again and again, to the Imperial bedchamber. Ling is no fool. She plays her own game, and she is winning. All these years, concubine after concubine has tried and failed to rise above the rest to become a favourite. All these years the Emperor has loved his Empress above all others. The rest of his women have been called to the bedchamber but without much favour. There is no pattern. But here comes Ling, called again and again, promoted twice in one year from a lady-in-waiting into a Concubine and then again to an Imperial Concubine, an unheard of rise in favour. She is not about to become Empress, for Fuca still lives, but certainly Fuca is not being called to the bedchamber quite as regularly as she once was. Ling's face has an air of calm to it, of security in the knowledge that she has been seen, has been chosen from the ranks of women available, and raised up above them. Whatever she does when she is alone with the Emperor, whatever she promises with her swaying walk, she knows that it works and she continues on her chosen path. The rest of us can only wonder at what might take place in the Imperial bedchamber between the two of them and wonder why none of us have succeeded in doing the same.

I receive word that my mother has died. I think of Shu Fang, how she will weep and weep, of my father and how he will manage without my mother's constant chatter, which he used to roll his eyes at, but which he will miss now it is gone. I wonder if she managed to control her pride at knowing I was named Consort to an Emperor, since she knew I was unhappy. I think of her fondness for Niu Lang and I weep.

It is time for the Festival of Hungry Ghosts. Feng and Ping busy themselves with an altar in my own courtyard, heaping it with both real food and paper offerings. I make my way there and burn what is to be burnt, bow and kneel, my eyes growing red with the clouds of incense surrounding me.

"There are ghosts who are good, our venerated ancestors," says Ping as darkness falls. "But there are those who remain forever hungry. A hungry ghost searches for what cannot be offered, for revenge or love, ever searching, never finding. It grows wasted, its belly always empty, its eyes always searching for what it cannot find. Such ghosts are not easily appeased."

"I am going to bed," I say, cutting her off.

Feng and I lie in the darkness, wrapped in a tight embrace, while outside ghosts walk the Forbidden City, welcomed for this one night only, invited back to our world to eat and drink their fill, to feel the warmth of our veneration and respect, to satiate and keep them at bay for one more year. I wonder if my mother walks close by me tonight, if she eats from the food I have offered, dresses in the paper clothing I have burnt, if her constant chattering annoys the other ghosts as much as it ever annoyed my father. I wonder, if I stepped into the darkness, if I would feel her arms about me one last time, but I am too afraid of Ping's stories of what else might lurk outside in the darkness.

Fourteen days later comes the time to light paper lanterns and float them on the waterways of the Forbidden City, each tiny light a flickering guide for any lost spirits to follow back to their own world, for fear that they should remain trapped in this one. As each light is extinguished, a ghost returns from whence it came and leaves us safe. I watch with my household as our tiny boats set sail, as Feng and Ping and the other servants' tiny candles burn out and go dark. Only mine shines on, even as the little boat turns out of sight we see its flame still burning.

"A hungry ghost still walks among us," declares Ping. "It has not returned to the other world."

The other servants murmur.

"Be quiet, you stupid old woman," I say. "You have spoken once too often."

I beat Ping myself, red weals rising on her wrinkled back, her knees giving way beneath her before I stop. I walk away from her and none of the servants dare step forward to raise her up. She lies there for some time and when she dies a month later, I turn my face away at the news and never speak her name again. A new maid rises to prominence among my servants but she knows better than to talk when she does not have to. My palace grows silent, the servants do not speak above a whisper for fear of being heard.

The court grows sombre. Lady Fuca's older son has died. He should have been heir to the throne and now that task will fall to his younger brother, her second son. Fuca's face when she has to appear at rituals and official events is white with grief. Qianlong treats her very gently, all of the court must tiptoe around her sadness.

I search for sorrow in my heart for the little prince and there is nothing there. I wonder how low I have sunk that I cannot mourn a dead child and yet there is still nothing, only a dull anger. Why should I feel sorry for Fuca? She still has Qianlong's heart. She still has another son, one whom we all know will be heir one day. The boy was under the care of another concubine, about whom nobody worries, even though she was more the boy's mother than Fuca. No one thinks of her grief for a child she has raised since he was born. Such is the way of the court. Such is the way of this world in which I live.

"You are to be promoted," says Feng.

"What?"

"You will be made a Noble Consort at the next promotion ceremony."

"Why?" I have not given the Emperor a son, have not given him pleasure. There is no reason for me to be promoted.

Feng shrugs. "I think they're afraid of you."

It's a possibility. I know full well that no-one at court is fond of me. Lady Wan perhaps may still speak my name with pity, but she has always been absurdly kind in her evaluations of people. Everyone else is afraid of me, shifts away from me if I stand too close, falls silent when I approach. No-one seeks me out, they would rather I were not here. Perhaps those who decide such things believe that I am overly ambitious and think that by promoting me to a higher rank they may soften me, take away whatever it is that makes me unhappy, for there are those who still tell the story of when I was chosen and begged Niuhuru not to take me.

The *ruyi* I receive at my promotion is made of black sandalwood inlaid with rubies. The wood is an odd choice of setting for the rubies, for it is so dark that the rubies do not shine pink or crimson but rather a dull red, like dried blood, their lustre lost without light shining through them. I place it on a silver stand beside the carved rosewood and stand looking at them for some time, unsure that this new piece is any better than the first, for all the gems embedded in it. Its darkness echoes the darkness inside me and does not promise change.

Green Jade

THEY PROMOTE ME AGAIN, AS though the title of Imperial Noble Consort, just one rank lower than Empress, is an offering to placate an evil spirit. There are whispers that Niuhuru herself asked for me to be promoted, desperate to atone for the past. The *ruyi* I receive this time is a weighty green jade, ornately carved by a master craftsman. I stand in my rooms after the ceremony, twisting it in my hands. It is grander by far than the rosewood, grander than the black sandalwood. I wonder whether it is enough, whether its weight can equal the weight in my heart, balance it in the scales of my life. I set it on the new, larger, more elaborate silver holder that has been sent to my rooms. I look at the three sceptres sitting side by side and swallow. It is not enough. I think of that flickering flame that would not go out, the hungry ghost still roaming the Forbidden City, wanting *enough* and never finding it. Nothing would be enough except to sit by Qianlong's side as Empress and that is not something that I can make happen: it lies in the hands of the Immortals and my whole life has been lived under their injustice. Why would they relent their cruelty now?

The dark days of winter come and with them a great fear. Smallpox. The word is on everyone's lips and there are stories everywhere: a maid, a eunuch, one of the dressmakers, not names that bother anyone. But then a new name is spoken. Fuca's second son, heir to the throne, has died.

The court falls silent. Qianlong disappears from view, as does Fuca, both wrapped in sadness. Fuca has no other sons and she is thirty-six now: it is unlikely she will bear more sons in any hurry. Suddenly, those concubines with sons spot an opportunity. They stand a little taller, they dress a little better, they make sure to mention their sons at every possible opportunity. The younger concubines, still at the peak of their fertility, hope to be blessed with children, for now there is a chance to be noticed, to vie for promotion based not just on beauty or desirability but on the ability to birth a healthy son.

I am unlikely ever to bear Qianlong a son, so this means nothing to me. It only means that my path to the top will be made harder, for there are women who can beat me by playing a game I do not have the pieces for.

Now Qianlong decides we must somehow cheer Fuca, take her mind off what has happened.

"The astrologers say there may be evil influences in her charts," says Feng, returning with gossip. "She is not to stay in the Forbidden City."

"It's too cold for the Garden of Perfect Brightness," I say. "Or the hunting grounds. Wrong time of year."

But Qianlong has in mind Shandong, in the south-east. We are to visit Mount Tai and the birthplace of Confucius.

"Well, that would make any grieving mother happy again, I'm sure," I say to Feng. "Did she agree to this?"

He shrugs, directing the packing of my clothes. For some reason I am one of the ladies chosen to go on the trip, along with Qing and Ying, Ling and some others.

"The Chief Eunuch told us that we are there to make merriment, to lift the spirits of the Empress," I say. "I'm sure what she wants is all of us with her," I add. "To be constantly reminded that there are plenty of ladies just snapping at her heels to fill Qianlong's bed at night and provide a son and heir. They must be mad, arranging this journey."

Spring has not even come when we leave the Forbidden City behind us. As I expected, the travel is long and tedious. We must move constantly from one resting place to the next, one unfamiliar set of rooms after another while bowing nobles and local officials try to ingratiate themselves with us when we stay in their palaces. They know nothing of court politics, they cannot tell a beloved concubine from one who has not been called on for years and so they creep and bow and flatter, hoping for favour. I ignore them all.

Qing and Ying, set free from their usual routines, feeling part of a privileged group for once, flower on this journey. They chatter and laugh, they play silly drinking games and spend time feeding fish in ornamental ponds and other such nonsense. I find myself watching them all the time. Ying knows what she is about, that much is clear, the way she looks at Qing is plain enough for any idiot to see it. Qing is more of an innocent, I am not sure she has yet put a name to what she feels for Ying, but it is there, in the shining eyes and sudden giggles, it is one word away from love, one glance, one kiss away from passion.

I cannot bear it. It twists my stomach when I see them together. I find myself taunting them, even in front of the other ladies, who draw back when they see me, pretend not to listen but hear every word I say and remember it next time they look at the two of them.

I commission Feng to find me a pillow book for Qing, one filled only with images of women together, for he says such things exist. Sure enough, when I provide the silver, I find in my hand a pillow book that suits my needs. I give it to Qing and watch her pull away from Ying the day after, holding herself stiff and apart and there is something base in me that is glad to see that shine gone from her eyes.

The tour is the bore that I knew it would be. Everything revolves around Fuca's wellbeing. Qianlong is with her all day, their heads pressed tenderly together, his voice low when he speaks to her, the rest of us are only there to make up the numbers. He is a hypocrite anyway, for as much as he spends time with Fuca by day, by night it is often Ling who is sent for. I see her setting off for his rooms time and again, returning late, her ruffled hair loose, her robes thrown on any which way. She looks relaxed when she returns, her skin rosy, her body loose-limbed with sated desire. I do not know if she sees my face at the window, but if she does, she shows no sign of seeing me. She only returns to her own room and spends each day in cheerful chatter with other ladies or leisurely dressing, certain of Qianlong's eyes on her that coming evening.

Feng is gleaming with a secret.

"Fuca is ill," he says.

"What with?"

He shrugs. "A chill, they said."

The last few days have been cold again, after a first glimpse of spring we seem to have retreated back to winter. "Is she at dinner?"

"No."

I brighten a little. I am the second ranked woman here. This means that I will sit close to Qianlong, which does not happen often. It is a chance to outdo Ling, to show her that she is still not winning this game. "Get out the other robe, then," I say. "The purple, not the blue."

I ensure that I am at my finest and make my way to the meal. There I take my place by the Emperor. I turn my face away from Ling, but not before I see the look of pity she gives me. I will not be pitied by a woman barely over her twenty-first year only because she is a slut in the bedchamber. She has yet to reach my own rank and if I had my way, she never would. Where I have put on my best robes and dressed my hair with care, Ling is in a robe better suited to an informal dinner with a friend, her hair loosely pinned. I think for a brief moment how easy it would be to undo her hair, how quickly it would tumble from its pins and spread over a pillow. No doubt this is exactly what Ling would like the Emperor to be thinking when he looks at her hair.

The other women chatter amongst themselves, making little effort to entertain the Emperor, since they can see for themselves that I intend to keep his attention on myself. Qing and Ying sit with their heads together, murmuring to one another in low voices that no one else can overhear. The servants scurry around us, busy bringing plates of food, while musicians play for us. But there is a doleful air in the room, a sense of something missing. I try to talk to Qianlong, but his face is grave and he does not respond much, only eating his way through the many plates offered, as though it were a task he must perform and one he would rather get over with as quickly as possible. I wonder why he did not just have his food taken to his own rooms, instead of insisting on a formal dinner surrounded by his women. Perhaps he does not wish to be left alone with his thoughts, since despite his efforts to cheer the Empress, he, too, has lost a child of late, one whom he had expected to favour as his future heir. He all but grunts when I speak to him of the day's various scenic visits we have all been forced to undertake.

"Is Lady Fuca well?" I ask at last and his eyes immediately focus on me.

"I am concerned for her," he says, frowning. "The physician said it is only a chill but it has been very cold today and in her present state of mind…"

I nod, as though I care about Fuca. "I will pray for her," I say perfunctorily and he smiles and pats my hand.

"Thank you, Ula Nara," he says. "That is a comfort to me."

The rest of the dinner proceeds without much further conversation. Ling catches

Qianlong's eye and we are promptly all dismissed, she no doubt making her way to his bedchamber again, since Fuca is not available.

Morning comes and Fuca is still ill, we are left to our own devices. I follow Qing and Ying, but lose them in the gardens and get turned away by Qing's over-officious eunuch. In the end I sit alone and watch the sun move through the sky, my mind empty, bored.

Another day passes and another and still we are stuck waiting for Fuca to recover. The physicians bustle back and forth, her servants will only say she is still unwell, but by the third day they are beginning to look afraid.

"Find out what is happening," I tell Feng. "Something is not right."

Local visits and banquets are suddenly cancelled. A message is sent to each of us to pray for Her Majesty's good health.

"She is very ill," says Feng. "The Emperor has decided we are to go back to Beijing."

"We left Beijing for the good of her health," I say.

He shrugs. "The Emperor is getting worried."

Our chests are packed up and we leave the fawning local nobles and officials behind, boarding the Imperial barge.

"Why aren't we moving?" I ask Feng, after darkness has fallen and still nothing has happened. The room I am in is stifling. The gentle rocking of the boat is making me feel nauseous. I wave away the snacks and drinks I am offered, afraid I will be sick.

He shrugs. No one knows anything. No one is saying anything.

"I am going to sleep," I tell him. "Do not wake me. With any luck when I wake up we will be on our way back to Beijing."

I try to sleep but the nausea I feel makes me twist and turn. From outside comes the low but endless and unmistakeable sound of monks chanting for Fuca's health. I wish they would be quiet and allow us to depart. If she wants to go back to Beijing, then we should go. The monks can chant in a temple for her good health. I try to plug my ears but nothing works. Then the door opens and I see Feng silhouetted in the light.

"I told you not to wake me," I hiss, forgetting that I have anyway not been asleep.

"Fuca is dead," he says.

Vomit spills out of me, a bitter yellow bile I have suppressed too long, staining my silken covers.

My hair hangs loose, jewellery and flowers are set aside. White robes arrive from the Imperial storerooms, our usual bright colours abandoned in mourning. The men of the court cut their queues. It makes them look like half-shaven monks.

In his grief, Qianlong gives absurd orders. We return by boat along the canal and when we reach Beijing thousands of men are called upon to line the streets with leaves to form a slippery surface. Then they are ordered to pull the whole barge up to the Forbidden City, so that Fuca's body should not be disturbed as they bring her home. The Palace of Eternal Spring, her residence, becomes a mausoleum for her body. Every member of the court visits, bowing to her stiff body, lying in state while Qianlong kneels by her side, weeping.

I stand by him, looking down on Fuca's empty face and his shuddering shoulders. I feel nothing for Fuca, but as soon as I think of Niu Lang dying, tears spring to my eyes. It seems I do have a heart left, after all. I kneel next to Qianlong and perform my kowtow. When I raise my face Qianlong is looking at me. He sees the tears in my eyes and takes my hand in his, nodding to me as though to recognise the grief we are sharing. I let him hold my hand and when he lets me go I leave.

Qianlong is now a target. Every woman in the court with even a shred of hope for securing the title of Empress has him in her sights. But he is oblivious to us all. His eyes are red-rimmed from tears, his face is white. He spends every day in the temples, praying for Fuca, his white robes a stark contrast to the orange-clad monks who surround him. Meanwhile the court whispers. It does not take long for them to decide who is in contention as the next empress. I know that two names are spoken. Mine. And Ling's.

"Ling," says Feng.

I look up at him, eyes narrowed. "Say her name again and I'll have you whipped," I snarl.

"He likes her," he says bluntly. "He doesn't like you. He loved Fuca, now that she's gone he'll have to find someone else to love. It would help if he liked the woman to start with."

"He doesn't have to love his empress," I object.

"Don't you know him at all?" asks Feng, exasperated. "He's a romantic. He chose Fuca's children as his heirs without even seeing how they would turn out. He was touched by her making him that stupid leather pouch like the old Manchus had to celebrate his heritage: he went on about it for months. He wants a woman he can love."

"I'm the highest-ranked woman at court," I say.

Feng shrugs. "He can promote Ling or anyone else to whatever rank he likes," he reminds me. "He doesn't need to pick the highest ranked woman. You have to do better than that."

I look down.

"What have you got?" asks Feng. "You have to come up with something. He doesn't love you and your rank counts for nothing."

"I am a Manchu," I say.

"So? Half the other women here are Manchu."

"Ling isn't. She's Han Chinese."

"Oh, so you do realise she is the most likely to be chosen," he says. "Her family have been made honorary Manchus."

"That's good enough for a concubine," I say. "Is it good enough for an empress?"

"I wouldn't risk it on that," says Feng. "Find something else."

We are silent for a while.

"What does he need from an empress?" asks Feng. "You can't offer love, he can get sons from any woman here, so what does an empress have that the rest of the bitches don't have?"

I think of walking one step behind Fuca for all these years, her grace and elegance, her faultless knowledge of every ritual and ceremony to carry out for the good of the empire. I think of the days and years I have spent studying so that I might equal her in this knowledge. "A partner," I say. "The rituals and ceremonies, they have to be carried out by an empress. They have to be flawless. An empress is not just a pretty face and a companion for the bedchamber, that's what the concubines are for. An empress is something more."

Feng considers this. "Better," he says doubtfully. "But is it enough?"

I lower my head. "Probably not."

"What have you got, Ula Nara?" he asks. "Think harder."

I think of the secrets I know, the whispers and rumours of the court, what I have seen and heard over the past few years. Most of them concern minor ladies-in-waiting or concubines, those with no power.

"You need someone with power on your side," Feng reminds me when I do not speak. "Someone who owes you something."

Slowly, I raise my head and meet his gaze.

"You have something," he says. "What is it?"

Niuhuru is always uncomfortable in my presence. When I am shown into her rooms she stands up, as though for a more senior-ranked woman. Her odd grey eyes flicker over my face.

"Are you well, Ula Nara?" she asks.

I don't engage in niceties. "I want to be made Empress," I say.

She blinks, then swallows. "I did not know you felt so strongly about my son," she says.

"I don't," I say.

Her personal maid Yan watches me from a corner of the room, her face very still. I would dismiss her but even I cannot dismiss the maid of the Empress Dowager.

Niuhuru swallows again. "Why do you wish to be Empress?" she asks.

"In compensation for all I lost when I was chosen by you," I say.

Her face grows paler, one hand flutters to her chest. Perhaps she cannot believe I would be so honest, but I do not care what she thinks. I have one chance to achieve what I believe I am owed and this is the only way I can make it happen.

"Qianlong does not wish for a new empress to be appointed," she says. "He says that it would dishonour Fuca's memory."

"Every court needs an empress," I say. "There is always an empress."

"I am sure in due course, when he has finished grieving..." she begins, but then trails off.

"Then he will choose another woman," I say. "He will choose Ling for whatever filthy tricks she performs in his bedchamber."

Niuhuru looks shocked, but I don't care. Now is not the time for politeness.

"Or he will fall for some new girl and have the romantic notion of making her Empress at once, of raising up a nobody to the very pinnacle of the court, like some sort of fairytale. I cannot wait for him to finish grieving. I need you to appoint a new empress now. You are his mother, you have the power to do so."

"And what reasons will I give for choosing you?" she tries.

"I am a Manchu," I say. "I am the highest-ranked woman at court. And you will find that I am well versed in court etiquette. I have walked one pace behind Fuca for long enough. I know all that should be done and how to do it. I will not disgrace you."

She looks away for a moment and then back at me. "And will this satisfy you?" she asks and her voice has a pleading note to it. "Will it make you happy, Ula Nara?" She wants me to smile and say that yes, if she does this all will be forgiven, that I will be happy and she can let go of the burden she carries every time she sees me.

"I do not know," I say and then I play my last, desperate, move, the only move I have left. "Does the Jesuit make you happy?"

There is a tiny gasp from Yan and Niuhuru's eyes widen before her face closes up entirely. For a moment I think I have lost the game, that my final move was too much, that she will hit out and send the board flying, the pieces scattered at my feet. But she only says, "It is time for you to go now," and turns away, leaving me alone in the room with Yan, who does not stand to show me out as she should do, only watches me in silence as I leave.

I wait for an announcement. The whole court waits. I hear the whispers, I know they watch Ling and I to see who will win this secret silent battle.

But Qianlong has the whole court gripped in fear. His grief is greater than any of us could have foretold, he cannot think of anything but Fuca and whether she is being adequately mourned. He has a list of over fifty names drawn up, officials and nobles whom he feels have not been sufficiently grief-stricken by Fuca's death. He has the Han Chinese ones demoted by two grades and the Manchu ones executed. The court tiptoes around him, shocked by his transformation from benevolent monarch to vengeful overlord.

"Cut my hair," I say to Feng.

"What?"

"Cut it off," I tell him.

"Why?"

"Mourning for Fuca," I say.

"You don't need to," he objects. "You would only need to if it was Qianlong or his mother."

"She outranked me," I say.

"She outranked everyone," says Feng. "Having your hair unbound and undecorated is sufficient."

"Qianlong is losing his mind over this," I tell him. "I need to be seen to be mourning her more than anyone else."

I watch the long locks of my black hair fall to the ground.

"Make it look rough," I say. "As though I have done it myself in desperation while grieving."

"Madness," says Feng.

I shake my head. It feels oddly light. "He will like it," I say.

He does. I see him note my hair the next time he sees me and the way he nods, as though satisfied. A few other concubines do the same, although it is too late now, they will only be seen to be copying me, sycophants with no sense of originality, of true sorrow.

My hair cut, I begin the next stage of my plan. I approach the Chief Eunuch and remind him that, as I am the most highly-ranked of Qianlong's woman, and as there is no empress, he, the Chief Eunuch, must be finding certain ceremonies very difficult to arrange. I will stand in for the role, I tell him.

"There are a great many rituals, my lady," he says doubtfully. "You may not wish for such a burden."

"It is no burden to help the Emperor at this time," I say. "I studied the late Empress Fuca for many years, I am well able to perform her duties. And you may brief me if needed."

He is right, of course. The rituals and ceremonies are tedious in the extreme. Mostly they consist in wearing the correct robes, being taken to certain temples on certain days at certain times and then ostentatiously praying. I pray for the empire, interceding with the Immortals. I pray for rain, sun, good crops, healthy livestock, strong backs and hands of the peasants. Sometimes I feel like a farmer. I hold vast bundles of smouldering incense sticks and learn not to choke in the trailing clouds of perfumed smoke that surround me as I bow to the four directions, kneel and pray. I was right, though. I have stood one step behind Fuca all these years and I know what to do. I do not falter, I do not stumble. I remember all the right words and gestures. The Chief Eunuch visibly relaxes as one ceremony after another proceeds with elegance and correct ritual. At least I can be relied on while the Emperor has lost his mind. He bows more deeply to me, treats me as though I were already Empress, whispers in Niuhuru's ear that all is taken care of, that Lady Ula Nara has proven more than worthy to be promoted.

"Ling has been called as the Emperor's companion tonight," says Feng.

I feel my stomach drop. Qianlong has not called for anyone since Fuca died. But now, it seems, his grief has lessened sufficiently that he has remembered more carnal desires which have not been assuaged for some time. And of course it would be Ling who is called, Ling with her confident smile and her swaying walk, her quick glance at him which always results in the rest of us being dismissed. What does she do with him? What games does she play, what skills of the bedchamber does she offer?

"You have lost," says Feng. "The time was before now, while he forgot which of his women he enjoyed the company of."

I think of Niuhuru's eyes widening when I spoke of the Jesuit. "I may still win," I say, but I am afraid. What if I have gone too far this time? How could a concubine accuse the Dowager Empress of any misdemeanour, let alone what I have threatened her about, and be believed? And if she decides to brazen it out, she may then decide to eliminate me as a threat altogether. I think of what she might find out about me. "I am cold," I tell Feng. "Fetch me a jacket."

His eyes tell me he knows full well that it is not the weather making me cold but he fetches me a padded jacket anyway and I huddle into it, but feel no warmer.

Ling is called for again. When I hear of it, I slam my hand down on a table in anger.

"But another girl was called," says Feng, standing in the doorway, watching my reaction to this news.

I frown. "You said Ling."

He nods, his dark eyes gleaming with something he knows. "*And* another girl."

"On the same night?"

He nods.

I think of the album I gave to Qing, the images of more than one woman with a man and my eyes flicker. "Report back to me tomorrow night. And every night."

Ling is summoned every night. But every night some other woman is also summoned. And those chosen do not crow over their popularity as they usually would, they do not hold their heads high and look with disdain at those of us not yet summoned. Instead they go about their days with lowered eyes and are silent. Only Ling smiles. Her smile grows even broader after the previously utterly unfavoured Qing and Ying are summoned on the same night.

"Three women?" I ask Feng, to be certain. "He had three women in his chambers at the same time?"

Feng grins. "Ling is no better than a brothel keeper," he says. "She is tantalising the Emperor with all the goods of the court but keeping his seed for herself."

"Don't be so vulgar," I say, but there is something in me that wants to hear more, my breath comes a little faster. This is akin to the nights that Feng and I spend together, our whispered descriptions of what others do. "They won't be called again, they're two of the most unpopular women he has."

But I am wrong. Now only three women are called to the Imperial bedchamber. Ling, Qing and Ying. Over and over again. "Why them?" I ask Feng. "Why are they suddenly in favour? He never cared for their company before. And the two of them only have eyes for one another, any fool can see it even if they can't."

Feng's eyes meet mine. "Oh, but I think they can," he says. "I think their eyes have been opened and now the two of them are enjoying each other's company. And the Emperor is enjoying their pleasure."

"And Ling?"

"Ling will get what she needs, never fear," says Feng.

"Empress?" I ask.

Feng shakes his head. "You only think of what you want, Ula Nara," he says. "You need a better imagination."

Feng shakes me awake, his hand rough on my shoulders.

"What?" I ask.

"There is to be an announcement," he says. "You are summoned to the throne room."

"I?"

"You and all the women of the court," says Feng.

There is a tension in the throne room. First Ying and then Qing are promoted. I look from one to the other of them but their faces are like stone, they do not look in the least pleased with these promotions, they seem more unhappy than anything else, which I cannot understand. They surely cannot harbour romantic feelings for Qianlong, knowing how they feel about one another. But they do not even seem to acknowledge one another, they pass one another rigidly, their bodies stiffly held apart. I frown. What has happened between them? Certainly they have been rewarded for their part in Ling's scheming. She must have got what she wanted from them.

Ling catches my eye. I glare at her and am about to look away but she smiles, as though she is a friend to me, then drops her hand to her belly where I see an unmistakeable curve. I feel a great wave of rage sweep through me and with it comes a cold understanding. The bitch is with child. She has used Qing and Ying to titillate Qianlong, shown him something forbidden, something new. She has used every woman at court as living pictures from a pillow book while drawing the Imperial seed into her own body to achieve the ultimate success: a child for the Emperor. I can feel my hands curl into fists, can feel my back muscles clench so tightly that my whole body is shaking.

But no-one is watching me. The Empress Dowager is on her feet and all the attention is on her.

"My son's loyal and wise first Empress has left us bereft at her passing," she announces, her voice loud in the vast room. "He is, naturally, full of grief at this loss. But a court without an empress is not a proper court and therefore I have chosen a new empress for my son."

Her eyes have been looking about the room but now they settle on me. I meet her gaze and know what is coming. She hopes to repay me with this, she believes that in taking this step she will give me back the happiness she took away when she chose me for her son. She hopes that my lips will stay closed on what I have seen, on the spark between herself and the Jesuit, a love so deeply forbidden it cannot even be hinted at.

The court is alive with anticipation. Every eye is on Niuhuru. I look at Qianlong but he is looking straight ahead. Probably he is thinking of Fuca, resenting his mother's intrusion on his endless mourning for her.

"Lady Ula Nara will be the successor to the first Empress," announces Niuhuru and I look towards Ling. Her eyes drop, she chews her lip as she thinks about what this means for her. She had better have a son in her belly, for if she does not then her gamble has been for nothing. The court rustles as everyone turns to look at me.

My long-overdue payment is about to be made. The hungry ghost inside me is waiting to be fed.

Gold

I MAKE LING PAY FOR HER rank-creeping, for the bedroom games she played with Qianlong in her efforts to be his favourite. I take Lady Ying as a 'companion,' have her moved close to my palace, as though I actually want the sulky-faced girl anywhere near me. I know that she would like to refuse but in the end she says nothing, only does as I command. She attends me in silence, her face white with misery. I see her cry silently for her lost love Qing and I think, *you do not know what it is to lose a true love.* After all, Qing is still nearby, if Ying had any guts at all she would walk barely three hundred paces to Qing's palace and declare what she feels, speak the name of this forbidden love and see what Qing has to say in return. But she does not, she is a coward under the outer show of bravado she likes to put on.

I see Qing creep to Ying's new palace under cover of darkness, her fluttering head eunuch accompanying her. I see them watch as Ying weeps and I take pleasure in the way they scurry away as soon as I step out of the shadows and stand guard over Ying's miserable crouched figure.

The ceremony to make me Empress is absurdly long but I am used to such rituals by now, I do not move, do not shift awkwardly on my cloud-climbing shoes. The stiff silk robe in Imperial yellow to which I am finally entitled hangs heavy and motionless around my frame. On my head is the Phoenix crown that Fuca once wore: excavated from the Imperial storerooms and brought to my own palace this morning. A heavy gold central headdress of pearls and gems, topped with three phoenixes created from blue kingfisher feathers finished with dangling ropes of pearls on either side. Its weight reassures me that this moment has finally come, that I am made Empress, that what I have worked for has come to pass. My payment is due.

Qianlong looks down at me from his throne, his mother's anxious face beside him. He does not look happy, but he is playing his part as required. Now he holds out the *ruyi* sceptre with which I will promoted. I reach out and take it from him. Intricate gold filigree studded with precious gems and characters, it is heavier than I imagined. I wait for the last part of the ceremony to be completed: the Chief Eunuch will announce my new title and then I will take my place in the empty throne by Qianlong's side, will turn to face the court as the highest-ranked of his ladies. I will meet Ling's gaze and relish her failure.

"Lady Ula Nara is promoted from Imperial Noble Consort. She is henceforth to be known as the Qianlong Emperor's Step Empress."

I should step forward, the empty throne is now mine, it waits only for me. I can hear the rustle behind me as the court kneels, ready to kowtow to me, ready to wish me ten thousand years. But I am unable to move. *Step* Empress? What is this title Qianlong has given me? No such title has ever been given to an empress, even one following a previous holder of the position. Each woman to take on the role has been known as Empress. No more, no less. With this title Qianlong is signalling, forever, that I am second choice, that his heart still lies with Fuca. I look to Niuhuru but she does not meet my gaze. I look at Qianlong but he only looks back at me and now everyone is waiting.

I take one step and then another. I have not spent all these years emulating Fuca for nothing. My every move is perfection, elegance personified. I reach the carved throne at Qianlong's side, turn, sit.

Sitting in Fuca's throne, I feel the weight of the gold *ruyi* in my hands, the Imperial yellow silk against my skin, the Phoenix crown weighing down my head. The court kowtows. I look down at the ranks of courtiers, see pregnant Ling on her knees to me and already I know: the payment I have received is not enough to feed the hungry ghost who lives inside me.

It will never be enough.

Ling has a son. Feng brings me the news.

"Bitch," I curse. "How does that woman always outrank me?"

"You are Empress," he reminds me.

"Step Empress. To an Emperor who spends his time sniffing after that bitch as though she were on heat," I snarl. "Watch how fast she is called back to the bedchamber to perform whatever services she has to offer and whelp another child. Watch how fast he promotes her for giving him a son."

Feng nods. "She has already given her son to Qing to bring up," he says.

"Oh, a reward for services rendered?" I sneer.

Feng shrugs. "Qing and Ying are living in the same palace," he says. "Do you want to report them?"

I shake my head. I know they are under Ling's protection now, she would speak up for them, not in the court but in Qianlong's ear, reminding him of the desire he felt in watching them together. His pleasure has cast a protective spell over them, to break it would only bring down his displeasure on my head. He dislikes me enough already, it would not take much to dislike me further.

Feng no longer sleeps beside me. As Empress, I am too surrounded by guards, by servants. There would be talk. I cannot risk whispers. Once, after the promotion, he tries to touch me when we are alone, his desire suppressed for many months, but I push him away, afraid of being found out and afraid of my own desire for him, angry that even now that I am Empress it is not enough to satisfy my desire to be held, to be touched.

He leaves the room without speaking and the next morning I hear a maid screaming.

When I follow the sound, I see for one moment, for one terrible moment, for one endless moment, Feng's body twisting in mid-air, his face turned away, his dark hair loose as it was on my pillows. I turn and run screaming away before his body turns to face me, for I cannot bear to see his face grown discoloured, the white silk scarf wrapped round his neck.

I mourn him in silence and secrecy. Perhaps what was between us was wrong, twisted and dark, forbidden, but it was all that either of us had to cling to here. I send money to his family, making sure that his role at the Palace should not be mentioned by the messenger, although I wonder if his wife knew, if she realised the sacrifice he had made for her and for his children and grieved for it, for what they had both lost.

I dream of him endlessly. Dreams in which I give him the silk scarf myself, dreams where he offers it to me, asking me to join him beyond this life. I dream of our nights together, our bodies pressed tightly together and then hear him choking and realise I am holding the white silk, slowly strangling him, my hands gripping so tightly that he cannot prise them open. I wake over and over again with a start, gasping as though I am suffocating. I cannot tell my servants what is wrong when they hear me scream and come running, I have to send them away and be left alone in the dark to dream again.

The summons had to come.

"When are Your Majesty's monthly courses?" enquires the Court Physician.

"Why do you need to know?" I ask.

"His Majesty has requested that his household be informed of when Your Majesty will be most fertile," he says.

Reluctantly, I give him the information. Sure enough, as the days approach when I am most likely to conceive a child, I am given warning that I will be called on as Qianlong's companion, something that has not taken place for more than a decade. I note with bitterness that Ling's courses are not remarked upon: she is called whenever Qianlong desires her, which is often, without worrying about whether or not she will birth a child. Of course she is nine years younger than I. At thirty-two, the chances of my having a first child now seem remote. She is only twenty-three and has already born an Imperial son, she has many more years ahead of her in which to birth still more.

Our encounter goes exactly as I expect it to. I am rigid with nerves and Qianlong is dutiful. He greets me with all courtesy and indicates the bed. Once I have awkwardly made my way onto it he joins me.

"Are you comfortable?" is all he asks and I nod stiffly. My body is laid on silk, my arms and legs have enough space around them. The fact that I feel cold despite the warmth of the *kang* under the bed and that I am almost shaking with tension is irrelevant. He does what he must do and I am dismissed with a nod of his head, a eunuch appearing so quickly to take me away that I think they must have been forewarned. I am called for each night for three nights and then no more until the next month. As soon as the Court Physician hears that I am suffering with nausea, Qianlong ceases to call for me.

I am the Empress, I am with child. All is as it should be. I see him only at the rituals and ceremonies that we complete together: in temples and the great receiving halls. As soon as I am too large to comfortably carry them out, I am excused all such tasks. Some other keen concubine will leap forward, beg for the chance to be seen and praised.

We are transferred to the Garden of Perfect Brightness for the summer and find ourselves without Qianlong, for he is much occupied with his generals, poring over maps in their ongoing battles to try and conquer the vast territory of Altishahr, to the West. With him gone, it feels as though the women of the court relax. There is no-one to impress, no-one to score points against as a rival. I walk through the gardens and see Qing and Ying walking ahead of me, their bodies close. Qing carries a bundle in her arms and I realise that it is Ling's son, whom she gave to Qing to raise. I hear their laughter and Qing's cooing to the child, see them come to their own palace and Qing's head eunuch waiting for them, stretching his arms out for the child as though it were his own, a beaming smile on his face. Most of the eunuchs are like this with children, they fuss over them as though they were their own mothers. I walk past them and Ying turns to look at me. She bows her head, as she must, but there is no love or loyalty in her gaze, only a defiant fear.

I sit alone in my rooms, my belly swelling, and weep again for Feng. Perhaps he would have softened at the idea of a child, since he missed his own children so greatly. Perhaps he would have been kind to a baby and we would have been something like a family together, would have felt something like the closeness that Qing and Ying have managed to create from nothing. Perhaps our darkness would have been lightened by a child. Perhaps mine will be.

Whether it might have been or not, I will not find out. I howl with the pain of birthing my son Yongji, the midwives hovering about me, concerned at my advanced age in birthing my first child. They think either I or the child will die, I hear them whispering it.

"Shut your mouths or I will see to it you never speak again," I scream at them and watch them draw back in fear. After that, they tend to me in silence broken only by my own screams and by the wailing of my healthy son as he enters this world.

I hold him in amazement. He is so tiny, so perfect. He is like a miniature copy of Qianlong and it is the first time I feel true tenderness towards him, seeing his image replicated here in my arms, so small, so trusting in my ability to love him, to mother him. I feel a great welling up of love and have to stop myself from snatching Yongji back from the wetnurse. My own breasts cry out to feed him, they swell up with milk and each time he cries they leak, staining the bindings my maids wrap about me, regardless of how many layers they wind around. I dandle him on my lap and smile at him when he awakens, touch his tiny hand and laugh as he makes a fist around my one finger. Qianlong visits us and beams at the sight of him, sends me flowers and jewels, his demeanour towards me somewhat softened at this proof of my further suitability to take on the role of Empress.

"Your Majesty will wish to choose the concubine who will raise the child, of course," says the Chief Eunuch. "I have taken the liberty of drawing up a list of suitable candidates."

I feel sick. "No," I say quickly. "I can raise him myself."

The Chief Eunuch's brows come together and I feel the room swirl about me, knowing that yet again I have come up against one of the rules of court that must be obeyed. I look at the list I am being offered and choose a name almost at random.

"But I must see him every day," I insist.

The chosen concubine kowtows and promises that of course, of course, she swears to bring the child up as her own, he will have every care...

I watch her leave my presence holding Yongji and wonder how many times a heart can be broken.

I see Yongji on the first day as promised, on the second day also, but then the Chief Eunuch returns me to my duties as Empress and first one day and then another goes by when I cannot see him because I must complete the right rituals, be present at the right ceremonies. I must sit by Qianlong's side and when at last I am free of my duties, then the baby is asleep or he is feeding, he is unsettled and must be kept quiet. If I think of him I weep, even in situations where to weep is unacceptable, and so eventually I try not to think of him. I pretend there has been no child, for to think of him is so painful I cannot bear it. I send word to the concubine that she does not need to worry herself, she must take every care of him but I will see my son only when it is convenient. This comes to mean hardly ever and meanwhile I am summoned back to the Emperor's bedchamber. One heir by the Empress is not enough, it seems, it would be most auspicious to have more and so I must lie still and wait for the day when the Court Physician pronounces me with child again.

There is a daughter the following year. It seems I am fertile after all, despite my advancing age. Who knows how many children Qianlong could have had by me if he had continued to call on me, all these past years. This time I turn my face away from the tiny dark head, I do not brush the little cheek, for I know what is coming. Another concubine kowtows at the vast honour of being given the Empress' child to raise, even if it is a girl. I have my breasts bound so tightly I can barely breath and the child is quickly taken away, so that I need never hear her cry out for her mother.

I do not hear her cry for me before she dies, either, when she is only two years old. I barely knew her. The hapless concubine who had the care of her kneels and weeps, begs my forgiveness and I turn my face away, say nothing. This woman was more the child's mother than I ever was, I think, and yet she is forced to beg my forgiveness for the loss and grief she has suffered in my place.

A year after my daughter dies I produce a second son, who again dies within two years. Another sobbing concubine shakes with fear as she kneels to tell me what has happened.

I look down on her from my throne, my face blank, silence the only thing that stops my tears from flowing.

"I have a ritual to attend," I say, rising, as though her news is irrelevant to me, an inconvenient interruption.

In the temple I speak words without knowing what I am saying. I keep my eyes on the nuns. Their heads shaved, their faces devoid of emotion as they chant the sacred texts, offering incense, their eyes closed in peaceful prayer. I try to keep my face like theirs, still and remote, not of this world.

Qianlong no longer calls for me. Apparently my surviving son Yongji grows well, he has taken his place among his living siblings to be educated as befits an Imperial prince.

I come across the Imperial children one day by accident as they learn archery in the Garden of Perfect Brightness. At my approach, they all stop what they are doing and make their obeisances, from the elegance of the older children to the clumsy attempts of the youngest.

"Come forward, Yongji," says the tutor, gesturing to one boy to step forward. "You must greet your mother, her Majesty the Empress."

I swallow. If I had been asked to choose Yongji from the group I would have struggled, I might even have failed. Now he stands before me, very upright, his bright eyes on me.

"Mother," he says, bowing deeply.

I think of the concubine who raises him and wonder what he calls her, if he calls me Mother. What name does he give to the woman who strokes his hair before he goes to sleep, what word does he cry out when he is afraid at night and wants her by his side?

He is waiting for me to say something. I do not know what to say. I know nothing of children, only what I remember from my own childhood. I do not know what Yongji likes to do best, what games he plays, whether he has been given a pet, if he chose a dog or a cat, perhaps a little cricket or a slow-plodding tortoise. I try to smile.

"Yongji," I say, aware of how often I have whispered his name through tears, how few times I have spoken it aloud. "Are you well?"

"Yes, Mother," he says politely.

I do not know what else to ask. I look to his tutor. "Does he do well at his studies?" I ask, as formal as though this were the Imperial Examinations rather than a mother asking how her son does.

The tutor bows. "He is an excellent archer," he says. "A true Manchu. Soon he will be learning to draw a bow on horseback, as his ancestors did."

I nod. I have barely heard what he said. I look back at Yongji, who waits expectantly for me to say something else. "You must obey your tutor in all matters," I say, as though he has been chastised, as though I have been informed that he is lagging in his studies.

He bows. "Yes, Mother."

"I must go now," I say, although in truth I have nowhere to go, nobody to see. Everyone bows again and I walk away. When I have gone a few steps I look back, thinking, hoping, that perhaps Yongji will still be watching me, but he has already turned back to the targets, eager for his turn.

Ling has a child every summer without fail for three years, her first son growing under the watchful eyes of Qing and Ying, who love him as their own. Any chance I might have had to find motherly love has been taken from me.

The summer that Ling provides the Emperor with another son the child's birth is celebrated with fireworks and glory, festivities and feasting.

"What news?"

The maid hovers. She does not want to say what I have asked her to tell.

"Well?"

"Lady Ling is delivered of a son, Your Majesty."

"You must think I'm a fool not to know that," I say. "There were fireworks all of last night. I could not sleep. I asked you to find out details."

"Yes, Majesty."

"Well?"

"He has been given to Lady Ying to raise, Majesty."

Slowly, I nod. Ling is still rewarding Qing and Ying for the services they performed in the Emperor's bedchamber, several years gone by now. Whatever they did, however they pleased him, it was Ling who benefitted, and she has not forgotten their service. Qing plays mother to Ling's first son, and now the family unit that Qing and Ying created together has been enhanced by this new addition, another princeling to raise, more favour shown to them by the Emperor's favourite.

"And?"

The maid hesitates.

"*And?*"

"And… Lady Ling has been made… Imperial Noble Consort."

And here is proof, if proof were needed, that Qianlong does indeed have a favourite, and she is Lady Ling. This title that has been given to her, this promotion, now ranks her as second only to the Empress, to me. It is only the rules of hierarchy that prevents him creating a second Empress. But there can be only one Empress, and I am still alive, therefore Ling is barred from the position he no doubt would have gifted to her, had he been able to. Had he had the chance to finish grieving for Lady Fuca, he would have chosen his Empress with more care. It would have been Ling sitting in the throne by his side, not I. He was bludgeoned into choosing me, by his mother, by court expectations, by years, decades, centuries of dynasties. And now Ling is ranked second only to me, ready to become Empress should anything befall me.

I become watchful, afraid, jumping at shadows. I fear assassins with knives in the dark, I fear poison in my food. I check the silver strips that are placed in every dish at my mealtimes, check them myself for any sign of staining, of darkening, of poison leaking out and making itself known in the shining surfaces of the tiny strips that are meant to protect me. My eunuch taster must taste everything before I put it in my mouth, sometimes more than once before I am satisfied. I cannot eat while the food is still hot, for perhaps the poison will not take effect for some time, and so my taster eats long before I do, and by the time I eat my food is cold and congealed on the plates. It loses its appeal, and so I find myself eating less and less. I pick at my food and swallow each morsel as though it may kill me. More servants must sleep in my rooms to protect me, until what ought to be my private bedchamber becomes a dormitory. None of my servants dare speak to me about my behaviour, but I see them look to one another as dish after dish is returned to the kitchens, as they wait for their chance to eat my leftovers and watch the food grow cold and stale. They exchange glances when they dress me, when they wash me, as I grow thinner. Sometimes I look down at my long bony hands, made longer still by the golden nail shields I wear, studded with gems, unable to hide the pallor of my skin, stretched out over bones. My robes must all be remade, for they hang on me, baggy and loose. I sit by the Emperor's side, heavy in my court silks and my jewels, high above the other women on my gilded throne, knowing that the man I sit beside would rather it was another woman beside him.

I am desperate to find a way out of this life, a freedom from what I feel, from what I have felt all these years. To be released from the grief of losing a distant love, to let the pain go and instead to feel nothing, to feel calm and free. To forget the child taken from me and made another's, to forget the two children lost to this world. To step away from the darkness inside me and the constrictions and horrors of the world around me, and instead live a life of simplicity and purity.

During another endless ceremony I notice the nuns again and suddenly I think that perhaps I could follow a new path. Perhaps I have come to it too late, unlike Niu Lang, who knew at once what steps to take to avoid the pain of our lost lives, but at least I have come to it now. I could become a nun. I think that the Emperor will not refuse me this, for there can be no shame in it. For an empress to choose a life of spiritual growth and piety cannot be an embarrassment to him. If he lets me go, I can become a nun and he may choose whomever he wishes to join him on the golden thrones. No doubt it will be Ling who sits by his side, but I find, much to my surprise, that I do not care. Let her have her time as Empress. Let her find out for herself that it is not the glorious role she thinks it is, as all the women here think it is. They look at the Imperial yellow silk that makes up my robes, they see all the jewels of the warehouses in my hair, and they imagine that to sit by the Emperor's side, bedecked in these treasures, must lead to happiness. As did I. But I have found that I was wrong, and now I have seen for myself a possible solution, the path I should have chosen long ago, if I had been as brave as Niu Lang was. I think that his choice to become a monk when the life he had planned was denied to him was a strong choice, a pure choice. He will not have grown bitter and dark in his thoughts and deeds, as I have. He will have found freedom over the years, will have meditated on our love and blessed it, will have let it go peacefully from his heart and risen above the pain. He will think of me sometimes, perhaps, and smile, he will wish me good things in the life destiny chose for me. He will have been taught acceptance by his religious masters, perhaps struggling at first but eventually coming to a place of harmony that cannot be disturbed by the petty concerns of daily life. I wonder if I, too, could make such a choice, could learn another way. I think of what it would be like to shed my silken robes and shave my head, to wear the simple robes of a nun and spend my days in prayer and contemplation. How slowly, over time, I would feel the pain of these past years leave me and instead find an inner peace, a way to accept what has been and let it go without judgement, to feel a lightness of being I have not known since I came to this place.

I request an audience alone with Qianlong and am shown into his private study. I kowtow.

"I have a boon to ask."

"Ask," he says, his tone benevolent, not looking up from his work, as though he will grant whatever I name without even thinking about it.

"I wish to become a nun," I say.

"What?" he asks, looking up from his papers, his attention suddenly on me.

"I wish to renounce my title as Step Empress and become a nun," I say. "I will leave the Forbidden City and go to a nunnery somewhere remote, I will pray for the good of the empire. I wish to take up a holy life."

"No," he says. I wait for him to ask why I do not wish to be Empress, but he does not ask this.

"There are plenty of other women who would be happy to take my place," I say. "Lady Ling, for example," I add, swallowing my pride to name his personal favourite, hoping that the thought of offering her such public favour will sway him.

"No," he says. "It would not be seemly. People would talk, they would suggest you are unhappy as Empress and that would be inauspicious."

"You can say that I have retired because of grief for my children," I suggest.

"No," he says. "And anyway, you have a living son."

I think of Lady Fuca, dying of a broken heart after losing two children, how tender he was with her. How I, too, have lost two children, but have not been shown the same tenderness. I stay on my knees.

"I beg you to let me go," I say and my voice shakes. "I will not cause trouble. No-one can object to an empress being devout. My sacrifice in becoming a nun can only bring favour to the Imperial Family."

"No," he says.

"But I – " I begin.

"No," he says. "This conversation is at an end, Ula Nara. Your request is refused." He is very calm. He does not need to raise his voice or be angry or upset at my request, he is the Emperor, he can simply refuse and know that his word must be obeyed. I leave the room in silence and he does not watch me go.

I try to accept the emptiness of my gilded life. I carry out all my official duties, the meaningless bowing and praying, the movements and costumes required for each occasion. I no longer have to listen to Ping's horror stories, I do not engage in the dark yearning of the nights with Feng. My three children are gone, one way or another. Every woman and servant at court fears me, including the Empress Dowager. Ling will never be Empress while I still live, even if one day her sons make a bid for the throne it will mean little to me, for my living son hardly seems my own.

I had not known such emptiness could exist, such deep loneliness even beyond yearning for a lost love. I wonder how many years it is possible to live like this, a hollow shell giving the appearance of life, like one of Qianlong's beloved Western clocks, exquisitely decorated, ticking and ringing, made up of only cogs and wheels inside, endlessly turning for the amusement of their master.

I ransack the Imperial storerooms to which only I, as Empress, have access. I can have anything I want sent to my rooms and so I plunder their contents. I fill up my rooms with exquisite furniture and priceless ornaments: vases, precious calligraphy, board games, fans, trinkets, jade carvings. My rooms do not have the sparsely luxurious air that Qianlong likes to cultivate about him, they grow crammed and heavy with wealth. I wear only Imperial court robes, not the more informal robes the other women wear, choosing colours to suit their moods or needs, instead I wear only the coveted Imperial yellow. I have the jewels to which I am entitled brought to me and I wear them all. I spend my days weighed down with jewellery, from ropes of pearls and gemstones to heavy jade pendants, headdresses which shiver with gold filigree strands and pearls, or wholly made up of the tiny, exquisitely gleaming, and highly prized kingfisher feathers. I do not know how many tiny darting kingfishers have been killed and plucked to create my hairpieces. I do not care. I know that behind my back the court compares me unfavourably to Lady Fuca's style of dress, how she preferred freshly-plucked flowers or little creations made from plaited straw, how Qianlong himself would place wild flowers in her hair, how she wore only simple robes unless called on to perform a formal ritual. I do not care. The Imperial storerooms are at my command day and night and there is not a jewel I might command that I have not worn. Anything and everything that is mine by right of my position, I take. When I dress each morning a third of my own bodyweight is added to my frame in the form of heavily embroidered robes, cloud-climbing shoes so high no other concubine can wear them, the crowns and jewels that adorn me. The weight is a comfort to me, it is like a burden I must bear each day, but one which can be supported physically rather than in my heart and mind. I wonder whether perhaps I have found a way to continue this life, balancing the emptiness within with the weight of clothes and jewels and rituals on the outside. Perhaps this is the best I can hope for, to keep this balance, to feel as little as possible, to act as a hollow adorned shell of a woman.

But news comes that disturbs my delicate balance. Altishahr, the Muslim territory bordering China to the West, has finally fallen, Qianlong's armies have won a battle that has been going on for decades. Renamed *Xinjiang*, New Territory, it is added to the empire, vastly expanding its size. Prisoners of war and huge quantities of jade, in which the new territory is rich, are brought to the capital. There is whispering among the ladies of the court. A new woman is to join our ranks, not through the Daughters' Draft but from this new territory. A noble family of the area turned traitor on their own people and joined us as allies. Now they are rewarded with access to Qianlong's very own bedchamber, for their daughter will become a concubine.

Qianlong is already half in love before she even arrives, he talks of nothing else but his New Territory and the woman who is to be sent here, he applies himself to studying her language so he can speak with her. He wants to revel in this glory. I can imagine that the idea of lying with a woman from this conquest fills him with desire, as though he will conquer the land over and over again each time she is brought to his bedchamber. I can see that even Ling, confident in her many healthy children, is a little anxious at the idea of this new arrival. She has new robes made, her children are drawn to Qianlong's attention more than usual, she even has the Jesuit paint her portrait with her little son, a permanent reminder of her ability to breed Imperial heirs.

I arrive in the vast receiving hall, dressed in Imperial yellow, my head weighed down with the kingfisher-feather and pearl Phoenix crown. The Chief Eunuch looks distressed at the sight of me.

"Your Majesty," he says, bowing very low.

"Is something wrong?" I ask.

He bows again, uncertain of what to say. The Chief Eunuch was chosen for his ability to know what to say and do in all circumstances, even how to deliver bad news to senior members of the Imperial Family. "His Majesty…"

"Yes?" I say. I look up at Qianlong and his mother, already seated. Qianlong is looking through papers. My empty throne awaits.

"His Majesty has asked that you stand with the other ladies today."

I don't ask why. I am not stupid. Qianlong is excited about this new arrival, this woman who stands as a much-anticipated symbol of a new conquest. He does not want to be reminded that he has an Empress already, he wants to believe this new woman promises a new romance about to blossom. I feel some of the emptiness that I have so carefully cultivated slip, emotion rising up in me. I try to crush it back down. I make my way forwards and find a place to stand, knowing that the other women have read this slight correctly, they are too well-versed in court etiquette not to notice that I am stood amongst them rather than being seated above them.

Wan arrives and smiles brightly at me. She is caked in too much makeup, as though to keep her status as Qianlong's youngest bride, even though she is by now forty-three and there are women here who could be her grandchildren. I have heard that she is now entirely bald, through some illness, though her eunuchs are experts in wig-making and dressing and therefore her hair is as silkily black and elegantly over-dressed as it ever was.

"I hope the new lady will speak Mandarin," breathes Wan. "I have tried to learn a few words of her own language but really, I cannot make it out at all. The Emperor has learnt it with no trouble at all, it seems! He is so learned. A true scholar."

I don't answer her. I have already arranged for a translator of the new woman's language to stand by my side, so that I will not be left out of any conversation she may have, so that I will have a ready-made spy to observe this new arrival's progress. I am watching Qing and Ying who have arrived together, as usual. They do not even hide their relationship, they go everywhere together. Ling is already here, well-dressed and smiling at the Emperor, who for once is not taking much notice of her, instead looking over papers while his mother sits by him, looking tired.

Behind me I can hear rustling and whispers, but what I am really listening to is the steady thump of feet from outside, the bearers of a palanquin running towards us. And then there is silence. The Chief Eunuch leaves Qianlong's side and makes his way out towards the doors where the woman will be waiting for his signal to make her entrance. There is an absurdly long pause. No doubt the Chief Eunuch has in mind some auspicious moment which must be exact, as though it will make any difference at all whether Qianlong sees her now or in several moments' time, as though it will somehow change their destinies.

Now one woman after another turns and although I want to keep my back turned I cannot. I turn to look at her.

She looks very odd to my eyes. She is dressed all in red, as befits a bride, but rather than our long, loose-fitting robes she wears a skirt of many layers that comes out from a tight waist. She has little shoes with high heels and a billowed-sleeved shirt with a waistcoat over the top, again fitted tightly to her form. The whole outfit hugely accentuates the curves of her body in a way that looks positively immodest. Her hair is long and black like ours but it is woven into many tiny plaits that fall to her waist, while on her head is a little embroidered cap.

She looks terrified.

Her own translator, a eunuch, is gesturing to her to move forwards, but she shakes her head, touches his sleeve as though to make him come with her. He shakes his head in turn and by now the Emperor has noticed her. He stands and comes towards her. She ought to kowtow, of course, but she hesitates as though she has not been told what to do.

"Welcome to court," says Qianlong in her own tongue, hastily translated in a whisper by the man at my side.

She looks astonished. He looks delighted at having made such a good first impression. Qianlong always did like to be praised, to be admired, I think wearily.

"I speak all the languages of my empire," he says. "I have been learning yours in preparation for meeting you."

She doesn't reply, only looks awkward. I think of the ceremonies when new women arrive following a Daughters' Draft, how polished each girl is, how they have been drilled for days, perhaps months, on how to behave at court, how to respond to pleasantries from the Emperor. This girl has all the polish of a peasant.

Qianlong, meanwhile, is looking her over. "Your clothes are not court dress," he remarks. He does not sound annoyed, only curious. He cannot visit his new dominion, so this girl is a symbol of it, something he can explore. He likes her odd appearance, I can tell, it shows he has conquered a truly far off and exotic land, not just some minor annex to China.

She blushes. "They're – they are the traditional clothes of… Xinjiang, Your Majesty. I thought it would please you to see them."

He smiles at once. "Of course. Turn around."

She turns awkwardly on the spot, like a piece of livestock for sale.

"Charming," says Qianlong, looking at her hair. "All those little plaits."

"There'll just be two tomorrow, Your Majesty," she says.

He frowns. "Why?"

Her cheeks grow scarlet. "I will be m-married," she says. "Married women wear only two plaits."

"Then I will look forward to seeing you with only two plaits," says Qianlong suggestively.

The courtiers titter. We women do not.

She looks as though she would like to leave, but Qianlong is not done with her yet. "One more thing."

She waits.

"I have been told that you have a special attribute."

She looks at him.

"I have heard that your body emits a natural fragrance."

She looks down.

"Is it true?"

"I've been told so, Your Majesty." It comes out as little more than a whisper.

He smiles. "Come closer."

She steps forward, still leaving a considerable gap between them.

"Closer than that," he says. "I am not a hunting dog, to scent you from so far away!"

The courtiers titter politely again. I can see Ling's face stiffening. If the Emperor wishes to flirt with a new lady, must we all be forced to bear witness?

She comes one step closer to him and he leans forward. He inhales loudly, putting on an amusing show for the courtiers, but clearly her perfume is of quality, for he closes his eyes for a moment. "It is your own scent? Not a perfume?"

"Yes, Your Majesty."

"Remarkable. It reminds me of lotus flowers."

Of course it is not her own scent, I think. *It is some perfume from her own land that half the women there wear and he does not know any better.*

There is a whispered consultation between the Chief Eunuch and Qianlong before the new arrival's court name, status and privileges are read out.

"We welcome the noblewoman of Xinjiang, now made an Honoured Lady and given the court name of Lady He."

He has named her after a lotus flower in honour of her supposed natural fragrance. Absurd. At least her rank is not high, she is sixth-ranked, she will have to work hard before she reaches the heights of Ling, who is looking relieved. But clearly the girl has no idea that she must now take on a new name for the rest of her life, she looks confused and her interpreter-eunuch has to murmur explanations before pushing her forward to perform a kowtow, which she stumbles over. As she stands, Qianlong holds out a *ruyi* carved from a dark wood inlaid with white jade panels. She takes it, looking mystified. Again I find myself wondering about how ill-informed she is over courtly customs.

The Emperor reaches out and traces the carved characters with his forefinger. "It says that all the world is now at peace," he says, smiling. "Now that Xinjiang is part of our empire's family and Lady He has joined the ladies of the court, the world is at peace."

The court applauds. The palms of my hands touch one another, though they make little noise.

A few more proclamations are made, covering additional gifts given to her family. Her father and brothers are to live in a newly-created Muslim quarter of Beijing, situated just outside the walls of the Forbidden City. The newly-named Lady He does not look happy about this. I wonder if she, like Wan, was ill-treated by her family. If she was, she can take comfort in the fact that she will never see them again.

Eventually, she is led away to her new palace and I return to mine. But I have a restless night. The deliberate lack of feeling I have tried to cultivate of late has been disturbed by this new arrival. Watching Qianlong flirt with her brought back a rush of unhappy memories of how he used to be with Fuca. And something about Lady He bothers me, there is something not right about her. I try to tell myself that she is from another country and culture, that she is unlikely to behave as I would expect her to, but still it is almost dawn before I sleep. The next day I am bad-tempered with the servants. They in turn grow skittish with nerves, remembering the bad old days when I would watch and wait for misdemeanours so that I could lash out with punishments out of all proportion to their faults. They prefer the numbness I have cultivated of late.

Now that the army has returned from Xinjiang, glorious from success in battle, rich with jade, gold and prisoners of war, there must be a large celebration, a parade. Slowly, I dress myself, and am carried in my palanquin to the seating that has been arranged, high above the Meridian Gate. The whole court is gathered, ready to celebrate the conquest, the enlargement of the empire.

I make my way to my allotted seat by the Emperor's side, I feel a little breathless and dizzy, for the seating is steeply raked.

"Ula Nara," says the Empress Dowager, bowing her head to me. It is I who should bow to her, but she is like this with me, anxious to please, able to see for herself that becoming Empress has done nothing for my happiness. I ignore her.

"Your Majesty," I say to the Emperor. He nods, as though to a common courtier, his attention wholly taken up with the procession below and the casket on which his hand rests. It is supposed to contain the left ears of two rebels, a gory trophy. I shift my attention to the people below, the prisoners of war. A few women, mostly men, dressed in the style we have seen on Lady He, little hats perched on their heads, the women with billowing skirts, all of them with colourful waistcoats. I look for Lady He in the crowd and spot her, looking back at me. Her face is anxious, her eyes flicker to me and then back to the procession, she looks as though she may cry. Perhaps she does not wish to see her countrymen as spoils of war, although she must be a fool not to realise that she is a prisoner of war herself, a trophy, although prettier than the ones in the Emperor's casket.

The Emperor has gone so far as to write a poem commemorating this celebration, as he likes to do for important events, thinking himself something of a poet.

> "The casketed Khodja's heads are brought from desert caves;
> The devoted Sultan knocks at the Palace gates…
> By Western lakes, the might of Qing Eternal is decided,
> At the Meridian Gate our triumph is thrice proclaimed.
> From this day forth, we no longer stay this military course.
> My people, sharing joyful plenitude, now shall take their rest."

There is applause. Lady He wipes away tears. I shift in my throne. Now that this is over, I hope that the Emperor will stop with his incessant talk of conquest. Although, from what I have been told, he has yet to conquer his new concubine.

Now that the procession is completed the court begins to disperse. I rise to leave. But the Empress Dowager, seated on the other side of the Emperor, has other plans. I see her speaking to a servant and realise she is about to summon Lady He. I wait, my head turned away, my ears straining to hear.

"You cried," Niuhuru says to Lady He, without any opening niceties. "When the prisoners of war were displayed."

I can barely hear the reply when Lady He answers, it emerges as half whisper. "Yes, Your Majesty."

"Why?"

"I – I am a little homesick, Your Majesty," she stutters.

Niuhuru is silent for a moment. Perhaps she is thinking of the day she chose me, wondering whether this concubine also has a secret love, a secret heartache. She speaks a little more kindly. "All the ladies are at first," she says. "You will grow accustomed to your new life and the world within these walls. Each lady finds her own way to be happy." She pauses and I know without looking that her eyes flickered towards me. "Or not."

"Yes, Your Majesty," Lady He replies, her voice soft.

The Dowager must make some gesture of dismissal. I watch as Lady He makes her way down the steeply raked seating to her palanquin. She stumbles as she enters it and is saved from falling only by the quick wits of her eunuch. There is something about the way she looks around quickly, as though afraid that her stumble is somehow reprehensible, a fault for which she can be chastised, that makes me curious, it echoes how she behaved when she arrived here and stirs something in me from the days when Feng and I whispered and watched together.

I ask for news of her, give little coins here and there, to receive reports of her days, of how she spends her time, of how the Emperor treats her. Oddly, it seems that the Emperor has forgotten her. He has not yet summoned her to his bedchamber, nor even visited her. I cannot understand why. His conquest of her homeland certainly stirred something within him, for he looked younger, stronger and happier than I had seen him in a long time. Surely, Lady He would stir such feelings in him also.

The news I have of her is not very interesting. She likes animals, it seems, for first she adopts a kitten, followed by caged birds that are hung in her garden and the walkways of her palace, as well as in her living rooms. She fills the pond in her garden with fish, and appears to enjoy feeding them. The little dogs that almost all the eunuchs seem to keep are allowed to roam about her palace and treated as though they were her own pets. Her palace quickly becomes known as a noisy place, full of the sounds of animals. Still the Emperor does not visit her. At last the second-hand information is not enough for me.

I send word that she is to come to my palace and meet with me. No doubt her eunuchs, if they are loyal to her, will warn her against me, will tell her of the secrets I have hunted down and the punishments I have ensured were meted out when they were discovered.

I can hear the sound of her palanquin's bearers, trotting into my courtyard. She will think my own garden different to hers, for I only allow white flowers in my garden, the colour of mourning, loss and grief. I hear footsteps coming towards me. I am not sure what makes me do it, perhaps a memory of waiting and watching with Feng, but at the last moment I hide behind a giant black and gold screen and wait for her to enter what appears to be an empty room. From where I stand, I cannot be seen, yet I can observe her.

The eunuch showing her into the room knows better than to comment on my absence. Instead, he indicates a chair by the window. She sits looking about her, a worried frown on her face. She gives a little nod to a maid who brings her tea and a small dish of sweets, but she does not touch them, only peers out of the window at my garden, as though she expects to see me there. She shifts in her seat, uncomfortable with the silence surrounding her and my absence.

I continue to watch her. A part of me thinks that I should show myself now, that I should step out from the screen and speak with her. Still, there is something about her that seems strange. I am not sure what it is, she does not remind me of the other concubines, something about the way she sits or the way she moves, seems wrong. Then again, of course, she is not one of us. Perhaps women in her country do things differently, behave differently. Still I watch.

She stands, as though unwilling to wait longer. I wonder if she will leave, or continue to wait for me. She walks about the room, pausing to look at the stand on which my four *ruyi* are displayed. The rosewood, the black sandalwood inlaid with rubies, the green jade, which perhaps reminds her of home. She pauses over the fourth, the one I received when I was made Empress, its intricate gold filigree weighed down with precious gems, characters for greatness spelled out across it. Whether she can read them or not, I do not know. She sits down again and sighs to herself.

What she does next confirms the strangeness I felt in her. First, she dips a finger into the cold tea and sniffs her finger as though expecting to smell something on it, perhaps poison if she mistrusts me. Her uncouth behaviour surprises me. Now she taps her feet, growing ever more restless as she waits for me. Just as I am about to speak, to reveal myself, she looks down her nose, making her almost cross eyed, and blows a spit bubble, something I have not seen someone do since I was a child, and saw ragged urchins in the street blowing them to amuse themselves. I am so shocked that I speak from behind the screen without even stepping out.

"Is this how they raise the daughters of Xinjiang's noble families? Or just you?"

She jumps to her feet, spit dribbling down her chin. She looks about her and wipes her chin with a shaking hand. She looks towards the door and takes a few quick steps to it, touches it but it is fully closed.

"Behind you."

She turns quickly but I am still hidden. Her breath comes loudly, she is panting with fear. She looks about her and suddenly her eyes fix on the screen, on the tiny gap between the panels, where she can see the glint of my eyes. I step out, move forwards, come close to her. She gasps at the sight of me.

"Answer me." She tries to take a step backwards, but there isn't much space between her and the door.

"W – what?"

"Are all the daughters of the noble houses of Xinjiang allowed to blow bubbles from spittle, or just you? Or are there no nobles in your cur-ridden land? Have we been sent nothing but a street rat, a flea-infested stray from the back alleys, a prisoner of war masquerading as a woman fit for an emperor's court?"

Her eyes widen with horror, rather than narrowing with outrage, as though what I am saying is true, rather than deliberately insulting. "Your – Your Majesty – I – I didn't know you were…"

"Clearly not," I say. I glance at the tea and sweets. "You have not partaken of the refreshments I offered you."

"N – no," she says her voice barely above a whisper.

"Why not?" I move slightly to one side, allowing her, if she wishes, to go back to her seat. Awkwardly, she does so, and stands looking down on the cold tea and sweets. I follow her. "Drink. Eat."

"I – I would rather…" Her voice trails off. Slowly, she reaches down without looking away from me and touches the small bowl of tea. She lifts it, her hand shaking so that a little tea spills over the side, but she does not react to it. She brings the bowl to her mouth and takes a little sip, then suddenly gulps it all down, with sounds more befitting to an old woman without teeth than a court lady. The tea finished, she sets the little bowl down.

I will not let her go so easily. "Eat," I say. I do not take my eyes off her.

She eats all of the sweets, one after another, choking a little, one hand over her mouth. When she has finished she stares at me, her eyes wide and terrified, like an animal waiting for the kill. I step one pace forwards, put my face so close to hers that she is blurred.

"Welcome to the Forbidden City, concubine," I say.

But she still stands there, as though unable to believe that she is free to go, that she could have left this room at any time, what could I have done to stop her? For a moment neither of us moves, until finally I speak again.

"Return to your rooms," I say at last.

She backs away, as though I am about to follow her, feels behind her for the door, then turns and runs. I hear her footsteps in the garden, turn to see her almost fall into her palanquin, see her shout something that I cannot hear to her bearers, who look up, startled, then quickly lift her and begin to run.

And she is gone. My garden is empty, full only of the white flowers and twisted black rocks that make up its sole ornamentation. I feel dizzy, afraid, as though it were she who threatened me, as though it were she who made me eat and drink, while insulting me. I have to lean against the wall for a moment, until my breath returns to normal. After that I stay away from her for as long as possible. I am not sure what I have seen in her, but it is something strange and because I cannot name it, I must bide my time.

Finally the Emperor visits her, but only briefly. Then he sees her again, and again. But she is not called to his bedchamber. It takes me a while before I understand what he's doing. He is courting her. The man who could summon her by turning over a bamboo chip on a silver tray to indicate her name to his servants, is courting her. As though she were some new romance, as though he were a young man falling in love for the first time, rather than an emperor, with dozens of women at his disposal. It is sickening; it makes me angry, that he should play this game, and worse, that she should believe it. I think of Feng, of how he described the Emperor as a romantic, a man who wishes to pretend that he must court his ladies, that they truly love him for himself and not because they must. No doubt this is why he does not love me, why he can barely abide me. It is because he knows full well that I do not love him, that I will not play his game of courtship and romance. That I know who and what I am, and who and what he is, and I cannot be persuaded otherwise.

Summer comes and we move to the Garden of Perfect Brightness, where the Emperor has Lady He installed in one of his beloved Western Palaces, as though the Western referred to her own homeland, rather than a place across the seas that she has never visited. He even gives her a second palace, in which she may pray, sometimes watching her as she does so, as though her prayers are some sort of exotic and charming behaviour singular to herself.

Hunting season comes. My furs are unpacked from perfumed storage chests and then repacked for the journey. As ever, the whole court must attend what is, effectively, the Emperor's private hobby. Certainly none of us ladies are interested in the hunt, for we do not take part, we are there only to marvel at Qianlong's prowess and applaud such prize kills as a tiger or a bear. We are expected to listen once again to the story of how a bear nearly killed him as a child, how his grandfather saw, then, the man he would one day become. A true Manchu, he likes to say, to repeat, endlessly.

Many thousands of men along with a few women make the journey to Chengde, the hunting grounds. Here, tents are laid out in a symmetry that matches the Forbidden City, and each of us must give up the comforts of our palaces for a tent, however luxuriously appointed. I retreat to mine, and resign myself to the many days of boredom ahead.

From the opening of my tent I spot Lady He, standing with the Jesuit painter, Giuseppe Castiglione. They are speaking together, smiling, as though they are old friends. I walk towards them. They do not notice me until I am almost behind them, when Giuseppe's expression alters at the sight of me. He bows deeply, his expression wary. I am certain that Niuhuru told him, years ago, the threat I made that bought me the Empress's crown. He has treated me with excessive caution ever after.

"Your Majesty," he says.

I ignore him and look at Lady He, who bows to me, her own expression fearful. Perhaps she thinks I am about to command her to my tent, to make her drink tea and eat sweets again. "Are you enjoying the hunt, Lady He?"

She flushes and her answer comes out as a stutter. "It's very interesting," she says.

"It's very dangerous," I say. "There are wild animals all around us and the hunters have been known to let fly an arrow in the wrong direction."

I wait for an answer, but she has none to give, she is all but trembling at being in my presence. The old darkness inside me rises up, a thrill of pleasure at her obvious fear of me. I turn and walk away, a smile on my lips.

But it seems the trembling concubine is not so stupid after all, not so fearful. Somehow, she finds a horse, somehow, she ends up in the middle of a hunt, and must be saved by the Emperor and his men, like something from a fairytale. I find myself wondering whether she is cunning, whether the show she puts on, of a homesick and delicate girl, is in fact a front.

For now the Emperor rides with her every day, he even neglects some of the hunting, an unheard of lack of interest. Her eunuchs work deep into the night to have her skirts altered, so that she may ride more easily, they plait her hair with tiny woodland creatures crafted from paper, which nevertheless are left dishevelled after her rides. Half the court wonders whether the Emperor has had her up against a tree or lying in a pile of leaves, like some street girl. He begins to show her other favours, having melons sent from Kashgar, in her homeland, to supposedly tempt her homesick palate. I watch her blush at a banquet when she realises the honour he has paid her, and the faces of the other ladies when they see this sign of favour. I do not taste them, only wave the platter away with disgust.

The nights grow too cold and even the Emperor must give way to the complaints of his women. We make our way back to the Forbidden City and now word reaches me that Lady He has been given another gift. A cook. Apparently, she is homesick for her own food and none of the servants in the vast Imperial kitchens have been able to feed her satisfactorily. I roll my eyes. But when I catch sight of the man, I almost gasp. He does not look like a eunuch, he looks like a man. He reminds me of Feng, his body muscular, his jaw pronounced.

"Find out everything you can about Lady He's new cook," I tell my spy.

He looks confused. "Her cook?"

"You heard me," I snap.

When he returns, the information he brings does not reassure me. His name is Nurmat, apparently, and he is a Muslim, a cook from her own country.

"He's a eunuch?" I cannot help asking.

"Of course," says the spy, looking surprised. "He sleeps in her bedroom, as a guard at night."

I pay and send him away, but something in me tells me that this is not right. This cook, I would swear, is a man, not a eunuch. And if he is a man, if Lady He has a man in her bedchamber every night, then I will ensure that the Emperor hears about it. But not yet. I need evidence.

The Emperor visits her again, this time wishing to try the work of the new cook. Briefly I wonder whether the girl, rather than belonging to our allies, does not in fact come from a family who have hidden their true nature in order to gain access to the Emperor. Is she a spy in our midst, a woman who might seek to harm the Emperor?

"Are you certain," I ask Qianlong on a rare occasion when we are alone, "that Lady He is everything she seems?"

He does not even look up, he only sighs. "I do not wish to hear of your jealousy, Ula Nara," he says. "It is not your business with whom I spend my time."

"You do not spend your nights with her," I say. "Do you mistrust her?"

"It is not becoming of you to know of such things," he says, looking up at last. His expression is cold. "An Empress should not be spying on which lady enters my bedchamber or not."

"I – " I begin.

"This is the end of our conversation," he says. "You may leave."

I have no choice. I have to bow and leave his presence.

Lady He has taken up with Qing and Ying, I see her walking through the gardens with them, watch them visit her palace, and see her visit theirs. What she makes of their forbidden alliance, I do not know, but clearly she has the ability to make friends here. I know she has visited Lady Wan, although Wan always did make friends with anybody.

It is the end of our time at the Garden of Perfect Brightness for the year, which heralds the day that I dread. When the Emperor uses the maze in the Western Palaces to show all of us who is his favourite.

The maze itself is beautiful, made of a grey stone, carved here and there with flowers. At its centre sits a pavilion, where the Emperor, during this event, will sit on a gilded throne, surrounded by lanterns. Here, in this shining, tiny palace, he will await the lady who can make her way through the dark twists and turns of the maze and ascend the steps of the pavilion at its centre. It has been an annual event, since the maze was completed. The outer walls of the maze are surrounded by Imperial yellow flowers, and on the night of this event, it is lit all around with shining lanterns of every shape and size. Each lady is given a lantern to hold, as she enters the maze, and as the first woman makes her way inside, all the lanterns, except those we carry, are extinguished. The maze will be plunged into darkness, and all we will have as our guide is the tiny flickering lanterns in our hands and the shining glow of the pavilion, which we all seek to enter.

As ever, half the court has arrived to watch the spectacle. They think it is charming to see our little lights bobbing amongst the maze, they find it romantic that one lady, one fortunate lady, will enter the Emperor's pavilion, and his arms, if she can walk the maze swiftly and surely. They do not think of the other women, those who are lost inside the maze and who suddenly see the lights of the pavilion go out, signalling that it is already too late, that a woman has made her way to the pavilion and is even now leaving with the Emperor, bound for his bedchamber. They do not think of the humiliation of those of us who must stand and wait within the maze for the eunuchs to find each lady and return us to our palaces.

I sit within my palanquin for longer than is necessary. I do not want to get out and face the court and the other women, take part in this exercise in humiliation. At last, however, I must leave my tiny cocoon and emerge to face what is about to happen. I step out, smoothing down the Imperial yellow silks that are my only protection, my only reminder that, supposedly, I am above these other women.

They are all here, of course. Even Lady Yehenara, who has recently lost a child, and is still grieving, is here. She has dressed in green, which the Emperor dislikes, and so perhaps will only pretend to walk the maze and wait quietly until this evening is over, when she can return to her palace to weep alone. I see Qing and Ying, standing nervously to one side, their hands clasped as though no one were watching. I know full well that they will make no attempt to reach the Emperor.

"Ula Nara." Ling. The only person who rarely calls me 'Your Majesty' as she ought to. I look her over. The embroidery on her robes is designed for one reason only. Bats, persimmons, peaches and cranes, all symbols of fertility, all designed to remind each and every one of us that she has given the Emperor not only two living sons but also daughters. Ling has chosen her own path. Accepting the fact that she cannot become Empress whilst I still live, instead she looks to the future, when she may become the Dowager Empress if her son is chosen as heir to the throne.

"You seem confident," I say. "Anyone would think that you knew the secrets of the maze."

"I have reached the pavilion for many years," she says.

"Since Fuca died," I remind her.

She smiles. "Indeed," she says. "Such a short time ago. And here I am, an Imperial Noble Consort already."

"It may not be so easy this year," I say.

"Really?"

I allow my eyes to flicker in the direction of Lady He, who has had the audacity to dress from head to toe in bridal red. "It looks as though someone else intends to reach the pavilion before any of us."

Ling's eyes follow mine and for a tiny moment a frown crosses her face. "Of course," she says evenly, "the Emperor likes to have a new romance, from time to time."

"He does," I agree. "And Lady He is such a young woman. Fertile, no doubt."

Again, the flicker of a frown crosses Ling's face. "Perhaps," she says. "But her fertility is untried, as yet."

"I am sure tonight will help with that," I say smiling as though I am saying something delightful and turning to leave.

"Ula Nara."

I turn back. "Yes, Ling?"

"There is no need, you know."

"Need?"

Ling sighs. "There are enough paths," she says wearily.

"Paths?"

"You are the Empress," she reminds me. "I wish to be the Dowager Empress." She pauses. "You do not seem ambitious for your... son," she adds, the tiny pause a reminder that one child is all I have left.

I step close enough that even Ling blinks and steps away. "Do not speak of my children," I hiss. "Or I will see you die."

She moves away then, head down, as though she has seen into the pain I carry for one brief moment and realised its burden. I am left with anger running through me, with a darkness that must be unleashed. I make my way to Lady He, signal her to come closer, which she does, unwillingly. I allow myself to look over every inch of her clothing and notice with pleasure the flush staining her collarbones.

"Red, Lady He?"

She bows. "Yes, Your Majesty." There is nothing else she can say.

"Do you know your way through the maze?" I ask.

She lowers her eyes and shakes her head, although there is something in the gesture that is too quick, suspiciously so.

"Have a care which path you choose tonight, Lady He," I say. "The maze is a dark place in which to be lost."

I watch her fear rising at the implied threat. It gives me some satisfaction, it takes away some of the pain that Ling's mention of my children has caused me. I move away, noting the Chief Eunuch's small gesture summoning me to take my place at the front of the women of the court, ready to enter the maze. He hands me a glowing yellow lantern and I stand, facing the dark entryway of the maze, aware of Ling behind me, and behind her all of the other concubines. I nod that I am ready and at once we are plunged into darkness. There is only the moon above our own flickering lanterns and ahead of us the Emperor's pavilion at the centre of the maze, glowing as a beacon to us. I step forward into the darkness, knowing full well that I have never learnt the ways of the maze, that I would be better off following Ling, who I am sure knows at least half of it. I hear the clatter of her shoes as she strides past me and turns right, but I cannot bear this. I cannot bear to follow her and be second. Instead I turn left, into further darkness and then left and left and left again, trying to make my way into the very darkest corners of the maze, as far away from the pavilion as it is possible to be.

I hear giggles here and there, little exclamations, sighs of exasperation and, somewhere, weeping. I stand still for a moment, resting one hand against the cold grey stone of the maze walls. Perhaps I should just stand here, I think, and wait for the pavilion's lanterns to be put out.

They are extinguished so quickly even I am surprised. Somehow one of the concubines has learned the secrets of the maze, for it is impossible to have reached the pavilion so quickly without doing so. Even Ling was never so fast. I reach up high above my head and place my lantern on the top of the wall, a signal to the eunuchs that I am here, lost in the darkness, awaiting rescue. One by one the lanterns appear, one by one they disappear again as each lady is taken from the maze back to her own palace. Some of them weep, some may rage. Some will be relieved. I do not know what I feel. A resignation, perhaps. A glimpse of the future, when year after year I will stand in the darkness of the maze and know that I have failed again at this game and that this moment will happen again and again and again, without end, until I depart this life.

It was Lady He who reached the Emperor so fast. Now he calls for her regularly, he has wooed and won her, has made her come to him of her own free will. He has created a romance and won the maiden's heart.

His gifts to Lady He become absurd. He has some notion that she is homesick. He takes this as a challenge, embarking on a quest to make her happy. First, he turns an old printing room into a bathhouse for her, insisting that we call it a *hammam*, some word from her country that no doubt pleases him with its exotic sound. I go to look at it, stand inside the small space and look up at the domed roof, run a hand across the gleaming tiles and then leave.

He goes a step further. He somehow believes that a noblewoman, if that is what she is, must miss the hustle and bustle of a street market. And so he constructs for her a *bazaar*, another exotic word for the folly he has undertaken. Eunuchs are dressed up in clothes from her home country, wearing mock beards and embroidered felt hats, the bright colours of her people. They have even been taught to pray, or at least pretend to, in a manner that mimics her own devotions. The other ladies of the court chatter over this extravagance, some even go so far as to have their hair dressed in plaits, as though they were common maids, in an effort to look like the Emperor's new favourite toy. I make my excuses. I plead illness, although no doubt everyone will whisper that I am jealous. But my curiosity cannot be held in check, and so I dress as a maid and scurry, head down, through the *bazaar* to see it for myself. No one sees me, no one expects me, they only play at their game, hoping to win the Emperor's favour by so doing. I see him with her, one arm about her waist, as though they were peasants, young lovers, instead of an emperor and his concubine. They laugh together, heads almost touching as she shows him first one delicacy and then another from her homeland. He eats the sweetmeats provided and is delighted with his illusion. I see Ling look away, lips tight, but I know that all that worries her is the possibility that Lady He might bear a child who could supersede her own as heirs. Ling plays the long game. I return to my rooms and feel the bile rising, the darkness inside me twisting. I had thought I could stay numb but I cannot. So Qianlong is to have not one but two great loves in his life and I am still denied even one? The Immortals must truly hate me, must have chosen my destiny based on some grave misdemeanour in a past life, to be so cruel in their mockery of my own desire for love.

I begin to avoid going out of my palace, I pass on my duties to other women. I am afraid of what I will do or say. The emptiness, the safe numbness, will come back, I think, I will reclaim it if I can only stay away from the sight of Qianlong and his new love.

"A visitor," announces a eunuch.

I look up. "I do not wish to receive a visitor," I tell him. I am still in my sleeping robe, my hair hangs down my back, unbrushed, unwashed.

The eunuch hovers in the doorway, uncertain of how to proceed. "It is Lady Wan," he says. "She is most insistent."

I frown. It is years since I have seen Wan socially. I see her at court gatherings and she always smiles. I nod to her in return, watching the wrinkles grow on her face, noting the rumours that she is still bald, although if she is, then her wigs are a masterpiece. I do not see her socially because I do not trust myself not to wound her with my words, lash out with the hurt that is within me.

"I do not wish to see her," I repeat. "You may tell her that I am ill."

"That is why I am here," says Wan, appearing just behind the eunuch and gesturing to him to leave. He glances at me but I do not respond and so he obeys her, closing the door behind him. Wan's dog is with her, an absurdly small creature who bounces around the room as though it cannot contain its pleasure in being alive. It licks my hand and then brushes back past my fingers as though to entice caresses from me but I do not respond. Its short curly fur is rough on my fingertips.

I look up at Wan. "I cannot imagine why you would want to see me," I say, trying to keep my voice polite.

"I am worried about you," she says. She comes closer, sits down next to me, our knees touching. She is still dressed as the young girl who first came here, in a light pink silk covered with cherry blossom embroidery, her hair full of flowers. Not for her the more formal robes or stronger, darker colours favoured by the more mature women of the court. No, Wan's heart is still girlish and her appearance matches her demeanour.

"I hear that you are unhappy," says Wan. "That the Emperor's interest in the fragrant concubine distresses you."

"The what?" I ask.

"Lady He."

"What did you call her?"

Wan laughs. "'The fragrant concubine'. The ladies call her that. Because of her personal fragrance. It comes from her own skin, it is astonishing."

"Don't be ridiculous, Wan," I say. "No-one naturally smells of perfume."

Wan smiles as though she has decided not to argue with me only to keep the peace. It grates.

"I am well enough," I say.

Wan looks at my tangled hair, down at my hands, which are grown skeletal, at my wrinkled sleeping robe, which should have been replaced by my day clothes far earlier this morning. "Oh my dear," she says, her voice trembling a little with unhappy kindness. "You are not well at all. You have not been well since you came here."

I try to laugh. "I have managed to become Empress," I say. "There are those who would say I have done well enough."

"But you have always remained unhappy," says Wan simply. "Your heart still aches."

I feel something rise up, the desire to weep at the simplicity and truth of her words, her good hearted understanding. But something warns me that there is so much to weep for that if I begin, I may never stop. Not only for the lost love of Niu Lang, but for the loss of my family and little sister, for the loss of my children, even for the loss of Feng, for Qianlong's eternal reminders that I am not loved. If I cried for everything I have been through since I was chosen, how could I ever stop? And so rather than lay my head on Wan's shoulder and let the tears fall, I only hold myself more tightly upright and give a pinched smile.

"I am sure everyone has heartache in their lives at some time or another," I say. "None of us can claim eternal happiness."

Wan only looks at me, her own eyes brimming with tears at the lie behind my words. One tear falls and she brushes it away, then rises and looks down on me. "I would always be glad to see you, whenever you cared to visit me or send for me," she says gently. "We all of us have heartache, Ula Nara, but heartache shared amongst friends is greatly lessened."

I do not answer. I do not even watch her as she leaves the room, her little dog gambolling behind her. Instead I spend several moments clenching every part of me so that the tears will not begin to fall.

So be it, I think. If I cannot rid myself of the darkness within, if I am not even free to become a nun and seek tranquillity and peace, then let the darkness rise again. I see the Emperor with Lady He. Knowing what fear I strike in her heart, I send for her again. When she arrives, I am standing looking down at my collection of *ruyis*. I see her kowtow out of the corner of my eye, but wait before I turn to face her.

"The Emperor shows you favour," I say.

"Yes, Your Majesty," she says. Her voice is very flat, she has been expecting this line of enquiry. "He has been gracious to me – as he is to all his ladies," she adds.

"I am concerned." I wait for her to ask why, but she only bows her head. "I have heard rumours," I say.

She looks up at once, frowning. Her eyes are filled with a fear I find interesting. "Rumours?"

"I have heard that the cook that His Majesty gave you is of your own country and that you speak often with him."

"He comes to me for his orders," she says, much too fast. "To agree on the dishes he should serve at my table."

I take a risk. "At night?"

Her eyes flicker. She does not deny my insinuation. "He's a eunuch," she says, then adds hastily, "there can be no harm in his attending me."

I think of Feng. I think of nights together in the dark, our bodies tearing at one another for comfort, for release, for revenge on our miserable lives. "There are many ways in which a eunuch may please his mistress," I say quietly. "It has been known before."

She gapes at me as though she cannot imagine what I am saying. "I – such things – how?" she stutters at last.

I frown. How is it she does not understand what I mean, yet her eyes are filled with fear at the idea of my questioning the status of her supposed eunuch? "Perhaps when you are older you will understand more of what can be between a woman and a man – or even a eunuch," I say. "You are still a child who believes the storytellers' lies of true love."

She says nothing. She does not deny, she does not pretend outrage, she does not try to protect herself. She only stands there, waiting.

I turn away. "Thank you for your visit, Lady He," I say. I hear her kowtowing behind me and then her steps as she reaches the door. I speak softly just as she is about to escape. "Lady He?"

"Your Majesty?"

"I will not fail to undo you if I find you are betraying the Emperor."

She does not answer, she only leaves me alone, gazing at the four *ruyi* as when she found me.

But her visit and my insinuations have frightened her. I hear that she has her servants whipped, that she has their rooms searched, which only turns up the fact that Ling has been spying on her also, wanting to know when she bleeds, whether she has fallen with child. This is what worries Ling. It does not worry me. I have no children, only a boy who does not even think of me as his mother. I have no-one's future to protect or fight for, not even my own.

I sit on my throne and watch.

"Lady He is promoted: she is made *Pin*, Imperial Concubine."

New allocations of silver, silks and servants are proclaimed. She stands, dressed in pink and gold, silk flowers in her hair, pearls dripping from her earrings. She is presented with a new *ruyi* in a white jade inlaid with coloured gems in the shape of flowers, which she holds as though it might break, smiling up at the Emperor, who beams back at her. She is about to complete a kowtow and leave, when he speaks.

"I have another gift for you," he says. "Something to mark the anniversary of you joining my court."

She smiles and bows. The rest of the court watches and waits. The gifts he has given her so far have been lavish, even by Imperial standards, but they have also been unusual. We wait to see what he is about to offer this time.

"I am honoured, Your Majesty. You have done more than enough," she says.

He shakes his head. "I believe your cook has been satisfactory," he says. "I have enjoyed good meals at your palace and I even hear your clothes have been altered to ensure you can continue to eat your fill." He chuckles.

Her eyes flicker. "Yes, Your Majesty. He is a most excellent cook."

"Very good," he says. "Now I have brought you a new servant. A maid."

I catch the expressions of some of the courtiers. A maid? What sort of a gift is a maid? The Forbidden City is full of maids, indeed, Lady He has just been granted more of them. Why mention one in particular?

"A maid," he clarifies, "from your own lands. One who will remind you of Xinjiang and help you feel more at home here."

He is delighted with his idea and the court murmurs with interest, but I am watching Lady He, whose face has drained white. Her legs seem to be trembling and her eunuch attendant puts one hand on her back, as though she is about to faint. She turns to look at a small, folded up figure in the doorway, but her face suggests she already knows who the person is, before they even lift their face from the kowtow they are performing.

The girl, this new maid, is scarred, an ugly scar that comes too close to her eye and cuts her cheek in half. She stands and makes her way towards Lady He, one foot dragging in an ungainly limp. A scarred, crippled maid might be occasion for disgust, not the fear that I see on Lady He's face. The maid is dressed correctly, in a plain blue robe, her hair in a long plait, tied with a small red ribbon. Her face, despite the scar, looks similar to Lady He's, but then they are from the same country, so I suppose that is to be expected.

Lady He has still not spoken. Now she swallows, and opens her mouth. "Your Majesty's generosity knows no bounds," she says. "Thank you." She kowtows, the Emperor smiles, and she is dismissed, making her way out of the great receiving hall, the crippled maid limping behind her.

I might have forgotten about the maid, but when I think about it, it is from the moment of the maid's arrival that Lady He begins to change. She makes strange requests, such as desiring a grove of oleaster trees to be sent from her homeland, to be planted in the gardens here, claiming that they would help with her homesickness, a strange thing to be homesick for. But the trees cause more trouble than they can possibly be worth. The porters rebel against transporting them. More than two hundred men use the trunks of the trees as clubs to attack the armed guards, before going on to kill local officials and install their own leaders. This, of course, only enrages the Emperor. More trees are sent for. The men are punished.

Lady He becomes changeable in her manner: sometimes displaying unexpected coldness or rudeness to people she knows quite well. I hear that she treats the new maid as though she is afraid of her, often requesting a different maid to serve her, although one would have thought she would like to have someone with whom she can easily speak or even reminisce with about her country. I think to set further spies on her, to understand what is going on, but I am saved the trouble.

It is nightfall when a eunuch announces that I have a visitor. "A servant of Lady He," he adds, foreseeing that I will refuse to see the person in question.

I am on my feet at once. "Show him in," I say. I do not know why the personal cook of another concubine should visit me, but such a visit can only confirm my feeling that something strange is going on.

The cook hovers in the doorway and again, particularly at close quarters, I am reminded of Feng. I am reminded of a man. I would be prepared to swear that he is no eunuch. He does not walk like them. He does not talk like them, he does not even smell like them.

"My name is Nurmat," he begins, his dark brown eyes flickering around the room as though to check we are alone. He falls silent as though he does not know how to go on.

"You are welcome," I say. "Sit down."

He blinks at this unexpected offer, then takes a seat at the far end of the room from me.

"Closer," I say.

He rises obediently and makes his way closer to me, pauses uncertainly before I wave him into a seat barely an arm's length from me. For a moment, we only look at each other, before I decide to risk all.

"You are not really a eunuch," I remark, as though it were a matter of no importance rather than a treasonous offence punishable by instant death.

He could protest. He could widen his eyes and be appalled at the suggestion. But he does not. "Your Majesty is perceptive," he says.

"And you are here because you wish me to know this," I say. "Because you wish your mistress harm?"

"It is she who wishes the Emperor harm," he says.

I feel my heart begin to race. "In what way does she wish the Emperor harm?" I ask. "As far as I can see, she enjoys his attentions. And he has been most generous with both his time and gifts."

"My mistress is not what she seems," says Nurmat.

"Tell me everything you know," I say.

"What do you know about the besieging of Yarkand?"

I shrug. "The final siege of the battle to conquer Xinjiang. The Sultan surrendered. He cut off the heads of the rebel leaders Burhan ad-Din and Khoja Jihan and showed their bodies to the commander of the Emperor's army as a gesture of goodwill. The Emperor was delighted. The Empire was made a third larger by his victory."

Nurmat nods. "The girl sent here, whom he has named Lady He... she is the daughter of the family who turned traitors and helped the Emperor to victory."

"Yes," I say. "Their treasonous act to their own country finally gave us victory. The girl being made a concubine was a reward, an acknowledgement of their loyalty to us."

"But what if they had a different plan?"

"Plan?"

Nurmat pauses.

"Speak," I urge him.

"What if they thought to harm the Emperor?"

"By surrendering?"

"By *seeming* to surrender. By asking for their loyalty to be rewarded with a daughter of their house coming to court."

"And what good would that do them? What good is a woman at court?"

"A woman who hates the Emperor, who would kill for her country?"

I swallow. "Are you saying Lady He is going to kill Qianlong?"

Nurmat kneels. "I beg you to have her sent away from the Forbidden City," he says. "All of us: Lady He, myself, her maid."

"Her maid?" I think of the scarred, limping woman.

"She is here to help Lady He," he says.

My head is pounding. I think of Lady He's bright eyes looking up at the Emperor, his arm about her waist. "Are you sure of what you are telling me?" I ask. "What is your part in all of this?"

"I was to bring weapons into the Forbidden City for her," he says. "I smuggled daggers to her. Her maid sewed them into the sleeves of her jackets, so that she might use them when she has a chance, when they are alone together."

"All the court ladies are stripped of their clothing before they enter the Emperor's bedchamber," I say. "For that very reason," I add.

"But the Emperor walks with her in the gardens, he takes her hunting," says Nurmat. "It would take only a moment."

"You must leave me now," I say.

"I beg you to send her away," he repeats.

"Why do you wish her plan to fail?" I ask, suddenly suspicious. I move away from him, thinking for a moment that perhaps he, too, has daggers on him, that while Lady He kills the Emperor, he will kill me.

He swallows. "I – I love – her," he says. "I do not wish harm to come to her because of this plan."

His eyes shine with unshed tears for a moment. "You wanted her for yourself and instead she was chosen for this plan?" I ask.

"Yes," he says and I recognise grief in him, the grief I have felt all these years.

"Leave me now," I repeat. "You will do something?" he asks.

"I will think on it," I say. "She is the Emperor's favourite, I cannot simply have her dismissed."

"I am afraid," he says, his voice very low. "I am afraid she will act soon."

I am frozen. I cannot think how to even suggest to Qianlong that his favourite concubine might wish him ill. But even if I did, something makes me pause. If Qianlong were to die… I would be free. As an Empress, I would not be banished to the back palaces as would the other concubines. I would become an Empress Dowager. I would be free of obligations, for it is unlikely that my son would be chosen as heir when Qianlong has always favoured Ling. Instead I would keep my palace but be set free of any obligations, of any expectations. I might even claim that my grief for Qianlong is so great that I wish to become a nun, and no one could stop me. But if for any reason Nurmat should talk, if it became known that I was told of the danger to Qianlong and did nothing, then I would be executed for treason. And if Nurmat has lied to me and I accuse Lady He without cause, Qianlong will believe me merely jealous or worse, mad. I wonder sometimes if I told Qianlong everything and was proven right if he would reward me by setting me free, allowing me to become a nun after all, but that seems an impossibility.

I wake and these thoughts go round in my head. I sleep and dream of Lady He, of Nurmat, of Qianlong dying. I wake gasping and once again the endless thoughts circle around my mind while I try to find a way forward.

I try to eat. At every meal, my table is covered in more than one hundred dishes, yet I cannot find anything that I can swallow. Food that was once pleasing to me is now tasteless, as though my mouth no longer recognises it as food but only as ashes or dirt. It is so extreme that I wonder if perhaps I have lost my sense of taste, of smell. Yet the incense that I must burn for rituals still chokes my nose and mouth, its rich sweet smell making me nauseous. I ask my cooks to provide ever-stronger tastes, from spicy peppers to heavily salted, sharp pickles, or cakes dripping in honey. I place them in my mouth and the taste that ought to be there is gone. I eat less and less, rising from my table when the food in front of me has been barely touched. No doubt my servants eat better than they have ever done before, gulping down the lavish remains from my table, while I grow thinner than ever. When I dress in the mornings my robes fall over my shrunken frame. I see the eunuchs who dress me glance at one another. They have my robes taken in, made smaller to fit my newly narrow body, but still I grow thinner. Now when I look down at my hands, clutching bundles of incense, I can see every bone, my golden nail shields as hard and pointed as the rest of my hands. My skin turns grey. My maids take it upon themselves to rub ever-richer creams into my skin, hoping to restore some of its natural lustre, but they do not work. Even my shoes grow loose, my hair loses its shine and hangs limply down my back as the eunuchs brush and pin it each morning. I feel dizzy when I stand up, and am unsurprised when my monthly bleeding does not come, heralding not a new life within me, for I have not been summoned to the Imperial bedchamber in some time, but instead, the weakness of my body made manifest, unable to perform its natural functions.

Along with the weakness that I feel and the dizziness when I rise comes a great weariness. Even when I wake in the morning, the only thing I can think about is sleep. Sometimes I refuse to rise altogether, if there are not rituals to be carried out, instead returning to my bed, waving away my expectant servants and burrowing into the warmth of my coverlets. I feel the cold, insisting on wearing furs even when the other ladies have packed theirs away for the summer. The old nightmares that I thought had left me return. All of Ping's stories come back to me now, waking me from slumber in a sweating gasp, clutching at my covers and calling for more lights. Soon I am sleeping with lanterns fully lit in my bedroom, many dozens of them, making the night brighter than the day. Still I dream. I see the Korean concubines, lying in pools of blood, or those lucky enough to escape such an end then finding themselves obliged to take their own lives to honour the life of the man whom they must have feared and despised in equal measure. I hear things that are not there, I see things that no one else sees, starting back from shadows and refusing to be left alone. I am afraid that Nurmat will have told his mistress what he did and that now she will think to kill me first, before I can warn Qianlong, if I can ever warn him. My servants grow accustomed to keeping watch over me all night, knowing they will be whipped if I wake and find them asleep. They set up shifts amongst themselves, ensuring that there are always two of them awake, sitting in my room, watching me sleep, or rather, watching me toss and turn in the grip of my nightmares. I doubt they feel sorry for me, why would they? I have earned a reputation as the harshest of mistresses. Eunuchs and maids alike blanch at the thought of serving me, even beg not to be assigned to my palace.

My dreams and fears unnerve them. At first, they say that it is my palace that is haunted, but then I hear the whispers. They remember what Ping said, for it has been passed down, maid to maid, eunuch to eunuch. I hear them whisper about a hungry ghost, who stalks the Empress, wanting something from her, always wanting and never satisfied. They speak in whispers of Ping, whipped to death, of Feng, who took his own life. I do not dissuade them, for I believe them, although I know that it is not a ghost who stalks me, but I myself that is the hungry ghost, who searches and searches for what will fill the gaping belly of my loneliness and grief and yet cannot, will not, ever find it. I wonder that no one can see this, that no one knows what and who I am, what I have become. There are days when I remove my robes and stand, naked, in front of a mirror. I see the bones that make up my body, the grey-white of my skin and the darkened circles under my eyes, and I think, *how can you not see what I am?*

We are to embark on a new Southern Tour. I cannot help thinking back to the last such tour, when Fuca died and I made the mistake of thinking that her throne would heal me. This tour is supposedly for the good of the health of Niuhuru, so that it can be seen as the Emperor's filial duty to take her on it, although everyone knows that it is Qianlong who loves to travel. The route will take us overland through Zhili and Shandong to Qingkou in Jiangsu, where we will cross the Yellow River and continue our journey on the Grand Canal. The Canal will take us to Yangzhou, Zhenjiang, Danyang, Changzhou and then Suzhou. After Zhenjiang, we will also go on to Jiaxing and Shimen before we reach Hangzhou, our last stop, on the Yellow Sea. On our return journey, the Emperor will wish to inspect the troops at Jiangning. We will travel constantly for four months. The very thought of it is exhausting. The Emperor intends to visit the Yellow River, to ensure that barrages and ocean levees are built to avoid disastrous floods such as have happened in the past. No doubt he will enjoy inspecting the works, while we ladies will be expected to accompany him on these dull visits. Meanwhile there will be processions, with special permission granted that common people may look upon the Emperor's face and ours as we pass by, unlike in Beijing where we travel with bamboo screens along the routes we take to avoid the Son of Heaven being seen by mere mortals. There will be thousands who come to see the Emperor and, of course, his ladies. My servants spend days packing, my richest and most beautiful robes will be displayed to peasants who may never have touched silk, let alone worn it.

The court gathers in readiness for the journey and I make my way to the Emperor.

"I ask you not to bring Lady He on this journey," I begin.

"It is not your place to even make such a request," he says, and his face is already angry.

"I do not trust her," I say.

He sighs in irritation. "You don't trust anybody," he says. "You are known for it. You are known for your spying, your punishments, your jealousy of every other woman at court. It is not becoming. It is not the behaviour of an Empress. Lady Fuca would not have stooped so low."

"Lady Fuca was loved," I say.

"Are you still clinging to the memory of your lost sweetheart?" he asks.

I gape at him.

"Did you think I did not know?" he asks, standing, coming closer to me so that I have to look up at him. "Oh, I was told, I was told at once. The whole court knew. That you begged my mother to let you return to some childhood sweetheart. That when your plea went unanswered and you joined my ladies, you set your mind to grieve forever. And nothing has pleased you since. I did not call you to my bedchamber and you were not satisfied, I promoted you twice and you were not satisfied, I made you Step Empress against my better judgement and you were not satisfied. I saw to it that you bore children and you were not satisfied. You have set your mind to be unhappy, and so you are. There is nothing I can do for you, for you will not be satisfied. Now you are determined to be jealous of a woman who has done nothing to you but choose to be happy here. Can you not allow others happiness, Ula Nara? Are you not capable of it yourself?"

"My children," I begin.

"We have all lost children," he cuts me off. "There is barely one of my ladies who has not lost a child, and all of them were my own sons and daughters. You still have a son, whom you never see. You could not have him by your side all the time, and so you refuse to see him at all. You could not have your sweetheart, and so you have refused every other possible chance of happiness in your life. Do you think he has done the same?"

"I – "

"He will be married by now, Ula Nara!" Qianlong says, his voice rising in anger. "He will be married, with a concubine of his own, or maybe several. He will have children. He will never think of you, except when he has drunk too much and boasts to his friends that he once kissed the cheek of an Imperial concubine, of the woman who has become Step Empress. That is the only time he will think of you."

"He became a monk!" I retort, my own voice rising almost to a shout. "He knew the meaning of loyalty! He swore to love me for ever, and if he could not have me, he would have no other."

"And if he did!" Qianlong says, throwing up his hands, "then by now his masters will have taught him to let go of a childish love, to see beyond it and look into the infinite, not tie himself forever to an earthly need. He is gone, Ula Nara. Whether married or a monk, he is gone. And you should let him go."

"I will never let him go!" I say. "He was my true love, as Fuca was yours. And I do not think she would care to see you wooing Lady He."

I have gone too far. His face changes from exasperation to anger.

"Do not speak her name," he hisses at me. "You are not fit to speak her name."

"*His* name was Niu Lang!" I scream. "His name was Niu Lang and we loved one another! And neither of us will ever forget our first and true love. Unlike you!"

"Get out," he says. "Get out of here, before I order you punished."

I weep in my rooms for many days, and of course the servants talk. They say I am jealous. They do not know that I weep because I am afraid. Afraid that what Qianlong said is true. That Niu Lang may have married after all. Or that, as befits a monk, he may have learnt to set aside all thoughts of me. In either case, I am alone with my love, a love that is not returned, but long forgotten by my beloved.

But the Southern Tour must go ahead. The vast courtyards of the Forbidden City are filled with courtiers and eunuchs, maids and guards, palanquins in every colour, as each lady of the court and her retinue struggles to find their place in the hierarchy of the procession that is about to make its way out of the gates. My own palanquin comes close to that of Lady He, who is not yet seated within it, but is stroking a horse on which is seated Ling's son Prince Yongyan, dressed in an orange silk with stripes, a tiger costume of which he is inordinately proud. He bares his teeth at her and she laughs and makes some answer, pretending to cower. Rage rises up inside me, at this woman who finds happiness so easily, so far from home. I put out my hand from the silken drapes that cover me and say, loudly enough for her to hear, "The dogs should be at the back of the procession, especially that mongrel cur." I know that to call people of her faith a dog is a great insult, and I watch her face flush. She turns and climbs into her palanquin, seeking safety from my gaze.

And so the Tour commences. We sway along, day after day, our resting places changed each night, the servants unpacking and packing again each day. As Empress, as part of this court, I am endlessly surrounded by fawning hosts, who hope to gain favour by their treatment of me, who do not realise that all I want is to be left alone. Many of the women plead 'Southern heat' in order to avoid attending the Emperor as he visits construction sites for dykes, levees, and barrages. But I am the Empress, I am not allowed respite. In every city I must perform rituals at the temples, side-by-side with the Emperor. Local deities, sacrificial ceremonies at the mausoleums of ancestral Emperors, commemorations for historical personages of note and officials, honouring their past memories if they are dead, presenting them with tokens of favour if they are alive. My days are spent within clouds of incense, so that my lungs ache and I develop a cough. I walk up and down endless steps of temples and memorials, kowtow so often that my muscles ache. When I look in the mirror at night, my wrinkles have grown more pronounced, and I am so tired I can barely eat at the banquets we must attend. I grow thinner, and this only makes my wrinkles more evident. I feel and look far older than I am, and still there is no chance to rest.

Today we enter the city of Suzhou, almost at the end of our journey. It is something like the Garden of Perfect Brightness, criss-crossed with waterways on which boats of all sizes travel, with tiny bridges everywhere. It is famous for its gardens, some of which are built around fairytales and legends, often made of the dark twisted rocks so beloved by the Imperial Family. Expert gardeners have created mazes and placed rocks to simulate the shapes of creatures, such as those found in the Lion Grove Garden. We enter the city sailing down the Grand Canal, lined with thousands of people come to see their Emperor. There are lanterns, singers and musicians, so that there is a cacophony of different pieces of music being played simultaneously. As we pass, the people throw themselves onto their knees and kowtow, before raising their heads again to gape at our splendour. Every lady of the court, conscious that they will be seen, has outdone themselves in their selection of robes, jewels, and flowers. We look like the Imperial warehouses come to life. I sit in my Imperial yellow, wearing a diadem of golden birds and dangling pearls. I feel so tired I can barely keep my eyes open. My stomach churns, whether from hunger or the rocking of the boat, I am unsure.

"Are you sick?" asks Niuhuru, when she sees me. "Smile," she adds, conscious of the show we must put on for the watching crowds.

I fix something approximating a smile on my face and look to one side and another, so that the onlookers will be able to say they have seen the Empress and be satisfied. I put one hand out and touch the Emperor's sleeve, hoping that he may see how unwell I feel and tell me that I do not need to attend all the events that have been arranged for today. But his attention is on the high-ranking officials who are awaiting our arrival ahead, and he makes his way to them as our boat docks. A trembling official helps me disembark, and I wearily follow him, while Lady He, all smiles, follows the Emperor.

It is my birthday. Qianlong has decided there will be a banquet in my honour, there will be local officials and dignitaries. But I am distracted. I can hear endless chanting from a nearby palace, wafts of incense smoke float past.

"Lady He is having an exorcism performed," says my eunuch.

"A what?"

"An exorcism. Her eunuchs believe they saw the ghost of her dead sister in her room. So an exorcism is being carried out."

I am so tired I cannot even think this through, what it means. Ghost of a dead sister? Appearing, suddenly, in her rooms when there has been no previous mention of such a person? "I need to sleep," I say. "Close the shutters and prepare my bed."

"The Emperor expects you at your birthday banquet tonight," says the eunuch. "The maids are waiting to bathe you."

I think of the bathing, the dressing, the elaborate ministrations to my hair, the heavy headdress I must wear, the high shoes that make my feet ache. I think of the toasts that will be made, wishing me ten thousand years of this miserable life. I bite my lip so hard to stop from crying that I taste blood. "Very well," I say, as though I am a child, or a servant, to be commanded in this manner. "I will attend the banquet. But I will visit the gardens first." I need to get away from everyone, from their endless watching and from my muddled thoughts about what Lady He is doing.

Tiger Hill is warm and muggy. I almost regret coming here. I pass by the Sword-Testing Rock and then the Pond of Swords, each named after some legend or other, some myth of great deeds or words immortalised in water and stone. There is even the Magpie Bridge, named for the tale of star-crossed lovers I have clung to all my life. I turn my face away from the sight of it and call out to the bearers that it is growing late and we must make our way to the banquet, I do not wish to walk in the gardens after all. The quickest way to our destination is to pass the maze of the Lion Grove Gardens, and so my bearers make their way along a small path and then into an open area, decorated with the twisted rocks of the region, a pond and some trees. The palanquin comes to a sudden halt, as though there is some impediment to us proceeding. I draw the drapes and then, my stomach lurching at what I have seen, step out of the palanquin. Somehow, I remember to gesture to the bearers to wait elsewhere. They trot away.

Lady He is standing with Nurmat by her side, both their faces flushed. Behind her, on the ground in the dust, is a crumpled jacket, as though they have been using it to lie on. But beyond the two of them stands Lady He's maid, who has turned to face me. I stare at her. She is not dressed as a maid, she is dressed in rich silks. Her scar has disappeared. What I am seeing is a near-double of Lady He. I look from one to the other in disbelief and yet what I am seeing is confirmation that Nurmat told me the truth, that there is a vast deception going on which can only mean something terrible is about to happen. A glint catches my eye and I see, at Lady He's feet, a pile of daggers, perhaps as many as seven, their blades uncovered. I step backwards, suddenly afraid for my own safety. My movement is echoed by the maid, who darts away, disappearing behind the rocks. Now I am alone with Lady He and Nurmat and I can feel my heart beating fast. Will they kill me, I wonder? Is the maid concealing herself nearby, ready to throw a dagger at me? But the two of them are kneeling to me and kowtowing, as though we are back in the Forbidden City, following the usual rules of protocol. Lady He rises, but Nurmat remains kneeling in the dust.

"How can there be so much treachery in one place?" I say at last, my voice hoarse with fear.

Neither of them answer. I turn to Nurmat, still kneeling before me. He, at least, I think, has not lied to me. "You have been loyal to me," I say. "I will not forget it."

Lady He frowns. "Your Majesty?"

"I live only to serve you, Your Majesty," Nurmat replies. His voice slurs. I think perhaps he is drunk, or maybe ill. Maybe Lady He has poisoned him, I think, has found out that he has betrayed her secrets and now means to be rid of him.

Lady He is still staring at him. "Nurmat?"

He looks up at her, his eyes bloodshot. "Now your ladyship will be punished for your transgressions," he says. "For attempting to seduce a eunuch servant of your household. For having treasonous intentions towards the Emperor, spurred on by traitorous rebels from Xinjiang with whom you secretly corresponded in Beijing. Her Majesty the Empress will see to it that you forfeit your life for these crimes."

Lady He gapes at him and then looks at me. "I—" she begins but I am already holding up a hand to stop her. There is nothing she can do to explain this situation. "You traitorous, lust-ridden bitch," I say. "I will have you executed for this and then the Emperor will see how wrong he was to care for you. He will reward those who are loyal to him."

"Your Majesty – " she begins.

"You can deny nothing," I say. "Your own servant has testified against you."

She puts out a hand but I step back. "Don't touch me," I say. "Or I will scream."

She draws back. Unsteadily, I make my way towards where my bearers have taken the palanquin, afraid that if I lose eye contact with her she will grab for the daggers at her feet and strike at me. The bearers approach as they see me coming towards them. Once I am safely inside, I address her again.

"Your country is a treacherous pit of mongrel dogs," I say, my heart still beating hard. "It does not surprise me that we have been sent two of its bitches to commit treason against the Emperor. You will all die for this."

I am carried away but as we leave the gardens I look out of my draped window and it seems to me I see the Emperor with Lady He at his side, walking together. For a moment I think of going back, of accusing Lady He in front of Qianlong but I know that my words will have more weight if there are witnesses.

I make the bearers run back to the palace. The birthday banquet will begin soon and I have not been prepared. My hands are shaking from the encounter with Lady He and her collaborators and my heart feels strange, as though wings are beating inside my chest, the rhythm of its beat uneven, first a slow beat and then two together, too fast. The maids try to wash me but I wave them away, there is no time, I will have to go as I am, even though I have been sweating, my skin feels clammy. I pull on a fresh robe, which is too large. The belt must be pulled tighter to try and shape it to my body. My hair takes a long time to style, made longer by the fact that I keep moving under the hands of my servants, my legs constantly shaking, one foot drumming out a nervous rhythm.

The eunuch painting my face does not look happy. He hesitates, before applying more pink to my cheeks, confirming what I already know, which is that I look ill. Additional trinkets are added to my hair, a longer string of pearls is hung around my neck, as though all of these things will magically make me look younger, healthier, happier.

"Enough," I say at last, seeing that he is about to put still more red on my lips.

I stagger towards the door. My head is spinning. What am I to do? Whatever the plan between Nurmat, Lady He and her maid, I believe they are about to strike. The Emperor's life is in danger. And I, who wish to be free of this life, am the only one who can save him. I stop, clutching the doorframe, and breathe heavily for a few moments. At last I raise my head. I will have to save him. There is no one else to do so and I am afraid of what will happen if their plan goes ahead. I would be a fool to think that an easy path to freedom would lie ahead for me were Qianlong to die. Why would they kill just the Emperor? They may well kill us all. I take a deep breath. I know that I look ill, but I must appear to be well enough to make this accusation against the Emperor's favourite concubine and not be thought mad or jealous. He must believe me. I begin walking towards my palanquin, when I become aware that my magpies, in their aviary, are making a strange noise. I hesitate. The banquet will already have begun, Qianlong will be angry with me for not appearing on time, and if he is angry, he may be even less likely to believe me.

But I have never heard the magpies cry like this, not even the time when one of their offspring fell out of the aviary and had to be rescued.

"One moment," I say to my hovering eunuchs. "I must see to the birds." I walk to the aviary and at once my heart falls.

Lying on the bottom of the aviary floor is the male magpie, its wings outstretched, its eyes lifeless. Above, the female magpie cries and cries again, her plaintive calling for her dead mate breaking my heart. My eyes fill with tears for her. These two birds have been my constant companions all these years. A sudden cold weight settles in my stomach. Is it a sign? Has Niu Lang died? He gave me the magpies as a sign of our love, and they have lived longer than I have ever heard of two birds in captivity living before. I had almost thought them immortal. And yet, here is the male magpie, lifeless, whilst the female grieves for her mate.

"Your Majesty," says a eunuch by my side. "We are very late. We must go."

"I cannot," I say, my voice shaking. "I cannot."

"We must," says the eunuch, "His Majesty will be expecting us."

I do not answer. I simply walk away from him, back into the palace rooms. Inside, I make my way to my dressing table, where I look in one drawer and box after another until I find what I am looking for. Scissors. The weighty golden headdress I am wearing is difficult to lift away from my hair, but I manage it. The gold and jade pins underneath are trickier. I tug and tug, feeling knots form under my fingers as I force the pins out of the elaborate hairstyle my servants have created. The floor is littered with pins, my headdress lies on its side on the dressing table, abandoned. The scissors are heavy and the metal feels cold in my hands. For a moment, I hesitate. But I am too well versed in etiquette not to know what is required of me now. The man I have considered my husband all these years is dead, and a grieving widow must take this step. The first sound of the scissors, the sharp snip of metal on metal shocks me, but I keep going. I do not look in the mirror until I have finished. When I do, I drop the scissors, which crash to the floor.

My hair is cut close to my scalp, ragged chunks still left here and there, where I could not see what I was doing. There is one long strand still left, but I am already on my feet and leaving the room. When I step out of the palace, the eunuchs turn to me. There is an audible grasp.

"We are late," I say calmly, as though nothing were amiss. "I must speak with the Emperor," I add. "We must hurry."

They do not dare to speak to me, they do not dare to ask what has happened. They will have seen me stare at the dead magpie and now they are to deliver me to the Emperor, to a formal birthday banquet in my honour, with my hair cropped by my own hand. They do not know, how can they know, that my hair has been cut for the sake of Niu Lang, the male magpie's demise a sign from Heaven that I am now a widow.

The banqueting hall is immense. I have already ignored the expressions on the faces of all the guards, servants, and minor officials whom I have passed on my way here. But when the doors are opened for me and my name is announced, there is a sudden silence as more than four hundred people turn their faces towards me and stop speaking. In the utter silence, I walk the length of the hall until I stand by Qianlong's side, with Niuhuru next to me. Slowly, I kneel, looking up into his face.

"Your Majesty," I say, my voice loud and clear, the voice I use when I must say prayers for the Empire in public, "your life is in danger."

He stares down at me. The Son of Heaven is lost for words, unable to believe what he is seeing. The Empress, disrespectfully late for a birthday banquet in her honour, kneeling at his side, her robe crumpled, her face powder caked with sweat and most shocking of all, her hair, cut as though for mourning. As Empress, there are only two people for whom I should cut my hair in mourning, and both of them are still alive, each of them only an arms' length from where I am kneeling. The silence seems never-ending.

It is Niuhuru who gathers herself first. She leans from her chair so that her mouth is close to my ear and hisses, "What are you doing, Ula Nara?"

I continue to speak loudly. Qianlong must be made aware of the gravity of the situation. "I am warning the Emperor that he is in grave danger from a woman whom he purports to love. He does not know that she is capable of treason, of taking his life in revenge for the wrongs he has done her."

I have barely finished speaking when I feel my arms pulled behind me by armed guards. I am hauled to my feet, the Emperor still gazing at me in disbelief, while the Dowager Empress quickly stands and addresses the gaping courtiers.

"Her Majesty is unwell," she announces. "You will continue the banquet without us, I must attend her."

Nobody speaks. They only stare.

"Please continue," says Niuhuru, her tone now one of command.

The courtiers look hastily back down at their plates, a few quick-witted ones begin to speak to others, in a formal and stilted manner. I admire their presence of mind.

I am being pulled backwards by the guards, towards the doors that I came through. Niuhuru is following us, her face white as carved jade, her eyes full of fear. Behind her, Qianlong has turned in his throne to watch us go.

I am manoeuvred into a palanquin and Niuhuru steps into one nearby. It takes only a few lurching moments, our bearers running at top speed, to reach my own rooms again.

"Leave us," says Niuhuru, once we are in my receiving hall. The eunuchs, their faces horrified at the sight of us, back away in silence. We are alone.

It takes Niuhuru a few moments before she speaks. Her hands are shaking when she turns to face me. "What is going on?" she asks at last.

I am so tired, so dizzy with all that has happened to me since sunset, that I sink to the floor and sit, knees folded beneath me. The room is cold, and I wrap my arms about me and rock myself a little. It feels comforting and I am badly in need of comfort.

"Ula Nara? Speak to me. What is going on?"

I can't help it, I laugh out loud. I had thought there would be questions, accusations, rebuttals. And yet no one has done any of this. They have only hustled me to this tiny shadowed room, away from everyone of importance. "I tried to tell you," I say. "The Emperor is in danger. From Lady He. Why won't you listen to me?"

Niuhuru gapes at me. "Lady He?"

"Yes."

"What are you talking about?"

"She has daggers," I say, rocking a little faster. "She means to kill the Emperor. There are two of them," I add.

"Two of what?"

"Two women," I say, realising that I have forgotten to explain this. "They look the same. But there are two of them. Lady He and her maid. Dressed the same. With daggers. And her cook," I add. "Although he is loyal to us. He warned me. He should not be punished. He loved her, you see." I add.

Niuhuru does not look as though she is listening to me. "And your hair?"

"My hair?"

"Why is your hair cut short?" asks Niuhuru.

I put a hand up, touch the ragged clumps. "Oh," I say. "No, that has nothing to do with it. I cut my hair because I am a widow now."

Niuhuru stares at me. "A widow?"

I nod.

There is silence for a few moments and then Niuhuru comes closer to me, squats down barely an arm's length from me and looks at me carefully. "You know that the Emperor is alive?" she asks.

I frown. "He is *now*," I point out. "But he is in grave danger, as I told you."

"From Lady He?"

I smile. Niuhuru is at last listening to me. "Yes," I say.

"Who you believe is aided by others?"

"Her maid and her cook," I say. "Although the cook told me what was going on, so he is loyal to us."

Niuhuru shakes her head. "Tell me again why you have cut your hair," she says.

"My husband has died," I say.

"Your husband is the Emperor," says Niuhuru, very slowly, as though explaining something to a child. "And he is alive and well, whatever danger you believe him to be in."

I shake my head. "I meant my real husband," I say.

"Your real husband?"

"Niu Lang," I say and it is strange to say his name. "You took me from him," I add, looking Niuhuru directly in the eyes. "I begged you to let me go home and you would not change your mind. You chose me for your son without wondering if my heart belonged to another."

Niuhuru's face is very pale. "I did not know..." she begins, stumbling over her words.

And suddenly the rage I have held against her all these years comes rushing out of me. I find myself gripping her face in my hands, my broken nail shields pressed into her immaculately powdered cheeks. "You knew!" I scream at her and the fear and pain I see in her eyes gives me a rush of pleasure. "You knew I did not wish to come here! I begged you to let me go back to my family, something no other girl has ever done. I was willing to bring dishonour on my family, I was so desperate not to be chosen! You knew something was wrong, you looked back and you hesitated and then you let the Chief Eunuch hurry you away, you let them drag me to join the other chosen girls, even though you saw me sobbing! You knew!"

I push her away, one of my broken nail shields dragging across her cheek as I do so, the jagged edge ripping into her skin, a line of blood welling up even as I release her. She topples backwards, her squatted stance unbalanced by the fury of my push, ending up on her backside on the floor. She puts up a hand to the stinging pain she must feel in her cheek and when she sees blood on her hand she stares at me in horror before crawling away from me as though I am about to attack her again. But I am rocking, my arms wrapped about my knees, tears rolling down my face, choking out Niu Lang's name over and over again.

"What is the meaning of this?"

I look up. Qianlong is standing over me. Behind him, Niuhuru gets to her feet, still keeping a distance, repeatedly touching her face and looking at the blood on her hand, which is shaking.

"Your life is in danger and I came to warn you even though I do not owe you any loyalty," I sob.

"What have you done to my mother?" he asks.

"It does not matter, it is no matter," says Niuhuru in a ragged whisper.

"What have you done to your hair?" he asks. "An Empress cuts her hair only for the Emperor or his mother's death. Are you cursing us? Wishing us dead?"

"I cut it for Niu Lang," I say. "He is dead."

"What are you talking about?" he asks.

"Niu Lang," I repeat. "He has died."

"You are in communication with a man outside of the Forbidden City?" asks Qianlong.

"No," I say. "I do not need to communicate with him. I know it because of my magpie."

Qianlong turns to his mother. "What is she talking about?" he asks.

Niuhuru shakes her head and does not answer.

"Is she mad?" he asks her. "Has she gone mad?"

She does not answer, only gives a tiny nod, a quick downwards jolt of her head.

"You lying bitch!" I scream at her. "I am not mad. I am trying to save your son's life even though you would not save me from the insanity of this life! I am showing you the mercy you should have shown me!"

"Be silent!" roars Qianlong suddenly. His mother whimpers while I crawl away from him, afraid. I have only seen Qianlong like this once, when Lady Fuca died and he ordered people executed for not mourning her sufficiently. I crouch in a corner, shaking, my head down, waiting for him to strike me or call the guards. But there is only silence. I hear Qianlong take a few steps and when I look up I see he has taken a seat in the receiving hall's throne. He is staring at me with an expression of combined disbelief and anger. I wait but he does not speak and now I hear running feet approaching, the familiar sound of a palanquin's bearers. There is a pause and then comes the hard click clack of heels, the sound of Lady He's shoes, a different sound to the shoes the rest of us wear. I look towards the door and there she is, framed in the light, hesitant. I do not know if Qianlong has summoned her here or whether she heard what happened, knows the accusations I have made against her. I wonder if she will strike now, if she is concealing weapons somewhere about her person.

"They want to kill you," I cry out, my voice hoarse. "I swear I am telling the truth! She has a twin, a sister! I saw them – first one with her lover the cook, both of them with daggers, embracing. And then the other one – walking with you. There are two of them and they mean to kill you!"

Lady He stares at me in horror, her eyes wide. Then she looks towards Qianlong. I wait for him to question her.

"The Empress is unwell," he says slowly, speaking only to Lady He, as though I am not even present. "She has been making accusations which I cannot believe are true. She says you are two different people, she accuses you of wishing to kill me, of drawing me close to you so that you might use these... daggers... to assassinate me in the Lion Grove."

Lady He's voice is little more than a whisper. "And you believe her?"

He shakes his head wearily. "She is unwell, as you can see," he says quietly. "I walked with you in the gardens and all was well between us, as you know. There is only one of you. She is hallucinating."

"She has hidden daggers in her clothing. Make her show you!" I scream, furious at Qianlong's dismissal. I throw myself at Lady He and grab at her jacket, tugging it off her. She fights to escape my clutches and the jacket comes away in my hands. Frantically, I turn it inside out, but still there are no daggers. I want to call for scissors but there are no servants so instead I claw at the silk with my hands and then, in desperation, with my teeth. The silk rips and the wadding inside is revealed, but still there are no daggers, no concealed weapons of any kind. I put my head to the floor and weep, rocking back and forth, still clutching at the torn silk with my bony hands. After a while, I look up at Qianlong but he is looking at me as though he barely knows me.

"You will be sent back to Beijing in disgrace," he says. His voice is low but carries as though he were shouting and suddenly I am truly afraid of him. I try to perform a kowtow, as though the ritual of the obeisance will somehow remind him of who I am. But I pitch my head forward too fast, knocking it hard on the stone floor. For a moment the room swims before my eyes and I think I will faint but I try to focus on Qianlong.

"Do not punish me, my lord," I beg through my sobs. "Punish her and her twin. They are treacherous bitches. I am your Empress and she is a nobody, a prisoner of war from a land ridden with mongrel curs." Tears roll down my cheeks. "I have been loyal to you," I half-whisper. "I have bound myself to you since I was chosen and I have done everything in my power to deserve your favour. Do not punish me."

Qianlong is not listening, he speaks to me as he does when passing judgement in his court rulings. "You will return to Beijing under guard," he says. "You will remain there until my return and then you will be sent to the Cold Palace where you will live until the end of your days. You will no longer live within my presence."

"I am the Empress!" I shriek. "You cannot do this to me!"

"You are no longer my Empress," he says and his voice is colder than I have ever heard it. "From this moment you are stripped of your titles and privileges."

Still kneeling, I twist towards Niuhuru, waiting for her to intervene, to speak up for me, to protect me, but she stays silent, her eyes on the floor. I feel a great pain from my cramped knees, so that I slide to the floor. I can hear myself moaning in pain. Looking up I see Lady He staring at me, but she startles when Qianlong speaks to her.

"Call the guards," he says. "And a maid."

Lady He nods and backs away. A few moments later a terrified young maid appears.

"Her Majesty needs new clothes," says Niuhuru, her voice shaking.

The maid runs to my bedroom and returns clutching an armful of clothes. She stands by my side, although keeping her distance, looking down at me as though I am a wild animal. Meanwhile Lady He has reappeared accompanied by eight guards. Niuhuru turns away, as though looking out of the window, so that her damaged face cannot be seen. The maid looks about as though hoping for guidance.

"Something plain," says Niuhuru to the maid.

The maid hovers, uncertain. As Empress of China, I have very few clothes that might be called plain. She holds up a few robes but even the few I own that are not official court robes are exquisite in their use of fine materials and embroidery.

Niuhuru waves her hand without looking. "A maid's robe," she says.

The maid gapes at her. The guards remain motionless, expressionless.

"Fetch one!"

The maid hurries away and returns with a pale blue cotton robe, cleaned so many times that it has faded, still crumpled from its latest wash.

Niuhuru nods and turns away. "Dress her," she says over her shoulder, her scratched face hidden.

The maid tries, but my body is limp. She fumbles with the fastenings of the robe I am wearing and in the end Lady He joins her, the two of them kneeling at my side. Together they strip off my Imperial yellow silk outer robe and cover up my sweat-stained inner robes in the faded blue cotton. I move like a child for them, allowing them to lift my arms and legs. I do not try to obstruct them but I feel so weak I cannot really help them in their task. At last it is done. Still sitting on the floor, I look down at my body. I have never worn such an outfit before.

"Take her back to Beijing," Qianlong says to the guards.

They daren't gape nor disobey but they hesitate before laying hands on me. Carefully, three of them lift me to my feet and guide me stumblingly to the door. I have only one shoe on, the other has dropped off my foot and the difference in height of one foot to the other is causing me trouble walking. They have to half-carry me towards my Imperial yellow palanquin, topped with golden phoenixes, shielded from curious eyes by silk drapes. I am half aware that Lady He is following us.

"Stop!"

At the Emperor's voice ringing out behind us, every servant falls to their knees, face down on the ground. The guards and I stand still, prostrate bodies all around us.

"She is no longer permitted to ride in that palanquin," Qianlong orders. "Fetch an orange chair."

A servant runs out of the courtyard and returns with an intercepted chair and its bearers. I stare at it and when the guards try to make me enter it I hang back. I am the Empress. I travel in a yellow silk palanquin. This chair is orange, it cannot be meant for me, whatever Qianlong says.

Lady He appears at my side and then crouches in front of me. "Give me your hand, Your Majesty," she says in a whisper. "Let me help you into the chair."

I look down into her wide brown eyes. "There were two of you in the garden," I say in a croak.

"There is only one of me here," she replies. "Will you give me your hand?"

I take her hand, which is warm and soft. Once I am in the palanquin she reaches in and pulls the gauze curtain across, so that my vision is blurred. As the palanquin moves away, I see her outline standing watching me go. A great weariness comes over me and I close my eyes. I must rest, I think. Soon I will be back in the Forbidden City and as Empress I will be called on for many tasks. I must be ready. I must sleep so that I can perform my many, many duties.

Mountain Pass

A LURCHING. A HEAVY-FOOTED SWAYING. A juddering mis-step and then back to the swaying, no smooth rhythm to it. Grunting, panting. A muttered curse.

I try to open my eyes but the light hurts them and I close them again, feel the swaying go on and on, not soothing but startling when it fails, my body suddenly slipping one way or another. More curses. I open my eyes again and narrow them against the brightness.

A palanquin. I am in a palanquin. I close my eyes again. Of course. I travel everywhere like this, so it is familiar to me. Although there is something not quite right about this one, something my mind cannot grasp. I open my eyes and peer again at my surroundings. A palanquin should be familiar but this one is not. Why? What is wrong with it, apart from its shuddering progress, which is not as it ought to be? My bearers are the best, they are used to keeping the palanquin's progress steady, no matter how uneven the ground beneath their feet.

The colour. Orange. A plain rusted orange. I put up a hand to touch the sides. The fabric is not silk.

The colour should be Imperial yellow. I earned that colour. The walls should be made of silk. My progress should be utterly smooth.

Another jolt. I put up a hand to steady myself.

What am I doing in a palanquin that is not Imperial yellow and not made of silk? My mind is unsteady, it judders through images and stumbles over thoughts, leaving them incomplete.

Something comes back to me. Wide grey eyes in a white face, a slash of red beneath.

Someone's face too close to mine, brown eyes filled with tears.

I feel cold. I look down at my lap and see blue cotton. I frown, touch it to be sure of what I am seeing. Blue cotton? I have never worn blue cotton. That is what a maid wears. A blue cotton robe, her hair in a single plait, tied with a red ribbon. Every maid in the Forbidden City wears this. I put up a hand as though I, too, might have a plait tied with a red ribbon. But I can only find one strand of my hair and it is loose. I feel about for more of it, wondering if this one strand has come undone from its pins. But my hand touches something else. Short, rough hair.

Wide grey eyes in a white face, a slash of red beneath. Niuhuru. The Empress Dowager.

I look down at my hand. It is bony but also dirty. My golden nail shields have disappeared, my nails are mostly broken, their jagged tips lined with dirt.

Outside the bearers change over. I know the feeling, the slight dip as one man takes over the pole from another bearer. And then the palanquin rocks again as we move forward. I can hear the first bearers spit, mutter to one another about something. A laugh, cut short. Onwards. The palanquin seems to be tilted backwards, as though the front bearers are too tall for the back ones. Bearers should be evenly matched in height to serve in the Forbidden City.

Wide grey eyes in a white face, a slash of red beneath. Niuhuru. The Empress Dowager. And then, towering over me, the Son of Heaven. Qianlong. Forcing me backwards and away from Niuhuru and then...

Screaming. Orders. A maid, her eyes frightened. The blue cotton. Guards. Dark brown eyes full of tears. Looking out from an orange palanquin as I was taken away somewhere.

Where am I?

I brace myself against the sloping jolting of the palanquin and use one hand to open the curtain shielding me from the outside world.

There is only sky. How can there be only sky? Where is the horizon? Buildings? People?

I lean further forward and then my stomach clenches at what I see. A terrifying cliff edge into nothingness, a drop down – down – down to far away greenness.

I am on a mountaintop. Higher than I have ever been in my life. Higher than any mountain I have ever been to. On a tiny path, so narrow it makes my stomach lurch. I cower back in the palanquin, huddle against its rough orange sides. I am cold, very cold. Only my feet, oddly, seem warm.

Now I see that there is a blanket in the palanquin with me, it has fallen to the floor. My feet are covered, leaving the rest of me chilled. I pull at it. It is a thick padded cotton, with a greasy feel to it. I pull it up around me, feel my body stop shaking.

Now my mind unfogs a little. The greasy cotton against my skin has drawn a clearer line of thought from me. Why am I dirty? Why am I dressed in cotton: not just any cotton but a maid's blue robe? Why am I in an orange palanquin? What am I doing on the top of a mountain? Something has happened. I hold the blanket tighter in my bony, dirty hands and try to remember. But the swaying has stopped, there is a final jolt. The palanquin has halted. I hear voices far away, then closer. A hand appears inside the palanquin. I hesitate, then take it.

Coordinating my body sufficiently to get out of the palanquin seems difficult, made worse because I am still clutching the blanket to me, as though it may protect me from whatever is happening outside. My eyesight does not feel right, emerging from the palanquin I blink, the bright light of day no longer filtered through the dusky orange walls. When I can look around me better, I stare.

I am standing in a small village. Huddled wooden houses are clustered around a tiny open space of packed earth in which stands an old gingko tree. The houses are tiny and very worn, their once-brown wood now a weathered grey. They have been patched over the years: the wood is not all the same colour and the walls and roofs are crooked, sagging. There is a stink of livestock in the air.

Next to my palanquin stand the bearers. They are not eunuchs from the Imperial household, they must be local men. Their skin is burnt brown, they have wide shoulders but are short in stature.

In front of me, gathered by their houses, stand a few dozen people: men and women, a few children who peep out from behind their mothers. A baby cries and is hushed. All of them are poorly dressed in what look like layers of rags, one item of clothing over another, the bottom layers poking through here and there. Their faces are as weathered as the wood of their houses. They stare back at me.

I stand, clutching my blanket, staring about me like a lost child. Turning my head, I catch sight of two guards. Their armour and clothing marks them out as Imperial guards and they look so familiar, in the midst of all this strangeness, that I smile broadly at them. They do not smile back. I look around me again and realise what it is that seems so strange. It has been many years since my arrival somewhere was not greeted with people on their knees, their faces hidden from me as they kowtow. I wonder if this is some strange play, if I have been dressed as a maid to play a part, that once I am revealed as the Empress all these people will fall to their knees and my court robes will magically reappear, Imperial yellow silk folds tumbling over me as jade pins and flowers pull my hair back into its usual place. I put my hand up and again all I feel is roughness. I cannot think what it reminds me of, until I think of Wan's little dog and its rough fur, short and a little curly. I am not sure why my own hair would feel like dog's fur.

The guards have moved, are speaking with a man who looks bewildered, but is nodding at whatever it is they are saying. I see them hand him a large leather pouch and know that it must contain payment for something. The man is awestruck at the weight of the pouch, his nods become quicker, more eager and the guards nod back, satisfied with his enthusiasm. They speak a little more, while I stand still. The bearers pick up the poles of the palanquin and I ready myself to climb back into it. Perhaps we have not arrived where we are headed, this is only a tiny mountain village and maybe the people here were in need of help from the Emperor. It is possible that I was sent here to give them confidence that they are not forgotten. I smile at them, hoping to convey confidence and benevolence, assurance that they are not forgotten, even by the Son of Heaven himself.

No one smiles back. One little boy sticks his tongue out at me from behind his father's legs.

The palanquin moves away from me. I expect it will turn around, for there is limited space here, and then it will be brought close to me so that I can step back in. But it continues to move, the men half-trotting away, down the path we must have just come up. I look to the guards but they do not seem to have noticed.

"My palanquin," I say, although my voice hurts when I speak, I feel as if I am hoarse with shouting, although I have no recollection of shouting. "My palanquin!" I add, more loudly, as I try to command my voice. One of the guards glances at me and at the rapidly disappearing men with my palanquin and then continues talking, uninterested.

"You," I say to the guards. "Come here."

One of the two comes towards me. I wait for him to bow, but he does not.

"Where are we?" I ask. "What is happening?"

"The Emperor has ordered that you be brought here," he says.

I look about me. The villagers are still staring at me. "Why?"

The guard looks at me oddly, as though I am stupid. "You have been sent to the Cold Palace," he says, as though reminding me of something obvious.

"The Cold Palace?" I repeat. For a moment I look about me, as though there is a palace here somewhere that has been given a poetic name. But the meaning of what he is saying is seeping into me. I look down at the greasy blue cotton and my broken nails. "The Cold Palace?"

"Yes," he says and it is only now, it is only him answering me without using my title, without saying *Your Majesty* or even *your ladyship*, that suddenly breaks through my confusion.

"The Emperor has exiled me from court?" I say. I have to be certain. I have to know that I have not misunderstood a phrase that I have only ever heard applied to others.

"Yes," he says. His face is very still, there is no emotion. He has been given his orders and he is carrying them out.

"Why?" I ask.

There is a flicker now, he cannot believe I am asking this question. I think of Niuhuru, her grey eyes in a white face, a scarlet streak across her cheek but only after my hand reached out, my already-broken nail shields ripping across the whiteness, the red rising in its wake.

"I struck the Dowager Empress?" I ask, my voice shaking.

He looks at me in disbelief. "You cut your hair," he says.

I put my hand up. The rough feel of Wan's little dog. "I cut my hair?" I repeat.

He nods.

I feel a great wave of cold. I am the Empress. The Empress cuts her hair only in mourning and only for those higher ranked than herself. There are only two people in the empire for whom I would have to cut my hair. Qianlong. And his mother, the Empress Dowager, Niuhuru. "Who died?" I ask and my voice shakes.

Again the look, the disbelief that I cannot remember what has brought me here. "No one," he says and walks away from me, back to the other guard. They speak together while I stand watching them in silence.

They leave. The two guards, in the uniform that has been a constant at the peripheries of my vision ever since I was chosen at the Imperial Daughters' Draft, are gone. They walk away, down the mountain path, without a backward glance. I think of running after them but my legs will not move. I stand as though I were a statue, frozen into place, watching the last glimpse of them disappear behind a tree on the path and then they are gone.

I turn back and find that the man with whom they were speaking, perhaps the head of the village, has approached me. I wait for him to kowtow but he does not.

"Ula Nara?"

I stare at him. No-one addresses me like this except the Emperor and his mother, or Ling if she is being deliberately rude.

"Your name is Ula Nara?" he perseveres.

I nod, a slow cautious nod.

"I have been given directions that you are to live here," he says.

"Where?" I ask. I cannot see anywhere that I could possibly live.

He indicates a house among the huddle. "My niece Min lives there. Her husband died last year, so she lives alone. She will care for you." He makes an involuntary gesture towards the leather pouch, now attached to his belt. "You have been provided for."

I say nothing.

"Come with me," he says.

He walks away and I take one step and then another, the rough ground under my feet coming through the thin soles of my cloth shoes. My knees ache from being bent for so long. The villagers part to let us pass, then close up behind us.

The man pushes the door open and leads me inside. I am vaguely aware that someone else has followed us inside. The door closes on the curious stares outside.

I am standing in a single-roomed house, dominated by a mud-brick stove and a niche in the wall beside it, in which is a bed just large enough for two people to lie side by side. The floor is made of packed earth, the ceiling is barely an arm's length above my head, made lower by all the things hanging from it: dried herbs, cooking utensils, clothes and more. There is a table and a low bench, a small wooden chest. The room smells of smoke and sweat.

"This is Min," says the man, indicating someone behind me.

I turn round to face the woman who has followed me here. She is quite young, I would say mid twenties at the very most, although her skin looks older and her hands are calloused. She stares at me with undisguised curiosity.

"This is Ula Nara," says the man. "She is to live here with us. She has been well provided for and will continue to be so. She has been unwell in her mind but it is hoped she will recover. She is of no harm to others. She will live with you, Min."

I stare at him.

"How long will she stay, Uncle?" asks Min.

"For the rest of her life," says the man.

Min nods, as though it is normal for the Empress of China to be brought to a tiny mountain top village and live out the rest of her days in a one-roomed wooden shack with a sagging roof, in the company of a widow.

The man nods back at her. "The village has been given silver for her," he says. "She is to be cared for as one of us."

Min nods again and the man leaves us, the door behind him closing quickly but not quickly enough that I cannot still see curious faces outside, waiting for another glimpse of me.

I wait for Min to kowtow, to address me as your ladyship, Your Majesty, but she does neither.

"You'll need boots up here," she says. "I'll ask my uncle to make sure you have some. He's not tight-fisted," she adds. "He'll look out for you, make sure the village takes care of you. But he's a man, he won't think of such things. A coat, too, for when winter comes.. I can sew you one if he can buy me some cloth, but I don't have a lot of time for sewing so I should start soon, even if it is spring. Winter comes early here," she adds with a smile, as though I am likely to know this.

I think of my furs, of the multiple layers of silk robes I wear in winter, of the beds with *kangs* under them, the stoves kept burning all night if necessary to avoid any Imperial lady catching cold. "Where am I?" I ask.

Min frowns. "Mount Hua Shan," she says.

The only thing that comes to mind is that the Daoists claim that the god of the underworld lives under Mount Hua Shan. I try to think of the maps Qianlong was so fond of looking at, showing his empire in all its glory, especially once he conquered Xinjiang. "The Qin Mountains?" I manage at last. "Xi'an?"

She nods.

I think of how far I have travelled from the South and how far it would be to Beijing. The man spoke of me staying here for the rest of my life, he cannot have meant it. Perhaps Qianlong means to frighten me, to show me what life away from court is like. Perhaps he finds me ungrateful for not being happy as his Step-Empress, perhaps he does not realise that even that title is a daily reminder to me that I am not his true love, just as he is not mine, of all I have given up to achieve that title and yet have achieved nothing at all.

Min is still standing watching me, expecting some sort of response.

"Do you know who I am?" I ask her, a thought coming to my mind. Perhaps they have not been told. Perhaps that is why they are not behaving as they ought to.

"Ula Nara," she says.

"But do you know who I *am*?" I persist.

She shakes her head.

"I am the Empress of China," I say.

She looks at my blue cotton robe and shorn hair, my dirty-nailed fingers still clutching the blanket I have not yet let fall. I can see her thinking of what her uncle said, that I have been unwell in my mind. "I think perhaps you are mistaken," she says and her voice is very kind. "I know you have not been well. But I am sure you will recover here. It is only a little village but the people here are good people. We do not go hungry and the houses may be plain but they have always kept us warm." She smiles. "The silver your family has provided will help all of us and we will make sure you are comfortable. Are you cold?"

I nod.

She comes closer, takes the blanket away from me, placing it on the bed with other worn blankets. Then she opens a small chest and pulls out an embroidered padded cotton jacket, which she holds out to me. "It was my wedding jacket," she says, smiling. "But it doesn't get much use. It will keep you warm."

I look down at it. It's bright red, as befits a bride, clumsily embroidered with flowers. I think of the Imperial dressmakers, what they would say if they saw it. They would have an apprentice whipped for this kind of needlework. "I can't wear this," I say. "I can't wear your wedding clothes."

Min keeps smiling but tears well up for a moment before she blinks them away. "Can't have it lying around useless in a chest," she says. "Not when you're cold."

Slowly, I pull the jacket on over my thin robe. It may be clumsily made but it is warm. I try to smile. It feels like an effort but Min smiles back readily, as though I have beamed at her.

I stay in the house all the rest of that day, sitting on the low bench at the table. Even though it is still daylight I do not leave the small room. I watch Min as she breaks kindling over her knee for the stove and feeds the flames, keeping the room warm. She chatters as she works, speaking of things I do not even understand, names of people and their histories, work that must be done. She chops up a piece of mutton and puts it on the stove to cook with vegetables, then fiercely kneads a small ball of dough until she is satisfied with it. As the darkness grows outside she lights another lantern and turns the dough into noodles, adding them to the simmering pot. When she brings me a bowl heaped with noodles and chunks of fatty mutton, the whole spiced with cumin and fiery hot with peppers, I eat as best I can, although my stomach feels shrivelled. When I slow down after only a few mouthfuls I can see Min's disappointed face and I try harder, eating until I feel overly full. I do not think I have ever eaten a meal made up of only one dish.

Hungry Ghost

I STAY IN THE HOUSE FOR many days, afraid of leaving the tiny interior, huddled against the unknown world outside. Min comes and goes, she cooks for us both and we eat together. Sometimes she does work inside, mostly she leaves me alone while she goes outside, returning with flour, firewood, vegetables, clothes that have been dried outside and are now ready to put away. She is always busy, always working. Whenever she leaves the house she asks if I want to accompany her and I always say no.

"Today you need to come outside," she says at last.

"No thank you," I say.

"You can't spend the rest of your life in one room," she says. "Come." She holds out her hand. Reluctantly I rise from the wooden bench and follow her. The light outside makes me blink, I have not been in daylight for so long I had forgotten how bright it can be.

Min has tasks that take her all over the village: first to pull up vegetables, then to take some tool back to a neighbour, followed by a visit to her uncle to ask him something about seeds. I walk a few paces behind her, uncomfortable with the stares I get from the villagers.

"They'll get used to you if they see you every day," says Min over her shoulder.

Behind me trails a little boy, the one who stuck his tongue out at me when I first arrived. He has a three-legged dog, a mutt with no pedigree, a far cry from the dainty lapdogs and noble hounds of the court and hunting grounds. This one hops along with an ungainly but enthusiastic gait, faithful to her small master.

"What's your name?" asks the little boy.

"Ula Nara," I tell him.

"I am Chen," he says.

I don't answer.

"Min says you said you were the Empress of China," he says.

"Yes," I say.

"If you're the Empress of China, where's your crown?" asks Chen. "And why aren't you wearing silk? Are you in disguise? Will you tell me about the guards in the Forbidden City? What weapons do they have?"

"Shush," says Min, emerging from her neighbour's house in time to hear him. "Be off with you."

"But an Empress *should* have a crown," insists Chen.

"Little boys *should* know better than to be cheeky to their elders," says Min. "Shoo."

Reluctantly, Chen and his dog stop following us.

"I don't want to go out again," I tell Min.

"You need to," she says firmly. "You must take a walk every day."

At first I only go outside and stand, awkwardly, in the centre of the village, all but clinging to the trunk of the ancient gingko tree. But everyone still stares at me and Chen and his dog hang around me asking endless questions until I retreat back into the dark warmth of Min's home. At last I decide to walk away from the village, a little way along the mountain. The view down into the ravines below still makes me afraid. I walk as though I might fall at any moment, occasionally clutching at a bush or small tree when I feel my balance deserting me. I walk only for a few moments each day, then return to Min's house, ignoring Chen, who seems fascinated with me.

"Do you want to come with me to see the monkeys in the woods?" he asks.

"No," I say.

"The first berries are getting ripe," he informs me the next day. "Do you want to come and pick some to eat?"

I shake my head.

"Look," he says one morning, holding up a brownish dried out husk. "It's a caterpillar's cocoon. Do you want to keep it and see the butterfly come out?"

"No, thank you," I say, retreating back into the house.

He makes such offers whenever he sees me and I always refuse, hoping that soon he will stop following me.

I see Min's uncle sometimes, usually carrying an axe on his way to chop firewood or with a dangling dead chicken in one hand, still twitching from having its neck wrung.

"You are well?" he always asks gruffly and seems relieved when I nod without replying, perhaps not wishing to engage in idle chatter with a madwoman, even if he has been appointed my guardian here.

Sitting alone with my thoughts does not make for a peaceful existence. I think of my life at court, still unsure whether this exile is a welcome release or a terrifying punishment. Sometimes I laugh out loud at the ludicrous comparison between my grand palace where every room was fragranced with expensive perfumes and over-filled with precious objects and this single-roomed house, dark and full of pungent smells. I rock back and forth, laughing till I cry, then tears fall for hours while my thoughts are a jumbled whirl of Niu Lang, of my lost children, of the pain and fears and bitterness that have made up what feels like the whole of my life. Min watches me silently when I laugh, sometimes she pats me when I cry, but mostly she continues her daily tasks as though I were hardly there, as though I were some strange pet whose odd behaviour cannot be explained, only watched with interest. Her uncle brings her good cloth from the village and she spends her evenings cutting and sewing, making me warm clothes for the winter: trousers, a padded jacket, a long robe.

"He even bought both of us new boots," she says, pleased, showing me sturdy knee-high boots for herself and me. I nod, although the idea of being here all winter seems impossible, Min and her uncle are planning for a future I cannot even imagine.

I sleep badly. I am unused to a snoring body pressed tightly against me, the night noises of the mountain. Often there are strong winds and the village dogs never tire of barking when they sense some wild animal nearby. One night I lie restless and at last I rise from the bed and make my way out into the village clearing. There is a full moon, it shines as brightly as though it were only twilight. I shush Chen's little dog who is making the most noise and she subsides, which calms some of the other dogs, if only temporarily.

I stand beneath the gingko tree for a few moments and wonder whether I might sleep now that the dogs are quiet, but I already know I will not, I am too wide awake. Instead, I find myself walking down the path that leads away from the village and down the mountain, the path I was carried up, the last time I rode in a palanquin. I have never gone this way before. The villagers use it a little, for when they roam the mountain to gather firewood, or when the men descend the long way down into the valleys below, to trade. The path is not well-made, only beaten out over the years by the footsteps of those who have gone before.

The ground is steep under my feet. More than once I stumble and have to try and regain my balance. A thick, half-buried tree root proves my undoing and I fall headlong into the undergrowth, hands outstretched to break my fall. My palms sting and as I clamber awkwardly to my feet I look down and see that I have scraped them on stones and brambles. The brambles are also clinging to the bottom of my robe and it takes me a few moments to break free of them. I brush away the dirt on my hands and use my tongue to clean one particularly bad scrape. I wonder whether I should go back, but just below me the path splits and one part curves away, turning across rather than down the mountain and I wonder where it leads, why it would not follow a more direct route. *I will follow just around the corner*, I think, *then I will return to the village.*

The wind picks up. I am on a more exposed part of the mountain here and I slip again but manage to keep my footing. The path I have followed is smaller than the main path that leads downwards, not so many feet walk here regularly. I cannot see much of interest and a sudden screech overhead frightens me before I realise it must be one of the monkeys I have sometimes heard further away, the monkeys that Chen is always talking about. I twist my head upwards and see a face in the upper branches of the tree, blurred in the grey light so that it might almost be the face of a baby, bright eyes watching me. I stand still and the monkey chatters at me and then hides away among the branches, perhaps reassured that I mean it no harm. I think that I should turn back, there is nothing here, but ahead I see a darker shadow and, curious, make my way towards it. I narrow my eyes, trying to understand what I am looking at before realising that it is a rocky cliff face under which is the opening to a cave. I think of wild animals, perhaps clouded leopards, and draw back, but the cliff face catches my attention. It seems to be marked with figures. I forget the possible danger and step closer. Daubed on the cliff in what looks like a dull blood-red are human figures, their legs bent into a wide-legged squat, their arms raised up above them to mirror their stance. In the poor light, as the faint shadows of the branches move across them, they make me think that they are alive, only waiting for a command to move. I back away, noticing as I do so that the cave is not natural but carved into the face of the cliff, its straight lines betraying its human origins. I wonder what kind of person would live here, immured in rock they have carved into a tiny shelter, close to these images from another time, another world. I wonder if they were as lonely as I have been. I find my way back to the main path and to the village, crawl into Min's bed and try again to sleep, but find my dreams filled with dark caves that go on forever and red-daubed figures that dance to music I cannot hear.

My night-time walks become a habit. I wander the side of the mountain, afraid of the darkness and yet drawn to it. Some nights I can barely see anything, when the clouds cross the sky and the moon shrinks down to a tiny sliver of silver, clutching at shrubs when I fall, returning to bed with scraped knees and a fast-beating heart. Once I hear the padding of heavy footsteps and see a leopard cross the path ahead of me. It turns its yellow eyes in my direction and I hold my breath thinking it may attack me, but it only looks me over and continues on its way. Often I return to the cliff top and the cave and stare at the figures as though they might speak and tell me something. Once I scramble to the top of the cliff, following the steep mountain side round until I stand, trembling, on the crumbling edge of the cliff and look down, down, down. I wonder what would happen if I jumped, wonder how the air would feel as I fell and who would find my lifeless body, whether a hungry leopard or one of the villagers. I take a step closer until my toes are on the very edge. One step more would find me falling. Only the sudden thought that it might be little Chen to find me, that he might be hunting for berries and instead find me and be afraid, makes me pause. I would not wish to frighten him. I step away from the cliff and find my way back to the village.

Min is not one for dates and times. I am used to the court astrologers guiding my every move, their insistence on the exact time, the exact day to complete rituals or take almost any action at all. Time in Min's mind is something different. It is the time to plant seeds, it is the time to harvest them. It is the time for the goats and sheep to give birth, it is the time to kill the kids and lambs. She and the other villagers do not wait for the astrologers to tell them when to do these things. They watch the moon for themselves, they smell the wind and touch the earth with their hands and know what should be done. Then they do it.

But she does know about festivals. "It is the Festival of Hungry Ghosts tomorrow," she says, taking an empty platter and piling up fruits and vegetables on it. Later she makes noodles for us to eat and puts a portion aside for the ghosts.

I think of the vast long tables set up in the ancestral hall of the Forbidden City, covered all over with hundreds upon hundreds of fine dishes heaped with food. The thick perfume of incense everywhere as one member of the Imperial Family after another bows and lights whole bunches of incense sticks to add to those already burning. The clouds of smoke everywhere, hiding and then revealing the ancestral portraits hanging above us. I watch Min prepare the simple platter with care, heaping up different foods and arranging them as best she can into a pleasing sight.

"I will leave it outside the door when night falls," she says. "Then we will not be disturbed by those that wander."

I nod.

"The village is grateful to your ancestors as well as ours," she says earnestly. "My uncle used some of the silver to buy more livestock for each of the families, so that all would benefit from you being here. Tonight we welcome your ancestors here as well as our own."

I nod, wondering if Qianlong imagined his silver would be used to buy pigs and goats. I am glad enough for the village, it seems a better use of silver than endless trinkets such as jade ornaments no-one even notices in their rooms.

Night falls and Min closes the door after setting out the platter. I lie beside her, but cannot sleep.

At last I get up and make my way to the door. It opens with a slight creak but Min is sound asleep, she does not stir. I slip outside and softly close the door behind me. By my feet, incense burns in Min's platter. Above me, the bright moon illuminates the village square, the gingko tree's leaves trembling in a slight breeze. On the ground in front of each doorway is a dish like Min's, heaped with whatever food each household can spare. A silent clearing, waiting for the ghosts to arrive. I think that the ghosts whom the villagers expect will be their own ancestors, the hardworking men and women of the past, come to see that all is well with their descendants, well-meaning spirits who bring only good intentions and well wishes. They do not know, the sleeping villagers, that they harbour amongst themselves a hungry ghost who cannot be fulfilled with their simple plates of good peasant food, who will only bring ill fortune to them the longer I stay here.

I walk away, down the tiny path into the woods. The moon is so bright I might as well be carrying a lantern in my hand. Despite the light, I slip more than once. Creatures scurry away from me in the underbrush and the steep path causes me to tumble several times, when loose pebbles slide under my feet. My forearms sting with grazes. But I keep going down, down, down. I have never ventured this far, have always returned before I reach the foothills. Now I continue. Ahead of me, I see lights and I head for them.

The village in the foothills is far bigger than the one on the mountaintop. It seems impossibly large to me after a summer spent with Min. So many houses. Many even have tiled rooftops, the grey tiles stretching out in every direction, one house and another and another and another as far as I can see. It feels like a city to me, the size of it overwhelms me.

There are lanterns here and there, but all is quiet. It is very late, it must have taken me a long time to make my way down. I hesitate, wondering what I am doing here. What did I intend to do? Did I want a temple to pray at? Am I trying to return to the

Forbidden City and Qianlong, to fall at his feet and beg forgiveness? I hesitate on the path, halfway between the mountain's forests and the first house in the village.

A chained dog barks at me. I shrink back but as it continues barking I hear its owner curse and tell it to be quiet. The dog looks at me with its ears flattened, angry at being told off for doing its duty, but it stays quiet and soon I can hear snores from the house, its owner quickly returning to their dreams. I step forward again and the dog watches me pass but does not bark again, only bares its teeth in a soundless growl.

I walk on to the next house. A lantern hangs outside, illuminating the platter of food that has been left here: a congealed meat stew, little dumplings, their white dough shining in the light, a flat bread.

The next house has skewers of meat, filled breads, dried fruits.

I feel my belly rumble. I have not eaten for many hours and in that time I have walked continuously. I am hungry. I look down at the food and wonder what will happen if I eat it. Will I be sick? Will the ghosts possess me? Will they follow me back to Min's house to reclaim what is rightfully theirs, bringing misery to the village? I shudder and walk on.

When I come to the end of the village I stop. I stand by the last house and look out across the rolling fields and hills. I could keep walking, could head for Beijing and return to the gates of the Forbidden City and ask for entry. I look down at what I am wearing and a laugh escapes me. No guard would ever let me in, they would be dismissed at once. And even if they did? I have no desire to be an empress any more. I gave everything I had to become Empress and I still could not oust Qianlong's memory of Fuca, just as he could not oust my memory of Niu Lang.

I could return to my family and beg them to take me in. My father may still be alive, perhaps Shu Fang will have a household I could join. But I think of their horror when they heard what has happened to me, their fear of retribution for their daughter's failings. They will have heard the news by now, they will know that the Empress has gone mad and cut off her hair, an unspeakable act. They will have been shocked and then ashamed to know that I have been exiled. They must have spoken my name with pride all these years, one promotion following another until the unthinkable happened and I was made Empress. Everyone in the empire knows my name, knows whose daughter I am and now everyone will know of my disgrace. I laugh again. Everyone of note, that is. To the villagers with whom I live I am no empress. I am a woman from a well to do family who has gone harmlessly but embarrassingly mad and has been sent to them so that I may live quietly out of the way, cared for but not seen by anyone of importance. I squat down for a moment, my legs are aching from the long walk. I wonder who I have left in this world. Perhaps I could find a temple where I can be a nun, as I asked Qianlong to let me be. But I do not know where I would find such a temple and it occurs to me that Min might be lonely if I were to leave. She is a widow and life is hard for a widow. I think of her sunburnt smiling face and Chen's endless questions, of Min's uncle who is always grumpy but nevertheless has not been stingy with the silver Qianlong provided him with. Perhaps the village has not been harmed by my coming after all. Perhaps if I stayed here willingly

I could be a part of their lives. Certainly, my chances of happiness are greater here than they would ever be if I were to find my way back to Beijing.

I stand up, my legs cramping at the new movement. Slowly I turn back the way I have come, back through the sleeping village, to begin the steep climb up the mountain.

It is dawn when I finally make my way, panting, back into the village clearing. One or two of the houses already have smoke coming from the chimneys and I hope that Min has not noticed my absence. I am almost at her door when I see Chen emerge from his own house, to be greeted enthusiastically by his dog. I can't help smiling at the welcome she gives him, as though he has been away for a month rather than asleep a few paces away.

"You're all muddy," Chen greets me.

I nod. "I went for a walk."

"In the dark?"

"Yes."

"All night?"

"Yes."

"Why?"

I shrug. "I don't know," I confess.

He nods as though this is an acceptable answer. "Are you hungry?"

"Yes," I say, feeling my stomach rumble again.

He takes a handful of berries and a piece of bread from the platter by his own door. "Here."

I am about to refuse. The food is not to be touched by humans, it is there for the dead. But Chen means well and I am hungry and too tired to explain. I hold out my hand and he pours the berries into my palm. I hesitate but then tip them into my mouth. Their sharpness brings a rush of saliva and the hard bread he passes me is sweetened by the fruit as I chew.

Min comes out of the house, her anxious expression relaxing when she sees me. "I didn't know where you were," she says. "Are you well?"

"Yes," I say.

Fourteen days later, it is time for the villagers to light the tiny floating lanterns that will guide the visiting spirits home. They set off at dawn, carrying their little lights to a mountain stream. I pretend to be asleep, afraid that if I light a lantern my flame might not go out and it would frighten the villagers. Min tries to stir me but gives up when I turn away and pull the blankets over my head.

Summer is short here on the mountain, I can feel the first chill of autumn. I see Chen's older sister sitting on the doorstep of their house day after day, embroidery in her lap. She seems to be outlining the shapes of butterflies.

"What is it for?" I ask.

She blushes. "My dowry."

Melissa Addey

I hear myself saying, "There is a stitch I could show you. For embroidering grass stems."

She passes me the cloth and watches me eagerly as I show her a stitch much favoured at court. Its delicacy brings to life waving grass stems beneath the floating butterflies. It takes her a little while, but she makes a good job of it.

"Thank you, Ula Nara!" she calls, as she hurries to show her friends. At least, I think, being Han Chinese she will not be summoned for the Imperial Daughters' Draft, she may marry whomever she wishes to, she need only seek her parents' blessing. I raise my hand to wave her off and she beams back at me.

I stop my night-time wanderings and instead walk in the daytime. The villagers are used to me by now, they do not stare so much when I pass, only raise their heads briefly from their work and nod when they see who it is. Much of the day I sit on the doorstep, enjoying the sun's waning warmth on my skin.

"Help me pod these, would you?" Min's old neighbour, a hunchbacked woman whose own doorstep is only a few paces away, holds out a basket filled with withered bean pods.

I fumble with the pods, dropping dried beans here and there, which the straying chickens try to steal before I can pick them up again, but I manage to beat them to it just in time.

"Quick-fingered," laughs the old woman and I laugh back, proud of myself for outwitting the hens, who cluck disappointedly and return to their scratching in the dirt.

"You are well?" asks Min's uncle, passing by. He has a couple of sacks thrown over his shoulder, he must have been down to the village for supplies of some sort.

"Yes," I say. "And you?"

"Well enough, well enough," he says. "For you," he adds, throwing a small bag my way.

I catch it and open it up to reveal dried dates. "Thank you," I exclaim, surprised.

He shrugs but looks pleased. "Min said you had a liking for them," he says and walks away. I hold out the bag to the neighbour and we both munch on the dates, the rich sweet taste an unexpected treat.

"I'm still dropping the beans," I confess, when we return to the work in hand.

"Be not afraid of growing slowly, be only afraid of standing still," chuckles the old neighbour, watching me boldly shoo away the chickens.

Snowfall

AUTUMN COMES AND THE LEAVES of the gingko tree in the clearing turn golden yellow. I watch them falling from my window at dawn and then turn to Min.

"I need brushes and inks," I tell her. "In different colours."

She looks awkward. "My uncle says that you are not permitted to write letters," she says, her eyes not quite meeting mine.

I want to laugh. To whom would I send letters? To Qianlong, to beg to return? To my family, to tell them of my disgrace? To the other ladies of the court, to warn them, as if they needed to be warned, of what can happen when you fall from favour?

"I do not want to write a letter," I say. "I want to paint."

She nods, relieved, and hurries away. I wonder where she will get brushes and inks from, perhaps from a local official or her uncle. I wonder if she has ever painted in her life, if her life has allowed for such luxuries. Perhaps as a child she might have crushed red berries and smeared them on white bark or a smooth rock.

When she returns she is clutching two brushes and a few inks: blue, red, black. She also has some paper.

"Thank you," I say. "I do not need the paper." I get up and pull on my jacket, then walk out into the cold air. I make my way to the gingko tree that stands in the centre of the village and begin to collect its leaves. Min has followed me. Now she stands frowning at me.

"Why do you need leaves?" she asks.

"I will show you," I say. "Help me pick up more."

We return to the room with our hands full of the golden leaves, more than a hundred between us. I sit down at the table and take one leaf in my hands.

"Watch," I say. I take the little stem at the top of the leaf and carefully split it in two with my short nails, then pull it apart so that it forms two tiny stems where there was only one before. Min frowns with concentration, watching me as though she might miss what I am doing.

I dip the brush in the red ink and add two bright circles to the lower parts of the leaf, one to each side. Then I take the blue ink and add tiny dots to the upper half. I twist the leaf round so that Min can see it better and her eyes suddenly widen.

"A butterfly!"

"Yes," I say, smiling at her amazed face.

She quickly learns to split the stems that make the antenna for each butterfly, while I paint one leaf after another with the colours I have. I even manage to mix the red and blue to make a beautiful purple, giving me a fourth colour. Soon the rough table in front of me is covered all over with painted butterflies, the leaves transformed. Min looks to me for guidance when we have used up all the leaves.

"Now we let them dry," I say.

"What are they for?" she asks, gazing at them in wonder.

"The children," I say.

The next morning it has grown still colder. Min and I shiver, even after cramming on as many layers of clothing as possible, our arms and legs stiff with padding.

It is Chen who sees me first.

"What are those?" he asks.

I hold one out, a golden body marked with bright blue patterns.

He stares and then reaches out a fingertip to touch the quivering antenna. "What is it?" he asks and his voice is a whisper.

"A leaf," I say. "A butterfly leaf."

Suddenly he sees what it is. He beams. "Did you make it?"

"Yes," I say.

"Who taught you?"

I think of the court painters, decorating gingko leaves in their thousands to be thrown for Qianlong's bustling street scene in the Garden of Perfect Brightness, how they were barely noticed by a court too used to such marvels.

"I saw ones like these a long time ago," I say. "They were thrown into the air, so that they looked as though they were flying."

"Who are they for?" he asks.

"You," I say.

"Me?"

"You," I say and I tip the bowl I am carrying towards him so that he can see that it is full. "You and your friends." I hold the bowl out towards him and he takes it, looks down into it with wide eyes.

"Thank you," he says.

"You are welcome," I say.

He turns from me and runs away, towards a group of children a little way off, engaged in a hopping game. I stand with my hands empty, Min behind me, watching him shout out to them.

"Look what I have! Look!"

They gather round him and I can hear them exclaiming, see their hands reaching into the bowl, retrieving the little scraps of colour.

I turn back to Min. "They like them," I say, smiling.

Someone is tugging at my jacket. I turn round to see Chen's face upturned to mine.

"Aren't you going to come and fly them with us?" he demands, as though it is unthinkable that I should not go with him.

And so I find myself following the ragged band of children through the village, Min a few steps behind me. They run ahead and I have to walk quickly to keep up. In the end, I find myself half-running behind them and when they look back and see that I am keeping pace they run faster, so that I must actually run to stay with them. The cold air rushes past and my feet feel suddenly light. I have not run anywhere for years. Why would a court lady, much less an empress, run? I run and run, until we are well beyond the village and have reached the narrow ridge.

"Be careful!" I call out, panting for breath, but of course the children are sure-footed, they have been this way many times before. They look like mountain goats, bouncing and twisting along the tiny path, uncaring of the drop on either side of them. At last they stop, at the point where they can look down into the valley. By now I am no longer running. I can barely breathe, my heart is pounding and my side hurts. An empress has no need to run.

When I reach them the children are already dipping their hands into the bowl and throwing up the tiny leaves. Each one twists in the wind, spiralling first upwards with the thrust of their arms and then gently floating downwards, sometimes catching in the wind and being lifted up again, twirling briefly in the air before sinking down again, bright sparks against the pale gold and pink rays of the early sun. Each butterfly has its turn, the children watch each one begin its flight before reaching for another, until the air is full of flying butterflies. I feel the first warmth of the day's sun on my face and find that I am laughing, shrieking with delight as one leaf touches my face on its way into the valley. I look to my side and Min is laughing, begging for a chance to throw one herself, which the children grant her. I find one pressed into my own hands and throw it up high, its tiny red and yellow body setting out on a voyage of discovery. I wonder whether the children in the villages of the valley below will find them, these strange autumn butterflies, these last colourful reminders of the summer behind us, if they will wonder where they came from and think them sent down from the realm of the Immortals.

The next day Chen is waiting outside the house as soon as I step out of the door.

"Do you want to come and pick nuts with us?" he asks.

"Nuts?"

"We're going to pick birch nuts. Before the monkeys finish them off. You can come with us."

I think of my little son the last time I spoke to him, how formal he was with me, how neither of us knew what to say to one another. I have to look away for a moment, up at the sharp blue sky, while my eyes clear. When I look back down Chen is still waiting.

"So will you come?" he asks.

I smile. "Yes," I say. "Yes. Thank you."

My autumn is spent with the children. We pick birch and pine nuts, forage for kindling for the fires, turn hundreds upon hundreds of gingko leaves into butterflies. We venture down as far as the foothills of the mountains and bring back walnuts, which stain our hands when we remove their husks before we put them away in storage for winter.

Min looks at me with surprise. "Not panting?" she says one day as we reach the village, having climbed up the steep side of the mountain.

I smile. "No," I say.

"Strong lungs," she says. "Strong hands, too," she adds, pointing at my hands, which have grown calloused from carrying wood and husking nuts.

"Brown skin," I say, looking down at my forearm when I push up my jacket sleeves to wash my hands. It's true. The once pure white of my skin has grown brown in the sun. I can see my face has done the same, even in the small chipped mirror that is all I have to look at myself in now.

There is a tiny temple I sometimes glimpse, its little swooping rooftop all I can make out of it, set on the far peak of the mountaintop.

"Do the villagers pray there?" I ask Min. I have never seen any people going that way.

"No," she says. "A Daoist monk lies there, a hermit. He prays. The men take him food every few days and he prays for our village."

"Can I go there?"

She shrugs. "If you want to," she says.

It's a cold morning with a low sky. I think of turning back, of going there another day when it's less likely to rain, but I woke this morning thinking of the temple and so I set off, waving to Chen and his friends. They follow me along the tight path for a while before losing interest and diving off into the woods, looking for wild animals. I can hear them making monkey noises, crashing through the underbrush below me and smile to myself, thinking that any wild animals will go to ground at once.

The narrow path still makes me nervous. One wrong step and I would find myself clutching at thin air to try and stop a fall down the cliff-like edges of the mountain, for there are few trees sturdy enough to grab at here. The few that have managed to survive, clinging on to the rocks with desperate strength, are tiny and would be uprooted in a moment by the weight of a person. But the woods no longer frighten me. I have roamed all over them with the children these past months and I feel more at home in them than when I came here. I hear the calls of the eagle as it stretches it wings high above me and spot a flash of red and gold, a golden pheasant in the undergrowth. I hear the screeches of the monkeys and wonder what has made them so excited. Perhaps the children are chasing them again.

The temple, when I reach it, is tiny. There is a small wooden building, which I assume houses the hermit monk, protecting him from the cold. It is not the kind of highly decorated temple I grew accustomed to in the Forbidden City. This is made of simple wood, only its swooping rooftop surmounted with tiny guardian statues adds any sense of beauty. Where there would usually be a large enclosed courtyard with grand cauldrons waist-high to a man, filled with sand for burning incense, here there is only a tiny paved area directly in front of the building. There is space to take perhaps ten steps and then, abruptly, the paving ends. Two more steps would have me falling through the air, to reach the valley below lifeless. I step back a little nervously. There is a very small stand for placing incense in, with some already burning and other sticks ready to be lit. I take one and touch it to the red tip of the already burning incense, thinking of the huge bunches of incense sticks I would once have gripped as I bowed in the name of the Imperial Family. Now I am alone it seems fitting to take only one stick. I watch the tip grow red and begin to smoulder, lift it away and bow once in each direction. As I turn towards the tiny building I briefly notice that the door has opened and the monk is standing there watching me, but I continue my bows and by the time I have placed the stick in the holder and knelt before the burner he has moved to one side of me and is kneeling himself, face down.

I wonder what to pray for. Before, I was always instructed as to what ritual we were carrying out. Fertile soil, rain, sun, good crops, the health of silkworms, the wellbeing of the empire seemed to rest entirely on my shoulders and my prayers. Now that I am no longer Empress, what do I pray for?

I pray that the village will have a safe winter and enough to eat, that Chen will grow up strong and healthy. I pray that next spring the crops will grow. I pray that the animals in the woods have good deep burrows and strong nests in which to huddle come the storms of winter. Then I raise my head and look across the open air to the far horizon and give thanks that I am here and happy, that the bitterness of my life has faded from me.

For it has. I had not known it before now. Perhaps it was when I laughed at the butterflies or even when I first thought to paint the golden leaves of the gingko tree. Perhaps it was when I saw Chen peering at me and saw something other than my own thoughts and misery. Or perhaps it was the day when I opened my eyes, looked out of a swaying palanquin and felt my heart drop with terror at the view below me. Perhaps that was the first true feeling I had had for many years, a feeling based in reality rather than the tortured twisting thoughts of my mind. I think back to my belief that I was a hungry ghost and the moment when Chen fed me from a platter intended to fill the bellies of the dead. I wonder if perhaps there was something magical in that food, if it truly fed the ghost in me, or whether it was the kindness and simplicity of Chen's offer that did the feeding. I take in the cold cold air and rise to my feet looking down at the monk. I cannot see his face, for he is prostrated deep in prayer, so I only bow to him and then walk back to the village as a fine mist of rain begins to fall on me.

The cold grows sharp now and even the children prefer to stay indoors. I sit near Min as she does her chores and help her when I can. The first time I do so she looks startled, and more startled still when she sees that I have never chopped vegetables in my life and that I am likely to cut my fingers. She shows me how to hold the sharp knife properly and slowly I grow more useful to her. I help her wash clothes and marvel at my wrinkled fingertips, chop mutton and learn to roll and hand-rip noodles for the fiery cumin-spiced stews she makes. I squeeze stored pomegranates for their juice and suck my fingers clean, the sweet-sharp taste a welcome reminder of summer's fruits, now that fresh fruits and vegetables are hard to come by.

I teach Chen to write his own name and to read a few characters. He wants to know how to write *horse* and *dog*, *sheep* and *house*, *monkey*, *berries* and *noodles*, the words that make up his life here. He does not want to compose poetry and read up on illustrious ancestors, for he has none. He wants the words that feed and house him, the words for friends and family, the words that tell of his adventures roaming across this mountain.

Every day I walk to the temple. I grow used to the pathway, although there are days when fierce winds remind me of my fears and with good reason. I take with me a stout stick, so that I can use it for balance if the path is slippery with rain. When I reach the temple I light a stick of incense, watch the red tip glow and breath in the sweet smell. I pray for little things: for Min's cut finger to heal, for Chen's mother's cold to get better soon. I give thanks for a full belly and for a warm hearth to sit by. It is a relief to pray for little things and not feel the weight of an empire's expectations crushing down on you.

From time to time I see the monk. Not every day. Sometimes I catch a glimpse of him practising his martial arts a little way off, or praying, more often I do not see him at all. He is often busy carrying or cutting firewood or making repairs to the wooden building. I do not speak to him, nor do I really look at him: he seems to want to keep himself apart and after all he is a hermit, so I do not wish to disturb him. But he is a comforting presence. Sometimes I bring the food from the village for him and leave it outside his door, where he will find it, taking back to the village the empty basket he leaves there. I like the silence and smallness of this temple and I like that there is only one monk here, that he cares for it as his own home. It seems a more humble way to approach the Immortals than with vast pomp and ceremony as though we were equal to them, as though the Emperor were indeed the Son of Heaven instead of what I know he really is: a man, like any other.

Thick snow falls. The children play in it, building up great heaps and trying to sculpt it into the shape of people, of little houses, of animals. I watch them from the window and then join them, only to be pelted with snowballs that they have made and stored up behind a snow wall. I give satisfying yelps as they hit me and they collapse laughing when my own poor attempts miss them entirely. Chen's three-legged dog barks hysterically, overexcited by the children's enthusiasm. I make more and more snowballs, my aim improving until I manage to get Chen exactly in the chest, at which he staggers and plays out a convincingly dramatic death scene, which has the dog worried.

The snow seems too thick to risk walking to the temple but after a few days I ask Min whether the monk will have enough supplies.

"He has enough for two or three more days," she says. "After that one of the men will have to make their way there or he will have to fast."

"I can go," I say.

She looks at me doubtfully. "If you slip now, we'll never find you," she says.

"I have my stick," I say. "And the poor man must have some food." I do not say what is also true, which is that I miss my walks to the temple. I can pray in the village of course, I can pray by the warmth of the fire if I wish, but the little temple draws me. I like to say prayers by the cliff edge, as though they have nowhere to go but straight to Heaven. I like to feel the cold air flowing over me as though it takes every bad feeling away, every fear and worry, every bad memory and replaces it only with the cold and purity of the air, sweeping away all that is not good and leaving a fresh surface, like new-fallen snow. I enjoy returning refreshed and purified, as though I have been blessed by the Immortals.

And so when a few more days have passed I take up my stick and Min helps me put a basket onto my back filled with food for the monk.

The snow has fallen more than once and it is thick. Each step I take pushes down layer upon layer of the snow with a satisfying crunching sound. Despite Min's worries, the thick fresh snow actually gives my boots something to grip onto, unlike the wet muddy days of autumn, although I think that if it turns to ice I will have to rethink my confidence in coming here.

The temple has almost disappeared into the snow, from a distance one might not even see it, or think it was just a hilly mound. The doorway and a tiny path has been cleared of snow, but the rest is entirely white. I twist round so that I can take off the basket, gratefully releasing its heavy weight onto the ground with a little grunt. I roll my shoulders and then consider whether or not to knock at the door. But I have never spoken with the monk and I do not want to disturb him if he is at prayer or meditating. So I simply leave the basket in front of the door and then turn to the little altar at the cliff's edge. There is no incense today, so I only stand before it and make my four bows, then kneel in the snow and kowtow. When I stand I brush down my clothing and stand for a few moments, looking out over the valley below and the mountains beyond. It is a scene of exquisite beauty. The mountains are endlessly white. The tiny villages that I know sit in the valleys below are gone, lost in the snow somewhere. It is as though a painting has been wiped away, the colours and shapes I knew taken away, revealing the white silk canvas beneath it, fresh and clean, ready for a brush again, for a new image to be painted. I feel the cold air rush through me, imagine it taking away everything that has happened in my life, taking me back to a moment in my life when all was good, to snowy mornings when Shu Fang would whisper in my ear that Niu Lang was waiting for me in our garden. I think of everything after that moment floating away from me, leaving me here in the white snow, purified and blessed, my burdens released. When I turn back to the tiny path, passing the hermit monk's hut, I am smiling.

Stormy days follow, with snow blizzards so heavy that we can see nothing at all and have to spend our days huddled indoors. Sometimes we scurry to a neighbour's house and spend time together, the old people telling stories while the children crack nuts between two stones at our feet, munching and giggling at funny stories from the past or sitting wide-eyed at legends featuring great deeds of heroes and Immortals. I hear the story of the Cowherd and the Weaver Girl and for once, it does not hurt my heart. My thoughts turn to Niu Lang, wherever he is, and I hope only that he is happy, that he is surrounded by good people, as I am.

At last, the storms clear and a sun-sharp day dawns, the glitter on the snow so bright that we have to shade our eyes, walking about like moles newly-emerged from the earth, bedazzled.

"The monk will need food," says Min and I nod. This job seems to have become mine and I am glad to do it, it pleases me to have a task that is mine, a task that otherwise someone else would have to do. I feel useful doing it, part of the village's life. I take my stick, hoist up the basket and set out.

When I get to the temple I leave the basket by the door, then make my way to the altar, which has been swept clean of snow. Set on it is a round object like a ball. It looks like something encased in ice, perhaps a forgotten tool or a stone. I get closer to it and set down my stick before reaching out my hand, which is shaking.

The ball is a carving in ice. Two magpies, their bodies intertwined to form a spherical shape. I stare down at it in disbelief.

"Ula Nara."

I don't turn. I don't need to. I would know his voice anywhere, even after more than thirty years. I look down at the carving in my hands, the two birds just as I remember them, trembling between my fingers as though they have come to life.

"Niu Lang."

The Bridge of Magpies

I DO NOT KNOW HOW LONG we stand on the cliff edge together. At first we stand side by side and do not speak, do not even look at one another. I look forward but I can see the shape of Niu Lang at my side, close enough that I could reach out my right hand and touch him. The cold wind blows through us and I wonder whether it has been sent down from the Immortals, if this snow is the magpie bridge that I have spent three decades waiting for, if the Immortals have finally relented.

"I thought I had learnt patience," he says at last. "I thought I would wait until you saw me for yourself." He laughs a little. "But you were too wrapped up in your own world, Ula Nara."

I think of the glimpses I saw of him: kneeling, carrying wood a little way off, his graceful movements as he practiced martial arts with his back turned to me. Now it seems incredible to me that I did not see it was him. "I was wrapped up in my own world," I echo. "I felt only my own pain."

"I have spent thirty years praying for your happiness," he says and his voice cracks.

"Your prayers are granted," I say.

"But only now," he says and I can hear the sadness in his voice.

I am about to say yes and then I pause. "Before now," I say at last. "Before now."

"When you came here?"

"Yes," I say.

I catch a movement of his head, a nod. "I saw you change," he says. "I could have waited for you to see me for yourself. But I was still too impatient, even after my years of training, even after all my masters have taught me. And the snow would have melted. I could not wait another year to make you an ice sculpture."

I laugh. I laugh out loud and then I turn to him even as he turns to me and I see him for the first time.

"You are the same," I say in surprise.

He laughs. "Older by thirty years. And without hair."

I shake my head. "You forgot the wrinkles," I tell him, still laughing. "But you are still you."

"Who did you think I would be?"

"A monk," I say.

He snorts with laughter, his eyes shining with tears. "I am."

"That is not what I meant."

"I know." He looks at me for a moment, then looks down. "Your hands must be frozen."

I am still holding the icy magpies. I place them back on the altar.

"Come inside and get warm," he says.

I follow him to the little building. Inside it is much like Min's house, but less cluttered. I sit on a little wooden bench while Niu Lang makes tea and serves it to me.

"When did you first see me?" I ask.

"In the woods."

"The woods?"

"You were walking in them alone, at night. I think you had only been here a little while."

"Did you recognise me?"

He looks at me in disbelief that I would even ask the question. "I thought it was your spirit. I thought you had died and that you had come to bid me farewell."

I think of the grief I felt when the male magpie died, my certainty that it was a sign that Niu Lang had died. "What did you do?"

"Watched you walk away and came back here."

I wait.

"And wept for you. For us."

I look down, my own eyes brimming. "I wanted to become a nun," I tell him. "As you became a monk."

"We do not all arrive at the same place by the same means," he says.

"You remained true to who you were," I say. "You remained pure in your mind and in your body. You practised a spiritual path that kept you whole. And sane," I add. "While I was dragged into court life, and all its darkness. It warped me. My love and grief for you became something twisted. It lost whatever was good and pure and became something bad. It made me into someone else, a dark person. A bad person." I shake my head, as though to release something stuck in it. "It drove me mad. I saw things that could not have been true, things I wanted to see. I saw the secrets that everyone keeps and hated them because I had secrets of my own that I could not speak of." I look down at my hands. "I became nothing but skin and bones, as though there was a terrible hunger in me. Gnawing at me all the time, begging to be fed and yet I could not find anything that would satisfy it. It made me ill."

He nods. "Ying is the spiritual self," he says. "Yang is the physical body. The two are equally important, they cannot be separated. Your feelings affect your body whilst your body affects your mind. They are two parts of the whole."

I give a little laugh. "You are a physician," I say. "Did becoming a monk make you happy?"

"Not at first. I was angry all the time, I refused to obey orders, I would try to pick fights with the other boys, even with my masters. At last my master taught me that we do not simply achieve peace. We must *practice* the Dao. We try to build a path between who we are and who we want to be, but it requires effort. It requires learning. It requires planning and thinking about who you want to be."

"Tell me about your training," I say. "About the early days."

"I started my training late. Many boys had already begun their training on Wu-Tang

Mountain by the time they were thirteen. It was exhausting. Before dawn we would run up and down the mountain carrying heavy sandbags before attending morning prayers. We spent more than nine hours every day learning ancient forms, drilling with weapons, stretching and praying again. We were taught herbal medicine and massage, even acupuncture. We chanted sacred texts. We had to study Daoist Scripture. We slept ten to a room and when we were not training we would walk in the mountain eating wild berries or play board games together in our dormitory. It took me many years to complete the training. Once ordained I left my master and became a wandering monk. I travelled from temple to temple, year after year. I sought out other masters, learned their skills and practised what I had been taught when I was alone. Along the way I learned to play the bamboo flute and cook for myself." He laughs. "I am not a bad cook now, Ula Nara."

"You live here all year round?"

"Yes."

"It is a hard life," I say.

"I am used to it. Most of our practice when I was a trainee was outside. We trained in the sun and in the cold. If it rained or snowed we could practice indoors." He looks around at the thick snow surrounding us. "Although I have always liked being in the snow," he smiles.

"It is such a tiny house," I say.

He laughs. "I have two sets of practice clothes, some street clothes, a bowl to eat from, and a cup to drink from. Bedding. A basin for washing myself. There is a bed, a table, the bench and a chest for my belongings, such as they are. I am not sure what I would do with a larger house."

"If you enjoyed the company of the other students," I say, "why did you leave the temple and come here? Wu-Tang Mountain is close enough, you could have returned there."

"I struggled to master my sense of loneliness," he says, looking away. "Even when I was surrounded by others, I thought of you and felt alone. In the end my master suggested that I explore what it is to be truly alone, with one's thoughts, one's feelings, one's physical body." He looks down into the valley below us. "And so I came here, to this tiny place."

"How long ago?"

"More than ten years." He grins. "I think the villagers thought I would not last the year, especially once the snows came. But I surprised myself, and them."

"What made you stay?"

"The people, at first. They were so kind. They brought me food, they watched out for me, the children were forever peeping at me from behind the bushes. They made me laugh."

I think of the children leaping in the air and shouting at the sight of the ginkgo butterflies and smile. "And then?"

"Then the mountain, I think."

"The mountain?"

"When I first came here, I spent days and days wandering all over the mountain. Months. I saw all its secrets and all its beauty. I saw the living spaces of hermits before me, who had come here and found peace. And before them, people from so long ago we do not even remember their names."

"The caves," I say. "And the paintings."

He nods. "Yes. At first they frightened me, I did not know what they were."

"Do you know what they are now?"

He laughs. "No, but they no longer frighten me."

"And what else?"

"Everything." He thinks for a moment. "The trees, the berries, the animals. The way the seasons pass and things change but are the same."

I think of the ginkgo leaves changing from green to gold and then into painted butterflies. Of the berries I ate from Chen's hand, so different from the over-ripe berries steeped in honey I was served at court, how their sharp-sweetness awoke something in me and laid something else to rest. I nod.

Spring comes. The snow and ice melts away. Tiny streams make their way down the mountain's sides, to join rivers in the valley below and make their way to the Yellow River. I have a cough, which Min fusses over, but I tell her it will be gone soon, it is only the change in weather.

"You shouldn't spend all that time out in the cold," says Min. "Let the men take food to the monk."

"It makes me happy to go there," I say. She calls me stubborn and has me wrap up more warmly, but she lets me go. Every few days I walk to the temple as I have done these past months and take food to Niu Lang. Then we sit together and look out over the valleys below, watching the seasons change.

"Tell me about your life," he says one day.

I think. We have never spoken of my years in the Forbidden City. What do I tell him about? The pomp and ritual? The splendour? My children, lost to me as soon as they were born? Feng? Ling? Qianlong? Lady He? All the petty rivalries, which now seem so meaningless even though they were all I had to live for? "I was a hungry ghost," I tell Niu Lang. "I wanted what I had lost and I did not know how to find it. I searched and searched but each time I thought I had found something to feed on it was only an empty bowl and my hunger grew greater."

He nods.

"I cut my hair because I thought you had died. I had come to the end of my search," I say. "I realised I would never fill that need. I was mourning for myself as much as for you."

We sit in silence for a little longer.

"I ate food from the bowls left out for the hungry ghosts last summer," I say. "I thought I was one of them."

"And then?"

I shake my head and smile. "Perhaps it fed the hungry ghost in me," I say. "I thought of going back to my family or to Beijing to beg for forgiveness. But I came back to the village that night because it felt like my home. One of the children offered me food from the ghost dishes and the food seemed meant for me, as though I belonged here. The people felt like my family. And they did not care about who I was before. They don't even know who I was," I add with a laugh.

"They know who you truly are," says Niu Lang.

I nod. "I was afraid that the hungry ghost would never leave me," I say. "There was a Hungry Ghost Festival many years ago in the Forbidden City and when we set candles afloat afterwards to guide the spirits home, my flame alone did not go out. I thought it was a sign that there was still a ghost wandering in my life and then I thought it must be me. That I *was* the ghost and that I would wander forever, unhappy and seeking what could not be found."

Niu Lang gets to his feet and walks away, to the little house. I wait for him, watching the clouds moving across the sky. When he comes back, he is holding a tiny round candle and a scrap of paper. He folds the paper this way and that until he has made a little boat, into which he sets the candle, wedging it firmly into place.

"What are you doing?" I ask.

He goes to the altar and lights the candle, brings it back to me and indicates the little stream running down past the altar, the last of the winter's snows.

I look down at the boat cupped in my hand. "The lanterns are supposed to be sent out fourteen days after the Festival of Hungry Ghosts," I say quietly. "It is too late."

"It is never too late to set a spirit free," says Niu Lang.

I take the boat with its tiny flame and kneel by the side of the stream. I set it gently in the fast running water and watch as it bobs its way around obstacles: a twig, a stone, moving now fast, now slow. It reaches the edge of the cliff and just as it tips over the edge a gust of wind catches it. The flame flickers and goes out.

I look up at Niu Lang, who smiles.

"It is never too late to be set free," he says.

Author's Note on History

Ula Nara features in all four of my books set in China, and I have mostly cast her as a villain: a frightening rival or presence for many other characters. But the more I wrote about her, the more I wanted her to have her own story. Her real name is lost to us, as most concubines did not have their real names recorded, only their clan names. I have therefore chosen to use her clan name as a given name rather than make one up.

Ula Nara came from a military family and was chosen as a concubine for the heir to the throne, known as Prince Bao (later the Qianlong Emperor) at the age of sixteen (he was twenty-three and his Primary Consort Lady Fuca was twenty-two). I always thought that there must have been many young girls attending the Imperial Daughters' Draft who were already in love with someone but who were then selected for the Imperial Family and had no choice in the matter, so I gave this back story to Ula Nara. To aid with the comparison between Ula Nara and Fuca's experiences, I have them enter Qianlong's life together, although in reality Fuca would have already been his Primary Consort for a few years when Ula Nara arrived.

Looking at her records suggests that Qianlong was not very interested in Ula Nara. She was promoted on the occasion of his coronation (this was standard) and then twice more for no obvious official reason. She had no children at all until two years after she became Empress, a full sixteen years after being married to Qianlong. She then had three children in only four years, which means she was not infertile but strongly suggests she had not been favoured until Qianlong felt he ought to call for her since she was now his Empress, indicating duty rather than fondness. Ula Nara lost two of her three children very young, while they were still toddlers. Her eldest child lived only into his early twenties, dying about ten years after she did. It was standard practice for a concubine's child to be raised by a different concubine.

Qianlong was very much in love with his Primary Consort Lady Fuca, who was made Empress after his coronation and whose sons had been chosen as heirs before they both died. Chinese emperors did not necessarily use primogeniture when choosing an heir: they chose the son they believed was the most appropriate for the role or the one of whom they were most fond. Qianlong did not wish to have a new empress appointed after the death of Lady Fuca, but his mother Niuhuru apparently intervened and insisted that a new lady be made Empress, forcefully backing Ula Nara, who was said to be extremely well versed in court etiquette. After a stubborn delay of two years of mourning, Qianlong gave Ula Nara the unheard-of title of Step Empress rather than Empress, again indicating a rather reluctant appointment.

On a trip to Southern China, Qianlong apparently celebrated Ula Nara's birthday but then suddenly and dramatically demoted her from Empress. She had cut off her hair, a huge breach of protocol, which could be interpreted as cursing the Emperor and his mother, as cutting off her hair suggested one of them had died. She was sent back to Beijing, where she had only two maids (what a very low-ranking consort would have had). She died a year later, aged forty-eight. To this day no-one is certain why this incident occurred. After her death she was buried with only minor ceremony more suited to a medium-ranked concubine. When, after her death, both a historian and a scholar pleaded with Qianlong to give her a better burial or re-instate her position, one was exiled and the other executed.

After Ula Nara's death Qianlong flatly refused to ever appoint another empress. Lady Ling acted as Empress where required but was not given the title. Her son (raised by Lady Qing) was chosen as the next Emperor (Jiaqing) but she did not live to see him on the throne.

Magpies have been known to live for more than twenty years, I stretched this a little further for Ula Nara's pet pair.

Lady Wan outlived Qianlong by eight years and lived to the grand old age of ninety. She was made a Dowager Noble Consort by his heir, the Jiaqing Emperor, in recognition of her age and service.

Lady Wang suffered demotions twice for being abusive to her maids. However, she was reinstated both times because she had a daughter of whom Qianlong was very fond, saying that she should have been his heir.

Being exiled from court, as Ula Nara was, was known as being sent to 'the Cold Palace', which is an expression, not a real place, but in this book I created a real exile for Ula Nara, so that I could re-unite her with her fictional long-lost love. I based her place of exile on a slightly-fictionalised Mount Hua Shan, a very beautiful but isolated place with terrifyingly narrow mountain-top ridge pathways, caves carved by hermits, strange red ochre paintings of human figures on rock faces (some of which are 16,000 years old) and temples set on the clifftops. The mountain is considered sacred by Daoists, whose mythology says that the god of the underworld lives under it.

I used the Qixi or Lovers' Festival as a structure and theme for Ula Nara's fictional love story, but also used the Hungry Ghost Festival (which takes place just after) because I felt there was something of the hungry ghost to Ula Nara's unhappiness, forever craving something that could not satisfy her. She died in August, the month in which both festivals take place.

We know so little about the women of the Forbidden City, yet the glimpses of their lives are fascinating. From what I could piece together I felt Ula Nara had an unhappy history. This book is partly my apology for always casting her as the villain, as well as an attempt at guessing what might have happened in her sad life from the tiny fragments left behind. It gave me pleasure to create a little fictional happiness and peace for her at the end of her life, however unlikely.

Your Free Book

The city of Kairouan in Tunisia, 1020. Hela has powers too strong for a child – both to feel the pain of those around her and to heal them. But when she is given a mysterious cup by a slave woman, its powers overtake her life, forcing her into a vow she cannot hope to keep. So begins a quartet of historical novels set in Morocco as the Almoravid Dynasty sweeps across Northern Africa and Spain, creating a Muslim Empire that endured for generations.

Download your free copy at www.melissaaddey.com

Review request

If you enjoyed this series and have a moment, I would really appreciate a brief review to help other readers find my stories. Thank you so much!

THE MOORISH EMPIRE

If you've enjoyed The Forbidden City series, I hope you'll try my second series, the Moorish Empire, due for completion in Winter 2019. It follows four women linked to the Almoravid Empire, which conquered the whole of North Africa and Spain. Follow the intertwining lives of Hela, a healer trapped by an impossible vow; Kella, a woman fighting for her freedom; Zaynab, a powerful queen searching for love and Isabella, a woman torn between her faith and her son's destiny. The first book in the series, *The Cup*, is free from my website or you can buy it on Amazon.

Thanks

My grateful thanks go to Professor James Millward for his expertise on the Qing era and encouragement. Mark Elliot's book *Qianlong: Son of Heaven, Man of the World* is a fascinating book for character information on members of the court and contains the poem Qianlong wrote to celebrate conquering Xinjiang. www.daoistgate.com and in particular the blog on the site was my main source for Niu Lang's life as a monk. Their collective scholarship gave my imagination a wonderful basis to work from, although of course all errors as well as deliberate fictional choices are mine alone.

Thank you to Rob Gifford, author of *China Road*, a great travelogue where I first read about the Chinese legend of the Fragrant Concubine, which kick-started this series.

Thank you to my beta readers for this book, Etain, Helen and Martin, for their questions, ideas and reminders that made the story and the writing better. To all the readers who review my books: I read every word and I am so grateful for your time in sharing your thoughts.

I am immensely grateful to the University of Surrey for funding my PhD: a very precious gift of three years of creative freedom to explore not only this series and my craft but many other creative outlets as well.

To all the scholars, artists and photographers on whose work I have drawn in the many years I have spent writing novels set in eighteenth century China: thank you for opening up the gates of the Forbidden City to me, it was a world beyond imagination and I am sorry to leave it behind as I complete this series.

Thank you to Streetlight Graphics and the illustrators who helped make the world come alive in my own books.

Thank you to my family and friends who continue to offer encouragement along the way. To my children, for their inspiring enthusiasm in writing their own books once they realised what I do for a living.

And always to Ryan, who makes all things possible.

Biography

I mainly write historical fiction: I have just completed The Forbidden City series and am about to complete a series set in Morocco and Spain in the 11th century. Next up will be a series set in 80AD in Ancient Rome.

I was the 2016 Leverhulme Trust Writer in Residence at the British Library and The Cold Palace won the 2019 Novel London award.

I am currently completing a PhD in Creative Writing at the University of Surrey.

I love using my writing to interact with people and run regular workshops at the British Library as well as coaching other writers on a one-to-one basis.

I live in London with my husband and two children.

For more information, visit my website www.melissaaddey.com

Current and forthcoming books include:

Historical Fiction

China

The Consorts (free on Amazon)
The Fragrant Concubine
The Garden of Perfect Brightness
The Cold Palace

Morocco

The Cup (free on my website)
A String of Silver Beads
None Such as She
Do Not Awaken Love

Picture Books for Children

Kameko and the Monkey-King

Non-Fiction

The Storytelling Entrepreneur
Merchandise for Authors
The Happy Commuter
100 Things to Do while Breastfeeding

Thoughts on research... and magic

As an author of historical fiction, I am used to treading the fine line between fact and fiction. I like my books to have solidly accurate historical settings, so I do a lot of research, which I enjoy. But then I allow myself a little freedom when it comes to the plot and the characters, sometimes because there are gaps in the historical record which leave me that freedom, sometimes because I feel that I am exploring an idea or a character in a way that requires the fictional element I have brought in. But sometimes something very odd happens, where I believe I have invented something and then find out that it is actually true. In my series set in China's Forbidden City during the eighteenth century, each of the four books focuses on the life of a particular concubine and the people who matter to her.

In the first book of the series, The Consorts, I described a newly-arrived concubine, Lady Ying, as looking like a wild eagle, being forcibly tamed for the gilded cage of the court. Several chapters later, I thought I would check the meanings of the main characters' names, just in case there was something interesting about them that I could work into the story. I do not speak or read Chinese. I looked up Lady Ying's name and found it meant... eagle.

For the second novel in the series, The Fragrant Concubine, I created a scene in which Lady He (the title character) went hunting with the Emperor. It is a crucial part of the plot, a turning point in which the Emperor and Lady He begin to fall in love. I felt that I was taking some artistic license, as the concubines rarely actually hunted, they simply attended the hunting grounds as spectators. But I felt that for my character it was important that she had this bolder, more active role and so I went ahead and wrote the scene. Only when I had finished the book did I come across a new painting from the era, that I had not focused on during my research, believing it to show a servant rather than a concubine. It is a small portrait, intended as a personal image, perhaps of emotional value, rather than a formal painting. In it, the Emperor gallops at full speed while shooting at a deer. Just behind him gallops a woman, leaning forward to pass him another arrow. Because of the particular ethnic hairstyle of the woman in the image, scholars have now determined that this painting portrays Lady He, my fragrant concubine, hunting with the Emperor.

The Garden of Perfect Brightness is the third book in the series and brings in an outsider: an Italian Jesuit painter by the name of Giuseppe Castiglione, who served at the Qing court for many decades and who managed to create an East-West fusion of painting styles that has been much admired since. For this book, I took a more dramatically inaccurate approach, by creating a fictional forbidden romance between Giuseppe and a concubine. I wanted it to stand as a symbol of the way Giuseppe managed to 'fall in love' with China and create a relationship with its culture in a way that none of his previous colleagues had succeeded in doing (several of them returned to Europe, unable to find a way to bridge the cultural divide: their Western painting style was considered 'inauspicious'). I did worry a little that the notion of a Jesuit painter falling in love with a local Chinese woman was a rather unlikely fictional element, but I decided to go ahead anyway as I felt it was an interesting approach. I had already written the whole of the first draft when a new academic paper was published. A set of diaries had been found in a church in Beijing, belonging to a certain Laura Biondecci. This previously unknown woman was in fact a female Jesuit painter, who was not listed in the Imperial records because of being a woman. Giuseppe Castiglione was her mentor and she served alongside him in the Qing court. Because of the similarity of their painting styles, some of her works may even have been mistakenly attributed to Giuseppe. In her diaries, Laura refers to a reciprocal romantic relationship with a Chinese woman named Guo. Somehow, I had written what seemed to be an unlikely story that turned out to be true, just that it belonged to a different person, although someone very close to Giuseppe. I felt I could not ignore this new evidence and so wrote Laura's story into the novel during the second draft.

What are these instances examples of? Perhaps they are just coincidences. But many writers, when they talk honestly about their writing process, will admit to strange things: writing about something that subsequently happens, describing people who then walk into their lives, and more. For myself, I like to think that perhaps, if you do enough good quality research about an era or a person, something unknown but true from the past makes its way to you. It makes me feel that these instances are a reward for having put in the hard work, for having thought long enough about the people, places and times that I have sensed something unknown about them.

The last book in the Forbidden City series, which I have entitled The Cold Palace, is about a concubine named Ula Nara, who rose to become Empress but apparently then 'went mad' and cut off her hair, a grave breach of etiquette which could be construed as cursing the Emperor or his mother. As a result, she was demoted from Empress and sent to 'the Cold Palace,' an expression for being exiled from court. To this day, no-one is certain of the reasons for Ula Nara's strange behaviour. In the novel, I give my own explanation. Now I'm waiting to see if the fictional reason I've given for her 'madness' will one day turn out to be true...

Printed in Great Britain
by Amazon

37758871R00381